Praise for *Some Sing, Some Cry*

"*Some Sing, Some Cry* is both MOVING and ARRESTING."
—Annette Gordon-Reed, Pulitzer Prize–winning author of
The Hemingses of Monticello: An American Family

"With music as a sustaining force, Shange and Bayeza's epic of courage, improvisation, and transcendence is GLORIOUS IN ITS SCOPE, LYRICISM, and spectrum of yearnings, convictions, and triumphs."
—Donna Seaman, *Booklist* (starred review)

"[A] complex poetic treatise on race, culture, love, and family, the use of regional vernacular, dialect, and pure song, resulting in a PROVOCA-TIVE fictional history."
—*Publishers Weekly*

Some Sing, Some Cry

Ntozake Shange 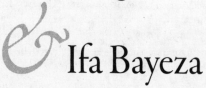 Ifa Bayeza

ST. MARTIN'S GRIFFIN

NEW YORK

SOME SING, SOME CRY. Copyright © 2010 by Ntozake Shange & Ifa Bayeza. All rights reserved. Printed in the United States of America. For information, address St. Martin's Press, 175 Fifth Avenue, New York, N.Y. 10010.

www.stmartins.com

Text design by Meryl Sussman Levavi

The Library of Congress has cataloged the hardcover edition as follows:

Shange, Ntozake.
    Some sing, some cry / Ntozake Shange & Ifa Bayeza.—1st ed.
        p. cm.
    ISBN 978-0-312-19899-2
    1. African American families—Fiction. I. Bayeza, Ifa. II. Title.
PS3569.H3324S66 2010
813'.54—dc22

2010022066

ISBN 978-0-312-55271-8 (trade paperback)

First St. Martin's Griffin Edition: October 2011

10 9 8 7 6 5 4 3 2 1

To Mom & Dad
Eloise Owens Williams
and
Paul Towbin Williams, M.D.

Simply the best

Some Sing, Some Cry

1

THE FIRST ORANGE LIGHT OF SUNRISE LEFT A FLUSH OF rose and lavender on Betty's hands as she fingered the likenesses of her children. There were tears she was holding back and cocks crowing, as well as her granddaughter's shouts, "Nana, you ready?" Betty sighed and closed the album reluctantly. Time had come for the last of the Mayfields to leave Sweet Tamarind, the plantation they'd known as home for generations. Talk was some carpetbaggers had bought all the land and paid the white Mayfields a smidgeon of what it was worth and left the poor blacks high and dry. A rough white man, whip and rifle in hand, had passed by a few days before, warning Betty and hers to be off the land by evening of this very day. So off they planned to be, not wanting to know another moment of the whites' wrath. The colored Mayfields were familiar with what that meant, and with no slavery to hold them back they were off to Charleston, where others awaited them.

There was nothing odd about two colored women racing the rhythm of cicadas and the tides at first light, busying themselves with order, a sense of the day to come and dreams of what it might bring, yet this day felt different. This day the cicadas were louder, purposely taunting Betty and her grandchild with their steadiness. Betty set her album down for a second and went to the window to be sure what she was hearing wasn't a band of washboards and gourds being played by some fool-ass folks with tongues in they cheeks. There was no one there. Only the density of Betty's imagination, the palms, some lily o' the valley and nightshade-snugglin' magnolia and giant oaks.

Well, music is not a bad omen, Betty thought to herself. Then she wondered did God mean for her to hear the glory of Gabriel in the morning machinations of insects, the breeze caressing dew on leaves left to themselves all the dark night, waves breaking how the drum popped if African Jeremiah wanted to change the gait of the ring shout, change the dancers' direction with three strong beats and a quick run of his palms on the face of the skin before beginning another rhythm demanding other movements, other oblations, and peace in the energies of the spirits spilling from his fingers to their bodies through the rings of soft clouds round the dawn moon. Sometimes the drums, fiddles, and washboards saluted the giant rose-orange sun, taking up the whole of the horizon like nobody had anywhere to go but to the center of the universe. Yes, the Lord's set the gulls to calling over the ocean's irrepressible going and coming, midst the cicadas' crescendo, to let her know to listen to this blessing, before she and Eudora made this wild—some would say this wild and thoroughly foolhardy—change in their lives. Moving to Charleston.

Why, on Sweet Tamarind everybody understood everybody else. The mélange of Yoruba, Wolof, Portuguese, French, Spanish, and a hint of English left the words of men, free or slave, soothing the air from mouth to mouth, left history in place, content with the comings and goings of her children. Nothing was lost, no one madly pounding gainst a vacuum of silence, nothingness that comes of being of nothing, nothing in particular. When she looked out from her tabby hut, oyster and clam shells cemented with sand thick enough to withstand the might of a cyclone, Betty saw the ruins of the Big House of Sweet Tamarind. She kicked something, not knowing what, thinking to herself, *I got no call to leave here. I belong right up there. We all do. Belong right here where I stand.*

And what was to become of the graves, the bittersweet memories of her mother, sisters who had been fortunate enough to pass over to the other world before the rigors of this island beat them down, smashed their spirits, left them but ghosts of themselves before it was time. She would have to go to their final resting place before she went anywhere. Sacrilege was not only the province of the white, but could fall upon the unmindful of any of God's children. This Betty believed with her whole body, her body knowing no separation from her soul, ever close to the breath, past and present, of all those whose blood was her own.

But she would have to hurry to pay her respects secretly and gather strength from the loved ones who were no more. Her grandchild Eudora had no sympathy for any who'd come before and had managed to find some joy in the throes of bondage, those who'd thrown away the rigid color codes and property laws to find warmth, love, passions too rich to suppress, so fertile that Eudora owed her own life to them. Perhaps it was this debt of her very being with which she was yet uncomfortable that led Eudora to reject all Betty held so close. *Don't for the life of me know why. What for? She 'most white, ain't she?* How could all of Africa get so deep in her granddaughter when Mayfield blood flowed just as readily in her veins? *How's all this come to be? And if she not all niggah, why not rejoice in that?* Eudora's cheeks had known the back of Betty's hand more than once for voicing her defiantly blasphemous thoughts. No matter. Both women were deeply rooted, like Carolinian cypress wondering and massive, to views of themselves that knew no connections other than the words Grandma and chile.

Slipping quietly from the house, Betty hid in her bosom her precious album of daguerreotypes and photographs from wandering carnival sideshow artists. She'd searched futilely for her apron pockets, but she wasn't in an apron. She wasn't going to be cooking in her very deliberate way in her own home anymore. She kept forgetting her future, but refused to forget her ancestors.

Betty swept by purple and white globe amaranth that clung to her skirts like weeping toddlers. She pushed further into the wooded areas she knew to be the resting places of her mother and sisters. Of course she didn't know for sure which of the mounds overgrown with wildflowers and weeds. Were wildflowers weeds? Betty'd asked herself that a thousand times. Was she a wildflower? Was her mother wild? Was she beauteous? *Was she full of life like good soil, or empty like dirt? There's a difference tween soil and dirt. There's a difference from coming from nothing and coming from something simply not known.* Betty's mother, Monday, was not known to her but she'd clearly come from something. It wasn't true that there was an emptiness. She felt her mother in the fiddle's melody, in the dried gourds ancient women shook until the spirits of somebody from somewhere drove secret sounds from mouths twisted in foreign shapes, squealing and growling a birth of a soul that had no choice but to shout. Then those shouts corralled the bent women and young heifers into a circle that shuffled along, weaving something like Spanish moss around some unseen skeleton the size of God's toe. Or she saw her mother possessed under the arch of God's foot, beating the air with her hips, the soles of her feet afire with the rhythm of the forbidden. Betty knew about the forbidden, therefore she knew her mother. She'd just picked a grave site and called to her. *Ma . . .*

When the azaleas or camellias rose up from the earth for the white folks to pick and pretend love of nature, Betty'd covered her mother's grave with flower petals and danced the dance of longing that became sated only when her body fell, fingers digging for arms to hold her, digging for a womb to bury her tears. But the grasses cut her face, left her limbs grimy with wishing for the impossible. Yet Betty made that real enough to hold sacred, to hold as her beginnings. She sang her mother. Betty let her fine dark hair hang from her head like a mantle of audacity.

She sang her mother when leading other blacker ones through the marshes cross to a safe boat on the way from where she belonged. The darker ones weren't left suspect of their very being. Least that's what Betty imagined. She had to imagine a lot because once she was free and then she was not. Once she wore satin and the finest lace, then she washed someone else's. Betty tried to imagine a reasonable world. She found that harmony by the graves she chose to call her family. She was entitled at least to that. All the others had kin, some that died or were sold away, but they existed somewhere. They knew the smell of magnolias and dogwood blossoms. They knew the songs she sang with them to calm the spirits, to move God's foot in time to the gourds, especially the fancy dangerous ones that woke glory in the tiniest child, the oldest mammy, the fastest picker, chopper, all succumbed to the glory gourds in their gleaming color-ful beads, their white feathers and blessed frog's legs. Betty let the music make her belong. She knew her mother. She knew her God danced.

That's what Eudora never found, a place she belonged, and now she was going to force the world to just accept her. Eudora could not bring herself to feel the fiddler's lyric, the gourd's invitations; her own limbs resisted harmony with anything that quelled the dissonance she knew to be herself. Betty jumped once, no twice, round and about the place where she knew her mother's bones waited for her words of love and reverence. She was saying good-bye in silence which broke her heart. Betty became the multitude of sounds and gestures she knew to be safe for those who'd crossed over. The music of a people tumbled from her till only sobs and a writhing body grabbed to hold on to her life. Betty rose weaker than she'd ever been when a child fell from her. Barely breathing she knew the song of her was, indeed, so much a part of her she'd be humming it in her own grave one day. So averse to silence she'd become, the butterflies were clapping bout her head, only no one else could hear them.

Her own daughters' graves were a bit more trouble to identify. Elma, so fair and pampered by the Mayfields she took to despising her mother and her mother's mother, simply disappeared one day. No more than seventeen, she determined that green eyes and silken hair made her ready for whatever the world had to offer. Heavens, no! Not the world of her mother and her mother's mother, but the world of the father, who thought her beauty set her free. *Pity.* How Betty saw her child's life or death depended on her mood when she looked at the clouds over the horizon. If the clouds were thick, white, billowing, Betty figured the white world was treating her daughter good. It was those thin fast-moving wisps of cloud that troubled Betty. *Didn't leave enough for a soul to hold on to.* The world was moving too fast and free with Elma, which to Betty signaled a mighty probability of stillness, the silence of the unmourned. And she'd just have to wait to get to Charleston to visit with her dear Blanche. Juliet, her youngest, was lost to her. Juliet, Eudora's mother, who simply had no song. She'd let love fly off with her voice and she had nothing to say to Eudora. Now Eudora was going to Charleston to set something straight that wasn't crooked, going to Charleston to make herself known to the world, when the world was full of young gals like her and dealt them no easy hand, no dance cards or honor.

Shame, Shame. She had to steal away, play half mad to get to the grave of her lover and owner, her master and partner, Julius Mayfield himself. How could he die fighting to keep his own enslaved, children he played with, inspected and vowed never to sell, but own was no contradiction. What kind of man had she shared so much of herself with, did he know she'd done that? Laid open her womanhood and soul as much as any wife anywhere ever had. Over and over she'd gifted him with healthy, never before seen children. Girls whose eyes suggested fog-laden dawns, whose skin was opalescent, whether bronze or ivory. Girls so wantonly free a sane soul couldn't conceive of them as some white's slaves. Yet they were property, like chattel or so much hog entrails, these girls, begat with joy sometimes, from power other times. Either way, how could he at the mere suggestion that she, Betty, the one who laid naked gainst the blond hair silken on his chest, whose legs entangled themselves with his arms and calves, have their mother re-enslaved because he, Mayfield, the planter, heard something about a wench close to him aiding troublemakers to make their way north? He'd heard. He'd heard her screams at childbirth. He knew her sighs of pleasure or terrible release from ecstasy. But what he'd heard from some anonymous white man or maybe a niggah was enough to take those same soft hands of hers that pulled the damp hair on his neck late in the night, holding on for a different kind of glory call, those same hands could now be shackled and set back to boiling lye, washing the undergarments of the white lady who thought she was his wife.

    It was not right. It was not wrong. It was. Like stars are. There. Like men and women are. No different from rivers or ravines, caves, hills. Betty didn't care about notions that divided men and women from rocks and fish. It was. She was. Her children were blessings because she had them. She couldn't watch her offspring with disdain the way she'd seen other women look at their master's broods. The pain of carrying hatred round in her body, in the hair that flowed down her back, was too ugly to leave any room for her. She had to be because her girls were, because the wind blows and stars decorate the night, sometimes falling into the laps of lovers, the currents of twisting creeks, the moist black of dream, and the song of her mother. Crepe myrtle spread over the grave of the father of her children like her arms and hair use'ta cover them after the act. He never touched her mean then, with the stinginess folks assumed. There was no hate between them. There was a chasm of fate, cowardice, and the inevitability of men and women seeing nothing but one another, smelling nothing but the scent of the other. That's all Betty understood. It was enough for her to curl neath the flowing crepe myrtle and let the pulse of his breath calm her. He was good for that.

She carefully laid the pictures of their children over the granite carved with the letters of his name, Julius Mayfield, and told him all she could about each child because he would hear from her no more.

I'm still amazed how somebody standing way from me that I never seen before, with his head under some black cloth, bad luck there for sure, makin' poofs, puffs, whatever, some dusting of the sky with soot, with smoke, with my soul maybe, hope not. Stranger come and we give up hard-earned money to look at pictures of ourselfs. Like mirrors wasn't enough. Like the reflection of you in my eyes to your eyes wasn't the Lord letting our insides out into the other. There are ways to remember and put back together whatever it was you want to recollect. Seems to me a laziness come over folks preventin' them from going deep down to the gut of all they ever been and tellin' somebody, if somebody want to know.

Don't know why Julius was so taken with these here whatchu call em, oh, photongraphs, no daguerrographs. Oh, who in the Lord's world want to know what they callt? All I know is Julius went to Paris, France, as a young man and came back besotted with this newfangled invention. Done built hisself a black room to fiddle around makin' em, an invited every wandering 'tographer on the road to the house to make more, talkin' bout they "art" all night long. But I found a path through them black-and-whites thinner than pastry dough, less supple than bark, more costly than lace, I say I found me a way to put some blood life back in the still of my children's eyes, they limbs caught in the air like dead folks shaped the way a fool wan to remember, with they smiles pained or pushed way past a lie. Oh, yes, Saints be praised, I can read some life into these pictures, make my family come back to life. Only funny thing bout it, they still coming back in black and white, that the only true thing bout em. Black n white. Niggahs n peckawoods. Enough to make me find some dark funny in all this. Can't get through my children's eyes. If you can't make your way through black and white in a heap of entanglement and haints, good and evil, always nearby to help us, or at least me, find my way through what all I done or what done come up with me. No matter.

Whoa! That's a tellin' one, this one with all them niggahs and white folks favorin' one nother. We relatives, but cain't tell nobody. All them fancy white women—they all cousins or aunts or some kin could be named for sure. The black one to the right in the muslin skirts, that's my Ma, but she paid for them skirts what was given to her by the white man, yes, the one in the center with authority like he God, he reignin' over the land. That's the world of a plantation, Sweet Tamarind, where this was took. My chirren there, too. His chirren, but cain't tell nobody (like you cain't tell by lookin'). Anyway, Ma she paid for all them slips and the lace by her wrists with plenty strap marks down her back. Some so raw the cloth stuck to her flesh where it turned inside out from the lash and the weft of the cloth liked to growed into her like she was a new kinda crop they playin' round with to see what's more productive. Well, you can see lookin' at her, lookin' at me and my young ones, we was sure nough productive. Shame. Shame on a man who is Grandpa and Pa to his own kith n kin. Then goin' to turn round an ignore em, like she wasn't his daughter cause she was dark like indigo, like the night quiet ringin' with sounds of water courtin' the winds, tree limbs rockin' niggahs to sleep or shakin' em wake if they gotta gal to visit fore sun-up. Keep tellin' myself ain't no sin in bearin' no child when there ain't no choice. And the Good Lord know, I got respect for the living and the dead. Cain't nobody come sayin' my babies ain't gotta right to live. Slave or free, they's the bounty of God. That makes em worth lovin' and lookin' after, whether you, Julius Mayfield, ever come to realize you wasn't the Almighty or not. My chirren deserved respect cause they alive. How could that be such a hard idea to get to? Even if we was jus' a pack of hounds. Folks love they dogs. I love my daughters. My ma loved me when she could, fore that witch Master Mayfield callt a wife most beat her to death and left her in her good dress bleedin' blue and no more a distraction to her than some dust on a table leg. Said she didn't notice no bleedin' negress nowhere. Couldn't recall any colored woman missin' that mornin' neither.

That's what threw my Pa, my lover, over the line, so he finally found some of himself in me and mine. That's why I saved this here picture of everybody. Cause everybody didn't last till the next harvest. That's a sad thing to say. It's a sad thing for me to remember, but it's the truth. Buried my ma and took her place for the next white man with black cloth over his head and flashes like bits of God's wrath come to capture our souls. Pa-lover said wasn't true, was darkie legend that souls end up in these here pictures. But if that's so, why am I cryin' now?

Gotta go on ahead and find myself somethin' else to do. Get tired visitin' the way back times, I do. Yet I cain't get to the nowadays less I go way back. Sides, I done enough for one woman in two or three lives of anybody. I guess I got me a right to set here and look at what I come from and what I beget to this world.

Now look at that stirrin' young gal! That ain't no show turkey vaudeville somebody. No. That ain't nobody's outside woman, either! That's me in my calico matchin' with my girls. Didn't mean to look over em so at first, just I surprised myself, so good-lookin' I forgot, anyway all three of those lil beauties is mine. Mayfields to the bone, I say. They all look so different I worry sometimes that a body might not put em all together as one. And that there hurts a woman's feelin's. I know. I seen folks peekin' to check if they all favor Julius Mayfield or not, or even if they favor me! I swear for glory I take for a wonderment a child God's done let out the heavens. Got no time to be creepin' bout the Devil's doorway, seein' if he been up to mischief or not. Besides, a Mayfield's a Mayfield however they turn out. Can spot em a mile away if you close to the right circle and got any idea of what blue-bloods is.

Look at how that rose from the sleeve of her dress bring out the red in Elma's lips, look to be painted but they not. I got me a mind to get me a brush or an embroidery needle so I can show all the colors them dresses bring out in my daughters' hair, they cheeks, even they eyes take on different kinds of lavender if they wearin' rose at dusk. There's always been more to my girls than black n white, else they faces wouldn't look chiseled like a Ethiop one day and flat like a Cherokee the next. They changin' constant, sorta how no one day come out jus' like some other day, but more like one day slips into another with a slower rhythm or a brighter sound to it. I live some muffled days now, when I barely hear anybody even when I listen close. Then I got days I could hear a stranger's dreams like they was my own. My girls are like that. One day Blanche the whitest niggah wench I ever set eyes on. Next day I find myself callin her "missie," cause I ain't sure if she French or Irish or whatever else kinda white done took to these parts. Now, Elma can look tawny, her eyes blue or purple dependin' on the time of day. And Juliet is a deep bronze with a set of veins all different colors pulsin', filled up with the spirit of her blood so she look like one of them twirlin' mirrors at the travelin' medicine show. But don't none of that matter cause I getta swellin' in my heart which is what the ol' folks say is truly a African heart if I hear any one

*of my chirren a-callin' for me. Ma, Mawmaw, Mama, I answer to every-
thin'. Girls gotta way of callin' for they mother let you know if they happy, in
trouble, in love, or foolin' with the haints or a wish they done felt crawl from
they toes to they mouth and out comes the call for me. Ma, Mawmaw,
Mama, and off I go without even turnin' my head round to see who might
be about. Slave or free, my girls got the best of me. If somebody don't like that
they can whup me later, if they dare. And sometimes, one of them evil niggahs or a white trash beyond they station might very well go on ahead and
do that very thing. All I got to say is nigh everythin' close to God can be beat
out a soul, but they cain't whip the Ma outcha. I know that.*

 *I'm just gonna sift through these here pictures a bit longer to see if any-
thing jumps out at me. Jesus knows my body's a vehicle for the Holy Ghost or
any other kind of somethin' we cain't actually see but can get right up on ya
and change your whole life. I never know what or when some creature from
the other side gonna need me to get somewhere or tell somebody somethin'.
That's why I keep those bottles hangin' round my porch, sometimes I want
just a little warnin' if a body from the other side or a African borned soul
needs to speak through me. Hard on a body to be in this world and the next
world, goin' back n forth at a stone's throw, like I ain't got enough to do. Oh,
I found me somethin' to be right proud of. Wish time didn't make sucha
brittleness in my bones and these here pictures. Life ain't like that, not really.
Well, got fits and starts, but memories don't break off at the edges, crack up
the middle leavin' scars where they weren't none. Pictures sure nough do
damage to a body's recollections, even though I could see how sometimes they
help me go back quicker to what's no more, yet close as breath. So, I guess
I'ma do my best to handle em more gentle. Cause this one right here got a
big markin' comin down Blanche's face, like a knife been took to her. My
chirren may have lived some full and dangerous lives, but that you cain't tell
by lookin'. Real seein' is a art, but like everythin' else you got to have a gift.
This is Blanche with her beloved Roswell Sr. A woman dressed in lace that
fine and coiffed just like somethin' from a New Orleans magazine don't have
no knife scar down her face. Look at my Blanche! Did so well for herself!
Though Roswell was a mite older than what I woulda picked, they's benefits
to taking up with a man what's settled. Got everybody in Charleston respec-
tin' the ground he walks on. There is somethin' could be said for that.*

 Oh my, cain't hide from the gaze of a sorrow-filled child. It shouldn't be but it is, my sweet Juliet with that Willie, Willie Chisolm to be exact. He didn't mean her no harm in the beginning, but the Lord's got a way of un-doin' deceit. I tried to tell my chile that, but she trusted in guile, not the truth. I know I couldn'ta laid up next to a man so all the time angry with me, hurt and wild with suspicions, while my lil one, Eudora, was there in the next room, never imagining her presence was like a venom nobody took the time to stop from poisoning . . . Oh, Juliet, however could you believe gainst the truth so much, or want the lie to be the truth so much, you'd write "Eudora is Happiness" neath that child's face. A Ma can set her eyes on only so much pain in her chirren, then comes time to do somethin' else. Leave em in the Lord's hands. Ask the ancestors for guidance. Tend to what I got cookin' in the kitchen. That works most of the time for me. Fussin' with my pots, turnin' down the fires.

Betty cupped her hand and swept a fistful of soil from Julius's grave into her purple satin pouch, tied it closed, and tucked it into her bosom. Then she slowly gathered up the pictures, inspecting them carefully to make sure nothing that didn't belong in there was there and wrapping the album back up in the cloth. With head held high she gazed at the headstone of Julius Mayfield, for whom she still held both an indignant passion and mightily felt connection. Then off she sauntered toward the shouts of her granddaughter, whom she had left shouting in the first place. Betty shook her head, chuckling about how a body could shout about the same thing with the same words for so long when it didn't bring an answer. Finally, Betty yelled back, "Heah I'ma comin'. Put your bonnet on. I'ma comin' to ya now."

* * *

"GOOD GRACIOUS, Nana! Where on the earth have you been? Don't you know we've got to get a move on or the ferry'll go right on without us? All this packing I've done, all this planning up to this very minute, and off you go without so much as a how-de-do." Eudora was vexed.

"Well, a body can't just up and leave without some good-byes here and there. A couple of thanks for years of friendship and such."

"Grandma, you didn't have time to go so far as to find a soul. Next folks downstream are more than an hour away, but judging by how you lookin' right now, maybe you did go crawlin' through the marsh to say a fare-thee-well to somebody. Don't know who. Don't know who'd receive you in a mess of briars and weeds as a bustle. Less you got a beau back up in them woods who don't know he's free yet."

"Young lady, mind your mouth first off. I got rights to go from hither to yon, if that's my choosin', and whatever kinda courtship I got goin' on is more than the one you ain't got goin' on anywhere."

Eudora smarted from her Nana's words, but pride pulled the pout of her lips back to her teeth, let the red blush fade fast enough for her to regain her composure. "Now, see here, Grandma, we've no call to taunt one another today. Why don't you make yourself presentable again. Then we'll be off to Charleston."

Betty pulled some of the red amaranth still tangled in her slips away from her comely but scarred legs. "I was lookin' just fine, and I wasn't tauntin' you. I was simply speakin' the truth. In the ol-timey days, a gal with your blessed health and keen smile'd be surrounded by young bucks hankering after a wife."

Eudora was losing her patience. "Nana, the ol-timey days, as you see fit to call them, were slavery days. And those young men, bucks as you choose to call them, weren't lookin' for a wife. They were lookin' for a good breeder. So they'd be more valuable to . . ."

"Julius Mayfield, that's who." Betty glanced at Eudora's frantic attempts to create order, seeing only a mass of confusion. "Can't bring yourself to say his name, I see. Well, huh, that surely tells me somethin'."

"And what might that be?" Eudora's anger was slipping out of her control. Her greatest desire at this moment was to pull her skin off and suck the Mayfield out of herself. Yet the best she could muster was to clamp her teeth like a hound on a niggah.

"You can't get very far, can't get nowhere, without takin' all your self. From the way you soundin' to me, looks like you plannin' on leaving your grandpa out of who you are. You telling me you some creature made outta smoke and mirrors? You best check yourself again, gal. If all this talk proves anything, proves you a Mayfield."

"Nana, please stop. They owned us. They owned us. That's not a family. It's . . . like harvestin' niggahs 'steada rice or cotton. Don't you see that, Grandma? We're some by-product of nights when decent white women would have not a thing to do with the likes of Julius Mayfield."

Before Eudora could get another word out, Betty grabbed a switch, took it to her granddaughter's cheeks, hands, any visible flesh. Thinkin' to finally break this girl of disrespect, living in a dream where folks was not folks just cause they allegedly belonged to somebody. *Don't a soul belong to nobody but God.* Betty knew that. She just been visitin' with her gods, her companions, the only family she knew about. The switch landed on Eudora more ferociously, but Eudora wouldn't give up insultin' her Nana. "Is this how he loved you, Nana, with the threat of the whip, a fist, being sent downriver? Am I here because you believed love and violence could sleep in the same bed?"

Betty raised the switch up once more. This time to teach this gal a lesson in respect, but somethin' held her hand back. She almost believed she felt Julius grab her wrist to stop her, sayin' *Enough is enough, my dusky love. Everthin' the chile says is not untrue.* Betty dropped the switch. Her eyes sought out the darkest corners of the room, not Eudora's eyes waitin' for her Nana to hold her. Too much'd been said, more razor-thin scars set to swellin' up. Betty's anger was spent. Her body seemed to shrivel right in front of Eudora, who reached for her grandma. A gesture of reconciliation, but Betty'd have none of it.

"Don't touch me, gal! I ain't got the strength to carry your misery away from what I love. Get yourself lookin' like somethin'. We can get on our way like you say, but you still takin' yourself and all this land, whatever come with it is in you, you takin' that to Charleston, too. All anybody'll have to do is look at you sideways and know you a Mayfield. You don't know you a loved one. You the only one don't know."

A diffident Eudora disappeared to tend to her wounds. Betty chuckled to herself. *That chile don't even know what a good beatin' is.*

* * *

LIJAH-LAH HANDLED his canoe like a woman's body he knew well. The weight of the Mayfield ladies' goods was a challenge, especially with Eudora all the time fidgeting this way and that, like her looking round would wind her in Charleston's harbor any sooner than the way folks always go, no faster than the breeze, no slower than the tide allowed. Lijah-Lah knew his waters from the Ashley to the Cooper rivers. His knowledge was formidable. Was born under the light of a different God, folks said.

Lijah-Lah came out his mammy praising the Infidel, but not the Devil. The Infidel made his mark on him and gave Lijah-Lah a firm hand on an oar, direction, and a quiet confidence that too many times nearly undid a white wanting to go someplace. Somehow Lijah-Lah could only understand where the whites wanted to go. After that he didn't respond to anything they went on about. Went back into his mother's spirit, they whispered, where the tongue of the Infidel had never been silenced, brought to praise the name of the Lord Jesus, Almighty, son of God and Savior of us all. No, Lijah-Lah was one of the last to know the other Holy Book. The one he read five times a day, prayed on and beseeched the souls of his ancestors to show him the true way. Lijah-Lah was, therefore, a man prone to long periods of introspection and meditations; the less he opened his mouth, the longer he would live to find his fate. There were only a few of his kind left, who didn't eat crab or pig's meat, who shied away from the jamborees likely to seduce every other river soul. Eudora found him peculiar, but Betty'd ride with no one else. Betty's reasoning was questionable, but consistent. "I like being in the company of those whose God protects em. Long as the oars in Lijah-Lah's hands I'ma get wherever I'm fixin' to be goin'."

Somehow, Eudora became the one who didn't speak or listen, least not to Betty and Lijah-Lah. Today, of all days, Eudora was full of voices in her head, smells of the marsh, the blackness of the water. If she could help it, she'd never come back here again so long as she lived. No matter the mystery of the whiteness of the lily pod, or was it truly white with its honey-colored center where its sweetness lay, in the sepia sway of the creek, rippled with shadows of ancient cypress, the surprise of silver moons winding toward the sun. Eudora felt herself part of all this, and that caused the auburn hair on her arms to stand on end. She was only from these islands, not of these patches of sand begging the salt marsh, rivulets, the rills, to let them join.

"Hey now! Hey!" swept through the air like the dance of dragonflies. Mama Sue-Sue 'long with all her kin were waving Betty and Lijah-Lah toward them. Eudora snapped, "Ignore them, just keep rowing."

"What you want I do, Mah Bette?" Lijah-Lah erased Eudora.

"I say we say good-bye to our neighbor folk, that's what I say." Betty almost got the canoe tipsy with her excitement.

"Mah Bette, please, let me get us there," replied Lijah-Lah. Betty had nothing to say to that. Her eyes, old as they were, wandered the glistening blue of Lijah-Lah's veins pulling the oars. Betty was enough of a woman to imagine Lijah-Lah pulling her toward him through the night, through sweat and weeping that blessed women are familiar with. Shaking her head, getting Lijah-Lah out of her bones, left Betty with nothing to concentrate on but Eudora, pouting so she competed with the Spanish moss, lips 'most dangling from her face.

"What on earth is on your mind, chile? We all set here to do what you got your heart set on and look at you. You look meaner than dirt."

"That's exactly what I'm talkin' bout, Nana. How're we going to have a new start if we carry all this back here with us? We don't have time to visit every soul you know on these islands if we want to get to Charleston at a decent hour. Brother Diggs and Blanche should be happy to see us, not come draggin' from their beds to greet their vagabond relatives."

"Speak for yourself, missy. Blanche presented her little blue-veined behind to me in the middle of the night. And she coming out backwards weren't no delight of mine either. I'm that girl's mother. The two of you may forget that, but God Almighty and I sure haven't."

"We most there, now. Mah Bette, don't worry yourself."

"Not me worrying, Lijah-Lah. It's this gal here thinks she can catch up to her future or outrun the past, I don't know which. Anyway Charleston's not going anywhere, and neither is Blanche, bless her poor shallow soul."

"Don't talk like that, Nana."

"Lijah-Lah, do you hear this, now my gran's gointa tell me I can't call upon the Lord for one of mine I know needs His help. Ain't that something?" Betty was amusing herself again with Eudora's anxiety, her fear of what to do with herself. They were doing just fine, the Lord saw to it. They were breathing. *What else that girl want?*

Long strokes and a few grits of his teeth, Lijah-Lah brought the overloaded canoe into Sue-Sue's landing. They made a number of other stops 'long the way to Charleston. Betty greeted her weaver friends, her basketmaking sisters, and the woodworkers who'd been kind enough over the years to fill her house with all manner of cypress and walnut furniture. Betty stopped to sanctify the kindness shown to her for so long. No matter what her children looked like, no matter who their pa was.

Eudora imagined herself in Brother Diggs's grand house in Charleston with Blanche, her aunt, to show her the finer way to live. To know the opera and the ballet that Charleston boasted before any other colonial center. Why, her Aunt Blanche was cultured, had escaped the sin of her birth, she thought. *All I have to do is refine my outside qualities and no one will ever know. They'll never know.* Not thinking, Eudora answered Sue-Sue's daughter, Maribel, in Gullah. She didn't even hear herself. The part of her that was the islands spoke at will, with ease. Eudora actually smiled every once in a while when they passed a tabby hut she recognized, but she'd never tell her Nana. *Nothin' rushes water but the water alone.* Eudora was no fool, simply a girl aching to feel dreams she could hold, that she could touch.

And there was a whole lot of holding of folks and plucking and beating of instruments every time Betty and Lijah-Lah stopped at a half-hidden old place set behind loping magnolia trees dressed in wax myrtle and nestled in circles of spartina and palmetto. The music'd get to going and Betty'd set to dancin' with young men and old, blue black and ivory, toothy or toothless, limbs whole or withered. The whole of the waterways knew something was up or over. The last of the Mayfield colored women was gettin' on away from here. The swamp sang 'long with the folk, and Eudora, still as she was, was singing because the choice was no longer hers. It was up to the growing things, the flying and biting creatures, now. Hurricane time come soon enough. Though brooding, Eudora knew she too was a force of nature like all the Mayfields. Time would come when the winds would sing her song.

✳ ✳ ✳

LIJAH-LAH WHISTLED to Max, the oyster man. Max, upon hearing, cocked his head and cooed back smiling to himself, knowing it was his friend Lijah-Lah even before he could see him. Through the darkness he made out three figures. By Gawd, one was Betty Mayfield, whose outline he knew as well as his own hand. So they were the cargo, the Mayfields. Max would be taking the last of the Mayfield clan from Tamarind to Charleston. No wonder Lijah-Lah had not mentioned who or what he wanted Max to carry. Betty Mayfield was leaving Tamarind!

On *Emilena,* the oyster man's bateau, the strange mixture of salt water and fresh gave the air Eudora huddled in a depth like a blanket everywhere she moved, stretched, arched her back. Max the oyster man was an industrious fellow, finding a way to make himself a bit more independent any old way he could. Folk talked bout that. Max was a bachelor, one past his prime, so what was he making a legacy for, who was to benefit from all his work beyond what had to be done? Max'd reply in his slow and sly way, never letting on whether he was joshing or no, "Can never tell who'll be in need, I looks at it this way." Betty knew Max most of her life and all of his, she wasn't surprised. If the Yankees could wipe clean the riches of planters, who knew what could disrupt a niggah's fortune? Best to have more. Wasn't nothing to be said about having enough.

Betty couldn't help herself. She started counting, picking out the green growing things she loved and might never see again. You could tell, she thought, almost exactly where you were by the growing things lacing your path, flirting with the tides, murmuring honest "forget-me-nots" to the bateau and her passengers. Betty wanted to share her good-byes with Eudora, but the child had decided to absent herself from her own life's turning-point, too full of tomorrow to pay homage to yesterday. Betty, missing conversation, decided to let her graying hair down out its braid. When she was through slowly unwinding the heavy mass rarely seen in public, never by menfolk, even Max, who paid women no mind at all, believing they didn't have any, was hankering to get his thick knobby fingers to running through that fine-looking old gal's head of hair. What nets he could design with the like of black and white strands Betty shook atop the water so they set the water lilies to dancing, got the wax myrtle giggling, the spartina and star marsh to putting on airs. Azaleas backed up gainst palmetto looking to mask themselves in the face of such wanton abundant growth. All this was goin' on, Betty smiling, feeling the energy from the river in the pit of her groin.

2

Blanche Mayfield Diggs was not pleased with the architect's new designs for her country home. She was so annoyed that she dropped the blueprints and had to call the girl for some smelling salts. She suddenly reminded herself of her mother, Betty, who all too often associated physical ailments with something gone asunder in life. This thought made Blanche Diggs even woozier. What else, what at all could she have in common with her mother?

The girl came running up the stairs to Blanche still pulling on the cord of dark violet. Maggie couldn't get the smelling salts close to Blanche quick enough. Blanche's mind and body flooded with a confusion of thoughts and feelings. Something terrible was going to happen to her or Roswell, one of the children. This was a sign. She knew sure as her mother. This was definitely a sign. Blanche shook her hand toward Maggie to pick up the blueprints. Then she indicated with some fingers to roll them up and lay them on her desk. Blanche loved that desk. It was very much the fashion, Oriental, with inlaid mother of pearl and gold trimming on the peacock's feathers. The wood—teak—brought up memories of the colors of those who'd peopled her childhood, comforting her, although of this she was unaware.

Just as she was managing to make her bedroom stop twirling about, leave Maggie with only one face, the peacocks no longer prancing, Blanche shook her head again. There was a great commotion coming from somewhere in her house. Loud voices, even peculiar smells. All this began to undo her composure. Now Blanche was becoming angry. She had no time to be losing her senses, lying about waiting for the world to come into focus. Maggie stood about waiting for God knows what else to happen, watching over her like she was some injured stray. Blanche took one deep breath. "Don't you think we ought to see what in heaven's name's taking place in this house, girl?"

"Yes, m'am," Maggie replied without moving.

"Oh, Maggie, sometimes . . ." Blanche muttered under her breath, pulling her skirts up to give herself room for a purposeful stride. "If I was the one who inherited your black behind, I'd disinherit you now. But Roswell, Roswell has obligations. Obligations. And as Roswell is obliged to keep you in service, so am I. So, am, I." Blanche turned suddenly, realizing Maggie was nowhere to be seen. "Maggie?" she screamed.

"M'am?" Maggie's head peeked from Blanche's doorway. Maggie knew to stay out of the way of Blanche's walking tirades.

"Let's go see what madness is overtaking the house you're to be keeping charge of, shall we?"

Blanche was red with rage. Who had the gall to inconvenience her? She was just now coming out of a spell. What on earth was that? What was wrong with Maggie? Even Blanche knew haints and spirits didn't come traipsing about in the daytime.

"Maggie, I said let's go."

"Yes, m'am." Maggie spurted with more liveliness. "That's right," the seasoned maid said under her breath, "I'm the one to keep order in this house. How could I forget that?"

Blanche was in a brisk yellow damask dress, her wasp waist natural and envied. Her skirts rustled with the determination of Napoleon's armies. Head high in the air, Blanche almost didn't see Maggie catching up to her going down the stairway. The two virtually flew down the last landing, but Blanche prevailed, presenting herself with grace and blazing blue eyes.

"Mama, Mama, Mama!" Benny and Francina ran toward her, forcing her to give up her stiff demeanor. "Mama, Mama, Mama, Mama, did Tobias come tell you? Did he? Did he?"

Blanche drew her children to her. Oh, how she loved them. Their faces were in a state of wonder and excitement. As if they'd been to the circus or Market Square with the island women telling them hocus-pocus tales while weaving their baskets and selling their wares of fruits and seafoods, all manner of whimsical concoctions. The children kept up the clamor until Blanche broke into laughter herself.

"Yes, I'm your mama, but I was your mama long before now. Are you telling me you are just now realizing who I am?"

"No, No. Mama, not you. Your mama. That's right, your mama is here. That means we've a Nana and a cousin."

"Mama, why didn't you tell us before?" Benny indignantly pulled at her arm.

"That's right, Benny," Francina chimed in. "Nanas are a precious lot." Blanche could hear her mother's voice tangled in the voices of her children. "Is that daughter number two I see?" This was not good, but Blanche was too caring a mother to simply push her children aside; they were not the problem.

"Oh, did I forget to mention my mother? Oh, I remember now. I thought you two were so smart that you knew, even I had to have a mama somewhere."

"Oh, Mama, I thought you never mentioned her because, well, because . . ." Francina's eyes started to water.

"She thought she was dead. And you missed her so much you never spoke of her, that's what," Benny said matter-of-factly.

"Yes, I thought so myself." The voice of her stepson Roswell Jr. hovered over her like a circle of vultures. Blanche had tried to love this boy, but his own mother never let go of him enough to leave room for her. Now, any closeness between them would be impossible. Nothing could shut Roswell Jr.'s mouth now. "Yes, I saw the whole thing myself. I can't wait to tell Father."

"Me, either," Francina blurted.

"Me, too," Benny echoed.

"Imagine a long-lost, taken-for-dead Nana appearing at the Diggs front door," marveled Roswell Jr.

"Who's that sayin' I'm dead when I'm right here on this earth?" Betty bellowed from the parlor, the French doors only serving to usher her indignation through the foyer where Blanche was trying very hard not to use some vigorously strong language directed to Roswell Jr.

The smartly tailored Roswell Jr. played affectionately with Francina's curls. "I saw the whole thing."

"What whole thing?" Blanche responded.

"Your children . . ."

"You mean, your brother and sister, don't you?"

"Why of course. Benny knows that's what I mean. Don't you, big fellow?" Benny nodded in eager agreement.

"My brother and little sister, here, were looking through the latticework of the library window because a strange carriage had pulled up to the front of the house with two women who were even stranger looking . . ."

Whatever else Roswell Jr. had to say, Blanche never heard. She'd already begun to trek to the parlor to see her mother and, maybe, her niece Eudora. But it could be anybody from out there on those islands. Could even be ones who still couldn't speak English and wore amulets and potions round their necks to ward off evil, disease, and such. Blanche began talking to herself. She lost sight of her children for just a few moments to ask, "How did they find this house? How could two creatures with no city ways find their way here?"

Following right behind her, Roswell whispered, "Well, she is your mother, Mama. And any fool could tell any other fool where the Diggs home is."

Roswell Jr. was enjoying himself so much. Blanche's azure eyes cut him into a thousand pieces, yet she restrained herself so she could greet her relatives. When Blanche entered the parlor, she didn't see her mother, Betty. She saw bags. Tied-together suitcases. Woven baskets with those godawful island patterns, jammed full of what apparently were all Betty's worldly possessions, her banjo atop, strung up with twine.

"Aw, Mother, what a surprise! And this must be Eudora!" Blanche feigned familiarity and happiness at the sight of the two who'd traveled so far.

"I ain't no surprise, gal. I'm your mama. And who else could that be but Eudora? You think I just run around the marsh lookin' for more responsibilities and gals with hard heads to raise? Do ya?"

Francina had never heard a soul speak to her mama like this before. She hid in her mother's skirts, but not for long. Uncharacteristically, Blanche yanked Francina to the fore. "Mother, this is your granddaughter, Francina. And, Francina, this is your cousin, Eudora."

"But she's so big, Mama!"

"Yes, she's almost a young lady, ready to go out on her own."

"What about me?" Benny whined.

"That's right, angel-baby, what about you?" Betty cooed. "C'mon right here to ya Nana." Betty opened her arms wide as love can, and Benny and Francina both fell laughing in her lap.

"Mother. You're their Grandmother, or Grandma. A nana is someone who works . . . well, is a servant."

"Are we not all servants of the Lord in this house?" Betty snapped.

"I'm Roswell Diggs Jr., Mrs. Mayfield. Welcome to our home for as long as you care to visit with us and the beautiful city of Charleston. We shall do our best to make your stay pleasurable."

The only thing Blanche could say to that and to Eudora's blank face was, "Francina, play something on the piano for your grandmother. Benny, get your violin."

Roswell saw an opportunity he hadn't expected. Eudora was a comely young woman with a hint of wild in her eyes. The way her shoulders sat easily on her muscular torso, so straight with pride, aroused him. "I apologize for my stepmother's neglect. I'm Roswell Diggs—"

"Yes, I heard, 'Junior.' You are very gracious, sir."

"You mustn't refer to me that way. I'm almost family."

"That's the truth and don't you two forget that." Betty raised her eyebrows and attempted to find a comfortable way to sit in Blanche's rigidly upholstered satin chaise. "Show some respect for these younguns. They are getting ready to perform for they Nana."

"Mother . . ." Blanche felt the need for the smelling salts again.

Roswell situated himself near Eudora while Francina and Benny displayed no talent at all. Betty carried on like she was at Black Patti's Minstrel Show. Francina was inspired now. She played every tune she knew and some she'd never seen before. Benny showed Betty how the marks on the staff corresponded to the notes they played.

"Leastways, my grans unnerstan they nothin' wrong with not knowin' somethin'. Just somethin' wrong when cain't nobody learn nothin' to a body."

Roswell, taking all this in, noticed that Blanche couldn't ground herself anywhere. She was like a loose buoy in her own parlor. "You know, Eudora, Mrs. Mayfield, my stepmother is so overwhelmed, she's forgotten to offer some sweet tea. Maggie, bring our family some tea and those delicious shortbread things with the raspberries that you make."

"I'd prefer coffee myself, black," Betty said.

"Then, coffee it shall be. Maggie, did you hear that?"

"Well, sir, Mr. Diggs Jr., I usually serve what Miss Blanche ask for?"

"That's all right, Maggie. Just bring something," Blanche said sharply.

"Yes, m'am."

"Why you got to speak to that gal like that, Blanche?"

"Mother, this is my house."

"How I'm goin' ta forget that, I'd like to know that now?"

"Nana, there's no need to be ornery with Mrs. Diggs." Eudora blushed and patted Betty's hand, heavy-veined as it was, delicate as she was.

"That ain't Mrs. Diggs, chile, that's Blanche."

In the corner of the parlor Roswell Jr. was about to split his sides. How could his stepmother have imagined she could escape what she was and where she came from. Some Geechee gal up outta the swamp. Then he recalled his face smarting from the palm of his father's hand. All he'd said was, "Papa, we used to own wenches like that." And his father's hand flew like an anvil through the Carolinian dusk.

"Those wenches, as you call them, were your cousins, aunts, and uncles. I slaved hard to buy them from the white folk. Are you a complete ingrate, a fool, or have I neglected some aspect of your upbringing, lil niggah?"

Maybe that was why the beautiful Blanche never shared her tenderness or lighthearted joy with him, only with her own children. She treated him like he was a white, really. Staying out of his way, saying only what had to be said. Roswell Jr. never stopped regretting that day. He'd wanted to call someone Mother. Now, how abruptly his wounded soul twisted that thought. He needed a Mammy, too. Maybe Blanche's mother would do.

"Let's go help Maggie bring Nana and Sistah Eudora some repast. What do you say to that?" Swiftly Roswell Jr. swept Francina and Benny to the pantry. Shouts of "Let's fix something for Nana" and "Sistah" curdled in Blanche's throat. Betty and Eudora began to relax. There was some family left in them, even if the instinct skipped Blanche and bloomed in the young ones, little Mayfields, whether they knew it or not.

Betty surveyed the white pine instead of the usual cypress used for the woodwork of the salon. Blanche's eyes never left her mother. Betty was unsettled by the pure lack of imagination and color in her daughter's home. Muted greens. Muted maroons. Muted and plain. "Those missionaries in the Freedmen's School taught you all everything but good taste, Blanche. You and this one here with me are still all muslin and gabardine, stiff white collars."

Francina ran in next to Maggie with a tray of scones and cucumber sandwiches. Blanche was tiring of this visit, of all she must remember not to say. Francina placed herself majestically at the gleaming piano. "And, now, Nana, I am going to play—"

"For heaven's sake, Francina, isn't there enough commotion going on already?" Blanche growled out of nowhere.

"I just wanted Nana—"

"Stop it. Stop it right now. You have no nana. You outgrew your nana. Nana is a woman who works for you, not your grandmother."

"But that's what the old lady asked me to call her."

"Young lady, I'd appreciate your referring to me with some respect in your voice," was Betty's stern counterpoint.

"Stay out of this, Mother."

"Now, who are you to tell me what to get into and what to stay out of? I birthed you and I'll be gall darned if you speak to me like I was what you think of as hired help."

Francina began to play Liszt as loudly as she could. Benny moved behind Roswell Jr. as if that might help him when the storm really riled itself. Eudora tried her best to keep her eyes on all the textures and fabrics of the room. Her grandmother was wrong about Blanche. There was a great deal of thought, delicacy, reflected in the décor Blanche created. Eudora also kept her eyes anywhere she could to avoid Roswell Jr., who was seeking any connection with her that he could make in polite society.

"I tell you, I won't have this, Mother. I will not stand for this under my own roof."

Perhaps auspiciously, Roswell Diggs Sr. entered the room he usually considered his refuge, now asunder with voices raised, cutting glances, suitors with nowhere to go, an angry Francina banging out something on the piano, Blanche on the verge of apoplexy, and two strangely dressed island women, as best he could make out.

"Is there anything I can do to calm this tumult?" Roswell Sr. jauntily interrupted. The piano quieted. Blanche breathed. Betty smiled. Eudora's eyes searched Roswell Sr.'s face for solace. Benny stepped to the side of his father. Betty extended her hand to her son-in-law. "Maybe you can make some sense of all of this, Roswell, bein' you the man of the house and all." She sweetly awaited her son-in-law's greeting.

"I know who's come calling now. And I know why the house is just about to come undone, as well." Walking toward his in-laws, Roswell Sr. leaned over to peck Betty on the cheek, caress her wizened hand, while raising Eudora's chin gently toward his that he might see what sort of young woman she'd become.

"Oh, Mother Betty, the two of you look splendid. There's something to be said for what the island air does for a woman's complexion, no matter what her age," he smiled.

Blanche groped for a sitting chair. The divan was filled with her mother, her niece, and peculiar woven baskets of all shapes and sizes. But at least her husband brought some peace to what had been verging on the Battle of Bull Run with bustles. What was she to do now? Surely her mother and that, that Eudora didn't plan to stay with her, in her house, with her beloved, cultured children, and her husband, surely the most prominent of Negro gentlemen in Charleston, an undertaker of high repute. Maybe she could put them in the country house. That was it. Her mother could cook for the workmen while Eudora would tidy up behind them. The country house was the answer. *Then nothing and no one in Charleston would associate Blanche Diggs with these hellified Geechees. Nobody.*

"Why, Roswell dear, I've an idea you simply won't believe."

"I doubt that, Blanche, but go ahead on."

"Since Mother and Eudora have come to Charleston to stay...I think that's right. Isn't it, Mother?"

Betty sucked her teeth, slowly moved her eyes from Blanche to Roswell.

She knew where the power lay in this house, and it wasn't on her daughter's lap.

"Well, Eudora, you are planning to visit here in Charleston, aren't you?"

"Not to visit, Aunty Blanche, I've come to stay, to make Charleston my home."

"Oh."

"Yes, Blanche?" Roswell Sr. gently prodded.

"It's the country house."

Finally, Roswell Jr. was able to hold Eudora's attention long enough for her to know that the country house was not a feasible notion. Between the two was some intense connection sealed only by the glance of an eye that Eudora startled herself by grasping. Roswell Jr. suavely moved closer to Eudora as Blanche virtually shrieked, "Yes, the right wing is finished. Truly it is, my dear."

"But, Blanche honey, there's nobody out there but a rough enough work crew, if I do say so myself. The country house isn't fit for living yet. If it were, we'd be lingering on the veranda this very moment."

Unswerved, even more determined, Blanche paced the parlor in a regal manner, lacking only a crown. "Well, I know Mother isn't prepared in any way for this coming social season. At the country house, she and Eudora can accustom themselves to our ways of doing things. This is a different experience for them, is it not? Roswell, do you understand what I'm saying?"

"But, Blanche, we've plenty of room right here—"

"Yes, darling, I know, but Mother has always been so independent, and Eudora is herself a grown woman."

"For sake of the Lord Almighty, would you please stop talking bout me like I was somewhere else, Blanche!" Betty said crossly. "We're comin' from the country. We don't want to go to some other part of the country. How would that make any sense?"

Eudora tried with everything she could muster to address her aunt Blanche, so forlorn and lifeless, but her eyes darted immediately to young Roswell Jr., whose eyes were waiting to meet hers.

"Yes, I'm plannin' to open a dress shop that will cater to all the best families in the whole of Charleston, in all South Carolina one day, maybe!"

Eudora was captured by her own vision. She saw tens upon tens of the best of society in fashions by Eudora.

Her brief version of her own success was cut short, but sweetly, by Roswell Jr.'s remark, "That's very enterprising of you, Eudora."

Francina, who was doing her best to comfort her mother as if to protect her from some unknown malady, innocently queried, "Mama, did you know people from the islands, those Geechee people, even knew the best families in Charleston?"

Blanche vaguely nodded her head.

"Eudora, do you know the best white ones or the best colored ones? Wouldn't it be a scandal if a white lady and a colored lady of distinction both showed up somewhere in the same fashion by Eudora?"

The younger Mayfields and Diggses enjoyed Francina's naivety, but Betty was not so charmed.

"First of all, missie, you can't always tell the colored women of distinction from high-class white ladies."

Blanche came to life to protect her child. "That's enough, Mother."

"I tend to agree with my wife, Mother Betty. Let's reserve this conversation for the adults in the family."

With focused indignation Betty retorted, "That's exactly who and what I'm talkin' bout. Family. There's nary a soul in the Low Country isn't familiar with Julius Mayfield, his property and his kinfolk. Now, a Mayfield, a chile, you can tell by lookin'. Any of em. A body just know a Mayfield, colored or white, when they walk through the door. From here to northern Georgia Julius Mayfield's influence, his seed, is sown—"

"Mother, please . . ." Blanche pleaded.

"The chile got a right to know who she is, daughter!"

"Oh, Nana, oops, Grandmother. Ma Dear, how is that, Mama?"

Blanche didn't respond.

"I know very well who I am. Francina Juliet Mayfield Diggs. Oh my, that means folks can tell who I am when I walk in the door! Right, Grandma?"

Blanche was furious, the Diggses a mite contrite to say the least, but none dared actually break the bond between Betty and her granddaughter, especially since she'd spoken nothing but the truth.

Then came the inevitable confoundment Blanche had been seeking all her life to avoid. Francina turned to Betty, Eudora, Roswell Sr., Roswell Jr., and Benny, surveying them closely. "Why don't we ever visit the white Mayfields then, Mama?"

When the question was met with silence and peculiar looks, Francina wondered why Mother Betty didn't go to the white Mayfields first, since she knew them so well. Then she shook her auburn hair about her shoulders as if acknowledging the inescapable Black Codes her family went out of the way to ignore, so much so she actually forgot. Blanche was exceedingly protective, to a point of danger to Roswell Jr.'s mind. He saw his half-sister's self-recrimination as evidence of his opinion, which held no sway with Blanche, and sauntered out of the room.

"Maggie, bring me a strong cognac that will go down smoothly, dear heart," said Roswell Jr. "Francina, Benny, why don't you come with me and help Maggie?"

A momentarily grateful Blanche chimed in, "Yes, children, it's past your naptime. Go help Maggie, then off to bed."

The young dandy exited with the children, their banter the last words anyone could hear. Blanche's face was so scarlet with anger or shame, or both, that Roswell Sr. took to conversing again.

"Although I'm only a Mayfield by marriage," Roswell Sr. went on, meaning to bring some jocularity back into his home, "I've a mind to extend myself as a Diggs and suggest that we might find the industrious Eudora and her Nana—if I may, Miss Betty—a set of very nice rooms where we could look out for you without being troublesome to you. How much were you planning on spending on lodging? There are a number of fine boardinghouses with impeccable reputations very near my businesses."

Eudora didn't have the gall to say she was planning on staying with the Diggses, not near them. Blanche was only a mite less beside herself, sensing her relative's disappointment.

"I hadn't a notion in my mind to pay for my lodgings or this child's at all." Betty rose and spoke with the volatility only Geechee women can muster in a hundredth of a second, least that's what folks said. Roswell Sr. cleared his throat, rang for Maggie, and walked closer to Betty, all at the same time. His eyes did not glance at Blanche. He could at last give himself credit. He knew his wife. This had to be stopped. "I could cer-

tainly advance you both some funds, no interest or other encumber-
ments, to facilitate your stay. Please don't misread me. I am truly offering
to be of service to you both. We've seen so little of you since Elma and
Juliet . . . Well, you understand, Miss Betty?"

Before Betty could get a word out of her mouth, Blanche rose as if
possessed by the spirit of an experienced auctioneer. "Oh, Mother would
never take money from a soul, Roswell, you know that. And the idea that
two independent Mayfields would need looking after is absolutely absurd. I do believe that modest flat we own near Shinnecock will suit the
two of them just fine. Room for sewing."

"For designing, Aunt Blanche," Eudora jumped in.

"Yes, designing, sewing, and living. A full enough day for two well-
brought-up Mayfields, if I do say so myself."

Roswell Sr. scratched the back of his neck, which was getting quite
hot under the collar.

"To my best recollection, 'twas I brought you up, missie."

"Mother, please! You know very well what I meant, mean . . ."

"Yes, Blanche, I'm afraid I do."

"You certainly could do worse here in Charleston, Miss Betty. I'm
very familiar with many of the families down that way." Roswell Sr. attempted to quell the storm looming in his well-appointed parlor.

"I don't mean to disappoint you, either of you, Roswell, but we came
here to live, not to be buried. You know folks down Mexico way. I know
what you call that neighborhood you're trying to push us toward, Mexico.
Well, you may make a living burying them for a song and a hog's head,
but Eudora and I have set our sights high. Higher maybe than you could
imagine. Seeing all Blanche can conjure up for a future is her own Low
Country plantation."

"Mother, stop it. Right this minute. We are trying our best to help
you both."

"I guess it's a good thing, then. First lesson I learned is that family
don't mean nothin' to you, Blanche, less we come with a silver spoon
attached to our tongues like those Ubangis white folks always gaping at
round Carnival. That's all right, Blanche. I ain't one to beg, and I won't
allow Eudora to grovel at the feet of her own mama's sister—"

"Why, I never . . ." Eudora protested.

"Stop engagin' with these folks, people, relatives, whatever Blanche calls herself these days. Let's get a move on. C'mon. I know you can hear me talkin' to you. Let's get goin' to our quarters. Slavery ain't killt me, for sho some colored high yellars won't."

"I'll get one of the hearses to carry along your luggage. Send a boy right this second to a Miss Aurelia, keeps a fine establishment down Mexico way," Roswell Sr. added, ignoring the rancor his wife had precipitated. If only she weren't so beautiful, so much like spun glass, he'd have been done with her long ago. But such was not the case. Blanche's whimsical as well as her diabolical notions were made real with a simple nod of her husband's regal head. She'd succeeded again, even though it was against every instinct in his bones to turn away family. Roswell could not bring himself to defy Blanche about her own.

Nursing the last of his cognac, Roswell Jr. re-entered the parlor, assaying the various states of shame, anger, embarrassment, and shock that had overtaken his relatives and his relatives once removed. If he were the patriarch, how different the welcome for the comely and imaginative Eudora would have been, how both the town home and the country estate would have warmed with her presence, her knowledge of the way of the common folks, and the magic his stepmother clumsily took to be below her station. One day all this would be his, God willing. Then maybe he might make amends for this crude and insulting reception. For now, there was little he could do but be of service in a quiet fashion, assisting the pair who'd need a man, even if a man like him or perhaps especially a man like him, down Shinnecock way, Mexico they liked to call it, bringing attention to the throngs of miscegenated abandoned population that was truly the essence of Charleston, the rough underside that supported the likes of the Diggses and many more of their ilk.

Settling his tongue round a fresh swig of warmed cognac, Roswell Jr. gently moved toward Eudora, offered his hand to Miss Betty: "I'll have my carriage ready for you two lovely ladies in the front momentarily. Maggie, call Tobias to fetch my carriage. We've a short journey ahead, Mother Blanche. Did you realize how truly near Mexico is? Why, there's no doubt that Miss Betty and Eudora will rarely be out of my sight. Certainly not out of my mind. Your well-being is my primary concern."

"Well, I never . . ." Blanche began, but then turned to her mother. "Mother, Eudora, I'm not feeling terribly well, if you'll excuse me. I'm going to check on the children and be off to my bed."

"She's not even going to let me say good-bye to my own grandchirren?"

"I'll see to it that you see so much of them, Mother Betty, you'll be beggin' for Maggie to relieve you," Roswell Sr. assured his mother-in-law. "Rooted in graciousness were many," as his own mother, Euialla, was accustomed to saying, Roswell mused. There were ways around his wife's obsessions. Roswell Diggs would keep his promise. Betty Mayfield would see her grandchildren as often as lovingly possible.

With great kissing and hugging of the two gentlemen of the house, Eudora and Betty were on their way with Roswell Jr.

"Young man, I want to thank you. I'd have walked to Mexico with these old feet rather than travel in the last riding place of the dead."

"I understand completely, Mother Betty. Besides, I couldn't see anything auspicious for Eudora's new enterprise ridin' in the car with the dead."

"Bless you, boy. I didn't know there was any colored left in your house."

"Well, Mother Betty, it's not so much left in the house as it is in me and the children, if we tend to them carefully."

Eudora's eyes scurried from her Sunday best shoes to Roswell's face, back and forth, back and forth, till she was almost dizzy. What kind of a Negro man was this?

"Tobias, what kind of scenic route are you taking us on? I want these ladies settled in before dusk. Get a move on, boy! Or you'll be sorrier than a she-bitch left in the rain."

Now Eudora was truly confused. Betty, on the other hand, was relieved. Folks who didn't reveal their shadow side early on could be dangerous. Now all the danger'd been smote down from the Diggs side. Now their new life was free, free of the malice that had been thrown in their path, attempts to shame them, to tear asunder that which was deigned by God. All that was gone.

Betty relaxed in the velvet corner of the Diggs carriage. Regal as it was, there was a stench they'd soon be rid of. Betty wasn't even studying young Roswell's interest in her Eudora. *Nothin' gon come of that. She-bitches left in the rain, huh?* Betty had a plenty of concoction to put a pounding on thoughts like that. Pound evil into the ground she would, whatever deal the Devil offered.

"Eudora, would you mind if I checked in on you tomorrow? To make sure all your needs are being met?"

"Why, certainly, cousin Roswell."

"You know we're not really kin, Eudora, not really."

"You know better than to be sweet-talkin' this chile after a day like today, young Mr. Diggs. I take it the tumult's gone to your head."

"Maybe you're right, Mother Betty. I'll give you both—"

"I know I'm right. We're in the Lord's hands now, son. You cain't do a thing bout that."

3

THE DIGGS CARRIAGE PULLED UP TO 32 ROSE TREE LANE. Eudora knew because Tobias announced it. "Thirty-two Rose Tree Lane, Mr. Roswell, sir."

And with a false sense of pleasure, Roswell Jr. smiled at his traveling companions for what seemed to be a mighty long time. Saying nothing, simply staring into space, Roswell Jr. apparently didn't hear Tobias ask if they were at the correct address. Eudora pulled at Betty's sleeve, telegraphing with each urgent tug. *Somebody must say or do something. The carriage can't simply stop in the middle of the street.* The whole of the street being the middle of the street, the lane hardly a street at all, more a thoroughfare for street peddlers, fancy women, men too beautiful and black to be husband material, children who sprouted from the cobblestones like wild mushrooms. How could there be an address here? There was no room for an address, a home. The narrow streets were crowded and dense, oozing heat like a sugar refinery.

The people of Lil Mexico were simmering with the spirit of get or get got, now's the time or never; the people of Mexico challenged a half-dozen rainbows, their raiment and languages scampering the horizon so bright, laced with Africa, Cuba, Georgia, and sweat, not telling exactly the origins of nobody, but revealing the bounty of the gods at every turn, even when the Devil was at work. It was true that Geechee women walked, if you could call that switch with an accent to each buttock a walk, with razors in the sides of their mouths, the gaiety and fervor of their speech mystifying. The singular definition of the men's muscles among the throngs of masons and day laborers bustling bout the Diggs carriage was humbling. Wasn't that these Charlestonians were blatantly different from the villagers Betty and Eudora had known all their lives, was the fact that they valued their beauty. Out on the islands white folk were just an oddity, nobody to revere and obey with awe. Here in Charleston, their foibles, passions, flaws, and meanness were too familiar to sustain an image of majesty. In the presence of the irrational, the people of Mexico found it necessary to hoist themselves into a realm of deeper color, denser implacability, more convoluted conventions and habits than the whites could keep track of. This way everyone was sure who everybody was, except of course in the borderline case of families brought high or low by bloodlines out of their control like the Mayfields and the Diggses.

Yet it was clear that Roswell Jr. knew his way around and about the folks of Mexico quite well. Any number of Magdalenes and Carmens flaunted themselves before him as he helped Eudora and Miss Betty out of the coach. Tobias seemed more ill-at-ease than young Diggs, who called everyone by their first name and asked and knew everyone's trade, or at least what was publicly accepted as their profession.

Literally putting his best foot forward, Roswell Jr. guided his charges up the none too stable stairs of the fairly dingy second-story flat at 32 Rose Tree Lane as if he were guiding two temperamental fillies back from a close quarter-mile race. Betty kept moving his hand off her arm. "You cain't hide me from nothin' I ain't seen before."

Eudora, trying not to let on how nervous she was, corrected, "Haven't seen, not ain't seen, Nana."

"Well, I seen it all then! How you feel bout that?"

Roswell nodded to Tobias to go back to the carriage. He had everything in hand now.

"You know, if you'd like, I can take it upon myself to place you two in a neighborhood more, huh, suited to your liking..." Roswell didn't look at the pale splintering wallpaper, nor the peculiarly warped window frames. He was unconsciously dusting his shoes, which had distributed a sediment of reddish gray that he found fascinating.

"I like it here just fine. Needs a bit a fixin', a lot of cleanin', is all. Right, Eudora?"

Eudora's disappointment showed in her body, no longer spry and eager, but in the process of erasing itself, falling into her own shadow. "If you'll excuse us now, cousin Roswell, we've a lot of work to do here, if I'm ever to become the most talked-about dressmaker in Charleston. Which I do intend to be. Oh, look at that, Roswell . . ." She ran to the largest window, and using the palm of her hand and her skirt, she wiped the pane. The sunset sky relaxed wantonly before their eyes. "Oh, no, we won't be moving from here for a while. You must thank your father sincerely for affording us these lodgings and such an exciting little area. Inspiration everywhere I turn! Right, Nana?"

"Oh, Lawd, yes, plenty of that."

"Yes, I'm sure that's true, but I could find you—"

"That's quite all right, Roswell. You must take me seriously when I speak. I'm not some Geechee gal with nothin' but Gullah and chicken feathers fallin' from me. You have been more than gracious, in fact exceedingly so. And I, uh, both Nana and I, appreciate your thoughtfulness. But the Diggses didn't invite us to Charleston. As far as I can tell, my mother's own sister never gave us a thought. Believe me, I am takin' to my heart all that you, who aren't even blood, least not my blood, have done. But we are not thinkin', in the least, of burdenin' you and yours with our problems. We really do thank you very much."

Although her voice began to crack, Eudora's eyes glistened with determination. Roswell wanted to hold her, out of tenderness and respect, but the ferocity of her vision left him only time to bid them a short farewell.

Once they were alone, Eudora's face wrestled with a cascade of tears she let flow freely. With her fingers she drew emblems for her line of clothes in the dust on the windows, emblems just like the magazines from the Continent, emblems just like the ones Betty made in front of the small house back home to keep evil spirits away.

Betty didn't feel a need to tend after Eudora right that moment. She was too busy hanging dried sage and eucalyptus in the corners of their quarters. "Won't no haints be comfortable up in here with us, I can say that." Eudora said not a thing. The only sounds from the Mayfield women's lodgings were the swish of brooms, the rustle of the sea.

* * *

EUDORA'D FALLEN into dream early and deep, but Betty'd kept on with the business of ridding the flat of unknown, possible errant spirits and restless souls. She sprinkled fresh spring water in every corner, left thick cigar smoke in the backs of closets, used a potion of her protection cleanser to do the floor, and left white flowers with something of her mother's or her aunt's behind every door. Just as she was beginning to tire, her gnarled arms aching, Betty heard, no she didn't hear, her body felt the rhythm of the streets. She got to twitchin' and hummin' until she had no desire to resist anymore. All her spells an magic'd been placed before midnight. She was free to join the celebrations that come with the black of night, the call of those whose true work was to make music out of nothing but the gusts of their small bedeviled lives.

Before she knew it men white enough to be her pa, others black enough to be her grands before that, mingling with no thought about the implications of their bonding ritual, were singing beneath her very windows. Betty stuck her head from the window and listened carefully as they haphazardly introduced themselves. The fellow sporting a black patch over his left eye was Rufus; Big Mingo wore a spotted red and white stevedore shirt and Lil Mingus a black and white one; Black Tad was tattooed from wrist to elbow; and Beau Jim was all his name proclaimed, bronze bones set like a statue you see in a picture. Deke, the scruffy young bootblack, tagged along, a brush in his hand, cleats on his shoes. Their singing reminded her of the islands, and she couldn't help but join in. The strings tinkled the breeze and egged on those who thought they'd heard it all.

Then her voice rang out with a crystal soprano taunting the wind and the surf to curve or twist her melodies. She didn't know anybody, but she knew everybody. She'd never heard the song, but she could sing it:

> "When it rain five days an de skies turned dark as night,
> When it rain five days an de skies turned dark as night,
> Then trouble taken place in the lowland that night,

I woke up this morning, cain't even get outa mah doah,
I woke up this morning, cain't even get outa mah doah,
Make a po gal wonder where she e're gon go,

O-o-o-oom, I cain't move no mo,
O-o-o-oom, I cain't move no mo,
There ain no place fo dis po ol gal to go."

Betty lost sight of Rufus, Big Mingo, Lil Mingo, Black Tad, Beau Jim, and Lil Deke, who had wandered on as she fingered her banjo, remembering the first time she'd held one, grabbed one from somebody. She was fighting off a heavy lostness, a wounded heart that came nowhere near the hellation she'd brought down on herself.

Before the banjo, her master and lover, Julius Mayfield, spent hours of flamingo golden dusks with her and their girls, Blanche and Elma, on the veranda of the house he had built just for her and her girls. "This house is like the ones I've seen in New Orleans, Betty. See, this wrought-iron design allows the breezes to cool you in the terrible summer heat, but these shutters, straight from France, close in the winter to warm you." Julius kept the black fiddlers up into the night playing waltzes and polkas. The hidden lovers danced through the night until Julius would notice the children, huddled on a maroon and gold chaise lounge, heads on each other's laps, legs akimbo in their lace stockings, shoes still a mystery to all but Fancy, the hunting hound Julius bade protect this, his other, family.

Other nights, her children safely tucked away on beds facing the rising sun, Betty fled to join the others like her yearning for a union with the wind and the drum, the fiddle and the bosom, stroking the night breezes in the tumult of a juba. Calves and arms flying, eagerly rushing to the spirits that they might ride to the other side, be strengthened and ride again. In the midst of this, Betty's arms flung by her torso every fourth beat, her back undulating until her heels almost touched her head. She knew a freedom beyond emancipation, or the Gates of Heaven. Somehow, a heat other than that of her own sweat and breath overtook her body. Not that she lost her step with the others dancing, or that the magnolia-accented night was any less dusky.

Then two other arms, two other legs caught her shadow in motion and would not release her, shade or soul. In some manner Betty's never been able to recall, only to revisit by touch and smell, she wound up in the pulsing veins, she'd say, the seed blue black, of the fresh one, she called him. Salt air still seeping from his skin. Just arrived here from Guine, she'd say. All she callt him was the fresh one or the Guine man, as if you'd recognize him from the wistful smile on her face. A face that blossomed as her womb began to grow the size of yellow watermelon, a fresh one from Guine, she'd think, patting her tummy.

Julius Mayfield caressed the bulging belly of his favored negress as well, imagining another one of his beautiful girls. At delivery time, come all the singing and clapping and whispering of the women, and the men, music off to itself, Betty carried a deep bronze child to the cradle by her bed with her master, Julius, who nearly crushed the child's skull when he threw the cradle over with his booted foot. "Takin' up with darkies, after all I've given you, black bitch!" His wrath willing Betty's frail body against the walls, under his feet, caught by his closed fist. Bloodied and not believing, Betty guided her two girls with her outstretched hands, the infant screaming in eerie harmony with her sister's cries for a return to peace. Instinctively Betty swept the baby into a sling over her back. Betty's back, bloodied now by Julius's whip and blows, served as a cushion for the infant trying to find her mother's breast. The sweetness of blood, thicker than that of mother's milk, came at a higher price as well. Betty stilled her pace for a moment, catching each blow as if on purpose. Julius's anger grew more furious as she refused to run from him.

Then suddenly, without Betty uttering a word, he fell weeping to his knees. "Oh, my darlin', I . . . I . . ." and he groped the air as if reaching for her. Betty did not move. Julius moved toward her still on his knees, dropping the whip and softening his hands that had beaten Betty like falling boulders. She did not look at him, but ran her hands through his hair when his body grew close to hers. She felt more tears welling up in her eyes. Julius Mayfield continued to cry, but could not bring himself to apologize. She heard a whimpering that was none of her children. She stepped outside to be soothed by the evening. Oaks and moss hung over her like death. The whimpering kept on. She walked toward the pens. Not even Fancy, his favorite hound, had escaped Julius Mayfield that night.

Lijah-Lah, then a young man, along with Pretty and Sabina, the weavers, helped her round the quarters, to an empty shack where she could raise all her children like any of the others on Sweet Tamarind. In a way, Betty was relieved. Now she could be an ordinary laundress, with ordinary pickanninies who looked like whoever anybody wanted to think they looked like. There were no china plates or silks from Calais, but Betty found an old beat-up banjo in the corner of her new home. She tuned it best she knew how, so it fit her feelings, she'd say. She played alone while her children slept, the laundress hands drawing beauty from those strings; at least that had not been taken from her command. Into the night, the sleeping families of the quarters were serenaded by Betty's melancholy tunes. Those too restless to sleep were comforted by them. Betty couldn't really hear what she played. She felt the strings vibrate 'neath her fingers and knew how rich her song, how sad sometimes, made Fancy howl.

> When it rain five days an de skies turned dark as night,
> When it rain five days an de skies turned dark as night,
> Then trouble taken place in the lowland that night.

Betty perked up from her sorrowful thoughts. Her new singing friends had meandered back her way. This time she was determined to shake the misery off her. She opened the window wide and sang as though she were one of the men, a coterie by the wharfs she felt in her soul. She grabbed her banjo and tickled the strings as if she'd always been a member of this band of seaside crooners. Lil Mingo waved for her to come on down and join them. It didn't take Betty but a second to get down to the street, banjo, tambourine, and all. Rufus picked up his fiddle. And Black Tad had garnered himself an accordion, albeit a small one. Three little urchins had found their way to the center of the group and were busy doing a jig when Betty pulled up her skirts and joined them for a while. When she felt herself tuckered out she threw her tambourine to Lil Deke, who could slap the daylights out of it. Smiles graced all the faces of this motley band as they wandered the streets and alleys of Mexico. Beau Jim turned out to have a voice like an Irish tenor and shared the upper registers with Betty, who was having a grand time her first night in

Charleston. The islands seemed to loosen their hold on her now. The quiet too much, too early. This new life of night music and dance was much more to her liking. No memories, no regrets, only joy, music, her daughters, and the sea.

Betty's fingers weren't nearly so spry now, nor lovely to look upon, but she held her own with the jackleg band by the wharf, that banjo still letting go of what she could not say or didn't know she wanted to say. *"Keepin' up with livin'! Music is just another way of keepin' up with livin'. Cain't find nothin' wrong with that.* Go on now, Lil Deke. Show me a thing or two. That's right! Let it go. Let all that's in ya come right on out. That's a way! That's a way. I say, come on, boys. Don't let the child scare us, now!"

4 🖋

*E*UDORA *MEANS HAPPINESS.* BUT IT WAS SORROW THAT clung to her heart. As Dora examined her new home, she felt it, the sorrow—an extra pump, a shade, a haint of longing. Smatterings of dialogue crowded out her thoughts. *Waxpaper. Grease stains. Why we come here?* Snatches of phrases melded with fragmented images of her new lodgings. *Daughter of Mah Bette's black chil'.* Dust. Duster. Mustee. Runaway. Her head bowed, she examined the room's loose uneven floorboards. A soot-drenched mouse ran along the corners of the tight close room. Things had not gone as planned. Dora stomped her foot. The startled intruder shot straight in the air and flew through the crack from which it came. "What done you expect? A reception?" Her face flushed, tinting its copper hue a rich red sienna. Instantly aware of her own deepened color, she bristled at the pervasiveness of the Codes—the legacy of slavery that judged her by the proximity to whiteness in fractions of sixty-fourths, the habitual practice, designed to increase the bounty of human livestock, now the source of standards to rank respectability. "Associate goodness wid good hair, proper wid property. Just cus I don't own nothin' don't mean I don't have nothin'. Or won't still!"

Blanche was her mother Juliet's sister, nearest in birth. Eudora had hoped, thought, she might find something of Juliet in her aunt's face, a smile, a smell. Instead, the porcelain mask was beautiful, smiling, and cold. "Your uncle I'm sure has found you a nice place in town. Roswell Jr. will show you."

Blanche's saccharine words now slashed across her cheek like a spring willow switch shorn of leaves. *Nice? Fuh who?* Gray dust coated the pine wood slats posing as walls; a few mismatched dishes sat atop a single crooked shelf. Beneath the propped-up boards posing for a table—a warped wooden bucket for slop and a rusty tin tub not big enough for a squat. Dora's full broad lips compressed into a thin straight line of rage. "Treatin' me like a common lowland lowlife. Seen bettuh in a sharecrop tabby shack. How could I be so stupid as tuh 'spect a welcome from my so-called fam'ly?" Words from her aunt and uncle's overheard chatter ricocheted in her brain. "Showed up in a basket. Mayn't even be a Mayfield. You wouldn't take her for one, 'cept for those eyes. True beauties, true Mayfields they are, for sure."

"True Mayfields. As if it t'were sumpin to be proud of. If that be true, I glad I not one!" The broken Gullah patois Dora had tried so hard to dispel rattled in her brain. *Mah Bette . . . tink cus she dark-eyed and tawny, she warn't his chile. She wanna believe that he love her, that him kindly, good and noble Massah Mayfield. That him only sell off she mama cuz she wild and not cuz he—"Him husbin to me eben when I slave," she say. When he try to mess wid she own daughters, you tink she'd see den? Twice-over shamed, she no want to. That why Juliet—that why they all gone from her. Then here I come, the shame lookin' em right in the eyes. Eyes dey call beauties. Got dey nerve. Call em true.* Those eyes, equally a source of wonder and derision, glowered at their current circumstance. Two half-moons of tears collected but refused to fall. "Place lookin' like this?" The cramped two-room flat closed in about her. Memory burned through her back, a taut steel strap of muscles. Mah Bette's oft-whispered stories, curling through the spires of smoke from a cob pipe, crackled in her ears, but Dora refused to hear them. "No! We make a new life. These eyes, they doan look back."

Each of Bette's daughters—Elma and Blanche, then Juliet—had left Sweet Tamarind, never to return. Mah Bette, whose silken strands circled her face like sea waves at dawn, kept a lock from each of the children born to her, stiff ash blond, auburn, and black-purple curls kept in a sack between her breasts. The old woman had made it all sound like music, a romance, made it seem that each daughter had been running toward something and not away from it. She painted Dora the prodigal grandchild, drawn back with a past scrawled on a scrap of paper. Swaddled in a bundle of rags, she had been carried back in an old fruit basket. A small yellowed picture of a mother and child was pinned to the corner of a tiny quilt wrap, dirty and singed at the corner. A note was attached to the basket handle in an uneven but bold script, *Eudora means happiness.*

"Sent back wid a huckster peddlin' pans," Mah Bette would tell her. "A white man walked up the way wid a carpetbag in one hand and a peach basket in th'other. Lijah-Lah brung him up from the way. I didn't believe you was no gran'baby of mine, till you opened them eyes. Like two pieces of sky, two little bits of heaven, changin' color with the wind," Bette mused. "My girl was lost, but you come back to me." Dora could almost hear the clanking of miscellaneous pots as her bearer ambled up the stone-strewn path to Mah Bette's tabby shack. Dora swayed, still hearing the syncopated stroke of pirogue oars against the low white-capped top currents of tidewater, where Lijah-Lah kept his small craft idling. The remembered sound calmed her. She missed the island already. *How stupid!*

* * *

"HOW STUPID! Dora May!" The refrain danced in her head as she winced at the streak of pain across her palm. At the Normal School, the sisters had often slapped her. "How stupid! You can do better," one would say, while the other wagged her head in agreement. The sisters, missionary teachers, had come to the parish after the soldiers and stayed. Miss Highgate was a colored lady from Niagara Falls, "A slight admixture of negro blood in my veins." The other, Miss Stubbins, had been an abolitionist, her zeal now transformed into a passion to uplift, to make righteous citizens of the slave population in one generation, "Bring them from the edges of savagery to the threshold of civilization in one mighty stroke, just as we have toppled the Confederacy!"

Shakers, they called themselves. Dora thought this was because of the way they shook the children who did not behave or perform to their standards. Or for the way they smacked their hands with the flat of the ruler.

Or used the pointer as a whipping stick. Or the way the children would shake when the two women walked down the aisles of wood-crate desks each Friday, with fists balled up, ready to pound an unsuspecting youth in the soft part of the spine between the shoulders. Each Friday, Eudora would huddle in her seat, her back hunched, trying desperately not to tremble. They took special interest in her.

"Child of sin threefold, they say."

"Odd colors to mark her."

"But clever. Bright."

"Maybe she's a Shaker, too."

Eudora Mayfield, or Dora May as she was known then, had been one of fifty parish children who had crowded into the barren main room of what had been the overseer's cottage. O'Brien had been killed on the stoop where he had attempted to hold his ground, defending his right to possibility as a white man. It was the children's habit to spit on the stain of blood where he had fallen. Barefoot and already wearing hardship on their faces, the children and grandchildren of Sweet Tamarind slaves had come in all ages. On that first day when the sisters opened the newly hewn door of the shack and stood, their two hands clasped, the setting orange of the afternoon sun aglow behind them, seven hundred and two prospective pupils gathered, their silence heavy with expectation. By the time Dora May strode in, book learning had lost to the fields and the necessity of extra hands to meet the growing crop liens that bound most families as tightly as a trader's knot. That or the wanderin', the lure of freedom's illusive call, drawing folks away from the island toward destinies unknown.

Dora had the same wild, nappy head tamed into plaits as the other Geechee children on the island, but she was distinguished by her unusual colors, the surprise encounter of genes that made her eyes the shifting hues of sky in a face the ruddy color of Sea Island topsoil.

They called her a Mustee and, in the hierarchy of colors from when the chain of Low Country manor houses had required a maintenance corps of servants, she would have been assigned the task of duster. The system had long broken down, had not recovered from the war, but the terms remained. Duster, meaning second-tier house slave, too dark to be a lady's maid, but bright enough to clean the banister. She resented the word, but not the placement. "Anything but field hand." She loathed putting her hands in the dirt, even, to Mah Bette's dismay, tending the old woman's small garden. Still, the girl was industrious and clever. She could make things and sell them at a fine price. When Lijah-Lah loaded up his catch of fish for the mainland market, Dora could be counted on to add some new bit of ambition. SWEET TAMARIND WILD HONEY, JARRED AND LABELED, TEN CENTS. STRAW MATS WITH PICNIC BASKET, BEST OFFER.

She preferred the potential peril of bees or the eyestrain from the intricate weaving of palm baskets and mats to laboring on the land, but neither enterprise held her attention like needlework. What began as small mending jobs and neighborly favors—a rag-doll, a hem, an alteration— soon became her primary industry. After she mended the itinerant preacher's frock so the stitches couldn't be seen and fashioned Miss Emma's daughter a true wedding dress, with a delicate eyelet making the calico look like lace, word spread. Taking note of her creativity and industry, the sisters taught her to use their Eldridge B sewing machine. It was a petite model, barely six inches across, and it was already twenty years old, but with its spidery filigree legs and floral decorations, it was a wonder to Dora every time she used it, the hand crank and feed occupying every muscle and all of her concentration. She would often work until the light failed. The sisters would find her hunched over, squinting, racing with the setting sun.

Her ambition followed the path of her shoes. She had a bold, sure walk. Whether on the island's brambled forest paths or the wet sand at low tide, she always wore shoes. She wandered the island, bartering her skill. Along with jars of honey she soon didn't have to gather herself, baskets, jams, clay pipes, tortoiseshell combs and buttons—all made their way across the stretch of sea to the city and returned as coins that she secreted away. The heavy imprint of her gait belied her size but befitted her purpose.

She and O'Brien's half-caste boy were the only children on Sweet Tamarind with shoes. Oversized and old, scuffed and run-down in the heels, hers had "belonged to one of the little misses." Mah Bette had given them to her, bestowed them upon her as if part of some pirate's trove. "Weren't hardly worn." Though the pointed toe squeezed her foot, which always slid down to the front, Dora wore them with a confused pride of inheritance. She had grown into the shoes, had mended them many times. Sealing the soles with tree sap and stitching the instep with heavy thread, she replaced the tie-string with twine coated in wax, a small cowrie on the ends.

Soon she wore them only on Sundays. Now she had even put them behind her. With her sewing handiwork Dora had earned enough to buy her own. "A decent pair of work shoes." Ordered from the Sears Roebuck catalogue, they arrived in a box wrapped and addressed. "To: Miss Dora May. To The Care Of: St. Simon's Island. Parish Normal School. Sweet Tamarind, S. C."

She had hesitated when placing the order. What name to use? May-field? Certainly not Field. Chisholm, maybe, for that after-the-war wanderer, the fiddler who swept my mama up in a dance? What name? When the package arrived she stared at the label. "May. Hope that don't sound too familiar." May, the month my mama run away, May, the first month after the fall, the first month after the war, the first month of freedom. New life. *I think it'll do juss fine. When I get me a huzbin, I'll make it the middle,* she thought to herself as she sniffed her new shoes and folded back the stiff, new tongues to try them on. They were brown and solid shoes with real laces and the smell of new leather and glue and they bore no history except the one that she would make. "Yes, May. Dora May."

"Real freedom must be earned," the sisters said. "Must be deserved."

"The way to freedom is to uplift!" Alas, these shoes also pinched her toes. Still, they pointed her in new directions.

✳ ✳ ✳

"MIND, GAL! Cain't sweep under ma feet. Gimme chance to move. Might take that broom and beat you wid it. I said, move way from hyeah!" Dora moved about the cabin in a frenzy of sweeping motions. Dirt specks danced in the air around them. Reading Dora's humiliation in her doggedness, Bette sucked her teeth. "My daughter Blanche think mighty much of herself. I 'member when I walked away from better than that!"

"Oh, please don't start! I doan wanna hear nun uh yuh stories!"

"You bettuh look see who you think you talkin' at, gal. I put my fist down your troat, I will, you gib me mo uh dat soss."

Dora never liked to display anger. She feared that if she let loose of it, the feeling would consume her, that fire would fly from her mouth if she spoke. How could she be mad at the woman who had cared for her and raised her, taken her in? She watched Mah Bette from the corners of her eyes. Alternately gloating or moping, the old woman mechanically fluffed the bed tick made of straw and settled in. To Dora, more like "settled fuh." Mah Bette sat heavily on the cot's edge and primed her pipe. Dora could see that her grandmother was winded. *Mo from sweepin fuh haints n fuh dust.*

Through the narrow curls of tobacco smoke, Mah Bette watched her granddaughter with bemused eyes. Dora wilted under the elder's silent, cryptic assessment. She pulled off her headrag to wipe her face and snatched up her bonnet. "I goin' for a walk."

"Suit yourself, city gal. Bring back some saltfish and a sense of humor while you at it."

* * *

LIFE IS in front of me, not behind. A good walk always helped Dora to think. She emerged from the small flat into the warm salt air of Charleston. As she followed the trail of day workers, noise assaulted her from every direction.

"Seconds!"

"Got brooms!"

"Pee-eEECHezEHsuh!"

"Porgy walk. Porgy talk. Porgy go wid uh knife an fork."

The crowd's movement gave her direction. The narrow, short, dusty streets of Charleston Neck gave way to the busy thoroughfare of King Street and Market, two blocks from the harbor. On the island, she could walk for hours with only bullfrogs and rice birds for company. Here in Charleston, the mixing of whites and colored on the street startled her. Eudora was used to seeing one or two people at a time, and—except for Miss Stubbins, the storekeeper, and the yearly census taker—all of them colored. In Charleston, the races mingled in swarms and waves. Careful never to touch, coloreds stepped off the sidewalk without losing stride. Watching the delicate reel, Dora felt clumsy and unsure, her head light from hunger and agitation.

A cacophony of market smells—saltfish and earthen yams, fresh berries and woodsy cane strips, encircling currents of musk, talc, and plump tobacco leaves—mingled with wafts of dank harbor water. A quartet of turkey buzzards, hovering over a feast of cast-off produce and horse dung, flung their gullets and rattled their wings at her. As she backed away, a centaur on a broomstick with goggles on his eyes, white silk scarf flapping round his neck, careened toward her. The young man blew furiously into the high-pitched whistle clamped between his teeth and honked the shiny goose horn on the handles. Dora froze. The bicycle zigzagged around her, throwing the rider into the squawking crew of scavenging birds. "Dumb country bitch! I oughta smack you upside yo haid!" Dora hesitated, not knowing whether to assist the young white man or run. She backed away and rounded the corner onto an even wider boulevard, where, clanging its bell, bellowing smoke, and spitting sparks from the rails, the King Street trolley screeched to a halt right at the tip of her newly bought shoes.

Her wobbly knees stepped to the side of the tracks, her shaking hand holding her country hat. A tiny bootblack, made to shine from tallow and sweat, dancing for pennies from passersby, set his workbox down and began to circle her, the metal bottle caps in his shoes in heated conversation with the wooden planks of the sidewalk. He mirrored her consternation with trembling hands and eyes popped wide, then turned in a pirouette and doffed his hat in flirtation, his sparkling eyes two black marbles of delight and mischief. The ebony cupid courting the pretty bronze lady in a swoon—a circle of pink speckled faces formed and bombarded them with laughter. As magically as he had appeared, the boy spun away from her and tapped his way around the perimeter of their audience, who tossed bright coins into his cap. He turned to her, preparing to go another round. A serious furrow formed across Dora's brow, a low-hanging cloud above her eyes. She hurried away as fast as she could. He followed her in pantomime, flexing the muscles in his buttocks to mimic the flapping bustle of her skirt, the crowd's laughter trailing.

No, things had not gone as planned. Rays of heat rose up from the cobblestones, and the white sky seared her eyes. The tall brick buildings loomed like tombstones, but Dora May refused defeat. "This is Charleston," she told herself. "Act as if ye have faith! Bound to be a few things of surprise. Take it in stride is all. If you never go back, you can only go forward." In honor of Miss Highgate's geography lesson, she bought a peach and placed it in her purse for later, repeating to herself, "The world is in reach of my fingertips." Her confidence restored by the memory of her teacher, she lifted her chin and continued her walk, now a journey of discovery.

She turned onto King Street, the city's main thoroughfare, and its row upon row of stores, each with unique signs, names, and merchandise— M. Lazarus Furnishings, Kerrison's Haberdashery, Land's Fine Linens— strings of kerosene lamps, suspended on invisible wire, arched across the boulevard, fine white ladies all equipped with parasols to shield their faces from the sun. At the corner of Ashmead, she stopped under the awning and attempted to adjust the brim of her bonnet to shield more of her face. Glancing to the side, she was startled, then fascinated by her own reflection in the display window. She had never seen herself, her full self. She had always felt herself to be large. Her shoulders were too broad for Miss Highgate's old Butterick patterns. She routinely had to widen the neckline, lengthen the sleeves, and trim the waist. Bloomers, too, were too short in the seam. Even her hat never fit, but sat atop her abundant hair like a teacup on a saucer. She was shocked to discover that she was not as large as she thought, not large at all nor as tall. Only then did she notice the golden letters of invitation painted on the glass across the street. FALK AND BENTSCHNER, HOUSE OF FABRICS. SILKS. WOOLENS. LINENS. COTTONS. VELVETS. MEN'S SUITING. BEADED LACES. EVERY IMAGINABLE FABRIC LACE AND TRIMMING FOR THE ENTIRE BRIDAL PARTY. SHOP AT HOME SERVICE, INCLUDING CUSTOM LABOR.

Dora had bought shoes from Sears and Roebuck, and so she felt that she knew about such things. But here was cloth come already on the bolt, towers of it, and thread already on the spindle. Colors, textures, and patterns she had never imagined. "I will inquire on employment," she said to herself with the stiff language of someone trying to be proper.

This time adjusting for the trolleys, wagons, pushcarts, and people, she strode boldly toward the entrance, only to be assaulted once again. Inside, a young white woman dressed in fine afternoon clothes was sitting in front of a delicate wasp-shaped machine mounted on a rosewood table fine enough to serve tea. The woman gently tapped her foot on an iron floor pedal between the curved cherrywood legs as if she were listening to music. Only the sound wasn't music, but the whir of a sewing machine powered by a small cylindrical electric motor attached to the side. Dora watched in disbelief and amazement as the woman stitched the seam of two pieces of thick brocade together in seconds, then held the fabric up to the window. The simple running stitch was straight and firm and fast. Then the woman held up two yard-length squares of heavy brocade and, after adjusting the knobs on the machine, aligned the fabric swatches beneath the machine's feeder pedal. To Dora's amazement the material seemed to move itself, needing only gentle guidance from the model's hand. Again, the task was done in a flash and the stitch, a different stitch this time, was clean and solid. Such tasks with Miss Stubbins's hand-me-down, hand-crank Eldridge B would have taken Dora a quarter of an hour. She had seen pictures of electric sewing machines, but until that moment she had no idea of their speed. Her mind a whirl of new possibilities, Dora floated through the brass-framed doors and reached over the tabletop to touch the instrument's gold embossed letters. Singer. *Ah, I could sing with this. I could make me a fortune!*

"Git yo hanz offuh dat." The store clerk had a tight nose and thin, withered lips that bespoke a natural parsimony.

"It says here, 'Purchase Plans Available.' What do that mean?"

"Nothin' for the likes of you. That's for white ladies. Where is yo' Miss?!"

"I have no Miss. I am a dressmaker."

"Not in here you ain't. Git yo uppity ass outta here fo I call somebody. And leave out the back!"

Enraged, humiliated, and dejected, Dora flew toward what she presumed was the back of the store. Not knowing which way to go or whom she now dared to ask, she spun in a slow circle of bewilderment, fighting with her tears, holding on to her hat. The screech of a chicken hawk, its talons bared to attack, dropped her to her knees. Still shielding her face and hair with her palms, she realized she was not in the woods or gathering eggs in the henhouse. The sound was not a hawk, but the grate of metal curtain rings. Dora had stumbled into the women's changing rooms. "You, gal, is you the fittuh?"

* * *

NOT GOOD *for a young colored gal to be goin' about by herself in the city. Some of dese young'uns could be my son, waggin' they tongues out the sides of they mouths at me.* Those would not do. Out among the peddlers and street singers, Mah Bette had been sizing up young men she considered appropriate matches for her Dora. Bette thought her granddaughter not bad to look at, but shy of knowin' it or showin' it. Not good for a young woman to stay single too long, be too ambitious. *My grandgal need a protector.* Bette quickly dismissed the smart-lipped, arrogant ones, yellow or brown made no mind to her. Then as she was making her way down the avenue, she saw uh upright, Dogon-Guine man for sho. *Got a buckboard, no ring on he finger, and respectable from the way folks call out.* That was the one. *Fuh now.*

Betty waved her hand ever so feebly in the air toward him and smiled meekly. She still had Oshun's power to draw the light of a man's eye with her own. "Good mornin', Mauma, surely there's somethin' I can do fuh you this beautiful, blessed day to match the sunshine of your smile." His dark chocolate skin flushed maroon when he smiled, revealing a perfect set of evenly spaced, strong white teeth.

Healthy, good bones, strong blood, ambitious. *Eyelashes so thick a gal could sit on em.* Betty could think of a few things he could do, but she voiced only one. "My granddaughter done slipped out of my sight. Went fuh a walk she say, got no idea where. Surely you musta seen her. No young man in his right mind coulda missed her. She a restless sort. We just got ch'here and now she done run off. I seen her goin' thataway."

"Toward the harbor most likely. S'where I'm headed. You wanna ride alongside, we'll find her." He jumped down and, extending his hand, helped her climb aboard the seat behind his. She liked him even more. "Right this way, Miz . . ."

"Mayfield," Mah Bette answered proudly.

"Look out now, I got royalty in my carriage! Make way, I got a Mayfield ridin'! There be a statue, a park, even a street named Mayfield, but this the first time I met a person by that name." Everyone in the Carolinas knew the name Mayfield, one of the oldest planter families in the state, but if this young man had a mind to treat her like royalty, she had no intention of dispelling the notion. She had been as much a wife as a wife could be to Julius Mayfield. That is how she understood herself. Mistress of the house, more than the white woman who called herself such. Julius Mayfield had chosen her, loved her, taken her and taken her back again. Wasn't cuz of no land or property—was a man made her his own.

"You so gracious, Mr. Winrow."

"How you know my name?"

"This old lady know a few things. I been watchin' you 'fore I spoke. I like how you do. It's hard these days to come across a nice gentleman of color like yourself, Mr. Winrow."

"Mister, I like the way that sound, but please call me Win, Mauma. Everyone do." Mah Bette became excited for Dora. She was anxious that her young charge show some interest in cohabiting. *Not dry up like those old Sesesh biddies, or choose wrongly like my girls. This one got some prospects. Strong bloodline, his. Oh yes, but humble. Still, wish he had a horse 'stead of a mule.*

When the buckboard turned onto Calhoun Street, Bette leaned over Win's shoulder and pointed to her granddaughter. When the wagon pulled up alongside her, Dora couldn't even see it. "Oh, chile, you sho nuf got too much on your hands this day. What is all this? Did you steal somethin'?"

Her arms ladened with uneven bolts of material, hat skewed to one side, one lock of hair sticking out like a spear, sweat streaming down the sides of her face, Dora had a mind to spit out something she would regret, so she held her tongue along with her parcels and temper. In reality, she was grateful to see her grandmother appear with a rescuer in tow. She could never figure how Bette always knew, how she would just mysteriously show up when she was needed. At that moment, Dora didn't much care. She was relieved to unburden herself and to reclaim her wardrobe and hair from disorder. What she did not like was the liveryman her grandmother had so obviously procured for her review. "No, no, gal. Sit up front wid me. Let yo Nana hab room to rest huh legs." *Callin' me a gal, axin' me to sit up front like I'm 'posed to be wid he. She ain't my Nana, she Mah Bette. Miss Bette to you!*

Dora soon realized that the driver had asked her to sit up front not to be forward but so he could collect other passengers along the route. Laundresses, day maids, doormen, and waiters on their way back to the Neckbone piled into the back of the buckboard. The pain in her head listed from side to side each time the wagon halted. The bootblack who had accosted her ran beside the wagon in his bare feet, his hardscrabble shoes flying by their laces over his shoulder. The fruit-monger who had sold her a peach hopped aboard. *The world at your fingertips. First month of freedom.* She pulled the peach from her purse. It had browned and bruised from her travails. She pulled back the skin and listlessly sucked on the warm sweet pulp.

An ancient indigo woman hailed the driver, her hand outstretched in supplication. Dora watched her approach the wagon with an off-balanced gait, syncopated stress on the right foot, the other one dragging beside, short quick glances over her shoulder, a tick of the jaw. "Whoa! Aunt Sibby! How you doin' tuhday, Aunt Sibby?" He jumped from the carriage and turned to Dora in one move. "Scuse me, m'am, but you got to ride to the back now. Aunt Sibby always git up front when she be ridin', much obliged."

The old woman smiled without parting her lips. Her wide, wizened eyes meeting Dora's gaze. Water-filled eyes, yellowed from too much memory. *Where you been, what you leff, Aunt Sibby? Bent bowed legs and shoulders hunched over. Jubilee come too late. Not goin' to be like that. I'm tryin' to move forward. Life is in front of me, not behind.* Dora slid to the driver's side and stepped down as the man steadied the old woman, whose high youthful voice surprised her, "Ebenin, Win, how's my luck today?"

"It's always good, Aunt Sibby, when you wid me. Got to be." With firm forearms, Win lifted up the petite woman and gingerly placed her on the seat. Before Win could assist her, Dora squeezed a spot in the back of the wagon next to the bootblack, who was swinging his dusty feet over the sideboard. The boy doffed his bowler hat. Holding tightly to her purse, Dora rode primly alongside, her feet involuntarily dangling next to his. He looked hungrily at her half-eaten peach. She gave it to him. He devoured it in one mouthful, his cheek bulging, then smiled at her with the pit between his teeth. *Aunt Sibby. Sabina . . .*

* * *

SABINA CALLED her an old soul, "Kin see it in she eyes. Done set she mine fo she got dere. Doan lea' much room fo change it." And Pretty, smiling through her purple gums in a speech impossible for all but the intimate to understand, "Cose, dat may mean she mayin git whenrother ony dream."

Almost every day coming to or from the Normal School, Dora circumnavigated the graying columns of wisteria to stop by the Weavers. Aunt Sabina and her daughter Pretty, the oldest family at Tamarind, had been given the name Weaver by the Union census takers. "I'm a weaver," Aunt Sabina had said, and what she did became who she was. In the hierarchy of Tamarind artisans, their weatherworn shack, the weaving house, was the middle ground between manor and field. It became a favorite place for Dora. She felt safe and welcome in the weaving house. The posts missing from the banister, leaning against the side of the house, clapboard shutters askew, the crooked chimney, all felt familiar.

The old women took more kindly to Dora than other former captives of Tamarind. 'Most everyone had a grudging respect for her grandmother, for Mah Bette's ability to read dreams and, on occasion, fix one's future. "She have a gift," they would say. "Only God choose upon whom it be bestowed." They didn't care much for the grandchild, though. "Left behind colored offspring." When Dora passed through what was still the quarters she sensed, in unspoken glances and stares, the curious knowledge of her family's past. *Reminder of times ebbody sooner forget.* Sometimes, though, Sabina's recollections as a young girl told her things.

Sabina had been a girl when the gin came to the islands. "That djinn, it the Devil. It come out the groun', spittin fire, make men crazy. Wid power. An yoah Great Gran'mama, that ol silly gal Monday, say, Maas say this here thin' gonna change the world. Maas say this here maa-chine gonna do alla work of a hunnerd slave. Maas say dis and Maas say dat. Maas say dis here thin' make my job easy as pie although I spec it ain't no pie Maas hisself be eatin. Maas say this here djinn gonna let him plow out de norf pasture and do the souf pasture and eben buy up dat swamp lan'. He eben sent dat ol lazy no-count brothuh uh his to Miss'sippi see bout mo lan'. Maas say, No mo rice! No mo indigo! No mo stompin' in dat swamp neck deep or stirrin' dem pots till yo han turn blue. From now on, eb'ting gon be diff'ent."

Overnight, it seemed, the arcane Sea Island culture, the grand barons of the South with their archipelago of great estates that unfurled along the ocean's edge, had been overthrown. Julius Mayfield, who through the partial humanity of his slaves constitutionally had the voting power of seven hundred men, now found he had to share that power with back-woods up-country hooligans, second sons, indentured servants, trappers and rogues, who ventured west by the throngs, seeking and making their fortunes in the formerly Choctaw-Creek territories of Mississippi and Alabama. The small cadre of men who had for years controlled the destiny of their state and most of the nation found themselves outdone by an invention, drummed up by a Yankee, no less! Some say stolen from a slave. Within ten years, the undulating, fulvous fields of rice and the steaming kettles of indigo, the scarlet blossoms of long-haired cotton, so bright as to seem silver, all gave way to acre after acre of the tight, speckled, scruffy breed, shorthair. The cotton that would be the new king was the scrappy kind. Wild like a weed, the new upland cotton could be culled in sand or delta or dirt. Prematurely sensing the approaching death of a ruling class, speculators appeared like buzzards. What was one to do with an over-abundance of labor and a shrinking market demand for one's product? What was one to do when there was simultaneously a demand for slave labor in the territories, a demand which could not be met, because the international trade had been outlawed?

To supplement his cash crop losses, Julius Mayfield, master of Sweet Tamarind, looked to his livestock to restore his profit and began experimenting with breeding. "Massa come roun' us up, made us strip all our clothes off, eben our head tie. An then thew us inna barn an lock the doah. Next spring, hyeah come sixty baby. Pretty made that way. Yuh granmama, Mah Bette, too. He do dat ebry harvest or so till he die inna war. Sometime he and he gentlemen frins git up on innere, galavantin', the bunch of em."

Though Sabina did not know her own age, she knew her daughter to be seventy-two because it had been written in the manor book, along with the birth of those sixty babies, and the sale of twenty of them. Pretty, it was noted, was Sabina's youngest, her twenty-second, twelfth born live. At the war's end, while others left, Sabina had stayed waiting for the return of her children, the sight of them, any of them. Pretty tended her.

Dora envied the life that mother and daughter shared—the warm sounds and scents of the two-storied, leaning shack, lifetimes humming in the spinning wheels, the steamy mixture of salt air and vinegar in the dyeing room. On occasion they allowed her to hold the paddle-stick and stir the simmering cast-iron pots, then hang the heavy hanks of thread on the thick ropes stretched between the house and neighboring trees. Drying in the sun, the tangled coils of yarn formed a muted rainbow of henna, purple, indigo, and evergreen.

The women took turns wrapping Dora's hair, twining each tuft to make it grow. While Bette fought to comb Dora's head by pulling and yanking, twisting and cussing, Sabina and Pretty carded it gently with tortoiseshell combs and arranged it in intricate patterned plaits, the light and dark interplay between scalp and hair part of its charm. Folks said they had the growin' hands. By the time Dora came of age, they had coaxed some length from her hair to match its thickness. Washing day she pranced around, the lioness!

This would not do for the parish school. The sisters insisted that her hair be pulled, slicked, and pressed down tight. "Anything but those pickaninny tie-strings!" they told her. There were new things to be learned. There were all kinds of new mechanisms to tame that wooly mess atop her head. "Magazines. Catalogues. Fine grooming," Miss Highgate would rail as her fingers flit through the years-old *Harper's Bazaar*s, whose pages she had taped so assiduously at the binding to keep them from flying about the room. "Good manners are the tools that we need. We are not mere brutes to pick, hoe, scrub, and clean! We must free our people from the burden and expectation put upon them by slavery! And it starts with those tie-strings!"

Mah Bette hadn't fancied Dora going by the Weavers' any more than she had approved her attending the parish school. "All them coals and fire. One misstep, pot turn ovuh an you ruin all you got. Don't nobody want no scarred-up heiffuh." All three Sweet Tamarind women bore the signs. Bette, who had done her time over steaming vats of lye soap, had keloid welts on her arms and neck from where the scalding water had splashed her. Sabina's hands were gnarled and twisted like the dry husk of a cotton boll. Miss Pretty was missing three fingers. Dora thought this was also from a weaving mishap. The women did not say, but Sabina herself had maimed her daughter to keep her near. An infant with a mangled hand would not sell.

They passed within days of each other, mother and daughter. One had prepared the body of the other, dressed in simple homespun with rosewater and a garland, a bright copper penny on her tongue. The other lay on a floor pallet of straw, curled upon herself as if sleeping. Dora arrived at the tin-roofed porch to find the wailing women who always appeared when someone died. She flew up the steps, but Bette caught her at the door. "Mother outlib even her baby chile. Gwon to find her again, Ah speck."

Dora made matching coverlets of damask, double woven and ornamented with intertwining hearts. She placed the quilted squares over their frail birdlike forms and silently watched as they were sealed in separate pine coffins. She took some hanks of their colorful thread, a few calabash buttons, and placed them in her Sears Roebuck shoebox next to the photograph of her mother, Juliet.

The sisters, too, had moved away. The school, which was never well off, got worse as the few Northern dollars upon which the teachers depended shifted to the cause of suffrage. The children did their addition and subtraction lessons in boxes of pressed dirt and strained ink from pokeberry juice and blanched sheets of newsprint for papers. Bible pages frayed, as did tempers.

Dora had thought to become a missionary teacher herself, and she looked to the sisters for encouragement, but Miss Stubbins, packing the books of Botany and Greek which she had never used, retreated into tight-lipped obstinacy, while Miss Highgate had responded to an advertisement. "Bride? What a waste of time," Miss Stubbins fumed. "While you were writing some lovestruck cowpoke, I have knit five pair of stockings. What age did you tell him you were? Thank God, we've given you the means to an honest living, Dora. Marry late, or better, not at all. Never depend upon anyone."

Such declarations would send Miss Highgate into a frenzy of tears. "Oh, you are heartless."

"And you are deranged. What do they call it? Brain fever? Illiterate sod-farmer. Does he know you're a colored woman? 'A slight admixture in my blood,' indeed." Miss Stubbins said she would return. "When I have found a more suitable and dependable companion and when we have achieved our needs as women, as equals."

Mah Bette simply folded her arms and watched from the comfortable distance of plantation talk. "Both of um need a good poke. Got neither chick nor child. Ain't natural."

"They work hard in devotion to our people, Mah Bette."

"What yuh say? I sittin' round inna rockin' chair? What they teach yuh, eh? Sewing with that Yankee cloth, cookin' with that store-bought flour? That old long-toof white one, try she carry fitty pound rice on she head stead of some book, she fold up into dust on duh ground. And dat colored gal, think she so somebody, somebody pozed to wait on huh. What she know?"

"Writing and arithmetic, the Lord's Prayer and the Ten Commandments, to start."

"Uh-hum. Don't you start wid me."

Dora ignored her grandmother's ill-temper and made parting gifts for her teachers. Miss Stubbins was easy—a traveling bag of brocade. For Miss Highgate Eudora could not think of an appropriate offering. Miss Highgate had taught her the first letters of the alphabet, the rotation of the earth on its axis with a peach perched on the tips of her fingers. "Think of it, Dora May. Columbus discovering a world and never to realize what world it was! Our fate is in the hands of the Almighty. But He has given us free will to shape it in accordance with His law. We must be forever fearless to discover what wonders He has in store. There is a world beyond this island and it is glorious. Emerald fields even for an autumn bride." The Weavers had taught her trust. Miss Highgate had taught her manners and poise and possibility. For her, Dora forswore the ancient paper patterns and created a design of her own invention. While Mah Bette gathered herbs and gossip in the woods and fields nearby, Dora scavenged patches of lace and silken threads and wallpaper scraps. pieces of doilies, table napkin trim, and the torn interior curtain that still blew in the breeze at the manor house—Tamarind, a moldering maze of scorched cathedral walls surrounding the last twist of a spiral stair. In one magical sitting, three days that seemed to pass as one, she fashioned an ivory gown, a patchwork scalloped sheath, gossamer in spots, laced with gold threads that glistened in the sunlight, and presented it to the sister soon to be married, who seemed now only capable of crying. "Why, Dora May! A frock to rival Titania. My mantua! It's perfect for my wedding night! You could open up a store!"

"I took the liberty, m'am."

The words had surprised her. Changed her. The dress—the act of making it had changed her. Out of pieces that were bits of nothing she had made something beautiful, designed from her own mind a garment like no other.

Bit by bit they be leavin', like sand eaten way from a tabby shack . . . She would not be sucked down. Taking liberty, she would seize it. Dressmaker! MISS DORA MAY'S FINE DRESSES AND MANTUAS, she envisioned the sign of her establishment. She went to check her spelling in the sisters' thick, six-inch dictionary, the last of the books to be packed away. "Mantua: A loose-fitting gown or robe, open to show the petticoat." She blushed. A fine seamstress, she knew nothing about womanhood.

✳ ✳ ✳

DORA WAITED impatiently for the buckboard driver, Tom Winrow, to unload her purchases. Rose Tree Lane was the last of his livery stops he said, or made it so. He smelled of musk and sweat as he chatted. Clearly taking his time so that he could talk to her, he lingered still. He hulked in the doorway, then finally stepped back. Dora thanked him brusquely and shut the door. She had things to do and dawdling was not one of them.

All evening, Dora busied herself cleaning the small rented rooms. She swept the ceiling of spiderwebs, banished the motes of dust, then scrubbed the walls, mopped, scraped, and burnished. Bette followed her around, sprinkling salt in the corners. "Sure you don't want me to do sumpin? You'll tire yourself out. Save some for tomorrow. You coulda had that nice young man do some of dis." Dora would have none of it. "I ain't thinking bout no man, Mah Bette. I'm thinking bout that thing I seen this morning. That thing sews faster than I kin think. Cost more money than we ever seen. Cost more than a hunnerd dollah, I bet. And they won't let no colored get it on the pay plan. I got to hab all the money up front."

"Don't worry bout dat. Money don't mean much uh nothin'. I seen a hunnerd dollah, missy. Seen me a whole mess of money a whole bunch of time. One of Maas Julius's frins try buy me fuh turty-tree hunnud dallah, but he say no mount worth what I give. I seent me a whole bunch of money a bunch of times. He come an hid all his loot when the Sesesh come. Pile upon pile of it. Not worth nuthin cuz it federate scrip. Dug it up and used it fuh kindlin, I did."

Dora's eyes rolled but she stayed silent. As much as Mah Bette talked of resistance, she had not left that time either. Dora was determined to get away, to get beyond that, to leave behind all that was painful, sordid, and ugly. Her mind awash with new thoughts, she intended to make her surroundings befit her ambition for herself. She assured Mah Bette she would rest, then waited for the old woman to drift off to begin the quiet tasks. *Hit that woodwork again, sew some curtains, then start on these orders. Look at this place. What you gon do with uh 'lectric Singer, don't even have 'lectricity?* Dora glowered at the slop pot. Remembering Blanche's indoor water closet with pearl tiles, she went looking for the outhouse.

Her skirts hiked over her narrow hips, Dora squatted in the dark and held her breath against the hot, fetid air. She didn't inhale again until she got back to the second-story landing. Leaning over the banister, she drew in a gust of cool night air. "I will own me a house with a privy and a front door that goes to the street, I will run a respectable business with my name on it," she declared to the one visible star, "and people will call me Miss."

Only then did Dora become aware of the music. This was the first night in her life that she could not hear the water, the soft gentle rhythm of ocean waves. Instead she heard music drifting on the soft late summer winds, tingling her face like the sea mist rolling off the bay. Drawn toward the sound, she descended the stairs and entered a narrow arched alleyway. A lone singer perched in a low porch window crooned while indifferently caning a chair. His voice trailed from words to a holler to a wail, the song, an invisible reel cast on the breeze, the music's changing arcs and pitch drawing her further down the darkened corridor.

The shadows gave way to a broad courtyard. The delicate pianissimo harmonies Dora had heard from a distance now pulsed with a ragged, raunchy rhythm. In the wee hours of the morning, the scene was loud as day. A motley pipe and drum team of children drilled in the dusty square, their bare feet marching in high, uneven steps. Quill and voice made two instruments—reed and horn—drums and feet, the rhythm. The young bootblack who had accosted her that afternoon was leading them. His taut black calves powdered with red dust, his face serious with pride, he pranced about with a piece of driftwood as his baton. Not wanting to repeat their encounters, Dora hurried in the direction of a tall shuttered building that sat across the courtyard, where the warm glow of lanterns beckoned from the windows.

One shutter on the third story hung on one hinge, others missing lattices. A piece of wrought-iron fencing, a section of the second-story balcony, leaned against the wall, chipped, rusting, and stained with lime. Suddenly, a quartet of dock workers burst out the door. Fresh from loading a harvest of timber logs, they celebrated with stevedore gusto, the gravel call of the lead man, three harmonies alone. "All Righty! Join the band! Huhn! All Righty! Join the band! Huhn! Come round and join the band! Huhn! Bo Bo-Boah, Bo Bo Bobo! BAM! Huhn! Bo Bo-Boah Bobo, Bo Bo Bobo! BAM! Join the band! HUHN!" The crew, their interlinked arms propping each other up, marched right toward her. The one on the end had gone to relax, win some money, and have him a woman. He had a little whiskey in him now and crashed into the wall. Before Dora could move, he spun out from the group and grabbed her. That "legomania" got him, the hip action. He was getting that Ashanti quickstep that would one day take on the city's name, Charleston. Needing a girl's hot waist in the cup of his hand, he danced a fast, furious scissors move around Dora's knees, bringing her dangerously close. The music, spilling out of the salon doors, rose into an up-tempo genuine grind, a percussive, poppin' brass horn drivin' the song to a frenzy. Her self-appointed partner's hard-soled boots shook the planks of the sidewalk and rattled the few panes of glass in the window, just when somebody's fist went through one. Dora pushed herself away. He lunged for her but fell into somebody else. The whole line of burly men went crashing to the ground. "Fight!" the bootblack yelled. Dora May flew back to her rooms.

She sat down on her sewing trunk, her hands between her knees and her feet turned on their ankles. Ringlets of sweat cascaded down her face, drenching her stiff round collar. She watched Mah Bette asleep on the single pallet. Her grandmother's breathing was heavy and deep, the mouth partly opened, gasping for the night air. Dora buried her face in her hands, then swept off her scarf of muslin and wiped her brow. *Some of everybody's colored folk, and some of everbody else livin' next doah.* "Stomp down, baby!" No, this was not the beginning Dora had imagined.

Opening her sewing trunk, Dora pulled out two of her patchwork quilts. She placed one over her grandmother, then folded the other into a cushion. She knelt wearily and began to pull Lijah-Lah's hand-carved tortoiseshell pins from her hair. Defying gravity, it spiraled out of its own accord into a crown of abstract auburn peaks, her mind still astir. *In instruction and construction is God's grace, spider-fingers.* Dora could lose herself in the movement of her hands, whirling together something whole out of random threads. A pattern, order, design. Her hands were strong, solid, and muscular, with no daintiness or fat. They were smooth and tough like the bark of a young elm. She grabbed random locks to make her plaits for the night and considered her plans for the future.

* * *

A GASH of light from the hot orange sun pressed against her eyelids. A sliver of light was shooting through an opening in the curtains she had just made, the hem of one panel a full half-inch shorter than the other. Dora did not realize she had fallen asleep, and she could not remember when she had so miscalculated a measurement. Mah Bette had risen at dawn as usual, banjo and herb basket in tow. Somehow the old woman had not let this strange new life alter her rhythm or her own way of doing things. Marching to the window, Dora snatched the fabric down, nails, dowel, and all.

Even through the bustling sounds of the Charleston weekday morning, music still wafted from the alleyway. "Dog-bite-it, they still at it!" The music was not stomping anymore, but a slight, low honky-tonk pick guitar. This was the last indignity. Roswell Diggs Jr. had told her, "Charleston's not like other places. White and colored always lived intermingled. Papa got this block for a steal after the earthquake in '86. That's when it turned colored, when they thought the ground was going to give out underneath it. The place has a lot of history. That's the Heyward-Washington house across the street, one of the oldest in the city, from before the War of Independence. Aaron Burr's daughter lived over there."

And round the corner is a bawdy house, don't you know? She understood now why Roswell had called the area Little Mexico. Just down the alley and through a trellised gate was a world outside the bounds and rules of the nation. Black men could be kings at music or cards or raising proud killing birds, and white men could excuse themselves from dinner and step out with the boys, south of the border without even leaving the city.

She would have to move, of course, find respectable lodgings on her own, but then how would she purchase the sewing machine? She had not the money to do anything but go back, and she would never do that. Never go backward. Always be movin', movin' forward. *Life is in front of me, not behind.*

5

Half the cost. And if you're not satisfied, you don't pay." What had possessed Dora to say that? "I am not a mere fittuh, m'am, but a dressmaker of such a quality you have never seen. Whatever you are havin' done, I can offer at half the price, twice the value, and three times the beauty." Dora had not only offered to make the dress alterations at half the cost, but to have it completed in half the time! "You must be outta your mind. Sometimes you just say things that are ridicullous," she fussed aloud to herself, mispronouncing the word as she would for the rest of her life. She pressed the wrinkles in her frock with her fingers, walked to the tin basin, splashed her face twice with water, pausing long enough to let the drops set on her cheeks and the metallic taste grace her tongue. Then she spread her comforter on the floor and the material upon it, then the pattern, one of the delicate paper stencils she had fashioned so she could cut the cloth as she had seen it in her mind. On her knees, she began to pin each cutout to the fabric. Dreaming of the Singer, she worked in silence.

The mystery of her mother Juliet's death hung over her. The memory of her mother's voice—every now and then Eudora thought she caught the memory of her voice in the morning birds or in the mists of the trees at dawn. Odd she remembered a woman singing, but she could not remember the sound, the melody. She did not understand how the sensation could be so vivid while the sound itself stayed hidden, lost.

"Oh, yo mama was a sanguh," Lijah-Lah would say. "Woo! She could sang! Song would come out. No words—and somebody say, 'Ma! That purdy.' An she face would turn all red all de time. An she not know she be singin' and no remember eben what't sound like. But don't yuh know, fuh long, she make up nuther un. A sweetness, too sweet for Tamarind. Too sweet fuh dis wuld she wuh, uh angel own stay wid us uh shoat time."

Since she had been a child, Dora had been aware of every sound—the rustle of her skirt as she lifted it to climb the stairwell, stifled giggles of plump children following her, "Outhouse, she asked for the outhouse," the soft friction of fabric as she prodded her gloves onto her fingers, the straw snapping in her hat, the crackle of her hair as she pushed it back in place. The contempt in Roswell's voice that had seeped beneath the crack in the door to his study as she passed. "Your sistuh run off with a field niggah for sure. That's the first burley-headed Mayfield I ever seen."

Aware of every sound, Dora never sang. She shut out the soundlessness with the whir of industry. *When one is idle, one is farther from God.* Silently she tacked across the floor on her knees, prodding the fabric with straight pins. Like teeth, they jutted from her lips, pursed in pure determination.

"Who could have such hands but a hummingbird?" The bold baritone voice startled her. Dora almost swallowed a mouthful of straight pins. Thomas Winrow, the driver her grandmother had insisted on calling a gentleman, laughing deep in his stomach, rested his elbows on the windowsill of her room, two arms' width from her. A pewter cornet, slung over his shoulder, nestled in the slant of his back. Instantly Dora knew that he had been the one leading all that ruckus last night. She snatched the pins from her mouth. "What you doing at my winduh, suh? No one ask fuh you to look in hyeah!"

"Whoa, sorry, m'am. You know I surely mean you no disrespect." He stumbled over his words. "I look out here just bout every mornin', yet I must say, never did I saw such busy hands with a face that did not eben look up. But now that I looks upon the face, I see that it be the most beautiful thang I seent in a long while! You truly is a dressmakuh?"

"Course I am. Now if you'll scuse me, I got work."

"Woman like you shouldn't have to woyk, shouldn't be on her knees."
I should have left those curtains up. Arms akimbo, Dora walked to the
window with the dowel in her hand.

"Tom Winrow, leave that gull alone! Leave that gull alone, I say. Ain't
nuttin but a chile." Dora looked down the narrow alley. A woman had
strolled up, her lips painted, her eyes lined with charcoal, her dress showing
far too much skin. A thick coat of powder nearly hid the red clay Cherokee
color at her temples.

"Ain't nobody's chile. She uh dressmakuh."

"I didn't know you went in for dresses, Win. Thought you only went
in fuh hats." Dora could tell from the casualness that the two were
friends and that she had already been the subject of some talk. The reference to a milliner, suggesting a woman of loose morals, did not escape
her.

"Shoot, woman, you ain't made no hats since you leff Jacksonville."

"I aim not from Jacksonville. I aim from Storyville. I tole you dot."

"Storyville, hunh? All y'all hinkty Creoles need to quit. Where my
money at?"

"I already pay you, Tomás, and you turn roun' and spend it. Way I
figure it, you the one owe me. Tu devais donner moi d'argent."

"Watch out now. I'ma have to hurt yuh. Put a hurtin' on yuh, Pilar.
Talkin' that mess."

"Don't pay him no mind, gull. He tink he big and bad, but he just
big." The woman had a strong, lean face, with eyes black and sharp and
angry at the sunlight.

Winrow laughed deep in his stomach. "Most women round here say
they make somethin', only make trouble." He turned abruptly to Dora. "I
mean what I say, m'am. No disrespect. Anything you need, I am here if
ever you needs me. Neighborly, seeing as we neighbors and all . . . My, you
got purty eyes. They almost purple."

"They just look like that in the shadow light is all, but—" Dora by
now had sheathed the straight pins in the cushion. She had forgotten his
name. "Mister . . ."

"Thomas Winrow. Call me Win. Everybody do. Bring you luck."

"If you are of a mind to be of assistance, Mr. Winrow, I would 'preciate a ride over to King Street on Thursday. I got three dresses to finish fo

then and could use all the time I can get to make em—uninterrupted. A ride for the 'livery would greatly help."

"You hear that, Pilar. She got three dresses to make by Thursday! And juss got hyeah."

The woman below fanned herself with her handkerchief. "Ah, une modiste! Ma petite, tu travail trop. Gull, you wuk too hod."

Dora's back stiffened. "The colored must earn their way."

The woman chuckled, "We done got some back pay already due on dot, je pense."

Even Dora had to smile. Right then she made an agreement with herself never to treat anyone with the indignity she had been shown, kin or stranger. *I don't know her story. She don't know mine.* "My name is Miss Dora, Dora May."

"I am Pilar . . . Madame Pilar to most. You can make me a dress, I fix you hair nice." Only then did Dora realize that her hair was still in its plaits. After her moment of restless sleep and the frantic movements of the morning, the spires stood on their own like the outstretched branches of a tree.

✳ ✳ ✳

"FITTIN DUH ax—fittin duh ax you sumpin, Miss Dora." Winrow had overpowered many obstacles. With his livery and hauling, he had freedom of movement. Freedom of assembly when playin' his music. He was welcome at Pilar's as well as the Temple of God. He was a good gambler, reading cards and faces, quiet as he kept it, relying more upon skill than the luck he often advertised. Dealing for the white gentlemen who came on Pilar's designated "society" nights or playing coon can with the brothers, he earned money easily. He had seen his share of the world, and railroad men, sailors, musicians still brought him news of it. With his cornet, Miss Lizzie, he could make music, pick up anything by ear.

He had everything, but the reading. He recognized some letters. If a storekeeper said, "Git down that flour!" he knew the "flour" sign looked like a bent cross, though he could not understand why ground meal had the same name as a daisy. The deficiency embarrassed him. He practiced getting up the nerve to ask Dora if she might tutor him. *Then you might get the nerve to speak open for yuhself.*

Win liked Miss Dora. The way she held her head up without treating people like they was less than her. The way she made things beautiful. Decorated her place with seashells and whatnots. Took care of her grandma, though that woman was a piece of work, he could tell. Though Dora had the face of a young girl, he could see that she was a good, strong woman. Win could spend the day configuring her in his mind. The shock of colors from hair to skin to eyes, reminding him of a spring meadow. He saw in Miss Dora May a drive and determination, a faith, "Colored people goin' get somewhere!" He greatly admired her for that. "Don't let that woman get an idea in her head!" he joked with Mah Bette. "Not that an idea belong most anyplace else, but don't let her git one in her head—Lawd have mercy, cuz then it done happen. Whether it be a good idea or not. Whether it be possible or not. Whether it foolish or wise, whether she done told you or not, it done happen."

Dora had got it into her mind to be a dressmaker, to open up a store as fine as the white ladies' on King Street, to be "une modiste," a maker of fine women's dresses and hats and to run a school to go with it for the young girls who had started collecting around her window when she worked. Thomas Winrow watched her pursue these goals with the same straight-backed determination that distinguished her walk. Every Thursday, Eudora marched up and down King Street with her head held high. She never let things stand in her way, never let things hold her back. Still, her quest was not without frustration. When Dora found out that Miss O'Malley, the wiry Falk and Bentschner clerk who had initially thrown her out of the store, was passing on the praise, but keeping Dora's tips, Dora promptly asked for her proper earnings and was fired from the Custom Order sewing department. Hair oiled, pulled, twisted, and tied down, her lips pursed and drawn in, Dora responded to an advertisement for a new position the very next day: WANTED—YOUNG LADY TO OPERATE SEWING MACHINE. SHIRTS MADE TO ORDER. 348 BUELER ST.

Mr. Yum Lee initially stood right over her shoulder, watching to see if she knew how to operate his equipment. Although this machine was not a Singer, she figured it had to work with the same principles. Her first try, she placed the spool on the top spindle and wound the thread through the cat's cradle of gears. When she pressed her foot to the pedal, joy graced through her body as the thread spun round the bobbin. She went into hire, doing piecework and tailoring on a steady basis. By night Yum Lee allowed her to use the machine for her own clients. Dora might have lost her tips, but she took all of her Falk and Bentschner customers with her. And Yum Lee's Custom Laundry had electricity and lights.

Before long, Dora had bought her own sewing machine, then a second for embroidery stitching, expanding her booth in the laundry to her own room. She soon had a mess of clients—white and colored—and was working for herself. Instead of taking orders from Miss O'Malley, she placed them. "I'm 'spectin' several bolts of satin from New York for Miss Bonneau's wedding next week, iffen you please, Miss O'Malley, thank yuh. And I'll have some of that pipin' trim today, thank yuh."

Win admired the way she talked to white and colored alike, but he worried about her boldness. A colored woman could get away with things he couldn't dream of doin', but still! Not allowed inside the store, he paced in the service alley and waited beside his red-chipped buckboard with Mr. Lee, a mule thought he was human. The moment Dora emerged from the store, Win jumped aboard the wagon and snapped the reins. "Lessin you fixin' on bein' sombody's gluepot, Mr. Lee, you better git, gitty-up." He tugged the straps to the right and forced a sharp turn at the corner, then bounded from his seat and scooped up Dora's parcels.

"Why is it, Mr. Winrow, every time I come out a stoah, I run into you?"

The sun at his back, his shadow engulfed her. His chest barreled out with a deep rounded laugh. "Just lucky, I told you. Although I don't know whether that luck be yours or mines. Most me, I guess. Figure a lady needs escortin'," he said, holding his hat so as to conceal the hole in it.

"I am much obliged, Mr. Winrow, but waitin' on me like this gon keep you from gettin' your other fares."

"I don't mind. I takes the time for what I thank important. Sides, most of my folk get picked up sunrise when the market open and sunset when it close." He dusted off the seat with his jacket elbow and hoisted her by the waist like a sack of grain. "You should ride up front. Mo comf'table."

She was flattered by his attention, but she did not intend to like him. She disapproved of his music and card playin'. "Least let me pay you something for your trouble," she demurred as he slid into the seat beside her.

"Ain't no trouble. Long as I'm back to cart Aunt Sibby, I be fine. Most folk don't pay me no money no way. Aunt Sibby fix a meal uh okra stew, put a hurt on yuh. We figure somethin' out."

"Playing that honky-tonk every night, I don't know how you find the time to haul no one at all."

"Never say I don't like to have some fun, now, Miss Dora. Playin' that honky-tonk is paying the note on my daddy's farm." This surprised her. He chuckled to himself. "You think a niggah make a livin' on day woyk, you livin' in another country." Seeing that he had offended her, he countered, "It's up past the Neck a way, a bit up King's Highway, then take Charleston-Camden Road . . . Got greens, tomatoes, mulberry trees, Japan plums. Three hogs, five pigs, and a sow, two sheep, a cow, and four old goats." His laugh was thick and raucous like a crashing wave. "Naw, it ain't all that, but it got promise. Ain't no forty acres, now, but I do got the mule. Ain't that right, Mr. Lee?" The mule whinnied and snorted, taking two steps forward and back. "Ain't that somethin'! Got me a dancin' mule! Thought perhaps you might like to see it someday. Got me the sweetest scuppernong grapes inna country."

"You got property, Mr. Winrow. Don't that mean you kin vote!"

This was not the response he had expected. "I stayin' out of that now, ain't not none of my affair. They mix up the ballot when you do go. Find you ain't got no credit at the stoah when you git back. Any niggah what go down there is marked fuh trouble for damn sure."

"I don't need you to cart me around if you gon cuss, Mr. Winrow."

"Fuss at you? I ain't doin' that, Miss Dora. Don't never want to . . . Maybe another way uh doin' things is all. Make a way my own way."

"I just ax a simple question."

"Well, lemme ax you one, Miss Always Goin' Somewhere, where we goin'?"

"Fifty-three twenty-five Everett Road. Wisdom Hall."

Win slowly drew the figures on his paper bag ledger. He took great pleasure in demonstrating that he could write numbers.

"Fifty-three," she repeated more slowly.

"Five . . . three . . . Oh, look at that. Just bout made him uh accident. Not lookin' at all where he goin'. Five . . . what was it?"

"Five, three."

"Five . . . three . . ."

"Two, five. Twenty-five."

"Two . . . five, twenty . . . five . . . What should I do when I git there?"

Let's juss get there fust.

✳ ✳ ✳

COLERIDGE MCKINLEY'S unflawed hands moved across the keys playing a gentle rag. With ease he blended standard parlor tunes with the new Negro sounds he had been hearing in his habitual visits to Pilar's house of pleasure. He intended later to delight his friends, classmates from Princeton, one of whom was soon to be family. Gazing out the upstairs window, Coleridge watched the weathered buckboard pull up to the alley entrance of what was left of the family estate, Wisdom Hall. "Cousin, I think your seamstress has arrived."

His cousin turned slightly. She had almost no chin, and her hair was pulled far off her forehead, suggesting an impish and suspicious nature. "You got relation with this gal?"

"My dear cousin Tildie! Such an unbecoming question! Do you want a wedding dress or not?" He poked at her slightly rounded belly.

She swatted at him as he passed. "Don't mess with me, Cole. I said is she one of your whores?"

"She's expert at alterations. Fastest seamstress in the city."

"She will have to do the cleanin' also. You know Mama."

Dora could now boast that she had secured employment at the home of Miss Matilda Bonneau. Through Pilar's intersession with one of her clients, Dora now worked for bona-fide quality white folk. *A little down from the olden days, but quality nonetheless.* She told herself it mattered not how she got the job, just that she had it. Despite being Blanche's relation, Dora had not been invited to any good colored Charleston homes yet. *Good enough to make they dresses but not to grace they parlors.* When word spread that she was designing the wedding party for the Bonneaus, one of the oldest of Charleston's white Huguenot families, Dora firmly believed she would surely gain entry to the higher class of colored Charleston society. There she could begin the next phase of her ambition, finding a suitable husband. Thick brick walls, sprouting azaleas, shielded the house. The iron gate stood open as Win's wagon pulled up.

"Miss Dora, I was fittin tuh ax—"

"You, boy, you! Git down from there and help!" An ancient white oversized, musty black suit stood before them, shrouding an odd old man, his angular face overpowered by a sculpted silver mustache that twitched with irritation.

"Yessuh. Tenkee, suh," Win said, shifting his being into someone else. "Scuse me, Miss Dora."

"Come on, boy, come down."

"Yes, yes, yessuh."

"Damned stutterin' fool."

The sloping sides of the estate driveway still held pools of water, reflecting rain from the night before. The carriage leaned to one side; the family jostled within. The frantic horse pranced and sputtered, threatening to ply his harness from the axle. Chewing on his bit, Mr. Lee looked warily at his owner, then over his shoulder haunch at the frantic mare. The anxious black coachman tried to soothe the old man. "She a race horse, Maas Bonneau, not use to livery."

"Go and get another horse from the stables, then."

"Ain't got another horse, Genrul."

"Don't tell me Wisdom Hall ain't got another horse!"

Voices spilled from inside the carriage. "Your grandfather's going to get us all killed. I told you not to let him have the reins. Oh, Mama, please. Look, he's frightened Brunetta!"

Win calmly approached the horse with tongue clicks and the stroke of his hand. He took the animal's face with both hands, leaned his forehead in till his brow was touching, and exhaled into the horse's nostrils, exchanging breath for breath. The animal flounced its head and quieted. Win opened the carriage door for the women inside to disembark. "There, there, Brunetta," said the younger one, holding a small brown hen. The old man barked at Winrow, "Don't even think bout hitchin' that filthy mule to my carriage. Get back there and push when I tell yuh."

Embarrassed for Win, angered for him, ashamed and infuriated at once, Dora darted her eyes away, only to be met by another pair. Gray and bemused, they were watching the scene through an upstairs curtain. Dora knew nothing of womanhood, but she knew what a look like that meant from a young white man. She shifted the angle of her seat and straightened her back in a defiant pride, her eyes lowered to conceal her raging contempt.

With the coachman looking on, his arms protectively folded over the one dress waistcoat he had left, Winrow fixed his shoulders beneath the rear bumper of the carriage chassis and in three heaves succeeded in releasing the vehicle from entrapment. The skittish horse bolted a few yards, then came to a stop, the cab without the driver listing to the side. Voices swooned in unanimous laughter as the cluster of young women resumed their seats. The old man waved his arm and angrily hobbled back toward the house in his shiny riding boots, dusted red with rage. The colored coachman nodded a perfunctory thanks to Win and snapped his whip. Two bits flew out the window of the carriage as it passed him. Feed to a chicken. Win brushed the spattered mud from his trousers in casual strokes. Small brown speckles dotted his dark face. "Tenkee, tenkee, m'am. Right smart, tenkee."

The coach disappeared out the gate. Winrow's broad smile faded. With one leg stiffened, he bent over and picked up the loose coins, examined them, and put them in his pocket. "I'ma walk like that someday. Walk knowin' everyone gon move out my way." Clacking his jaw, Win walked back to his wagon. He patted Mr. Lee on the neck and began to check the bit and harness as Mr. Lee bristled and backed into the wagon. Win jerked the bit sharply and held the reins tight. "Watch out now or might get some Broken Bone Fevuh. Johnnie Reb gon find out niggahs won't die so fast . . . I sorry, Miss Dora, I forgot muhself."

He extended his hand to help Dora step down. She thought to wipe his face with her handkerchief, but she did not want him to consider her forward. "What were you fittin to ax, Mr. Winrow?"

"Some other time, maybe."

✻ ✻ ✻

PROMISING TO return before dark, Win had left her standing in the pockmarked driveway. Sesesh leftovers—the shattered Confederacy put back together, peculiar and misshapen. Still riddled with mortar holes from the siege, the garden a riot of jonquils, bluebells, and weeds, Wisdom Hall wore defeat like a garland.

The interior was no better. A Parisian clock with silver bells graced the mantel, the hour hand frozen, the minute hand darting forward, then back at the quarter hour. A crystal chandelier hung low, its golden brackets empty of candles. Velvet couches, worn on the arms, were covered with doilies that were ratty at the corners. The portraits and photographs that lined the hallway hung crooked and covered with dust in their gilded frames.

"Are you the stand-in maid? Regular gal say she took sick, don't believe it a minute."

"M'am, I'm the dressmaker. Come for the custom alterations for Miss Matilda."

"Let all the servants enter and see." Wearing a cap with black feathers and a garish plaid jacket over a shirt and trousers, Miss Matilda jumped on the kitchen table, dressed as a man. "I am she. But don't call me that! Call me Miss Tildie or Mattie, but never Matilda, or this is what I shall wear to my wedding!" The young woman squatted down so her face was even with Dora's. "Don't look so startled, gal. I'm not serious. That yo' boyfriend who dropped yuh?"

"No, Miss Tildie. A neighbor, is all."

"Your gentleman friend?"

"He is a friend and a gentleman, yes, m'am."

"She's not a m'am yet." Her betrothed entered. Cigar in his mouth, he burped. Crab cakes, fried chicken, green peas, cakes, strawberries, ice cream, and beer. The house was a riot of smells, voices and people.

The mother, thin-faced and bulbous-eyed with rolls of fat beneath sour strained folds of fabric, ignored her except to bark orders. "I say, girl, are you the switch maid? The carpet has not been swept, the mantel has not been cleaned. Look at the dirt on my fingertips. The doors throughout the house are smudged with many, many fingerprints. When I arrived home today, there was a chicken breast, a chicken bone right in front of the door. It was there yesterday, too. This is not acceptable."

The youngest collected pets—rabbits, guinea hens. The miniature menagerie pecked and poked about the room; an ancient white peacock stood sentry outside the chipped French doors. "My Brunetta has died. Oh my poor hen. Whatever shall we do?" The old man, oblivious to all but his own rage, paced and ranted, "Burning, bursting brain! What am I to do? What is Wisdom Hall without a master?" Tildie knelt on the table and conspired, tête-à-tête, with her future husband. "The Cozzens and the Sproles and the Bairds, I'll seat them at table number six. They deserve each other."

"Matilda, get down off that table at once. Who's goin' to the ice house? And who placed flowers there? You, girl, put those things down and do somethin' round here."

Dora immediately disliked them all. She did not see among them the one she had caught staring. She presumed he was the gentleman of whom Pilar had spoken, a gentleman in quick need of a seamstress for his cousin. She intended him to know right fast that, though she was a friend to Pilar, she was her own person and a respectable one. *I am nobody's maid. I am a dressmaker. Pilar juss my neighbor. My business ain't hers.*

* * *

PILAR'S PALACE of Pleasure was a ramshackle three-story French-style town house with two floors of gals for any type of persuasion and a dirt floor saloon, known for good music, authentic Chinese lanterns, raw whiskey, and honest gambling. Sullivan slapped the deck on the table and tapped the surface. He never did catch Thomas Winrow "carryin' a cub," stacking a winning card close to the bottom of the deck to draw it at his choosing; still, the wily railroad porter, pistol in the back pocket of his uniform, preferred to deal when playing against his friend.

Win deftly triple-cut the cards with his cornet-fingering hand. Sullivan shook his head in silent marvel and dealt out ten cards each. "Deuces," Win called out to Sullivan's jack, knowing his match cards would turn up first. The two friends played each other only for sport. When the cotton harvest was in, or when trade ships pulled into the harbor, the two of them were a formidable pair. Against the itinerant workers looking to stretch their earnings with a little luck at poker or skin, they were peers. But in the one-on-one game of coon can, Win was the best in the city, hands down. Already ahead with a pair, three queens, and a spread of diamonds, Win drew a redheaded jack. In disgust, Sullivan relinquished his hold card and threw up his hands, once again leaving his partner with the winning eleventh card. "Some coons can. Some coons can't," Winrow crooned. "I'm the coon that drug the can. Give it up, Sullivan! Less you wanna go nuther round?"

Sullivan pushed away from the table, the lantern swinging overhead. "Caulkers and menders now got to give they pay to the owners. Brakemen used to run the railroad gettin' fired. They be comin' aftuh me next. Cain't be throwin' my pennies at you. You a magician, Win. Lucky you my friend."

"Lucky in general, Cap'n. It's my nature. Doggone!" He jumped up, leaving his winnings of fifteen cents on the table. "I gotta pick up Miss Dora."

He needed little sleep, three, four hours tops. After the early morning farm chores, he would instantly fall into a black forgotten sleep. Awakened by the nine o'clock sun, he would check the new scuppernong bottles and drive into town to service his regular customers, the afternoon taken up with hauling and his jitney service. He then freshened up and was back at Pilar's, playin' music till three and cards between sets.

He had been in love, or what he would call love, perhaps twice. Both were carried off. One by the fever. The other by a railroad porter who promised her free fares and fancy places. Sex he regarded as an activity between friends, a friendly business transaction, a necessity of life like food or shelter. He thought himself content until he met Dora. Until Dora, he had not contemplated his future.

He saw the way men looked at her. Ungentlemanly talk, though, he would not tolerate. The regulars at Pilar's who saw him carting her around joked that she was not his usual kinda woman. The stokers and firemen on the Atlantic Limited already had a bet going. As Win bolted for the door, Sullivan cackled, "Win gon get hisself some Red Bone tail tonight."

Win stopped and held the swinging saloon door. Gracious but firm, he turned and faced his old friend. "We'll have none of that business," he told Sullivan. "I'm gon marry that gal. Marriage by the book."

Sullivan shook his head in dismay and dropped Win's forgotten loose change into his pocket. "Young gal done got him right by the nose. His luck done run out now. Gon git Bap Tized."

* * *

A STUD deal had produced Thomas Winrow. Milk from his mother's breasts never touched his lips. Upon birth, he was put in the slave nursery with twelve other foundlings. Rocked by the foot in a tray of cradles, he drank from a trough with piglets and chicks. Destined for the fields and a three-hundred-pound cotton sack, he was rescued by a smile—his own. The big dark dimples in each of his plump cheeks and his round black eyes brought him notice. The four-year-old whose job was to chase birds and cart water was sent off to Charleston, to the city house, as a gift to his owner's daughter. His new job title was shoo-fly. Dressed in powder blue knickers and a ruffled shirt, he fanned the buzzing black pests away from his white folk with a spray of peacock feathers, delighting them on occasion with a jig or shout. He felt like a gift, somethin' special and pretty. The blue satin looked so beautiful against his black skin he was dazzling even to himself.

The war was at its climax then. Win's transfer had been a gesture of desperation. Two years into the Union siege of the city, the tidewater family that owned him, like many others, had refused to abandon their way of life. Though the dinner was seven courses, the main dish of horsemeat and plum cakes baked with watermelon juice scratched their throats and soured their stomachs as it went down. The gentlemen were missing limbs and eyes. The mistress bit her lip between chatter. While they braced themselves for the North's revenge for the assault on Fort Sumter, their faithful slaves one by one stole themselves away each year as the war went on. Those who remained, the old, the young, the addled and unsure, were put on triple shifts. Turning five, Win had added to his tasks shoveling the horse droppings and cleaning the chimneys. "Roo-Roo-Roorey!" he cried when he got to the top, ash up his nose, his face smudged with soot, his pantaloons exchanged for a raggedy homespun shift. By the time he got to the dinner chores, he could barely lift his arms. As he stood beside his mistress, the metallic blue wash of feathers lulled him to sleep and he let the fan drift into her plate. "Son of a bitch!" Startled awake, he steadied himself on the edge of the table. The master's daughter closed her fist around her fork and plunged it through his hand, pinning his palm to the wood. A red aureole of blood swelled around the wound, the scream still making its way to his consciousness.

The mulatto butler pried his hand loose and rushed him through the kitchen to the outside water pump. The old man knelt over him and directed the water over the gushing wound. The child's jagged screeches of panic and outrage called forth great, rolling roars of thunder. The sky began to rain fire, the winter night lit up bright as day. "Lawd God Ahmighty!" the butler cried. "It be Jubilation!" The young boy fainted straightaway.

When Win awoke in his bed-tick cot on the pantry floor, he was looking at a swift-moving patchwork of turquoise sky with billows of pink-orange clouds. Just as the preacher had predicted, he thought, the wrath of God had come down on slaves who failed to honor their masters. But if he was dead and this was heaven, why was his hand stiff with pain and bandaged? He rose and called out. The house was empty, Cook, Missus, everybody gone. Half the roof was torn away. The chimney he had so often cleaned was rubble. The walls were cracked and the windows blown out. From over his shoulder a huge shadow fell upon him and stretched across the cratered parquet floor. Framed in the sunlight, a blue black man in blue black clothes, buttons shining, stood before him, three stripes of lightning on each arm, hat cocked to one side, his sword a silver shaft. Momentarily the master of the house, the little boy thought he would be bold. "Is you Lawd God? Cuz if you ain't, why you come to the front doah, niggah!"

"Your name Winrow!"

"Yessuh."

The tall man squatted down and gripped his shoulders. "I am your father."

* * *

WIN'S FATHER nursed his hand and talked to him in shards and fragments. "Drew fire at Jacksonville, 'Kill the Goddamn sons of bitches!' James Island, Wagner, and Olustee. Warn't never no colored prisonuh. This cut hyeah ain't nuthin. I seen a bayonet rip a niggah up the gut to the chin. We Winrows both lucky, I guess. It be our nature." A runaway, barefoot and near naked "contraband," the elder Winrow had enlisted, then taken his uniform from the dead. Shoes from one, hat from another, and the prize—a bugle pried from the severed limb of a boy not much older than his son.

He purchased land at auction with his overdue soldier's wages, built a lean-to, and every evening in the dim campfire light he dealt his son a weathered deck of cards. "I'ma teach yuh to play a game call coon can. It be so hard, only coons can play it." He laughed with the same baritone staccato Win would later recognize as his own. The card games forced the boy to exercise his hand until the withered muscles became strong, the fingers dexterous, and the eye sharp. Three years later, his father built a cabin and brought a woman home. "This yo Ma." Chest sunken and belly rounded, she smiled with joyless eyes, revealing the same distinctive dimple that graced her son's cheeks. She spoke simply of being paired with Win's father as a favor to a farmer whose wife was coughing up blood. "He was in need of a wet nurse, he say, who could still cook and keep to the fields. Gib my baby way so milk be good fuh his, but," she chuckled deep in her belly, "it dry up." She spoke little of the other places and owners, but dictated notices and had them printed by the Freedmen's Bureau for the children. Winrow was the only one she found. They would not allow the young boy to work at all. "Just set up there and make us some music, Win. Play us sumpin purty." He would march around with the bugle to his lips, making squawks and notes with his voice. The instrument had no mouthpiece, but from their radiance he thought himself Gabriel.

From his father's old bugle, Win advanced to a cornet, won off a minstrel sideman with a passion for absinthe and a poor face for poker. The man had called the horn Miss Lizzie, and Win soon knew why. "Miss Lizzie can school you, rule you, and conversate. Miss Lizzie can spit, growl, and cry, patter, pout, and shout." From reveille to mournful taps, that horn shared stories of almost everywhere she had been. "Second Line?" she wailed. "I was lead cornet at Dr. Buzzard's wake! I done bust out the workhouse of eighteen states! Wharf dens, whorehouse, street parades. Field gang, tent show, jamborees. I can walk, talk, croon, and cuss, strut, cut, and testify! What you got?" He carried the mouthpiece in the pocket near his heart and polished the silver bell till it had to be hidden from the sun.

He kept the land because his daddy wanted it. "This lan' belong to you. Was promised and fought fuh," his father had said. And his mother, "Promise me you won't be like yo pah n leab me wid no way to fend." Out of loyalty, Winrow worked off the debt accrued against the land where he had buried them, but like Miss Lizzie, he lived for the night. He liked the city. Even as a child he loved it, the big streets and houses. He didn't miss shoveling shit or getting soot up his nose, he didn't miss that. But the sounds, the voices, the music, the people, the night! He never thought to find something as fascinating till Dora.

* * *

EVEN WHEN she could afford it, Dora decided not to move from Rose Tree Lane. She knew the neighborhood now. Aunt Sibby's slow-movin' ways had become a kind of grace, and the street urchin Deke who lived under the porch at Pilar's always devoured the plates of food she set out for him. Yum Lee's laundry was conveniently located a few blocks away. She also realized that Winrow's attention might not be so easily available if she didn't live across the street from his city room. She was frugal with her earnings, mindful of every penny. She had her savings and, through her uncle, burial insurance for both herself and Mah Bette. Time enough for big things later. When she did spend, it was with relish. She particularly enjoyed being implacably polite and cold paying her rent and rubbing her relatives' noses in their original discourtesy to her without ever mentioning it.

Blanche softened, especially after she had seen Dora retool some of her hand-me-downs to look brand-new and better designed, and when inadvertently Roswell Jr., who had so flaunted his fine broadcloth linen suits and his plump soft hands stuffed in kid gloves, brought her some new customers. Dora had stopped by the funeral parlor to pay her weekly rent. Roswell Jr. was propped up behind his desk in the stairwell. His father obviously had about as much respect for him as she did. Dora considered it a ritual of pride to put the money directly into her cousin's hand, which was softer than her own. She removed her macramed glove with emphasis at each finger. "Cousin, I was thinking, perhaps, I could pay my rent on a monthly basis."

"And deprive me of an opportunity to see you?" Though the light scent of talc from her body and the swanlike slope of her neck and throat enthralled him, he was inhibited by their familial relation and her lack of standing, the tight kink of hair at the nape of her neck, and her washerwoman's hands. *Someone's in the kitchen wid Dinah.* She could feel his lurid thoughts creepin' toward her.

"I am sure if you wish to see me more often, Roswell, there are more

'propriate circumstances than a stairwell. Is your father in? I might speak
with him."

"... Well, I ..."

She saw that she had embarrassed him, then chastised herself for enjoying the sensation a bit too much. He cleared his throat and pulled his
stomach in. "I'll see if he's free." Young Roswell turned to exit, then, as an
afterthought, held the door for her to follow. Dora graced through the
portal. *Put him in his place I did.*

The two ran directly into the bereaved relatives of the late deceased
Joseph Marivale. Roswell clasped her hand and introduced her as "a relation from the Low Country, a seamstress." Taking his tone in stride, she
corrected, "I prefer to speak of myself as a modiste, a maker of fine dresses,
mantuas, and hats. I do outfits for the bereaved, wedding gowns, and, of
course, christening frocks." The young Mrs. Marivale, her stomach already showing, was immediately taken with the notion.

The gown was to be worn the following Sunday at the Emmanuel
A.M.E. Church. Dora was delighted. The Marivales were an important
family, the best of Charleston colored society. "Oh, oh, oh, they massuhs
was Frinch," Mah Bette joked. The Marivales were part of the old colored
elite, descendants of free people of color, mostly mulattos, with long-
standing ties to the wealthy white Charleston families. Their source of
pride and economic advantage was one that might have been afforded to
Mah Bette, had she not so betrayed her owner by conceiving her third
daughter, Juliet, with a saltwater African and aiding a group of swamp
niggah runaways with saltmeat lifted from his smokehouse. For decades
after the war's end, the Marivales, De Saussures, Pettigrews, and Hugers
socialized and married among themselves. If none of them could technically be called mulatto, that is, one-half white, they all looked that way.

It was a pedigree even the Diggses respected. Although Roswell's
family mingled with this crowd, their claim to standing was tenuously
based on his marriage to the first Mrs. Diggs more than his recently acquired personal wealth. Of the three Diggs brothers—Lee tended bar at
the Charleston Club, while Hiram marked billiard scores—Roswell Sr.
had been the one to strike out on his own. Picking up on the unusual passion the newly freed had for goin' to heaven in a dignified way, he sold
burial insurance. A long-term policy at a penny a week guaranteed a pine

box, a lot, and a marker. Flowers were extra. When they paid on time, he buried them proper. When they didn't, he foreclosed on their worldly goods. "Well, at least he was good for something," snapped Bette as Dora helped her up the chapel steps to the balcony.

The church had a revolutionary history. It was there that Denmark Vesey, a free man, conspired to liberate Charleston's slaves. The failed insurrection so panicked slave-owners that all colored churches were outlawed, so that the congregants had to practice their faith in secret until the war's end. It was there that the new freedmen's Union Club met to debate the Constitution, governance, and law in the heady days of Reconstruction. It was to their faith that the families retreated when the bloody red shirts of terror tore away the thin raiments of the just-born democracy, replacing it with gunfire, demons, and threats of death. The families of the old colored Charleston society retreated into a world of self-delusion. Like the nobles in King Louis's court, they fawned and fought for favor in a cloistered world they could control, deriving status from having a pew on the chapel floor, vying for its distance from the back. The Diggses were seated by the middle window, the Marivales in the second pew. Dora leaned over the balcony rail to view the gown she had made for the child. Bette folded her arms and went to sleep.

The gown hung nearly to the ground in a gentle scalloped train of Alsace lace with a ribboned bonnet to match. The priest with long white fingers dabbed holy water on the baby's forehead. The baby winced and fussed in her mother's arms. At the start of the squall, Bette opened one eye momentarily. "Piscopals. Even too rarified fuh she."

At the conclusion of the services, Dora was lost among the swell of well-wishers and relatives and promptly forgotten. She stood awkwardly in the cloying heat of the mid-July day, the threat of her own sweat challenging her hair's Creole masquerade. Church members whispered among themselves that the odd-looking girl was Blanche Diggs's niece and, indeed, a Mayfield.

Old Bette raised her eyes to the sky in gratitude as they descended the church steps, for there was Tom Winrow, silently waiting, his buckboard in tow. She poked Dora in her rib. "Come on, gal, let's get us some real spirit. Need some Revival!"

Didn't tell me he were gon be here. Dora didn't really want to be seen boarding such a low-class carriage, but Bette had grabbed her by the arm, and she followed dutifully.

＊ ＊ ＊

"AND IT shall come to pass, that I will pour out my spirit upon all flesh; and your sons and your daughters shall prophesy, your old men shall dream dreams, your young men shall see visions." The itinerant preacher held the Bible as a weapon or talisman in his outstretched hand, the leather binding curled around the feathered pages. His eyes closed, his face raised to heaven, his voice, at once growling and clarion, traveled to the far ends of the meadow in a great rolling wave of sound.

To this sloping field of marsh grass and wildflowers rimmed by white oak they were still coming, drawn to his call. Being a Gullah-talkin' Geechee anyway, Mah Bette found this gathering more to her liking than her granddaughter's high yellow High Episcopalians. "Church of the Living God! Hallelujah!" Bette threw her hands above her head and ran toward the white-frocked throng of ebony faces, one hundred voices singing, one hundred tongues speaking at once. An old man muttered and chanted a prayer. A woman spat a plosive percussive rambling text that forced her head back with its power. Another fell to her knees and crawled upon them weeping, her body wracked with invisible currents. The Revival's practice of "talking in tongues" shielded the much older tradition of the hijacked saltwater Africans who called upon the forbidden gods who could not be controlled, who danced beyond the grasp of their captors. A high-stepping young man, his arms darting and distending out, up, and behind as he bellowed commands, the dark of his eyes rolled up to his soul, transformed pain into rapture, the long-sought gift of freedom discovered in surrender.

Dora stood aloof as the preacher railed, "And also upon the servants and the handmaids in those days will I pour out my spirit. And I will show wonders in the heavens and in the earth, blood and fire and pillars of smoke!" She resisted the voice meandering through the strange, spontaneous harmonies of the growing congregation, the shouts, hands clappin', feet stompin', bodies rockin' to and fro, the sound like a great ship cracking under gale winds, at once whole and separated into siren voices. She scowled and tugged at her bodice. *This ain't eben Christian!* Ring shouts and work songs were to her the signs of lingering barbarism that needed to be replaced with good old New England rectitude. The sisters had often said at Sabbath school catechism, "To hear that still small voice, one must be still." But here, the people danced their faith and hollered hosannas, shaking with fervor and fainting straight away.

"The Sun shall be turned into darkness and the Moon into blood, before the great and terrible day of the Lord come! Whosoever shall call on the name of the Lord shall be delivered!" One by one, initiates placed their head in the cradle of the preacher's palm and were thrust backwards into the trembling waters, made fierce by those dancing on the river's ten thousand points of light. She was drawn in as one standing on an unfamiliar shore finds her knees enveloped by the tide. "Hallelujah!"

In the shade under a tree, Tom played his cornet with a fellow on guitar and another on drum. He tried to look casual, draining the instrument of spittle, as Dora approached. "I didn't figure you for the holy-rollin' kind, Miss Dora May."

"You figured right bout that." She fussed about her skirt and attempted to wring out the hem. "Didn't figure no trumpet playin' was neither."

"Shoot, woman, you know how many time the trumpet inna Bible? . . . The horn be a powerful instrument of Gawd. Number Ten, verses one to ten. Signal of there gonna be danger. Signal for the people of Israel to gather together. Blow on feast day and the Sabbath. No work till Monday! Celebrate when you win a battle and honor the dead. Joshua used it in Jericho. Gideon in the victory over the Midianites. When Solomon was made king, a hundred twenty priests sounding trumpets. That's a lot of sound. Revelations, the trumpet will sound and the dead will rise and the Lord Hisself will descend. Sides, this be a cornet."

"I didn't figure you to be so studied up on the Bible, Mr. Winrow."

"I ain't that easy to figure out now. Look like Preachuh needed a little help this mornin'," he joked, then continued. "I don't go in much fuh the prayin' part myself, but I likes the music . . . I figured a good woman wouldn't much go wid nuttin but a church man, sose I might as well find a church what likes music." His humor was greeted with silence from both women. Dora liked Win, and his waiting upon her she found very convenient and flattering. Still she dreaded his advances. She preferred her relationship with Win just the way it was. Neighborly.

"I would much been wantin' to inquire, Miss Dora. I see you real good at readin' and writin'. I kin do figurin' well enough, but eben a grown man could use some schoolin'. I been fittin to ax iffen you had some time, could set aside some time, to teach me book learnin' in private—never too old, but nobody's business you doin' it juss the same."

Dora sighed with relief that Win's request was not a proposal. "Cose I don't mind tutorin' you, Mr. Winrow. Readin' is a powerful thing. You are a courageous and wise man to recognize that. It would be my pleasure."

"I would consider that more than exchange for the livery and would like to do sompin fuh you . . . and your grandmammy."

In the span of a country sermon, Mah Bette had decided she didn't like Thomas Winrow anymore. A musician had stolen her Juliet and brought her to a bad end, and she did not want that fate for Dora. Bette sucked her teeth and retorted, "You doan have to pay me no mind. I be juss fine."

"I know that, Mah Bette. Seen you wid yo banjo. Got a nice strum to it. But you know, Callendar's Minstrels be in town in a fortnight. Got thirty pickers inna band. If you never seen a real traveling show, this the one! All colored. Got they own railroad car." Bette perked up. He boasted further, "Some of my buddies inna band. Won Miss Lizzie offa one. Oh, that my horn, not no other woman."

Dora hesitated. "I should think you'd wanna take Miss Pilar."

"Pilar ain't no nevermind to me. Useta keep comny, but not for no permanent purpose, and that was a long way back. She juss a good bidness partner, card games and such, is all. But I don't plays much no more. Hardly even think about it. Cuz I done found God, I has. I done seent me a bit of heaven the first day I laid eyes on you. I would like to 'scort you, if I may."

Dora had never seen a real minstrel show. And even she knew of Callendar's and their trademark song, "Oh Dem Golden Slippers." She could wear her precious lace boots for the occasion. "I don't rightly know, Mr. Winrow. I will consider it, I guess. I will consider to consider it, I reckon."

"Gotta hab some fun sometime, Miss Dora."

"Well, yes, I spose I could. We—Mah Bette and me."

"Great day in the mornin'!" Thomas Winrow rubbed his palms together, threw them above his head and out into the shape of wings.

* * *

BETTE WAITED until they were back at Rose Tree Lane to fuss. She followed Dora up the narrow stairs to their flat. "Don't hitch up to him just yet. You might wait till he's got some hired help or something. You don't haveta marry him at all. He ain't paid that lien yet, and you want a man who's got something of his own."

"Oh, fuh goodness sakes! I ain't marryin' nobody. Juss goin' to the show." They opened the door and found young Roswell Jr. seated at the kitchen table, now reinforced and shellacked. He stood upon their entrance. Dora folded her hands together in indignation.

"You have done wonders with this place, Dora."

"Thank you. I wonder should I invest in some new locks."

"Don't shoot the messenger. Seems you've made an impression on quite a few people." He handed her a small square envelope. "Miranda Marivale has sent me on a mission. You've arrived, my dear cousin."

With Bette plying her for what it said, Dora could barely read the note. "It's an invitation. The Brown Society of Charleston . . . Cordially invites you to a reading by Miss Ida B. Wells . . . Grandma, I've been invited to a book party."

Bette put her hands on her hips. "Who ever heard of a party fuh uh book?"

6

I RECKON I RECOMMEND A RUFFLE AT THE COWL, MISS Tildie, to set off your figure, and a ribbon brooch around your neck to match your cameo earrings, with your hair up like so. With perhaps a few curls in the front to show off—"

"My forehead, I know." Tildie Bonneau squinted in the looking-glass.

Dora peered out from behind her. "I kin show you how to make the curl tuh stay."

"Kin yuh, Dora?"

"Oh yes, of course, Miss Tildie, my pleasure." *Somethin' gotta make this dress look right.*

For weeks, Dora had been preparing gowns for Tildie Bonneau's trousseau and wedding party. The harvest party season presented a perfect framing for Miss Bonneau's announcement of engagement—dinners, balls, and casual gatherings designed to impress her fiancé's family with her social prominence and her privileged Charleston elite friends with his money. Tildie and her bridesmaid gossiped shamelessly, both of them prisoners of straight pins, while Dora finished their fitting. Dora had learned to ignore their chatter.

"Other than his bein' from Delaware, he's the perfect pedigree. Princeton—old Yankee money—Mayflower. One Southern grandma. All he needs now is a young Southern wife. Young, Southern, virginal, and pure," Tildie went on.

"When is Cole going to find me a Princeton classmate?" Dora heard one of the bridesmaids whine. The entourage—Nimmie, Ginny, Nancy P., and Annie—were interchangeable. Dora could never tell them apart.

"They've gotta let him back in first."

"I'm young, Southern, virginal, and pure, bein' goddaughter to Julius Mayfield oughta count fuh, ow! What's wrong wid you—nig—"

"Dora, where is yo' mind today? Go an' get me somethin' to drink."

"Yes, m'am."

"Do not call me m'am! Call me Tildie or Tootie or Miss Tootie. Anything but m'am!"

"Yes, miss."

As she exited, the bridesmaid jiggled on the hem stool. "Tildie, I gotta go to the potty."

"Dora! Where is your silly ass? Get us outta these pins, please!"

Dora ignored them and continued down the hall. The wedding dress and the bridesmaids' gowns would surely make an impression. Business would grow. That was the plan. And now it had gone awry again. How they just presumed she was there to wait on them! She had not expected her own pedigree to come up, but if the Mayfields were still a prominent family, there was no indication of their relation to her. Even so, the comment had unnerved her.

"Miss Matilda would like some mint tea," she announced to the regular maid, the kitchen swing door swaying loudly behind her. The young girl folded her arms across her chest, announcing she had no intention of budging. "Git it yoseff." Dora gritted her teeth and got the glasses from the cupboard. She pulled apart the sprigs of mint, doused the water pitcher with sugar, then placed the whole saccharine presentation on a silver serving tray. The maid snickered as she left. The swing door popped her in the back. Sparks pricked at her woolen stockings as she marched across the hallway Persian carpet and up the stairs.

The day had collected static, distracting Dora from other concerns. She had put off telling Winrow that she could not go to the minstrel show with him. She had practiced several versions—lies, the truth, the truth with different emphases, part of the truth. *Maybe won't say nothin'. Maybe somethin'll happen and won't be no need.* But nothing had happened and now she only had two days left. How was she going to tell him that the minstrel show was the same day as the book party? *When he come over for his readin' lesson, why din't you tell him then?* Her confusion was turning her whole day into a medley of irritations.

Oh dem golden slippers, oh dem golden slippers, golden slippers I'se goin' to wear, because they look so neat . . . She had wanted to hear that music, but an invitation to the Marivales' was an entrée to colored society, one that had not been offered by her own blood kin. It not only meant business opportunity, but the opportunity to meet some more suitable partners. *No, cain't say that.* She didn't actually believe that. She hated the presumptions of entitlement, worth, and acceptance that her aunt's social group assigned to color. Nevertheless, as strongly as she disdained their practice of exclusion, she wanted so very much to pass their judgment. Her desires were torn. She so wanted to hear the music and to wear her lace-tipped shoes. *Oh dem golden slippers, oh dem golden slippers, golden slippers I'se goin' to wear, to walk the golden street . . .* Suddenly Dora realized that the song's refrain wasn't in her head but was emanating from across the upstairs hall.

Following the music, she ascended the stairs and crossed the hall, then stood transfixed in the doorway, the tray of mint tea juleps in her hand. Coleridge McKinley was seated with his papers and cigar. She moved away wordlessly, her back straight as a pin as always, her head a little bowed. "No, Dora, it's fine really. It's just a piano. Plays by itself. Come see." The new player piano had brought the bird to his perch. He cranked up the handle and a medley of tinny chords danced across the keys. Like magic!

"I bes' get back to yo' cousin Miss Tildie."

Languishing in his rooms, Coleridge was in dread of his own dementia. His grandfather, who had lived in baronial splendor, now wandered around a withered old fool in gray homespun and soiled tights. The sight disgusted him, the slobbering excuses for defeat. He found it all so tedious. He blocked her path. "You needn't go just yet." Mid-afternoon and he had already been drinking.

"Please let me pass."

"Why, Miss High and Mighty?"

"Get away from me, suh."

"Bring you something nice."

"Get away."

He leaned against the door frame and stroked her cheek with the back of his hand. "I seen yo grandmammy on the docks. Sellin' charms. Crab claw under the tongue. Where's your charm, huh? Let me see?" When his palm graced her lips, she bit him good. The tray went flying. Green crystal glass and sprigs of mint crashed to the floor. Coleridge retreated back to his room as Tildie came running out, followed by her entourage—Nimmie, Ginny, Nancy P., and Annie.

"Goddammit, Dora, clean that up! Takin' it out yoah wages, yuh know."

Dora determined from thenceforth to finish up early and get on home. *Come back inna morning is better. His ol' drunk ass be sleep.*

*   *   *

SHE WALKED back to her home that day, marching off her fury. As she approached the two-story row house, narrow alleys closed in on her. Less space than the quarters. *Slave street.* Was there no escape? She was still sputtering fury when Winrow arrived. Sweat poured from her forehead as she ironed a batch of dress shirts for Yum Lee. *How stupid!*

"Whyn't you wait fuh me to fetch yuh?"

"What is it of your business, Win? I am doin' my work."

"A woman of mine wouldn't do no work."

"I am my own woman, not one uh yourn."

Her sharpness took him aback. "... You got the niggah's attention, Miss Dora. What's wrong? Sumpin happen at that house?"

"No, nuthin happen. Why you ax sumpin like that?"

"Things is changin', that's all. Times mo dangerous. Sully got pulled off the railroad n beat up. Stoah got shot up in Allendale, dragged the colored sheriff through the street back of his own wagon. Lynchin' up the way at—"

"That's lowlife white trash cuttin' up, not respectable folk. I have a respectable job."

"Look around. Rights stripped away, more every week it seem. They even trying to say I cain't do livery no mo. Axing where my license, sayin' they a new law an cullud cain't cart no people, only produce n livestock. It's raining fire, Dora. And you just walkin' through it blind. I juss wanna make sure you safe."

She slapped the hot iron upright on the table. "I kin see juss fine. Everybody kin see it's the women that's gettin' the work. I got to get this money. That's how I be safe. That's what people respect." She did not tell Win anything of the incident. She felt confident that she could handle it herself. Her back was strong from lifting bolts of material, her fingers nimble enough to gouge, pinch, and scratch.

"I didn't come to fight wit yuh, I used too strong words. Just let me pick you up is all I ax."

"All right then." She watched him, fingering his hat. "But I ain't goin' to the minstrel show with you. I cain't . . . I been invited somewheres else."

"If you wanna miss the bess band inna country, don't understand that. But I'll go wherever you wants."

"The invitation was just for me, Win. It is a private function, but it's a chance to improve my condition, my situation in life. There'll be a lot of clients for work. It's important for my business, really. But you go on to the show. And I'm sure Mah Bette still wanna go."

"Well, awright then. I kin understand that. But you got to take some time to have some fun sometime, Miss Dora."

"I kin have fun latuh. I gotta make sumpin of my life right now."

"Well . . . how you goin' git to this thing? I could drop you on my way if you needin' transport?"

"Thank yuh, but my cousin Mr. Diggs has kindly offered me a ride."

"Oh I see. Show's in two days, you juss findin' this out? . . . Oh I see."

"No, Mr. Winrow, you don't," she lied. "I just need to go to this event. It will help me make my livin'. I would like to go with you to the show, but I must look out for Ma Bette and myself. I'm sorry I did not give you much notice, but I struggled to tell you."

"You don't ever need to struggle to tell me nothin', Miss Dora." He broke into a wide bright grin. "Yo granmammy an me gon have us a good ol' time. Now, I bettuh git my lesson or Aunt Sibby be mean as a snake, I ain't there to pick her up."

* * *

EUDORA COULD not catch her breath. *Dear Lord, please help me. When I get to askin', you know I'm serious.* That morning, the sky still dark, she had already started working on her hair, scenting the cooking oil to grease it with tea rose water. She had left her hair plaited in thick sections for three days to get it to look wavy, and coated it nightly to make it shine, all the while praying that the sea fog would not envelop the city on this most important day. Each strand bristled as if terrified. Dora was always trying to improve herself, but no effort was ever good enough. Embarrassed by both sides—the mothuh's, the phantom fathuh's—she was as wracked by doubt as she was stoked with determination. *They's all gonna be high, high-toned. God the Fathuh sent me these trials to prepare me for His Kingdom.*

Dora made herself respectable with meticulous attention to detail. Collar buttoned, hands gloved. Hat, purse, posture. She had decorated her old straw sunbonnet with wildflowers that Win had brought her from his farm. A perfectly symmetrical bouquet of pansies, poppies, bluebells, and lilies tied to a wreath of sea grass arched across the front brim. She wore it tilted forward to accommodate the rather large folds of hair, which she had swept into an asymmetrical sculpture. Saucer on a teacup. She suddenly regretted the flurry of imagination. *How stupid!*

She was beside herself. A woman living without a father, husband, or male relative. This was black Charleston's cream of the crop and its café au lait. A woman who made clothes for a living. No education, no money. The thinnest grasp on respectability. *My pride, their shame, their pride, mine.* She thirsted for air, then stopped breathing altogether. Sitting on the banister beside the reception table was a small brown paper bag. The torn edges of paper fluttered and buzzed in the breeze. *Brown Society? That's what it is?* She bristled at the prospect of her flesh tone being compared to a paper bag. Her chest constricted with pain, her breath shallow. The last stair. Dora stepped up, lowered her gaze, and steeled herself before looking up.

The young men at the reception table froze in wonder. She had no concept of her beauty or its impact. *There is something wrong, I did not pass, I did not pass, this doggone hat has too many flowers . . .* Her eyes startled everyone. "I am a guest of Miranda Marivale, Miss Dora May." She stood with her back perfectly straight as the young gentleman rifled through the list and found her name handwritten on the bottom. "Ah yes, of course," he chirped and held the bag up to her face. She almost fainted.

"Bon-bon?"

"Put that away, John Lake," the elder Mrs. Marivale interceded.

"Madame, if I must man the table, I am entitled to some nourishment."

"At least let me get you a dish."

"I prefer the bag. That way I can share with whom I wish." He smiled at Dora. Roswell Jr. bumped her bustle with his plump torso as he reached over her and swiped one of the small candies. "So nice of you to offer, John Lake." Roswell took another. "But my cousin is not interested in any of your bon-bons."

The elder Mrs. Marivale rescued her and whisked her into the house. "I can see why Roswell's son has kept you to himself. My dear, you are simply beautiful! Never put any anything on your face!"

It was a three-storied mansion, each room larger than the last. The walls were oddly covered with mural paintings of near naked cherubim and women embracing, draped in flowing swatches of cloth, frolicking in dense amber foliage. "My nephew's. He studied in Paris." Mrs. Marivale had the demeanor of one accustomed to privilege. Her gracious, jeweled hands waved about in small swirls as she maneuvered Dora through the vestibule crowd. "We'll be discussing the latest missive from the hand of Ida B. Wells, a colored female journalist out of Alabama. Quite something, a first for us, a woman writer. That hat is splendid!" Her fine strands of silver hair swept into a chignon, her rounded shoulders consumed in a lace cravat, Mrs. Constance Marivale looked whiter and richer than any of the Bonneaus. "The christening gown was a work of art. You must meet my nephew. He is artistic, too. Oh, there's the assemblyman, excuse me, dear."

Dora tried to take stock of everything. A garland of pond lilies tied with blue satin ribbon graced the serving table. Dresses of silk, brocade, satin, velvet, moire, and tulle. She noticed also that, although the men were of many different hues, the women were not. Excluding the servants, as invisible as she was at the Bonneaus, she was the darkest. *Diamonds! Pearls, fresh flowers, someone else has flowers. Blue surrah lace overdress. Cloak $15. Saque hat $3.* She now thought the houndstooth plaid of the waistcoat she had thought so smart was too casual for the occasion, and the flowers a transparent attempt to draw attention to herself. *Ridicullous.*

From the corner of her eye, she caught two women, their eyes laughing, their hands cupped over their mouths. She saw one pointing to her shoes. *My cowrie shoes from the Miss.* Her feet were pointed east and west. *Country Lowland Geechee.* Beads of sweat dotted her nose, bluebells and hyacinth dancing just above.

Roswell approached, his cheeks already rosy from the flask of brandy he used to wash down the bon-bons. "Let's see. Blanche and Juliet were sisters. That would make us cousins, I suppose. No such thing as a step-cousin. My stepmother's niece. Blanche does hate for me to call her that. Mother. If I said Mama, she would probably asphyxiate."

"You may just continue to call me a relation if that suits you better."

"In actuality, we are not related at all really. You are cousin to Francina and the boy. There's no blood between us."

Whiskey, chocolate, and bile. "My, it's close." She waved her handkerchief. "Might I have some punch?"

She watched Roswell toddle off, then began moving in a direction away from him. The less said about her relations the better. *And who is your mother again? Where are your people from?* She dreaded the questions. She wanted just to start fresh. *Why can't life be what you make of it yourself? Who cares where you come from?* "What is it you're doin' for yourself?" she blurted aloud.

"Makin' it, but could do a might bettuh." Sullivan, the railroad porter, appeared at her side.

Her eyes widened. "Mr. Sullivan, I did not expect to see you here."

"Indeed. Nor I you, Miss Dora," he said wryly. She knew Sullivan only as one of Winrow's gambling buddies. "I had understood that Win was taking you to the Callendar's minstrel show."

"He has spoken of me?"

"Not out of turn. He has great admiration for you." Sullivan would relish the next time he saw Win.

"What brings you to the Brown Society?"

"Railroad gets around," he smiled. "And you?"

Roswell returned with a small crystal cup of punch. Dora introduced the two men, wishing they would both go away. The handle was so petite, the punch spilt from the cup the moment Dora brought it to her lips. Her fingers in her newly macramed gloves felt like ten bound beings. She rested the cup in her palm and turned to Sullivan. "I made the christening frock for Mrs. Marivale's baby. As I am a professional woman, she thought the discussion of a woman writer would interest me."

"Indeed."

His terseness infuriated her. "A colored woman author, you must admit that is something."

"Yes, but did you see her hair?" Roswell chuckled.

If she could have fit her fingers around the handle, Dora would have thrown the cup in his face. The both of em! One of the maids detected her distress and appeared with a serving tray. "M'am, may I take that for you?" The two women had often ridden Tom Winrow's livery together. "I believe Miss Marivale lookin' fuh yuh." She winked and directed Dora toward the next room.

The idea of a woman on her own, writing, going all across the country, exposing the horrors of which no one else would speak—the audacity, the courage thrilled her, yet here she was, panic-stricken at walking across a room, at even speaking.

"Race interests before party interests."

"But we are down to two state senators alone."

"A Negro is hanged who stole a box of cigars and a bottle of whiskey? A white man stole six thousand dollars and is pardoned? You aren't still thinking that we can achieve anything through government, are you?" She was fascinated by the conversation—as much of it as she could follow. The sisters had taught her, "One must speak up to have one's thoughts considered," but the conversation was so heady, the people so confident in their thoughts, their speech unflawed to her ears. She hesitated at each turn. *Literacy, poll tax? Eight-box ballot? Colored, Afro-American, Negro?*

"You do not identify with the poor members of the race when you benefit from their earnings to sustain your own."

"Their experience is so far removed, it's like . . . it's like a picture on the wall."

Pictures don't talk, people do. What they need, what they want, and none of yuh doin' much talking to em, much less askin'. People got mouths. People got ideas. She was beginning to feel that this venture was a terrible mistake. *Could be tappin' my foot to a good music show, and here I am walkin' round, dressed up like a dummy, feet flappin' on the parquet floor.*

Winrow was right. The Charlestonian colored aristocracy continued to live in a world of their own. The way they earned their money—the barbers, caterers, morticians, lawyers, and the few government positions that remained available to them—protected them against the change in times. It would be two more years before Homer Plessy would discover that their country regarded them just as unequal and unentitled as regular black folk. Sheltered from the rapidity and severity of the descent into Jim Crow that the laundrywomen, dock workers, street cleaners, and maids knew only too well, they were living on the vapors of history, just as much as the Bonneaus.

They were decent enough. Teacher in the freedmen's school, tailor, small shopkeeper, pastor in a stone-hewn church, steamboat operator. Like Roswell, they served their people in necessary ways. Like his brothers, they still had intimate ties with their white tidewater families, their fortunes as interwoven as their bloodlines. Freeborn forebears—tradesmen, craftsmen, artisans, and lots of mistresses, concubines—were as dependent upon the slaving South as the slaveholders. Fear of the black slaves' freedom had more than once put theirs in jeopardy. Dora, with her foot in each world, belonged to neither.

Another guest watched her as she moved. He had been wandering around the party—a colored de Tocqueville, observing the provincials. He noticed her immediately—so different from the others, so beautiful. "Mademoiselle, vous êtes une fleur, vient en vie."

Dora did not know how to react. The only person she knew who spoke French was Madame Pilar, and that friendship was hardly one to which she wanted to call attention. "Beg pardon?"

"The way you are standing. In Paris, I would take you for a ballerina."

Ballerina . . . what that mean?

Mrs. Marivale floated in behind her. "Ah, I see you have met our other islander, Monsieur Dessalines. Eudora Mayfield, monsieur, is niece to my good friend Blanche Diggs. Comes to us from St. Simon's."

Dora May! "It's a small island just off the coast," Dora explained.

"Monsieur Dessalines is from Hayti," Mrs. Marivale said conspiratorially, "where the late Mr. Marivale served as ambassador in the years when our people had their few moments of glory."

"Like yours, mine is a small island, too." His eyes flirted with her, caressed her as he kissed her glove. The sensation raced up her arm, ricocheted through her body, and exited out her toes. She barely heard his words.

"An island which astonished the world by winning its own freedom," Mrs. Marivale added, as she put her slender veined hand on his shoulder.

"Yes, and we have paid a price for that arrogance."

"You are faring better than the colored are here, Monsieur Dessalines. From eleven congressmen, we are down to two. Dessalines and my nephew became acquainted in Paris, Dora."

"Mr. Dessalines."

"Please call me Yves. As in temptation."

In the nick of time, Blanche approached with Roswell Sr., forever late to social affairs. Blanche squeezed Dora's hand in a show of filial affection and placed her cheek on the young woman's face and made an audible kiss to the air. "Forgive our tardiness, my dear. Roswell had three services today."

Miranda Marivale descended the stairs, holding her newborn. Blanche, with her flaxen locks, golden skin, and a practiced grace, scooped the infant in her arms and cooed, "I must see this Miss Wells. I heard Senator Bruce of Mississippi pursued her and she turned him down."

"Don't believe it for a minute. Pursued, yes," her husband corrected, "but not in that manner. He has absolutely castigated her in the press. We must ask her about that."

"Miss Wells could not join us as planned," Mrs. Marivale interjected in a near whisper. "She is in seclusion. There is a death threat on her head across the South for publishing her book. We will have to settle for the autographed copies Mr. Sullivan was kind enough to smuggle in."

Dora wandered again into the vestibule to examine Miss Wells's new book for herself. Copies were stacked on the mantel and one was open for display. She leafed through it and found the inset photograph of the author. Dora stared at the image. The crown of African hair which Roswell had so derided, her broad, sculpted features, the solid, dark proud eyes fixed on some faraway future or past, reminded Dora of the one picture she had of her mother, Juliet.

She flipped to an interior page and began reading. "...neck...Death came...for fully ten minutes after he was strung up the chest...convulsive movements of the limbs...threw his body into a fire and watched as it burned . . . heart and liver cut into pieces . . . bones crushed for souvenirs, 25 cents, piece of cooked liver for ten. A noted senator bought a slice of the heart." In Charleston, she had been shielded from the severity of the South's retrenching terror. The coastal lowlands, still majority black, were being defeated by the legislature, not by lynchings. Dora dropped the book on the mantel and covered her face with her hands. She pushed her hat back off her brow. The lace collar she had knitted herself suddenly was tight around her neck, the floral pattern on the walls she had so admired now nauseated. She stepped quickly to the wide front porch to breathe in some air and sunlight. She could not move her fingers. She felt heat, smelled flesh, heard screams.

Dessalines caught her by the waist and eased her to a porch chair. The confident tenor melody of his voice brought her back. "It is quite gruesome what one human being can do to another."

"I had not a notion. All these stories. All these people killed!"

His eyes narrowed and his gaze turned inward. "That is nothing."

"How can you say that? How can you possibly say such a thing?"

"I am from Hayti." His laugh was incredulous. "The depths of depravity that I have witnessed, the generations of stories I was told all of my young life, my nation's bloody and furious hundred years' war for freedom allows me." He wanted to sound worldly, to impress these colored Americans, who, twenty years out of slavery, fretted that liberty was still elusive, but when he turned to her, the ardor in her eyes, the flush of her cheeks, the passion in her lips, her honesty as unnerving as her beauty, he was speechless. His confident, Continental visage dissolved. He wanted to kiss her.

"Oh, there you are, Dora!" Mrs. Marivale had finally found her nephew and was dragging him beside her, their short arms intertwined. "I wanted you two to meet. You're both artistic."

Mrs. Marivale's nephew lifted the stem of his sherry glass with his whole fist. "Aunt Constance tells me you have a good head for business."

Dessallines clicked his heels and faded away.

✳ ✳ ✳

DORA HAD purchased her first book. Now she had three. The Bible, a hand-me-down dictionary. *And now Miss Wells. First one of my own.* The world it seemed was much bigger than a peach. Miss Wells had demonstrated capabilities that made Dora feel her own ambition meager and selfish. The small children who gathered round her window. Perhaps she could give them some rudimentary instruction and start that sewing school. Fights on the railroad and over the erasure of colored people's rights. People dying too often. Flare-ups of violence. What was she to do about this? And what of Aunt Sibby, the generation that had borne the yoke of enslavement, who would tend them? Miss Wells's book had opened her eyes to the threat of random violence besieging her people at every turn. There were too many problems to contemplate, too many people to help when she could barely make a way for herself.

The next day Dora arrived home from Yum Lee's with her weekly piecework order. "Got somethin' for yuh," Bette announced and pointed to a long balsa wood box on the table. Since getting her first pair of shoes from Sears Roebuck, Dora always liked boxes. She opened it quickly and unwrapped the white tissue. A shimmer of sun caught the fabric inside, a bolt of Andalusian lace, linen and silk gossamer threads spun by butterflies!

"It came all the way from New Orleans, and before that Paris, France. Know where that is, gal?"

"Yes, I know where that is. I have seen it on a globe, Mah Bette. How did you get this?"

"I didn't get it. You got it. Read the card, Miss Smart Nose."

" 'For someone as delicate and graceful as this lace, with hopes that I might see you soon.' "

Dora unwound the bolt of fabric and wrapped a piece round her waist. Mah Bette squinted at the card. "Yives . . ."

"It's Eve, Mah Bette, Eve Dessalines," Dora corrected as she swayed, modeling the fabric to herself, holding it to the light.

"Name sounds like a woman." Winrow, who had entered for his lesson, put his hat on the table as if, having shellacked it, he was entitled to do so. Sullivan had told him all about the book party. "You missed a great show at Callendar's, Miss Dora. Bert King got a new act, put a whole cup an' saucer in he mouf. They played up a might of they hit tune. Me and Miss Lizzie sat in wid em. It was a good time."

"I'm accustomed to someone knockin', Mr. Winrow."

"Doah was open," he said, standing at it.

Bette threw her white braid over her shoulder and placed her hands on her hips and wiggled a bit girlishly as she retired to her sleeping area behind the curtain. "He sure don't look like no woman."

Predictably alarmed, Dora followed. *Always knows somethin'.* "How you know, Mah Bette? You seen him?" she whispered.

"Fuh sho," Bette answered quietly. "He bring me some things for my business from time to time. He be captain of a great ship. He seen you talkin with your ole Mah Bette and inquired about you. I told him where we lived and I promised to bring you this package." She folded her arms across her chest and giggled. "I give him a charm to keep him fuh yuh."

"No you dint!" Dora hissed. "I know you dint do that!"

"He don't know what it fuh. He a sea captain, own his own boat. Dot what I talkin' bout. Got people workin' for him. His business takes him to Haiti, Savannah City, Cuba, New Orleans, even New York. A true gentleman." Bette moved closer. "Winrow's nice enough for when you first got here, for you to get to thinking somethin' of yourself, but that was all that I intended."

"Well, I'll not accept such a gift. This will have to go back. I'll have to tell him thankee, but he'll have to take it back."

"Tell him yourself," Bette replied, pulling back the curtain.

There at the door was Yves Dessalines. Both he and Tom stood at the entryway. Two pole cats.

Mah Bette was delighted. Here was a man more to her liking than that mule driver musician who fancied her grandgal. Though not one to make her true feelings known, Bette readily acted upon them. *Every gal need to have suitors.* "Mr. Dessalines, a pleasure to see you again!"

Dora rewrapped the material and approached him. "I cannot accept this."

"But je ne comprends pas. I understood you were open for business."

"Hey, wait a minute!" Win interjected, thinking his girl insulted.

"You are a dressmaker, non? Best in Charleston, I am told. I brought the lace for you to make me a dress. A dress for my affianced, my bride-to-be."

"Oh, oh . . . oh. Forgive me." *How stupid!*

A quartet of voices followed.

"You have money for this?"

"Win, I can handle my own affairs."

"Why yes, of course. I will leave this as deposit. Spare no expense."

"I cannot begin work on the dress today."

"Of course, I do not mean to intrude."

"Siddown, stay fuh dinnuh."

"I cannot, Maum Elizabette, but thank you. I must get back to my ship. I have already intruded upon you for too long. I will return tomorrow to discuss the design, if I may."

"Why yes, of course."

"What time?" Win intruded.

"Is this gentleman someone to you?"

"He is my neighbor and friend. Forgive me. Mr. Winrow, Thomas, Mister . . . Monsieur Dessalines."

"Yves."

"I heard."

"Yes, what time?"

"Round two o'clock?"

"I reckon that will be fine."

"À deux heures, bien." Dessalines clicked his heels and bowed, then crisply nodded to Winrow, the challenge clearly on.

* * *

DESSALINES. HIS lips were broad, soft, and unlined, always in a faint smile. Chestnut skin, hair of raven ringlets close to the scalp, he had the eyes of a ladies' man, and smelled of scented water used for linens. His body was robust and lean like a swimmer.

Sired of a cane wench during the Grand March of Dessalines, he was a road bastard born of a marun brought down from the mountains, a Dahomette warrior who had drunk blood to free herself, only to be splayed across the table for the pleasure of the new king of a new nation. "Dessalines!" she cursed and named her bastard after him.

He liked to tell that story to impress, but he knew no more of his ancestry than a dog or cat. He was a harbor rat as a boy, begging for coins, diving for wrecks, singing for the few foreign vessels that still docked at the rotting piers, scorched black wood spires scratching at the sky.

Dessalines could dive deeper than most boys, could hold his breath like a fish. He discovered a world beneath the glimmer of the surface water. The algae-laced wreckage of a lost world—caravels, men-of-war, brigantines, schooners, and clippers—great sailing ships, collapsed like a game of pick-up sticks on the ocean floor. Slavers coming to port, rum dealers leaving, gens de couleur traveling to Europe, French colonists coming to settle stolen lands with stolen people. Soldier fleets of the revolution for liberty, disembarking to battle slaves. Shackles, cane rounds, coffee sacks, cocoa beans, rum barrels, and jugs of molasses—Hayti, the land of mountains, the richest colony in the New World for two centuries, now arched her bare rib cage for schools of fish and curious boys.

* * *

DESSALINES APPEARED a week late, and he did not come at two, but at three thirty. "I stopped to pick some apologies," he said with a bouquet. Flowers picked from the road. Golden jasmine, deep yellow with crimson tips.

"Mr. Dessalines. This is not 'propriate. Your appointment was a week ago."

"Mais prie, don't take it out on the flowers."

She put them in a tin can. "It seem odd, not right, you should gib flowers to someone and you are affianced."

"Because one picks a rose one cannot admire a garden?"

When he did not appear, she had cried herself to sleep two nights in a row. And here she was, delirious with longing. She determined not to display an inkling of it. "So tell me what did you have in mind about the dress."

"Well, it would be about your size."

"I'll make it so you can adjust when you take it to her. And the style?"

"Whatever you would choose."

"Forgive me for saying, Mr. Dessalines. I would think a woman would like to pick out her own wedding dress. I think I know that much by now."

"She is from a respected family, but they have fallen on difficult times. My returning with the dress will indicate respect for their standing and discretion. She herself knows nothing of her own beauty. She is young."

At all of twenty, the intimation that Dora was not "young" disturbed her. "You say she is about my size?"

"Exactement."

"Anything I think is best? Perhaps off the shoulder, with a train, scalloped."

"In two weeks, I shall return to see how the work fares. I sail again tonight."

AN AMSTERDAM outrigger, last of the clipper ships, making short runs for low-volume goods like Blue Mountain coffee, Indonesian hashish, and Ethiopian red amber, docked in the bay of Gonaïves. As a young boy Dessalines had impressed the Dutch captain with his ability to hold his breath. "I stay under water long time, you take me with you," he said and progressed quickly from cabin boy to first mate to navigator. The sea had taken him to Paris, The Hague, Liverpool, London, Bordeaux, Cape Verde, Zanzibar, even Cairo. But he had escaped one dying world and entered another. Sailing ships, the three- and four-mast silhouettes that had dominated the seas for three centuries, were disappearing, defeated by diesel and steam. To stay in business sailors sometimes resorted to smuggling.

Winrow knew him to be a scoundrel, a modern-day pirate, with the presumptuous airs of a gens de couleur. Away from Dora's view, Win caught him by the arm in the street. "You leave her alone. She a decent gal. I hold her mighty high in my book. Don't wanna see her brought down by no port trash like you."

Dessalines contemplated which blade he carried. The short poniard, the grooved stiletto, or the kris. "Come at me with a sword, monsieur, you shall get the end of it."

7

WHEN DESSALINES RETURNED, DORA MAY WAS IN A WHIRL. *Stitches too tight, décolletage too busy, poorly sewn.* Since she was making the dress for some other woman, she was trying too hard, thinking too much and not at all. "It is only a basting stitch. I didn't use the good fabric. Just calico, until the design is right." His head was tilted to the side, his hand on his chin. "You don't like it."

"Yes, but . . . something is lacking. Get dressed quickly. I will show you."

"But I am dressed."

"Not for sailing."

Dora ran behind the curtain and changed three times. She had gone on a ferry to Fort Sumter for the church picnic. She had ridden pirogues on the islands, fished in a rowboat, but she had no idea what "dressed for sailing" meant. She put on her Missy's shoes, then changed back into her sturdy browns. Then ran back for her hat, ripping off the dry brown flowers from the party. She wore it plain, but still forward on her forehead.

Triangle sails dotted the cobalt sea as they walked along the pier. It had been a long time since she had seen the sea. Though she walked along the Charleston harbor market district weekly, her eyes were focused on the future, rarely on the sights around her. They stopped at a Baltimore, a trim twenty-foot sloop named *L'Heureux.* She watched herself take his hand. *You are making a mistake. You will lose sight of your ambitions.* The boat was much bigger than the hauling pirogue Lijah-Lah used to maneuver around St. Simon's canals and waterways, but it was sleek and new. Unlike the mosquito fleet of rowboats, flat-tops, skiffs, and tugs that daily supplied Charleston's fish markets, this one was built for racing. It cut fast through the waves, shifting the winds on her cheeks and around the curves of her neck and through the winding coils of her hair. It stole her breath, the rhythm on her chest a whispered heartbeat. Her hat flew away and cakewalked on the waves, a high-steppin' reel. The winds parted her fingers as she held her arms out to them. The salt air tasted of freedom. Erzulie risen, she leaned on the stern laughing as the waves kissed her feet. "What kind of man can go sailing in the middle of the week? What is it you do, Monsieur Dessalines?"

"But please, call me Yves."

"*Yes, I remember, as in temptation!* What is your trade? What business you have with Mah Bette?"

"None I think that needs concern you." He had said the wrong thing. She frowned. Her chin buckled like a chicken's. She turned away, mumbling to herself under the wind. He laughed and mimicked her, put his arms astride, leaned against her and, in the heave of the bow, just graced her lips. "I am a sailor, by trade."

"Mah Bette says you are a captain."

"Of my fate, yes."

"No, of a boat."

"A ship. I am first mate of *Les Marassa,* and being first, I am more essential than a captain. This is her deck sloop. I take it out when we come to port." She felt the sweet warmth of his breath, then caught her wits again. He backed away from her. "But that is a secret between us, my being first mate. In Charleston, I must declare myself a cook or spend my land time in the brig, for by law no 'colored' may hold such a position. Alas, that makes me an outlaw. A pirate. Born of a cane wench during the Grand March of Dessalines's black Jacobeans through the mountains."

They buoyed on one of the temporary island sandbars the autumn storms would bring, a miniature dune, a few shrubs, an oasis in the sea.

As he spoke of his youth, his chestnut eyes drew her into another world. Recounting the history of his people in an afternoon, he strutted about as the stocky Napoleon, outraged that a band of blacks could outwit his Sons of Revolution. He mimicked the languid Southern drawl of the American slaveholder statesman, offering the young new republic, instead of celebration, the stranglehold of embargo and intrigue. He staggered, embodying a colony intoxicated by liberty and exhausted from battle, feeding upon itself. "As whites had upon blacks, blacks and colored upon each other." As she sat beside him on the cool sand, Dessalines spoke of his mother, caught in the maelstrom. "Danced in a palace, then swung from the gallows, garroted, and hung from her heels . . . I don't know why I tell you this. I am not accustomed to revealing so much of myself."

"It is the water. The setting perhaps. The sound of the ocean. You cannot look upon it, listen to it, and deceive. It pulls the truth out of you."

"What is your truth? A beautiful woman like you, laboring away over gowns for others far less fair."

"It is an honest living, upon which I can depend."

"But what do you dream, Dora?"

"I don't much bother with that. I just do. Don't have time for dreamin'."

"If you did, what would it be?"

"Well, I don't much know. I dreamed of gettin' my own sewing machine. Already done that . . . Of course, I dream of family. Havin' a home. Bein' an honorable free woman of color with respect, I reckon."

"Respect? How do you think to get this?"

"Are you my schoolmaster, now?"

"You are a free woman. You should have no master but yourself."

"How you vex me! Monsieur Dessalines—I—"

"Ah, I have been demoted. Yves."

"Yves . . ." Her knees drawn to her chest, she watched him build a small fire, then produce a handful of wild yams from the sack slung over his shoulder. He delicately maneuvered them into the embers with a piece of driftwood, all the while humming a soft tenor merengue that blended with the chords of salt air, his voice merging with the sea in serenade.

> "Oh, I had a girl in Port-au-Prince,
> I loved her so and was convinced,
> She was the only girl for me,

And I gave that girl a golden ring,
I promised her 'most everything,
But then I heard your melody,
And sitting here beside you now,
This to you I vow,
Whenever, wherever, forever,
I am your,
Mon amour, je t'adore,
Toujours, tu as mon coeur . . .

He the Devil meant to steer you off yo' course, she cautioned herself. *What sort of man have no home but the sea?*

As he poked at the edges of the flame, he turned, laughing. "Your shoes. They are quite formidable."

"Yes, I bought them myself. From the Sears Roebuck catalogue. My work shoes, for work."

"Perhaps you should give them some air, non?"

Fussing with herself, she roughly unlaced her shoes and placed them upright beside her, then struggled to remove her cotton stockings without raising her dress. The fine sand drizzled between her toes. "Mons— Yves, you bring me out here to explain something about the dress?"

He took her feet by the ankles and held them by the arches, beheld them. "Is there no part of you that is not beautiful?"

"Just what is it you want of me?"

"I wanted to spend time alone with you."

"What of your affianced? The one that you would marry?"

"She is a long way away and I do not believe that I will see her again. I have written her a letter declaring that I have found the woman of my dreams."

"But you hardly know me." She pulled her feet back and, brushing off the sand, tucked her knees under her dress.

"Aha, I have not yet mailed the letter."

He sat beside her. The cup of his hand drew her mouth to his. "I am not the sort of man you get involved with, but when I look at you I don't care. From the moment I saw you gazing at the world, I knew. I want you to come away with me, Dora."

"What?"

"Tell me where you would like to go, anywhere in the world. Command me and I will take you there."

"I think I would like to go back to Charleston."

"A free woman of color, free to choose any place in the world, and you choose Charleston? Before we have even had our feast?"

"We must go, please." Her heart raced. She fought like a swimmer in undertow.

"You should sing again with me."

"What'd make you say such a thing? I cannot, I do not sing. I would frighten the sunlight."

"Nonsense, I heard you singing on the boat. 'I gave that girl a golden ring and promised her 'most everything, but sitting here beside you now, this to you I vow . . .' The dress you make for my bride, you make for yourself."

✳ ✳ ✳

"FOLKS BE talkin'."

"Why, whatever could you think, Winrow! What is it of your business? Monsieur Dessalines was trying to show me something of the dress he wants for his affianced."

"Some . . . thing?"

"What can I tell you, Tom? He wanted me to get a sense of the dress, so it would feel like sailing. And since when do I have to explain myself to you?" She sat back on her buttocks and rocked to and fro, self-content. She had done nothing improper and would not act so. "I am making a dress."

"Folks be talkin' is all I'm sayin'," Tom said softly, his teeth clenched.

If there is no leaving, there is no coming back, Yves had said. She had allowed him to caress her, he had declared himself, and yet now he had sailed again. What was she to make of this? It had stormed the night long, the thunder rousing her from sleep, her dreams punishing her with doubt. On her way to the Bonneaus' when she was sitting beside Win, the buckboard passed a tree shorn clean of bark. It had been struck naked by lightning. *Someone should gather that bark, make good kindling,* she thought as she walked into the Bonneau mansion.

Miss Tildie greeted her at the door. "We have very important visitors coming, an important connection for my fiancé's fathuh. Regular gal took sick again. Mama says you will stand in as the servin' maid." Before Dora could respond, Tildie turned her back and moved up the stairs, gesturing dismissal with her hand over her shoulder. "Go on in the kitchen. Cook'll tell you what to do. We'll finish up the fittin' tomorruh."

Grimfaced, Dora quickly decided that she had no choice but to put up with the indignity. She had forgone other clients to work on this wedding, and she had purchased some of the special elements—pearl buttons, décolletage—from her own pocket. *These gowns gotta look like they come from France, high class, high society.* The Bonneaus had excellent social standing, but—holes in the carpet, hens in the house, crazy old man think the war still on—they were holding on to that, it seemed, by Dora's needle and thread. She knew the only reason she had been hired was so that the Bonneaus could save cost. She couldn't tell with these white folks what their reaction would be to her refusing their request to "help out." She cringed at the thought of Dessalines seeing her ambition so compromised. *I will own me a house with a privy and a front door that goes to the street. I will run a respectable business with my name on it, and people will call me Miss.* The refrain ran in her head like a mantra as she wove between the seats, efficiently removing soup bowls and replenishing dinner rolls with silver tongs it had taken her twenty minutes to polish. More than ever she needed to prove that she could succeed at her design, that she could make her way on her own. *You will not succumb to this man, this man who offers faraway worlds and song and sweet yams. He doesn't offer you freedom. He mocks you, toys with you.* His was a freedom she didn't dare fathom. Hers she held firmly in her hands. Yet here she was, clearing the table for the next course, doing something she swore she would never do—wait on white folk. She ground her teeth with every pass.

The intimate dinner of twenty was a motley assemblage: Tildie and her bourbon-swooned beau, pink-cheeked at noon; his father, Woodson Sr., a portly stiff New Yorker stuffed into his waistcoat, and his Delaware-bred mother with crinolined hair, the railroad baron and his gilded wife; two of Tildie's bridesmaids and their beaus; her poet brother, her Confederate grandfather in his mildewed dress grays, and her mother with the constant downturned smile and arched eyebrow, Charlestonian aristocracy, the heart of a fallen empire—first to secede, first to fire, first to fall. The constellation was rounded out by an empty chair, opposite a talking mouth full of food, bits and flecks of it in its mustache, teeth dribbled with tobacco, the governor of their fair state, a small farm husbandman from the Cumberland piney woods who went by the name of Pitchfork. Ben Tillman had come to get support for his new registration law. He had journeyed to the city of Charleston to arrange a sit-down, a political union between the old-time gentry, represented by the empty chair, Northern capital, represented by Tildie's affianced, and himself and his kind. He longed to bring these arrogant tidewater bastards with their crusted power and influence to their knees, but first he needed them. He intended to be the new senator from South Carolina, to reclaim the state not for its former masters, but for the new ones.

"We have got the Negro down, we are going to keep him down."

"But Governor Tillman, we have already initiated the eight-box, gerrymandered all colored voters into one district, and reduced representation of the Low Country by a third—they have only two delegates left—Miller and Whipper. For all intents and purposes, the Negro has already been stripped of power, what more can you ask?"

"Perhaps that we not discuss politics at the table," snapped the household's dour matriarch.

He wasn't askin'. He didn't have to. Talkin' bout the colored as if I ain't even here! Like the chair got ears and I don't. He look juss like the Devil. Poll tax, eight-box, gerrymander. She didn't understand any of it. *Democrat, Republican. Be the dickens gettin' home at this hour.*

Tillman turned toward Woodie. "The North misunderstands us. We want investment from industry, diversification of our crops, modernization of agriculture, increased trade. We welcome competitive bidding so that we are no longer hostage to the usury of a few Charleston bankers and merchants and dreamers who owe their power to the past, not the present." Tillman suppressed his ire that the guest of honor still had not shown up. Julius Mayfield, Son, was deliberately keeping him waiting. Tillman had never been invited to the home of one of the old families before. Though he had amassed two thousand acres of his own up-country, his holdings still did not compare to the wealth of the islanders or the stranglehold they still had over the politics of his state. He took the absence as a snub, deliberate and personal. An unusually long nose, thick wild eyebrows, one shiny eye, the other a sunken hollow, Tillman watched Dora wordlessly circle around the table. *Mongrel bitch*. Her ears prickled.

"I seek complete elimination. Refuse registration to any Negro applicant."

"But why?"

"The principle. The principle of power. Unless we crush the Negro totally, they will rise to rape our women and murder us in our beds." Cole had to keep from snorting in his wineglass as the visitor continued, "I say follow Mississippi and extend suffrage to every male in South Carolina—lived in the state for two years, county for one and precinct for four months. And as for the colored," he said with a snarl, "hit em with a poll tax, and typical niggah crimes: vagrancy, adultery, attempted rape—and you won't find nary none of em left to vote. Any that sneak through, make em read and write a section of the Constitution, say that blasted Fourteenth Amendment. If that fails, shoot em. Gentlemen, I seek complete separation of the races. Railroads, schools—everything. Fraternization leads to mongrelization and utter degeneracy," he spat, his one eye following Dora every time she passed.

"Shall I clear the setting, m'am?" Dora asked politely.

"Did I ask you to speak?" Mrs. Bonneau said without looking in her direction. Cole leaned back. Tildie glowered at him, ready to pounce. Cole's delicate hands, so unused to toil, placed his fork and knife across his plate. Dora wordlessly removed it. His soft lips, used to exerting no more energy than persuasion, curled in a half-smile. His ancestors had weathered a century of assault—from the British, from the cotton gin, from the North, from their own niggahs—and now they had to suffer this invasion from this poor white, up-country-come-downtown redneck. "That poses an interesting dilemma, Governor. What you propose would eliminate whites, too. Some of our best families might be denied rights under your new laws. Quiet as it's kept, there's scarcely any person of pure Caucasian blood in all of Carolina. Even with your new law, we would still have a Negro majority."

Tillman grew red and silent, then wiped the sides of his mustache with the napkin tucked in his collar. "For all practical purposes a person of color would be declared one-eighth or more. The black race is two thousand years behind and they should stay that way. We must eliminate the vote, restrict the fields of labor open to them, and demolish their schools. Every lil nigger in the state going to school and the state paying for it! Plain and simple, it spoils them for work."

Tildie's future father-in-law stirred in his chair. "You just don't trust free labor, Governor."

"Slavery is the ultimate free labor." Cole chuckled, dabbing his lips with the corner of his napkin. "You wouldn't let us keep it."

The governor glowered. "You find this humorous, son?"

"The schools would be fine if the colored raised the money themselves," Tildie interjected, picking bits from her dinner roll.

"Did just that in Columbia," Tillman clipped. "Raised all the revenue in the church. Built the school. Then wanted all black teachers. Put white teachers out of a job."

Tildie's eyes rolled up in her head. "Another croquette, Governor?"

"We need to make sure this district follows suit with the others," he continued, turning his one cold eye toward the empty dining chair. "I was under the impression that I would have the opportunity to discuss these issues with your guest, who has so unfortunately decided to absent himself from the present company. You assured me he would be here. I consented to attend this affair in the spirit of honorable cooperation and partnership."

Cole sighed with the largess of unearned privilege and stood. "May I propose a toast to the partnership at hand? I raise my glass to my fair cousin and to my esteemed former classmate, to this fine new union of North and South in a new decade of prosperity."

The old colonel came to from his stupor. "North and South? Who dares mention the North in this house? Fetch my horse!" He turned and blurted to the governor, "How'd you lose your eye? What battle? What field?"

Tillman's face flushed scarlet. Tillman had ridden the back of the bloody Red Shirts into the governor's mansion. The champion spokesman for "the average white man," he had lorded over those marauding bands that had terrorized Carolina for three decades. Emboldened by his success, he was poised to take his agenda national—looting, shooting, defrauding, and ultimately disenfranchising the nation's colored citizens en masse. Still, he was sensitive about his absence from the battlefield. "I lost my eye to illness, sir. I did not fight in the war. I fight for the cause now."

The doorbell chimed from the hallway, allowing Dora a brief escape. *Chickens, cats, bunnies, pigeons. Nimmie, Ginny, Nancy P., and Annie. Lord, just let me finish this day! Polishin' the silvuh, servin' drinks, then waitin' on the table. Now walkin' to the gate cuz the gateman's out. They such liars. Ain't got no gateman.* Dora pushed the heavy wrought-iron gate open with both hands and stood, waiting. The carriage passed, the door crested with the state seal. From the carriage window, the same bright blaze of sky that made others stare at her was staring back.

Miss Matilda Bonneau's late-arriving dinner guest, Julius Mayfield III, the heir apparent of the political oligarchy of old Carolina, appeared at the door, extended his apology, and left just as abruptly as he had arrived. Tildie was mortified. She realized immediately what her missing guest had already discerned—that Dora May was short for Mayfield.

* * *

BETTE'S HEAD bobbed in the breeze. Selling charms on the docks, she had dozed off. In sleep, the warm moist sun became candlelight. Bette could hear chamber music mingled with laughter from the banquet below—violins in the vestibule played a delicate allegro for entry music, while the Tamarind string band played a quick-stepping reel quarter dance in the main room. She was helping her white half-sister prepare for the ball. The notes wound up the spiral stair in an intoxication of harmony and melody, toppling one another as she flew about the room like a firefly. The candlelight became the myriad reflections of a chandelier, jeweled circles of light dancing on the walls. As she cleared the table of dirty china and silver, her tiny fingers just reaching the top, Massa extended his hand, inviting her to dance. Musicians played in the distance, not an orchestra, but two, maybe three trusted accompanists. While Julius twirled the child around and around, the child became a woman, spinning herself at a Juba, the clandestine ring dance practiced among her own. Candlelight to pitch torches deep in the swamp where Lijah-Lah played a new banjar and African Jeremiah pounded a hollowed-out log with flat palms, his fingers commanding her feet to lose themselves to the webbed fury of his song. Juba, Jewel, Jewel. "I can see," he said, "from how high she rides in your belly that she will be a girl. We will name the child Juliet." The name became wide dark eyes, encircled by a honey-glazed face, always a steady gaze as Bette suckled her, the mother's smile broken by the back of a hand cracked against her jaw. "Sell that bastard! The bitch and the bastard, both!"

Bette stirred from her slumber, the crackling squeal of a seagull startling her back to time. A stevedore, cap in hand, bent down beside her, in obeisance. "Mah Bette. Mauma?"

"You are troubled, my son."

In her waking state, Mah Bette didn't remember much of her childhood. Snatches of things mostly—a turn of a fiddle in the evening harbor winds, a figure dancing in the movement of the leaves. She didn't remember much of nothing but a hearty laugh that shook the boards of the floor and, to this day, her chest bones. In her old age, Bette always told her family that she had been purchased. "Mr. Julius seen me at auction in Virginia and brought me to the house. He brought me to the house as a gift to his new wife, who was barely more than a girl herself. Then I were scrubbed, fussed about, gived a little uniform. Harr all curled, a cinnamon doll, I were. Then schooled in service." Her favorite chore, she said, was to sweep the ceiling of cobwebs with a cloth-covered broom. Monday, the cook, would hoist her onto the mahogany dining table, so that she was big as the grown-ups in the room, on her toes even taller. Cook would give her a warm bath in a tiny tin tub. Then she would warm the bed. She would slip under the Missus's covers and warm the rosewater sheets with her body, for the Missus said the bed iron left the smell of coal in the threads. Her final job was to brush the Missus's hair, which was thin and straight and fine, not at all like Bette's, which sprang from her scalp in great heaping coils. Cook called it, "Your crownin' glory." The Missus made Cook cover it up. Cook brusquely fussed at the task, jerking Bette's neck as she adjusted the topknot to sit proper. But by the end of the day, the tie had always slipped off or to the side and Bette's shock of curls would spill out on their own like wild forest vines. This would infuriate the Missus, who would stomp her foot and hiss, "Git that little niggah lookin' right!" Cook would laugh and, more gently this time, fix the topknot just so.

Cook, again fat with child, was proud of the beautiful daughter she had produced, who had earned her entry into the manor house. She was content, even vain, until she saw them dancing, until she saw her master dancing with her child's feet curled around his shoes. She realized then that she had given birth to her replacement, a tiny chambermaid for his wife and himself. Monday began to beat the child, "I not your mama, you not my child," then hold her tightly to her breast. "Lawd, what we to do? Somebody ax you anyting, no speak. Nevuh." When she was delivered of her newborn, Monday tried to run away with her children, but the winter rains came early. The ground was wet and her daughter had grown. The weight of the child in her arms and the one she held fast by the wrist slowed her. She never made it to the shore, to where a boat was hidden. She was caught, branded, then sold off.

O'Brien burned the sign into her forehead. Bette clutched her own arm above the elbow, the fingers digging into the skin until it bled. Monday fainted backward into the dust. Her head snapped as O'Brien loosed his hand. "Tangled in the naps, it was," he said. "Damned niggahs." Her mouth lay open and her knees flopped to either side of her hips like a child sits sometime. Her palms were up, one hand was twitching, the fingers dancing by themselves. Bette thought that she was dead. Already, a fly circled round the blister. It landed on her cheek, cleaned its legs, and tiptoed to the edge of her lip. A faint breath startled it and blew it away. She was not dead, but scarred for good, a crooked *x* on her brow, a curved *t* for Tamarind.

The overseer was still barkin', still holding the iron in his hand, whirling it round when he spoke. "This is what'll happen if anyone attempts to steal Mayfield property or destroy it. Let it be a lesson to you all." Nobody hear him. Nobody lookin' at him. They all gone way. Standing there, eyes glazed over. Lookin' to the groun or inna far off way. Not one of em there. All run away only way they could or dared.

The circle of stunned onlookers began to fade away. Bette, in her confusion, followed a woman who looked like Cook, smelled like her, the starch and suds and flour. The woman turned around and spat.

Next dawn, a new woman, wearing Cook's clothes, came into the pantry door where Bette still sat on her palette. The new housekeeper made a clicking sound with her tongue. The child had soiled herself. Moving through the haze of habit and memory, Bette rose and set the table, laid out clothes, emptied slop, brought coffee and chicory, and brushed the Missus's hair. But there was no one to lift her onto the mantel when she was done.

Master asked her to dance, instructed the fiddler to play, twirled her around till dizzy. She clung to him. He stooped down and cupped her face in his hands. Through the double image, pale blue-gray eyes framed by golden hair that fell across his forehead, she saw the fractured angles of her own face. "This is not to go outside the house," he said and kissed her lips and drew her body into his. Bette shuttered at the memory, in longing and in loathing. She went inside herself and found a song, a wordless melody, inventing memories. Purchased she said in 1836 if anyone asked. There was no record to prove her wrong. Sherman had seen to that. Her mother, she said, she did not know, and this was not untrue.

She never saw Monday after that day. She went out to the quarter where her mother had lain. The shape of the body still showed in the dust, and a two-lined curved trail where she had been dragged away by the heels and thrown in a buckboard. O'Brien said she had been shipped back to the Indies, "To die of a sweet tooth in the sugar fields." But Bette imagined Monday had escaped again. Disappeared into the wilderness, melted into the emerald green leaves and brown bark of the forest.

Miscellaneous women attended her then with a rough mechanical coldness. Herbs to soothe, reduce the cramping, stop the bleeding. She learned quickly how to tend herself, and showed a knack for harvesting medicines and herbs. This eased her relationship with the others.

She did not linger in the past or much contemplate her future. She lived for the present. Monday had sacrificed so that she might live, so she squeezed her joy from every moment. A well-cooked stew, a beautiful morning, the mellow blend of hemp and tobacco and her children—daughters born close together, Elma, Blanche, and Juliet.

Her children were a source of pride and vengeance. Julius had children by his wife, but three were stillborn. Two died in infancy, one at five. His wife's reaction was one of denial and hysteria. The Missus hated Tamarind, the isolation, the fevers and mosquitos. The hot heavy air that hung on her clothes, the sea of slaves everywhere, most of them looking like they still tasted of salt. She exhibited such fits of rage that Bette automatically was sent to the laundry when she visited the island estate. Bette hated the laundry, working next to Sabina, the withered old woman who had spat at her as a child.

When the Missus's young daughter Rosalie, stricken with the fever, passed at the age of five, the Missus took sick herself and received condolences in her bedchamber. Female guests at the wake marveled in silent awe as the women and children who looked so much like the frail corpse waited so kindly upon them. Between her chores, Bette's firstborn, Elma, had often played with Rosalie, now so still. She watched the Missus snip a curl from her daughter's hair and asked Bette if she, too, could part with a lock. Bette's eyes glazed wide. "Don't ever let no one have yo' harr. Else they hold yo' soul."

A veil parted in the Missus's awareness that day. When she came back from riding, the black mesh netting on her face blew above her eyes as she looked around at the slave children, in particular the child sweeping the veranda. Elma had been crying, missing her playmate. As the Missus mounted the steps, she caught sight of the tear-polished eyes that in the twilight sun were unmistakably the exact same downturned oval shape and color as her husband's.

She raised her riding crop and began beating Elma with it. At the wail of her child, Bette flew from the kitchen house and showered the woman with blows from her broom, backed her away like a maddened dog. Max dropped his basket of oysters and ran to separate the two battling women. He held Bette back by the shoulders, shielding her with his body from the Missus, spewing curses and screaming for O'Brien, their chests heaving with mutual fury.

O'Brien dragged Bette away and, with thoroughness coupling envy, he stripped Bette, bound her wrists, and hoisted her to a tree. Just as he had done the mother, he now beat the daughter. Elma lay crouched beneath the porch, her knees drawn to her chin, chewing on her hair, her body a mass of tics and grunts.

Julius banished his wife to a second plantation, which he rarely visited. A vast tract of up-country land inherited from her father, it lay on the western frontier of the state near Allendale. He tended the business of his growing land interests and the wounded hearts of both of his ladies. He teased Bette with talk of freedom.

Both the white wife and the slave wife delivered of a son the winter of

1852, but this time, it was Bette's child who died. Julius consoled her with words of rekindled love, of apology. "What would have been his fate? It is God's will," he said. "For the girls there is a place. The next one we will name Juliet. Our Jewel." Then he fled Tamarind, rode in the dead of night, driving the carriage with whip and howls, so that when his wife awakened, he could present her with a bouquet of rare orchids to celebrate the birth of his heir.

Bette could not believe her child had died. They had not let her see him, touch him. She knew in her heart that her child had been stolen. The grief—all of it bundled together—drove her to the forest of mangroves and the Juba, her feet remembering the attempted escape of her mother years before. She came upon the clandestine ceremony, her soles bleeding, muslin gown rimmed in mud. The bandanna lost to the branches, her braid uncoiled like a snake and languished on her shoulder. Her eyes were wide, darting, mad, seeing too much, too fast. The drums stopped. The black and ebony faces aglow in the flames of pitch torches reflected orange in the forest light. She sank to her knees, her legs splayed to each side like a child, her back caved from the weight of her heart.

Softly, the rhythm began again. The beat of the gourd drum drawing her body upward. The women drew her slowly to her feet, helping her to stand. Limply, stumbling in a circle dance, she joined in. The song of her mother came upon her. "Jemaya-ahhh-ah-ah-ahhh-ah-ah-ahh-ahh-ahhhh!"

As she danced, the near-dawn sky suddenly darkened and cracked open. The tears that she could not shed fell from heaven in a torrent. The prayer gatherers scattered as great balls of lightning rolled onto the earthen middens surrounding the clearing. Shango had entered. The supplicants watched her dance a solo in ancient fury, her feet a stuttering whir, her back undulating, when the one who rose up from the salt began to sing. The African, newly named Jeremiah, held her fast as the sorrow burst forth.

When Bette returned at dawn, the sky had cleared. She was greeted at the kitchen door by the old hound dog Fancy, twitching his nostrils, sensing a difference. She stared him down. He turned and walked away.

A dark amber baby with black garnet hair and tiger's eyes, Juliet was born the following cotton harvest. Her master went mad. He banished his slave wife and, this time, beat her with his own hand. This time there was no tear, no sound. He threw her aside and took her two daughters into the house. Bette sensed that Blanche was the strong one, but Elma was bold. "Stand at the gate," she would say. "Tell somebody to buy you. Get away from here any way you can."

Then the war came. Julius, dressed in a bright, new uniform, stitched by his very own people, rode off to Virginia with his favorite horse and manservant. He didn't last long. He abandoned the assault on the North and returned to join the local militia to defend the honor of his state, he said, but always the mercenary, he connived to amass the spoils of fellow Confederates desperate for any barter, then ran the blockade off the coast, sailing toward the Indies. Upon each return trip, he distributed a meager, cosmetic profit to his neighbors, then dug holes all over Tamarind, depositing his stashes of loot.

Bette was the only one he trusted. Others vanished as soon as they had word of emancipation, abandoned him to become contraband, stolen property of war. Even the invalid and the one with one leg. Even Elma and Blanche, whom he had taken into his own house. "Union troops are fast approaching," he rambled on, tossing the dirt to either side of his britches. Bette spiked the torch in the soft marl. Her trembling hands steeling one another, she plunged a kitchen knife into his back. He whirled around to strike her, but was stunned by a sudden explosion of blood in his chest as she struck him again. "Ah Bette, Mah Bette." Palm-upturned, his hand reached out and he took a last halting step toward her as if still dancing. Her foot moved backward. "Who is Massa now?"

He fell forward, toward her. His hand graced her foot and curved round her ankle, clutching it. He pulled his body up to her knees, the crimson halo of his life pouring into her dress. She stabbed him again in the neck until the hilt of the blade broke. Blood speckled her face and streamed down her arms and legs. She fell back against the tree, the whipping tree, and thought she heard in the brush footsteps of an animal or spirit. Fancy.

When the Union troops arrived—the First South Carolina Colored Battalion—she held Juliet at her side and watched Sweet Tamarind burn to the ground. Julius Mayfield was declared a hero. Died, they said, defending his family and honor.

Mah Bette cloaked her wisdom in a folksy humor, hid her pain behind a wry half-smile. She could look at someone and know they were going to die. She could see the illness before it came on. She knew someone was coming by a scent that twitched her nose. Her left eye jumping forebode ill. The forest would tell her things, the clouds, reflections in a bowl of water. Sometimes pestering souls would scratch at her back. In the voice of thunder, she heard the call of unnamed gods, of spirits who were not at rest.

The wind on the docks turned cold and awakened Bette. Business was good. Cabinetmakers, tinsmiths, hostler's helpers, all came to her for aid, the plaintive stories all too familiar. Negroes were suddenly forbidden to ride horses, forbidden to hire out as porters, laborers, even fishermen. They couldn't be peddlers with a packhorse. Couldn't carry a cane. She heard black men say they weren't going to take it that easy. They had tasted freedom, the promise of it, all the worse to have it trammeled again. Gov't gib lan to railroad, how come not to us? She could see times getting harsher, the tribulation was not over.

Bette consoled herself with a gentle humming, a song she made up or remembered only slightly—like a glint of hair in the copper sun, a smell and a lightness that sometimes still entered the old woman's heart. But this time she knew something was amiss.

8

DORA HAD BEEN FIRED ON THE SPOT. MISS TILDIE TOLD her blankly, "Get your things and get out. I can't have you around upsettin' my guests. One of his nieces is my bridesmaid . . . Goddam it, Cole! Who's gon finish my dress?"

All morning, Dora paced up and down the back stoop of the Bonneau house, until in the bright daylight of afternoon, she bit her lip, turned, and knocked on the door three loud times. "Somebody come to this door. Miss Mattie, Miss Tildie, whatevuh yuh name is, you gotta pay fuh the wuk I done. It ain't right you don't pay me nothin'." Mr. McKinley finally agreed to see her.

"You bastard, Cole, juss smilin' n lisnin to her complain."

"Maddie, this woman says you owe her some money."

"You pay huh. I don't want huh here."

"Let her finish the dresses and you never have to see her again."

"All right. But I don't want to have tuh look at huh."

Dora sewed like a demon, cussin' and fussin', marching on her knees across the redwood floor. *This all a ruse to git outa payin' me what's due. Just git the job done and git outta this madhouse.* She forgot about the time. And worked well into the night until she finished.

She walked toward the shaft of light in the study and waited in the doorway. "Come in, Dora."

"The outfits, I hope, are to Miss Matilda's satisfaction."

"I am sure they will be. What is it that we owe you?"

"Fifty-three dollars, Mr. McKinley, suh."

"I shall give you thirty."

". . . Thank you, suh."

✳ ✳ ✳

"LAST NIGHT of freedom, gentlemen."

"Let the Regulators ride again!"

"Rise, Oh ancient Saxon Stag Kings!"

To impress and remove the irritation over the debacle dinner party, Cole had taken the groomsmen down to Little Mexico, to Pilar's on one of the white nights. The loud, raucous music with the slurping beat intoxicated them. That and the liberties they could take for cheap and some healthy doses of Winrow's moonshine and scuppernong wine. Anglo-Saxon Stag Kings, future presidents, senators, men of means, the bachelor party. Woodie, his best man, and two other frat brothers from the Ivy League campus that Cole had quit before he was expelled for nonpayment. Cole was to plan it. Drinking since ten, they were singing a blues they had heard at Pilar's. "Ev' since I been yo' man/ I been yo' dawg/ Well, I'll be yo' dawg/ But not be yo' slave." They found Cole's grandfather quaint and would scramble and squat around the house with him, imagining the enemy behind the broom closet or under the table. Cole had taken them to Little Mexico to regain control, an upper hand with cockfights, niggah bitches, and music that vibrated inside their bones. What more? The best man still singing to a rag, the second passed out with vomit in his hair. Woodie, the groom, leaned over. "You had Agassiz for science, didn't you?"

"Of course, everybody did. Freshman biology."

"You ever go to his office?"

"Had no cause. That's the only class I got an A in."

"Not for grades, boy, for the pictures." Cole sat quietly as Woodie explained what he presumed everybody knew. Agassiz had gone south to prove his theory that the Negro race was another species, inferior to humans. He also went at the behest of a certain gentleman farmer who was interested in his theories of maximum yield and who shared his love of the new camera arts. In exchange for his expertise in breeding, Agassiz was allowed to take photographs of certain subjects in hopes of substantiating his theory with physical evidence. The women were stripped to the navel and of their headdresses. They were made to sit thus and to be very, very still while Agassiz and his host huddled under a black sheet, fiddled with some knobs and exploded into white light and smoke. "I remember distinctly," Woodie recounted, " 'Woman Weaver, Sweet Tamarind, home of Julius Mayfield.' Was that the Mayfield who came to the house?"

"No, that was his son."

The puke-haired youth sat up for a moment. "What kind of name is Agassiz, anyway?"

"Hey, Cole," Woodie continued, "how's the bachelor for a one-night favor? That girl? The one that made Tildie's dress?"

* * *

DORA WALKED proudly down the path to the street. She strode with a country stride toward the gate. "Thirty dollars. Coulda been worse."

"Someone's in the kitchen with Dinah/ Someone's in the kitchen I kno-o-o-ow . . ." She paused, looked around, a big-eyed doe, ears distended . . . "Oh dem golden slippers, oh dem golden slippers . . ."

Dora grabbed her skirt and ran down the road, but an arm grabbed her by the neck and pulled her down, took hold of her hair and pulled her across the ground. Briars cut, briars cut her face—*draggin' me in the, where we—uh uh—my face! Uh—Pl—ease!* They dragged her into a shed. Her head struck the door. She clung to the post and, groping, found a shovel handle and struck at something, him, them. Another took hold of her and pressed his walking stick onto her neck. He stripped her to the waist, clothes drawn up. She kicked and squirmed. The choke hold got tighter. "Goddam you, open your legs!" "Pour liquor down huh!" "Why you trembling? We got us a Shaker!" "Splittin' a nigga woman." "Suck my privates." "Buck her down. Open your eyes. Open your eyes, yuh goddam yellah bitch! Shut your damned mouth or I'll knock your goddam brains out!"

"Make a good girl of yuh," a voice said calmly. It was husky, contemptuous. "Where you headed, fancy girl? Why fight your blood? I seen you walkin' down the way. Why act so high n mighty when you come here? Buy you somethin' nice. Bet you ain't seen nothin' nice like this. Where's your charm? How come you ain't wearin' one? Let's see."

The dress, the patch, the tear. Finish the gown fore nightfall. Things tore up n nowhere to go. Didn't know where to of went. Tears me all to pieces. Draggin' me down, draggin' me back. NO! Fight, kick, bite, scrape get up   get up

✳ ✳ ✳

BLANCHE WAS thinking of her new Harvest Ball outfit. No one else's design would compete, she was sure, with cousin Dora's—she insisted Dora call her cousin. Aunty sounded so . . . mature, old-timey. After a time, it was only right that she look after her less fortunate relation, especially since the girl didn't charge her for the dresses. For this occasion, Dora had outdone herself. Gold embroidered panels over the most delicate shade of olive, lace pelerine, rhinestone posts, bustle tied tight around the waist, overlapped with frills and bound with steel. Blanche would be the envy of maidens and matrons alike. She sat in bed beside her husband, enjoying their Thursday evening reading for self-improvement, when Dora arrived at their home.

"Din't know where to of went. Din't want word gettin' round. Couldn't risk no doctuh." She collapsed on the steps, her dress in shreds, blood crusted to her thighs. Blood run down to her heels, clear down.

Roswell Sr. fetched Bette to the house. He wanted no news of the incident to spread. When she saw Eudora's bloodied body, swollen jaw with a studded ring emblem embedded in it, Bette threw up her hands, fell on her knees, and poured dirt on her head. Blanche kicked a watering can and folded her arms. "Get up off your knees, Mama! Where was all your powers and potions to see this coming?"

Mah Bette steeled her face and replied, "Dis no your affair. Was part my doin'. Mine to undo."

Bette arranged with Roswell to take Dora back to the island, back to Tamarind. Aunt Sibby rode along silently. While Lijah-Lah docked in the twilight, Roswell carried the girl to the pirogue. In her delirium, Dora still fought, striking feebly at the air, at his chest with her fists and broken nails. As the oarsman pushed off the shore, the gentle waves seemed to bring comfort to her sleep.

Mah Bette threw off the brambles of her tabby shack and, still wise in the healing ways, she sent Lijah-Lah on a quest. "Tansy root rue enh, penny royal enh, cedar berries enh, camphor enh," for herbs, poultice, and prayer. Aunt Sibby came in, white shirt round her head, veins in her brow in the shape of a great winged bird. The eyes, once large and almond, now narrow slits, lids heavy, almost forcing them closed. Deep furrows in her cheeks beneath her eyes and around her mouth, her mouth curled and upper teeth forgotten. Despite the heat, she wore white stockings with holes and runs, her top button tight around her neck, and a worn blue velvet waistcoat over her two skirts of wrinkled cloth, plaid over paisley. On her knee, one hand was folded over the other, fingers interlocking, odd twisted bends at the end joints, indigo veins visible through her skin, still soft as a newborn's. Though you could not see her eyes at all, you could tell she was staring deep into Dora's soul. "I cotched many baby, ax under the straw. Brought in many white as culled. Neber loss one."

Preparing to assist, Aunt Sibby rumbled through her medicine bag of jars and cans. "The gull hoverin' tween the worlds. You kin call her back or let her gwon." Bette nodded understanding.

On the fifth day Aunt Sibby told Dora to walk around the house once and come in. The sky was yellow white with sunlight. A gray-backed sparrow scratched his belly in the dust. When Dora returned, Bette was humming. Aloe had dulled the swelling, and steaming poultices of cider vinegar had made the scabs then fall away, leaving her skin once again smooth, if discolored in places.

Weeks later when Dora came back to the flat on Rose Tree Lane, she told her neighbors Bette had nursed her through a touch of the fever and shingles. She insisted on holding her regular reading lesson with Win. "Glad to see you is feelin' bettuh."

"Thank you, Mr. Winrow. 'Preciate it." She seemed distracted. He could see where the fever had caused her skin to peel. He did not correct her on the formal use of his name, but began reading slowly from "King James, Saint Mark . . . You was working too hard, Miss Dora."

To his surprise, she agreed. "I thought I might take some time to myself, thought I might like to see that farm you talk about. Mmm, a ride in the country where it's quiet. Flowers. Lots of birds singing. Not so many people."

He was somewhere between proud and embarrassed when they arrived.

Seeing all of the flaws of his roughshod place, Win tripped over himself and his words, trying to impress her. "Don't look like much. Of cose, I don't git out here that often. But I would, I mean if I had a reason. I'm a hardwukkin' man, I told you that. But I try to be smart about it." He straightened up just like his father. *Your name Winrow?* He laughed awkwardly. "I have a confess to make, Miss Dora. I use them scuppernong grapes to make wine. I bottles it and sells it to Miss Pilar and a few other folk. Ain't no hard likker, now, but it do make you happy." She was acting peculiar, her face to the ground, smelling the soil. She touched the flowers with her fingers, examining them as if she had never seen one before, tilting her head to one side as if she were hearing something far away.

A permanent reminder of the grip on her neck, a sharp shaft of pain shot down her spine and inhaled her smile. "Might I taste some, this wine?"

"Who? . . . Why sure, cose. Uh, wait a minute. Lemme fine a cup or sumpin." He rinsed a tin cup at the water pump, all the while talking to himself. "Woman say she want a taste, don't mean nothin'. Maybe a full moon or sumpin." He sat on the porch steps beside her. She wrapped her arms around her knees. He poured a sip's worth and a little more. She took the cup in both hands like a child. He watched her swallow and react, a slight dart of her chest forward.

"Sweet."

"Yes," he laughed, "yes. Too sweet?"

"No, just takes some getting used to . . . I will be your wife, Thomas Winrow, if you will have me."

He knelt down beside her and took her hand. "I will make you proud to be my wife, Dora May. Won't be no reason for you not to hold your head up high."

They were married in a simple ceremony at Azula Street, the small frame church Win's preacher friend had managed to build. Dora packed up her things and moved out to Win's small farm on Camden Road, and they began to make a home. Dora scrubbed, burnished, and polished and brought it into some order. She relished the solitude. Mah Bette explored the woods, hunting herbs and mushrooms. Win was patient. He thought to give her time. He thought a visit with Miss Sibby might cheer her. The old woman took one look at the young bride. "My dear, you is havin' a baby."

No, no, no, no. This couldn't be. She had not thought, did not realize, could not believe. Win was delighted. He beamed, "Gon buy him a bugle."

* * *

DESSALINES RETURNED from his voyage to Montreal. He had found a small community there that spoke French and English. Though the weather was fierce, the frozen St. Lawrence Seaway locking him in port for months, he believed he could make a living there and live free. Now that they had no imperial aspirations in the New World, the French let you breathe. The British enjoyed their moral superiority, and the colored were strengthened by a core of families who had risked death to escape their enslavement. Fishing was good, and in the spring and summer months the skiff would make a healthy business of lessons for leisure-class sailors. He returned to Charleston full-chested, with a new song for Dora.

He found her flat empty. New people were moving in. He went to Pilar. "She got the fevuh, then up n marry Tommy Winrow," she said. "Married tree munt ahgo. They livin' out by he farm up Camden Road the way." Dessalines turned and marched back to his ship, his boot heels digging in the ground. "You say you want Charleston, well now you have it." Determined to leave the city as quickly as possible, Dessalines offered spring pleasure outings and racing on *L'Heureux* while his captain bartered goods from the main ship.

* * *

COLE THOUGHT to make up to his cousin with a jaunt down to Savannah. Abandoned at the altar, Matilda Bonneau months later was still salty that her whole carefully orchestrated political arrangement had fallen apart. Woodie's family had whisked him out of town and married him off to a New York debutante. Ben Tillman managed to get himself elected to the U.S. Senate without the influence of Julius Mayfield, wrestling the seat of power from the tidewater families permanently. While Julius Mayfield and his class of planter statesmen retreated from public life, Ben Tillman took his brawling ways to the halls of Congress and remained in the Senate seat he had stolen well into the First World War.

None of Tildie's former bridesmaids was speaking to her. "Oh for Chrissakes, why didn't you take bettuh care of him, Cole? He looked terrible, his face all blanched and scratched up. You bastard. What happened? He said he didn't remember a thing. What'd you do?"

To make amends, Cole brought home a new batch of Robber Baron sons looking for social connections, and Tildie soon tired of her anger. She turned the debacle of the prior summer into entertaining chatter. "No more dinner parties," Matilda chirped in her best bawdy voice. "Last summer's was absolutely awful. The bunny died. The servants took sick. My guests hated each other. The guest of honor was two hours late and turned around at the threshold cuz my maid was his relation."

They had rented the sloop and were eating fresh clams on the deck. "All because Cole wanted to show them a good time." Cole seduced the new recruits with his songs of the South. "Someone's in the kitchen with Dinah, Someone's in the kitchen I kno-o-o-ow . . . The blacker the berry, the sweeter the juice, gentlemen, but, you ain't tasted nothin' till you had yourself a sweet Geechee peach, ripe for the pluckin', ready to pop out its skin."

Yves Dessalines veered the boat on a sharp angle. It keeled to the side. The pleasure passengers toppled onto each other, almost falling overboard. Yves hollered, "Storm's comin'," and despite their protests and threats, he headed back for the harbor.

Back in Charleston, Yves rode straightaway to the Winrow farm. There he found Dora, her apron wide around her bulging stomach. "Mr. Dessalines . . . so nice to see you . . . I finished the dress . . . would you like to see it?" He slammed his hand on the porch in aggravation. "I took young Master McKinley on a boat ride. Your boyfriend's got a loose tongue."

She flew at him, a fury of unleashed ferocity. Her teeth bared, screaming and growling deep in her throat, she overturned tables, benches, the cooking pot. He caught her by the wrists. Her clawed fingers balled into fists and drew blood from her palms as she struck him and struck him again in the chest, then sank to her knees, sobbing in great rolling heaves. "Please, go away. Go." Her hands shook and she stammered, "It don't matter what you do. We're all the same. No better than dirt . . ."

Yves instantly moved toward her. "Why didn't you come to me?"

"Where was you? Do not speak of it again, to me or anyone. You must promise me that."

"Something must be done."

"Nothin' to be done, but go on. It is forgotten."

"When are you due?"

"In three months or so."

"May I call again?"

"I do not believe that would be 'propriate."

He began to reply. She placed two fingers on his lips. He turned them over and kissed them slowly, then walked away, his boot heels digging in the ground. When he had gone a few yards, he pirouetted and, looking toward her, bowed like a gentleman. "Perhaps I will have another dress made, or a fine waistcoat, madame." Later in Charleston, he passed Tom Winrow unloading his buckboard across the boulevard. Dessalines doffed his cap to the victor.

* * *

DORA DISTRACTED herself from Dessalines' visit by preparing a good meal for her husband—okra and rice with sweet corn and shrimp. Win came in with his weekly earnings and talk from the town. "One of them Bonneau servants, that stuck-up colored coachman, come in. You wanna hear somethin' funny?" he asked as she heaped the stew from the okra pot over a steaming pile of rice. "Talk from the servants outside the stoah was somethin'. Word is, that cousin at the Bonneaus' what keep company with the colored over to Pilar's sometime, someone caught him on the wharf and toah his ass up. They say he got cut up wid a razor, got his hands stomped on." Dora covered her mouth and started to gag. Tom caught her and eased her onto the kitchen chair, placing the plate on the table untended. "If havin' a baby is gonna change you like this, we ain't havin' no more."

"Win, I need to sit down. I cain't be no longer on my feet these days." She started to tell him but the words would not leave her body.

"Sure, baby, sure. I serves you fuh a change. I sorry, Dora, just talkin' plain is all. That's one rich crackuh won't be camptown racin' for a while. Police out lookin' for the person what did it." He rinsed his hands in the bucket on the counter and sat down to eat. "They pickin' up niggahs for vagrancy just waitin' fuh a fare." Winrow reached over the table and hugged her. "But you not gonna have to work for white folks no more, you hear me? From now on, you my wife."

He is so proud. She wished she could be like Mah Bette and hear voices in the thunder, spirits in the wind. She went into the forest, with her Sears Roebuck shoebox, and sat on a blanket of fallen leaves. She opened the box lid and fingered the locks of hair. Withdrawing the picture of Juliet with her newborn in her arms, Dora pleaded with God.

Mah Bette came upon her. The old woman counseled, "He a good man, you should tell him."

* * *

IT WAS a difficult birth. Panic made Dora sick with fever. The women kept turns on the watch. Blanche, Aunt Sibby, Mah Bette, Pilar. In the candor of the ritual, they traded stories.

"Married to a soldjah, I wus. Lousiana when he found me," Pilar recounted, her legs splayed before her. "Had another wife by then. Next one I marry, come say 'Stay home, cut de grass.' I say, 'Let it grow up under yuh, I leavin'.'"

"Those sistuhs—Miss Stubbins and Miss Highgate. Shakers and Movers of the World!" Mah Bette went on, "The brown gal, Miss Highgate. Said she was runnin' off to Kansas. She say when she really messin' with that Union Jack Bureau man's son—one that wrote poetry. Humph. Runnin' off to hide her shame she was. Din't git fuh."

Blanche filled in some of the missing pieces of Dora's birth. "Your aunt Elma brought me to Charleston, told me, 'I'll come back for you,' but she never did. Suitcase full of dreams we had. Elma went on over to white. Never saw her again. Mrs. Diggs took me in, treated me kindly. When she passed, seemed natural for me to take her place."

Late into the night when the others had tired of their vigil, Mah Bette would tell her stories, curling through the spires of smoke from her corncob pipe. "Man come bring you, sayin' a woman instructed him to bring you here. How was I to believe this was my daughter's chile, when never seen he nor you before. You ain't had no harr, no harr at all. An' you was toasty. I could tell by your ears, you was gonna be golden brown like a fresh autumn leaf. Cryin', eyes close tight, little fists flailing about and me an old woman. 'What I'ma do wid dis,' I say. He say, 'That yo bidness, cuz I done finished wid mine.' I went to look you over and seen the note. Ax the man could he read it and tell me what it say. Just then you stop crying and open up your eyes. Just then I know, before he even say, 'Eudora means happiness.' You was a pretty lil ol' baby, but no harr at all. When all my babies had a whole mess of harr right out the womb. How was I to believe this was my daughter's chile. Never seen no Mayfield sleep so. Eyes just as shut. I got to look you over. Sabina say tap you on your toes. Then you open your eyes and I know."

Bette talked to Dora, squeezing her hand. "We got nothin' but to choose life. Find the honor in it. Make it so. Will it so. You a fighter, Eudora May—in life there is hope. In life—choose not to give up. New day mean a new day's battle begun. This child is the child of your womb, and if she is born of this hell all the more power to deliver us from it. To the seventh generation."

The old midwife Sibby motioned that it was time. "Git uh ax n put up unnuh duh straw tick, ease em blood flow." She worked quickly, coaxing the reluctant newborn. "Think you fallin'. Not know where. Dat's arright. Aunt Sibby gon cotcha." The child came out the color of pound cake, hair straight and black as a crow. "Juss like the China doll I seen at Yum Lee." The old woman grinned as she held the baby for the women to see.

"Like Elma come back." Blanche sighed.

Winrow hovered at the door. Mah Bette beckoned him forward. "She may be a might bright fuh yuh, Winrow, but she a fine gal. Right smart." Winrow took the tiny infant in his arms and sat down on the porch. Bette sat down beside him. "Mayfield blood is strong. Chirren come out lookin' any which way."

* * *

BEFORE ELMA Thomasine was even weaned, Dora was back at work. She went back to Miss O'Malley. Offered to work on consignment again. Her posture of pride became a rigid rectitude, an upturned chin which she could not move. Winrow also returned to his routine, struggling with the farm by day and hittin' it at Pilar's at night and on the weekends. They argued about it furiously on Saturday and attended the small Azula Street church together on Sunday. Dora preferred it to Emmanuel, where the wealthy colored attended. To be seen was not her goal. While others sunk further into dependency and borrowed lands, lent in shares, their combined income met the payments on Win's land.

Win came home from Pilar's drunk again, singing a tune bout romancin' some woman. Three-year-old Elma ran from the porch and greeted him, a clothesline rope tied around her waist, she halted and pranced like a puppy when the rope went taut. Frowning, Winrow unloosed the tie and looked around. "Where yo' mama?"

"She at service. Gettin' Revival!"

"Where yo' granmama?"

"She inna woods. Told me tuh stay put."

"How's my girl?" He smiled and tossed Elma into the air. She erupted with laughter. He tossed her higher, teasing her, asking, "Do you know where your daddy at?" Tossing her up, shouting, "Where could he be, I wonduh? . . . Can you find him in the dark?" Catching her, he smiled, "Here I is!"

Dora came from service and saw Win playing roughly with their child. "Stop it, this instant! Put her down!" Winrow gently set his daughter down and approached his wife. She turned her head away from the smell of liquor on his breath. "Got somethin' fuh yuh. Postman give it to me at the stoah." He pulled from his pocket a letter from Dessalines. It was torn in half. "You betrayed me with that high-tone nigga, come in here have the nerve to turn yo' nose to me?" He pulled out three more and threw them on the ground.

"Where did you get those? Going through my things!"

"I got 'em in my house. In my goddam house! You think I gonna be a fool an' let you keep this up on me? Huh?"

"Those letters three years old. Never opened."

"If they so old, why you keep 'em? Where this one from, Paris? Where this one from, Havana? I cain't read 'em, you tell me!" He hurled the letters at her chest. "Why you keep 'em, huh? An what's this one? Keep it cuz you in love with him. Keep 'em cuz of this bastard yelluh chile!"

"Don't you call her that! Don't you call her that!" They fought. Little Elma began to cry, trying to get between them.

"You betrayed me, made a mockery of me. Tricked me into marryin' yuh after that no-count nigga thew you off!"

"Is that what you think? How stupid!"

"What'd you say? What you call me?!"

Dora began to laugh. Before he could catch himself, the back of his hand had struck her face. "Damn, woman!"

A single tear rolled down her cheek. "It is fit to punish me, but please, please don't hurt Elma. Please."

She took her daughter in her arms and carried the child inside. When she had calmed the girl to sleep, she returned to Winrow, who sat on the porch step, his world shattered. She leaned against the post. "I was too proud. I shoulda seen it. Shoulda knowed." She told him of the dress and the walk and the tree with no bark. "I shoulda knowed, shoulda knowed when I seen it. So busy makin' my future, I couldn't see it."

"Oh Dora, sweet Dora." He took her in his arms and carried her to bed.

She wanted to show him love, wanted to comfort, to close her eyes and feel whole, but his hands were rough. When he entered her she was aware again of her separateness, the chafing of his skin against hers as he moved inside her, reminding her again and again of the ruptures in her flesh—the heat of his breath on her neck—sweat of his body dripping on her face—not like the sea but thick and sour. "Look at me, Dora. Tell me you love me. Tell me you love me. Look at me, Dora." But she could not, would not open her eyes until he was spent, the chaotic rhythms of his heart knocking in spasms of longing and anger.

Just like a baby, wants his milk. A smile brushed her lips and she raised her delicate fingers to stroke the knobby waves of his hair, but before she could soothe him, he had turned away and rolled off her body, his back to her side. The sweat left on her chest and breasts turned cold. She marveled at her hand, still raised from the elbow, her fingers dancing in the shard of light cast from the amber moon, hanging low in the twilight.

* * *

HER TRAY of charms covered with a checkered napkin, Mah Bette attempted again to pinch Lizzie May's nose, but the screaming infant, Dora's second child, wasn't having it. Before the old woman knew it, the baby had scrambled around in her arms and was nudging her in the mouth with her tiny feet, screaming for the whole neighborhood to hear. Bette turned little Lizzie over and roughly jostled the girl on her knees. "All right, Miss Nosey, time fuh some sleep." Yum Lee looked on from the counter and called behind him for Dora to go to her newborn. Bette clucked her teeth at him. "I know how to do this. Had children, grandchildren, now greats." She bounced the child hard with slight irritation as the screams subsided. A sailor approached and handed her a package. She slung Lizzie to her shoulder and went to where Dora was working in the back.

Little Elma sat on the stoop by the door, fanning herself with her hands and jiggling her knees. Outside the shop she could hear Deke, now a husky youth, leading his troupe of beggar children, dancing and doing their hambone routines. "All Righty! Join the band! HUNH! All Righty! Join the band! Come round and Join the band! HUNH! Bo Bobo, Bo Bo Bobo! BAM! Bo Bobo, Bo Bo Bobo! BAM! Join the band! HUNH!" She could hear the coins jiggle when white passersby tossed them into his old stovepipe hat. Elma tapped her foot to the rhythms and hummed along. "Elma, come way from there," Dora cautioned without looking up from her needlework.

Bette patted the head of her first great-grand and handed the package to Dora. It bore the familiar mark of Yves Dessalines. Eudora turned the letter around in her hands and headed for the pier. When she got to the water's edge, her dry, wide eyes the purple haze of sunset, she released the unopened letter to the sea. In a gentle call and response, the surf just grazed the tips of her shoes, in the echo of the waves, a faint dulcimer lullaby, *"What kinda name for muh child is best? Eudora, I b'lieve, for happiness."*

Dora ran her fingers through her upswept hair and leaned against a weathered pylon jutting up from the sand. She thought of Tom. *Funny, he used to be the one who sweat. Now, here I sit, a faucet in plaid. Sweatin' and cryin' alike. Get on back to work. The past is the past. The future, make somethin' of that.* She rose and headed back to her sewing station. Heavy heart, cloaked in sorrow, eyes downturned, she began again at the task before her. She would make a life for the girls. Respectable girls. Women of dignity, class, and ambition. Whatever her life had wrought, she had two fine daughters, her Elma and her Liz. They would have the life that she was promised.

9

ELMA OPENED HER WINDOW WIDE, EMBRACING THE GENTLE breeze that calmed her excitement. Lettin' some air in might reduce the lightness in her head, help steady her for the evening: the Fisk Jubilee Singers concert! As she gazed out at the green lawns, everything seemed to smile back at her—the grass, the leaves, the dots of clouds—beautiful in full anticipation of this evening.

And how long Elma had waited for this day, too! She hugged herself with both arms just thinking about it. From the country to Charleston and now here she stood, a Jubilee singer. Blushing mightily she felt so proud. The feeling started deep inside and grew a bit, to a broad smile that laughed and laughed, the giggling ringing out like the peal of church bells, announcing, "Here I am, here I come, I am making my debut and taking on this stage as if it belonged to only me, just like Black Patti! I am singing, singing, singing!"

The image of Black Patti prompted Elma to go search out her photographs. She rummaged through her hope chest, pushing aside the baptism gown and worn baby socks, respectfully displacing her first Bible and her old colored school primer. There it was. The lace-covered book of daguerreotypes and photographs lay on the bottom of the chest. Taking it out gently, Elma held the book between both hands as if praying. Her Mama had crocheted the lace covering. She opened the book and a rush of memories came flooding forth. The photographs weren't glued in place, and Elma traced each one with her fingers before lifting one up to study closer.

That's when Mama and Pa took me to see Sissieretta Jones, "Black Patti" to everybody else. Why, Ma Bette put the ticket stub right next to the picture of me with Black Patti. What a proud day that was! I wish I could remember what she sang. All I know is the notes from her body were like the wind blowing in major chords on a damp Charleston night. Not that I really lived in Charleston to know, but I imagine if the country, well, the farm, was never silent, always singing, then the city must have been like a choir of colored angels all the day long. Sounds making music out of every turn of a corner, wink of an eye, mule passing, kicking, the white folks' banter, and the glower of the stevedores, even the silly rhymes of the fruit sellers all mixed in with the melody of frangipani and magnolia, sweat and fast-beating niggah hearts wondering if, or what, was wrong now.

A single sound from Sissieretta Jones just bout lifted Elma off her feet that night. Her voice could rumble like an angry ocean or soar sweetly as a drifting cloud. Elma imagined herself singing with Black Patti, their voices dancing like the gulls just hovering over the crest of each wave only to rush toward the clouds again, leaving her to wonder what the next beautiful arc would feel like.

Mama could sit on me, but she could not get Pa to hush up. He was so full of himself and somebody's corn whiskey he went about courting Black Patti from the crowd. I was so embarrassed. I thought I hated him. I'd hate him forever for piercing and smearing the magic of that voice. Folks didn't just look at us funny, while we tried to leave invisible, with Pa making all that racket. "Ya sho' lookin' good for a black one, Miz Patti. This black daddy got something'll make you sing, too. Don'tcha want to see? I got Gabriel's trumpet. That's God talkin'. Ya hear me, I say God's talkin' to ya, heifer!" Mama was trying to hold her head up like she could hear nothing, a void, an emptiness around her thick as new cotton, but I could never have held my head up, knowing I had some relation to the ugliness pounding the glory out of Black Patti's triumph over the clumsiness of the human tongue, the human voice so accustomed to the mire of brittle, quacking sounds. And he was my father, like a murderer of the sacred touch of life.

Had nothin' to do with bein' colored, nothin' at all, Mama told me later.

But it did have somethin' to do with bein' like my pa. Anythin' like my pa is
bound to bring hurt. That's all he ever did to my mother: hurt her. Why
won't the sounds of Black Patti's voice come back to me? Mama said I could
always hear them. "I was there," she said. "You are not your pa. He's gotta
answer to the Lord for himself." For himself, not me, not me. But I never
believed that, Mama. I've always answered for Pa's ways.

Before she put the album away Elma came cross a picture of herself
with Lizzie and Bette on the front porch. Lizzie, small bones and hair
wild as ever, looking like she'd just stopped running somewhere. Elma
wondered how Lizzie had grown, was she still sneaking into Miss Pilar's
to hear music. Elma looked at a younger Ma Bette next to the tree bent by
all the dangling bottles to bring good luck, to keep haints away, to protect souls.

Elma carefully folded the yellowing album, trying to wipe her tears
while she tied the satin bow around the book Eudora had kept so meticu-
lously for her daughter, for her to remember them while she was away.
Somehow Elma always forgot. She forgot what she actually did remember,
beguiled by the ribbons, the class photographs and school reports all done
up in her mother's lace work. Her life looked like a fine French lace with
the spices of the tropics, her Nana, her sister Lizzie, Mama and Pa dancing
'tween the frenzy of looped threads. *Yes, this is what you come from, this is*
who you are. This is why you sing, Elma thought to herself. And now she
was going to do just that with the Fisk Jubilee Singers. But first she had to
sing for herself—a devilish bluesy number she learned as a girl from her Pa.

> "I'm goin' away, baby, I won't be back till fall,
>   Lord, Lord, Lord!
> Goin' away, baby, won't be back till fall,
>   If I find me a good man, I won't be back at all.
> See See Rider, where did you stay last night?
>   Lord, Lord, Lord!
> Your shoes ain't buttoned, clothes don't fit you right,
>   You didn't come home till the sun was shinin' bright!"

Elma swayed as if she were on some ship taking her far away from
the mournful tones she knew to be her own. Her face was a clutter of

tear-strewn blotches, gray as the sky when the sun hides way up inside the clouds, making a mockery of dawn. Elma slid her album back between the sheets at the bottom of her chest at the foot of her bed where she said her prayers and hummed to make sleep come peacefully for once. But not now, not today, Elma decided, as she'd decided as a child to start her day again on her own terms, with her own phrasing and nuance. *This is going to be a fine day. A lovely day.* All she had to do was hang on to the last clear crescendo of Black Patti's voice. The last pure beauty she knew.

Elma herself was a beauty. All of the Cherokee, European, and African blood of her forebears blended into a tawny translucent ochre with a tinge of azure or rose depending on her mood. Her hair fell in cascades of black henna ringlets she futilely attempted to train into a bun at the nape of her neck. She knew nothing of how fetching she appeared to others. She knew nothing of the envy the stream of young women of color from all parts of the United States hid from her. After all, they were what Du-Bois called the Talented Tenth, which unfortunately meant to too many the well-to-do and white-looking tenth of the harried Negro population. Room was made for Elma to be one of them because of her voice, the voice that led the sorority song of the Alpha Kappa Alphas to victory in 1915. Each soror more demure, comely, and coy than the next. In Jubilee Hall they gathered for the last ritual of the summer, attracting possible suitors from as far away as Morehouse and Tuskegee. There was nothing like a Fisk girl to carry home to Mama. Nobody at Spelman or Bennett could hold a candle to them—or a brown paper bag—without seeing the difference.

Somehow Elma had negotiated her place among these aquiline-nosed females without actually knowing she had. No Diggs had to prove anything to anybody. Ask any black person from Chicago to Baltimore, or St. Augustine, for that matter. All she had to do was say her cousins' name. The more malicious of her classmates couldn't even say she was money poor and high yellow. She wasn't. There was simply something foreign in her countenance, something foreign and regal, even though she could sing the gospel or a low-down blues like any dirt farmer's daughter, which she was.

In her sheer pink gown Angeline Ducet from Baton Rouge hurried over to Elma to tug her arm and whisper about the number of fellows from Meharry Medical School across the way who'd made it their business to hear the girls sing.

Angeline couldn't contain herself. "Elma, wait till you see them. I hear Meharry men will be sitting in the first five rows of center seats in the auditorium. Sing to them, Elma. Sing like your future doctor husband is out there just waiting for the sound of your voice. You are so lucky to have the solo." Angeline was referring to Elma's three-octave range that allowed her to shine in every selection.

Every shade of pink and green, every version of coquette rustled from the podium to meet with family and suitors. Elma was not looking to meet anyone. Her family could barely get her to Fisk, let alone get themselves here to celebrate her successes. Nevertheless a gaiety and relief swept through the hall like sweet scents of summer blossoms hang in the air as the sun goes down. Fisk house-mothers watched their brood carefully, looking for untoward glances, a touch or a couple dashing off behind a willow tree. But since Elma was not looking for anyone, she didn't realize folks were looking for her, to congratulate her on the quality of her voice and the fine direction she'd given the other girls. Mrs. Waites, her vocal coach, almost squeezed the living daylights out of her, exclaiming, "Oh, Elma, you are blessed! The Lord has put his finger on you, child, I'm telling you! A voice like yours and your feeling for every sound is what makes working with tone-deaf colored folks year after year worth it all. You must never take this gift lightly. Do you hear me?"

Elma was still reeling from the emphatic embrace of Mrs. Waites when she was approached by Dr. Simeon Minor, her biology professor and advisor, who was just as dismayed with Elma's brilliance as Mrs. Waites was elated. "Elma, you mustn't let this gloating over a song here or there sway you from a very lucrative and stable career in nursing or teaching. Beggin' your pardon, but what 'niggah' do you know who can't sing? Tell me that. We need talent like yours to help our people. They don't need any more entertainin'. What do you want to be, another 'Black Patti and the Colored Troubadours'?"

Elma's heart sank deep toward her spine at the mention of her beloved Black Patti, but she simply replied, "Dr. Minor, you know the kind of profession you're pointing me toward is much too taxing for a woman, even dangerous in the countryside. Plus, it will take half my lifetime just to finish the required studies, and I can't ask my family to sacrifice any more than they have already. Surely you can understand that. Though I must say that I am flattered by your confidence in me as servant to our people."

Overhearing more of the conversation than she should have allowed, Mrs. Waites burst in. "Dr. Minor, you keep your hands off God's handiwork! This child will die if she doesn't sing. Can't you tell that? Wasn't that concert you just heard scientific proof enough?"

Dr. Minor's chest puffed up like he was about to implode at the strange mixture of theology and science that Mrs. Waites was arguing. Elma thought that a fine moment to intervene, and something made her need to respond.

"I want to sing," she murmured as matter-of-factly as she could. "Really, I don't rightly know if it's my calling or not, but I'm no fool either. Singing is a gift from the Lord, not a profession. I don't want to live off of something so precious to me. I want my voice to be free of the pressures of this world. My singing's not to pay the rent or a grocer's bill. It is my pleasure and my hope, it's my love, it's family. My voice is as natural as a sprig of honeysuckle. We don't pay for that. We sip it, like God's nectar, a bit at a time."

"Well, then, Miss . . . uh . . ."

"Diggs, Elma Diggs."

"How do you plan to earn your keep, if not by singing for your supper?"

The young man to whom this melodious baritone voice belonged was cocksure of himself and not a mite less handsome than Adonis, or some pure Seminole buck out of Florida. Only the mass of blue-black waves curling 'round his cheekbones gave away his hybrid genealogy. Everything about him was blue-black, his suit, his hair, his eyes. Everything but his color. Elma was taken aback just by the sight of him, let alone the familiarity of his initial contact.

"Well, I certainly do not intend to sing for my supper, uh . . . uh."

At that moment, Dr. Minor looked at Elma as though he wanted to apologize. Instead he stared hard into the eyes of the cavalier interloper, saying, "Miss Diggs, I, ah. Well, to get to the point, this is my nephew, Raymond Minor." Dr. Minor looked at the boy like he wanted to spit on his slightly too elegant attire and gesture, but his chest puffed up again and he walked away as if nothing would help him do anything but acknowledge the young man as his kin.

Mrs. Waites had no hesitation about interrupting the young dandy's obvious intentions toward her prodigy. "Yes, Raymond Minor. This is Elma Diggs of the Charleston Diggses. And the last thing she'll ever have to do is sing for her supper, or for the likes of you," she grumbled. Elma stood mute and slightly amused.

"Mrs. Waites, you know how much I hold you in esteem. I certainly had no way of knowing this lovely woman was one of the Diggses of Charleston."

Mrs. Waites was now truly annoyed. "You certainly wouldn't. She doesn't go around flaunting her background. She was as hard a scholar and a credit to the race as any student Fisk's ever turned out. You, young man, could learn something from her about how the truly genteel class of Negro people conduct themselves." With that, Mrs. Waites seemed to regain her composure. "Now, Elma, you just stay your sweet self. Don't let this young whippersnapper turn your head," and off she went.

Elma couldn't help but chuckle a little. "We surely have stirred up a little bit of temperament, don't you think?"

"Elma, my classmate at Tuskegee was a Benjamen Diggs, but I had thought his sister was much, much older than you."

Elma's body released her from gravity, and she reached for Raymond's arm, which he gladly offered. "Are you feeling all right, Miss Diggs?" he asked, very concerned.

"I most certainly am. It must be all this excitement, and the joy singing gives me does sometimes lift me right off my feet," Elma tried to joke.

There was a brief but dense moment when the two said not a word. Then Elma confided to Raymond in an almost singing sotto voce, "I'm Benjamen's, uh, cousin. A ward of his father."

Ebullient, Raymond grabbed Elma's hand to join in the dancing. "Listen to me, my sweet Southern belle, a Diggs is a Diggs. That's all you ever need to think about. I don't ever want to hear you excuse your right to your own name, not ever again! And I intend to know you, Miss Elma Diggs, for a long, long time."

Then Raymond, in true character, had Elma swirling about the dance floor as if they had partnered each other for years. Elma discovered then and there that her voice wasn't the only gift the Lord had bestowed upon her. She learned that in the arms of Raymond Minor she could fly to music as well. The farmer's daughter in her even found room for a jazzy two-step Raymond coaxed her to do. Neither Mrs. Waites nor the disgruntled Dr. Minor was able to come between the couple. Elma had found a new beauteous thing, the melody of romance, the magic of a star-strewn Tennessee night.

* * *

THE SAME orange-rose dawn that Elma sleepily flirted with in Nashville nudged little Lizzie Winrow from one chore to the next back on the Carolina farm. Lizzie's favorite hen, Turkey, kept sneaking 'tween her legs, trying to get lifted off the barnyard grounds and back to Lizzie's soft bed where the child had hidden her for so many months. She was called Turkey 'cause Tom Winrow had shouted, "That's what that damn hen woulda been, one dead turkey if she wasn't a chicken."

That drunken logic sometimes confused Lizzie, but most of the time it worked to her favor. Since Turkey wasn't a turkey but a chicken, Turkey wouldn't have her neck wrung for Thanksgiving, which was a fine outcome to the noisy commotion Turkey created when Tom and Eudora came to put Lizzie to bed one night and found a chicken instead of their sweet baby girl nestled all comfy on the pillow like a reg'lar human bein'. This while the real child was out trying to break in her pony, Amarillo, which was a nice name for Lizzie's yellow-red skin that mean folks callt rhiny or red-boned, but Amarillo and Lizzie blended together just fine, only Lizzie couldn't get the pony to hold still long enough for her to get a good cantor goin', so Lizzie put Turkey to bed in her nightshirt and went about breaking Amarillo whenever the moonlight allowed.

Tom knew he was bewitched 'cause he had a chicken callt Turkey and a child and a horse looked like one creature from a distance, like a bronze statue from near town where the white folks paraded their translucent-skinned offspring under parasols and fans. Ever since he'd married that woman, everything or some one small thing seemed to go wrong, or if not wrong, then funny in a bad way. Eudora might have meant happiness to somebody, but it sho' 'nough bought Tom Winrow a lotta grief, 'cept for his darlin' Lizzie who was as wily as he was but he'd never say that. Always blame it on the Mama, that was safer.

Lizzie was sliding from right to left on Amarillo's back, but managing to hold on as the pony meandered toward the barn. Lizzie wasn't falling off the animal, losing control, she was falling asleep, but Tom Winrow was wide awake, deciding if he should act like he was coming from the barn or going to it. No matter what he did, he couldn't keep the blazing morning sun from playing darts with his eyes. Blinking, holding his left hand just above his ebony eyebrows that curled inward toward his nose, Tom made out some figures moving toward him sometimes and sometimes 'way from him. Not sure if he'd come upon a haint or an interloper, Tom seized Lizzie by the waist. The drowsy little girl instinctively wrestled the wind, the arm 'round her body keeping her from doing what her mind told her to do: "Get up on your feet and run away from here fast as ya can." Amarillo, unaccustomed to his touch, pulled her head back from Tom's grasp, his unsteady lead, while Lizzie callt out to Jesus and Mary and her Pa to come to her aid. When she recognized Tom's laughter she relaxed. "Oh, Pa, I thought you was a evil somebody come to carry me off."

Tom set his child on the dry, dusty ground and Lizzie's knees 'most buckled right under her. Tom caught her, stood her up straight, and said ever so proudly, "Well, it looks like I've got me a brand-new pony! Whatchu think I should call him?"

Lizzie futilely rammed Tom's body with her head, punching him with her small fists. "You can't have my pony, Pa. That's my pony. Give him back to me now. Please, Pa. That's my pony."

Tom saw Lizzie's face get redder and redder, tears streaking down her cheeks, and relented.

"Okay, the pony's yours this time. But remember, you can't ride no horse with your eyes closed. That's always been true. Why, I came right up 'longside you, bold as could be, took your animal's reins, and was 'bout to be on my way, I was."

Lizzie was not too impressed with Tom's feat, just annoyed that she'd been had and her pony almost taken. "Aw, Pa, you wasn't going nowhere, were you?"

"No, but that's 'cause I love you and I just didn't, not 'cause I couldn't've if I'd wanted."

Lizzie really didn't like that notion, and kicked the dirt 'neath her till the dust almost surrounded her wild mane of hair. "Whoa, there, girl. It's not my fault you nodded off to dreamland and I just came along and did the natural thing—took your animal right from under you. Why, you're not the first person something like this has happened to."

"I'm not?" Lizzie asked, dejected, feeling terribly foolish.

"'Course not."

"How do you know, Pa?"

"Well, once there was a boy . . ."

"What was his name, Pa?"

"Well, I'm not rightly sho' I know that," Tom said, as he helped Lizzie brush her pony down, being sure not to be too expert or too quick, leaving the child some pride. "Anyway, he was just some ol' farmhand who was ever so sleepy till he got woke up by the Devil."

"The Devil?" Lizzie dropped the brush and was reaching 'tween Amarillo's legs for it. When her father brusquely interrupted, "What'd I tell you 'bout gettin' 'tween a horse and his legs, Lizzie? You move the horse, not yourself. You hear me?"

"Yes, Pa."

"Anyway, this ol' boy is shaking in his boots 'cause he's looking right at the Devil, you know?"

"Uh huh?"

"And the Devil takes his good time 'fore he says a thing. And that scared the ol' boy even more. Then the Devil gets to flappin' his mouth. 'Well, youngun, if you want me to let you go, you've got to give me somethin'. I think I want some grain.' And the ol' boy replies, 'Ain't got no grain, the field's dried up, sir.'"

Tom hesitated a moment, and looked out at his own fields, which he imagined were just as dried up as the boy's must have been. Then, bringing himself back for Lizzie's sake, he went on, "So, the Devil says, 'Then give me some eggs.' And a bit more fearful, the ol' boy says, 'Oh, Mistah Devil, sir, I got no eggs neither. The hen ain't laid none.'"

"Just like Turkey, huh, Pa?"

"Hold on there, girl. The Devil's not through yet. 'So, fetch me a bucket of milk,' he says. Once again the ol' boy thinks he's really gointa make the Devil mad this time. 'There ain't no milk. The cow died.' Now the Devil is turnin' redder and redder and the air floatin' round him is gettin' hotter and hotter. 'Awright, just get me a bale of cotton.' When the boy heard that he knew he was in trouble. 'Boll weevil already done took dat. As a matter of fact, Mistah Devil, sir, I cain't think of nothin' I got that you want.'"

"Oh no," Lizzie whispered.

"Yep, the ol' boy knows he's in trouble now. And all the time he's shiverin', he's justa thinkin', 'I got somethin' more better for your taste. Light and airy and not too fillin' and as close as you can get.' 'And what could that be?' the Devil asks. 'My Shadow!'" And quickly tying Amarillo to his gate, off Tom ran toward the house, guffawing and slapping his thighs, Lizzie right behind him.

When he reached the front porch, Tom surveyed his land sadly. *Crop comin' in look poorly and sparse.* He shook his head, thinking all he could give the bankers was his ol' black shadow, too. But when Lizzie jumped into his arms, Tom hauled her torso up toward the skies, saying, "The moral of that story is don't be sleepin' on the job. You never know who's watchin'. And if you get in trouble, don't be lookin' for nobody to bail you out, neither. Keep on a-steppin' and don't never look back."

Giggling, Lizzie wiggled from Tom's arms and ran into the house. Alone, Tom leaned against the porch railing, jumped back with a huge splinter in his palm. "Damn, place needs paint. Needs new porch steps for sho', and now the railing, too. Things just fallin' apart every time I look around. I'm afraid to look at the chimney."

The morning rays of sun left stark, isolated black cutouts of his home stretching across the fields. The day would be ablaze with heat, letting swirls of red dust burn up his face if he wasn't careful out in the fields. Tom raised his arm to wipe his brow, surprised his sleeve was sweat-soaked immediately.

The slap of the sagging screen door let everyone in the kitchen know what Tom would not say aloud. The day was goin' to be as hard and fruitless as the last few months had been. Eudora'd been up all the night wrestling with the trimming of a tea gown for one of her best clients. She was tired from that, and tired of Tom's resentment squashing every attempt she made to keep her home free of rancor and silences.

"Why don't you shut the door like a normal person just closes the door, Tom Winrow?"

"I didn't shut the door, Eudora, I slammed it. Do you hear me?"

"You need to stop botherin' me, for Christ's sake! What?!"

"I ain't botherin' you. You been workin' on that damned dress all night, is what!"

"Somebody's gotta bring some money in here—"

"Don't start, Eudora—"

"Here's something for you to eat this mornin', Tom," Bette interrupted with a very tender tone. "It's so early in the Lord's day to be fussin' 'bout what's in His hands."

"Yes, ma'am, you're right there. I can't make rain. And my looking at a seedling sho' don't make it grow."

"That's right," Bette reassured him. She knew Tom was fraught with the demons of the Devil, drink, women, that crazy music and gamblin', all addin' up to a stormy man whose tongue or fist might strike out like a lightnin' bolt at any moment. *No tellin' when. No tellin' who. Best to be gentle with a wild thing.*

Tom swished his eggs and grits 'round his plate, thinkin' 'bout when he and Eudora'd first married and joy wasn't feigned or forced, when Ma Bette's fingers were truly limber and her skin smooth as a youngster's. Now Ma Bette was afflicted with the arthritis, her knuckles sore too much of the time, her mind wandering unexpectedly when he was trying to tell her, since he couldn't tell his wife or child, he was trying to tell the one somebody who'd listen without scowlin' at him that the crops were ruined, the bank note due, he owed too much at Haggerty's general store. Only Ma Bette'd hear him out, though she secretly made offerings to some spirits for the rains to come and didn't mention Eudora's belief that only God could help them, that there wasn't anythin' he, Tom, could do to wrest them from losing everythin'.

"You know, Tom, I'm workin' with some mighty powerful forces to approach the Lord. Ask him for some rains to come on here. Not some showers or sprinkles here and there, but a full rain, what makes things grow and clears the spirit for blessings. That's what I'ma doin', Tom Winrow, cain't fault me there, now."

"No, Ma Bette, I sho' 'nough cain't."

"We got to work on all fronts, you see. Can't put all your eggs in one basket . . . Come over here, chile, let me do somethin' with that head of yours." Ma Bette suddenly focused on Lizzie, who was finishing off her grits slowly, trying to put off this very moment.

"Naw, Nana. Nobody cares 'bout my hair 'ceptin' you. My hair is fine just the way it is. Look, I combed it yesterday—"

"Girl, get your lil behind over here before I haveta come get you."

Lizzie was beginning to squirm and resist, even though her grandma hadn't even moved. "Ain't no company comin' today, Nana," she said, so emphatically that her hand pushed her plate of grits smashing to the floor, which set Tom to laughing, Bette to cussin', and Eudora to a frenzy.

"Would you all hush up, please! How do you expect me to do anything at all with this carryin' on 'round me. Look, I've even pricked my finger tryin' to just live 'round you all! Now hush up, I say. I don't wanta hear another sound from a soul. And I mean that, too."

Almost furtively, Bette shook her finger at Lizzie to come sit down and have her head looked after. Lizzie looked at the mess of grits on the floor with the shattered heavy pottery covered in them like that's what she should tend to. Bette just cut her eyes at Lizzie once, and the grits became a matter to be dealt with later, some other time, just not now.

Once she got Lizzie situated on the floor 'tween her legs, Bette started goin' on 'bout the War of Secession—well, not exactly the War, but the bounty and the beauty of the land before the Northerners terrorized everyone livin' and everythin' growin' till wasn't nothin' left worth lookin' at. Just a beat-down people on a beat-down earth. Things were just so different since then. Since freedom came. She spoke in that particularly genteel voice she took on when she thought about the times before freedom, and Tom's throat grew tight. The veins in his forearms stood out like each one of them remembered the pickin' and the hoein' for some white man somewhere who could tell him when to eat, when to sleep, whom he could sleep with, where he could go on his own two feet, and so many things swirled in his head and his body till he just burst.

"Ma Bette, are you really goin' outta your head? Don't you remember nothin' at all?"

"Boy, set down. Talkin' to me in such a way! I remember plenty . . . I been here longer than you could spit at. Now set your self down and let me tell you how it was . . ."

"I don't need you to tell me what bein' a slave was like. I know all I wanta know about that. We didn't have nothin', not even our own selves. We were just like a hog or a horse or a mule, somethin' to be used till it dropped dead! Stop your lyin' to my daughter. Stop lyin' to yourself. We didn't own anythin'. We was owned."

Startled, Lizzie asked, "Pa, what'd you mean? We didn't have the farm or nothin'?"

Bette answered for him. "Depends on how you look at it, darlin', and where you were lookin' from." She grimaced at Tom.

"Don't contradict me in my own house, ol' woman. Lizzie, no, we couldn't even have owned this piece of farm."

Bette was so mad now she started pulling Lizzie's hair like it really was cotton. "Ow!" Lizzie screamed, and then howled.

"Shut up, all of ya!" Eudora suddenly stood, yelling at the top of her lungs. "Shut up. Sit down. Leave it be. Do you hear? Leave it be! I've got to finish this dress, or we won't even have food on the table."

"Well, ain't that somethin'," spat Tom, "Now we won't have food on the table if you don't work your fingers to the bone all night for us. Stop lyin'. Your 'sacrifices' have nothin' more to do with us than those letters you sneak off to Elma so she could make believe she's not a po' niggah farmer's daughter. Down there tryin' to be somethin' she ain't. Why, I don't even see half the money I make, and I know you don't tell me nothin' of the truth 'bout what you send to Nashville, to the dirt farmer's daughter in dresses too fine for a body who can just barely afford to be where she's at. Why cain't you be satisfied with what we got, huh?"

"I want more for my daughters than this!" Eudora spoke with such force and bitterness that her words even pierced Tom's rage. There wasn't really any need to go through this again. The walls of the house probably ached with the weight of the repeated accusations and upbraidings. At least once every two days Tom and Eudora would have at it. To the unfamiliar, only their daughter Elma's aspirations came between them, but the mortar and wood of the Winrow place, the windowsills, the carefully laid floor, and the door knew the trouble was that Eudora was who she was and what she dreamed, and Tom the same. And nowhere in a Carolinian dawn, any Low Country space or time, did the dreams of Eudora and Tom intersect. Actually their understandings of being alive and colored were in fierce combat, and the battles were always ugly, if not bloody.

"You want! You want anythin' you ain't got that you think those rich cousins of yours may have . . ." Tom began his retreat from this implacable woman, this wife he didn't really touch when he thought he was touching her, Eudora, whose body wasn't actual, even when he lay with her. Tom withdrew till his spine was curled like the valves of the cornet he wished he had in his hands, at his mouth, so he could say what he meant and be understood. Nothin' he said in the words he exchanged with Eudora made sense like the sounds he could get to come out of that cornet. But Tom knew better than to get his horn now, while Eudora was on one of her Elma sieges. No music he could play could penetrate, harmonize, or resemble anything but noise in the face of Eudora's devotion to Elma. It had always been that way.

"I can't make out who this chile takes after," Bette mused softly, edging the rancor from the kitchen. Maybe it flew out the door as she finally, gently finished braiding Lizzie's hair. Nevertheless, Bette was still confounded by the color of her great-grandchild's skin, so ruddy, so red and opaque. "Cain't figure out how this happened," she mumbled very seriously, patting the child on her shoulder to let her know she was finished. Lizzie jumped up to run outdoors when Bette really got nervous for her. "Child, you too marhiney to be in the sun for long. Shouldn't be in the sun at all, if you ask me. And you need to clean up that plate!" But Lizzie was gone.

Bette had done her best, but Eudora was on her feet now walking toward Tom with deliberate, measured steps that punctuated her words like a pop of high hat on a set of traps: "Tom, Elma is a beautiful girl, and she can marry into somethin'. I don't ask you for the shirt off your damned black back to help better the lives of my children, and you know that. I'm so glad Lizzie isn't in here right now. Do you begrudge the support cousin Diggs has offered for both of them to get good schooling, refine their manners, and be somebody of substance in this world? Is that it? If you can't give it to them, you'd rather they just have nothin'? Well, Elma's at

Fisk University and Lizzie's gointa go, do you understand me? Why, hell, even Francina can't say that about her own self."

Tom's veins got to pulsing again, and his leg moved compulsively to some unheard blues beat; he just got into the swing of it. He threw words at Eudora like he'd been signaled to take a solo at the height of a hot tune.

"What you be sayin' to me, Eudora? If no damned crackuh blood flowed through your high-toned blue veins, huh? Would you be talkin' to me 'bout the hoein' or the bank note, Miss Mayfield? What would fall out your mouth if you had no ties to those grave-diggin' nigguhs? Diggs so much better 'n Winrow? That fam'ly ain't got so much to be puffed up about, far as I can see. Blanche ain't seen a smile cross her face in fifteen years. Francina so scared of livin', she make a real old maid look like the life of the party. And let's not forget the dear ole cousin Roswell, evuh the gentleman, ain't figured out perfumed handkerchiefs is for ladies. That fluff break a sweat, he'd fall out."

"He at least takes care of his family. They don't want for anything at all."

"There you go again with that word, 'want.'"

At that moment, Lizzie came skipping in with Turkey. "What do you want, Pa?"

"He wants you and that gall-darned hen to go to your room immediately. We're having grown-up talk here."

"Yes, ma'am," and Lizzie scampered away, looking up to Bette and Tom for some clue as to what she might have said or done to warrant all this serious grown-up talk. But she could not read their faces. They didn't even seem to see her.

"No, Eudora," Bette said, "you didn't have to snap at the chile like that. She can hear 'bout her own kin. All they do is get rich sellin' the colored burial insurance, waits till they die, and lead them straight to the dead folks' beauty parlor so they can fancy em up for the worms to get em. Too bad he can't do something for em while they're alive."

Eudora rolled her eyes at her mother and Tom, who she thought had turned his back to her, but Tom had turned to look at his land. Tears he fought with the music in his head took control for a second, and a growling sound jumped out of his mouth suddenly.

"Bless you," Bette chirped.

"Lizzie, get down here or you'll be late to school. And that's something I won't have." Eudora angrily gathered her things, reciting this litany to the walls. Lizzie was nowhere to be seen. "Where's that child anyway?"

"Here I am, Mama," Lizzie perkily announced.

"Oh my, you haven't done a thing I asked."

"Lizzie, your mama is in a bad humor this mornin'. She's all high strung today cause your sister Elma is comin' home. Ain't that right, Eudora?" Tom attempted to sweeten the air between the mother and daughter before it soured beyond countenance. He knew when Eudora looked at Lizzie, gangly and free of spirit as she was, yellow as she was, she saw his features, his eyes, his absolute connection to her through this little girl till the day they died. He knew that fact. The fact of their closeness once, the innocent Lizzie, was enough to ruin Eudora's day. He'd bet money on it.

Luckily Lizzie was too busy running out the door with a piece of bread and a piece of cheese to be concerned with her parents' goings-on. In a minute, all Tom could see and hear of his daughter was Lizzie's wild red hair and her holler "Look, Mama, I'm eatin' and walkin' at the same time. We don't be late, I promise."

Eudora sighed in exasperation, adjusting her hat. "I'm going to go on now, Tom, but you're right, Elma is coming home tomorrow and I do want us to make her feel welcome. All of us. That's the least her family could do, you know. Oh, I almost forgot. Don't forget to pick up that fabric shipment at Mr. Haggerty's for me and those things I ordered for Elma's dinner. And stop for Lizzie 'fore the day is out, all right?"

"Well, I don't know, I'm thinkin' 'bout movin' on to Oklahoma this afternoon. Good prime lands out there, dirt cheap, and enough of us to have whole towns of colored. That's what I might be doin' this afternoon—"

Eudora coyly interrupted, "Why move, Tom, dear. We've all that right here. Girl, don't run—you'll sweat yourself up." Eudora stepped out the door with the impossible task of catching up to Lizzie.

Tom shouted after them, "Don't forget, I may be goin' to Oklahoma!"

Lizzie shouted back, "I wanta go to Oklahoma with you, Pa!"

Eudora hurried to catch her daughter before more of Tom's foolish ideas got into her head. But Tom kept right on, "If we didn't spend so much, we could hire a hand and maybe make the land pay off."

Just as she reached Lizzie, the child yelled back at her father, "Ho, Pa, let's go to Oklahoma. Oklahoma, I say. That's my choice, Pa."

With Lizzie yelling all this nonsense, Eudora jerked the girl's shoulder a bit too hard. Lizzie gritted her teeth and shut her mouth, but her mind was on her pa, the land, Oklahoma, and her big sister Elma comin' home. Having Elma around made her mama happy, sweet. Good reason for Elma to get home real soon. Bring the laughter from her mother that she could not.

Not much passed between daughter and mother as they rushed past tall curved bamboo, Japanese wisteria that left lavender pollen dotting their hair, and dogwoods that were so whimsical even Eudora wanted to stop and enjoy them. But she did not. No, even climbing silver moons lacing grand old buildings with the kind of detail Eudora was proud of in her own designs couldn't sway Lizzie's mama. Eudora was going to get her child to that school before her cousin Francina could run back to Charleston with tales of how Lizzie was not only a troublemaker but had a leaning toward truancy as well, unheard of in the family before. The "before" was what stuck in Eudora's throat. Before they came from the islands, before they worked their way out of Little Mexico, before she married the likes of Tom Winrow. Yet Lizzie and Eudora managed to be late for the commencing of the day at the colored school, fondly referred to as the "True Freedom School" in whispers among their own kind. And Francina was waiting for them in the doorway as if she knew who'd denied themselves the luxury of fallen camellias and azaleas teasing the breadth of rainbows just so they could avoid this moment.

Eudora could hear the other youngsters already reciting their multiplication tables in different groups. There was a canonic crescendo to the simple task, which luckily muffled her curses at her situation, her husband, her cousin's ever-so-sweet smiling face masking disdain and the Lord only knew what.

"I'm so sorry we're late again, Francina, things just got to be a bit much at the farm today. Run along in, Lizzie. Catch up with the others. Say good mornin' to Cousin Francina." Lizzie gladly nodded her wild-eyed head and rushed to her classmates.

"Go along now like your mama told you." Francina spoke without noticing Lizzie was gone already. "Besides, I'm used to your family's tendency to tardiness."

"Well, Francina, I did have to complete all my own work on I don't even know how many dresses, do farm chores, get this child ready to go, and get myself some free time for Elma's return. You know, she's comin' home tomorrow. I can't wait to talk to her. From all her letters, she most surely has her hands full of suitors. I am certain she's to marry soon."

Self-consciously assuming Eudora was remarking on her own status as an unmarried woman of means, Francina snapped, "Well, don't stay up making wedding plans for your youngest one over there. She is totally lacking in couth, she lies, fights, put a junebug down that lovely Emerald Grieson's dress. I truly believe she was actually out back with the boys smoking a cigarette. For your sake, I try not to make too much of her, uh, 'activities.' I know how much you value the family's reputation."

Taken aback but not cowed, Eudora gasped, "Are you really discussin' my baby? If what you say is true, and I've no cause to doubt you, Francina, don't you be afraid to use the rod whenever necessary."

"I appreciate your understanding, cousin, but even belts and the paddle don't work on children born in a stormy house. I must tell you, everyone in town is talkin' 'bout your husband, Win . . ." Francina slurred the name with obvious relish at her cousin's discomfort.

"You mean Tom. His name is Tom."

"Yes, that's right, Tom. Well, his constant carousin' and gamblin' when he doesn't have a . . . oh my."

"Yes, Francina, the crop is not a good one this season," Eudora slowly explained.

"That's true, Eudora, but I must tell you what I myself truly believe."

"What could that be, cousin?"

"I think, uh, Tom is, uh . . . how can I say . . ."

"Francina, why don't you not say another thing. Only one I ever hear talkin' is you. I don't have time for idle tongues who've not a thing better to do than bad-mouth decent folks."

"Eudora, I was just trying to—"

"I understand, Francina. Why don't you try to come hear Elma sing at the church this Sunday? She just gave a performance at Fisk. She sent me the program. I'll bring it to you Sunday. You'll be so proud of her. The whole family will be, I'm sure."

Just then Lizzie poked her head out the door. "You still here, Mama?"

"Lizzie, see to your lessons," Francina snapped sternly.

"I saw my mama and I wanted to say good-bye, is all." For this once, in spite of herself, Eudora reached out for Lizzie and held her close.

"You be good today, Lizzie, for me, okay?"

"Yes, ma'am." Lizzie hugged Eudora so hard that Eudora's eyes widened and she thought, *My Lord, this child's strong.*

The little schoolhouse was spick-and-span, but stark and tight. Next to the American flag, Booker T. Washington's face loomed over the children, and Francina kept a smaller portrait of DuBois on her desk near the piano, which is exactly where Lizzie headed, her heart pounding and her feet itching with excitement. There was music in there, in the piano, her piano, if she could get to it. She pushed her way through the class, focused on the black and white keys grinning at her. She didn't notice who fell over or shouted, "Watch where you're goin'!" and "Don't put your hands on me, gal." Lizzie heard none of that. She heard the music even before her fingers graced the keys with a sassy touch, pulling a syncopated lyric from the lonely instrument usually restricted to spirituals and patriotic songs. The other children forgot how peeved she'd made them and began to clap their hands. A couple even hooted and hollered from the joy and raunchiness of Lizzie's playing, her body moving with the music like she was part of the melody, the rhythm. Annie Louise, the class monitor, began to get nervous. Francina Diggs didn't take to disorder. "Lizzie, stop cuttin' up. You got everybody actin' a fool. What if Miss Diggs comes in? Lizzie, please?"

"Young lady, get away from that piano with that nasty music comin' out of your fingers," rasped Miss Diggs as she glared at the children from the doorway.

Annie Louise piped in with, "I tol' her to stop, Miss Diggs, I did. I knew you wouldn't like it."

"Tattletale!" Lizzie hollered.

Francina was overwhelmed by the chaos Lizzie had started. "Everyone shut up! Lizzie, my days in this room are so much more civilized when you're not here."

The next moment Lizzie was in her seat in a beatific state. Music of any kind, no matter how low-down, was sacred in her eyes, brought out what was holy in her, eased her mind, and set her soul aglow. Francina turned away, exasperated, murmuring something about what the race was coming to. Lizzie, on the other hand, was motioning to Annie Louise that she was going to black her eyes good. Annie stuck her tongue out. The others, her classmates who'd had such a good time, were in her corner: "Miss Diggs, she was just lettin' us have some fun." "Lizzie didn't do no wrong, Miss Diggs."

Lizzie was sent to the cloakroom as punishment. She sat still for a minute, then spied the open window just above the coat hooks and climbed right on out into the freedom of the early morning air. "Woo-wee!" Lizzie exclaimed as quietly as she could. She'd fallen a whole eight feet to the ground and landed right on her behind. She looked back up at the window, dustin' her backside at the same time. As she realized from whence she had come, her head started weavin' and bobbin' to an as-yet unwritten tune. "Yeah, that's right, 'She can fall from the top of a tall oak tree, dust herself off, and come on home to me.' Yep, I'm gointa sing that to Pa, see if that's got the feel of the blues for real. Pa'll know right off. Then we could work on it together. I think Pa'll like that. An original Winrow tune. Maybe even with our faces on the sheet music. We could forget about the damned crops and sing an' be rich as them other relatives, and won't nobody have to die, either." Laughing and humming new words to her song, Lizzie dashed into the woods. *Trumpeter Tommy Winrow and His Amazin' Singin' Dancin' Daughter!*

* * *

OF COURSE, Tom had no thoughts of Lizzie communin' with the low-down spirit of the blues as he passed by the schoolhouse on his way to town in his buckboard empty of produce, a strange sight for that time of year. The load so light the horses were free to prance along almost as if they were loose from bridles and reins. Tom felt their relief and envied them. He glanced back at the wagon, feeling powerless and pitiful, while the animals moved forward with élan. "Boll weevil where did you come from, Boll weevil . . ." He didn't even wanna sing about it. He was tired, the normal energy he was used to sucked up by this life he was livin'. *This lie.*

How a man so good at readin' a card-playin' stranger cross the table could be so bad at seein' the woman who shares his bed. "The woman I love," he sneared. *Did love. My Dora.* The very thing that made his heart dance just at seeing her now made him recoil, her passion a simmering rage, her ambition turned desperate, leaving no room for a partner, no tolerance for failure. *Eyes, those beautiful strange eyes, a wonder and surprise, lookin' like they didn't belong there, if they looked his way at all lately, were un-blinking, uncaring, blamin' him—even for the weather.* It had gotten so he couldn't talk to her straight, but had taken to regarding her askance, squinting as if in the glare of the sun.

He daren't curse the land for fear it would turn on him some more. It had broken his folks and now it was breaking him. All morning he had pressed Mr. Lee into one more day of belligerent service, turning over the sandy red earth to reveal even more dry dirt, him workin' harder than the mule to coax the plow through another barren row. *Nothin' to do but turn it over.* He chuckled to himself, sweat streaming down his brow. Funny, when he hadn't cared nothin' 'bout it, the land just seemed to blossom for him, a fancy girl trying to make herself pretty, doll herself up with berries, peaches, wildflowers, a garland of grapes in her hair. Now that he depended upon her, she shrank from his touch, her red purple flowers falling early, the green bolls that would burst white with new cotton, crawling with hairy pincered bugs, poking their long snouts at him, birthing their white wrinkled larvae, yield after yield. He bent over the reins as a shard of pain coursed through his torso. "Damn, cain't even drink no moah."

The contradiction left an ache in his arms. He wanted to punish the horses, Willie and Sue, for being so gall-darned free of his dilemma. He had to have something to carry to market, and soon. He had to pile that buckboard with hay, potatoes, cotton, beans, anything that would force the horses to trudge slowly down the road, weighed down by the bounty of his fields. Tom burst into a fierce sweat on top of the light layer of per-spiration that had already left his back and underarms ringed and soiled-looking. But he didn't look nearly as unkempt as this white man on the side of the road waving his hand in the air, like a body wouldn't see a lone white man right away. Sometimes Tom actually believed he could sense white folks near him, so he was a bit put off by the agitated gyrations of this figure who couldn't possibly be a Carolinian. White Carolinians assumed black folks' lives revolved around them, that their needs were to be catered to anywhere, anytime, even by the side of the road in the heat of the day, even if they were dirty and close to trash as rotting hog entrails. Whoever this white man was, he wasn't local.

But Tom was local and knew better than to just ride on by. He pulled the reins hard on Willie and Sue, finally getting back at them for being so carefree. The white man was white enough to hop up next to him before Tom could get a "Good day, sir" out of his mouth. Not wanting to be too familiar, even with a white man whose suit was frayed and torn, face unshaven and bruised, Tom moved over as far as he could. *Give the man some space.*

"Which way you headed, sir?" Tom asked in a mild voice, though his passenger's eyes darted wildly in all directions, not unlike a wounded animal.

"Well, brother, I'm trying to get to Charleston. Is that on your way?" The white man tried to sound more relaxed than he was, which set Tom on edge.

"If you say so, Sir."

"Brother, don't take it that way. I really didn't mean to sound like you had to go there. Name's Marcus Singleton," he said with a quick nasal speech that was decidedly not Southern. "Where I come from we don't force the colored to do what's not on their minds to do. So if you're not headed for Charleston, I'll just jump right off your wagon, and you can go on about your day as you planned, although I do wish I had some time to talk with you about my business in these parts. I've got some very interesting opportunities for a man like you, uh . . . what did you say your name was, again?"

Tom took a deep breath and raised his eyes a little, looking as far away from this crazy white man as he could manage. "I didn't get a chance to tell you, sir—"

"Brother, drop all that sir business. We're just workers together like anybody else. Color makes no nevermind where I come from."

"Well, it does down here, sir. I could get myself in a heap of a mess if anybody else was to hear me talkin' to a white man out of my place, so please, I'ma keep on callin' you sir. Name's Winrow, most everbody call me Win."

"Win? I like that."

"Wish it was true," he chuckled, "and I am on my natural way to Charleston, though I can't 'xactly say what for—ain't got nothin' to take to market."

"Well, Mr. Win, I think I can help on both those counts." Marcus Singleton thought he'd found a hook to reel in another fish. He was a former carnie barker, the pitch rolled off his tongue. "If you take heed to what I have to say, you won't have to concern yourself with talking low to any old white person or worry about a good crop coming in."

"I like my life here just fine, sir. Traditions are traditions and they don't bother them what's used to 'em, plus worryin' 'bout a crop comin' in is just about as much a part of a farmer's life as breathin', which you should be real glad you doin'." Tom looked cynically at the bruises and scabs on the white man, whose shredded clothes rivaled those of any po' niggah he'd ever seen. "So they gave you a good enough welcome, I see."

Singleton hesitantly and quietly admitted, "Yes, brother, I did have some trouble in Wheeler. There's a fear of workers thinkin' for themselves up there that I wasn't prepared for. Seems to me a man ought to be able to work where he wants and demand to be paid adequately for his labor. Now that's what I think, but I couldn't get that idea through to anyone 'round there. All I got was their idea, which seems to be beatin' the livin' hell outta anyone who isn't one of them, even if they don't have a pot to piss in.

"It's fear, brother. I don't hold nothin' against them. The notions I was introducin' scared them more than the pitiful way they're forced to live, makin' a quota of a crop for somebody else, bein' forced to feed other folks 'fore they feed themselves, and always fearin' they'll lose their land or the plot they're workin' for somebody who doesn't give one damn whether they live or die."

Singleton had Tom's interest now. He was thinkin' how much he feared losin' his land just like this white man was talkin' 'bout.

"Say, what's a quota?" Tom asked tentatively, which was all Singleton needed to launch his agenda of taking black workers away from farmin' and sharecroppin' to luring them to the mountain regions of West Virginia to work in the mines. The owners of the Consolidated Coal Company had sent him south in search of scab labor to break the back of the fledgling United Mine Workers Union. By persuasion or otherwise, he had a quota he had to meet. So many niggahs for so many dollars.

Tom didn't know this. All he wanted to know was what a quota was.

"Hold on heah a minute, would you? I got my mind a bit confused. What'd ya say we was workin' for? A quota? What's that there? What's it got to do with me? I got my own land!"

Singleton was getting excited. "Brother, that's exactly what I'm talkin' about. You don't have your land. The banks have got your land. And if you don't bring in a certain kinda harvest, they'll take that land right from under your feet and sell anythin' that ain't nailed down before you can blink your eyes. And I know you could tell that's the truth way down in your soul. Look at the state of the farms 'round here. No rain. Scrawny corn. Little bits of cotton. Weevils eatin' at that. You know how close you are to bein' out of your land as I do!"

"Winrows always had they land," is all Tom had to say. "I'll find some way to deal with the bank."

"Brother, if you listen to me, you could pay off that note in less than a year, I bet."

Tom chuckled. "How's that, brothah?"

"Well, fellas I got jobs for up my way are makin' a dollar fifty a day, sending it homeward. Next thing they know, they've paid for their land, or some even bought new land right there! I'll tell yuh, most take to livin' up north so keen they send for their families and leave the dangers of livin' down here to the colored willin' to put up with it."

"You're right about that," Tom said, dead serious. "The two of us just ridin' in this buckboard together is enough to get us killt. Ya bettah keep yourself out the backcountry or might be nobody'll ever see ya again. You was really lucky this time, they left ya livin'. That ain't always the case. But stop this nonsense talk about a dollar 'n a half a day; a hardworking man down here might make that in a whole week. What, ya thought I was born yesterday?"

"Naw, brother, I'm sayin' you can be born again, a new man. Where I hail from, a man can live with some respect, not talk low to a livin' soul, and give his family more than white folks down in these parts dream about for themselves. And that's the God's honest truth."

Tom felt his stomach churning; his throat was dry. What this white man was sayin' was the answer to alla his problems with Eudora and her dreams, his dreams for Lizzie, Miz Bette's care, and a future for the

Winrow clan. Keep the land and still be free of Carolinian white fools in they white sheets and burnin' crosses, their crooked liens, take it or leave it. Tom didn't let on, but he took Singleton's suggestions earnestly. *Decision-makin' time is comin'* was what he thought. *New hand, change the rhythm of the game.* He relaxed a bit as they approached Charleston proper. "You best be gettin' on now, mista," he murmured. "I cain't ride up into the city with you, but you best get yourself to Miz Bette in Lil Mexico. She got a basket down there, sellin' herbs and what-not. She'll work some hoodoo on them bruises and won't nobody know for lookin' how dangerous could be talkin' with you. Dollah fifty a day you say, huh?" Tom asked, squinting his eyes, still leery. "Listen, for my family's sake, don't come lookin' for me. I'll find you if I got a mind to. Don't know right now. Just try to keep a little to yourself for a few days. Don't want to find you dead out in the swamp somewhere cause you tol' us colored we didn't haveta be slaves to no bank quota! Dollah fifty?" Tom laughed deep in his belly as if just told a good joke and clicked his teeth to get his horses goin' again.

Singleton was a bit dismayed he hadn't snapped Tom up immediately, but his body hurt so much from the beating and weakness from hunger, all he could manage to call out to Tom was, "Where is this Miz Bette?"

"Ask anybody!" Tom hollered back, the horses at a run now. "Tell her Tommy Winrow sent ya."

"Thank you, thank you kindly, Mr. Winrow. I'll be seeing you."

The summer sun had given way to a little breeze. As he watched the odd stranger amble down the boulevard, Tom sat up and let the air cool his skin. The pain in his side was gone. *Mistah, I like that.* His misgivings vanished. Tom had figured out a way to flee from what was ailin' him. Suddenly failure was a long way from this colored man. He laughed at his own excitement just contemplating the prospect of earning a decent wage for a man. He would speak to Mr. Singleton again. He looked up at the sun and howled, then drove the horses with the fury of a man who'd discovered he was the son of gods. His bellowing singing voice faded into the bustle of Charlestonians in the midst of their day. With an itch in his fingers, he headed for Pilar's.

10

LIZZIE DIDN'T LIKE TO ADMIT IT, BUT THE SHEER SIGHT OF Charleston made her joyful. Staving off a lone truant's boredom, she ran up and down the vaulted staircases colored were never to encounter. She could relax a bit more by the Diggs house, though. She wound her body through tulip balustrades imagining herself a raucous wildflower, a vision to behold, her tanned skin turned peach, tender and innocent smelling. If she found a guard rail detailed with the forms of the iris, she lingered, no longer imagining herself a flower but being one.

She had to be careful because the Diggses had surrounded themselves with all sorts of flowers and imaginary creatures, like horses with wings and birds with teeth, who looked all the more beautiful because of the ebony shine of the ironwork itself. There was one flying stallion, just before the lock to the front gate, whose open mouth held the key. Lizzie couldn't reach this key without possible injury, though she tried anyway. Somehow that key represented the secret, some secret that held her family and her relatives at bay, a dark, unknown fact that would be released to her if only she could reach it. She'd thought maybe a treasure existed somewhere down in the harbor where the Diggses got their money from. They weren't actually all that smart they could live this much better than her family, especially Ma Bette, who claimed to have some gold bullion stashed away somewhere. All these thoughts and whimsies passed through her tough little body before she neared the Diggses' front door. There she said a curse, mimicking the Gullah that she had often heard Ma Bette speak, and she scampered off.

A bit winded, but full of energy from the early day, Lizzie decided to go visit Osceola, her friend down at Pilar's place. That'd fix her relatives, the Diggses—a girl frequenting a dive like Pilar's and being familiar to them as well. That was a great compensation for her not being able to reach the key to the secret of the family, whatever it was.

Lizzie never knew which Osceola she'd find. He was enigmatic in a childlike way, wavering from Snake-Boy to the Beaver's grandson or just another half-Cherokee colored from Lil Mexico. Never could tell which one. Snake-Boy took over Osceola's bronze body with the flat, high cheekbones whenever he felt unappreciated, when he was not treated fairly. When he was angry, Snake-Boy appeared, glaring out of Osceola's eyes. According to what Osceola'd told her when he was in a good mood one day, Snake-Boy was an excellent hunter who brought so much game back to his elders that his brothers and cousins got jealous of him and began to treat him contemptuously, so Snake-Boy stopped huntin'. That was it. He just didn't hunt anymore, but he did go back to the woods, where he said his mother came from, and returned to the camp with a pair of deer horns and immediately went to the hothouse, the asi, where he explained to his grandma that he'd have to stay alone that night. So he stayed in the asi alone all night, while all the others were carousing and having family tradition in the cabin. Come mornin' time the grandma went back to the asi to get her favorite grandson and found a huge serpent on two human legs that made an awful sound when it moved about. The creature mulled around the family for a while, but finally made its way to the river, where it stayed for many years. Then one day a fisherman caught a strange animal in the river and he brought it to the village for everyone to see. It hung huge and lifeless in the fisherman's net as Snake-Boy's grandmother came out to peer at it. As she reached out to touch the skin of the fisherman's prize, the creature sprang to life. It was Snake-Boy! His eyes never leaving the grandmother, Snake-Boy scratched himself out of the netting, hissing and wriggling, and jumped back into the river. As if in a trance, Snake-Boy's grandmother jumped into the water after him and was never seen again. So if Osceola was Snake-Boy today, then Lizzie's job was to stay out of his anger and keep her own life intact, not get swallowed up in Osceola's problems. If he was the Beaver's grandson, that was somethin' entirely different, but Lizzie could tell from the way Osceola was throwing crates around that Snake-Boy was out. In his form as Osceola, the youngster was not quite a year older than Lizzie and 'bout as wild and dreamy.

"What devil brought yo' behin' down heah?" Osceola grumbled.

Lizzie ignored his gruff greeting and jumped right in the midst of the sawdust Osceola had begun to sweep up.

"Damn Geechee witch! Look what you've done now!"

Lizzie just laughed and started to do a soft shoe in the mess of sawdust that finally made Osceola smile. This sparked Lizzie to invite the loosened-up Snake-boy to go take a quick swim with her. "Don't you wanna walk on down by the bay and go in the water with me? Salt do you good."

Osceola shook his mane of thick-licked black hair, the only hair on his body Lizzie'd ever seen anyway, he shook his head no vehemently. "How can I go be in the water with you when I got to set up the whole place for tonight, tables n all? I got to get glasses cleaned, billiards set right, cards counted, the band rounded up. Just how'm I gonna take a swim?"

Lizzie felt Snake-Boy rearing his head. "Oh, we don't haveta. I'll tell you what I'll do, I'll stay and help yo' half-breed behin', so there."

With that, Lizzie jumped into a vigorous time-step that spread the sawdust all over the floor as well as Osceola.

"Deke's gointa get us good if he sees us foolin' 'round out heah," Osceola said seriously, referring to his brother, who ran the honky-tonk the children were 'sposed to be cleanin' since the musicians were starting to drift in.

"Look, heah come Mr. Jocelyn and the others with their instruments. Cain't wait for them to start practicin'," Lizzie exclaimed. "And yo' lazy brothuh ain't even up yet!"

Osceola stopped sweepin' for a minute to address Lizzie in a firm voice. "Listen heah, Deke is up all night runnin' this joint. He's gointa be a really big man down here in Lil Mexico. He'll soon take over when Miss Pilar let it loose. And that's gonna be sooner than you think, too. A man like Deke needs his rest."

"He needs a fool like you to do alla his work for him, too," Lizzie teased and ran into the club.

Mingo had already started the bass line of the popular "Ball and the Jack" while the other fellas were tunin' their instruments. While it was true that only Jocelyn and Thibedeaux from New Orleans could actually read music, the guys knew how to harmonize perfectly. They had perfect pitch, which Jocelyn claimed was more important than readin' music. They could get the folks roused and 'side themselves with the rhythms of the drums and the syncopated choruses of the trumpets and trombones, the ticklin' solos of the clarinet and fiddles. Lizzie was havin' such a good time, even while the cacophony drowned Osceola's voice screamin', "Lizzie Winrow, get outta there. That ain't no place for girls." Instead, Lizzie'd made herself comfortable on the piano bench next to Jocelyn, who'd broken into a sweat already. Lizzie played right along with him on the rag, but had to follow more carefully when Jocelyn cued the band to begin a slow drag.

Even though he still smelled of whiskey and musk, the high brown Jocelyn felt Lizzie's passion for the music. Encouraging her, he said in a whisper, "Slow songs are always hard, baby, put yo' ear to it like you been doin' and you'll get it."

Osceola heard a dirty, raunchy blues from inside, shook his head and his jaws got tight. He felt responsible for Lizzie in a way and was riled that she'd go on ahead against his wishes into a honky-tonk, even his brothuh's, in broad daylight—well, in any kinda light. He stormed over to Lizzie, who was so focused on her piano playin' she didn't feel Snake-Boy's presence till he grabbed her right hand off the pearly keys.

"I've told you a thousand times you cain't be seen in heah. This ain't no place for ladies, especially not for little girls."

Lizzie retorted, "I go where I want and I want to be heah. The Professor's showin' me how to play the piano real good and I ain't movin' nowhere now!"

The whole band fell out laughin'. Skipper Lou made his trombone howl at Lizzie's smart response. Big Joe let his trumpet heehaw. Sam the Main Man slammed his high hat on the drums. Lizzie's gumption got goin' again. "Why you ol-fashioned thingamajig, women all over the country dance and smoke and gamble and sing in places just like this." Lizzie looked around the barroom, which wasn't as fancy as the ones she imagined playing in. Where she was gointa be someday, there'd be no sawdust on the floor or men in any kinda getup they saw fit. No. One day, Lizzie thought to herself, she'd play the piano where folks were grand, just like her sister Elma. The thought of Elma got her goin' again.

"Hey, Ossie, you don't even know what you're talkin' 'bout. Why, my sister Elma's been halfway 'round the world by this time. England, France. Name a country and she probably been there. New Orleans, Baltimore, Paris. She goes with the Fisk Jubilee Singers everywhere."

Osceola held his head in his hands, exasperated by his friend's pronouncements. Slowly and quietly he turned away from the band and Lizzie's taunts. Then his voice almost catapulted his friend to the ceiling. "Lizzie, why? Why do you lie so much? All the time lyin'. Yo' sistuh ain't been gon' but fuh a year. Cain't uh been all them places. You ain't never been none of those places and you should be glad you ain't. It's no place for a girl, not here or anywhere. Talkin' like you know somethin' 'bout somethin', New Orleans, Baltimore, now Paris! You ain't even been all over Charleston, let alone the rest of the whole world."

Used to their frequent comic spats, the band went back to their rehearsal. Ossie went back to sweeping, Lizzie following behind him, getting in the way.

"Well, I intend to go all over the world as well as all Charleston. If you'd stop makin' jokes with me and be serious, you could go, too! . . . Find someplace where we're 'preciated. Someplace fuh people just like us. Like my mama says, the world at our fingertips." She wiggled her ten as if playin' a mad scale.

"What d'you mean? Ain't no country where folks look like you! You sho' nuf don't look like anyone from 'round here. and I cain't 'magine bein' surrounded by a whole gang of folks look like you!"

Lizzie was galled now. Then Osceola added, "Maybe that's where Elma comes from, too? Yo' country, all to yo'self."

Lizzie had been at the piano with the withered, drinkin' Mr. Jocelyn until now. She'd left the work of setting up to Osceola, the music so much more enchanting than pushing heavy tables and chairs through

sawdust that fell through the air like snowflakes when Osceola shook out
the checkered red-and-white tablecloths. The band's interest in the children's squabblin' waned, even though Lizzie's face burned with anger.

"You tryin' to say somethin' 'bout my family?" It was that secret again,
curdlin' in Lizzie's stomach. That hunch she had that folks knew somethin' 'bout the Winrows that she didn't, somethin' that made folks look
at her funny.

"I ain't sayin' nothin' that ain't been said before—" Osceola never got
a chance to finish his thought. Lizzie got ta chasin' him and he moved.
The band jumped in with a raucous nasty rag to underscore the touch-
and-go chase Lizzie and Osceola were executin' with life and death vigor.

"You take that back, you half-breed niggah!" Lizzie yelled.

"I will when you really know who's the daddies in yo' family."

The two were a tangle of limbs and fists when Deke burst out of his
upstairs office. "Osceola, get yo' girlfriend outta my establishment right
this actual second!"

A woman with a painted face like the dolls on jars for pomades and
skin bleach, on her tip-toes, rested her chin on Deke's shoulder to see what
the commotion was. The musicians were layin' bets on which of the two
young fighters would come out the winner. But Sam the Main Man
pulled 'em apart before Deke got to 'em. He didn't want to see Osceola
get another beatin' on top of the one Lizzie'd just delivered.

"I do believe it's a draw, ladies and gents," Mr. Jocelyn quipped, as Sam
held both youngsters. Deke came on down the stairs, with his stocking
cap and the painted woman hangin' on him. Lizzie was strugglin' to get
free of Sam, while still tryin' to get to Osceola. "You take that back about
my family! And you!" she squealed at Deke, "You take that back about
me! I ain't no girlfriend of his."

Osceola tried one more lunge at Lizzie. This time Deke caught him
and lifted him in the air, virtually droppin' the boy on the floor. Osceola
tried to regain face by sayin' to Lizzie, "You better listen to my brothuh.
He's gointa be a big man in Charleston one of these days."

Deke lovingly grabbed Osceola's shoulders, startlin' the boy. "Who's
to say we're not big in Charleston now, brothuh?" Then Deke looked at
Lizzie, who was a scraped and scratched mess of a girl at this point. He
indicated to the painted woman he called Billie, "Do somethin' with Lil

Red 'fore her daddy gets a mind to come and whip my behind." The whole bar laughed at that, knowing all Tom Winrow could do was halfway carry himself home after a night of drinkin' and mishandled gamblin'. Lizzie thought the patrons and musicians were laughin' at her because Deke called her Red. "My name ain't Red! It's Elizabeth May-field Winrow."

Deke laughed, fussin' with his stockin' cap. "Umph. Winrow, is it? I'd never have known," he said slyly. "Musta got your backbone from you mother's side." And the whole bar started laughin' again—even Mr. Jocelyn, whom Lizzie counted as a friend, was chucklin' away. Now Lizzie was truly piqued.

"Doesn't matter where my backbone comes from, long as it works."

Billie added coyly, "That does come in handy, chile. Now come with me and we'll get you fixed on up so you can go home respectable like." Then Billie took her hand, as if she were the handmaiden of a princess, and led Lizzie to her room up the stairs.

"Really, Miss Billie, I should be gettin' home, or my ma will know I cut from school."

"I think it's a bit late to be concerned about that, darlin'. You spent half the day on the piano with Jocelyn. I heard you myself. Sounded good, too. Hot music comin' from a lil bitty thing like you. That's some-thin' to see, I tell you. Now set down and let me wash some of this dirt off and get to those bruises."

Downstairs Deke was plannin' his future, which included Osceola's. That was why he was sometimes hard on the chile. Nothin' Deke ever did to Osceola was as bad as what white folks could do. He wanted him hard as a rock on every level, including with women. "Osceola, how'd you let that lil gal get you in a tussle, boy?"

Osceola didn't like Lizzie bein' referred to as his "gal." Right now he didn't like his brother at all. Only thing on Osceola's mind as he became his other self, the Grandson of the Beaver, was to apologize for Deke and yes, for what he'd done as Snake-Boy to embarrass and hurt Lizzie. Snake-Boy knew from the way folks treated him they didn't respect the time he spent with his Cherokee mother up in the mountains and what he learned from his people, the ones they called Injun or redskins. He knew his origins weren't respected either, and folks could tell by lookin' at him that he was a half-breed. And no, he didn't know the whole story of Lizzie's family, but he knew enough to know talkin' about it hurt her. So, when Lizzie came down the stairs lookin' a little timid—though neat enough—Osceola said, "I'm sorry. I shouldn't have said those things, or let Deke talk to you like that."

From her time with Miss Billie, Lizzie'd discovered a new part of herself, the girl Lizzie, so she just nodded her head, accepting the regrets of her very best friend. But then, the ol' Lizzie jumped out just to warn him, in case he thought she was gettin' soft on him, "Leave me alone! I don't have to take nothin' off you. I don't haveta take nothin' off nobody."

Osceola, miffed since Lizzie had rebuffed the Beaver Boy's entreaty, scoffed, "Save that for your ma. It's way past time for you to meet her."

Lizzie felt a sharp tingle up her spine. *Late for Ma, oh no!* As she ran out of the bar Osceola just smiled to himself, thinking how much a little girl Lizzie still was.

She ran right past the scruffy Marcus Singleton, white and wrong to be where he was. The whole bar took on a hostile quiet. Folks lowered their voices. Nobody knew what this white man was listening for or who he was looking for or why. No reason to tell him either. Just a lowering of voices accomplished this feat. At Pilar's, whites had their special hours and this wasn't one of them. Singleton could feel the fear and the anger his presence generated to the extent that Jocelyn over at his piano played such a slow blues, everybody in the place looked like they were moving in slow motion. But Singleton was not put off. He was familiar with the colored, he liked to think, knew the ways and reasons why, he thought.

Deke broke the mood first, though. He'd never let a white somebody determine what went on when he was in charge. He just could not allow that to happen. He wanted folks to move when he said move. And a nasty-looking white man with run-down heels wasn't gointa determine nothin'. Pilar's Palace was his kingdom.

"What do you want in heah, sir?" Deke asked, with his face so straight his jaws were tight. His blood rose up in his cheeks and his temple was pulsing, his broad flat face ancient, almost Olmec.

"Why, brothah, I'm glad you asked me that," Singleton replied in his happy-go-lucky voice. "I've got some things I'd like to talk to you and your friends about—"

Deke interrupted, "You come on with me to my office. I need to know what you're fixin' to get my friends into before there's trouble. Shoot, white man down here is trouble enough awready." As an afterthought, Deke commanded Lou, the trombone player, "Tell Billie to bring us a bit of whiskey."

Deke's "office" was the gamblin' room behind the kitchen. When Singleton was finally settled in, Deke said very frankly, "You must be that recruiter folks been talkin' 'bout?"

Singleton was taken aback. "Well, brothah, what makes you say that?"

"Word gets to me about everythin' unusual 'round here. You a unusual white man, always chasin' after the colored to go north, leave they families on your word and your word alone. Must make ya feel powerful to get folks to give up everything they know."

Now Singleton was seized with a passion. "But what is it they know? Bein' dirt poor? Spit poor, really. Havin' to live in fear of every white soul they see? You think I didn't feel the atmosphere down there change when I came in your place? That's no way to live, brother, poor and scared."

Deke took out one of his Cuban cigars and stared at Singleton. "Do I look afraid of somethin' to you?"

Singleton backed off his soapbox a bit. He didn't want to irritate. Clearly, this fellow was a powerful black man in Lil Mexico. "Listen, you know men—and women, for that matter—who are losin' their farms, businesses, everythin' right from under them, and banks are foreclosing and auctioning off all their possessions. Those are the folks I'm here to help, not folks who are doin' just fine down here in Dixie. And you look like the man who can help me."

Deke rolled his eyes at that remark. "And why should I do that?" he asked.

"Opportunity, my friend, opportunity." Singleton took off his bowler hat and drew a money clip from within the same secret pocket where he kept his pistol. "I'm recruiting men for some valuable labor up north. I love for 'em to see the light of day on their own. In case they don't, I sometimes have to procure their talents by other means. I give two bits for every ni . . . colored man we get. That's all."

Deke thought for a minute. Then he said very seriously, "Two dollahs a head."

Singleton wavered, taken aback by this darkey's audacity. "Brother, you drive a hard bargain."

"Two dollahs a head or it ain't worth my time." Deke got tired of the game and held out his hand to Singleton. "Two dollahs, it's a deal. You can get to work right now if you like. There's a fella goes by the name of Tom Winrow, comes in Pilar's most every night, 'bout to lose his farm." Singleton's impulse was to claim Tom Winrow off-limits to Deke's cut, but he decided to let it go. Deke knew too many men livin' on the edge of a dime or a one-cent piece. Best not to rile him at the very start.

* * *

LIZZIE WALTZED down the streets towards the vines that grew as wild as she, red berries hidden in dark leaves caressing the grand houses like your grandma's hand is apt to do. Everywhere Lizzie looked was white and forbidden, white and precious. Even though she danced with the wind like a cloud, she was not white and precious. Never would be. Yet she knew where to go in the midst of all this. She ran into the back door of a Georgian mansion, rushing through the roses and camellias as she hollered, "I's Lizzie May Winrow." A bulbous, brown-skinned woman, a cook, opened the door. She smelled of vanilla and cinnamon, onion and cumin, and Lizzie recognized the aroma, tantalizing it was to her, just like the cook would recognize that red hair anywhere.

"Lizzie, must you make such a fuss every time you come 'round this way? You gointa get me fired. Folks'll think I cain't even handle a chile."

"Miss Mary, you not 'sposed to handle chirren. You 'sposed to cook."

"Well, Miss Smartmouth, cook I do, but right now I'm gointa see to you. You look like you been runnin' through the swamps. Where you been?"

"On my way here. I had such a good time runnin'! Thought I was racin' the very sun itself."

"Well, that's how you look, too. Come on in and let me get that paint off yo' face and tidy you up a bit 'fore your mama sees ya. I swear I nevah in my life seen two chirren as different as you and Elma. She nevah even sweat far as I could tell. I oughta hang these clothes on you back in the air 'fore I let you in the house."

"No, Miss Mary, I don't stink that bad."

"Oh, yes you do. Now come over here."

Lizzie did as she was told, but even this reception didn't quell her ram-
bunctiousness. Miss Mary was beside herself trying to clean up Lizzie before Mrs. Calhoun came in asking about dinner. She braced Lizzie under
one arm, scrubbed her face, ears, and neck clean with the dishwater
soap. Still holding her shoulders, she shook Lizzie so hard that her recently braided hair came loose.

Just then Eudora entered the kitchen followed by Mrs. Calhoun
carrying a bundle of clothes. "Lizzie, Mrs. Calhoun has some dresses she
wants to give you. Isn't that thoughtful?"

"Mama, I don't wan no used, hand-me-down clothes," Lizzie replied,
as Mrs. Calhoun turned red and left the kitchen, embarrassed.

"Lizzie, don't you evah insult white folks like that again. I could lose
my position. You could get us all killed, if your pa had to defend us from
some white folks lookin' to maintain their 'honor.' I just don't know
what I'm going to do with you, Lizzie."

Mr. Calhoun's voice in the vestibule interrupted Lizzie's chastise-
ment. Eudora stilled suddenly, let go of Lizzie, and strained to hear the
conversation. Mrs. Calhoun was telling her husband how she'd spent the
whole day with the wonderful colored seamstress Eudora Winrow, Tom
Winrow's wife. Hearing the Winrow name caused Mr. Calhoun to pause
a moment, but when he entered the kitchen, he greeted Eudora as if she
were an old and close family servant. "It certainly is good to see you
again, Eudora. You keep my wife looking so very lovely in the dresses you
make for her."

Keeping her distance from Lizzie, Mrs. Calhoun chimed in, "And
Eudora's got a daughter finishing college."

"That's excellent. The Negro people need their women to have education and their men to learn a little more about agriculture. Although every man in the South should know more about how to turn this land
around. Why even my younger brother, Joel, is studying agronomy at the
University of Virginia. We all need our good sons, like my brother and
your husband, Tom. By the way, how is Tom these days? I know it's been
a rough year for small farmers in these parts. It'll be tough for Tom, too.
I'm certain of that."

Eudora saw a chance to make up for her child's insolence. In these
hard times, Mrs. Calhoun was a steady customer, and her husband sat on

the board of the bank. "I expect Mr. Winrow'll be able to pay off our note in a couple more years." Lizzie couldn't believe her mother's humiliating herself to the Calhouns like that. She didn't understand what hold these people had over her family, or the other colored people. They were just white, not gods. Why couldn't her mother see that?

Eudora and Lizzie walked toward the center of town with a terrible rift between them. Eudora's head was now held high and Lizzie's lowered, as her mother solemnly and firmly said, "If you ever act up like that again, I swear I'll beat you to death."

* * *

TOM HAD been 'round to Deke's, but nobody mentioned Lizzie's earlier escapade, which was good because Tom'd had a rough day. He couldn't even get any day labor by the wharf. He wanted to have something in his pockets when Elma came home, make his wife happy, and have a nice supper, maybe even a new dress or something. Although he had a hard time accepting what she was doing with her life, he still wanted to show Elma that he was proud of her, too. So, with his pockets empty and with a desperate hollow 'round his heart, praying he could gather up some things for his family on credit, Tom entered Haggerty's General Dry Goods. Old man Haggerty took one look at the yearning in Tom's eyes and just shook his head no. Tom had only managed to get a "But, sir . . ." out of his mouth when Haggerty's response was to call the clerk, Jody, a red-faced piece of a man, to get out the books.

"Look up Tom Winrow's account. Show it to him and see him out the door."

Jody fumbled with the book, a thick leather-bound ledger that measured people's lives. Tom was hoping against hope that he wasn't in arrears so much that his trip had not only been in vain, but embarrassing as well. Jody called Tom over to the counter. "Look here, boy. You owe us so much, we gonna put a lien on those fields of yours if you don't start producing some crops to sell."

But Mrs. Haggerty, a sweet cherub of an Irish woman, recognized Tom as Eudora's husband. "Oh, Jody, let the man have whatever he wants. Mrs. Winrow always makes good on her debts."

Hearing that, Tom's heart was not only desperately hollow, but seared with anger. "Never mind. I'll get me some money and pay cash." He turned and walked back to his buckboard.

Hat in his hands, Tom sat in the empty wagon, waiting for Eudora and Lizzie. *No groceries. No money. Nothin' for Elma's homecomin'.* He could hear Eudora's complaints before she and the girl appeared and right he was. "All I asked you to do was pick up a few little things so that we could celebrate Elma's return, and you're sitting here in an empty buckboard right in front of the store. I've been on my knees all day, sewing, fitting, smiling at the Calhouns till my cheeks hurt. What in the hell have you been doin'? Sittin' here waitin' for money to fall from the sky?"

Tom wanted to tell her how he'd been all over town tryin' to do anythin' a man could do to come up with some money. He'd failed, but not from not trying, not caring. But he couldn't say these things. His tongue went violently silent. Eudora knew that look. She knew her husband hadn't been sittin' around all day. Sometimes she just said things that she wished she hadn't. She leaned over to Tom and caressed his cheek.

"Was it an awful day for you, too? Must've been, or else you'd have those groceries. I know that, darlin'." Then she slipped the money she earned at the Calhouns' into his pocket, telling him all the fine things Mr. Calhoun had to say about him, callin' him a son of the South and a great farmer. How he worked the land better than anyone else. Exasperated, Tom mumbled, "It'd be easier if he took his foot off of my back."

Eudora felt her husband's frustration and said nothing. Lizzie only remembered how just a while ago, her mother had been making up to the very people who were wearing her father down. She slid away from Eudora so that when her father came back she could sit next to him, not her mother, who had no pride to Lizzie's mind.

Before Tom could get back through Haggerty's doorway, Singleton the Northerner appeared from out of nowhere. "Hello again, Mr. Winrow." Tom nodded his head. He'd warned the fellow already about being too familiar. Tom came back to the buckboard to act as if he was leaving, so that Singleton would go on by.

Eudora asked, "Who's that white man bein' so friendly?"

"None of your concern, that's who," Tom snapped.

Eudora, incensed, retorted, "Must be one of your gamblin' buddies to

be so happy to see you. Is he the one with all your money? Did he wipe
you out today?"

"Listen, you get on home. I'll come in later, ya hear me?"

"Why? What are you gointa do?"

"Right now I've got some business to take care of."

"What business?"

"My own goddam business! Get on, now."

Eudora, furious, shouted, "Did you even ask about the fabric order?"
She watched her husband walk on without responding. "A fine homecoming this is!" she blurted, and drove the buckboard away with a very
sad Lizzie next to her.

* * *

IN NASHVILLE the day was bright as Elma was about to board the train
for Charleston. The Colored car was hardly posh, but Elma looked as
grand as any of the white women at the station. She felt so good about
herself she even posed for a picture with her sorors who'd come to see her
off. They were hugging and kissing her good-bye when Raymond sauntered up. The other girls cleared a path for him, almost like a parting of
the waters. Elma blushed as Raymond kissed her hand.

"Oh, ever the gentleman!" she laughed.

"I came to tell you that I refuse to let you go."

"How can you 'refuse' to let me go home to my family, Mr. Minor?"

"Because I'll have no idea what to do with all the hours and minutes
of every day you're away from me, that's how."

Elma smiled coyly. "You do go on so."

"No, seriously, Elma, I only came to visit my uncle for a couple of days
and you've dazzled me so that I stayed two weeks. I think about you constantly. I even dream about you, and I hadn't planned to tell you that, but
you have a wondrous effect on me. I don't want to do anything more than
think about you, be near you if possible. Nothing else but Elma Diggs has
been on my mind."

"Maybe you'll have a chance to think about other things, like getting
meaningful employment, since I am leaving on this train today to go
home. If you let your mind wander away from visions of me, you might
be able to put some of your fine education to use instead of wasting it."

"But I really do want to see you again."

"But I'm leaving for Charleston any moment."

"Then I'll come to Charleston and court you like a proper lady should be courted."

Elma persisted, "Mr. Minor, Raymond, the first thing my mother will ask is where is your place of employment."

"Well, Elma, I thought I'd go to work for your cousin, Mr. Diggs. I don't know much about undertaking, and I'm not terribly fond of corpses, but I'm excellent with sympathy and decorum."

Elma was tickled by Raymond's wit and had an impulse to stay right there with him, but the train whistle blew. The conductor was shouting, "All aboard!"

"Elma, I do have career plans, honestly. I'm going to work in New York. That's where the market is for my skills. They're building skyscrapers faster than you can imagine, and they need good architects and engineers. I'd love to take you with me."

The train was starting to pull off, but Elma managed to say demurely, "I've never even thought of leaving the South," over the roar of the train's engine. She looked carefully at this dapper Raymond, whose lips were repeating, "I love you, I love you, Elma."

She blurted, "Will you write? Your uncle knows how to reach me." She waved to him and boldly blew him a kiss and she watched him watch her till he disappeared from her view.

Once on board, Elma was startled that she'd gotten onto the wrong section of the train, the White section. As she tried to gather her things and go where she belonged, she was spotted by the porter. "I'm sorry, sir. I didn't realize I was in the wrong car. I'm moving right now."

"I don't think anyone will notice any more than a pretty young woman riding along. And if somebody says something, you just let me handle it."

"Oh, sir, that's so very kind of you. I just had so many things on my mind I didn't know what I was doing."

"No need to worry. Enjoy your trip to Charleston, miss."

Elma's head was filled with Raymond's voice; his eyes and laugh whirled about her as the Southern countryside slipped past. She thought she heard Raymond's "I love you," but then realized that a sweet harmonica was being played in the Colored car just ahead. While the music delighted her, the cackle of chickens and black voices gave her pause. She laughed at the contradictions and said out loud to herself as if she were still talking to the debonair Mr. Raymond Minor, "I've never thought of leaving the South, never."

* * *

PILAR'S PLACE was jumping that night. The music was going. Jocelyn and the band had everybody up dancing who wasn't in the card game in the back room. Tom was losing badly, but talking big about how his luck was about to change. Deke was annoyed with Tom's attitude and his request for more credit. Deke had always backed him before. What was the problem tonight? Deke was thinking about the business of taking over Pilar's. He needed to make money and keep making money. Losers like Tom weren't good for his image. "I'm tired of carryin' folks. You can't pay, then don't play. Simple as that." Tom's anger stirred. Folks all day telling him no to every simple request he made. He was a man. He didn't need to beg for groceries. He needed to stay in this game to turn his luck around. "Look heah, Deke, I got me some money." He took the money Eudora'd given him from the Calhouns and handed it to Deke, who laughed at him and threw the meager sum on the floor.

"You owe me a lot more than that, man, and I want it soon. Or somethin' pretty terrible might happen to your black pitiful ass or that wild little girl of yours. Don't know which, but I do know that." Then Deke pulled one of Lizzie's pigtail ribbons from his pocket and dangled it in front of Tom's face. Tom was on the floor trying to gather up his money, since Deke didn't want it, but the sight of Lizzie's ribbon alarmed him. *How'd Deke get hold of that?* Tom went to grab the ribbon from Deke, but Deke put the ribbon back in his pocket. "Get outta heah before I put you out. You don't want me to have to do that."

Osceola'd been watching this scene from the bar. Deke's mention of harm coming to Lizzie stunned him and made him wonder what kind of man his brother really was. It made him even more determined to watch over Lizzie, since it was obvious her father couldn't.

Tom could hardly walk, but he stumbled his way home just singin'. "It takes a tall brown gal to make a preacher put his Bible dow-own/ You in the wrong town pal if you think you gonna mess around. . . ."

Lizzie heard her father singin' and knew there would be terrible words between her parents. She curled up in her bed, listening to Eudora scream, "All I do is work, try to keep a decent house, raise your children, and try to keep a good name, and you do your best to destroy it. Do you want to be the laughingstock of Charleston? Is that what you want the girls to think of you? A drunken, gamblin', no-account niggah." Then with all the might he could muster, Tom slapped Eudora so hard she fell against the wall. Lizzie hummed loudly, blocking out the rest.

* * *

THE NEXT morning Eudora went to her little church on Azula Street, allegedly to do some tailoring of the choir robes, but she went to pray as well. To pray for Tom, herself, her children. She asked the Lord for patience and strength. She asked the Lord to lift her burdens before she lost her faith. The welt on her face didn't go unnoticed by the Reverend, who gently placed his hand on her shoulder. Even so, Eudora winced, her whole body a tangle of pain.

"Eudora, is there anything I can do for you? Is there somethin' you want to talk about? The Lord's put me here as his instrument, to tend after his flock. Nothin' is too great for the Lord to handle."

"Oh, no, Reverend. Everything's fine. I've just been working too hard lately, I guess. But I did notice that in the program for next Sunday, you didn't list Elma's solo. Did Tom forget to tell you?"

As compassionately as he could, Reverend Caldwell said, "Eudora, Tom hasn't been comin' to choir rehearsal for quite some time now. We miss his playin', we surely do."

Eudora didn't know what to say, but she turned to the Reverend and smiled. "I must have forgotten that Tom told me the farm was taking so much of his time that he had to cut back on his church activities. I must've simply forgotten he told me that."

* * *

LIZZIE WAS laughing with Osceola at their favorite watering hole not far from her farm. The water was clear and cool and the rocks they lounged upon were smooth and warmed by the sun. They'd been coming here for years, and felt it was their own private domain. That's why they talked about important things here and nowhere else. Osceola liked to talk about love.

Lizzie didn't.

"I'm never gointa fall in love, and I'm never, ever gointa get married."

"Oh, Lizzie, you're just saying that 'cause you've never been in love. When you are, you'll change your mind for sho. Besides, how're you gointa have any chirren if you don't fall in love?"

"Who said I wanted to have chirren anyway? I don't want them either. And what's love gotta do with havin' chirren anyway?"

"I'll show you."

"Boy, everythin' you got to show I done seen."

"That was different. We were little then."

"Well, how different is it? Let me see."

Osceola was losing patience with his best friend. "Girl, you downright nasty."

"I am not. Ain't nothin' nasty 'bout lookin'."

"Well, all right, but first you've got to close your eyes."

Then Osceola did what he'd been contemplating for a good long while. Lizzie wasn't really a little girl anymore, and he was almost a man. Osceola kissed Lizzie on the lips, which threw her into a rage. "What's wrong with you, boy?" Then she did what she knew her father would want her to do and slapped her friend straight across the face.

Osceola lost his balance and fell backwards into the water. Tickled with herself, Lizzie laughed and jumped in after him, but Osceola would have no truck with her. He climbed out of the waterhole, picked his clothes off the tree, and angrily walked away, not even looking back. When Lizzie came up for air, poking her head out of the water, Osceola was already yards away.

"I'm sorry, Osceola. Don't be like that. Don't just leave me here. Please."

When she got no response but Osceola's back, she shouted, "You hard-headed half-breed!" Then she went back to swimming to cool off and think about having been kissed for the first time. There was a small smile on her face when she re-emerged from the water, but it disappeared quickly when she saw Deke and the white man, the same white man who spoke to her father in front of Haggerty's store. She paddled closer and hid in the brush to hear.

Deke gave the man a sheet of paper, looked like a list. "All these fellas are havin' a hard way to go right through here. They should be good marks for you," Deke assured the white man, who then gave him a wad of money.

"That's two dollahs a head from now on," Deke told the man.

"What if these guys don't pan out? I have no way of knowing if you're playing straight with me."

Deke chuckled, putting the money in his pocket. "I'm the only game in town for you, and what do you care so long as you get niggahs interested in leaving town? Anyway, I'll have some more names next week, but I'm gonna need some more money."

Singleton, convinced he was being had, shook his head vehemently. "No more money."

Deke turned to leave and said, "Okay, no more names. I don't have time to play with you."

Lizzie was perplexed and very still.

The white man called after Deke, "All right, I'll see you here again next week. But all these men better be on their way north within a week."

Deke replied, "That's your job. I done mine."

Lizzie stayed in the water until she was sure both men were well on their way. Then she ran all the way home. Elma was coming.

* * *

THAT EVENING, the Winrow house was a discordant discontent. Eudora was livid because there was nothing special for Elma. "The chile's been gone 'most a year and I don't know what I'm gointa feed her tomorrow."

Ma Bette said, "Oh, I'll get something together, believe you me. My great-grandchile is not comin' home to an empty plate."

There was not much food on the table this night, either. Tom saw this. Eudora tried to ignore it. When there was finally some quiet as they ate what there was to eat, Tom saw an opportunity to show he did have initiative and ideas. Maybe Eudora'd stop fussing so much if he showed a bit of progress.

"You know, Eudora, there's a lot of talk about folks moving up north, where there's plenty of work for a healthy Negro man, and more opportunities for Negroes in general."

Eudora looked at Tom as if he'd lost his mind. "What's that got to do with us?"

Tom got really excited now. "I've been talking to this fella who says he can guarantee me a job in West Virginia for a whole lot of money. More than I could ever make on this farm, or working for some white man down here."

Eudora almost dropped her fork. "Are you drunk again, or crazy?"

Lizzie tried to join the discussion, if it could be called that. "Pa, I saw Deke."

Tom turned at the mention of Deke's name from his baby girl. "I don't want you seeing Deke at all, for any reason! Is that clear?"

"Yes, but what I want to tell you—"

"I don't want to hear another thing from you. Just do as I say."

"Yes, Pa."

"Now finish eating your supper."

"I am finished, Pa. But I'm still hungry."

Tom was touched by Lizzie's honesty and handed her his plate. "Oh, thanks, Pa, but wait for me so I can go to church rehearsal with you."

Eudora glared at her husband, but he didn't see her. He was caught up in explaining to Lizzie that he couldn't take her that night.

Lizzie whined, "Oh, please, Pa. You know how I love to hear you play with the choir. Please let me go with you."

Tom still said she couldn't go, but promised her something even more exciting. "You know what, since I can't take you with me tonight, I'll make it up to you by taking you to the minstrel show next week."

Eudora jumped up from the table. "Tom, are you truly losing your mind? We don't even have enough food to get through the next week, and you're fillin' her head with all this nonsense."

Ma Bette grumbled, "They's bad blood in this house now." She started to sweep the corners of the ceiling in circular motions, an old purifying ritual she learned from her ma, who'd learned it from her ma.

Eudora was fit to be tied. "Mama, stop that heathen mess in my house."

Ma Bette paid her no mind and said, "Somebody's gotta do something to bring some healing spirits 'round heah."

* * *

THAT NIGHT sat on Tom's shoulders like a boulder. He didn't go to choir rehearsal—as Eudora knew he wouldn't—but he wasn't fumbling through the night without purpose or thoughtfulness. Tom went directly to the Calhouns' house. Mr. Calhoun was surprised to see him at that hour, but welcomed him in. Tom felt uncomfortable in the white man's house and wanted to get his business over with soon. Mr. Calhoun did not offer him a seat.

"Mr. Calhoun, excuse me for disturbing you like this, but I've got some very serious business to talk to you about, sir."

Calhoun replied, "Whatever it is, it must be very pressing, Tom, to bring you here at this hour."

"Yes, sir. I want to sell my land."

"What?"

"I want to sell my land. Now. Tonight."

Calhoun was taken aback. "Listen, Tom, I realize things have been very bad for small farmers like you, especially the colored ones, but it's not like you to give up."

"Sometimes it's time to give up, sir. Do you want to buy my land or not? That's all I need to know."

It didn't take Mr. Calhoun but a minute to agree to purchase the Winrow farm. The land was good, only waiting out a bad season or two was beyond the grasp of these colored people, he thought.

So Calhoun suggested, "Why don't you sell me the land, Tom, and continue to work it as a tenant farmer?"

"No, sir. That's not what I want to do."

Puzzled, Calhoun asked, "What are you planning to do to support your family, then?"

"Oh, Mr. Calhoun, that's not gointa be a problem. I've got contract work out of town. We'll be fine."

Mr. Calhoun nodded. "Yes, I've heard they are hiring in the mills, but Tom, once you get yourself straightened out, consider my offer. I can really use good boys like you."

Tom pulled a crumpled paper from his jacket. It was the deed to the land he loved so much, land that had turned on him, made him less of a man than he ever wanted to be. Tom signed the deed over to Calhoun, fighting back tears, his hand trembling. Mr. Calhoun went to a safe and counted out the agreed-upon amount of money. He started to give Tom the envelope of money, but Tom stopped him.

"I'll just take a few dollars, sir. I don't want to carry that much on me. It's a distance home and dark out there. Eudora will be comin' to fit your wife on Monday. You can give it to her then. And I think my wife and children will be movin' back to town as soon as arrangements can be made."

Calhoun assured Tom that his family could take as much time as they needed to resettle. "But Tom, I'd always be glad to have you back. Boys like you with a feel for the earth are hard to find."

Tom didn't respond. He moved slowly to the door and went into the night, his vision blurred by tears. He'd lost his land, given it up, and his heart believed it was raining.

*   *   *

TOM MADE his way to Lil Mexico to find Singleton. He'd heard that the recruiter was staying at a boardinghouse not far from Pilar's place. Lil Mexico was alive with every illegal and bawdy activity imaginable, but on this night, Tom was not seduced by revelry. He found a shabby boarding-house known for hosting transients and women of disrepute. He humbly asked the landlady if there was a man named Singleton there.

"Top of the stairs, to the right," was all she said. Tom climbed the stairs with trepidation, but he climbed them. When he got to Singleton's door, he pulled himself together enough to sound enthusiastic.

"Hello there, brother," Singleton greeted Tom. "Won't you come on in?" Tom stepped through the door and saw a bottle of whiskey on a small table. His glance at the whiskey was not missed by Singleton, who immediately offered him a drink. Much easier to handle niggahs when they've got a bit of sauce in them, was his philosophy.

"So what can I do for you, Tom?"

"Well, I've been thinkin' 'bout what you said about goin' north, and I think I'm ready to go."

"Well, brother, you've seen the light! Made a great decision. I'll get you all the help you need to get yourself situated once you get up there. You'll never be sorry, brother, for deciding to take this step." Tom finished the shot of whiskey Singleton had poured him, took the papers for his employment, and headed for Pilar's place.

Suddenly Tom had a new sense of himself. He had a future. He had some money. He didn't have to beg for anything anymore. He wasn't gointa to be the laughin'stock of the town after all. He was gointa be a success. Emboldened, he walked into Pilar's. When Deke saw Tom, a broad smile came across his face. Here was the fool he could have some fun with. Tom just didn't know when to stop. But Tom had a surprise for him.

"Here's all your money. Now I don't owe you a thing. And I didn't come here to gamble, either. I just want to play some music and relax myself. Maybe I'll even buy me a drink."

Deke was dumbfounded. Tom took a seat next to Mr. Jocelyn and began to sing and then, pulling his horn from the sack slung over his shoulder, he played Dixieland. The rhythm was fast, but there was a melancholy aura about his solo that no one missed. Osceola sat right up and watched him. He loved Tom's music just like Lizzie did.

When Tom saw Osceola, he stopped playing and took the boy aside, right in front of Deke. "Osceola, I want you to look after Lizzie for me, ya hear?"

"What do you mean, Mr. Winrow? I always look after Lizzie."

"I know it, just keep on doin' it, all right?"

"Yes, sir."

Osceola and Tom went back to the bandstand, and Tom played all night long. He wanted to hear music till he got on the train in the morning. Osceola fell asleep at his feet, but Tom Winrow was on that train north at dawn.

11

DAYBREAK COULDN'T COME SOON ENOUGH FOR EUDORA. Her darlin', her blessed Elma was on her way home. The sun obliged, leaving traces of lilac and tangerine lingering in the skies as Eudora checked to make sure everything in Elma's room was perfectly appointed. The sheets fresh, the woodwork spotless, and the curtains flowing to the floor with such grace that Elma'd be sure to know how cherished she was. Eudora's next task was to ready Lizzie, who was always tardy and such a mess that Eudora was sure she fought with great ferocity somethin' not human in her sleep. Lizzie woke up out of breath, eyes blazing and ready to do battle. Sometimes this took Eudora aback and she'd tell her child that it was time to start a new day with some caution in her voice, or if Lizzie'd been routed by the demons she fought off each night, Eudora'd shake her and shake her till she wearily opened her eyes, totally shocked that there was relief from her tormentors. This morning, however, Lizzie was up and donning her Sunday best before Eudora could get so much as a "How's my baby today?" out of her mouth.

"Oh, Mama, Elma's comin' home today, aren't you excited? Isn't it wonderful? Do you think she'll recognize me? I've grown so much. Do you think she'll be different after living in the city on her own? Oh, Mama. Elma's comin' home and I do love her so."

Eudora couldn't help but laugh at Lizzie's torrent of questions and exclamations. The most important thing was that her daughters loved each other tremendously. With all the problems posed in her family, this was one thing she'd succeeded in doing. "All right, all right, but put some of that energy into gettin' yourself ready to go to the station. Elma's train is arriving shortly."

"Yes, Mama, I'll be right on time. Wheee! Elma's comin' home and I'll have someone to talk to again."

Eudora shut the door to Lizzie's room and moved toward the downstairs. She wisht her child could talk to her, but Lizzie'd always been drawn more toward Tom. Never understood why that was. Never put up a fight against it. But it hurt Eudora that Lizzie seemed to feel closer to anybody but her own mother, and it especially hurt that she so clearly preferred Tom. Pushing that thought from her mind did Eudora no good, for the next issue was where was Tom? Even he knew today was the day that Elma returned from Nashville. Yet Tom was nowhere to be found. Eudora stood in the middle of the kitchen and prayed, "Lord, please let this be a day of grace, a day of rejoicing, and thanks for all Thy bounty. Lord, we are so grateful for Elma's safe return and good experience at college. We've worked hard, Lord, to do Thy will."

Just as she finished, Eudora heard Bette mumble, " 'Bout time somebody did some thankin' 'round heah."

Eudora rolled her eyes at her grandmother, who insisted on havin' the last word, even if it had to do with talking with the Lord. "That's right, Mama. Today's a day to be thankful for. You are absolutely right today."

Bette poured Eudora some coffee and placed some cornpone by her saucer. "Well, there's no news in that, chile. I'm thankful every day and I'm always as right."

Eudora surprised her mother and didn't even respond, except to say, "Mama, this coffee is delicious, thank you so much. I don't know what I'd do without you." Seemed like all the daughters had surprises for their mothers today. In fact, Lizzie got the horses and the buckboard ready before she came in for her breakfast.

Eudora was glowing on the way towards Charleston. She'd forget from time to time that Tom was late. She settled on the notion that he was waiting for them at the station. In fact she imagined he'd gone on ahead and bought Elma some flowers for her welcome. There were some things about her husband that Eudora liked, even though she kept that close.

The women of this family were so colorful and happy they turned heads at the train station. Eudora in a red and white gingham dress with a bonnet sporting a matchin' ribbon, Lizzie in a paisley dress with just enough flounce for her to be her rollicking self, and Bette in a concoction that's virtually indescribable except that she mix-matched whatever she could and held her head high while her ears nigh touched her shoulders weighed down as they were with heavy gold hooped earrings she saved for special occasions. The three waited toward the end of the railroad platform where the Colored section of the train usually stopped, but they attracted attention nonetheless. They had about them a dignity not expected from Negroes that did not set well with white patrons.

When the train pulled in, Eudora kept her eye out for Elma in the Colored car, but was astonished when her daughter's head poked from the First Class Whites Only car. Now Eudora couldn't hold back her fury with Tom. How were they to fetch Elma's bags way up in the White section without drawing attention? At least if Tom were there he could act like a porter for any old white somebody and get them out of this mess. Eudora tried to grab aholdt to Lizzie but she was too late. Lizzie ran up in front of the white folks and grabbed her sister, held her tight and led her through the crowd to where Eudora was waiting alone.

"Oh Elma, welcome home, sweetheart." Eudora nervously hugged her daughter. Ma Bette was next with a peck on both cheeks for her arriving grandchild. Her arms still strong, Bette pushed Elma back from her to get a good look. Yes, Elma seemed healthy enough, her skin was clear, her hands warm. Yep, seemed to Bette that Elma'd taken good care of herself.

"Oh, I'm so glad to be home, to see all of you. I've missed y'all so much."

Before Eudora could say a word about her bags being in an awfully precarious place for a colored passenger, Osceola came lumbering under the weight of Elma's things. "M'am, I think I got em all. Didn't want to draw attention, but Miz Elma's name was on what all I carried ovah heah."

Eudora's heart was touched. Osceola knew how much she resented his friendship with Lizzie, but he knew what an awkward situation they were in without Tom to carry Elma's things. Some things in Charleston had to be feigned, pretended, or the city wouldn't work. A Negro girl couldn't get out of the Whites Only car, even if everybody saw her. Her family couldn't be there waiting for her, even if they were. Some things had to be overlooked, dressed up, and ignored or hellish inclinations were indulged. Even on Sundays, such things were known to happen. Thanks to Osceola, Eudora's family'd been spared. This all but set Eudora's bonnet on fire. Where was her good-for-nothin' husband to leave them in such a position that a mere boy had to come to their rescue! Osceola set about loading the wagon with Elma's bags. There weren't that many but Osceola couldn't for the life of him figure out where Lizzie's Pa'd gone to, or was this what he meant by "lookin' after Lizzie"? Osceola caught Ma Bette staring straight at him, so he hurried more. No reason to get that old woman on his wrong side, everybody knew she worked roots, even if nobody liked to talk about it. No sireee, no reason to get Ma Bette on your bad side. Just brings trouble, and Osceola thought he had enough of that 'tween his brother Deke and Lizzie, 'tween his brother and her father, too. After he set the bags in the wagon, he doffed his straw hat and stepped aside, fading into the noonday crowd.

Elma craned her neck, looking about. "Where's Pa?"

This was the question Eudora'd hoped she wouldn't have to answer. "Oh, he'll be along." Ma Bette said in a rather sing-songy voice. "Ya'll bet he'll be 'long once he gets a sniff of the gumbo I got in store for us today. Oh, he'll be 'long for sho'."

Elma couldn't get over her homecoming. She'd missed her family more than she realized. She couldn't help thinking of all the sacrifices they'd made to keep her in school, to live out her dreams, but here they were, and gumbo, too!

"That's right, chile, gumbo wit shrimps, clams, lobster, wild rice, and scuppernong wine."

Lizzie got excited just hearin' about it. "It's all for you, Elma, on accounta you comin' back home."

Ma Bette tried to calm her youngest great-grand. "Yep, I went and got my own harvest together. Oh, chile, what ya cryin' fo'?" Ma Bette pulled the weepy Elma close to her. "Ya only come home, baby, you didn't get to heaven yet. Ya jus' got brought home to ya folks is all. Now quit alla that sobbin'. Eudora, come talk to this chile of yourn."

Eudora pulled Elma from Ma Bette's fragile arms and led her towards the wagon.

"Where's Pa, Mama? Is he still mad at me for costin' the family so much?"

Eudora pursed her lips and whispered in her daughter's ear, "Oh, he'll be along shortly, I'm sure. He's so proud of you, baby. We all are." With that said Eudora beat her anger with her husband further down so she felt her toes prickling and her fingers boiling. *Where in the world could that fool be?* Didn't he realize his very own child was due home? Of course he knew. *What a stupid question!* The tautness in her belly choked back a vague feeling of dread welling up inside her. *Could something have happened to him?* Was Tom hurt? Had violence struck him somewhere no one else had seen? *No, couldn't be.* It was easier, more comfortable for Eudora to imagine herself the victim, not Tom. This was Eudora's moment, and Tom's not being there had to be Eudora's crisis—certainly not his. That's what vexed Eudora most. Didn't he have any respect for any of them? They didn't have much, but they'd always been a family. Now Tom seemed set on taking that away from them as well. But, as always, when it came to her daughter, Eudora masked her anger with her husband.

"Come along, darlin', we've gotta million and one things to talk 'bout. Why, what's it like at Fisk? Where all have ya been? Oh I'm just so tickled to have ya back with us." Though it was against her better judgment, Eudora let Lizzie handle the reins. They were going home.

Eudora had done all she could to make her house inviting and open to Elma. Sometimes when a child goes off to school, the rhythms and song of the house take over the child's place, leaving no room for her return. This was not the case for Elma.

"Oh, Mama, it's like I never left at all. Thank you. Thank you."

Eudora blushed, so thrilled she was that her child felt home.

"Well, ya'll cain't oooh and aaah all the day long. C'mon down heah for some of my gumbo," Ma Bette chastised.

Lizzie was the first at the table. Her wild hair had found its way out of its plaits, but Lizzie still had a dress on and that was something. "I'm ready, Nana."

"Yep, but you ain't the onliest one eatin', are ya?" Ma Bette chimed finally when Elma and Eudora joined them.

Ma Bette turned to the kitchen as Eudora said the blessing. "Lord, you know how grateful we are for Elma's return to us. How we rejoice in her health and happiness and all the new experiences you afforded her this past year. Lord, we thank you for our health, our food prepared in your Spirit, and the coming together of our whole family this day. Amen."

As everyone added their amens, Lizzie ran up behind Ma Bette, who was carrying a huge tureen of gumbo to the table. Lizzie could see the crab claws, the lobster tails, and clams steaming on top.

"Oh, I cain't wait! Elma, you gotta come home more often. Ma Bette never puts all this in my gumbo."

"Oh, hush up, chile, and get from under my feet 'fore I don't offer you none of this masterpiece I done made for my oldest great-grand." Ma Bette served Elma first and was so full of questions about the travels of the Fisk Jubilee Singers that Elma hardly had a chance to eat. In the midst of all this Eudora thought she heard horses outside, but shook her head. No, not on Sunday at suppertime. Nobody came visiting at such an hour, but when Lizzie's head turned toward the front door too, Eudora figured she'd better go see what was going on. Sure enough there was a rider in the front yard. Mr. Calhoun's manager, a mangy-lookin' white man by the name of Granger, was on horseback just beyond the front porch Eudora'd covered with flowering plants. What could he want? They didn't owe any money, hadn't asked the Calhouns for any advances on crop produce.

"Afternoon, Mr. Granger," Eudora said, pushin' the screen door open. The rest of the family followed behind her from the dining table.

"Afternoon, Eudora," Granger replied. Lizzie hated it when white folks referred to her mother by her first name instead of by her proper name, Mrs. Winrow. Nonetheless, the mystery of the white man's appearance grabbed all their attention. Ma Bette lit up her pipe. The girls stood by their mother. This was a time that demanded the presence of the man of the house. Eudora cursed Tom under her breath. Why of all days did he decide to disappear?

"What can I do for you, Mr. Granger?"

"Well, I got a piece of paper here saying y'all got to clear clean out by Monday."

Ma Bette rolled her eyes and went over to the side of the porch where she could see the breadth of the land cradling her old soul. Eudora took a deep breath, holding Elma and Lizzie back from saying anything to Granger, who was known to be mean-spirited.

"Why, Mr. Granger, you must be mistaken. We own our land. Why, we've owned it since the War."

"Not no more, Eudora." Granger smiled licentiously. "I got the deed right heah in my hand. Your man come by to see Mr. Calhoun last night, sold the whole of the farm off to Mr. Calhoun. Said he was headin' north on the next train rollin', he did. If you ask me, he needed to go on up north, he didn't belong round heah. Too ornery."

At this Eudora almost lost control of Lizzie, who was screamin', "My Pa didn't leave, he didn't go nowhere!"

Luckily, Lizzie didn't run at the white man, but out into the scrawny fields that had so frustrated her father. Lizzie's screams of "No, Pa, no!" could be heard over all the rest of the transaction. Ma Bette quietly went back into the house humming "His Eye Is on the Sparrow." That left Eudora and Elma to deal with Granger.

"I don't have all day, Eudora, y'all got to be out by Monday. That's all there is to it. You should be grateful Mr. Calhoun sent me out heah to let you know. I coulda waited to Monday, ya know."

"Why, yes, sir, Mr. Granger, and I thank you for that, but could I see the deeds?"

"What, you doubtin' my word, gal?"

"Why, no, sir, I just wanted to see Tom's signature to know what he's done to us."

Mr. Granger was getting irritated now. "Jus' be outta heah by Monday dusk. 'Course I'll be glad to be of any assistance if it's too much for a whole house of women."

Eudora could sense the danger in Granger's offer. "Well, no. We'll be just fine, sir, but I do thank you for your kindness. We'll manage, though."

Miffed that his entreaty had been rebuffed, Granger turned to ride off, yelling, "Monday dusk, off this Calhoun land."

Eudora could hear what she imagined was Granger's deranged laugh for hours after he left. The dust from his galloping horse clouded her eyes for days. She didn't understand. *The Calhouns?* She had been working for Mrs. Calhoun for years. They had just said what a fine family she had.

Ma Bette was in the house clearing the table as though nothing out of the ordinary had happened. "Mama, what're we gointa do?" Eudora asked in desperation.

Ma Bette replied. "Seems like we're gointa move," is all she had to say.

Elma found Lizzie in the cornfield screaming and running errantly past the withered stalks of her father's farm. "It's a lie! It's a lie. Pa didn't. He didn't leave. He didn't leave us. It's a lie. Elma, you know it's a lie."

Elma didn't know much more than what Granger had said and what she could piece together of her parents' marriage. All she was concerned about now was her sister, whose pain was infectious. Elma found herself sittin' in a furrow cryin', Lizzie runnin' in circles around her.

"Elma, tell me it's not true! It cain't be true! Pa wouldn't leave me. He might leave her. But he wouldn't leave me. I'm his baby. Elma, I'm Pa's baby." Lizzie eventually grew tired and crawled into Elma's arms.

Some homecoming this was, coming home to a home with no Pa. Now a home that wasn't even theirs anymore. Elma rocked Lizzie for a long time. All she could think to do was sing. She found the words of "My Lord, What a Morning" falling from her lips all over her sister's body in spasms of sorrow. The words of the spiritual fell upon the land like rain, bringing peace to the parched fields and welcoming the setting sun.

* * *

EUDORA SAT straight up in the kitchen, a stone of a woman. What strength she had was wound so tight she couldn't even speak. Ma Bette didn't say anything either. The clatter of dishes and Ma Bette's feet moving about was all that could be heard. Finally, Eudora let loose of a cry like a wounded animal. Ma Bette went for the brandy she kept secreted. Eudora reluctantly took a swig and said, "Mama, what are we to do?"

"Well, don't you want to know what Tom did?" Ma Bette replied.

"I don't give a rat's ass what Tom did. Right now I just want to know what we're to do."

In her matter-of-fact way, Ma Bette replied, "We gotta move on, is what."

The sunset paid no mind to the tumult at the Winrow farm, gliding easily into night, ablaze with scarlet and purple streamers to embrace the earth.

* * *

RAYMOND MINOR, Elma's beau from Nashville, approached the Diggs home in Charleston expecting to find Elma at home. The horseshoe-shaped stairway left Raymond a choice of which side to take up to the double-doored mansion. He flipped a coin and decided the right side was for him. Then he'd lead Elma down the left side covering all his bets straight to her heart. He took the heavy doorknocker in his hand and beat out a rag on the impressive mahogany door. Dah-dah-dadada was the heavy knock the Diggses heard. What street pickaninny had made it his business to come begging now, was the thought that flashed through Francina's head. About to give him a livid piece of her mind, Francina opened the heavy door only to be greeted by a fine-looking young gentlemen with no niggah to him, if Francina was any judge of character.

"Why, good evening, sir. Can I help you?" Francina cooed.

"Why yes, you may, Mrs. . . . ?"

"It's Miss Francina Diggs, sir. And what may I call you? Why don't you step in? It's so colored to tend to one's business in public."

Raymond didn't quite know how to take that comment, but he entered the dense beauty of the Diggs home in his quest for Elma. "I'm Raymond Minor, an acquaintance of Elma Diggs, from Fisk. We met in Nashville. I've come to call on her, if it's not too late."

"You came to call on Elma?" Francina asked in disbelief. What kind of charade had Elma played at Fisk, that she would be expected to reside at Francina's home?

Unabashed, Raymond repeated, "Yes, I'm looking for Miss Diggs of the Diggses of Charleston."

"Well, Mr. Minor, you've found the Diggses of Charleston, but Elma Winrow certainly doesn't live here. She's out on her family's farm. Surely she's mentioned the farm to you?"

Raymond couldn't grasp what Francina was trying to say to him. He just couldn't figure why Miss Francina Diggs didn't just call Elma to let her know she had company. "What farm? I've come to call on Elma at her home," Raymond replied.

"Well, Mr. Minor, the mistake you've made, or that someone has made, is not to inform you of the fact that Elma Winrow lives on the farm. She most certainly does not live here."

Resenting Francina's tone, Raymond nevertheless remained gracious. "Well then, you'll hopefully forgive my intrusion. And I'll take my leave. Good evening then."

Francina, vaguely aware that she'd said something to cause Mr. Minor discomfort, quickly tried to make amends. "Won't you stay for a light repast? I'm sure Cook can manage to prepare you something. After all, you've come all the way from Nashville. What a journey, you must be exhausted."

"Thank you, but no, I must be on my way. Do you think you could direct me toward the Winrow place, then?"

"Oh, ask any livery driver. They've all hauled that Tom Winrow out there in the middle of the night."

Raymond could feel his temper rising. His ears started to burn. It was best he be on his way quickly.

"I thank you again, Miss Diggs. I really must be on my way."

Francina was so involved with insulting Elma's family she barely realized that Raymond was way out the door as she continued, "If you must, but I'm sure Cook can . . ." She saw she was talking to no one. Raymond Minor was gone. When Francina shut the door, the weight of it pulled her back. She leaned against it, repeating to herself alone, "Well, she does live on a farm, if you can call it a farm, she lives on a sharecroppers' vision of a farm she does, acting like she lives here with us. Wait till I tell Papa Elma's up at Fisk passing herself off as one of us. Ah, she is tough, she is, I can't take that away from her. How I wish there was something I could do. Let him go on out to the farm, it's no skin off my back, if he's been fooled by that no-count gambler's daughter."

Raymond was puzzled by Elma's deception, if indeed it had been deception. Raymond's thoughts leapfrogged through his memories of Elma's mentions of home. Perhaps it was he, Raymond Minor, who'd presumed. He had made assumptions that revealed more about himself than he cared to know. All colored folks were living precariously so long as the Jim Crow laws were in effect, so be it a farm or a grand house with a portico, all Raymond was interested in was Elma herself. Her family raised her, and whatever their circumstances, they'd done a wonderful job. The thought of Elma being so close caused his palms to dampen and his heart to beat faster. After Francina's less than tender remarks about Elma and her family, he was more resolute than ever. He'd come to Charleston to court the woman of his dreams. He even had a surprise for her, tickets to Phil Smith's Colored Minstrel Show.

Raymond hired a carriage to take him to the Winrow farm, as Francina had suggested it was too far out of the way for a gentleman to walk, plus with night coming on it might be dangerous as well. And just as she'd said, the carriage driver was familiar with the Winrow place.

"Ya goin' to git ol' Tom to pay a debt, we could turn us round right heah, suh. Tom ain't got no money fo' ya. I can say that right na'."

Raymond didn't want to engage in conversation that derided his girl. "Would you kindly just take me there," he replied.

"Out to the Winrows?"

"Yes," Raymond instructed.

What was it with every Charlestonian he encountered that they had a need to disparage the Winrows? Raymond could barely make out the houses he passed on the way to his darling Elma. Rather than houses they appeared like growths from the soil, some tilted, some spreading like an overgrown root over the land. He could make out colors of the clapboard and the roofs that teetered toward the sky like tilt-a-whirls in saucy pastels and dim ivory. Every once in a while he heard someone singing or a banjo strumming. The world he'd entered was somehow of another time, an unlikely place for a modern girl like Elma, he thought. But nothing he saw of the impoverished countryside was daunting enough to make him reconsider his choice to make Elma his bride. Francina could have said that Elma was a sharecropper's daughter and he wouldn't have changed his mind. Tonight he was going to meet the Winrows, whoever and whatever their circumstances. When the carriage finally stopped, Raymond paid the driver a handsome sum, he was that happy. It occurred to him that the mighty Miss Diggs might have to reconsider her perception of him if she knew he'd come barreling into Charleston with a minstrel show. Yes, the handsome and dignified Mr. Minor had been the guest of the Phil Smith Colored Minstrels. That's how he'd got to her front door.

Maybe Miss Diggs might not have asked him in, if she knew Mr. Minor was probably no better off than the Elma Winrow she'd so mercilessly dismissed. Colored folks had such a problem accepting the idea that looks can be deceiving. But now, Raymond Minor really wanted to make a good impression. He wanted to appear to be a man of substance, not just another Creole dandy. He wanted to be taken seriously by Elma's folks, especially Elma's mother, of whom she spoke so constantly and highly. He imagined Eudora's fingers to be laced and golden from the way Elma spoke of her mother's craft.

The path to the Winrows' was narrow and beaten down. There was no light other than that leaking from inside the small windows beyond the porch. Raymond took off his hat so as not to seem so citified and extraneous. Here every object had a function, had to be necessary, nothing frivolous, nothing simply for fancy's sake. He wondered if that was why he had a hard time getting Elma to laugh easily. Was laughter a rarified commodity in the Winrow house? At the door Raymond heard what he thought to be an altercation. But he certainly couldn't vouch for that when Elma came to the door. Her face was frozen with astonishment; she didn't seem able to move her lips to say a word, like "Hello, Raymond, I'm awfully glad to see you." The first words Raymond heard were from Ma Bette. "Elma, chile, who's to the door? Don't let jus' anybody in heah. The family's goin through enough as tis."

Since Elma was incapable of answering her grandmother, Raymond simply introduced himself as he shut the door behind him. "I'm Raymond Minor, a friend of Elma's from Fisk, and you must be Ma Bette."

The sound of Raymond's voice drew life out of Elma. "Oh Raymond, what a surprise! Ma Bette, this is the young man I talked to you about. Mama, Mama, Raymond Minor's here to visit," Elma said loudly, warning her mother not to be quarrelsome now no matter what. There was no need to involve Raymond in the family's catastrophe.

"Well, bring the young man in, Elma, and offer him some coffee," Eudora shouted from the second floor.

There was no getting around the pall that sat in the kitchen, no matter how Elma tried to banter as she'd seen her Fisk cronies do. "I wish I'd had some notion you were coming this way, Raymond. Why, I would have held dinner for you. We had a delicious gumbo."

Raymond, who had never heard Elma talk so fast, couldn't get a word in, but he managed to guide Elma to the porch where they could be alone for a second or two. "Sweetheart, what's the matter? What were you goin' on so about in the kitchen?" Raymond asked.

Finally, believing she'd found safe harbor, Elma flooded Raymond's ears with the whole story about how her father had packed up and left without so much as a fare-thee-well, how Lizzie had run off somewhere on the farm screaming like a banshee, and how as if that wasn't enough, "Here comes some white man who says we have till Monday to be off our own land. Oh, Raymond, this is the most perfect time and the worst time for you to show up. Not what you expected, huh?"

Raymond drew Elma close to him. "I came to see you, not your pa or your ridiculous cousins."

"Oh, no. You've seen Francina?"

"Of course, Miss Diggs of Charleston."

Elma blushed. "What you must think of me!"

Raymond shook his head, "It was I who made all of the presumptions."

"I never denied it either." She looked down, pursing her lips, embarrassed.

"But there's nothing to deny. As far as I can see, the Winrows are nobody to look down upon. They are high-class God-fearing folk who've been dealt a hand of bad weather and an equally bad hand by Fate, who is known to have a quirky sense of humor."

Elma's back straightened. "You think it funny?"

"Well, I was rather amused to meet the real Miss Diggs." Raymond's eyes twinkled. "To tell the truth, I much prefer the pretender." He took her hand and kissed it. He smiled, drawing her close again. "It seems like you could use some help getting everything ready for the move. Is there anything I can do?"

Elma shook her head vigorously, "Oh no, Raymond. Mama would die before we let a stranger come to our aid, but thank you for offering."

Raymond wanted to say more. He wanted to say that without a man to help them they were making things harder on themselves for no good reason, but Raymond could imagine Eudora's pride.

Elma hesitated. "Raymond . . ."

"Yes, Elma," Raymond responded.

"Raymond, there is one thing you can help me with."

"You name it," Raymond beamed.

"We've got to find Lizzie. She's run off somewhere round here and we need to find her. She's taking this whole thing about Pa very hard. What do you think, Raymond? Is it like a man to take off like this? Oh, there must be some mistake—"

Suddenly a voice came from under the porch. "You're darn right. There's some mistake! Pa didn't go anywhere without takin' me."

It was Lizzie, whose head popped out from her hiding place full of bristles and dust now. Who'd have thought to look for her so close? Everyone assumed she'd run off to the farthest reaches of the land in search of her father, but no, she'd stayed close at hand as if she was waiting for her father's footsteps.

"Who's that?" Lizzie asked, gesturing to Raymond.

Elma couldn't help laughing. "Lizzie, where are your manners? That's a good friend of mine from school. Raymond, this is my sister, Elizabeth."

"My name is Lizzie. That's what I answer to, even at school I made Francina call me Lizzie too." With that Lizzie presented herself.

"Well, Lizzie, I'm Raymond Minor."

"Oh, I know 'bout you already. I can hear everything from under the house. You came all the way from Nashville to visit us, but you went to the wrong house, didn't you?"

"Well, I like to think that I've found the right house, Lizzie, cause I've got something for the Winrow girls that they don't know about yet."

Elma covered her face with her hands. "Oh, not another surprise. I can't take another surprise today."

Sensing her sister's nervousness, Lizzie tried to calm Elma. "This might be a good surprise, Elma. After all, he says he's a friend of yours. Friends bring good surprises." Then Lizzie looked at Raymond so hard he believed he might turn to stone if his surprise didn't live up to Lizzie's expectations.

"Well, now, I've got three bona fide tickets to Phil Smith's Colored Minstrel Show for this very evening. Do I have any takers?"

At that very moment Eudora appeared at the door. "Good evening, Mr. Minor. I see you're prepared to take my girls out for the night. Well, that's mighty thoughtful of you. Takes a hardworking man to come up with niceties these days. Just what is it that you do, if you don't mind my asking?"

"Why, I'm an architect by training, a builder."

Relieved that Raymond practiced some recognizable trade, Eudora repressed her natural inclination to hold on to money and not spend it on foolishness the way her husband did. She wanted her children out of her hair this one night. She needed time to think. "Just give them a few minutes to ready themselves, Mr. Minor, and they'll both be lookin' pretty as can be." Elma couldn't believe her ears.

Lizzie flat-out refused to go. "I'm stayin' right heah till Pa comes home," she stubbornly announced.

Eudora wanted to say that might be a very long time, but instead she honeyed her tongue. "Lizzie, for all we know your Papa may well be playin' with the Phil Smith band. Now that's a real possibility, isn't it?"

That sounded to Lizzie like a real idea, as opposed to these folks' silly notions that her pa had deserted them. Of course, her father wouldn't miss an opportunity like this, to play with the renowned Phil Smith Band. Why, she should look her best. For the first time in hours Lizzie smiled. She smiled at Nana. She smiled at Eudora. Lizzie smiled in the mirror and up the stairs. She knew where her father was, even if the rest of them didn't have a clue. He was with the minstrel show. How many times had she and her papa talked about leaving everything in Charleston to go make music. Now the day had arrived.

12

THE PHIL SMITH COLORED MINSTREL SHOW HAD SET UP its tent outside Charleston about five miles from the Winrows' on a piece of land owned by one Leo Carruthers, who proudly stood next to the hawker selling tickets.

"Ladies and Gentlemen, come this way to hear the most beautiful voices and music of the colored world today. If you miss this performance you've one more chance. Two shows, but no more! The finest warbling black voices this side of the Mason-Dixon Line are waiting to entertain you. Come right this way!"

The hawker caught sight of Raymond and waved toward him to step right up. "How many tickets you need, brother? Phil says you really saved the show when you fixed his violin on the way down here."

Raymond blushed. He'd wanted Elma to think he was just a friend of Phil Smith, which he had become, but only after a choice feat of refined woodwork on Phil's fiddle. Actually Elma was impressed that Raymond had made himself useful. She had been concerned about how seriously Raymond took life's responsibilities.

"Step right on in, brother. Here's three tickets for you. I'll be sure to tell Phil you came with two dazzling lady friends."

Elma smiled, but Lizzie's eyes cut at the hawker. She wasn't a dazzling lady, she was a hard-working farm girl and she had the calluses to prove it. She wanted to give the hawker a talkin' to, but Elma whispered that the man was trying to pay her a compliment and the best way to take a compliment was to smile, nod, and keep on going. Dazzling lady, indeed! But Lizzie was in for a surprise.

The music started before they got to their seats. A semicircle of colored men in blackface were singing, "O, oh, didn't he rumble" with tambourines justa-goin' and Phil's fiddle ringing out the melody. Lizzie was enchanted. The show was a mixture of jokes, skits, and song, all designed to show off the many talents of the troupe. Lizzie found herself clapping all the time. Beside her, Elma was a study in contrasts. She sat erect, refined and distant, her mind still reeling from the tumult caused by Tom's disappearance. The minstrel players jammin' before her appeared a grotesque, dark pantomime of joy, bawdy yet melodious, loud and loving, laughing through grit. It was all too much for Elma to decipher tonight. She measured each breath and endured the show.

Lizzie only got upset when a clown with extra-large shoes and a yellow and white polka-dotted jacket became the brunt of all the jokes. The blackface he sported was ten times darker than the others and there wasn't one redeeming quality to him, but he drew the most laughs from the crowd. Lizzie was disturbed. *My pa is naturally black, and he is nobody's fool!* Some of the slapstick reminded Lizzie of how white folks treated her when she went to meet her mother at the houses where Eudora sewed. But once the entertainers invited the audience to do the cakewalk, Lizzie couldn't help but join in. This was something she and Osceola had mastered at Deke's during the day when no one was around. Lizzie wished her father and Osceola both could be with her to see her legs cut through the air with all the other colored legs. Maybe Lizzie liked this show business more than she thought.

Afterward, Lizzie and Elma were introduced to the company by Raymond, who'd made friends with everybody from the clowns to the crooners on the way down from Nashville.

Lizzie watched the performers taking off the blackface, revealing fine-looking colored men, and asked Phil, "Since you're colored already, why do you wear blackface?"

Phil was taken aback. "Cause we're a minstrel show, kid."

That was not much of an answer to Lizzie's mind, but the serious tone of Phil's voice led her to believe that was not something he wanted to continue to discuss. But he said he would teach her a tap routine and some songs if she liked. So Phil and Lizzie were so busy, they didn't really miss Elma and Raymond, who had gone for a walk behind the tent.

Raymond thought the new moon boded well for his plans for the evening. Elma's hand was soft and warm and fit his so perfectly. Elma looked at the sky and didn't see the moon. All she saw was the darkness. She saw in the sky an unknown chaos that had enveloped her family.

Raymond finally began to speak to her about the true intentions for his surprise visit. Raymond's voice brought her back from panic. "Elma, I know I'm just comin' out of school, and though I call myself an architect, I'm really a master carpenter, but I can build anything, Elma. There's a lot of building construction goin' on in New York City, and that's where I want to take you as my bride. Elma, will you marry me?"

Elma fell into Raymond's arms, her fists clenched against his back. "Yes, yes, I can't, I can't, but yes!" and they kissed as they never had before. Both were relieved and confused.

"Elma, you're saying you will marry me then?" Raymond asked tentatively.

"Yes, but I can't. I do love you, Raymond, and everything in me says go to New York with you this very minute, but there's so much I haven't told you. I can't. So yes, I want to marry you, but I just can't, not now."

"But why, Elma? This makes no sense. What you're sayin' to me makes no sense at all," Raymond said, while holding Elma even closer to him.

"It makes sense if you've been told to get off your land by Monday sundown, if your pa has hightailed it to God only knows where and there's an ol, ol woman and a child to look after. It makes sense then, Raymond. Yes, I want to marry you, but I can't. Do you understand now? I can't get married. I can't finish school. I've got to stay here with my family." Elma tried to turn away from Raymond, but he caught her arm and drew her to him. Her taut clenched fists opened and she relaxed into his embrace.

"So I have a fiancée, but not right now. Is that it?"

"Yes, Raymond, that's it."

"Well, once I get settled in New York, soon as I can help out, I will."

Elma gently stepped back from Raymond. She couldn't bring herself to look him in the eye, but she found the courage to say, "Oh, no, Raymond, I wouldn't want that. Neither would my mother. We'll take care of ourselves somehow. Let's go back now. We've left Lizzie on her own with strangers, you know." With that the two lovers sought one last glimpse of passion in one another and then headed toward the tent.

Lizzie and Phil were in rare form when they entered; fiddling away, Phil played against the rhythm of Lizzie's feet. Elma knew the melody—it was "Swing Along"—and joined in, her voice belying the tumult of her emotions. Elma found peace somewhere between the notes of the song so heartfelt and vibrant. Raymond inched in a little on Lizzie and the two became dance partners immediately, Lizzie trying to outdo Phil at every turn. Finally, out of breath and laughing, the quintet said their good-byes and the Winrow girls were escorted back to the farm.

In the back of the wagon Lizzie's eyes kept searching the horizon for her father. She'd been so sure he'd be there. She hadn't forgotten all the hateful things her mother had said about him, nor the disgust on Ma Bette's face when she had to say his name, Tom. How Lizzie wanted to hear her pa answer to "Tom." She wanted to hear his gruff voice singing; she wanted his cornet to blare through the night and wake all the neighbors, letting them know Tom Winrow didn't go anywhere. He was with his family like any good man. Lizzie wanted her father's singing to wake them up, wake them all up who looked down on him and felt sorry for her. *Wake em up, Pa,* she felt her insides crying. *Wake em up!* And Lizzie's face was covered with tears as they pulled up to the house. She shot like a crazed child up the stairs to her room where she could cry without being told how her father wasn't worth it. Nobody was fooled. Nobody tried to stop her.

It was late, the kitchen and parlor strewn with boxes and crates, half-filled baskets and overstuffed trunks. Eudora whirled about, her energy and rage focused on her tasks. Raymond attempted to speak to her. Out of the side of her eye, Eudora saw Elma catch his hand.

"Will one of you tell me what is goin' on here? I've no time for foolishness now."

"It's nothing, Mama."

Raymond interrupted Elma. "Now Mrs. Winrow, I hate to break it like this, but I have asked Elma to marry me. Not now, we know we can't marry until things are more calm here, but once I get set up in New York, I intend to send for her."

Eudora's face tightened as she heard these words. This was not what she had planned, not at all. Though she hadn't mentioned her plan to Elma, this was not it. "But young man, you've nothing to offer my child but tickets to a minstrel show." This was cruel, but Eudora didn't care anymore. She showed no response to Raymond's promises or his credentials. Finally Elma stepped over to him and whispered that enough had been said and he should go.

"Good evening, Mrs. Winrow, I hope to see you again soon. Please give my best to Ma Bette and Lizzie. You'll be hearin' from me soon."

"Good-bye, Mr. Minor," is all Eudora had to say.

Elma's eyes, fierce and determined, cut at her mother. There was no need to be rude. Elma knew she couldn't marry soon. What was wrong with her mother? On the porch a disappointed couple tried to say their farewell with hope, but Eudora's cold stance made that hard.

"Don't forget, I love you. We are engaged. Don't forget that, Elma. Don't forget that no matter what." Elma nestled her head on Raymond's shoulder.

"I won't forget, my sweetheart. I'll never forget. Now you go along before we upset her some more."

Elma reluctantly entered the house only to find Eudora packing away in silence. "Mama, have you ever been happy? I mean truly happy like I am tonight?"

Eudora without pausing for a moment said frankly, "I don't remember."

* * *

BEFORE THE crack of dawn Ma Bette was fixing herself for church. Her great-grandchild was to sing. Eudora'd arranged with the minister for Elma to perform one of the pieces she did at Fisk for the congregation. Being turned out of one's home was no reason to miss praising the Lord. She knew Eudora felt the same. Besides, with Tom disappeared and the town whispering loud as thunder, it was important to hold one's head high no matter what.

When she saw that Eudora had entered the kitchen, Ma Bette asked, "Anythin' I can get for ya?"

"Why, yes, Grandma, some coffee is all." The two women sat quietly for a minute, then simultaneously said, "How . . ."

Then Eudora finished the thought. "Are we goin' to move by tomorrow?"

"Aw, darlin', don't you worry none, the Lawd is gointa find a way."

Elma entered the room, curious about the moodiness of it. "What's got you two so bothered this beautiful mornin', besides movin' tomorrow?"

Eudora pulled herself out of doubting the Lord and replied, "Eager to hear you sing today."

"Who sing? What? I'm on vacation," Elma teased.

"You're too young to realize now, but colored women don't get 'vacation,' missy. Now get ready for church and check on your sister."

Elma took a deep breath, let it out. What her mother didn't realize was that she had grown accustomed to making her own decisions, determining on her own what was best. Elma followed Eudora's instructions only because they were being tossed out of their home. In any other situation Eudora would have to take the lead from Elma herself.

* * *

AT THE small Azula Street church more eyes were set on the Winrow family than on the deacon greeting folks. Black, brown, and hazel eyes fixed themselves on Ma Bette, Eudora, and the girls, then quickly turned away. No one could bring themselves to talk out loud about the fact of Tom Winrow abandoning his family and them not having a roof over their heads, but they all wanted to ask Eudora what was she planning to do now. Where were they going to go? How were they going to live? Could Elma go back to college or not? In their bonnets and gloves the women all came to say "Good morning," but left unsaid their true interest. All this was laid to rest once the preacher gave his sermon on loving your neighbor, as if he too were drawn to the calamity that beset the Winrows. Nevertheless, the entire assembly was spellbound when Elma sang "Amazing Grace."

With the first few notes, Elma's voice filled the church. She released each word as if singing itself were for her an act of sacrament and rapture. Her voice took on colors and textures, moistened the church women's faces, massaged the ache out of the necks and shoulders of the working men who wondered at this wisp of a thing who sang like a woman much larger than she was, much older than she was, and in more pain than the young Elma could possibly have known. The congregation which had arrived curious about Tom Winrow and his family found itself in humble reverence as Elma laid her heart open.

> "I once was lost but now am found,
>> Was blind but now I see.
>> 'Twas grace that taught my heart to fear . . ."

Lizzie was probably the only parishioner whose thoughts were ablaze. She wanted to find her father. Suddenly in the middle of the second verse Lizzie bolted out of the church. She ran as far as she could, hoping to leave the staring eyes far in the distance, and off her face. She had to get those pitying eyes off her face.

After the service, Elma wanted to go after Lizzie, but Eudora said, "No, leave her be. The child's lost the only parent she adores. She'll be along, or down by the wharf. Oh, by the way, I thought we might stop to visit with cousin Diggs this afternoon."

"Must we, Mother?" Elma pleaded. "I'm not so sure I want to visit with them."

"Well, I know for sho' that I won't be," Ma Bette interrupted. "I'll get a ride home with the Beltons. They was always nice folks."

"Well, whatever suits you, Mother," Eudora said.

Lizzie wandered back, her eyes red and cheeks flushed. Elma wiped the child's face with her handkerchief and pulled her up close. "We'll find Pa, Lizzie. Don't you worry." And Lizzie began to cry again.

"You two stop sniveling so. We've got things to do, and folks don't want us being pitiful on their Sunday afternoon."

"Where are we going, Mama? Shouldn't we go home in case Pa comes back?" Lizzie asked.

"Not today, Lizzie, we've got to go see our cousins."

"The Diggses? Aw, Mama, not today."

"Yes today. We've got business to settle with them." And with that, Eudora clucked the horse. They were on their way to Charleston.

The Diggses were just preparing to sit down for Sunday dinner by the time the Winrows arrived. True to form, the Diggses invited them to join in. There was plenty to go around. While the rest of the state suffered through a crippling drought, there was a boom in the undertaking business, and how well the Diggses were doing! Eudora didn't fail to notice Roswell Jr. eyeing Elma, which made sense for an unattached middle-aged man and fit right into Eudora's plans. She guided the conversation toward Elma's achievements and her return to Charleston, "leaving her one of the most accomplished young Negro women in the area." Roswell Jr. nodded yes to everything Eudora said and would then smile vacantly at Elma, who now began to see through her mother's plans.

"Excuse me, Mother, but may I have a word with you in private?" Elma said curtly.

Mother and daughter met in the pantry, Elma a whirlwind of emotion. "You're thinking to marry me off to that sorry excuse for a man, Mama? Why? We can make it on our own without selling my soul. Or don't you have your faith anymore?"

Trying to calm her daughter, Eudora said softly, "Now, it's not the worst idea in the world. You could have anything you wanted, even voice lessons!"

"For what, Mama? So I could sing to Roswell, huh?"

Eudora felt her anger rising. "Now you listen to me, girl. I've worked my fingers to the bone to make sure you always got what you wanted. Now the family needs you to sacrifice something to keep a roof over our heads."

"Sacrifice? Sacrifice? Go beggin' for favors from that good-for-nothin'? Well, I can do that in Lil Mexico, too. Is that what we've come to, Mama?"

That did it. Eudora slapped Elma with all her might. "Don't you ever speak to me like that again!" The ruckus brought the rest of the family running for the pantry.

"What are you staring at, huh?" Elma fumed, her cheek still burning with her mother's palm print. "Well, I tell you, we're homeless. Pa's run off and sold the farm. We've got to be off our land by Monday dusk. Mama was hoping you'd help us a little, seeing as how she's done for you and charged way below what she should have. Any aid you care to give at this time would be greatly appreciated. But marriage between cousin Roswell and me is out of the question. Now if you'll excuse me."

Elma let the pantry door slam and looked for Lizzie. So much was happening to that little girl that a child so young shouldn't have to bear. But Lizzie was nowhere to be seen.

"See what you've done now, Mama? Lizzie's run off again," Elma said accusingly to her mother.

Blanche Diggs, the matriarch of the family, had come from the dining room, roused by all the commotion in her usually quiet domain. "Why, Eudora, Elma, why are you all closeted up in here? Lord knows we so rarely see you, do come out and be with us. You'll have time to be with each other by and by. Roswell, tell Cook to bring the coffee and dessert for our guests. Now let's all sit down and talk."

Francina was only too happy to bring her mother up to date on the problems presented by Eudora's situation. "Well, we can't have our family living in the street, now can we? Eudora, what could we do to be most helpful to getting you back on your feet, if you're sure you don't want to move in with us?"

When Francina heard this, she glared at her mother. "Surely you don't mean that, Mother."

"I most certainly do. How would it look to the whole community if we're willing to help strangers and not our own? Francina, watch that you are never in need."

Eudora remembered Blanche's cold reception years before when she had first arrived from the island. She didn't want to accept her aunt's help now, didn't want to need the help, but she had no choice. *Just as before, twice before, the only ones to turn to. Fam'ly, fuh better or worse.* Blanche assured the dispossessed women that they would have a decent roof over their heads and some help with the packing and moving. Tempers cooled.

Throughout the evening, Roswell Jr. kept saying that he would be delighted to take Elma's hand in marriage. Finally his stepmother reminded him, "Roswell, you're old enough to be that girl's father. Surely you don't believe there is no young man courting her right this minute."

Roswell joked, "Mother Blanche, you mean to say I've lost my charm?"

"Yes, you've still not any substance to you. Now, get Cook for coffee."

Blanche looked around and realized only she and Eudora were left. "Now, Eudora, since it's just you and me, we can talk reasonably. I know we've never been close, but I won't have a Diggs in need and not be of any assistance. I've great respect for what you've done for your girls in spite of that husband of yours. Maybe you are better off without him. Yes, let's think of it that way. Things may be looking up for you now."

Eudora was simply trying to keep her head from floating away from her body. Too much emotion. Too many accusations. Too much need. Eudora was used to mending small intricate tears, not huge ruptures in cloth. This thing with Tom was going to drive her mad. After all her years with Tom, she'd always believed that he would never abandon them. It was their tacit agreement. Between working hard and loving the same way, Tom recognized that Eudora had "married beneath her" and he'd tried to compensate for that. But now this. This was even a greater cause for embarrassment—to leave the family with nothing. Not even a note or a last good-bye. Eudora thought Tom at least cared enough for her as a woman that he'd want a last embrace. *All those years for nothin'.* Her family was a brood of paupers. Eudora sat trance-like near Blanche, whom she had always despised, and was grateful for family.

* * *

GUITARS STRUMMING in time to the blues licks of drums graced the night, and Lizzie let the music carry her off to wherever her pa was. Blues music was in her heart this night, even though she was a child.

> "Backwater blues done cause me to pack mah things an' go,
> Backwater blues done cause me to pack mah things an' go,
> Cause mah house fell down an I cain' live there no mo',
> O-o-ooom, I cain' move no mo',
> O'o-o-oom, I cain' move no mo',
> There ain' no place fo' a po' ol' gal to go . . ."

Lizzie sat on the porch in front of Pilar's bar soaking in the music and the smells of beer, bluesy women, and pipe tobacco. Osceola saw her crying there. Puzzled, he came up to her quietly. "What's a matter, Lizzie?"

As if he'd unleashed a cyclone, Lizzie grabbed Osceola's legs and wept and wept. All he could put together was that Tom was gone. "But Lizzie, what you don't understand is that your pa had debts. He owed some big men a lot of money. Pretty soon things was bound to get ugly. Maybe it's best he's gone," Osceola explained.

"Naw, Pa didn't go on his own. It was your brother. I seen him down at the waterhole plotting with that dirty-lookin' white man. He was trickin' folks into losin', so they sign up wit him and go north."

Osceola thought for a minute. "Maybe that's why your pa tol' me to look out for y'all."

All of a sudden a gruff intimidating voice cracked the air. "Y'all best keep your mouths shut. I don' wanta hear bout none of that from nobody nowhere evah."

It was Deke himself looming over them, but Osceola challenged him anyway. "Is it true? Did you do that? Trick folks into losin' their pay to gamblin' so they could sell themselves to the Northerner?"

"What if I did, what's it matter to you?"

Elma had appeared from around the corner. Her search for Lizzie had brought her to this place she'd heard so much about. "A lot of folks would be interested in that information, Deke."

"Well, now look at Miss Susie-Q come callin'. Was ya lookin' to dance tonight or find yourself a fella?" Elma ignored Deke's crude remarks. "Listen, your pa was a good-for-nothin' loser. If ya asked me, you're bettah off without him."

Realizing she was a bit out of her league, Elma retorted, "Our pa is a good man, and if you know how to find him, would you please tell us. Deke, that's not asking too much."

"Naw, Missy Near White, I ain' tellin' you nothin' 'cept your pa was good for nothin' and he's long gone by now. I'm tellin' you, you're bettah off without him."

Now Elma was really furious. "We'd be bettah off if you hadn't stole the money off him with your cheatin' ways. You better give it back to me right now, Deke, I mean it. Give me my pa's money, right now!"

Now Deke smiled a curious smile. He took a wad of money from his pocket, unfolded each bill slowly, then ran the money gently but with malice across Elma's cheek. "You gon' play wit me, baby, you gotta get the facts first."

Before Deke could do anything, Elma grabbed the money from his hand, looking him straight in the eye as if daring him to move against her.

"Come along, Lizzie, right now," she said.

Deke grabbed for Elma's arm, but Osceola jumped him. Deke's fury roused, he simply threw Osceola off and walked back into the bar. Lizzie was at Osceola's side immediately. "Oh, ain't nothin' wrong wit me, Lizzie. Get off me now," Osceola grumbled and got up limping.

Elma gathered the youngsters around her and led them to a safer place. She kept repeating, "I wish I knew what to do now. I guess I should take this money to Mama first."

"No, no, Elma, use that money to go to New York and marry Raymond. Then you can send for me."

"Oh, darlin', Raymond's probably left by now."

"Oh no, Elma, we know where he is."

And Lizzie and Osceola took Elma to find her beau.

* * *

WITHOUT HER granddaughter around to chastise her, Ma Bette donned the white lace skirts and cotton shirt she called her "goin' out" clothes. Even her hat was white with a large brim sporting blue trim of satin. Off to the wharf she was, aiming to see her "customers." Over the years Ma Bette had built up quite a clientele of folks who believed she had the power to remove hexes, cast spells, change the course of human affairs. Now was their time to pay up. Her family was in need. There was the crush of time upon them now as never before. Tomorrow by dusk they must be out of their home and going someplace. The first young woman she approached was fashioning a woven basket to hold her fruits on Monday.

Ma Bette said, "Ya know I cain't rightly tell how much it is you owe me for bringin' yo' man back to ya, but whatever ya could spare today I'd appreciate."

With fear in her eyes, the girl came back with just under a dollar. "I'll have the rest fo' ya Tuesday next, Ma Bette. Ya know it ain't like me to forget how good ya been to me."

Ma Bette dropped the coins in the little hoodoo bag 'round her neck, nodded, smiled, and went on her way. Most of her customers were duly accommodating, except for one young stevedore. He wanted to argue with Ma Bette. "You promised that woman would get all the way out of my life, but she still comes round pesterin' me. Naw, I don't owe ya nothin', Ma Bette."

Ma Bette thought for a minute, then turned back to him and said, "As I recall that was a two-part hex and you only paid me for one-half of it, so she's only half out of your life. Pay up on your bill and ya'll never see her again. If ya don' pay up, I'm likely to work some roots on ya for bein' so honery. An she be on you like yo' shadow."

The young stevedore tore through his pockets as if they were filled with red ants to give Ma Bette whatever money he had. Finally Ma Bette found a lonesome spot 'long the sea to count her money. Not enough. Not near enough to get them out of the mess they were in. That meant only one thing.

* * *

THE INTERSECTION of Meeting Street with Ashmead, where the magnolias and bougainvillea guarded the wealth of Charleston with grace and a peculiarly intimidating beauty, was where Ma Bette was headed. She was an apparition along the pathway, a throwback to other times, other places, in her white lace and her hat. She fit in among the color of Little Mexico, but here colored people were assumed, like the landscape, something to pass through, walk on, lean on, and use at will. Ma Bette walking along with her song brought the life of her people to bear among the weeping willows and grand oaks.

At one very imposing mansion she stopped. There are people and things no one ever wants to think about. This house was such a place, where time is caught in its tracks and memory waltzes wildly with the present. Ma Bette had to steel her nerves and catch her breath, which was irregular. All her children, all her children had been touched by the people in this house, the white folks, who looked upon her and hers as some phenomenon of nature like the sea, low tide, high tide, dependable and unfeeling. She gathered her skirts and headed for the massive front doors, where a white butler answered, saying, "You, you must go to the back door, nigger."

Bette caught the door with her arm. "I ain't accustomed to goin' round to no back door. I came to see Miz Mayfield."

The butler looked at Bette and her raiment with disdain. "Who shall I say is calling?"

Looking him right in the eye, Ma Bette said simply, "The other Miz Mayfield."

"Let her in," a drawl of a voice instructed the butler.

Then Julius Mayfield's auburn- and white-haired wife appeared in the foyer.

"Why Bette, I haven't seen you since Sweet Tamarind, when we were all together . . ." Her voice trailed off as if the sentence could never be finished.

Ma Bette was silent.

"What is it you want?" the white Miz Mayfield asked pointedly. "Bette, I spoke to you. What do you want? What is it I can do for you?"

Finally Bette said, "There's something we can do for each other, I do believe."

Taken aback and more than a little angered, Mrs. Mayfield started out of the foyer. "Follow me, then," she said, leading Bette to the study, an oval room flushed with golden light filtering through the shuttered French windows. She sat primly on a couch, leaving Bette standing.

"Well, now we're alone. I want to know what you want, bold enough to walk to my front door."

Ma Bette remained composed. "Miz Mayfield, I don't and didn't never mean you no disrespect. And I've never asked you Mayfields for anything after serving Master Julius all his natural-born life, but now we're in a terribleness of trouble. And I needs your help."

Sitting back and arranging her skirt, the white Mrs. Mayfield surveyed the colored woman whom she'd resented for so many years. All she saw was a weathered old woman in an outlandish outfit befitting a child's first communion. "You want me to give you money?" she laughed.

And as Mrs. Mayfield laughed, Bette began to lay out on the couch photographs of Julius's colored family: Julius with Bette by a swing, Julius with Blanche on his knee, Elma and Juliet making flower garlands. The next picture was Ma Bette with a baby boy child swaddled in a little blanket the weaver women had made special, lying in the simple crib Lijah-Lah crafted, then last Julius and the white Mrs. Mayfield with the same boy child wrapped in the same blanket, but his bonnet with ribbons and silk.

Ma Bette bitterly fingered the photograph of Mrs. Mayfield with the baby in her arms, the picture she'd taken off Julius after she'd killed him. "Your youngest, I b'lieve, your only son, our baby boy."

Mrs. Mayfield reached for the couch back to steady herself before she collapsed. Bette smiled. "Ain't it funny to ya that Julius never thought he could have himself a son by either one of us, but I fooled him, didn't I?"

All of a sudden the white Mrs. Mayfield bolted up. "Get out of here, you nigger bitch! Get out of my house this minute!"

Bette didn't move. She only said, "Don't never call me out of my name again."

Mrs. Mayfield, whose hair seemed to turn wholly white in seconds, fell back into the comfort of the chaise. Bette was not yet finished with her task, however.

"Been so long now I almost forgot I had myself a boy chile, but Julius III is most an old man hisself. He nevah knew nothin' 'bout me, 'cept I was Massa's fancy gal. What's that to think about your mama?"

Mrs. Mayfield started up at the thought that Julius might discover that his mother was a nigger wench. Bette ignored her fury and continued, "Besides, I always liked girl chirren. They sensible, easier to deal with. Your son's a important man now. And I don't want to see any bad things befall him or your family."

"You want money?" Mrs. Mayfield blurted with venom.

"Just enough to help my granddaughter get back on her feet and take care of her two chirren. They father deserted . . . You can keep the pictures. I don't look my best in them anyway," Bette casually replied.

"How do I know that there aren't any more of these?" Mrs. Mayfield asked.

"I tol' you I don't look good. There ain't no more," Bette said forcefully.

"How much do you want, nigger?" Mrs. Mayfield asked with contempt.

Ma Bette answered matter-of-factly, "Massa Julius says he had uh offer fuh me once. Said em could fetch turty-tree hunnud dollah, but dis niggah wort more 'n dot. I reckon it'll do 'bout now." Acting as quickly as she could to remove this blight from her home, Mrs. Mayfield left Bette in the study only as long as it took her to get the money.

Bette said sweetly, "Thank you, m'am, I won't be troublin' you again."

Family's more 'n blood, blood more 'n family. And she departed as she entered, out the front door.

✳ ✳ ✳

TENDING AFTER Osceola, Lizzie, and Elma overwhelmed Raymond with their talk of Deke and the recruiter, but Lizzie's intention that her sister get out of Charleston with Raymond had not dimished. Lizzie and Osceola together were almost more enthusiastic about the coupling of Elma and Raymond than were the two lovers themselves. Almost magically the four arrived at the Reverend Caldwell's door, knocking loudly and calling out to him they had an emergency. The Reverend came to the door to see to the ruckus. Raymond in his inimitable way quieted the group and explained, "We wish to be married so that we can continue on to New York to make our home."

The Reverend scratched his head, puzzled. "Does your mother know about this, Elma?"

"Well, no sir, not yet. I haven't had a chance to talk to her yet, but she's certainly met Raymond, sir."

Lizzie was growing restless with all this talk. She jumped in front of Elma and Raymond and whispered loudly to the Reverend, "They have to get married! Don't you understand?"

Thinking that Elma must be with child, the Reverend hurried the quartet into his small parlor to perform the ceremony. Enough had happened to the Winrow family, Eudora didn't need a daughter with so much promise to disgrace her as well. Elma could only hear the murmuring of the minister's voice, "Do you Elma take this man Raymond to be your lawful wedded husband to love and to cherish, in sickness and in health, to honor and obey for all the days of your life, till death do you part?"

Elma heard herself say "I do" resolutely. Raymond looked at her with such intensity when he said his vows that Elma believed the Holy Spirit had truly visited them.

Lizzie and Osceola eyed each other and the newly wedded couple, blushing. Was this what the future held for them as well? Elma and Raymond were kissing everyone, the Reverend, Lizzie and Osceola, each other. They almost forgot they had a train to catch and a mother to see. A mother whose hard work and dreams had intended for Elma to finish college. What were they going to say? All they knew was they were in love and legally married.

Eudora could tell them a thing or two about love, about working till you couldn't stand, sewing till your fingers bled, doing without so long you couldn't imagine plenty, staying with a man more like the Devil than a husband for the good of the family. Eudora could tell them about love all right, but what love were they showing her to get married at a time like this? These were Elma's thoughts as they headed towards their farm, or what used to be their farm.

One of Bette's clients had given her a ride back to the Winrow place, where Eudora was busy packing the years of sacrifice away with every article she touched. She came across dresses that both Lizzie and Elma had worn, old bonnets, and quilt upon quilt that had kept them warm. "Well, I wondered what had happened to you, Mama, when you know how much we have to do before the move. I spoke to Blanche. We can stay there with her, all those Diggses, for a few weeks till we get on our feet."

Eudora brushed her hair out of her face, waiting for some answer from Ma Bette, who simply took the money out and placed it on the table. Eudora stopped what she was doing, dumbfounded.

"Mama, where'd this come from?"

Ma Bette, enjoying Eudora's surprise, said, "A rainy day. Never you mind and don't ask me no more questions. Just be grateful to the spirits. Now we don't haveta spend no time with those Diggs people at all. You're free, Eudora, to do what you must, but hold on to it, 'cause there won't be no more luck like this for us in a long while."

Eudora, who hoarded her hugs so often now, almost squeezed the life out of her grandmother, "I love you, Granma," and wept all her troubles from her taut body.

Lizzie burst into the room like a cyclone, only to stop on a dime. She'd never seen her mother cry.

Lizzie approached her mother to soothe her, but Eudora only reached out to her, gently trying to let Lizzie know that nothing was wrong. "I'm all right, darlin'. Don't you bother yourself about me."

Thinking that her mother was crying about losing the farm, Lizzie confusedly began, "Mama, we're gointa be just fine, Elma's going to New York and she and Raymond are gointa send money down here to us, and

I'm gointa get a job and me and Osceola are gointa give you all our money. Ain't that right, Osceola?"

Eudora laughed and pointed to the money on the table. Lizzie's eyes just about popped out of her head. Eudora assured Lizzie that there was nothing to worry about.

"Cuz Pa is comin' back to us, I know he is!"

Eudora didn't raise her voice, she merely put her finger to her mouth, leaving Lizzie to think all she needed to do was hush for now. No more chatter. Only a peace Lizzie'd never seen on her mother's face.

Lizzie's exclamation brought Elma and Raymond into the room. Eudora roused herself. "Listen everyone, we're going to be all right. We can move into Charleston like proper folks."

The entire brood fell into congratulating hugs and kisses. Betty invited Raymond and Osceola to join them for a repast that they could now truly enjoy. "Late supper," she chuckled, "not the last."

Elma pulled away from the celebrants to talk quietly with her mother. "Mama, I've got something to tell you." Finally, with Eudora's full attention fixed on her, Elma said, "Mama, Raymond and I were married this evening. We're married and in love, Mama. Please be happy for me."

Elma stood absolutely still waiting for a barrage of anger from her mother, but instead Eudora stroked her daughter's face and hugged her fiercely. "Oh Elma, I'm so glad for you. You don't know what a blessing that is to be married and in love. I wish you years of happiness. Where is my new son, Raymond? Come on over here. Do you promise me to love Elma and care for her gently? That's all I ask."

Raymond nodded yes. And Eudora hugged Raymond, too. She was on her way to hugging Osceola when Lizzie, not trusting her mama's change in temperament, jumped between them. So Eudora hugged Lizzie again. It felt awkward to be held so close by her mother. Lizzie was used to Tom's loose hugs and affectionate kisses, but her mother had always been so standoffish. Raymond, too, was startled by Eudora's response to the marriage. He told his bride, "See, she's not that bad, Elma. Everyone wants you to be happy, and I intend to do just that, make you happy."

There was such commotion Lizzie couldn't decide which of her stories to tell Eudora and Ma Bette first. There was the duet with Phil Smith, the fight with Deke, and the Reverend marrying the lovers. Lizzie had more to talk about than there was air in the room. Raymond and Elma were trying to explain their plans for New York. Eudora shook her head yes to everything they said. The calm emanating from Eudora enveloped the whole house. The quieter it got, the more Lizzie felt estranged. The house she was used to had been full of fury and music. But the cause of that, her father, had disappeared, and this new Winrow household felt unnatural to her. Lizzie walked with Osceola to the porch, where she waved goodbye to him as he captured fireflies and then freed them in her direction. Only Ma Bette was outside with the land now. Suddenly looking mature for a child her age, Lizzie sat next to her great-grandmother.

"Ma Bette," she said quietly, "he ain't comin' back, is he?"

"Don't seem likely."

"Moon's got a cloud 'round it."

"Rain's comin'."

13

WHEN TOM WINROW DISAPPEARED, DORA HAD TO THINK of the practical things—how to make ends meet, how to position the family in society, regain dignity. Since Elma had decided to settle in New York, Dora moved with Mah Bette and Lizzie into the old flat on Rose Tree Lane, which she was now buying over time from her cousin Roswell Diggs. *Married down and brought down further, right back where I started.* Dora consumed herself with industry. She took on extra work from Yum Lee, added a sideline millinery business around the holiday season, clandestinely sold piece-work to the mail-order catalogue mills, and hoarded her savings against every imagined calamity. Another earthquake, or a hurricane! *Readymade clothes just ruinin' my trade!*

In those years, she had little time to attend to her second daughter. She was too busy puttin' a roof over their heads and food on the table to realize that her child lived outdoors. It didn't help that Lizzie, with her muscular build, her broad flat face and wide smile, was an impish facsimile of the man who had abandoned them. By the time Dora looked up from her Singer sewing machine, her daughter had grown up—wild.

Lizzie Winrow had an energy that could not be contained by bows, straps, buckles, or belts. Dresses cut the stride of her run. Buttons resisted wrestling bouts. Seams were meant to be split. Fifteen minutes after Mah

Bette pulled her hair straight, she looked as if she had just arisen, the edges at her temples in gossamer spikes and her crown the crest of a cockatoo. She could run faster, throw further, spit longer, and hollah louder than any boy she knew. "Evuh!" Only difference she could see was that she couldn't pee in an arc. She tried a couple of times to invent a technique for girls, only to decide that such a contest was a waste of her time. "What a peein' contest got to do with progress?"

Lizzie never did like to do things she was supposed to, never liked to be caught in the ranks of what the respected expected. Since her pa was gone, she felt disobliged to obey anyone. She was full of anger with no place to put it but into trouble. She could win most any fight, but she rarely had to. She'd made an early discovery—get loud and improvise a barrage of epithets to make your assailant shrink from blows of pure sound. Expert at the dozens, she turned her hostility into pearls of wit, salting the pain of her victim with the complicit mockery of the crowd, her jocular slander, the parry, thrust, and contact. With military precision, she had an instinct for detecting the path straight to the heart. Audience was her armor, laughter reinforcement. An audience insured she would never feel abandoned again. She would never risk trusting her feelings to any one person again. But a crowd? That was a different story. With a wild shock of red and blond hair, a splash of freckles across her nose, her broad juicy mouth always had somethin' to say. Talking trash, she tried to claim her place in the world by announcing, "I am here!"

Most often Lizzie could be found rambling with her two friends, Osceola and Flip. "I forbid you to associate with either of them," her mother had said. As a consequence, Lizzie made the two boys her best buddies. While Lizzie knew Ossie from Pilar's, his official home was the Orange Street Orphanage Asylum, or what folks fondly used to call Crook School. By the turn of the century, the shelter was no more than four damp walls and rows of tattered cots shared with rats and waterbugs. Like most, Ossie, when he could, scrambled out the shutterless windows onto the street, down to the harbor and market district where the ambitious could make money. At twelve he left the home altogether and, following his older brother Deke, made his living on the streets. He had learned some music fundamentals from Mr. Mikell, the music teacher at the home. The rest of his musical education he picked up from the veterans who frequented Pilar's Palace of Pleasure—Professor Jocelyn on stride, Tom Winrow on cornet before he left, the Pullman porter Doc Sullivan, sittin' in sometimes on drums, and the regulars like Mingo and Black Tad, with Deke's girl Tillie on vocals when she wasn't juiced. Osceola Turner grew up sitting on the piano bench next to Mr. Jocelyn, watching the Professor's webbed fingers hitting a thousand notes. Being "forbidden to set foot in that place," Lizzie would watch the band and pick up what she could out the side window. Deke stood at the door as manager and bouncer, his wide chest sporting custom-made suits. She had seen Deke threaten her pa the day he disappeared and she vowed he would one day answer for that. Deke Turner was the last one to see her father. *He knows something.* But Deke's malevolence intimidated her. She had seen him drag a patron from Pilar's and beat his face to a pulp, gut-punch the girl who had caused the trouble, then straighten his suit and walk back in as if nothing had happened. She steered clear, with one exception, her friendship with Ossie, Deke's little brother, but the thought of revenge always resided in the back of her mind. One day she would steal away something he loved. *Show you how it feels.*

If Osceola was her best friend, Flip was their white man. Standing on the corner, arms akimbo in a striped tee-shirt and corduroys worn at the knees, the young Flip had introduced himself, saying, "Let me be your white man. Every colored act need a white man to get along. I'm offerin' to be yorn." Flip was the eventual son of Tildie Bonneau and Coleridge McKinley. After Tildie was stood up at the altar by "that Northern scoundrel," her first cousin Cole, "tragically infirmed by a hooligan who was never apprehended," married her as a token of honor and affection and mutual necessity. A month later they produced a daughter and some years later a son, Coleridge IV, whom everyone called Flip. Some years after that the elder Cole bought an old theater and converted it to a movie palace, just in time for the 1915 Charleston premiere of *The Birth of a Nation.* Flip grew up spending half of his time at the family home on Everett Street and half in the alleys behind the Bijoux on King. True to family history, Flip liked runnin' wild with Negroes.

By the summer of 1917 the trio had created rituals of behavior. Hitching a ride on the back of the Red Line trolley, Ossie and Lizzie could easily get from the Neckbone down to the market district and the Bijoux. With

Flip as the "Interlocutor," the rag-tag trio regularly entertained patrons leaving the movie house. "Ladies and Gentlemen! Lizzie Winrow and Osceola Turner's Colored Troubadours! The Girl made of Rubberbands and the Rubberband Band!"

In the alley behind the Bijoux, Osceola imitated the stride with a comb and a piece of tissue paper while slapping his feet for the rhythm, punctuating it with a bass boom grunt from the back of his throat. Lizzie invented dances and made up lyrics or scat a tight-harmony counterpoint to his instrumental. In exchange for Lizzie showing Flip how to shimmy and walk on his hands and Ossie teaching him to play a little drums, Flip let them sneak into the Bijoux to see the weekly picture show. Since colored weren't allowed except on "Colored Day," they hid in the last row in the balcony, where Lizzie demonstrated how to squeeze under the seat until the lights went down.

On other occasions, in the waning days of summer, they would go swimming not far from Lizzie's old homestead. Dora had rented out a small plot from the Hendersons, the itinerant white family that had bid on and settled on Tom Winrow's land. There Mah Bette still kept her garden, where the herbs mingled with vegetables and wildflowers.

The Hendersons had proved right decent white folk. They allowed Dora to board the mule and keep some chickens and a fattening hog. They built their own shotgun shack, though, for they didn't want to live in a house after colored. Except for an old stove, a broken cot, and a wobbly table and chair, the farmhouse where Lizzie was born stood empty, taking on years, the paint chipped away, the shutters fallen to the side and the door disappeared. Lizzie tromped around as if she still lived there. *Put out by some low-count, red clay rednecks! Sold off the property and he just gone!* That day so long ago.

Reclining on her treetop branch, Lizzie could still see the rooftop in the distance. One leg dangling, she twirled a sprig of lavender against her cheek, breathing in the scent. In these woods, she and her pa had played Union Jack and Johnny Reb. In these woods, he had told her about her grandpa's pickin' up a bugle from a dead boy's hand. "In this land our people are buried. Strangers they were, came and found me, found each other." *Running away, leavin' behind what you love, Pa, what made you?* She could not believe her pa would do that. Every day she expected to see him, every posting she expected to hear. Every time Mr. Sullivan came through the railroad yard, she pried and plied, asking Win's old friend where he'd been, what he'd seen, was there news, but it was as if Tom Winrow had died. Not even that. Disappeared, vanished like smoke from a chimney, fog off the lake. She couldn't grieve, daren't hope, never believed he would leave like that with no word, no reason, nothing, how with no explanation he would just walk away.

"Hey Lizzie, you spozed to be the lookout. What you doin' up there, daydreamin?" Flip protested, his neck craned toward the perch where she lay.

"Smellin' up one of her famous pomades," Ossie laughed. His dimples blossomed when he smiled. "Always experimentin', lookin' for the cure-all invention to tackle her hair." He trilled the air with one finger and with his voice mimicked a trumpet with the mute tight on the bell, signaling delight with a slight jab of his neck. After gorging themselves on wild peaches, the threesome had set up shop on King's Highway, where it was still a one-lane road. They watched for automobiles cruising down to Florida or the Carolina coast or rumrunner convoys piping their weekend medicine to the city.

Flip and Osceola would disguise a mud slick with palmetto leaves and sand, then watch the city-slickers get their front or back wheels stuck up to the spokes. Flip would then negotiate a tow for a fee. Mr. Lee, the ancient gray-haired mule Lizzie had inherited, had given up being a dancin' mule in the mature years of his ornery life, but he was pliant only in Ossie's gentle hands. The single reminder of her life as a child was Mr. Lee. While Ossie harnessed him up, Flip brokered the deal. Lizzie lingered in the treetops as the lookout. She became expert at the makes of cars and the potential for loot. She could easily spot a "Ford, Stutz White, leather seats, tight two-seater!" or a "Buick Touring, B-25! No, a Cadillac Landaulette!" Watching Ossie labor away with Mr. Lee and Flip wrangle the payment, she would idle in her branch and bat the breeze with the wayfarers, getting all the latest news from Savannah or Philly or New York.

These days the road was just as likely to bear military vehicles and work crews as lost vacationers and local moonshiners. The war raging in Europe for three years had finally spilled over to the U.S. Passersby had less time for small talk and adolescent pranks. "Trucks, flatbeds, red spokes," she called out. "These here don't look too friendly."

"Let me do the talkin'," Flip admonished. "And you!" he rasped, pointing his skinny finger at her, "stay outta sight."

Flip had his mother's big forehead and fine, thin hair the color of dirty dishwater. He compensated for his nondescript face and short stature with a twangy bluster and a presumption of privilege. Lizzie didn't pay him no mind and was about to let him know as much before Ossie interceded. A lanky, tall youth with a rich sienna complexion, he was uncomfortably thin with a straight narrow frame, his baritone voice a shock to hear. "Flip's right, you don't wanna be messin' with fellahs got war on they minds. Let us men handle dis."

As the boys walked toward the approaching caravan, warding them off from the slick, Lizzie crossed her eyes and chided them, "Men? Hah!"

* * *

FROM THE movie house to the farm to the wharf to the depot past the two-flat on Rose Tree Lane that her mother called home to the workroom behind Yum Lee's Laundry, her feet were a whir. "Hey, Mah Bette!" Rivulets of sweat cascading down her flushed tawny cheeks, Lizzie placed a big kiss on her great-grandmother's cheek and gave her a rough tight hug, startling the old woman awake. "Mr. Sullivan sent you this snuff and a little taste just like you asked, and the colored newspaper to boot." She untucked her blouse from her skirt and removed the prize tobacco, a pint of Irish whiskey, and a wilted folded newspaper. "*Chicago Defender*! Tellin' people to go north. Got good jobs with the war comin'," she added.

"Plenty of work right here. The North ain't all of that someplace," her mother scowled without looking up from her worktable. Lizzie saw that another letter had arrived in the post from New York. From Elma. It was no secret that Elma was her mother's favorite. Elma with her long silky hair and swanlike grace. *Always the pretty one, always the praise. Swan uh mean old nasty bird. Pretty on the outside, ugly in.* Even in her absence, it seemed Elma sucked up all the glory. Lizzie was a good singer with a strong, husky, belting voice, but Elma's high soprano with the quivering birdsong vibrato was the one that still garnered all the compliments. "My what a voice yoah sistuh has! So sweet!" church members would marvel, as if Lizzie, the loudest in the choir, had none at all. She shrugged off the slights. Since the church congregation saw no favor in her singing, she saw no reason to favor them with her presence.

"Gone to the Devil!" she laughed to herself. At all cost, she avoided direct comparison with her older sister's talent, deciding that she preferred instead to dance and dabble with various musical instruments—Mah Bette's old banjo, spoons, harmonica, and piano, when she could get her hands on one. Once she even had tried playing the old bugle her father had left behind. She wound up killing that ambition with enthusiasm. Trying to get good at it overnight, she played it too long. Whole mouth swole up like a paw-paw. "Nebber pwayin' dot dang no mo', look mah lips!"

Poking them out now nearly as far, she stealthily watched Yum Lee toggling back and forth, never sayin' nothin', while her cousin Roswell waited at the counter for his order of linens. Now that he had taken over the family funeral business, the younger Roswell was even more intolerable. *Some cousin. He shoulda gived that house to us a hundred years ago.* She hated the way Roswell leered at her, as if her father's not bein' there gave him license. *Claimin' he fam'ly, always tryin' to kiss me.* She gave him a short closed-lip smile.

The steam and sweat and noise, her mother hunched over that machine like a demon at work—it all made her fidget, stuffing her shirt back in, rolling her ankles to the sides. She hated the way her people tiptoed around their lives, hated how her mother kowtowed to whites and even with Roswell changed her demeanor and tone, hated how her mother preached disdain for white folk, then turned around and valued everything that was most like them. She hated her sister for pretending she had found happiness when the sorrow washed right through the words in her letters, hated how her once proud and mysterious Mah Bette would now occasionally lose her way, wandering around with goober dust and crab claws until Lizzie found her or the police brought her home. She hated the side glances of grown men lusting after the woman she was becoming and sometimes the child that she still was.

"Lizabeth." Roswell tipped his hat, his laundry package stuffed tightly under his arm.

"It's Lizzie," she glowered and stepped back with emphasis, allowing him free room to exit.

"Don't stand on the sides of your shoes like that," Dora snapped when the three women were alone. "They cost good money."

"I'm goin' out."

"You stay right there till I say you could move."

In defiance of her mother and to Mah Bette's secret delight, Lizzie jabbed her neck back and forth in rapid staccato, perfectly capturing a chicken pecking at grain. Mah Bette laughed aloud. The sewing machine stopped abruptly. Dora flashed a silent glare. Lizzie poked her neck back in place and stood still as a statue.

Each make up she own mind bout tings, Mah Bette mused. *Each tink she need nuttin' from th'other, an expect less. Dora hold she head up high. Folks tink she nose inna air. My Lizzie, stickin' she nose all de time where it got no place bein'.*

Lizzie casually palmed her sister's letter from the side of the table. Turning away from her mother, she plied it from the envelope and began to read it. Elma's letters were always cheerful and short. Life with Raymond was getting better. New York, where buildings touched the sky, things were always looking up. Lizzie could read through the lines. She could see within the picture, a photo from Easter—two toddlers by her side, another one on the way, Elma standing on a Manhattan rooftop framed by the New York City skyline. Her sister was gaunt, a smile forced on her thin lips, her large dark eyes wide and frightened, one fist clenched at the end of an arm seemingly bound to her side, her beautiful mane of hair pulled close to her head. Elma, too proud to ask, but always tacitly accepting the few dollars her mother dutifully sent.

Dora had overpowered her shame and shaped her older daughter with a fierce, unbending pride. Perforce, she had overlooked Lizzie, did not have room to see her. "Make yourself useful and fold some of those pieces for packin'."

Lizzie quickly put the letter back on the table, then flexed her feet and dug her heels into the floor. As she slapped the sleeve parts together sloppily her mother started in on her again. "It wouldn't hurt to be civil to your cousin. Don't you roll your eyes at me! The idea!"

Sensing a brewing summer storm, Yum Lee looked to Mah Bette and silently glided from the room. The sewing machine stopped and started as Dora stomped on the pedal with each new thought building to crescendo. "You want people to talk!? I always held my head up high. Made sure if people was gonna talk, I was looking straight at them and now! Waltzin' in here. Lookin' like that! My own daughter? Gallavantin' with that no-count waterfront trash!"

"We ain't no trash! We got us a good act! We gon be famous!"

"That nigguh ain't eben thinking 'bout you," Dora snapped, her shoulders hunched over the sewing machine. "When I was your age, I had my own growing business. I slave like crazy to make a decent life and what do I get? My own daughter! Hangin' inna trees like a monkey! Smellin' like a mule! Singin' on street corners like a common heiffuh!"

"I make good money same as you!"

Dora slammed her hand on the table. "Oh, you are a headstrong, willful, good-for-nuthin'! I swear you take after your father for spite!"

"I take after my daddy cuz he's my daddy. I should take after him for real and leave this doggone place!"

"Chile, you better not let me get up from here and get my hands on you. You ain't makin' nothin' but a mess outta that. Go on and refill the kerosene for the lamp."

"Ain't you never heard of 'lectricity?"

Dora made a gesture as if she would rise up from her chair. Lizzie darted out.

"No-good heiffuh."

"That's hoofuh!" Lizzie retorted and stomped an angry rhythm pattern on the landing as Dora's sewing box hit the screen door. Lizzie hated when her mother worked late for the Chinaman, the room close and hot, stinking of sweat and starch. Her eyes brimming with tears and fury, she stomped round back the building to the storm cellar. "Bending over that machine till she nearly blind! He so cheap won't even turn on no lights!" All had gone. All she knew as her family. Her father, never to be seen again. Then Elma. Elma used to send letters addressed especially to her. The last was in April and here it was July. She lifted one of the heavy cellar doors. The air within was cool and clammy. The cellar would be damp with soot and cobwebs. "Wouldn't have to cart no lamp up the steps if you'd git some doggone lights. I'mo get outta this backward doggone beat-up town."

She left the unfilled lamp on the ledge and in the last hint of twilight ran off to find Ossie at Pilar's.

* * *

OSCEOLA WATCHED her create an improvised dance, her body lithe with no seeming rules of behavior as she scaled the brick wall like a cat. Her feet disappeared through the jimmied window. He hesitated. "Don't think it's right, dancin' up where the dead lay."

"Ain't no dead people in here tonight. Besides, is that all you want to do—walk around behind Mr. Jocelyn, carryin' his hat? Where you gon go with that?" She flashed him the prize possession concealed under her shirt. "Looky hyeah, a Victrola attachment!" Her knees propped on the sill, she extended her hand, "Come on, reach!" she whispered. "We gon make some music of our own tonight."

They had snuck into the private office of her cousin Roswell's funeral parlor. Roswell had bought a Victrola to entertain his men friends with the latest Jass recordings when their wives thought they were having a Brown Society Benevolence Committee meeting. Twisting his lanky body to get through the tiny stairwell window, Ossie cautiously lowered himself onto the landing. Lizzie arched her back and pursed her lips. "Cousin Roswell be ovuh to Sundie dinnuh, sayin', 'Jass is the Ruination!' Then he sneak over here, snapping his finguhs and smokin' cigars."

Lizzie considered this minor breaking and entry a repayment for the grief Roswell regularly bestowed upon her family. Her first efforts were foiled. Roswell had kept the stylus attachment locked and hidden away in his roller desk. Without it, the mahogany box with its golden rimmed horn was beautiful to behold, but unplayable. Now that Lizzie had procured the exclusive Victrola attachment from Mr. Sullivan, "only for one dollah," she was ecstatic.

"A dollah?! Lizzie, we need be savin' our money. I'll keep it, 'fo you spend it on somethin' else stupid like them tap shoes."

"I need these shoes," she protested as she clicked her new patent leather, black-bowed flats around the sparkling parquet floors of the funeral parlor.

"Put bottle caps on the bottom like everybody else," Ossie rebutted.

"I ain't like everybody else. I'm Lizzie Winrow."

Her kinship with Ossie was genuine. He was a natural. He played multiple instruments, as adept at rhythm as melody as she was, and he laughed at her jokes, admired her dances. She could be herself. "Just the same," he said, "I'll keep the money."

"Whatever. We gon have us our own Victrola Party tonight!" Ossie's contribution to the evening was a new set of treasured Red Seal records. He had procured them off a sailor who owed his brother Deke some money. The two vandals watched transfixed as the needle rested against the rotating black disc. Miraculously, a cornucopia of sound washed over the room.

Ossie's hands went up in panic. "Oh Lawd, they gon hear us!"

Lizzie transformed her voice into a ducklike churl, crossed her eyes, and drew her knees together. Enunciating each syllable with exaggeration, she conjured her spinster cousin Francina to a tee. "Osceola! I know for a verifiable fact that cousin Rrrrrosssssswell is burying Mr. Portas tonight. I know, also for a fact," she shifted to her regular slang, "he buryin' the husband an sleepin' widda widda."

Ossie frowned in embarrassment. "You got a dirty mouf, you know."

"I tell the truth, is all. Can't help if it hurt to hear it. Come to think of it, Roswell and the widow Portas? Hurt to think about that!"

A selection called the Castle Walk began.

"These folks—the Castles—goin' all over the world teachin' folks how to dance our dances," she continued.

"It say Castle Walk, Lizzie, not Cake Walk."

Lizzie fanned herself with the box cover. "White folks, dancin' roun' the world—got a colored band leader."

"You lyin'. Lemme see."

"Why, you cain't read."

"Gimme it."

"You wish."

"Who told you he was colored? Ain't no colored people makin' no records."

"Uh-huh! Mr. Sullivan say when I brung him Mah Bette's charm and he give me the Victrola needle I asked him fuh. 'Same one as usual, Lizzie. Gimme Spell Number Seven,' he say." She handed him the weathered, folded newspaper that had been read by people many times over and continued, "These folks here, the Castles, goin' all over country, national tour, teachin' folks how to dance. Got a colored band leader on stage with em. Come on!" She held out her arms, expecting Ossie to dance with her.

"Ain't no sech a thing as a colored band leader for a white act. Colored act need a white man. Ain't no white act need a colored one." Osceola had stopped to examine the front page. He looked at the masthead and spelled out, "*Chi-ca-go . . . Defender.*"

"Say so right there. A symphony of one hundred instruments, including eleven pianos."

Ossie sucked his teeth. "Sullivan's a drunk and a liar. Ain't no nigguh got eleven pianos," but he flipped the page and saw that it was true. A full picture spread of a colored band graced the center pages of the smuggled Chicago daily. "Vernon and Irene Castle and Conductor James Europe." Ossie studied the pictures—Jim Europe standing between the Castles, standing with his horn section, standing next to the King of England! James Reese Europe, in fine black tails, a colored man named after a continent!

Osceola immediately saw the possibilities. The Victrola players had been selling for a decade, but still people were suspicious. The old stride player, Mr. Jocelyn, so prideful when Osceola would carry his hat and instrument case, was scared of this new sound. "Who gon come hear us, if they kin take the band home? Who gon wanna hear us play if they done heard the song over and over?" But Ossie could see now that the music could go anywhere, it was going everywhere, and colored musicians were riding first class. It was one thing to hear a coin slot phonograph in a penny arcade, it was another to have a full orchestra sittin' up in your parlor. White folks dancing with a colored band? That was nothing new. White folks paying a colored band leader, both of em standin' on stage together? That was something else!

Lizzie tried to match her steps to the foot patterns diagrammed in the paper. "Most of the decent bands not even comin' south no more. Far south as I'm goin is Baltimo they say. St. Louis in a pinch. Only ones come down hyeah is them tired old minstrel shows. Black Patti comin' to town next week. She a hundred years old. Come on. Let's walk like rich folk. No mo' Cake Walk. We doin' the Castle."

Osceola squinted in the half-light of the room. Lizzie approached and stood beside him. He could feel her breath on his neck. The article said that both Vernon Castle and Jim Europe had set aside their careers to support the war effort, Castle becoming an airman with the Royal Canadians and Europe becoming an officer with Harlem's 369th Infantry and leader of its military band.

Ossie studied the band picture in disbelief. In the last row of musicians, he recognized Herbie Wright, standing proud with his drumsticks, his bass drum emblazoned boldly THE PERCUSSION TWINS. Jim Europe had innovated again, amplifying his sound with two trap drummers, who only by coincidence had the same last name. Europe took a cue from Kittyhawk and dubbed them The Wright Brothers. Ossie was more than familiar with one of them. Herbie Wright was from Crook School, just like him! Herbie had taken lessons from Mr. Mikell and withstood his advances just like him. And just like him, Herbie had run off and gotten his start in Deke's street band. Even now Ossie could hear their marching rhythms and the sound of coins dropping into Deke's bowler hat. But Herbie had a temper, and when he tried on his own to collect on the band's popularity, Deke disabused him of that notion, pummeling him every time the boy attempted to stand back up. Dispossessed of all but his hide, Herbie left Charleston for good. Next thing Ossie sees, Herbie is being called one half of the Percussion Twins, sittin' in with the legendary Clef Club Band of James Reese Europe, drum set flanked by grand pianos.

Europe's matte ebony visage dominated the page. Suited up in perfectly cut formal black tails, he stood before a massive ensemble of banjos, reeds, fiddles, and brass—trumpets and tubas, trombones and horns curled around themselves with serpentine splendor. In the center of it all a black man, his almond-shaped eyes, piercing through his rimless round glasses, baton in hand, lookin' like Moses! Herbie Wright had not only resurfaced, he was resurrected, playin' in what had to be the grandest band in the world!

"Castle Walk. This dance don't look like nothin'," Lizzie complained. "Gimme a rag or somethin' jukin'."

Osceola barely heard her. He couldn't believe it. *Orange Street, same as me! Callin' theyselves Percussion Twins. Bet I kin outplay the both of em put together. Me and Lizzie like twins. Got talent and each other, just like them. We would run them off the bandstand. Cain't b'lieve, Herbie got out, got away, and wound up on the cover of the newspapuh!* While he could easily read notes on a piece of sheet music, he struggled silently with the words on the page.

Lizzie intuited his struggle and to distract him improvised a lyric while bumping her hips.

> "Told my mama I was sick, that I got the croup,
> Snuck out of the back to join a colored Jass troupe,
> But Mama put her foot down and this is what she say,
> I don't care if you got pneumonia, you gwine to school today!
> I hollahed right back at huh and this is what I say,
> You wanna catch up wid me, Mama, let me school you my way!
> You wanna lay some learnin' on me but it ain't no use,
> Less it's some fast jukin' Jass or a barrelhouse Blues!"

Tapping out the melody with a buck and time step, Lizzie slid into a skating scotch step to a crossover double tap to a broken leg and her old man's dance with one leg short and a dip and a wobble.

Their plan was to get in a little olio, the variety sketches that came after the comedy sets in most traveling shows, and, by way of entertainment, earn a ticket out of Charleston and make their way to New York.

*   *   *

IN THE wee hours of the morning the following week, Lizzie and Ossie approached the private railcar, the traveling troupe 'most packed up after their last set. A bright orange stripe of dawn had just cracked the night sky.

"Say, we're here to see Black Patti."

"Sister Sissieretta ain't, isn't seeing anyone."

"She seein' us! "Mah daddy and Black Patti was like this." Lizzie held her two fingers tight together. "Mah daddy come to see Black Patti. Turnt the show out! I'm Tommy Winrow's daughter."

"Who?"

"Tom Winrow, the cornet playuh!"

"Never heard of him."

"Yeah? So who are you?" Lizzie snapped.

"Please, mistuh," Osceola interjected, "she's just excited is all. We really got somethin'. I play the piano, she sing and dance."

The headliner Black Patti stepped out of the shadows and walked toward the couple. She was a giant woman, an earth goddess bedecked with sequined splendor of the sun and moon, one on each breast, a crest of waves atop her head, her chiseled brown face regal if worn. Osceola stepped forward to meet her and bowed. "We have created an act in your honor, Miss Sissieretta, and we would like to show it to you."

"What is it you do?"

"She sing and I uh . . . I uh, uh . . ."

"It's a song and dance. Uh olio, brand-new, never been seen," chirped Lizzie.

Intrigued by the earnestness of the young man's large languid eyes and the contours of his youthful body, the songstress turned to him, the sun of her left breast blotting out Lizzie's presence. "New song?"

"Yessum."

"You wrote it?"

"Yessum. Well I—mostly uh some . . ."

"Lemme hear it." Osceola moved swiftly and sat down at the upright piano. As Lizzie started shaking her shoulders in preparation, surveying the railcar to determine how much room she had for her moves, Sissieretta followed Ossie to the piano bench and sat beside him. "Lemme hear you sing it."

"Well, I just play. Lizzie Mae do the sangin', song part."

"I like to hear the composer sing the song," Sissieretta purred. "Tells me if it's true."

Lizzie didn't like the way this was going at all. She was not accustomed to some woman showing that kind of attention to her friend and partner, let alone a legend!

Osceola felt his heart racing. His face was flushed. A room full of people and he was fine, but with a giant goddess looming over him and the band members standing round, the hint of tobacco smoke, alcohol, and reefer clinging to the air, he panicked, couldn't move. When he played at cuttin' contests at Pilar's, he always lasted to the final round, but sitting there so close beside Black Patti he felt his whole body quivering like a puddle in a rain shower. His hands trembled. Dismissing him with a soft grunt, Sissieretta shifted her weight and turned indifferently toward Lizzie. "Lemme see yo' dance, then."

"Me and my partner come as a duet," Lizzie snapped. "Didn't come for no solo." With bold long steps, she marched toward Ossie, grabbed him by the elbow, and dragged him down the car and out the train door. Laughter followed them, jabbing at their ribs, Lizzie's fingernails digging into Ossie's arm.

Only when they were down the street and out of sight of the railyard did she let go of his elbow. "Osceola Turner, what wrong wid you? Yuh know you play bettern that."

"Oh leave me alone. I juss froze up."

"Just froze up?! Shit. North Pole ain't that cold."

"Don't be messin' with me, Lizzie. Doan be messin' wid me."

"I don't know why I bother messin' witchu at tall. I sneak out the house and for what? We ain't neber gon git nowhere talkin' 'bout 'just froze up.' A block of ice could just froze up. Snowstorm just froze up. Eskimo in uh igloo just froze up. Dead body got rigor mortis just froze up. How is a musician what wrote a song talkin' 'bout just froze up? What the people poze to do, imagine how it sound?"

"Oh shut up and leave me alone."

"Then there be two of us 'just froze up.'"

"One of these days yo' mouf gonna get you in a lotta trouble."

"Least it open when I want it to."

"She warnt interested in yo' singin' no way."

"Now he got something to say!"

He turned and left without speaking another word.

✳ ✳ ✳

THROUGH A wall of mirrors, Deke could scan the whole floor from the entrance to the bandstand. They were angled so he could even see the balcony ringing the saloon floor. He tracked all of the business like a musical score, the intricate weaving of human enterprise. Respectable vice. No crimps or dips. No snake juice. Only the devious and perverse. Only in this world could a black man assume some measure of equality—the underground that connected Pilar's to the wharf. South Carolina being a dry state since 1916 had produced in Charleston a healthy enclave for sin and abundant opportunity for ambition. Be it the white action on Beresford and Clifford Street or Pilar's Palace of Pleasure, Deke was the man to see.

Pilar's had three doors—one for the girls, one for white men, and one for colored. Sailors, scuffs, dock boys, clerks, stevedores, ruffians. Gentlemen who preferred the darker pleasures, he escorted to Pilar's— pillars of society he could break into twigs. He had paid his dues. Occasionally he had to clean up a mess—a slit throat, stabbing, suicide—but usually the whiskey was free and easy flowin', camphor and cocaine and cunt abundant and a fair fightin' game good for five bucks a purse. Deke was a large man with a quiet, still demeanor. Music kept him easy, his coolness serene.

He liked to keep things organized. Cards in the back: rotating games of poker, faro, gin, and blackjack, old-timers like Winrow playin' coon. *Bringin' in his homemade wine like it was an offering from God.* "Made up for you just right. Persimmon beer, corn liquor. Scuppernong! *Tommy Winrow's wine divine!*" Deke remembered Win's laugh the most, loud with joy he didn't deserve havin'. *Lookin' like a Sambo in a pichuh show.* Deke wanted to wipe that grin off his face, but he couldn't put it out his mind. *Lost his laugh, went lookin' for it in a slug of cough syrup. Rapture. Smack, thunder, hell dust, nose drops.* Even now, years later, *Deke couldn't get the sound out his ear.* The hollow laughter would beckon from a corner, or in the notes of an itinerant horn player's casual tune. Even after Deke had squelched him, played him, beat him, distilled him down to emptiness, Win was still laughin'. *Haunted, even now, in the face of that girl.*

Traveling the back roads through Hell Hole Swamp, Deke would store local moonshine and bootleg labeled liquor at Hiram's Barbershop, but he steered clear of the stuff himself. Anything that altered his attention. The whores had tried to feed him sweet water as a kid, a little whiskey mixed in with sugar water. He had turned his head even then. *Prize for the best picker, soldier's haze, double shot for a good hand.* He saw too many people swallowed. *Either by the spirits or by the smoke. Snow, juice, death. Even Tommy Winrow. Tricked out by his own hand.* "Made up for you, Deke, just right." How'd that happen?

Deke always liked to keep his mind sharp, calculating. He had a system: pickpocket—broken fingers; card cheat—gouge out an eye. If someone beat up one of the girls, he broke their nose and jaw. Confidence? Busted kneecaps. He carried three guns, one in his pocket, one behind his back, one in his sock garter, a shiv up his sleeve. Blackjack, brass knuckles, didn't need those. Reputation was enough.

Trade: opium from Chinamen, cocaine in packets from Sully, whiskey up the backwoods routes. Girls always in from somewhere.

Pilar was older now, her bloated hands tippin' her cough syrup brownlaced with heroin to her sunken lips, toenails curved around, couldn't fit in her red-topped boots. He stood to inherit, thought to expand, any day now. Then the war came. MPs everywhere, the girls gettin' surly, cuttin' deals on their own, up-country crackers struttin' their arrogance, banning fraternization, crimping his trade.

❋ ❋ ❋

OSSIE'S FACE was still hot when he got back to Pilar's. He headed for the backstair pantry where Pilar often let him sack out during the day. The old madame puffed on her cigar. Her weathered hands still graceful, her nails still pink, she cupped her mouth and hollered toward the back, "Deke? Got company." Ossie pulled back the pantry curtain. His meager belongings were scattered about. Deke's hulking frame huddled over the loose floorboard under which Ossie had concealed his stash. Ossie charged at his brother and whipped him around only to be confronted with a pearl-handled pistol at his cheek, the trigger pulled back.

"Better sleep with it from now on," Ossie spat.

"I always do," Deke chuckled, and slowly let the trigger ease, releasing him. Deke casually tucked the pistol back up his sleeve. "Hold out on me again and see what happen." In the silence, Ossie felt a trickle of urine run down his leg. The cigar box where he had secreted his and Lizzie's hard-won earnings was dashed, broken and emptied.

"That money belong to me and Lizzie. You ain't got no right to it."

"I got a right to anything you got, little brother. I brought you into this world, I'll take you out."

Ossie bolted out the door and ran.

"Come back here! Get back here, you lil nigguh!"

❋ ❋ ❋

OSSIE HID in an empty freight train all that day and night. He grabbed the truss rods of a livestock car and hoisted himself up. Retreating to the corner, he crumbled to the floor. *How'm I gonna tell Lizzie?* He beat his hat to his knee in fury and curled himself into a fetus, not even noticing when the train started up. The earthen smell and the swaying movement of the car finally lulled him to sleep.

He bolted awake just as the moving shadow of a train patrolman rushed him. The club came crashing down. He crouched and instinctively stuffed his hands in his armpits to protect his fingers. Better his head and back, he thought, than his hands.

He wound up in the Spartanburg County lockup, three hundred miles into the piney woods, cracker country. The cell next to his was occupied by a crew of colored soldiers. Five of 'em. Uniforms pressed, hair slicked, mustaches clipped. One of them was standing leisurely, taking a drag off a hand-rolled cigarette.

"Hey, I told you nigguhs, no smoking in hyeah!" The soldier coolly looked at the red-faced white guard, dropped the cigarette, and stepped on it. "Y'all coons bettuh loyn, this ain't New Yawk."

The soldier let out a smooth trail of smoke. "No kiddin'. We don't want no sparks in Spartanburg."

As soon as the iron jail door clanked shut and the men were alone, Osceola jumped up and held on to the bars. "Y'all real soljahs? Never seen colored ones befoah. Charleston full of 'em, but no colored to speak of. Just a couple of messengers and sech."

A chubby dark one seated on a cot replied, "Last time I looked we was colored."

A reddish-brown soldier with small black eyes paced in a circle and nervously slicked down his hair. He spoke with a staccato accent Osceola could not place. "I dint sign up to be no soljah. I juss play bassoon, okay?" he protested. "I sign up to be inna inna inna band. Five hundred dollah a month, that's what he say, that's what Jimmy told me. I sign up to be inna band, not no army. I don't wanna be no soljah. I play bassoon!"

"You a bassoon-playin' muthafuckin' soljah now, Romero," the fat one teased. "Ain't you heard? We got a war to fight."

"With who, a newspaper boy?"

"Shut the fuck up, both of you." A thin, wide-eyed caramel man grabbed the bars and shouted at the empty hallway. "Hey! We want to speak to the colonel! We have our rights!"

"You know they lynch nigguhs down here for mess like this," blurted the fat one. He leaned back, his hands folded over his round stomach as if in prayer. He closed his eyes while speaking. "In Houston, the colored troops and the locals got into it, and afterward, sixteen of the nigguhs was hanged."

"I ain't no nigguh. I'm Puerto Rican."

"Well 'scuse me for breathin', *mon señor.*"

"That'll do, guys," cautioned the one with the cigarette. He stood apart from the rest and moved slowly as if on his own time. The older man met Ossie's gaze. "Where you from, kid?"

"Charleston, thereabouts. Jumped a freight." Ossie chuckled wearily, bashfully. "Jumped the wrong train."

The man smoothly rolled a new blunt. "Didn't we all, brother. Didn't we all? Name's Mitchell, Mitch Jackson."

"Ossie . . . Osceola Turner."

"Hoss–SEE–o–lah." Mitch rolled the word over, shifting the accent, and set the seal of a new cigarette with the moist tip of his tongue. "Great, ancient war chief. Lover of black women, defender to the last." Hoss–SEE–o–lah . . . Hoss, hoss, hoss."

With each syllable Mitch emitted a perfect smoke ring. In successive sizes, they floated to the center of the jail cell and hovered. He shifted the conversation back to his comrades. "The lieutenant will be along directly. He's trying to get us reassigned."

"Never thought I'd say it, but I would give my right toe to be in Detroit right about now."

"Aw, gimme a beach in San Juan!"

There had already been a few incidents in town. Mitch wondered how the lieutenant was going to take this new situation: the drum major, lead trumpet, oboist, and the entire imported Puerto Rican reed section sitting in the county jail.

"On the positive side, we have not been arrested, only 'detained.' "

"On the positive side, we have not been lynched!"

"We still in jail."

The local sheriff was holding them he said for their own protection, but how long that safeguard was going to last was anybody's guess.

The thin caramel man approached. Noble Sissle, the great songwriter-singer, reduced to a twitter. "You think they've even notified the camp? Where's Jimmy? Where's Colonel Heyward for that matter?" His face was bruised and swollen on one side, his eyelid drooping and black. "What are we going to tell him?"

"Our drum major has to learn to remove his cap," Mitch teased.

"Wait till the shit happens to you, Jackson!"

"We're all here, Noble. We're all here," Mitch responded wryly.

At that moment, the bandmaster himself entered with papers for their release. The one called Sissle jumped up. "Jimmy!" He stepped back and saluted. "Lieutenant, I mean. I only went into the hotel to buy a newspaper!"

Jim Europe, his arms folded, head lowered into a straight gaze of disapproval, listened patiently as the guard unlocked the cell door and his men exited single file, saluting their lieutenant as they passed. Mitch, the last, casually explained, "Noble got into it with the local hotelier. Claiming he couldn't stand to be away from New York, he had to have a newspaper."

"I went to buy a newspaper, damn it!"

"Watch your language, Sergeant Sissle."

"Damned cracker told me to take my hat off . . . sir." The reedlike man enunciated every syllable in a crisp high tenor. "I had the paper in one hand and the change in the other. He knocked my hat off!"

"Knocked his hat off," echoed Mitch.

"I went to pick it up, and he kicked me. Kicked me, Jimmy! Almost took out my eye. Chipped my tooth! Like he wanted to take my head off. If the fellahs hadn't come in, he might have killed me!"

"Came in to see what was taking you so long, Sis."

"Go on, keep laughing. I broke a tooth!"

The lieutenant responded like a weary father with a houseful of children, the men clustered around him. "Pull yourselves together, soldiers. We have a gig in two hours. We're playing the local country club tonight."

No, uh-uh, the universal cry went up. "I no playin' in no goddam country club inna inna inna goddam country like these!"

"You have a problem understanding the command, Romero?"

"No sir, Lieutenant Europe, sir."

Osceola suddenly realized that he was standing before James Reese Europe in the flesh. A Negro, an officer, and leader of the finest band in the world! "Sergeant Sissle can sit out until he gets that tooth fixed," the

lieutenant continued. "If it's any consolation, the boys back at the barracks stand ready to tear up the town on your behalf, but I have to have
your word. No retaliation."

"No newspaper neither," mumbled the drum major as he exited the
jail.

Mitch idled and gestured with a slant of his head. "Chief, can you
spring the kid, too? Don't think you wanna leave him here."

The sheriff was only too happy to let Osceola go. Should the good
citizens of Spartanburg decide to pay him a visit, he wanted his jail emptied of any colored. Wanted his town that way, too. He spat after them a
thick sludge of well-chewed tobacco.

Their hands tucked into their pockets, the band members spilled into
the sunlit street. Mitch mimicked a slide trombone wail of George M.'s
"Over There!" shifted into a minor key. His fellow band members picked
up the variation.

That night before an all-white crowd of Spartanburg's finest and the
country club's all-colored waitstaff, James Reese Europe took the bandstand. Dressed in their military finest, pressed and polished, the band
members, forty-eight strong, sat forward at attention. Europe crisply called
out the number, then leaned into the hotspot and whispered, smiling,
"You know, gentlemen, a funny thing about war you'll discover—it
condenses and compresses a whole lotta manhood into a very short
period of time. A lotta people wanna know what kind of men are we?"
Jim Europe, chest round and tall, his cap cocked low to the head so the
men could see his bespectacled eyes without glare, raised his baton and
spoke in a barely audible nonchalant baritone. "They tell me they got a
medal over there of a naked white woman chained to a big black dick.
They wear it round their necks like the iron cross, two, three, four."

The ensemble struck up a hot tempo that increased in speed and volume and complexity with each riff. James Reese Europe's 369th. They
were soon to be known as Hellfighters. Already Osceola could hear it in
their sound. Already the music said they were a tough breed of city cat,
out from the shackles of Jim Crow, feeling their own power, feedin' on it,
"Harlem!" the horns howled, a part of town that black people owned or
felt like it—livin' it, smellin' it, soundin' it, lovin' it, tastin' it, movin'
breathin' bein' free! Had they own taverns, tailors, shoe parlors, barbers,

broad avenues, newspapers, societies, wage jobs, even unions! By steamer, by wagon, by foot they came, from country to small town to the black metropolis, the field hollahs and the moanin' blues travelin' up the New England Constitution, blending with the fast, loud urban rhythms of the factories. Jacksonville to Durham to D.C. to Philly to New York, the Tenderloin, baby, Hell's Kitchen, and from there to Harlem!! And Music! Bending the notes, spitting them out, diesel fuel gushed forth in great arcs of golden sound with so much power it got everybody movin'! Urban wildcatters, prospectin' for their future, their tools trumpets, cornets, sax and tuba, violins, clarinets, bass, flute, and drums. Hellfighters—shoot, even before the war, they was raisin' Cain and the roof! Their leader called himself a continent and built a band to suit the size. When the standard was twenty-eight, Jimmy had forty-eight. He insisted on forty-eight, with Noble Sissle as drum major. Went to Puerto Rico and Cuba to recruit the reed section. While the armies of the world were at stalemate, this big band from Harlem would conquer everywhere it went, killin' em with the music. While the great world seemed to crumble and fall, they offered the possibility of a wholly unimagined new one, sayin', "This is what freedom feel like—this, how it sound!"

The country club's Negro waiters bustled about, unsure of what to make of this bold new music. Ossie was quiet. He stepped out of the truck and stood at the fence listening. A sound so full it could not be contained, a power so rich it could not be resisted. He was a changed man. He had a whole new way of hearing.

When the band struck for the evening, Osceola was surprised that neither Herbie nor Stevie seemed to recognize him. Their drums were drivin'! He intended to tell them as much. Stoking himself, he patted a nervous tempo on his thighs. Herbie stopped packing his gear and cut him a look. When they had left, he was a kid. Now he was almost eyeballin' them. Maybe that was it. Maybe they remembered him as Deke's kin and thus no friend to them. Ossie smiled back. *Yeah, my friend, I'm coming after you. Osceola Turner's cuttin' in.*

The next morning, he joined the army, signed up right there in Spartanburg. Though he was not yet seventeen, he told the recruiter he was a home birth and gave his age as twenty. They told him he had a week to set his affairs in order. He thought he had signed up for the band.

* * *

AT FIRST the war had been good to Deke Turner. He provided protection for Pilar's girls and kept the musicians happy with whatever made them so. The pink-faced new recruits who crowded into the city, the doughboys, flush with innocence and fat with cash, kept the gambling tables busy. For a short while, he was king of the joint, Little Mexico's chief bandito. But as soon as the country actually entered the fight, things changed. Though the sailors roamed the streets three abreast and twelve deep, there was no action. Little Mexico was near shut down. "They say it because my gals hab VD," Pilar moaned. "My gals is clean. Got VD? Dem dam sailors brought it widdem. What we gon do, Deke?"

"Goddam white folks messin' up everythin'. Half the girls locked up." Deke had needed that money that Ossie had hidden away. A few months back, he had gotten himself detained in Georgia. Just travelin' through as he always did with hard cash and half pints to bribe the deputies at the state border, he ran into a roadblock manned by military police with rifles drawn. They commandeered his automobile, put him in cuffs, and threw him in the back of his own car. Before they could discover the seat's false bottom, he escaped—punched out the driver from behind, jumped out, and rolled into the thick country foliage just in time to see his car, along with five crates of good bourbon, crash into the sentries. He convinced a neighborly sharecropper's wife to bust the manacles with an ax, then, following the moonlit backroads to Savannah, he hitched a shrimp hauler up the coast to Charleston. He stayed in the Neckbone now, away from the harbor. Now that the U.S. had entered the war, the city was thick with military police. With an out-of-state warrant, he had double cause for concern. He had to make himself scarce, invisible, sittin' up in Pilar's like some washed-up pimp. Lost his car, his money, workin' on his reputation.

Through the curtain of Pilar's second-floor window, Deke saw his little brother disembark from the trolley and start walking through the square. He watched that gal run and hug up on him. Then she put her hands on her hips and fussed, flirting, he could tell. "Where you been at five whole days?" Osceola grabbed her by the shoulders and spun her around as if he had something to tell her. Deke was glad to see the kid was all right, but furious with Osceola for running off. He watched

Lizzie put her arms around him. Still grasping hands, they walked toward Pilar's together.

Deke flew down the steps and met Ossie at the door. He went to crack Ossie in the jaw with the back of his hand, but Osceola blocked the blow and pushed him back.

"Git yo' hands offa me. I ain't got to take that from you." Stunned, Deke started toward Ossie again, but his opponent stood firm. "You lay a hand to a soljah, you goin' to jail today. I don't answer to you no mo'. I am property of the United States Army. I enlisted!"

Lizzie grabbed Ossie's arm and spun him around, "You what?!"

Deke laughed, "You cain't enlist in nothin', you dumbass. You underage."

"Go tell somebody, why don't you? I signed up in Spartanburg. Gonna serve my country. Gonna join Jim Europe's band." Ossie smiled triumphantly.

Deke responded without emotion, "Your girlfriend don't seem to be too happy 'bout it." Ossie glanced behind him. Lizzie, a swirl of color, had already disappeared.

Deke sprang. He grabbed the front of Ossie's shirt and threw him against the wall. "I'll show you who you serve awright." He pressed a steel forearm against Ossie's throat.

Ossie clinched his teeth and spat back, "I'm goin' inna mornin'. Ain't nothin' you can do."

"Givin' me lip, boy, huh?" Deke released his hold. Ossie bent over, coughing, massaging his windpipe. "You goin' down to that office right now and clear this mess up," Deke continued as he shoved Ossie toward the saloon's swinging doors. Osceola landed hard on the sawdust floor and scurried to his feet. He skipped off in pain, running after Lizzie. Deke bellowed after him, "Come back here, you little shit! Goddam nigguh, I said come back!"

* * *

OSSIE DIDN'T find her at Yum Lee's. He peeked in the barbershop, but didn't ask. Didn't need any more folks all up in his business. He checked at the Bijoux. Flip had not seen her. He searched under the wharf where they first examined each other's changing anatomies, but he couldn't find her. He had outgrown Lizzie by five inches, but he still couldn't catch her, especially if she had a head start, especially if she was mad.

He hitched a ride out King's Highway, past Lizzie's scoutin' tree, the last artifact of their childhood. He found her, sitting on the front stoop of her family's run-down homestead. Hands in his pockets, he walked up the path flanked by Mah Bette's garden of herbs, vegetables, and wildflowers. Lizzie was combing her hair, having just washed it. The cans of cotton seed oil, beeswax, and petroleum jelly scented with sandalwood were lined up next to her, denying him a seat. She sectioned off a quadrant of the coppery mesh atop her head and began the process of braiding it. She layered on the oil and the scent and dried the section with a dishtowel, then pulling it taut divided it into three prongs that she laced through the fingers of her two hands. Picking through each dense, resilient lock in silence, she braided nine tight fat plaits that looked like half-smoked cigars. Her movements were slow and deliberate. When she finished, she twisted one braid on top of another till they ringed her skull in a crown.

Ossie stood there the whole time. He scuffed at the dusty soil. "I didn't mean fuh yuh to find out like that, Lizzie. Meant to tell you myself. I had to do somethin', somethin' to get away from Deke."

"From me too, look like."

"I just know this is the right thing to do. Yo' Mah Bette always talkin' 'bout signs. I seen Jim Europe and I signed up. I'ma git inna band. You watch!"

"I ain't watchin nothin'. Leave my great-gran'mama outta this! We coulda had a job with Black Patti if not for yo' sorry behind. Shiverin' like a yellah dawg. I don't need you, Osceola Turner. You was holdin' me back."

"I just come to say good-bye, then."

"Why? I got nothin' to say to you. Nobody give a shit about you."

". . . Ain't like I'mo be gone forever."

"Just give me my half of our money."

"Deke took it."

"What?"

"That's why I run off in the first place. I—"

She jumped up. "You let that nigguh take our money!"

"Don't do nothin' stupid!"

"Stupid? You got that pretty much covered on your own. You told me you was the best one to be keepin' it. What kinda moron leave a stash so easy to find?! You just gonna let him do that?"

He stood beside her and grabbed her arms. She squirmed and tried to pull away. He held her fast, his eyes piercing and earnest. "Listen, Lizzie, I can do this. We won't have to stash no money. In New York, Jim Europe got a musicians' union. Colored run every band in the city. That's a better connection than waitin' for any ol' touring show comin' through town. Black Patti's the past, Jim Europe's the future. We could make it to New York on our own! New York, Lizzie. You dancin' and me leadin' the band? Our band. Be just like the Castles and James Reese Europe. Lizzie Winrow and Osceola Turner's Colored Troubadours!"

"What about our money? You just gon run?"

"I ain't runnin' no more. I'm just goin' cross the water for a minute. I'll be back. I'll send you my earnings."

"Keep it." She pulled away, collected her things, and marched off toward the woods. "You're goin' to chase your dream, Osceola Turner, didn't ask nothin' 'bout mine."

That night he couldn't sleep. He wanted to keep his anger at her fresh, but it plagued him through the night and into the morning. His drumsticks in his back pocket, he beat out his anxiety with a hambone, quick-paced paradiddles and syncopated wordless speech, till his thighs and ribs were bruised. He stayed out of Deke's sight until the birds announced a new day.

Waiting on the depot platform for the local train to take him to camp, he saw her approaching. She stood beside him without looking at him, the air dancing between them.

"I got a letter from muh sister yesterday," she began, "from New York. She got two girls and a baby boy now. I thought to myself, Mama kin send me up there to help out. I'll be in New York and see my sister, too. But then I thought, naw, I'mo stay here with Ossie. We gon have us a show. We gon work on it. I was willing to give up what I wanted for you. You didn't think so much of me, I spose."

She was carrying the regular charm to deliver to Sullivan when he arrived on the 5:15 Daybreaker from Richmond. She reached inside her blouse and gave the charm to Osceola instead. "Mah Bette sent this for to keep you safe."

14

Absurdity and its consequences. Nations fell into war like stampeding cattle over a cliff. No retreat or advance, just a perpetual stalemate, the lines of defense and offense shifting back and forth a mere two hundred miles in four years. Four years and four million dead. By the time Private Osceola Turner hit the shore, the Germans had pulled in the Turks, the Brits the Australians, the French the Senegalese, and Europe was punch-drunk and weary, staggering at the prospect of relief. The Americans arrived, so fresh, they called them doughboys. The black ones they called sable for the shine of their skin in the sunlight.

Hard livin' and hittin' full force on the coasts of France, the original four hundred colored stevedores working the port towns of Brest, Navarre, Marseilles, and Nice swelled to fifty thousand in a matter of three months. But this was no tour of the Riviera, the colored soldiers joked. The Service and Supply Corps stood for "S.O.S.! Niggas need he'p! Stead of a rifle or a shiv, give you a shovel an a pick," they chanted, "Say, Service and Supply, mean S.O.S.! Niggas need he'p!"

They unloaded five thousand tons a day in twenty-four-hour shifts. The French were stunned by their capacity and by their song. Together, the men sounded one note that was simultaneously a chord, in harmonies so close they were dissonant though whole, broken but holding as one great rolling arc of power—the baritone voices of a hundred men, a palimpsest. Might was subverted into song. Like the clay figures of saints cloaking the aura of orishas, the words spoke another language in the tones. Locked in the harmonies and rhythms, the hammer of Ogun cracked, driving them onward.

These were rhythms and a unity of action Osceola was used to. He had heard these harmonies all his life from the stevedores and draymen on the docks of Charleston. Most of the fellows in his unit were frightened backwoods, up-country boys, scared conscripts out of county lockup or sharecroppers taking the place of a planter's son. A few were independent farmers, who would find their land stolen upon return.

> "Pickin' the Cotton, Cuttin' the Cane,
> Haulin' Tobacco, Prayin' fo' Rain,
> Listen up Cap'n, Ain't it a Shame,
> We in this Fight but, Nothin' Ain't Changed."

Their song, a slow bent-note dirge marking the rhythms of field labor blended with the faster-paced waterfront jig rhythms, emitted a whole new sound that fascinated and intoxicated him.

Some had come to fight, to show that black men deserved respect. Others saw no reason to go off and defend a country that terrorized them. "Say President gon make de world safe fo' democracy. He got the dem part right." The vast majority were draftees. A handful, like Osceola, had enlisted. All, regardless, were consigned, confined to the work of slaves—digging latrines, building barracks, hauling, peelin' potatoes, mess duty, and digging graves. They were manual laborers again, marched and drilled in coffles, bossed by poor white, tobacco-sluggin' gang leaders shipped over from bayou work camps and transformed into sergeants. The officers, who were also white and mostly from the South, publicly humiliated the Negro troops. Example—the order for mandatory VD treatment for the colored: "Short arm inspection!"

Osceola stood in line, listening to the disgruntled banter. "It's the officers theyselves got the highest count. Got they own private whorehouse givin' em the clap, won't let nigguhs eben into the town." The American command made sure the French understood their policy toward Negroes. Colored troops were forbidden to fraternize with the French. You could get jailed for complaining, shot for doing it. Osceola braced himself as the duty nurse washed his penis with bichloride of mercury and gritted his teeth through the five-minute injection of argyrol. Just as the real pain hit him, they slathered his johnson with two grams of calomel ointment and pronounced him good to go. His legs in a momentary bow, he hobbled out of the infirmary cursing under his breath, "Ain't never even had no woman. How I'mo get VD? Didn't sign up for this!"

Such had been Osceola's naivety, he had thought "signing up" with the army meant that he could sign up for wherever he wanted to go. His goal was to find James Reese Europe and that band from New Yawk. Word of their musical prowess had spread to all of the colored units throughout France. There were other military bands out of Chicago, Texas, and D.C., but hands down, Europe's troupe was a cut above, a breed unto itself, the King's musicians! Osceola had met the man once, but he had been so in awe, he had not even said he could play. He wasn't going to allow that to happen again. Convinced he could cut it, he practiced numbers in his mind. "Take that! Top this!" He still held out hope that he could get to Lieutenant Europe and play for the man and prove his mettle in a face-off, but now his only thought was to make it back to the barracks without fainting from fear, relief, or pain, take your pick. Handling the silk-pouched talisman round his neck, he spoke under his breath, "Juss what kinda charm this pozed to be, Mah Bette?"

Just then, a military sedan sped by, stopped abruptly, and backed up. Osceola stood at attention thinking, *If another one of these crackuhs mess wid me today . . .* as a thin, delicate youth with an oversized cap and a crisp new officer's uniform hopped out of the vehicle and approached him. He was a full head shorter than Osceola; his cap grazed dangerously close to his eyelashes. "At ease, soldier! . . . Hey Ossie, it's me," the cap whispered, "Flip." Osceola remained at attention, eying his boyhood partner in crime, now a commissioned officer out of the Citadel, "One of South Carolina's finest!" Still intent upon being Osceola's one and only white man, Flip had a new scheme.

"With you in the saddle, I could ride in one of those little sidecars—hopefully away from the front and toward gay Paree." Flip put his petite hand on Ossie's shoulder and clucked, as he pulled the tarp off the spanking new bike. "A Triumph Model H Dispatch—English! American-issued Harleys only go sixty. This baby clocks in at seventy-five."

When Ossie first got a look at the bike, he stood mute. Sitting astride it, he fell in love! Flip's plan to get him reassigned to the U.S. Army motorcycle corps, which by some strange stroke of military fate was primarily colored, sounded fine, but no big city car on the road, no Buick 25 or Cadillac Landaulette had prepared him for the sensation of straddling the curved leather seat, gripping the sculpted handlebars, and imagining the sleek, spoked wheels spin beneath him in perfect symmetry. It was the most beautiful assemblage of polished metal and chrome with a wasp waist and high behind, luscious curved arms, silver slippers and a poundin', pumpin' heart. He knew immediately the bike was his Miss Lizzie.

"You owe me big-time, brothuh," Flip chimed.

"How I'm to learn to drive it?"

"Already told 'em you could."

McKinley never did make a very good plan by himself. Fast as the scheme got cooked, the fire got too hot. Flip's dreams for Paris were dashed when the commanding general of the 2nd Army, General Robert Bullard, decided to embarrass the standing colonel of the 92nd, Charles Ballou, whom he hated. "Bullard and Ballou," scowled Flip, "sound like a bad minstrel act." General Bullard chose to seal his disdain for Colonel Ballou's nigguh troops by proving them incapable of battle and the colored officers under his command unfit for service. Orders came down that the new colored divisions coming in were to be sent directly to the front. As soon as Flip surmised that the courier routes would take him in the wrong direction—toward the battle—he immediately determined that his driver could make it on his own.

Country boys—draftees, from Texas, Oklahoma, Alabama, the Carolinas—were hit the first night at 2:30 A.M., with a rolling artillery barrage of three thousand seven hundred guns, twenty to thirty shells a minute. Sounded like the Devil's freight train roarin' straight outta Hell. Airplanes, machine guns, and cannon with trajectories a hundred times the distance capability of weapons used two years before were complemented by a new arsenal of barbed wire, tanks, and gas. In the strobe flashes of gunfire, the night sky was alight with a ghostly, pastel cluster of clouds. Mustard gas, named after the color of its mists, lingered with the smell of a perfumed bath, and after twelve hours caused the body to blister and rot from the outside in, the pain so excruciating the stricken had to be strapped to the stretchers. The second wave of gas, smelling of rotten fish, would drown its victims in their own lungs, while the pineapple pepper chlorine caused a slow conscious death, mixed with streams of delirium. The scene was madness.

As his motorcycle sped toward the front—headlights off—Osceola saw a surge of men running, falling back, their eyes round with terror or grimaced in fear. The roadway was clogged with sidelined trucks, the drivers squawking in terror out the windows. Behind them a fleet of flatbeds loaded with the heavy howitzer guns that were to provide the fire cover for the assault had taken a direct hit and were strewn about like the toys of a tempestuous child. The sky exploded, bursting stars of flame, cataracts of bullets. The night rained fire. The bike zigzagged, skidded, and tumbled on its side, ripping the side carriage from the wheel. As it spun off behind him, Ossie wailed, "Whoa, Miss Lizzie! Shake, shake that shimmy!" He righted the bike and pressed on. His body crouched low and shoulders hunched, he pushed up the fuel full throttle. Miss Lizzie growled, bucked, and screamed, the engine turning red hot. The sounds locked in his mind, a furious, relentless percussion. In the thick of battle, riding sixty-five miles per hour, with no headlights, his helmet knocked back by the wind, out from under Deke's thumb, holding tight to his firecracker of a girl, Osceola felt himself a man among men. Gray shrouds of smoke gave way to giant yellow bulging clouds, pushing the winds back. "Gas! Damn! Hit it, baby!" Holding on to his Lizzie, he could outrun God—outrun the wind, outrun death—"Shit yeah! Go girl!"

The troops at the front had lost contact. Isolated, they were now in the center of the siege. Ordered to go forward at all costs, they charged in waves over the top of the bunkers and evaporated like beads of water on a hot skillet. Osceola sought an authority in the chaos. He pulled a folded message from his satchel and stood before a white officer, his face covered with soot, his body instinctively flinching at the assault of sounds, making the very ground tremble.

"What do they mean, 'Advance'? They just gave us an order to retreat!"

"Yes, sir."

The wide-eyed officer crumpled the missive in disgust. "Advance, retreat. Advance, retreat. Four times we've tried to attack! What do they think we—" A machine gun bullet richocheted off the ground, blasted through the officer's forehead and out the back of his skull, burrowing into the mudbank.

"Jesus!" Osceola grabbed the message from the still-quivering hand. Holding his helmet fast to his head, he crouched low and moved swiftly through the maze of trenches, his nimble legs skipping past the singular scenes of war, Elegua's crooked dance of death among the dazed, wounded, and gassed. A boy squatted, shaking and praying on his knees, "Help me, please help me, Lawd, Jesus, uh Mama!" The soldier beside him writhed in solitary agony, a hole blown through his shoulder the size of a softball. A pair of legs dangled from the top of the trench. Another rookie enlistee leaned against the earthen wall laughing, holding a rifle he had first beheld only three weeks before. The noise shook the earth like rolling thunder, the sky of misted smoke bright as a day with a thousand exploding suns.

"Who's in charge here? Commander? Com . . . holy!" He came upon another officer. His tight jaws clenching the stub of an unlit cigarette, the young captain stepped over and through the tumult of men, checking to see who was dead, wounded, or stable enough to go on. Osceola fell in behind him and barked over the din, "Courier Corps, sir! With an urgent message from General Bullard."

"Where yuh been?"

"Command lost contact."

"Yuh think?"

"The troops are to stage another advance, sir. I'm to return with your response."

"Sent us into barbed wire with no wire cutters. Rifles with no bayonets. No fire cover, not one grenade, not even a friggin' signal flare. Advance with what?!"

"Sir? Your commander, sir."

"How's the song go? Over there!"

Ossie came upon the major, squatting in a ditch . . . crying.

"Sir, I'm in the Courier Corps. I have to return with your reply. My orders are to report back to central command the state of your—"

The world went silent. A trench mortar clipped his sentence and blew his body into the air with the power of a freight train. The bursting shell created a vacuum of silence that sucked up the air, then released it in a rush of wind, pulling the fluids from his spine into his brain. When his body hit the ground, his bones made the sound of a light bulb breaking. Then everything went white.

> Miss Lizzie Mae had her a way,
> Of walkin' down the street,
> That would make the sidewalk sizzle beneath her feet,
> Yes, Lizzie Mae had her a way,
> Of walkin' down the street,
> That could make a hungry fellah forget to eat . . .

Snatches of song, flashes of memory and conversation mixed with the pain, the gulps for breath, and the blinding whiteness of the sun as it split the horizon. The fierce night battle had lulled, it was quiet now. An incongruous symphony of forest birds heralded the day from the trees. Ossie awakened. Not dead. He opened his eyes cautiously, the slight traces of pepper gas still lingering. The landscape beneath the ashen morning sun revealed a field of slain and wounded, heaps of torn contorted sculptures emerging from water-filled shell-holes or fused with the broken carcasses of trees and split boulders. Abandoned and mangled artillery was draped with scraps of flesh, some still quivering with life. A tumbleweed spiral of barbed wire rolled of its own will. Amidst the pitched battle of the rats and crows over the bounty of corpses and the undulating whine of the flies, a defiant crimson poppy arched against the wind. The patient maggots gnawing through flesh made the sound of drying sheets, rustling in the breeze.

His head dropped back. While machine guns spat in competing languages, the whistle of metal sliced through the wind and the distant crack of sniper fire imploded in his head. A piece of metal was twisted into his leg, pinning him down. The drone of a high-flying squadron alerted him to the prickly smell of pineapples that soon invaded the air. Osceola tore at his uniform and ripped off a strip. He quickly urinated into the cloth and held it to his face, pressing it into his nose, mouth, and eyes as one of the old guys from the S.O.S. had told him, "It the only way to shield against the gas what smell like pineapple. Smoke helmit ain't no good again' it and they ain't gon give colored no smoke helmit no way. Come to say, they dint eben gib most boys no reglar helmit." Breathing in the rank, lifesaving smell of his own piss, Osceola smiled and drifted off.

Memories, the music, the trumpet and drums of a hot-tempoed band, blended with Lizzie's voice and she swirled her hips and sashayed away to the jungle beat of the drum.

> Miss Lizzie Mae had her a way,
> Of walkin' down the street,
> That would make the sidewalk sizzle beneath her feet.
> Yes, Lizzie Mae had her a way,
> Of walkin' down the street,
> That could make a hungry fellah forget to eat . . .

* * *

HE HAD been lying there for three nights. German patrols were nearing. It was their policy, when they came across black wounded, to shoot them, then bayonet the heart and private parts. In the darkness he heard them whispering in German. Their boots sank into the mud and their bayonets made sticking sounds. His eyes glazed, he lay there, not breathing as they slowly moved toward him. A band of pain squeezed his ribs, stemming his cough. A heaviness sat on his chest, challenging his breath. It was Lizzie or her spirit, vexing him, just like when they were children. She had his arms pinned down to each side.

"A starin' contest," she said.

"What the heck is that?"

"A starin' contest. You look straight at me and I look straight at you. Whoever can stare the longest win. Cain't smile, cain't laugh, cain't blink. Go!"

"I ain't doin' no sech thang," Ossie muttered.

"Yes you is. First one blinks loses, or I'll just sit here all day."

A young German replacement paused over his body. A flaxen lock fell over the youth's brow. Osceola held fast to his breath and stared like a dead man. Though he did not move, his eyes began to tear. The youth bent down and whispered, "I like your music, I like the Jass." The youth smiled and chuckled, with the hint of a wheeze and, for the second time in his life, death passed Osceola by.

"Remember the first time we snuck in the Bijoux and seen a motion picture show? Was about uh army on horses comin' in a charge, they swords raised and the dust flyin'. We bolt out that theater, thinkin' they was comin' straight fuh us."

"No, baby, it ain't nothin' like that. This war ain't nuthin' like no picture show."

Lizzie laughed. "Alla this to git inna band?"

He was aware that he might be left there to die, but he couldn't move his legs, couldn't get them out from under the twisted carcass of metal that had fallen upon him.

In the whirls of smoke, Lizzie's face appeared again, bright with freckles across her broad button nose. "Awrite, they goan. Now gib me yo han'." She was kneeling on the edge of a tree limb. They must have been no more than seven or eight, stealin' peaches from Yum Lee's. She was on the limb and he was on the ground, his arm outstretched but not quite touching her distended fingers. "Come on, reach!" Slowly, with his one good arm, Osceola dragged his broken body backward toward the bunker.

✳ ✳ ✳

"HOW COME y'ain't in uniform, nigguh?"

"Got flat feet. Say I cain't walk fah." Deke kept his eyes cast to the ground and lumbered in place with fake humility. He couldn't bring himself to say "sir."

"Flat feet or no, where yo papuhs?" Deke had gone out in the day, looking for his brother. The military police brought him in for not registering and discovered the year-old outstanding warrant from Georgia. He had escaped then, only to be returned, his feet and legs double-bound in chains that were looped through heavy iron wrist shackles that bit into his skin. His fingers tingled. To keep them from losing sensation, he kept drawing his palms into fists.

For years, it had been standard practice for many a Southern sheriff to lease out his prisoners to neighboring plantation owners. Farmers could

supplement the local field labor with vagrants, charged with miscellaneous crimes, committed or invented, such as walking down the road or,
in Deacon's case, driving. Between the draft and the colored runnin' off
to the North to the tales of jobs and fast free livin', as the war dragged on,
scores of Southern planters found themselves short of workers. Before he
could think of how to get word to Pilar of his whereabouts, Deke's "time"
had been sold to a turpentine plantation. In a lot with twelve others,
he was shipped off to some God-knows-where swampland, harvesting
pine sap for a crackuh with a thick, crusty mustache and eyes with no
color at all—called himself the Keeper. *They posed to be buying yoah time.
Time be yoah life.*

Weak from fever and hunger, a young inmate had slackened in his duties. The Keeper had Deke and another bulky captive hold the man down
while he laid the snake strokes of a whip across the prisoner's back.
"Please, boss, please, why don't you juss kill me?" he whimpered, the thick
grooves of broken skin already swelling with blood and pus. Without
speaking, the Keeper took out his pistol and shot the youth through the
temple. The body spasmed and went slack in Deke's hands. *That gal done
this. Come between me and my brothuh.*

Thinking only of escape, each day he methodically harvested the
thick amber resin from the scruffy pine groves that encircled the marsh-
lands. First breaking the bark, then cutting the groove, then screwing the
pipes into the pulp, Deke seemed a productive worker. He then "set the
box," boring more deeply into the stringy heart of the tree, draining it of
its blood, the glutinous sap that made paint thinner rosin, and enamel for
battleships. The slowness of the rhythm bothered him, the closeness of
the swamp pulled on his lungs. The thickness of the fumes made his breathing short. Sometimes the mud came up to his hips, the acrid juice burning his fingers so the skin turned to scales. His nails, once buffed and
polished weekly, were cracked and yellowed on the surface, blackened at
the tips. The rhythm of captive voices pulled him down like an undertow,
biting at him like the water moccasins, whose black flashing bodies slithered beneath the swamp water's surface. Deacon Turner, who used to
wear polished spats, now wore shoes handmade from old tires. The resin
from the trees stuck to the treads in the soles and made crackling sounds
as he walked.

His first pair of shoes had had metal caps from sarsaparilla bottles. He had danced the feelings down then—hammered them down with speed, whirling within the circle that always formed around him and ending on one knee with his cap extended, ready for coin, prayin' for paper. The morning that Dora May pranced by him, she walked right through his circle of patrons as if it were not there, as if he were not there. Her straw hat tipped low, purse held with both hands, and her skirt rustling at her heels, she stepped out of the way of white folk in a solo doseydoe, oblivious to all but her own dream. By compulsion and habit, he followed her. He was thinking he might snatch that purse she held so tightly, but when he came upon her, when he came near, he wanted only to impress her, to bring joy to her startling blue eyes and somehow to his own heart. He came alert in his hammock and shook off the reverie. The sodden hemp ties slung between two iron hooks, whined with his weight. He brought his arm to his forehead. *Got to keep focused. Go over the plan again in your head.*

"Hey Lawdeh, Lawdeh, Lawd! Don't you know I'm in bad shape tonight. Me an dat gull sho gon have a fight!" Rawley was rattlin' drunk from the hooch, slurring his words through the hiccups. Even in jail, Deke was ambitious. Tom Winrow had schooled him back in the day when he was a youngster. "You kin make the shine outta anything," Win had boasted, "grapes, potato—any growin' thing kin ferment, most anythin' once livin'." Deke used this knowledge now to befriend the old-timer. Tomato soup and potato rinds made a potent, if bitter brew.

> "I puttin' ev'day, money in yo' hand,
> Spect you to say I'mo be yo'man,
> Prettieh woman Ah evuh seen,
> I declare nah, she run down to New Orleans,
> Yuh go down juss tuh show yo' gold,
> Yuh gonna die someplace now nice n low . . ."

Rawley stayed in his cups. He had been locked up so long, he was a trustee. Too old to do much hard labor, he still had the sharp, piercing voice that drove the gangs forward. With rhythm and wit, he painted shorthand pictures of the outside, wrote unsent letters to sweethearts, cussed the cheaters and backstabbers and laughed. The simplicity of his phrases told bits of stories that each man knew to be his own.

> "I putting ev'day money in yo hand,
>   Come own, pretty woman, let me be yoah man,
>   Prettieh woman that ah evuh seen,
>   I declare now she run down to New Orleans,
>   Yuh go down just tuh show yo gold,
>   Yuh gonna die someplace now nice and low . . ."

Stackin' the tins in the predawn setup for mess, Rawley was still drunk from the shine Deke had passed him the night before. The Keeper wandered over, asking, "You think it's nice work doin' yo singin'? Think you can do moah if you slack off?"

"Nah suh . . . It what makes it go mo bettah when you singin', you don't have, you uh, you can forgit, you see, an the time pass on way, but if you juss get yosef devoted on somethin', it look like it be hard for you to make it, so you make a day, day be longer it look like, so to keep his mind from bein', keep his mind from bein', keep his mind from bein' . . ."

Deke cursed silently, without flinching, "Crazy redbone still toah up, gon be too juiced to hit it." This was the morning the Keeper chose to hold a conversation.

"I learn dat song in Florida."

"On the farm?"

"Yeah, county farm."

"What it take . . . to be a good leader, Rawley?"

"What you mean, Keep?"

"Yoah singin', lead singuh?"

"Stay in time wid duh ax, is mose potent part, I spoze."

Runnin' off at the goddam mouf, dat old man gon get us both kilt. Deke had no choice in the partnership. Rawley coughed blood like his mama used to do, but the old man knew the swamps. He was the last of the Yamassee, a descendant of natives who first roamed the land. As a trustee Rawley walked on his own without shackles, and he had an outside woman who cooked for the camp sometimes. She had helped plot the escape. Rawley knew where the boat was hidden. He knew the landscape. Deacon was counting on him to steer through the channels, the acres of Georgia bayou that surrounded the camp. "The turns kin git you turnt round so you wind up runnin' right back to Charlie." Rawley continued, "They keep the dogs hungry and set em on the trail as well, ringin' the outlands. You kin forgit swimmin'. If the snakes doan git yuh, gators will. Buddy almost made it once. Hid 'neath the watuh wid a reed as a breathin' straw. They pour kerosene atop the water and set it afire. He come up fuh air, torched hisself each time. Burnin' n drownin', both." Rawley's cautionary tale did not dissuade him. Deke had his mind set. As if sensing the plan, the Keeper kept pressing Rawley with small talk. "Been on line long time, spoze?"

"Seventeen yeah, come Monday, Keep, mighty long time."

Deke's Asiatic eyes watched without looking. Skin stretched taut over the muscle and bone of his face, square and full—Benin or Olmec. His head shaved to keep off the lice, sweat streaming down his face in the noonday sun, he shone like silver. The sound of hammer on bedrock, the saw blade, whiplash rhythm of his feet, his heartbeat.

"Monday it is then. Two days . . . Take care of baby and baby will take care of you."

✳ ✳ ✳

DEACON TURNER grew up a feral child. His own mah died when he was three or six, depending upon how he counted. She had come to work for Pilar, doing laundry and cleanin'. "She pretty nuff, but nommo good on she back," Pilar had casually surmised. He took charge, dancing in the streets for pennies. He lived under the plank walk beneath the docks and ran the wards at Orange Street Orphanage. Among the stray and abandoned children on the wharf, he was the leader. Before he was ten, he had lost three of his merry band. Justine was hit by a milk wagon, Ori got the influenza. Robert, whose rickets curled his body against its own will, finally could not feed himself, his wizened eyes confessing that he had not the heart for survival. Deke, on the other hand, tore into the discarded bones and greens from the garbage with no thought at all but that. Surviving. He had to. Be strong or die.

Then one of the new gals—a redbone from the hills, puree-blood some said—got knocked up. Had hid it till her water broke mid-day.

Deke set out to find Aunt Sibby, now so old she walked with her cane handle by her breast, raising her head in intervals to see where she was going. Just as he ushered her into the tiny shuttered room, the whore started gushing blood, screaming, her skin turning gray and the sweat turning cold. The old woman instructed Deke to hold the girl down as she examined her. "Birth cord wrapped round the baby neck," she pronounced. "The more she push, she gon strangle him. Stay in the chamber an gon drown. My hands too old fuh dis. You gon hab to help me, Deacon."

Following the midwife's instructions, he eased his small hand along the birth canal wall and felt for the baby's shoulder and head, then loosened the cord from around the unborn child's neck with his fingers. The baby shot out, floating on a thick black-red flood that seeped into the worn straw tick mattress and formed a corona around the new mother as she breathed her last. Deke took the baby in his small, stocky arms. His skin mottled, bruised blue and purple from his trials, the infant convulsed in a jagged, coughing outrage. Sibby took no challenges in the naming, "Call dis em Osceola. Em uh fightuh."

"Em muh brother."

"Now you done brought em here, make sure nuthin' happen to he."

"Why you call me Deacon?"

The old seer smiled, her watery eyes turned blue-gray from seeing far beyond the world of that room. "I seen you watchin'. Standin' there like you in church. You got sompin to watch over now. Your whole life."

* * *

DEKE DID watch over Osceola. He enjoyed seeing the boy progress with the music. Jocelyn and the band men took to schoolin' him. Deke had outgrown the music, himself, the dancin'. He did, however, enjoy the art of enforcement, protection. His wide chest sporting custom suits, his eyes so narrow they sometimes looked shut, he had so perfected his skill that he rarely had to use force, seldom had to raise his voice. "We can do this my way, or the hard way. It's up to you."

Tom Winrow had taught him a few things besides the secret to making good hooch. "I'ma teach you what my daddy taught me," Win had said. "I kin teach yuh how to read cards front an back and mark a new deck, but knowin' how to read people is moah important. Tug of a sleeve means he bout to lie. Twitch of the eye or cheek, it be a bluff. Slight cough mean he don't really wanna give up. Folk what eyes dart to the side is hidin.' " Deke's narrow eyes watched as he was told, only to see his teacher lose his way. Soon as she was born, soon as the color set, all the Neckbone knew that Elma, his firstborn, warnt his child. "A China doll, maybe the Chinaman's," people would laugh behind Win's back. Deke had grown up around whores and crooks. He knew duplicity, but he never understood why Win had stayed with the seamstress, how he walked proud with one step, broken with the next. *Soft, over a woman. Weak, over a trick.*

The fog was hanging low in the trees. The crescent-shaped moon, low in the sky, sliced through the stream of jagged clouds. He was on the run, crouched low to the ground, putting on speed. From childhood, Deke could run the fastest of anyone, forward or back. Lifting his legs up, his arms movin', like wings, low to the ground, he flew, his feet barely touching the ground. It was a sacred long run, following old Yamassee trails.

Rawley held up, panting, grabbing his chest, holding himself up with his hands on his knees, panic in his voice, "What I'm to do?" Deke slung the old man over his shoulder like a bag of sticks and pressed on, Rawley directing him with his loose arm as they made their way through the underbrush. But then he stumbled, slipping over mounds of sodden leaves and roots, the hounds in his ear, on his heels, crossing his scent. The two men toppled over each other. Rawley wound up almost sitting. He waved Deke on with his hand.

"I ain't leavin' you," Deke insisted.

"Stay, and we both worse'n dead."

"I don't know the way," pleaded Deke.

"Then you will not succeed."

Deke set out alone. His feet and legs sank into the earth. He could feel hands, pulling him down, clutching at his feet, the vines curling round his ankles, as he stole away. "Take me, take me, don't leave me," grabbing at his ankles, sucking him into the mud, bringing him to his knees. His bulky body fell to the side and he went spinning, tumbling down a ravine to an algae-cloaked stream. Surrendering to his instincts, he knelt, rubbing the green, thick mulch from the water on his arms and chest, smearing his bare flesh with blood-soaked earth mixed with tears. He wrapped himself in the cloak of clinging leaves, taking on the scent of the bayou, then continued low to the ground, his feet skimming the surface of the stream, hurdling the felled trees, dancing atop the bones and rotten flesh of lost souls. He dragged himself up and pressed on into the night, the rain, the sweet heavenly rain covering his escape—the thunder shaking the ground in syncopated time. A ball of lightning burst across his path. He could hear the dogs in the distance, yelping like children. The lightning had frightened them. The black sky cracked open and took him in. He ran with the wind's howling in his ears. He had traveled up the back roads. Hell Hole Swamp, this weren't nuthin'—he was free.

He awoke the next day in the boat, the bright sun in the yellow white sky burning his eyes. He dragged his leg over the side and collapsed by the oar and slept. The dugout rocked to the gentle rhythm of waves in open water. He had reached the river. He lay flat till the night struck, then paddled slowly with a sure shoulder stride, making good time. The clang and hammer of the sickle and pick breaking rocks into stone, the crack of an ax 'gainst the pulp of a tree, still hung in his ear. Scanning the shore, he spied a colored vagrant, a wanderer washing his face. Deke paddled downstream, then doubled back by foot, tracking the unsuspecting stranger. Boulder in hand, he swiped the man's skull from behind, spinning him around as he fell, then leaned over the stranger and smashed in his face. He exchanged clothes with the dead man and nestled the body in the hollow of the dugout. As he set the canoe afloat downstream again, he cursed the hobo for having no shoes. He would have to wear the tire treads a bit longer.

At the crossroads Rawley had described, Deke found the woman waiting. She spoke to him in her language, knowing, by the absence of the old man, that Rawley was all but dead to her. In a tongue Deke could not understand, she cursed him and walked away. He straightened his jacket and moved on, staying out of sight of the main road until he got to the state line. "By the time I reach Charleston, I'll have me a new suit, a new money clip, and a new woman." He got back to Charleston, and found Pilar's, the whole red light district, shut down and boarded up by order of the United States Navy. No place he could run, no place safe. He retreated to a sanctuary from his youth, back to the Neckbone. Every time he ran away from Orange Street, the sewing lady had given him food. Would set it right there on the stoop for him. *Hide out under there. The storm cellar. Wait for the night train or steamer maybe.* A December chill in the air, he could see his breath. White like a dead man's.

* * *

LIZZIE HAD no intention of following in her mother's footsteps, workin' up under Yum Lee. Still, being a duet of one wasn't much fun. Pilar was not too fond of her, blaming her not just for Ossie but for her father and Deke runnin' off as well. Even the Bijoux was a bust. With Flip gone, she had to sit in the crowded colored peanut gallery section like everyone else, nothing special. Dancing on the street she was more likely to get catcalls than loose change and a rough arm-twistin' from the police. Her lithe adolescent body was giving way to something else. If it wasn't the police it was the mattress girls harassing her for clogging the trade. Makin' money, havin' fun? She wasn't doing much of either on her own. Still, she had no intention of following in her mother's footsteps.

She stomped down the crooked wooden steps. Her father, then Elma, now Ossie. Gone since August and here it was December and she had not heard from him. The confusion of anger and worry distressed her even more. The night air was brisk. She hurried toward the cellar door. "Firewood, the woman want firewood. Ain't you never heard of no coal?! Or gas?!" She alternately imitated Mah Bette and her mother, both fussing at her. "I won't stand for this, one say. Help your mother out some, the other say. Ol' yelluh Yummy Lee sittin' up there not sayin' nothin'! Just once, could one of you act like you could give a good goddamn about me?" She sucked her teeth. The wick of the lamp began to flicker in the glass as she lifted the heavy cellar door. The air within was cool and clammy. The cellar would be damp with soot and cobwebs and rats scurrying. She didn't like the feel of it. She thought to turn around, but she defied her fear and loudly descended the stairs. *Lizzie Winrow 'fraid of the dark? I ain't 'fraid of nothin'!*

She stepped onto the damp cellar floor and immediately felt something sticking like gum or glue to the soles of her shoes. It made a crackling sound and tugged at the weight of each foot as she walked. The sound was odd, like the rattling of bones beneath her feet. The air smelled of turpentine. The lantern hit Deke's eyes. "Whatchu doin' here?" she asked, startled.

"I need you to bring me some clothes and some money."

She scoffed, "I ain't bringin' you nothin'."

He grabbed her by the neck and pushed her against the wall. The lantern clattered to the ground, sputtering out. "You my brother's woman. That make us family." He kissed her hard on the lips. She bit him. He slapped her and kissed her again. Full on the lips. Pressed his mouth to hers, breathing her in, frantic. He pulled her to the ground, pushing her against the cold stones, and got on top of her. He placed his hand over her mouth. "Sh Sh shshsh." Her skin was soft. Her breast smelled of salt and sweat and flowers. Her breath was hot, steaming through his fingers in muzzled screams. He tore at her, pushed up her skirt, pushed inside her. She squirmed beneath him, attempting to scratch, claw, her arms pinned down by his size. He pressed his wrists against her neck. Let her know he would break it. She was tight, unyielding, then gave way. Holding her, he thrust himself inside her. She stopped the muted screams. His hand slipped from her mouth, agape.

Outside, sailors headed back to their ships bound for war, their singing in unison. He had not known she was untouched. He laughed to himself, as he stood up and adjusted his clothes. She didn't move but lay in the position he left her. Girls at the parlor, he had seen all types—sex fiends, addicts, cutters, fucked by they daddies, ruined by a white man, waifs, dummies, business women, entertainers. Never anything pure. Untouched. What a fool his brother had been. *Wasn't even bangin' huh.*

He found Sully in the rail yard, bummed some clothes and cash, hitched a ride to Charlotte. *Travel up and work the mines for a while. Nobody to ask questions.* He made a little on the side, good for a new suit and a haircut. Didn't know how he would deal with the girl.

15

OSCEOLA CAME TO IN A FRENCH ARMY HOSPITAL, WHITE-habited nuns bustling silently through the colored ward. He quickly learned from the GI beside him that one of the patients was Lieutenant Europe, recovering from a gas attack. The wounded officer, separated only by a surgical curtain, wandered in and out of delirium. "Come on boys, over the top! Steadfast, keep your proper distance. Minenwafer comin'—look out! Don't start bombin' with those hand grenades. Rat-tat-tat-tat. Machine guns! Holy spades! Alert! Gas! Put on your mask!" Despite having one arm in a sling and his leg in a full cast, Osceola was determined to see his idol again. When the room seemed quiet, he cajoled a young novitiate to help him into a vacant wheelchair and roll him toward the end of the ward where the officer lay. Osceola saw that the lieutenant's eyes were heavily bandaged, and backed away.

"Who's there?" The lieutenant's head turned, his two gauzed eyes pinned squarely on Ossie.

"Private Osceola Turner, sir. You must don't remember me, but . . ."

"Hoss-SEE-o-lah," the voice perfectly recalled their first encounter. "Wait'll I tell Mitch. Come forward, then." Heartened by the reception, Ossie maneuvered his chair close to Europe's bedside. "I'm from Orange Street, sir. Orange Street Asylum, same as Herbie Wright."

"I wouldn't take that as a recommendation, my boy."

Ossie marveled at how calm the man was with the threat of not having his sight. Europe seemed to read his apprehension. "It's only for a couple of weeks, I'm told . . . Orange Street, huh? You're not by any chance a drummer too?"

"I play juss bout everything. Drums, clarinet, and trumpet. Piano in the main, though."

"Could be a big band by yourself! You say you play all those instruments. Are you any good at one?"

"Oh, I can play, now. I can surely play!"

"Do you read?"

"Not so much in letters, sir, but music pretty good."

"Then pull up a chair."

"Already got one, wheels included."

"Find a piece of paper, then. Gotta write this down. Music's been rattlin' round my head for days. Gotta get it out. Mademoiselles!" Europe bellowed in no particular direction, "Nous avons besoin du papier pour écrire!" A bevy of the angelic attendants appeared, shooshing him to no avail. "Le papier. Nous sommes pleines de la musique! Le Jass!" He growled the word, making the petite nuns flutter with laughter as they scurried to accommodate him. In search of this man, Osceola had entered the war and had nearly gotten himself blown to bits. And here he was in the cut already! Bracing the clipboard on his cast and holding the paper down with his sling, Osceola scratched out a few crude pages of musical bars and started scribbling notations as Europe blurted out ideas for a new song from his hospital bed. He called it "No Man's Land."

Europe talked in fragments, his mind rolling faster than his speech. "Drum roll like thunder, No Man's Land starts creeping . . ." Ossie picked up instruments with his voice. With remarkable precision, he mimicked a drum roll for thunder with accents of cannon fire. A whining clarinet emerged from the back of his throat and broke into a pursed-lip trumpet call to arms. The intro slid effortlessly into Europe's jaunty rag. The composition took shape as did the friendship, the memories of battle transformed to song.

"Alert! Gas! Put on your mask!
  Adjust it correctly and hurry up fast,

Drop! There's a rocket from the Boche barrage!
Down, hug the ground, close as you can, don't stand,
Creep and crawl, follow me, that's all,
What do you hear? Nothing near?
Don't fear, all's clear,
That's the life of a stroll,
When you take a patrol,
Out on No Man's Land,
Ain't it grand? Out on No Man's Land!"

"No Man's Land. You bettuh believe that!" Osceola said when they had finished. "Wasn't no place for nobody. When my body crashed, it shook my bones down to my teeth. But here it all come together. New rhythms—airplane whirs and train pistons and exploding missiles, machine gun clatter rat-tat-tat-tat—fast, shifting, and it all come together."

"The world is changing, Osceola. Somehow what has captured it is the music—our music. It changes up, improvises, shines, groans and growls—it speaks to the soul—because it comes from there." The lieutenant's body shook violently as if another spell or frenzy were about to descend upon him, but it was a rapture. "Take away from a man everything that he knows, his family, his name, his land, his language"—Europe drew up his arms as if shackled—"his freedom—what is he to do? — He sings. He dances. He play duh bones. He wails ... It's our path, our way out, Osceola. It is the door and the key. Ain't it grand?"

Even with his eyes bandaged, Jim Europe conveyed an intense awareness, hunger, and confidence. He was the Cat. "What do you do when you face the Devil, Ossie? I say, burn him up with your music. Give 'em hell! ... Even hell presents an opportunity, Osceola. This war has shown prejudice can be wiped out—through music! We must prepare."

Ossie nodded, silently contemplating his mentor's words and passion. Coming back to himself, the band leader shifted to casual talk. "You got a girl?"

"Sort of. Don't know if she know it, though. Been knowin' her all my life ... You? I mean, if you don't mind askin'."

"Got two," the elder man laughed, "not a situation I would recommend."

"I got one feel like two. She have big dreams. Work our way north in a medicine show, she say. Face-makin' her specialty, but she could do 'most anything. She actually dance with a broom, a mop, and pail an make you thank she got three partners. Pretendin' she got a partner, it the funniest! Her body do thangs you never 'spect . . . I don't know what to tell you bout Lizzie. She different is all."

"I think you're in love, my boy."

"Git out. I been knowin' Lizzie May ever since I been knowin'."

"Such is the love by which you will judge all others, my young friend."

"Song come to me while I was out there, too," he blushed and smiled, "bout the way she walk."

* * *

"PUT CLOTHES on yo back n food in yo mouf," Dora mumbled and folded her arms across her chest. She looked at her daughter with complete disgust. "Disgraceful! Knocked up by some gutter trash in the navy!"

"He's in the army!"

"Don't talk back to me, gal! I could kill yuh!"

"Now we got to find you a husband," Mah Bette chimed in.

"I ain't marryin' nobody."

"You lowlife lil heiffuh! You'll do as I say!"

"Go on and hit me. Go on. Hit me—I dare yuh!"

Eudora's fist froze midair above her head. "Git out mah house."

"I got no problem leavin' your house. This ain't never been mah house. Was always yoah house, yoah dream, yoah world! This ain't nevuh been mah house. You ain't nevuh loved me!" Lizzie turned her back. "You want me to pay for it? Here!" She slapped a silver dollar on the table. "That's my rent for this life!"

"Get out! Just get out of my sight!"

Lizzie ran down the steps and disappeared in a whir.

Dora froze like a stone, a woman of salt. "Put clothes on yo back n food in yo mouf," she mumbled and folded her arms across her chest. When she realized her daughter wasn't coming back, Dora fell on her knees and mauled the floor with clawed fingers till they bled.

* * *

THE 369TH was midway through its victory tour throughout the French countryside, accompanying the French high command, expecting to hit Paris. From province to province, the euphoria of the war's ending brought everyone into the streets. Villagers emerged from the rubble of their townships with wine and flowers and cheers. Old women lifted their skirts, and veterans stood, their eyes glazed with tears. The wheels of two buckboards locked together, a mortal combat of sound—the band men playin' they soul, they memories, they heart, they song, they history, divine! People just got possessed! Children marched and conducted the air with stray sticks as batons. Women pressed warm kisses onto their lips. When the band broke into their final jazz number, the whole village danced. Currents of music moved through the crowd with the voltage of lightning, the syncopated thunder of feet learning to stomp down the past and dust up a sawdust floor with this new American sound, Le Jazz. The war had come to an end. It was now the music that blew them away.

Osceola experienced this pandemonium from afar. As the newest member of the band, he was assigned to shine shoes, press shirts, polish the instruments, and arrange the chairs on the bandstand. Traveling in their exclusive three-car train, emptying ashtrays, he was still carrying their hats. The men talked around him, a cascade of rotating solos, each one cuttin' the last.

"Twenty-four hours' leave, that's all we got. The prescribed YMCA for the colored troops is one hundred miles away," Sissle went on, the perpetual complainer. "And check it out, there were three welcome women for three thousand colored guys. And those broads wasn't given up nuthin!"

"Mira, you guys son increíbles! Always talkin' like the only language inna inna inna world is inglés. Cabrones!"

"Aw, shut up, Romero."

"Nada. We are in France. The country that taught the world to kiss! How we gonna miss it? Por favor, I got no use for YMCA less I need a room or la piscina."

"Trumpet, trombone, traps, sax, clarinet, fiddle, and bass." Europe entered and broke up the banter, handing out new sheet music. He had written out Ossie's tune for him, broken it into parts. Europe placed the freshly crafted sheet music by the fellows who could read while the others gathered around. "Say, Herbie, gimme a beat."

To the rhythm of the maestro's hands, the drummer started tappin' on the metal pipes of the heater and countering it on the table rim. Mitch tried the first lines of the melody, his voice mimicking a brassy trombone, spitting growls and elongating notes into wails and bird trills and even a New York taxi horn. The leads played it straight, others just joined in, picking up what they could and adding. Once they caught the central thread, the whole band began to improvise a cappella. When the groove was solid, Europe impatiently waved his fingers at Ossie, who sheepishly relinquished a battered notebook page of lyrics. Noble Sissle's clear tenor completed the ensemble as the train sped down the tracks.

> "Miss Lizzie Mae had her a way,
>   Of walkin down the street,
>   That would make the sidewalk sizzle beneath her feet.
>   Yes, Lizzie Mae had her a way,
>   Of walkin down the street,
>   That could make a hungry fellah forget to eat . . ."

The band perfectly captured Lizzie's way of dancing. Sassy, brash, and defiant, they sang! And the tune? Wild with the freedom of mastery, it swang!

As the jam broke up in laughter, Europe took Osceola aside. "What do you think?"

"Writin' all that stuff in, I don't know. It's hard."

"That's a dilemma only gets better with practice. See, I cleaned it up some, but it's a smart tune. You've got an ear." The lieutenant's enlarged eyes seemed more intense, stuffed in their sockets. "You have some new sections to tap, here." He pointed to a bar on the page and quickly exited.

Jim Europe stood straddling the two train cars as Mitch joined him, sheltering a cigarette with his own damaged hand. "You all right, chief?"

"The rush of air relieves the breathing, effects of the gas, they say. That kid has a good mind, Mitch, only needs training. Just the way he constructs the parts, I can tell he hears orchestration."

"Takin' in another stray?"

"Got to. We gotta pull in every able-bodied musician we can find. We could lock down the whole of modern sound, Mitch. Foundation. Best in the world . . . at somethin'. You think I'm crazy? I might be, you know. When you are, everybody knows it but you."

"Naw, you ain't crazy, chief. You just colored. Kinda the same thing when it comes down to it."

Back inside the car, Herbie grumbled as he shuffled cards. "No-talent muthuhfuckuh. Cain't sing, cain't dance, clumsy as a drunk rooster."

Noble razzed him, "Jimmy was crazy enough to take you in. When you started, you was so green, Herbie, you was sproutin' leaves. Herbie couldn't buy him a job."

Fat Ivan turned to Ossie, "Listen at Sissle talkin' 'bout leaves. Yeah, what about it, Sissle? Slingin' a rope of flowers round yo' neck, tryin' to look Havaiian, big six-foot nigguh from Oakland." The men laughed easily as Ossie moved among them.

"They are called leis," Sissle countered, "your 'rope of flowers.' I might as well be Hawaiian. That pickaninny dialect of yourn is just as much a foreign language as French. A whole panoply of invented malapropisms. You should preserve 'em on account yo' granchilluns."

Herbie rose up from his seat. His temper was as quick to flare as his stick to hit the drumskin. Ossie's voice eased out, a perfect solo entrance, "Come on, now. No need fuh alla that. I don't think you should talk that way about other colored people, Sergeant Sissle." The men looked up in silent surprise. "Excuse me, suh, fuh speakin' but . . . but most colored folk ain't had the same opportunities as you. You's fortunate to hab come from someplace . . . what showed a man a different sense of hisself. Most of us felluhs just seein' it for the fust tam."

While Noble simply stared at the lad, Herbie smiled, his two front teeth crowned in gold. "Siddown, kid, I'll teach you some can."

Ossie's body relaxed with self-assurance. "Coon can? You cain't teach me no coon can, Herbie Wright. I do b'lieve teachuh gon to school on that." The whole railcar laughed as tensions eased. Ossie whipped a crate around, straddling his legs over the sides.

"Why you do your legs like that?" Romero queried.

"So I kin git away clean after I done cleaned out all yoah money! Some coons can. Some coons can't. I'm the coon that drug the can. Give it up!"

Ossie deftly shuffled the cards. "I was taught by the King of Coon Can. Went by the name of Win. Luckiest man alive till he met me. Cut." The game began. He was finally admitted, finally a member of the band.

"Jimmy say he got dates lined up already—Chicago, Boston. First stop, New York!" Romero smiled. "Spanish Harlem!"

"Shoot, I'm stayin' in Paris." Fat Ivan rubbed his gut and studied his hand. "Sid Pate already opened up a club. In Mo Mart. Northern part of the city, just like Harlem, they say. Working class in the day. Magic at night. Corsicans, Polish gangsters runnin' round wid deposed Russian royalty. Top of the hill, Sacre Coeur. Bottom of it, all the hashish, opium, cocaine, reefuh, black coffee, champagne, and pussy you can get!"

"Sound like my kinda place!"

"Hey, hey, hey, Herbie, I heard a guy took up drums, didn't even play, man," Sissle teased, "making moneeeee! Even you could get a gig."

"Bettuh quit ridin' me, Sissle."

"I'm not going back. Em-mmm, not me," said Ivan. "They givin' me a hard time, but I'm not going back. Got a date wid my destiny, mes amis."

"How bout you, youngblood? Headin' home?"

"Oh yeah," Osceola smiled. "I got me somebody to see."

✳ ✳ ✳

"WASTED HALF the mushrooms, too old. Oh, got string beans." Mah Bette pulled out the last clove of garlic. "Red pepper still half good, some good-smellin' onion, what lef', herb from the garden, spice from the forest, and a tech of Maum Bette's elderberry wine n let simmuh while the rice cook." Mah Bette was slower now, but from what others would discard, she still knew how to wring the last bit of nourishment and delight. Everyone was celebrating. "The war, the war is over!" She didn't know exactly who was coming to dinner, but she knew it was someone. With soldiers coming home every day, she sensed an opportunity to heal the rift between Dora and her younger daughter, who was now near ready to bear her own child.

Bette had struck a good bargain with the Hendersons, Rosa and Val. For a portion for themselves, they would slaughter the fattening hog. The whole family took part. Val hung the scalded animal up by the legs, and his sons all scraped the bristles. He then cut the still-steaming carcass open from head to tail and let the intestines fall into a deep wooden tub, so Mah Bette could instruct the girls on cleaning them. Val butchered the carcass with maximum efficiency. Bacon, ribs, steaks, chops, pigtail, feet, brain, testicles into mountain oysters, the head gristle for hogshead cheese. Mah Bette collected the backbones and tossed them in the rice. The tail, ears, and nose, Rosa boiled and ground into sausage. The feet, Mah Bette thought, she would pickle for New Year's.

They worked way into the night, the rag wicks of the flambeaus glowing softly, the fireflies syncopating. Mah Bette stirred a three-legged iron pot cooked over the fireplace. While hoecakes cackled, biscuits baked into the flames. She sprinkled white sand on the floor and began sweeping. *Muh great-grand fixed up this old place pretty nice.* She worked way into the night, as Lizzie sat in the corner watching her. In the back of her throat, she hummed softly to herself. The melody drifted over the air and floated on the night breeze.

✳ ✳ ✳

WHEN MITCH and Ossie arrived in Charleston, members of the Brown Society had their whole itinerary planned: a picnic at Goose Creek, a reception at Jehu Jones, followed by a parade at the Battery. Though it was only May, activities were planned all the way to the Fourth of July. Colored of every hue were feeling different about themselves and quite different about Osceola Turner. Formerly viewed as wharf-rat trash, he was now the toast of the town. "A hero has returned!" All he wanted to do was to see Lizzie. He had a brand-new dress from Paris for her, one like Irene Castle wore. She wasn't at the train station, wasn't at the gathering, wasn't down by the barbershop or even in front of the Bijoux.

He ducked away from the Welcome Committee, and he and Mitch started walking down Camden Road, alternating duets of music and talk. When they arrived at the small Winrow homestead, Miss Dora was sitting on the porch with her cousin, the funeral director. Lizzie's mother walked straight toward him and slapped him hard in the mouth. Roswell Diggs ran after her and pulled her away. Born and raised in New York, Mitch was not sure what to make of these Geechees. The last and only other time he had been south was for army camp, and he was there only long enough to get roughed up, jailed, then shipped off to war. He relieved Osceola of the dress box and stepped back to roll a cigarette.

Lizzie emerged from the cabin, her body swollen, her face a pushed-in pregnant pug. She stopped on the middle stair, her expression changing from anxiety to shame to anguish to joy that Osceola was alive in one piece and looking so fine! His face matched hers in metamorphosis—shock to betrayal to dismissal to realizing that this was his Lizzie May still. He ran off, leaving Mitch standing there with the box. Lizzie came quickly down the path and started after Osceola. Mitch grabbed her arm, his cigarette still lit. She jerked away. "You don't understand."

"I understand, sistuh. I understand everything."

Bette saved the day. She caught Osceola in the roadway with her hand full of sage. "Oseola Turner, zat you? Cain't b'lieve't."

"E'en, Mah Bette."

"Juss look at em! All full-out handsome. Got colors on he chess and stripe on he arm. Dog bite it, ain't dot sump!" Bette linked her arm into Osceola's and leaned on him a bit to slow his pace and heart. "An'm who em dis brought wid em, so good-lookin' n standin' tall?"

"Mitchell Jackson, m'am."

"Call me Mah Bette. Eb'body do."

"He one of the original Hellfighters, Mah Bette!" Osceola announced proudly.

"I could see dot."

"Now, I got to tell you, Osceola did his share of hell-raisin' on his own," Mitch added hastily.

"Well, we got hyeah 'bout it, got hyeah 'bout it all! Em stayin' fuh sup, of cose."

"We don't want to put you to no trouble," Mitch said.

"What kinda hell-raisuh don't wanna raise no trouble? Come, come." Mah Bette's broad arms ushered them in. They walked past Lizzie, who took on a slow stride behind them. Lizzie and Ossie found themselves on the top porch step, standing at arm's length, side by side.

Lizzie and Ossie. Lizzie stretched out her legs and curled her arches, straightened her back and sighed. Osceola leaned by the post, his hand in his pocket, one leg bent. Both wondering what to say, how to start. She sat down on the top step. He wandered over and sat beside her. Both looked straight ahead. Her hands resting on her knees, she turned to look at him. He lowered his head, then turned his eyes to meet hers. They stared at each other a long time, the wind dancing between them, quiet, unrevealing of the depth of their wounds.

＊ ＊ ＊

BOSTON'S MECHANICS Hall was packed. Detective Delaney sat uncomfortably in the double-letter section of the drafty old concert hall. He didn't like this jazz band stuff, white and colored sitting together! But what could you say, they were war heroes. He had to admit, he had never seen anything like it.

After the Brazilian number by Gomez, Europe left the bandstand. His eyes were smarting again, so he motioned to Sissle to stand in while he took a quick break. Herbie slapped his drumstick on the rim, got up from his seat, and followed the band leader off stage. He caught Europe just beyond the wings.

"Go back on stage, Herbie. What did I tell you about doing that?"

"What did you say to me back there?"

"I told you put more pep in your sticks. You're off tempo."

"Quit ridin' me, Europe. You tryin' to show me up."

Jim rubbed his eyes with impatience. "Listen, son, I told you, go away from me. I'm a sick man. I don't want to argue with you. Go on back on stage. And when we get to New York, you're fired. I'll get that other kid from Charleston," he said, walking off.

Herbie Wright followed Jim Europe into his dressing room, grabbed him from behind, and swiped a penknife across his jugular. Clutching his neck, Europe sank to the ground in amazement. Walking backstage for a quick bathroom break, Sissle saw the assault. He hollered out and charged at the crazed drummer, crouched with his shoulders hunched forward, his arm slashing wildly, the knife bloody up to the hilt. In a panic, the stage manager ran to the wings and motioned to the detective stationed in the audience.

"And for our next number, ladies and gentlemen, Al Johns will present a pianologue of song and stories . . ."

"Where's Europe? Where's Lieutenant Europe! We want Jim! We want Jim! WE WANT JIM!" the audience clamored, stomping and clapping.

"Lieutenant Europe is indisposed and will not be able to conduct the rest of the program."

* * *

OSSIE HAD invited Mitch to Charleston to see the other South, the South he loved, the place the music came from, to meet his girl. Now he was shamed into silence on their walk back. The older man considered how to offer solace. Their pace was slow, Ossie, for the first time, favoring the cane he was issued by the medics. The May air was hot and weighted, a hundred percent humidity, no breeze. Arriving in town, the two buddies ambled over to Hiram's Barbershop. Mitch peered in the galley storefront window, his face partially masked behind the painted letters. As usual every seat was taken. The shop was alive with customers, awaiting their turn for a haircut.

Mr. Sullivan, his weathered hand dipped in manicure suds, recognized Osceola immediately and drew attention to the young man standing by the door with his corporal's uniform and a couple of medals on his chest. The returning soldiers were greeted with a joyous hail of shouts and laughter. No one mentioned the cane, the stiffness of his knee. Osceola was still brooding over Lizzie, but his mood shifted as he introduced Mitch and the two began to regale the elders and small boys with tales of war and the new sense of freedom it had brought.

"They eat the egg of the fish? I thought only Negroes be eatin' everythin'! They eat the egg of the fish?"

"Caviar, my friend, caviar. Nothin' like it. French women and caviar. It's an aphrodisiac."

Conversation percolated about the room. "So we're assigned to the French. Overnight, the 15th Regiment of the United States Army becomes the 369th Regiment of the French 16th Division! Trained for ten weeks on French equipment and—boom! Sent to the front. Ninety-one days. Longer than any American unit, colored or white. Ain't like here. There's places in the world the black man's got respect."

Sullivan prodded them. "I heard 372nd Illinois, the Pioneers, gave your band a run fuh the money."

"They was National Guard," Ossie retorted. "We was Army! We was stacked! James Europe's band was all super selective, band members even from Puerto Rico. Illinois's shit was raw. Right from the source, come up from the Mississippi. But the Hellfightuhs had the brassiest brass and the sassiest rag, original jazz, man. Our music was the real thing! I watched it hypnotize a whole village!"

Mitch jumped in, "Language says it all. Sure they was the Pioneers, but we was the Hellfighters. They were first, but we were the finest, the finish. General Fouco comes up to the lieutenant and says, 'It's Hell, monsieur,' just like that, 'It is like fighting Hell.' Jimmy looks straight at the cat with these big, looming eyes, and says, 'Then we should do all right,' just like that. Shit, we from Harlem! 'The War is Hell out there,' the Frenchman say, but Big Jim, he say, 'Well shit, that ain't nothin'. We fight Hell every day!'"

"James Reese Europe, I didn't get to fight with em, but played some," Ossie continued. "He even helped me chart out one of my songs. You shoulda seen it, Sully. No more carryin' Jocelyn's hat, wrote out some charts. Been learnin' orch-es-tra-tion. The music! People just streamin' out, screamin' for it. It's a new world out there." Ossie looked down at his shoes, trying hard to stave off his lingering fury, the picture of Lizzie still burning through his brain. "New world here, too, it look like. . . . Say, Sullivan, seen Deke?" he asked as the banter lulled. "Satdie night, thought sure to see him at Hiram's."

"We under new management, kid. I mean, sir," Hiram chuckled.

"Ain't we all, ain't we all?"

Shifting a hot steamed towel from his face, Sullivan spoke cautiously as he examined the newly glossed neat nails of his dealin' hand. "Deke ain't been round since you left, son. Had some trouble. The law and what not. Couple of folks say they seen him, but he ain't been round, elst I'd know. Layin' low still, I suppose."

"I'm in no hurry to find him," Ossie spoke casually and looked up. "He'll find me direct . . ."

Lizzie came through the door, her stomach about to burst. The room quieted. Everyone thinking, *Bold little hussy.*

She looked straight at Osceola. "May I speak with you, please?"

He grabbed her upper arm and brusquely escorted her out of the shop and out of earshot. "What are yuh thinkin', comin' down here like that! I'll talk wid you later." But he didn't know what to say to her. He knew all the things he felt and mourned. He longed to hear her voice, but nothing she could say. "Get on the trolley and go home."

"I don't need no trolley. I got Mr. Lee."

"Get on the trolley, I said. It's dangerous tonight. I'll bring Mr. Lee to you tomorrow. Go home to your ma's." He grabbed her wrist and slapped a quarter in her palm, then walked back to the shop.

* * *

CHARLESTON WAS once again bustling with commerce. The sailors and soldiers returning on the SS *Wichita* were not the illustrious bourbon kings, but farm hicks and college boys, puffed up with victory. "We come early and we stay late!" hollered Coleridge McKinley IV after treating everyone to a discount at the movie house. Standing atop a table, Flip now had a crooked crap game going. Roswell's relatives still ran the billiard tables at the white tavern downtown, but the crowd from 1919 was not like the crowd from 1890. Just as Flip went to announce the participants in the next round, a billiard cue broke over someone's head, then a chair went flying. A bottle cracked a skull right next to him, then he got stabbed in the gut. Tables overturned. Pumped-up sailors were comin' home wantin', sensing it, feelin' it—something changed. Colored weren't colored. They were "Negroes." On the street, they looked new, acted new, proud and entitled. Expecting the war over there would change something over here, they had a new way of walking in the world, and these Southern soldier-boy soldiers weren't havin' it. They trashed the billiard hall, then like bees, a swarm of blue jackets came flying down the boulevard. They stormed out the tavern, knocking black fellahs in the head, throwin' them to the ground. They then spilled into the side streets and alleys, looking for anybody black. Their numbers grew to a thousand. The swarm blew over the city and formed a swath of rage and lust and fun. A phalanx of bobbing torches appeared outside the barbershop window.

The first thing Ossie thought about was Lizzie! Despite the stents in his leg, he ran out of the shop and made a dash in the direction he had last seen her walking. Mitch and Sully followed him into the street. The rest of the customers retreated to the back. The owners snuffed the lights.

By the time the trio got to the trolley, a pack of hooligans had surrounded it, rocking the carriage, pushing it on its side, lifting the wheels from the tracks. The driver was screaming for the colored to "Get off, get out and run!" Sparks and screeches flew from the wires above, the passengers thrown about the cabin. A few managed to get to the door. Others were pulled from the windows, and beaten with rocks and clubs and fists. Using the patrol technique they had learned at the front, Ossie and Mitch, joined by old Sullivan, fought their way to the car. Mitch's feint, thrust, and parry matched Sully's agile prizefighting moves. They shielded Osceola as he found Lizzie, crouched beneath a seat. Osceola carried her, flew with her, to a hiding place. Under the wharf. "Go, go in. You'll be safe."

"Osceola, don't leave me."

"Gotta help Mitch and Sully. Don't come out till I say ... Bought you something. From Paris." He smiled and let go her hand.

When Osceola turned the corner to rejoin his friends, he found Deke standing in his path. They had traveled the same alleys, the same escape routes as boys—stealing, hiding out from the asylum warden. Of course, Deke was headed for the hideout under the planks, but why had Sullivan lied? Osceola looked into his brother's eyes and knew. *Lizzie. It was you.* Deke also understood this. This boy he had birthed with his own hands, whom he had sworn to protect, meant to kill him. How would he defend himself? *How survive? How? Survive.*

Ossie's lust for blood was overpowered by his need to protect. He steered Deke away from where Lizzie was hiding. "I got guys need help out there."

"Fuck you," Deke scoffed, attempting to push the youth aside. Osceola held fast to his arm. This boy he had birthed with his own hands was ordering him. Before Deke could react, the mob was upon them. Like the old days, they were forced to defend themselves together. Trying to escape, they were nearly overrun, Osceola felled by a rock to his thigh. The injured leg buckled. The swarm encircled him, pounding, kicking, a dozen feet kicking, the blood in his mouth mixed with bile. Deke threw the assailant nearest him onto the gang attacking Ossie. Like John Henry, he lifted the man and tossed the body at a rush of them, then, stepping among the fallen and pummeling, twisting necks and arms, he broke the grasp of a youth with a lock around his neck like a noose. A limp sailor scampered, falling down as he fled in terror at the sight of a black man fighting back.

Deke pulled Ossie up and the two made their escape again, clutching each other in a three-legged race for their lives. Deke dragging him, his toes skimming the ground. The mob didn't care which was which, who was who. "Kill the niggahs! Kill the goddamn sons of bitches!"

When they were in sight of the barbershop, Deke broke loose and charged his pursuers. He waved Osceola on, awaiting their attackers, but the mob veered to another street, another random sighting.

As Osceola and Deke stumbled in, Mitch finished blocking the windows with benches and drew his pistol. Deke squared off at another window, drawing his gun from an ankle holster. A shotgun by his side, Sully wrapped his knuckles in wet towels to get good traction. As fast as Hiram, the barber, could fill bottles with kerosene, his brother stuffed them with face towels. "I can lob one of these with the force of a mean right fielder." An explosion of blue and white flames sent the rabblers yelpin' for cover in all directions. "They ain't takin' my shop. Not no mo'. Not this time."

When the mob retreated, the men sat quiet. *Shit, I fight Hell every day,* Osceola remembered as he sat quietly down in the barber's chair. The pin in his leg had snapped again. His shinbone bent at an odd angle. His eyes were open, but his breathing was shallow. He couldn't get his wind. The ribs had fractured and ruptured an artery. He was bleeding to death inside. He looked at each of them, these men crouched in the darkness, then closed his eyes. In the darkness, he heard music. In the darkness, he caught sight of the future he would never have and smiled, hearing the music. *Nothing could match Lizzie's dancin', nothing could match the way she danced!*

"He's going into shock," Mitch shouted, all too familiar with the symptoms.

"Stay wid me, Ossie. Stay wid me," Deke screamed. "You cain't leave!"

Nothin' could match the way she, nothin' could match, nothin' could . . . way she danced . . . Oddly, he could hear Deke wailing and cursing in the background, he could feel Deke cradling him in his arms, cryin', "Mama, no . . . No," tears running down his face like the many veins of a river. *One last look. Liz—* And he was still.

Deke grabbed the amulet round Ossie's neck and dashed it to the ground.

* * *

"WHAT A strange way to die. Machine gun unit, bandstand leader, consummate diplomat. Broke it all open. The whole array of instruments can fit—violin, bass, sax, strings, reed, brass, percussion, all in one glorious . . ." Europe's voice drifted off.

"Jim. Jimmy. Stay with me," Sissle insisted, talking his friend back from death.

Jim Europe watched his life force gush through his fingers in the dressing room mirror, and turned to Sissle. "Celebration of a new— Rhythms you cannot anticipate, but instantly . . . remember." He drifted between lucidity and dream. "Don't forget to have the band down to the statehouse at nine o'clock tomorrow morning. I'll be out in time to conduct. See that the rest of the program is gone through. Take away from a man—everything that he knows—his family, his name, his land, his language." He drew up his arms as if shackled, his blood-washed hands closed into fists grabbing at Sissle's jacket. "His . . . his freedom . . . what is he to do? — He sings, Noble, he sings . . . Two celli, four violins, four banjos, four bass, alto banjo, two sax, four clarinets, plus three, six, eight trumpets, four French horns, four English horns, two tuba, three trombones, and Castle is fined one case of champagne. Wearing brown shoes in the pit? You're late! My, look at all those stars . . ."

* * *

A THOUSAND hooves thundered above Lizzie, spewing dirt and grit in her face and eyes. A force in the dark grabbed her by the head and pushed her down. Her hair, her dress stick to the floor. He pounds her jaw, chin, and eye. Deacon, his face a black mask of rage, tears her open—

Lizzie jumped awake with a start. At first she thought herself entombed, but the muffled voices reassured her. They were quiet and calm. "It's a wonder she alive."

"She seem all right."

"Thank God."

"Osceola? Ossie?" She squinted at the sun's glare, her voice cracked and dry as strangers lifted her up.

Members of the search committee in their white armbands eased her from the cramped hiding space. Slowly the remains of the night's carnage came into view. "Osceola!"

"They taken him to yoah cousin's. Mr. Diggs takin' care of him now. There's no comfort in the world I can give you, child, but you got to think of yoah baby, Osceola's baby."

* * *

THE BOYS from Orange Street Asylum carried their instruments at their sides. Miss Francina, Roswell Diggs, all the people who had mocked and shunned him marched in silence. The pattern swept across the country. Tulsa, East St. Louis, Pittsburgh. Red Summer they called it. For all the colored blood runnin' in the streets. Charleston, the first, was a small affair. Only four dead. Mitch buried his friend and boarded a steamer for New York—Europe and Osceola, his father and his son, his brother and his friend, both slain.

Lizzie did not attend Ossie's funeral. She went instead to the woods ringing her childhood home. Her body swollen with life, she dug a hole and filled it with a soft bed of pine needles and spring grass. As she worked, she sang a strange meandering melody the birds seemed to know, their song blending with hers in counterpoint. She sang to her love a song of memories and laughter. She sang to her friend, she did. Sang to Osceola that day—a melody she made up as she went along. She dropped her arms and let her palms face front as a dirge rose from her womb to her tongue and through her lips, an aria of sorrow, a cryin' song for her beloved. The wisteria-draped trees as witness, she dropped to her knees from the weight of her heart. As the first wave of labor washed over her, she squatted over the earthen cradle and delivered of her loins a new life.

She looked at the baby a long time, considering whether she would let it live. The child's screams were so loud, her fit so furious, she won her mother over. Lizzie cut the umbilical with a razor, then tucked it back inside her braid. She bathed them both in the creek, then strapped the newborn to her breast and walked back toward the city, the harbor, the sea.

* * *

EUDORA WIPED her hands of dishwater and joined Mah Bette on the porch. In the evening light the old woman's skin still glowed. Dora squatted on her haunches and stretched her arms forward to ease her back, then brought her laced fingers back to her chest in prayer, silently shaking them at her God.

Bette let the breeze caress her face. "She be fine. She uh Seeker."

16

At first when faced with the funerals, the two diminutive caskets set in the middle of the room, Elma found comfort in the collection of old women mourners from her church. With their rambling talk offering remedies for her condition, they seemed by their own longevity to hold death back. "Liver, ginger, and some tonic, baby," one elder counseled. "Don't bind 'em to you till they passed the sixth year," added another. "Take that baby boy of yours outside. He'll do jus' fine. You will have your family yet," the last solo voice added, accompanied by the choir, "Uhn hmm, yes, that's right." *Yet . . . there my daughters lay. Stiff curls, powdered skin, painted lips,* Elma mused sadly, *China dolls.* The ritual circle of Bethel A.M.E. women with their wrinkled, down-turned eyes, so consoling when she thought she could not face the day, reminded her of Mah Bette. *Old women,* Elma thought, dismissing her sorrow as something that would dissolve like sugar in a hot cup of tea.

"No m'am, thank you. I cannot eat another one, Miss Tavineer." Elma feigned a smile, eschewing the last of her downstairs neighbor's crystal plate of cinnamon rolls. The weekly prayer circle that had tried to ease Elma through her children's illness and death was now reduced to one, Miss Tavineer, who lived on the second floor of the four-story Tenderloin walk-up Elma called home. Because the older woman often watched her surviving son, Jesse, while Elma ran her daily errands, she patiently suffered the woman's company and talentless baking. "Seems the whole congregation, all the good colored folk movin' on to Harlem," Miss Tavineer muttered, then heaved a sigh. "Now even the church itself."

"Yes, they're making fine progress. It's hard to believe the groundbreaking was only last spring," Elma replied. "Raymond tells me they've already started on the chapel interior." She added with a tight-lipped Cheshire smile, "He designed it, you know."

"It was hard enough getting down to 15th Street," Miss Tavineer grumbled and shifted in her seat. "I don't know how I'll make it to 135th. I don't know how you manage, raisin' a child with such troubles on your own in a city as difficult as this. Jesse's gettin' so heavy, I cain't hardly cart him up and down those steps. Maybe you should take the boy and go on back home, least for the rest of the winter."

Elma stood, indicating that the conversation was done, and saw her neighbor to the door. "You needn't cart him, Miss Tavineer. I will drop him off and come to fetch him myself as need be, if you can still oblige lookin' after him from time to time. I'm sure Raymond and I will soon be able to provide some compensation for your trouble."

In her weekly letter to Lizzie, Elma reiterated the conversation, emboldening her speech. "No sirree! I told her. We'll not be goin' back south for a while, or anytime." Elma resented the old woman's intrusive advice. Of course she recognized that the crowded mid-Manhattan streets were difficult with Jesse, but she wasn't about to let anyone else tell her what was best for him. *Least of all, some nosy old lady got neither chick nor child.* "Though I have lost Benna and Gabby," she continued in her letter, "many others have suffered greater. Fortunately, our Jesse has come through," she wished, prayed, lied. *This place is loud and cold, gray most every day.* "New York!" she went on. "The streets are so colorful. Different languages and smells. People are always taking me for something else, asking Do you speak English? Every day you are greeted with the unexpected. Yesterday, at the bakery, I caught a Chinese man staring at me from the street. I counted to ten like Yum Lee taught us as children—yut, gni, som, se, ng, luk, chut, bak, gow, sup—his eyes went round like silver dollars!" Elma rubbed her own eyes, feathered with lines of worry, and closed the note with borrowed optimism, "As Raymond says, here is where the nation is being built! This is our home." She sealed the letter and bundled herself up to head out for her morning chores.

She left Jesse with Miss Tavineer, making sure that the "fresh diapers, a change of clothes in case he soils himself, and something for him to nibble on, mashed the way he likes it," were noted. She decided to get her neighbor some peppermints to make amends for her shortness earlier and descended the narrow stairs to the street.

Asa Jolly and his wife were just opening up for business. Ray's old partner owned the building and ran a galley-style saloon on the ground floor. "Asa, Lille," Elma greeted her nominal landlord with a nod through the plate glass window. Asa waved as he taped a handmade sign to the glass, "Last Stop for Your Last Drop!"

"Thank the Lord Raymond's done with that life," she thought to herself, "soon to be done with Hell's Kitchen altogether!"

She stuck her hands into her muff and headed into the crowded 52nd Street thoroughfare, enveloped by the cacophonous patois of Irish, Russian, Polish, Italian, Yiddish, Southern Negro, and the quick, nasal, percussive speech of Tenderloin natives. She navigated the troughs of ice and sludge, slippery cobblestone, horse shit, and trolley tracks, a hopscotch across the street. Automobile fumes, ash, garbage, sweat, and dreams intermingled, the neighborhood loud and dissonant with impatience.

Routine was her salvation. First, the groceries and produce, then she picked up Raymond's laundry. "A luxury at ten cents a week, Raymond Minor, but a professional man needs to look the part," she spoke to the shirt, making sure that the cuff and collars were board stiff and white like he liked them. The visit to the kosher poultry house she saved for last. "Where yah been?" Mr. Ingerman always greeted her. "How's those beautiful little girls?" he used to add, asking after Gabby and Benna. Elma was thinner and paler and her eyes bespoke the grief she still carried, but she was a stunning woman, a beauty of indeterminate origin. The butcher still flirted with her unabashedly, the normalcy of his banter an awkward gesture of consolation. He always assured her that the hen that she picked was his fattest and the price he quoted was always "a good price, only for you. Okay you turn now," he announced, amused at her discomfort with the slaughter. Though she had seen her mother and great-grandmother handle the task scores of times, Elma hated the screeching wild rustle of wings, the fierce hysterical pinpoint eyes. She always averted her own as the jocular butcher snatched the hen, wrung its neck, and doused the still-trembling carcass in scalding water. "Plucked clean, only for you, Mrs. Minor."

"Just enough time to fricassee," she swallowed and replied, finally opening her eyes to the butcher's quizzical look. "That's French, Mr. Ingerman." She invented a story a ways off from her colored past. "A family recipe for stewed chicken."

The butcher looked aghast. "Stew! You gonna put this beautiful bird into a pot and turn it into a soup?"

She smiled and held the grocery bag aloft and allowed the delicate aromas to escape. "A rich savory sauce, Mr. Ingerman, with winter vegetables, clove, marjoram, and thyme. The meat just falls off the bone," she teased. "It's a feast in a pot. My husband's favorite."

The butcher leaned over the counter, mesmerized. "He is a lucky man, your husband, to have a beautiful wife and one who cares what he likes."

Returning to her building, Elma retrieved her son from Miss Tavineer's and made her way up the four flights of steep wooden steps with the shopping bag cushioned by the muff in one hand, the laundry under her arm, and Jesse slung on the opposite hip. Her body bent from the weight, she shifted the motionless toddler, hoisting him so that his chin rested more cleanly on her shoulder. "I can see what Miss Tavineer meant, Mr. Minor. You're gettin' to be quite a bundle, but we almost there, we almost there . . . A little bit higher, a little bit higher . . ." she began to sing, "I hear music in the air, just above my head, Oh, oh, oh, I hear music in the air, just above my head." With the creaks in the steps as her chorus, she crooned the familiar spiritual, modulating to a new key with each successive flight. "Each step a bit closer . . . to heaven . . ." She paused at the final stair landing. "Least we got sky, hunh, baby? We still got sky."

Ridges of frost glazed the windows, the world beyond a pale gray haze. The three-room, top-floor flat at 473 West 52nd Street seemed cavernous in its silence. Her fingers still tingling from the frost, Elma bustled quickly through the living room to the narrow kitchen and propped Jesse up in the corner of his crib so that she could see him while she busied herself preparing dinner.

The skin of the bird had blanched, a few belligerent feathers still wet and limp, the severed neck clotted with blood. She pulled out the innards, then set the bird atop a cutting board and with great efficiency severed the legs and wings at the joints, then cleaved away the rib, back, and breast bones. She dropped the parts into a bubbling broth of onions, spices, rice, and peas. Leaving the dish to simmer, she pushed Jesse's crib away from the window and opened it wide to take in the afternoon wash of hand-scrubbed laundry among the scalloped rows of clotheslines that ribboned the back alley. The wind bit at her fingers. The clothesline wheel squealed and whined an eerie mechanical protest as Elma drew in the stiff dry clothes, frozen to the touch.

She surveyed the rows of empty, frost-sealed windows. In the fluid community of immigrant women around her, who had the cleanest wash had once been a fierce competition, but she had lost more of her neighbors across the alley, women whose chiding boastful laughter and waves she had grown to anticipate and enjoy. She heard Kitty had gotten a job as a secretary and Mrs. Marrano now worked in the garment district. Little Demetrice, who had occasionally babysat for Gabby and Benna, was now a salesgirl at Gimbels. They could buy things, go to the nickelodeon or café. Even Jolly's wife worked at the tavern. But Raymond wouldn't allow her, wouldn't think of it. How could she anyway? *Money for the household but none of my own. Ten cents for collars and cuffs.* Her hands cracked and tingled as she folded and sorted the clothes. Her knuckles looked weathered and gnarled. *My beautiful hands just like Mama's now.* Red with flecks of skin peeling away, her hands used to glide across a piano. The melody of a sonata she used to play drifted into her mind, reminiscent of her year at Fisk, her year of promise—when she soloed with the Jubilee Singers, her crisp wool skirt, taken in at the waist, white ruffled blouse with a broad straw hat ribboned in the colors of the school, marching in line with the other girls, her long braid whipping behind her.

Beyond the occasional, ephemeral image, she had lost any sensation of that confident student. She had seen in Jolly's newspaper that one of her old choir mates from college had moved to New York. She thought for a moment to make contact, but *What would I say, what would I wear?* Instinctively, Elma adjusted an errant lock that had fallen into her eye. Mrs. Marrano, already selling clothes boosted off the racks from her new job in the garment district, had shown her a pink satin dress with a ruffle collar about four inches wide around and cloth-covered buttons down the front. The scalloped skirt had framed her body like a flower, revealing a hint of ankle. How beautiful it would have looked with the garnet earrings, Ray's present to her on their wedding day. She had stifled her urge to possess it and disdained the purchase. That pink was too youthful, the collar too low, the price too high, and the dress was probably stolen. Besides, who would wear pink in New York? She reddened at the confused rush of desire, guilt, anger. *Educated for grace, trained to do nothing. Shouldn't even be thinking of myself.* "Jesse? You awake?"

She checked on her silent child and patted his stomach, "Always hungry, that's one thing," then doggedly continued about her tasks. "I know you hear me over there playin' possum. Don't pretend you don't. You can fool someone else, but not me, Jesse Minor, not your mother," she called over her shoulder. As she sifted flour, she softly sang to him, "I hear music in the air/ Just above my head/ Oh-oh-oh, I hear music in the air/ Just above my head . . ." While the rumbling subterranean trains rattled the windowpanes, Elma pounded the lump of sugar into a fine powder, and ground the spice for the cobbler. Buoyed by the upbeat rhythm of the spiritual, the harmonies that accompanied her in her mind, she sat down to pare the apples, consuming the bruised parts and skin, preserving the clean white slices in lemon juice. Humming to herself, she rocked side to side in her seat, the motion mirroring an internal tension of defiance and surrender.

Raymond had told her that he wanted to build things—that he was putting himself through school by working the show circuit, but she came to understand that he actually liked that life on the road, the street life: *Common people.* Common had been such a bad word back in Charleston. As a girl in Charleston she had been forbidden to play with the children in the street, and even go near Miss Pilar's. Now here she was a grown woman with a husband and a child still livin' above a saloon. "Just till we get settled," Raymond had said, years ago. *Hell's Kitchen. For the damned.* She hated it when these thoughts invaded her. She would dispel them with a flash of lightning from her crown of raven hair. *Vow don't say maybe. Vow say forever.* She had burdened him, she decided. *Babies dyin', me laid up for weeks, now Jesse.* Distracted, she nicked her thumb. Instinctively, she drew the small pool of blood to her lips. The dank green smell of the hospital corridor for the colored wafted through her memory. A rat had nearly run over her foot the last visit. A whole crew of them zigzagged across the sidewalk in a devil's reel, a feral taunt. This was their home, too. The indifferent attendant sat her next to a pair of bent shoulders coughing up blood, then four hours later gave her a cream for Jesse's mottled skin and sent her home, pity and disgust in her eyes, not for the boy, but for Elma. "Colored. What a shame."

The dinner tasks completed, she heated the water for Jesse's bath and sat down to scour the daily newspaper borrowed from Mr. Jolly, looking for any advice or news on childcare. The information was so conflicting. One article had said babies needed rest and quiet, another that they needed exercise. "Children grow best when breastfed," this one said, but her milk had dried from worry. "When weaning, you may want to mix the milk with barley. Milk from Holstein cows is preferred to that of Jersey cows." Elma laughed once in her belly and folded the paper. None of this spoke to her concern. Could her son even hear her? Surviving scarlet fever right behind the influenza, her one remaining child now was over two and did not speak, walk, or smile. The fever had left him with no voice although he used to stand on his tiptoes at the window, announcing, "Daddy come home."

While his bath water cooled, Elma walked her son around the corners of the living room, crooning to him softly, avoiding the center where the caskets had sat.

> "There's a very pretty moon tonight,
> And I never saw a prettier sight,
> Than the girl upon my arm,
> I am smitten by her charm,
> And the very pretty moon tonight . . ."

She danced the two-step with her tiny partner, holding his diapered bottom as Raymond had held her waist, her cheek on the slope of his neck, his free hand bracing her back. She conjured the Raymond she fell in love with, their meeting and courtship, the rush of sensations in her body as he swirled her around and around, his liquid voice bearing love's nectar to her lips. The child slumped in her arms, his breathing heavy.

Elma cradled her son's head and lowered him into a tin tub beside the kitchen sink. Dimpled rolls of fat spilled over the sides of the basin, and his feet slouched limply on the counter. If not in mind, he was certainly grow-ing in body. She changed him into his bedclothes by the stove, then, having warmed his sheets with a hot water bottle, placed him under the covers of the oversized cradle Raymond had made at her insistence. She gazed at her son for a moment, hoping for some sign of recognition, then turned to check the table setting and reheat the dinner. The hour was late, but her courage would not be dampened. Elma Winrow Minor was a warrior. "Where's your chutzpah?" she demanded, appropriating the neighbor-hood Yiddish phrase. She would use the lace cloth and the silverware Mah Bette had given her from the remains of Sweet Tamarind, the uten-sils, if unmatched, at least two to each side. *Tonight is a celebration. De-liverance is at hand!*

When Bethel A.M.E.'s move to Harlem was just talk, Elma had dragged Raymond to the church on 15th Street. During the fellowship after the service, Elma mentioned to her pastor that Raymond had stud-ied the building trades in college. "Near the top of his class, you know." The intercession had led to an introduction to Arthur Landry, founder of Landry and Sons, one of only three Negro architectural firms in the city. Mr. Landry sat on the church board. "I know of your uncle," Landry had said to Raymond, "a fine teacher and scholar."

It was the break that Raymond needed, that she had prayed for. Though she had prodded him to accompany her to the service and guided him through the songs in the hymnal, Ray had needed no prompting to talk up his ideas. Landry had been so impressed that he offered Ray an associate position. Now, after all the false starts, in less than a year, Ray was poised to take on the premiere assignment of supervising the con-struction of the church's new home in Harlem. Elma straightened the doily on the armchair where Miss Tavineer had sat earlier. *I can't wait to offer that old biddy some good news for a change.* Once construction was under way, she was sure her family could relocate to an uptown address like the respectable people were doing. The anticipation filled her with a joy that verged on the devilish. *The Lord works in mysterious ways!* Elma laughed to herself. If only the congregation knew that Raymond had actually gotten his ideas for their new House of God from his stint in burlesque.

"Run-down, no-count, secondhand place fulluh nigguhs!" he would fume. The few months she had shared with him on the road, she often huddled in a cold-water flat, awaiting his return, only to endure his fussing about the construction of the colored circuit houses where he and Jolly most often played. He would bluster and pace. "Wing space, the place had no wing space! Dressing room's a broom closet." He often complained that people who built the theaters didn't have to work in them. "No depth of stage, and those seats! No room for your knees. Aisles on the outside! Every latecomer makes a bigger scene than me and Jolly put together. Complete parallel walls. The sound bounced around like a pool shark's eight ball."

"Raymond, the things you say!"

While Raymond was speaking with Landry at the fellowship dinner, Elma fluttered and hovered nearby, praying Ray would just talk about his ideas and not where they came from. And her husband had ideas! "Harlem has promise," he said. "Harlem could be that great invention," he went on, "the showplace of the Negro people!" Elma was filled with hope that he had finally found his stride. *Each step, a bit closer. A little bit higher, a little bit higher . . .*

They had taken the whole family to the spring groundbreaking ceremony, Elma's face shielded by a broad summer hat. Gabby and Benna raced down the small hills in the cleared corner lot while Jesse squawked loudly in her arms. She watched proudly as Raymond, with his dark brows glowering in the sun, stood with the design team of Harlem's only colored architect, his foot on the shovel next to the assistant pastor. After the ceremony, Mr. Landry invited the family for a private toast "for a few close associates" at his home around the corner.

Elma gathered their brood. Raymond bounced Jesse, already wanting to catch up to his sisters gaily skipping ahead of them. They strolled onto a block lined with carefully potted young trees. The row of neat, connected brownstones looked unassuming and small, but Ray explained they were Stanford White's, brilliant in simplicity and line, deceptive in size. When she entered the mahogany vestibule, as the stained glass inlays caught the last rays of the morning sun, the housewife from a fourth-floor Hell's Kitchen walk-up felt herself delivered to heaven. Brass sconces lined the intricately carved, wood-paneled halls. Chandelier crystals danced in the light. Elma couldn't wait to move to Harlem! She took Jesse from Raymond and watched their two little daughters shadow their father around the gathering. Though she had not been able to afford a new dress, she wore her hair in a crown, wound into spiral coils over each ear like Guinevere, the garnet-drop earrings Raymond had given her just visible. Mr. Landry approached her and gushed, "My dear, I don't believe you realize you're the most beautiful woman in the room."

"My husband is due far greater compliments than I, sir."

"Yes, but he's not my type," Landry quipped mischievously. To her look of bewilderment, he chuckled, "Call me Arthur, please."

On the subway ride home, while her cheeks were still warm from the sip of sherry she allowed herself, Raymond paced the car. "What did you call yourself doing?"

"I was just singing your praises."

That was spring, a world ago. Elma gazed out the kitchen window at the darkening twilight, crystal veins of frost forming on the panes.

* * *

EARLY TURNS of fortune in his Chesapeake childhood created in Raymond Minor a fundamental imbalance that made him prone to pendulum swings of action most of his life. While his grandfather had held a lesser federal Reconstruction office, Raymond's mother was a Baltimore whore. She died when he was seven and he was brought to Washington to live with his high-toned colored relatives, the Minors—respectable, high-class folks descended of Reconstruction legislators, freedmen and mechanics, scholars and teachers, men of letters and breeding and ladies of class and culture. "All refined, all free people of color," his grandmother would say as she stooped to hang her own wash in the brown grass backyard, "not a slave among them!" All the while covering her barely brown arms with long white gloves so as never to darken.

The whole family, a guarded people within the narrow range from taupe to alabaster, could not accept, refused to discuss, didn't dare imagine his parents' union. However brief and whatever the circumstances, which he never came to know, it had shaken the very foundation upon which their reality was built. Raymond's grandmother took every opportunity to berate him for his father's "shackin' up with that low-bred, street-walkin' mother of yours," as if the fall from grace were a disease he had brought upon the whole family, tree rot down to the root.

By the time Raymond was twelve, his grandfather had shrunk in stature as well. The old man squandered his pennies in drink and golden tales of olden days, bewailing the Jim Crow squeeze that had removed even peripheral government jobs from colored hands, even as his had given over to tremors. Reduced to managing a neighborhood burlesque house that featured dames just like Raymond's mother, his grandpap could be found most often by the stage door, a soused and passed-out sentry.

His uncle, who had matriculated through a small Southern college and remained there as professor of music, rescued him. Childless himself, his uncle, Professor Minor, sought to steer Raymond away from his forebears' profligate course toward the next generation of Negro leadership, but Ray chafed under the insular rigidity, the pastoral setting, and the chasms of caste and class between the light-skinned self-designated Talented Tenth and their darker-hued brethren demanding autonomy and a share of authority. He discovered in the small land grant colored college the same pretentious posturing of his grandparents, the same small-minded, narrow vision, the same pattern of mistrust and betrayal that had so bedeviled his youth. "Nigguhs in a haystack, crabs in a barrel."

He was invited to join the No Nations Club, those so fair-skinned that their racial path required decision. Every year a dozen or so disappeared into whiteness. Instead, Ray quit the college, thumbed his nose at his uncle's expectation that he would become a builder for a fling at a life in song and dance, staving off his ambivalence with a lacquer treatment of burnt cork, cavalierly aiming to travel, a white-faced fraud by day, a black-faced clown by night, following the rambling path of his confusion, a drunkard sailor stumbling along from one strange foreign port to another. Then he saw Elma, then he heard her sing, a melody like a breeze across his face. *That damned singing.*

They lost their first child in stillbirth, on a stopover in Cleveland. Raymond came back to the boarding house to find Elma sitting in a tub of cold crimson water. He had not even realized. Clearly she was too frag-ile for the road. His commitment to show business being faint, when his partner Jolly decided to pull out—"Got myself this brownstone," he said, "gon' turn the bottom floor into a saloon, a men's drinking joint"—Raymond followed and settled in New York, letting the upstairs flat. Then Gabriela was born with rich purple curls and golden Benna, named after his grandfather. Then Jesse, who would peek out the window, al-ready trying to stand up.

At the funeral, Elma sat on the side of the bed, her crying incessant, her face unrecognizable. He tried as he knew to reach her, to help her get dressed. "We should make another child," he said as he held her by the shoulders. She fell upon the ground, her body quaking, her back arched, hands distended till the bones nearly popped from her skin. "Another, a-nuth-er ch-child!" she stuttered. "Don't touch me! Lord! Don't! Leave me be!" then curled up like a stone and never cried again. The loss of iron, they said, had turned Elma's once warm skin to a sallow bruised hue, deep circles under her wide dry eyes. Like the sirens offering rescue, then dashing mariners to their deaths, the passion that she riled in him had brought only misery, guilt, and anger.

As he walked home from Landry's office in Harlem, traces of her melody teased him through the howling January winds. Iced wind-shears cracked his skin. White breath caps punctuated his heavy stride. Ray crossed the near abandoned intersection of 52nd and Eighth, the neigh-borhood gypsters, whores, gypsies, garage attendants, and pushcart own-ers having taken shelter in the ubiquitous taverns and saloons, and arrived at Jolly's Place.

His nostrils reluctantly breathed in the familiar, warm, musky tavern air. Jolly was telling one of his stories, looking for a chorus. "Face the or-chestra, damn it! I'd say," he hollered above the din. "Never used to un-derstand it. He'd stand there with that big old silver head of wiry hair of his and conduct just as graceful." Jolly waved his arms above his head in pert comical curlicues. Beckoning Ray with two middle fingers, he con-tinued one of his standard tales of the "World's worst pit conductor! Fac-ing the audience, his back to the band, like he was the star!" Laughter sidled through the chain of men, punctuated with clicks and taps and shouting.

Ray eased his way through the crowd. The narrow galley could neatly accommodate fifty customers. They were two and three deep tonight, leaning over the counter. It was January 1920. The Volstead Act was due to take effect in a few days. Both regulars and newcomers were guzzling mugs of beer and throwing down shots as if their bodies could stock up. The joint was bulging. The room had the loud boisterous gaiety of a blue-collar wake. "Another round?! — Aye! — Drink up, boys! Make room for my partner, so's he can catch up!"

"Man's gotta right," a regular halfheartedly argued. "It's interfering with the states. New York got rights." He hiccupped. "Won't hold."

"Damn hillbillies," Jolly snapped as he mopped down the mahogany bar top and slapped a shot on the counter for Ray, "moonshinin' for a hunnud years, now gonna dictate to the nation! Just got the joint goin' and here they come, pullin' the rug right from under me like a bad comedy routine."

In their show act, Ray, the straight man, had always followed the wise-cracking Jolly onto the stage. When Jolly gave up the life, Ray did like-wise. Ray told himself it was for Elma's sake. For Jolly the reason was simpler. Between road feuds and living hand to mouth, he couldn't take the food. "Hospital stay in Cincinnati and some bad barbecue in Denver, after that, took my earnings and bought me something steady," he would tell anybody. He ran a saloon with regular eats at 52nd, between Seventh and Eighth. Jolly contentedly cooked for himself and the small world of show people, mostly musicians, who often stopped by. Bookended by Marshall's and the Clef Club on 53rd Street, his tavern was becoming the hub of the colored music scene until Irish dives like Bucket of Blood moving up from the Five Points and the push south from San Juan Hill started squeezing out the colored from the Tenderloin. "Colored feelin' unwelcome, even in the slum," Jolly joked. The old German Jewish neighborhood of Harlem on the Upper West Side had begun to lure the upscale folk, their churches, and the few remaining high rollers. Still, Jolly owned his build-ing square and was reluctant to leave. Always a realist, he kept a billy club and a shotgun behind the counter and a pistol in the garter of his sock.

"Fellah from Rothsteins' come in yestiddy, say could keep me in supply—told me tuh serve it in teacups. Say cops, city already hooked up. Trucks loaded and routes mapped out. Business as usual."

His wife, Lille, looked up, frowning.

"What you looking at, missy?" he joked. "Can't you see we got customers here?" He leaned into Ray, "Gotta treat em like that to keep em sassy," then reared back and bellowed, "When my illustrious colleagues go to Tin Pan Alley to get fleeced, here in Hell's Kitchen, we got eats which they can still afford. Call it Ten-der-loin!" He elongated the word with relish and laughed so that his shoulders shook. Jolly, who was stocky and muscular, walked on his toes, not so much to compensate for his height, but more to demonstrate a quickness and sharpness. He was tight. Even with his protruding belly, you could still see the curve of his haunch through his pants.

Lille methodically rinsed glasses and mugs, then just as methodically dried them, then turned to dish up plates of Jolly's famous rib-tips. Tall, with a turned-up nose, she talked little. To her consternation, her common-law husband Asa "Ace" Jolly used to play a decent stride piano, and even then talked all the time.

"You gonna take the offer?" Ray asked.

"Don't much think so. Considering opening up a little grocery store, though. Say, you could design it for me! Drawing it up and such . . . Last round before supper, everybody! Last round, Last Supper!" he shouted down the galley. He slapped Ray on the side of the arm and served him a sympathy shot on the house. "Drink up, my friend. Two more days of freedom, then we all got to think another game."

Ray slugged down the shot in one angry motion. "Got fired today."

Jolly rolled his eyes. "Again?" Jolly, who presumed all people were cut-throat and out to destroy, seemed to contradict himself with his loyalty to Ray. He stuck by his old partner—"Rubbing shoulders with the aristocracy," he called it, "the golden days of Reconstruction, first taste of liberty, schools, gov'ment, and all that, when black folks walked the halls of Congress as lawmakers, not as butlers"—while he secretly delighted in Ray's floundering. The dependency seemed a marker of his own increased capacity.

But then there was Elma, rare and delicate as an orchid. Raymond had no appreciation, he was sure. "College man ain't got a clue what to do with that." When she started losing the children, Asa's envy turned to pity. Everybody lost children, especially in the Tenderloin, but the couple's inability to recover he attributed to a weakness in their blood, an inherited self-absorption he found fascinating.

Ray huddled over the bar; his long legs straddled the corner seat. "What am I going to tell Elle?"

"Fuck that. What you gonna do?" Jolly retorted, his dishrag balled up in his fist. Jolly looked over toward his wife, then palmed Ray some cash. "Just till you get straight. Consider it a down payment on the build. My new grocery store." He threw up his hands to Ray's refusal. "I'm good, I'm good. Till it goes into effect, Prohibition's the best thing ever happened to me."

* * *

THE TENDERLOIN, despite its poverty and reputation, or maybe because of it, offered mobility. During the war, with immigration down and single men on the front, Ray got work easily. With his swarthy looks and his knack for capturing accents, he could fall in with various pick-up crews. He spoke a few phrases of Italian and a lovely Irish brogue. Black Irish, they called him, not knowing the half. Redeploying his theatrical skills, he navigated around the unions' barring of blacks and the clannishness of the trade guilds, inventing characters and backgrounds to suit the moment. The masquerade worked beautifully when work was plentiful and the skilled labor pool scarce.

A wave of great inventions—electric lights, moving pictures, telephones, phonographs, human flight, automobiles for the common man—had made the world suddenly exhilarated and confusing, wide-eyed with hope and an unconditional faith in possibility, speeding into the future. Intoxicated by these new ways of thinking, Raymond chose experiences that gave him the best exposure, new ways of seeing space and structure—subway tunneling, bridge construction, skyscrapers. While others quaked at the thought of working the tall girders, arms akimbo, Ray stood flat-footed on the steel beams, breathing in the light atmospheric clouds like ether. His dream of becoming an architect rekindled, Raymond volunteered to make the blueprint copies and change orders, listening, observing, asking questions, practicing his drafting. He had ideas, but invariably he would undercut himself and irritate the wrong guy, threaten with the wrong question, challenge at the wrong time. Man of No Nation, when he got to the portal of choice, he would freeze or fold or turn trickster on himself, a skyscraper worker who could trip up a flight of stairs.

Harlem was Elma's choice, not his, but Landry's firm, one of three Negro architects in the city, had appeared to be the opportunity he was seeking.

The construction of A.M.E. Bethel was well ahead of schedule. Even unfinished it had become a showplace. Standing in the frame of the steeple, Ray had watched Landry take a group of church and city representatives on a tour of the construction site. He could tell from the hand gestures that Landry clearly had absorbed some of Raymond's ideas. He was even using Raymond's language. "The pulpit will be extended to thirty feet, and the audience will have a center aisle and two to each side. Notice how the walls are beveled to improve acoustics." As winter set in, work on the plans had given Raymond grounding, a focus outside the mourning. Breath.

"Mr. Minor." Landry's secretary, a flat pancake-faced girl with sly eyes, stood at the entrance to Landry's inner office, her hand on the knob, a heel balanced on the opposite shoe. "Mr. Landry will see you now."

He sat down, determining when he would speak. Landry began first. "Next project, Minor, I'm putting Bainbridge in charge. From now on, you should report to him."

"Bainbridge?" Ray said in disbelief. Maybe he hadn't heard right. "You want me to work under Bainbridge? A junior staffer, barely twenty?"

"Well, you're both junior staff. He's twenty-five, fresh out of the army, focused. Bethel is a fast-track project. If we're to be done before Easter, there'll be a lot of late nights. You have a family to attend."

"That has nothing to do with it. How can you make him the lead on a project that is my design?"

"Now see here, Minor, you made some notes on a blueprint. That hardly constitutes a design. I took you in because you showed a promise, which frankly has barely panned out. I've kept you as long as I have out of deference to your family's situation."

"I beg your pardon."

"I am sorry you lost your children, especially sorry for your wife—"

"You leave her out of this."

"I've made my decision."

"You wouldn't have a decision to make were it not for the work that I already did for you."

Landry's mouth twitched. He brusquely twisted the curled end of his mustache.

"My dear demented fellow, you seem to think that because you are a Minor, you are somehow entitled. I make decisions based on merit, on what makes for the best team, and you, frankly, are not fitting into it. I was prepared to keep you on in a position, but with this—"

"To hell with your position!" *Nigguhs in a haystack. Crabs in a barrel. Pincers clawing at my neck.* "You've stolen my design without crediting me."

Landry's eyebrows rose. "You credit yourself too much, Mr. Minor. Your check will be mailed. Good day."

Raymond pondered the state of his world going up the wooden back steps. *No job. No Nation. Now what? . . . Why not just cross over?* He could, on occasion, spot someone he knew was passing—by hair, aura, features, gesture, walk. He would often stroll with his little girl Gabby through the department stores. People marveled at her dark hair and onyx eyes, never knowing, but with Jesse, his mute, clearly colored child, this was not possible. Ray had been so happy to get a son. The ruddy complexion, thick kinky hair, and broad stubborn jaw of his grandfather bound him to an identity, but he loved his boy, right down to the turned-out, flat, narrow feet just like Pap's. Jesse had been so gleeful, so animated. His one remaining child. *Daddy's home. Now nothing.*

Ray had it all the spring before. Job, family, even the flu. It laid him up a couple of days, then he was back to work. When the same bug returned in September, he thought nothing of it as he left for the site. The kids were sniffling a bit, but Elma was there. He stayed late, determined to get the church steeple frame built before the onset of cold. She sent word by Jolly.

He found her flying from child to child. Gabby's red eyes darted in panic, her shivering face turned purple, gasping for breath. Jesse, with ugly, red welts, skin so hot, he was boiling inside. The little red bubbles in Benna's saliva flowed like a string of Venetian beads from the corner of her mouth on a bare thread of fetid air. His golden child a grimaced old troll, drowned in his arms. Jesse alone survived, the welts peeled away, a dying man's skin.

Some scratchy Victrola crooned through the window frozen open on the stairwell, a delta Yellow Dawg ballad, notes hangin' in the air like crystal.

> "He had it all before,
>   Then Death come knockin' at the door,
>   Life looked so good in June,
>   Then Death come stalkin' by the winter moon . . ."

Before the key touched the lock, Elma had swung the door open and quickly cupped her arm under Jesse's stubby thighs as she shifted the boy on her hips. "Look, Jesse, Dah-dah's home." The baby's eyes were vacant. His head jerked backward in an involuntary spasm while his neck, struggling to keep upright, bobbled as a slow spinning plate would on a stick.

"Old man Landry had to cancel the meeting," hat in hand, he lied, not wanting to hear about a move uptown, apartment with a yard—air. "How is he?"

"His name's Jesse," Elma said firmly. "Your son has a name." Ray put his hand to his forehead, pressed the middle finger on the space between his brows, and closed his eyes. "You should call him by his name," she softened. "It helps him. Call him by his name." Straining her shoulders, she handed Ray the child, a jostling sack of loose potatoes.

"It would help if you talked straight to him. I'm not Dah-dah. I'm . . . his father."

She had retreated to the stove. "I've got fricassee, your favorite."

Raymond approached her from behind, nuzzled his face in her hair. She turned to him and squeezed his hand. He was amazed that she still blushed. The yellow gaslight hit the timbre of her skin, the pitch of the air a fine-tuned cymbal. Tendrils of black hair framed her neck and face, delicate and fierce as a swan's.

17

"Look here, she say don't come north till spring," Lizzie pointed to Elma's underlined hand, "specially with a baby." She lifted her daughter Cinnamon off her lap, her nipple dislodging from the child's hungry feeding. "Listen, we can't have no more of that when we get to the city. You goin' on two, got to be independent." Lizzie folded the year-old letter and stuffed it in her pocket. It had taken her two springs to get out of Charleston, two years to get the money. Two years to leave behind the memories of her assault, the riot, and Osceola's death. Nineteen nineteen, a year she wanted to forget, was supposed to have been a good year—soldiers returning, peace, prosperity. It turned out anything but for Lizzie, for most colored folks as a matter of fact. The spring riot that left Ossie and four others dead proved just a taste of the summer terror in store for black folks naïve enough to think that the "war for democracy" would make a place for them at the table. Instead, white ire at such audacity ignited riots across the country that made the flare-up in Charleston look like a barbecue.

The city that had been the gem of the South was never the same afterwards. Charleston's busy seaport shrank to half. Scores of wharf joints stayed closed after the riot. More when the troops tapered off. Pilar's was long boarded up. Lizzie found work sparse at the few spots left. People who expected her to play the grieving wife couldn't see her as the notorious, swivel-hipped hoochie dancer, the Yamma Mamma. And Prohibition put a cramp in her program completely.

She refused to work in the laundry. Mr. Yum Lee wouldn't have it anyway. "You near burn my place down! Go way, go!" She turned to Flip McKinley, who now ran both the movie theater and the hotel. For old times' sake, he sometimes gave her work. When the piano tickler for the cinema got tight, she stood in, puttin' the pedal to the floor, jazzin' up the movie score. Occasionally she worked as a dishwasher at the hotel. She told him, "Cleanin' rooms is out, but dishes I'll do." The kitchen was next to the garage. Tooling around with the mechanics, she finally bummed a ride with a rumrunner. For once, her having a kid came in handy. Who was going to suspect a family man traveling with wife and child? The bootlegger took them as far as Baltimore. When he finished his last load, the joker told her, "New Yawk's just a short ways." By short, Lizzie thought he meant walking distance. She walked for two weeks. "Crossed the whole state of Delaware, as a mattuh uh fact," but had only gotten as far as Philly.

Picking up income where she could—street performing in Philly, a short gig in Chester, a little bait and switch in the Trenton train washroom—Lizzie finally arrived at her destination. The train pulled into New York's Penn Station in the spring of 1921.

"Couldn't leave you with Mah Bette," Lizzie chattered to her daughter, sitting beside her. "Jars of snakes by the door. Mass's big toe, petrified in the drawer. Haints seepin' through. We through wid all that slave time hoodoo. We inna trunteth cintry! We gettin' out of here. We goin' places! The modern world!"

"Charleston, Durham, Kittyhawk! / Norfolk, Richmond, New Yawk!" the duo sang and giggled together. Lizzie pedaled her legs in the seat as the train slowed and the city skyline came into view. "Look at that, Cinn, look at that! That's what I'm missin'—New Yawk!" An alchemist's combination of grease, water, and men's aftershave on her plaits gave her a Creole crinkle of curls, peaking out of a stolen cloche. "Four dollars." She patted the rolled paper inside her bra and picked up her twine-held suitcase, a sack of songs on her back. "So what do you think?" she asked the silent tot, standing broad-legged beside her. "We in New Yawk! Harlem, baby! Here I come!" Shafts of sunlight washed through the lattices of the glass-domed station as Lizzie warily mounted the wide granite staircase, the child riding her mother's hip like an ol' rockin' chair. Baby in one arm, suitcase hanging from the other, she twirled in an accelerated medley of steps when they got to the top.

A few feet away, Dakota Sparrow had been waiting for Huey Jones's late-ass train, talking to himself. He had told Big Ed that he would stop by the train station on the way from Tin Pan Alley and escort the new player to the club. "That's fine, but not if the nigguh gonna miss the— Whew!" Dakota Sparrow lost his thought and any memory of his mission as Lizzie Winrow Turner whirled past.

A series of quick-time pirouettes and a perfectly sequenced foxtrot across the marble floor left Lizzie's child dizzy and giggling, the world meshed into a wash of liquid colors, dancing to the timbre of bells. Someone had tossed them a quarter. Lizzie squeezed her daughter tight, then stooped to pick up the coin. A red-faced rotund policeman approached her from behind and poked her in the side. "Git a move on, girlie." The child took one look at his big, snarling face and let out a high piercing cry that made people from all directions look toward theirs. "Say! Whatza mattuh!" He threw up his hands, arrested, then collected himself. "Get that brat outta here! Tyke at stoof uptayne. Aff wid yuh."

Scooting her suitcase before her with her foot, Lizzie sat down and pulled the bag toward her with her calf. She flipped her baby onto her stomach and bounced the wailing small body on her knee, simultaneously leaning to her side to fix her stocking at the toe seam. Lizzie so wanted to impress her citified sister that she had splurged on the skin-toned stockings at two bits a pair. She had greased her legs with Vasoline, removing the excess with a barber's towel before putting the new stockings on. Her taut, sinewy limbs really did look like silk, she thought, but the toe seam had been bothering her since Newark.

The toddler's screams quickly descended to a rhythmic self-absorbed chant. "Look, Cinn, the floor shines." She tapped her toe rhythmically, reached in her purse, and pulled out a cigarette. Her child's head popped up like a periscope. Cinnamon Turner squirreled off her mother's lap and attempted to scamper forward on her own. Cigarette dangling from her mouth, Lizzie reached for her child, collected her things, and stood up in one fluid motion. Cinnamon protested by pushing away, planting her sturdy feet on Lizzie's stomach. Lizzie slapped her into the hip saddle and pointed her finger sternly. "Don't start!"

"Well, stop a fellah in his tracks! Who is this little pot of gold walkin' straight into the gaze of one Stretch Dakota Sparrow, talent scout?" The lanky chocolate dandy who had spied them dancing off the escalator now approached Lizzie as she walked ahead of him. "Georgia Peach!"

"Wrong state."

"Pecan pie."

"That's New Orleans." She stopped and turned, halting him in his tracks with a cold dead stare. "You ain't never been nowhere South."

"Been to New Jersey. That's South enough . . . Hey!" He jumped in front of her. "Flo Ziegfeld roamed New York to find the most beautiful girls in the world for his Follies—I do the same for Harlem!"

"That so?"

He had her attention. "You dance. I can tell by the shape of your legs." Her eyes rolled up, but she lingered. "And the way you danced around that cop. Pretty good, ain't yuh?"

"Some say."

"Ain't gonna git nowhere with a shorty on yo' hip, though. Barron Wilkins is hiring sharpies, but no babies allowed—you gotta be twenty-one, which I doesn't suppose you is neithuh. Hey! I'm trying to give you a break."

"How's that? You don't know a thing about me."

"I seen the way you dance down the sidewalk with the kid, how you can hoof it, and if your lungs are anything like hers, you can sing, you gotta sing good—total package—I got the eye for talent . . . Hey!"

"What part of get lost don't you understand?"

"That little part right there where you sorta like me. Side of your upper lip right here."

"Come on, Cinn," Lizzie snapped, the still unlit cigarette dangling from her lips.

"Sin, that's different."

Lizzie pivoted and strutted away, her hips bumping of their own volition. Riding sidesaddle as nonchalant as Buddha, the kid stared him down over her mother's shoulder. He stood with his hat over his chest.

"That's Dakota Sparrow. Eye for talent! Name's Stretch . . . Friendly, ain't yuh. Say!"

* * *

AFTER DITCHING the scarecrow, Lizzie emerged from the station to a wide avenue, congested with model T's, trucks, garment pushcarts and racks, double-decker buses and crisscrossing trolleys. People were moving fast, talking fast, but the blocks were only two steps long. *All slicked down, when she hit the town, Miss Lizzie strutted uptown.* She got to Elma's walk-up in no time. Mr. Jolly greeted her while his wife went to fetch Elma from upstairs. It was a real dumpy place. Elma had described it as a lively tavern, but with Prohibition in effect, it was just a cramped Mom and Pop joint, complete with Mom and Pop. Hardly enough stock on the shelves to make it worth their while. The only traffic seemed to be the delivery boys rolling boxes to the back, giving her the once-over as they passed, their skin sour and pale.

Elma emerged from the back, black stockings and long housedress to her ankles, her hair swooped over her ears in a tangled bun, held with the butcher's pencil. Her sister looked thin, her once radiant eyes dull with worry, but Lizzie busted out a face-splitting grin, propped Cinnamon on the counter, dropped her bag, and opened her arms. The two women embraced and rocked from side to side, squealing unintelligible delight. Elma pulled back in awe. "Don't tell me. This your baby?" Little Cinnamon almost fell off the counter, reaching for them. Elma darted and caught her in an embrace.

"Seventeen months," Lizzie affirmed. "Trying to walk by herself. Trying to dance too. Got her own mind. Almost got us arrested." Elma kissed Cinnamon's plump cheek. The little girl startled her with a deep-dimpled, full-lipped smile. When Lizzie tried to take her, Cinnamon shooed her mother away with a grunt. "Well, stay then. Meet your aunt."

Mrs. Jolly looked on sternly as Asa folded his arms, mesmerized. *Then here come the sister, a completely different kettle of fish. Slew-footed, red-boned heiffuh, been around and announcing it. Carrying that plump round-eyed chocolate drop of a kid, danglin' a cigarette from her lips, lipstick turned purple, jagged ring 'round the tip she done smoked down to the stub.*

None on her finger. A line of grime on her neck, beat-up patent leather shoes . . . and new silk stockings . . .

As is the Southern custom, Jolly invited the sisters to dinner with him and the missis, an instant welcome meal of leftover red beans. "My people from Tennessee and favor red beans over your Geechee black-eye peas . . . served over my very own dirty rice. The recipe shall never part my lips." Chicken necks in a fine jerk sauce, the bones cooked down to their softness, and stewed cabbage rounded off the meal. "Mrs. Jolly fixed the biscuits," Asa acknowledged of his taciturn wife.

Elma ate daintily, mashing food for Jesse, who was seated in her lap. Lizzie ate for three people and told of her plans. Sitting atop a stack of newspapers propped on a chair, Cinnamon stalwartly attempted to eat by herself with a spoon. Raymond joined them toward the end of the meal, his eyes still tearing from sleep. "Had to see what all this disturbing laughter was down here."

Elma joked, "Jolly's secret recipe It's the spice."

"You should have some. It's too good," Lizzie added with her mouth full as she reached over and fed her baby from her fork. Elma dabbed the sides of her mouth with her napkin to suggest the practice to Lizzie, who was too animated to pay attention. Lizzie paddled her legs under the table. "I'm looking for some work fast, Mr. Jolly. Y'all been in the business, I thought you could help." Raymond declined any food, not that there was much left. Cinnamon picked up the fork from his place setting and attempted to spear a series of red beans.

"You could get work as a nice housemaid or body servant, maybe even a nurse," Mrs. Jolly suggested, observing Lizzie's pert, full breasts.

"I'm not looking for that. I'm a show artist."

Ray crossed his legs and leaned back in his chair, wrapping his arm around El. "Any good?"

"I aim to find out!"

"What's your act?" Jolly interceded. "I can maybe recommend a couple of spots uptown."

"I'm a 'total package'—clown, sing, banjo, trumpet. Piano. I do everything."

"A regular virtuoso."

"Oh, I forgot to say I dance. Dancin's my specialty. I sing, too. Not like Elma, but I can get a crowd goin'. Do standards and my own songs—some me and Osceola did together."

"War widow and all, I should think you'd be getting benefits," Raymond wondered.

"Now, Ray—"

Jolly jumped in, "That's for the white folks, Minor. Where you been? Seen in the paper yestiddy bout that ship for mothers of guys killed over there. Some say, colored couldn't go. Colored gotta ride inna second ship. Gotta go steerage. Like they sons shed blood in another color. Only benefit we got is benefit of a doubt." He laughed at his own joke and slugged down a teacup of whiskey.

Lizzie scooped her child in her arms and rocked her roughly. "Well, I aim to be a first-class performer. That's the best I can do in his memory. My husband Ossie used to say, 'Don't sit there and wait for it. Go out there and make it happen.' Ain't that right, Cinn?" Mrs. Jolly's back straightened. Lizzie rolled her eyes. "It's Cinnamon, like her color! I didn't know I was gonna name her that. Can of spice fell off the shelf and there it was. Ain't she beautiful?" Lizzie rubbed noses with her brown-skinned child, playfully snubbing her nose at the table of would-be Creoles.

"In the old days, if you was a fellah I could send you right up to Marshall's or the Clef Club," Jolly advised, sucking on the marrow of a bone, "but when Jim Europe died alla that went. Ray and me been out the life for a while. Action's shifted uptown. Back in the day had to suffer through coon songs. You too young to know bout that. Me and Minor had a quality act. Ahead of our time. Ain't that right, Minor?"

Lizzie tapped her foot impatiently, tearing the few last chunks of a biscuit back and stuffing it into her mouth. She watched Ray out of the corner of her eye as Jolly paused, then launched anew, "Minor and Jolly. Class act. Nowdays, any heiffuh can barrel a tune, then cut a record. Call it Blues, and"—he rubbed his fingers together like he was sprinklin' salt and slithered the word out his mouth—"Jass. Nope. I'm out of it. Action's movin' uptown. All this Prohibition stuff. Too much fuh me. Me and the wife opened up a grocery store." At this, he hugged Mrs. Jolly's shoulder. She nodded a thin-lipped smile, her nose the perfect angle of a teapot spout. "Irish crew offered to buy me out." Dropping his voice to a whisper, he mocked his new investors, " 'Really tink about where we'se comin' frum,' says the quiet one—one with the bad skin, the one called, uh, Cappy Meeks. Little rough town scruff with lifts in his shoes. Fond of pistols, though. Cap yuh soon as whistle. Cap happy," he laughed. "I said, listen, I don't wanna know. Asa Jolly is foldin'. It's a new game now. Action's uptown where the colored still got some say."

"Your game still sound pretty good to me, Mr. Jolly."

Duly flattered, Jolly wrote out the directions uptown with pencil over a news page of stock prices, mapped out New York for her, posturing his knowledge as some influence he still might have. "There's Happy Rhone's on 143rd Street and Lenox, black and white, upstairs club. Got a nice floor show. Big white folks I hear comin up in there. Barrymore, Chaplin. Sissle's the MC. You don't wanna go up 'fore him till you got some seasonin', sugar. Same wid PJs, P&J Catagonia. Willie the Lion will eat you alive if you ain't ready. White musicians play for free just to learn! The Jungle's at 133rd, Bank's and Brownie's, and Leroy's. Lybia's fading. Small's Paradise got a wait list. Can you roller skate? . . . Well, forget that then. Cotton Club, started off as the Douglas, Jack Johnson's joint. White gangstas got to it, changed the name to Cotton. You know that weren't no colored folks' doin'. Don't think you light enough for them, though. They like 'em like yoah sistuh. If you got talent though, hell, try it. You can take the 35 straight uptown or catch the train at Broadway to 59th and transfer. It's the simplest city in the world."

While Elma made a pallet for Lizzie on the living room couch, Ray got Gabby's old milk crate cradle from the back of the pantry. He had crafted and sanded it himself. Elma threw her arms around him and hugged him from behind. She laid her head on his shoulder blade, next to his heart, beating fast.

"I don't think she was ever married to that fellah," Ray said.

"People grieve different, Raymond. She's young. It was a terrible blow seeing Osceola die like that. More terror in your own country than over there. She just needs a little time to get on her feet." He patted her hands across his chest. "Please say she can stay," she pleaded, leaning into the contours of his back.

"She still doesn't act like a war widow."

"She's family, Raymond. I am sworn to believe in her no matter what."

Ray brought Gabby's old cradle out to Lizzie, who was changing Cinnamon into an old slip, two sizes too big, the straps shortened with slipknots. She thanked him coolly, complimented its beauty, but waited until he had left to set it aside and cuddle her child in her arms. She heard Mah Bette in her thoughts. *Death done slept in there.*

"Pay panno on my tummy, Mama." Cinn pulled at Lizzie's fingers, urging they play the ritual game Lizzie had made up, each different note a different tickling spot. "Charleston, Durham, Kittyhawk! Norfolk, Richmond, New Yawk!" Cinn could sing like a mockingbird, anticipating where each tickle would fall until she laughed herself to sleep.

Night came restless for her mother. A force in the dark grabbed her by the face and pushed her down. Her hair, her dress stuck to the floor. Her body bolted back from a punch to the jaw and another to the chin. Her eye tore open, her body tore in half. She woke with a start at every crack or shift in the wind, a knock or hiss of steam. Likewise, the child often awakened, gasping at an unknown terror.

* * *

ELMA SAT feeding Jesse, spooning the cereal that spilled from his lips back into his mouth. A shadow passed through a shaft of morning light. "Gabby?" Elma looked up, for a moment expecting to see her second daughter. Cinnamon appeared in the kitchen doorway. Holding the night-slip with her chubby fingers, her wispy curls spiked around her head, a sleepy frown stuck to her brow, she seemed a princess shrunken by a spell.

"Well, good morning."

"Goo mowin'," the child responded with Elma's exact same pitch and rhythm. At the sound of a child, Elma's heart jumped. "Would you like to meet your cousin?" Cinnamon toddled toward her aunt and climbed upon a neighboring chair. "Cinnamon, this is Jesse."

"Yessee," the little girl repeated and clapped with delight, then took his hand in hers and released it. Jesse's arms dropped motionless. Elma joked, as she slipped Cinnamon's chair closer, "He's on the quiet side, but he's very observant. Aren't you, Jesse?" Cinn put her hands on her hips and brought her face close to his, nose to nose, examining him, then put her arms around the boy as if she would lift him. Jesse's arms popped up in a seeming reaction, a reflex memory of his reaching for his sisters. Elma felt a fresh surprise of tears collect in her eyes.

Lizzie entered groggily, her night-scarf askew. "Coffee?"

"Morning to you, too."

Grown up and grown apart, the sisters circled around each other with envy and longing. Elma, not being born into the high-tone class, abandoned by her father, mother a seamstress, had the look to suggest her path was different. She struggled through her pedigree-conscious college freshman year. She had the color, of course, and the hair—"your crown and glory," Mah Bette would repeat like a mantra as if Elma's assets were all on the outside. Obviously Tom was not her father, but she never challenged her mother's stoic silence on the circumstances of her birth. From childhood, Elma exercised a willful ignorance and passivity while Dora used the Diggs family connections to wedge her daughter into acceptable colored circles. Elma thought herself incapable of impulsiveness. Even her elopement with Raymond had calculation. She now had the Minor name, which could have been a stepping stone had Raymond lived up to it.

Lizzie, by contrast, had no one to make her way. Her father's disappearance had hit her hard, but in losing the parent who favored her, she developed a resiliency and independence of thought Elma would never possess. Lizzie seemed so comfortable with herself. She was a "bold, impudent heiffuh" according to Bette and a "spiteful, ungrateful wench" in Dora's opinion. While Elma suffered from too much expectation, Lizzie was burdened with none but her own. The more Dora hurled invectives, the stronger her defiance, a brazen helmet of red hair and a splash of freckles across her sun-bronzed skin. She attached herself to no one but Cinn, and that was a wary partnership, tumbleweed to a dandelion. "Yo Boo," she greeted her daughter like a pal.

Both sisters, like their mother and great-grandmother before them, simply erased from consciousness facts and experiences they could not face, inventing stories more to their liking and needs. As to talent, each possessed it in abundance, but while Elma sang for comfort and for her children and for God's glory, Lizzie, with the lesser range, sang anytime—and for money, she would put on a show! Elma sang absently and performed only when asked or prodded. Lizzie used every opportunity to practice. Every experience was fodder for material, every setting a potential audience.

"So I whip around, and it's the biggest policeman I ever seen, pokin' me in the ribs like that. Now I had told Cinn, anytime somebody touch you, anytime you see somebody come upon Mama, you hollah, you hollah good. Taught her to squeal like Papa used to when he was callin' to the pigs. She takes one look at this big joker, sizes him up, poking me with that stick, and lets out a hollah you could hear back on King's Highway, Charleston!" Lizzie sipped the last of her second cup, flailing her hands around, imitating her daughter, who now giggled with delight and clapped her hands, squealing in high decibels. "Talk about making a scene. Fifteen minutes in New Yawk and we gon' get arrested. White folks looking at me, saying what she doin' to that child. Colored passin' by, movin' out the way, sayin' she bettuh shut her up!" Cinnamon stood beside her, the perfect partner in the reenactment.

Elma, still holding Jesse in her lap, simultaneously laughed and shushed them. Cinn looked to her in confusion. "Your uncle Raymond's asleep," Elma cautioned quietly. "He's got the night shift, workin' on a tunnel to New Jersey."

Lizzie crossed her eyes and explained the dampening of their fun, "Aunty Elma has a huzbin."

"How's Mama?"

"Mama's fine." Lizzie sat down. "Mama's always fine. Cousin Diggs is just fit to be tied, though. He's been escortin' Mama for years now."

"Better her than me," Elma replied, still wincing from her mother's attempt to pawn her off to their wealthy cousin.

"Amen to that, sistuh. But, you know, the Chinaman's building a house next door."

"Get out!" Elma laughed, a parakeet with bells on its swing.

"Mama says she don't know who to choose, the undertaker or the laundryman." Lizzie put her hands to her face in mock dismay.

"After all these years? Yum Lee?"

"Yut, gni, som, se, ng, luk, chut, bak, gow, sup!" Expecting applause, Cinnamon glowed at how well she had repeated the phrase taught to yet another generation of Mayfield girls, reminding them that the laundry owner's business and friendship had been one of the most consistent the family had known. The two sisters simply gawked in amazement and burst out laughing anew. Elma put her fingers to her lips, "Shhh! Sh! Ray . . ."

Cinnamon immediately mimicked her, shooshing Lizzie with firmness, an erect pudgy index finger pressed to her lips, "Aunty El say Shhh!"

Elma marveled, "Oh, Lizzie, she's so smart."

"Thank God for that! You know, otherwise Mah Bette couldn't take no brown-skinned child. As much as she loved her baby, she have her ways. I came home, found my child with a clothespin on her nose. Woman say, jus' get a little bridge up there and she'll be fine. I told her, this bridge is closed. Her nose is just wonderfully pugnacious as it is."

Lizzie saw her sister's countenance change. Elma had not prepared her for Jesse. Lizzie reached for her nephew and picked him up. "Now this little bundle would be more to her liking. You a handsome son of a gun, Jesse Minor. We ain't never had no men in our family. That stayed for no time, anyway." Cinnamon started crying, reaching for Jesse and stomping her feet. "Your cousin think you her baby doll. That's what I'ma call you, Baby Doll . . . That's all right?" looking to Elma.

"Oh Liz . . ." Elma's body crumpled where she sat.

"Listen, your fam'ly's here now. Things gon change."

"Each day, prayin' for a miracle."

"Never know. Miracles happen every day. You watch, I'ma get one today. By the time I come back tonight, I'll have me a job. Gotta find someone to look after my pal, though."

"Don't worry about that. Miss Cinnamon and I are already good friends. Don't think you oughta call her Cinn, though. You see how people misunderstand."

"Yeah, well, that ain't my problem."

* * *

JOLLY REITERATED his maxim, "Easiest city in the world," as Lizzie walked out into the late morning rush. The loudness, the rhythms, the cacophony delighted her. As soon as she got to the corner, she balled up Jolly's directions, threw them into the gutter, and struck out on foot. She figured if the streets were all numbered, all she had to do was follow them uptown.

Maneuvering through the bustle, she suddenly understood the changes in Osceola's music, the sheet music recovered from his duffle bag. There were traces of her melodies, songs they had crafted together, but there were full orchestrations—horns, drums, brass—modern, wild, jazzed. In the drone and percussion of the traffic, the point and counterpoint of the city's rhythms, she heard the band in his thinking. In the traps of a sputtering motorcar, the timpani of a delivery truck, the warbling whistle of a street cop's ballad, Caruso bellowing from a tenement window, the blue note stride of a Beale Street sideman, in the stray notes of barkers, newsboys, and bagmen—"Hot dogs, Sauerkraut! Now, you listen! HellooooooOOOH, Temptation! Extrah!"—she saw where he was headed had he lived. A song of wandering outcasts, people of faith in a minor key, the tempo of the street, it was hot. She was home! "Ossie, you was right. We could have owned this town."

She ran into Sparrow, on 72nd Street, walking a string of West Side collared dogs in his green and yellow bellhop suit, the little pillbox hat sitting on the side of his head. "Hey Charleston!"

"Eye for talent, eh?" She stopped with her hands on her hips. "You book dogs, too?"

"This just my day gig. But you never know. That's Irene Castle's Pekinese right there. Hey, where you goin'?"

"Harlem, where you think?"

"You cain't walk to Harlem!" She continued walking uptown as he followed, dragging the mélange of pets with him. "You new in town, you need to know the layout. And something called the transit system. Besides, it's too dangerous. You walkin' in some neighborhoods they as soon cut you as speak."

"I can take care of myself, Scarecrow."

"That's Sparrow. I can't believe—you walked through San Juan Hill? You crazy? African boxer went up in there, world champion of the world—Sipi—with a leopard. Walked up in there, they killed him and the cat! . . . Wait, wait, wait, wait, wait, you need to save those legs for to-night! Wait till I git off work at six o'clock."

"Six? What I'ma do fuh foah hours?"

He looked at her with his eyes to one side. "Got uh empty ballroom with a piano. You could practice . . . Hardwood floors . . ." He did a quick time step. "Great for taps."

She looked him up and down. Sparrow's chiseled body seemed at-tached with wrenches. Smoothly oiled, moving gears, he was all angles. "Let's get one thing straight," she said, "I don't mess around."

"So where you get the shorty, then . . . No, no, no. Come on, come on, come on. I promise, just dancin' and singin', legit. Strictly hands off." With that he raised both hands as if under arrest. Impatient canines flew in all directions, their leashes snaking behind them.

Lizzie sat on the stone wall rimming the park while Sparrow collected his charges—she wasn't about to risk a run in her new stockings. She didn't know this guy, but figured she could handle him and she could use a little touching up before her first tryouts in Harlem. She followed him to the servant entrance of the upscale residential hotel where he worked. Waiting for him to let her in from the inside, she quickly grew impatient. "I didn't come to New Yawk to stand in no alley." She briefly entertained the notion of practicing some trapeze flips on the low-hanging fire es-cape, but the thought of her stockings got the better of her again. "Lizzie Turner, what are you doin'?!" Just as she started to bolt, the heavy kitchen entrance door flew open. Sparrow popped out like a jack-in-the-box.

"Come on, sugar."

"Don't call me sugar," she blurted as she brushed by him. "My name's Lizzie Turner."

She emerged from the washroom, her dance clothes concealed with an unbuttoned, oversized maid's outfit. Sparrow ushered her into a small, empty mirrored room with a shiny black baby grand. He crossed his legs and arms and leaned against its hollow. "Let's see what you got."

Lizzie tried not to act impressed, but her mouth salivated over the patent leather finish of the instrument's body. She ran her left hand across the keys, a lover stroking a long-missed cheek, her right foot angled on the volume pedal. Her first pounding set of chords threw Sparrow across the room. She launched into a strong left-hand stride, skating over the ivories, her voice clear as a bell, her command absolute, her sass-talking, brass-squawkin' Yamma Mama's Zombie Stomp! Not realizing that she would be that loud, Sparrow nervously looked toward the door, but then it got good to him, too good for him to care. His head commenced to wigglin', his foot tappin', fingers snappin', the boogie coming out of every pore. Suddenly, Lizzie stopped time, shifting pace and pitch. Her body arched into a backwards C and she snapped off the uniform.

"Damn!"

"This is where I go into my dance," she paused to explain, encouraging Sparrow to keep up the rhythm as she scatted through the next verse, imitating her backup band. She was just a green bean of a girl, but doggone if she didn't have the shapeliest legs he had ever seen move in more directions than he thought humanly possible. Though her hips were slim, the way she bumped em around sure made you wanna watch. Dakota Stretch Sparrow tipped his cap back. "To heck with the job. I got me a star!"

On their way uptown—on the bus this time—he considered the future of his client. "Lizzie Turner? Cain't go with a name like that. Gotta have something better than Turner. Every nigguh from North Carolina named Turner. Look. Mae West, Sophie Tucker, everybody change they name. Artie Flegenheimer, name Dutch Schultz. Lizzie Turner! Ladies and Gentlemen, Lizzie Turner! That don't sound like nothin'. You need a good stage name. Somethin' got a ring, somethin' say Boom!"

"Bessie Smith. Bessie Smith ain't no big name."

"But Bessie uh Big Woman. She come on stage an open up and nobody care what her name is! You ain't but fifteen pounds. You gotta hab sumpin up in front uh yuh. What your mama's name?"

"Leave my mama outta this."

* * *

EVEN THOUGH colored folks had started moving to uptown Manhattan just after the turn of the century, black Harlem, by the early twenties, was still a small, compact area, 130th to 140th Street between Fifth and Seventh. The famous 125th Street was still all white, the strip of Jewish merchants staying on despite their residential counterparts' gradual departure. As the colored continued to crowd into the uptown zone, fondly known as "the campus," the class of clubs followed an inverted pattern. Barron Wilkins for high society and Leroy's for the middle class, Harry Pyles and Connie's scaled down from 143rd. By the time you got to the lowest 130s, you hit the Black Bottom, literally—the Jungle, Basement, and the New Bucket of Blood—Coal Pit, the Airshaft, and Jonah's. Twenty-four hours, Live! This is where Lizzie's career was launched, a downstairs dive called the Turf Club. This was where Sparrow took her, where he had "connections."

"Mayfield Turner, Mayfield Turner everybody! Just arrived from Chicago! Coming through!" Sparrow's high, fast holler pierced through the crowd noise as he dragged Lizzie through the tight-packed line down the narrow steps. She fussed at him from behind, saying she hadn't given him permission to change her name, the crowd pushing them against each other. "The rule, keep playin'! We'll deal with that later."

"No we'll deal with it right now. My name is—"

"Lizzie!" he turned his head and hollered out. "Hey Lizzie, you here?!"

"What! Somebody call me?!" Random voices came from far back in the line outside the door.

"See, they two, three Lizzies already up in here. And ain't none of 'em gettin' in Big Ed's tonight. Stick with me, kid. I know my business. Now act like you somebody." Pouting, Lizzie quieted and followed him down the crowded narrow stairs to a steel door with a grated hatch. "Stretch Dakota Sparrow to see Big Ed. Escorting Miss Mayfield Turner."

The bouncer at the door spoke gruffly through the grate, his one eye fixed on the couple. "You need to know the password plus have fiddy cent."

Before Lizzie could open her mouth, he countered, "Be cool, I'll handle this." He turned back to the mean eye still staring at him through the tiny bars and said with great emphasis, "This is Mayfield Turner, here to audition for Big Ed."

"Auditions Tuesday."

"We ain't talking bout Tuesday! Big Ed sent me to the train to pick her up. We here tonight!" he scammed. "This Mayfield Turner, just come from Chicago! Ask him didn't he send me to pick somebody up from Chicago. Keep him waitin' if you want to."

Lizzie responded with a stance of self-importance and expectation of service that startled both agent and blocker. The bolt clanked and the fortress door swung open. Now, it was Sparrow who followed her. "Coming through!"

Big Ed sat in the back, a huge plate of food before him. His stomach bulged over and under the table. "Big Ed, Big Ed, here go your package from Chicago!"

"Get on outta here, Stretch." He poked at Lizzie with his fork, a diamond stud on his pinky. "I sent you to pick up a trumpet playuh."

"I am a trumpet playuh. Singer, dancer. Everything. I'm a virtuoso."

"Ain't gon find no virtue up in here. You wanna work the pussy, do it outside."

"I'm tellin' you, Ed," Sparrow commenced his pitch again, close to the man's ear in a stage whisper over the din of the club, "you gotta see her. If you don't, you gon lose her to somebody else and you gon be cryin' right in that spaghetti. She got the goods, I'm tellin' you. If my life depended on it."

"It could . . . Okay, sistuh. Show me somethin'. You got five minutes foah the stripper come on."

Big Ed watched indifferently as Sparrow chittered through the crowd like a gnat on some day-old food and handed out Lizzie's sheet music to the band members lookin' out the sides of their eyes. "Don't she know no standards?" the sax player whined. "What this shit say?"

"It starts off," Lizzie began.

"Why don't you just sing it, sistuh—we'll follow along."

"Okayyyy," Sparrow chimed and hopped on the small bandstand. He threw up his long angular hands and stooped to speak into the mike. "Ladies and Gentlemen!" The crowd ignored him. "Dukes and Ducheye! It is my great pleasure to introduce to you, straight from Chi-CAH-Go! Exclusive here, only at the Turf Club! The one and only Yamma Mama, Miss Mayfield Turner!"

As the combo struck up the first chorus, Sparrow extended his hand and Lizzie gingerly stepped into the light. There was barely enough room for the two of them on the bandstand, let alone for any dancin'. The bandleader softened, leaning in. "The chart's pretty decent. We gotcha."

Flashing a seductive smile, she belted as hard as she could.

> "Miss Lizzie Mae had her a way
> Of walkin' down the street
> That would make the sidewalk sizzle beneath her feet . . .
> Yes, Lizzie Mae had her a way
> Of walkin' down the street
> That could make a hungry fellah forget to eat . . .
> When she stepped in the lane
> All the necks would crane
> Just to name
> That funny way she had of wah-wah-wahl-kin'
> Baby, when she hit the street
> Lemme tell you it was somethin' sweet
> Made your heart just skip a beat,
> When Miss Lizzie Mae hit the street,
> When she what?
> Strut, Miss Lizzie, strut!"

Moving the microphone to the side, she broke out of the song and signaled for the band to keep going while she approached various members of the audience and with seductive swats of her hips motioned for them to move their tables back. The drummer followed her lead with some rolls and a pop with each of her undulating combinations.

Picking up on his cue, she mimed a kewpie starlet, caught in a sudden shower, apparently oblivious to the attention she was drawing and the havoc that it caused. She noticed a few drops of rain and popped open an imaginary parasol and a gust of wind blowing it inside out. Protruding her behind in curious, provocative ways, rolling her hips with each imaginary blast of air, each strident trumpet blare, she tried to hold on to that errant umbrella, swivel-hip backbends round and round, a crazy top. Strutting backwards and in place, she made space where there was none and pranced right up to Big Ed's table, shimmied off the drops of rain just enough for him to glimpse her pert and perfect cleavage, then spun around by the wind again, she shook her fanny at him like a duck.

The audience howled. The band got into the improv, talkin' to each other through the licks. "Oh, you see her comin' it's bad news—But it's bad news I can use—The kinda news you just can't wait to get—Make the muscles in your eyeballs sweat! Aw, go Miss Lizzie! Shim sham shimmy! Say what? Strut, Miss Lizzie, strut!" A vibrant, crazy, chaotic rumble, they threw it to the velvet!"

Three yards of upholstery trim sewn onto her mother's cut-down corset, spangles all shimmering, Lizzie launched into mad twirls, loose lunatic fringe going everywhere, a mad spider on the dance floor—every skin particle aquiver, closing with full split, scissor kick drop spin cross-legged bow to the floah, prostrate before Big Ed's table. Just like the song said, the audience was craning to see. Sparrow jostled around the floor picking up the coins folks had tossed her way. Lizzie attempted to quiet her breathing before she looked up at Big Ed, who stuffed a greasy dollar in her bra.

"Two fifty a night. Tips, sixty-forty split with the house. House get sixty." Ed gestured to his bouncer with his fork to relieve Sparrow of his bounty.

"Say, that ain't fair. She brought down the coin."

"So write your commissioner. Listen, kid," he turned to Lizzie, "you come up here to go to school, I'ma give you the tuition."

"When do I start?"

"Fifteen minutes. You come up here to sing, you sing."

"What'd I tell you, Ed," Sparrow interjected, "Dakota Sparrow? Eye for talent?"

"Get this ponce outta here."

For all the tuxedo-clad, slick-haired impresarios the twenties would come to be known for, black music was still the backdoor mistress and the shake-dancing, snake-hipped, pastie-taped, spangled, two-dollar whore, not the wife. But tonight Lizzie Mae Mayfield Turner didn't care.

Six nights, fifteen dollars a week plus tips! Even with the house split, it was more than she had ever made. In the funk-filled dressing room with just enough space for her to sit, Lizzie fastened tee-strapped, sequined tap shoes over fishnet stockings, sat up, and gazed in the mirror, framed by feathered G-strings, sweat-stained bras, and cardboard-backed tiaras. Much pleased with herself, she fantasized entertaining the skins of privilege—lords, ladies, starlets, gigolos, gangsters, and aldermen—band leaders, bootleggers, and bag men—prophets, pigfoot hawkers, and professional partiers who came to gawk at the busboys, elevator operators, and sailors—the maids, errand boys, messengers, and bellhops who frequented the Turf Club.

"When the ritzy places all closed down/ The dukes and duchesses comin' uptown/ To see and hear the world-renowned—Mayfield Turner!" she sang to herself. The set was little more than a floor show bordello with a strictly no-touch policy. It was Lizzie Mae's letter of introduction. She threw her legs up, pointed her toes, wound her arms round the backs of her knees, and held the position in a perfect pike. Bronze legs bedecked with silver slippers, a tight crown of sequined mesh above her brow, rhinestone arm bracelet and all her teeth!

After the gig, she was starvin'! Her appetite would later become notorious. Sparrow took two of the quarters she had earned in the showering gold of bandstand tips and introduced her to another Harlem tradition. "Rent Party! Rent Party!" Although colored folk considered Harlem a world unto itself, it was one they didn't, for the most part, own. The Mecca of the colored world was a rental property but the prices were twice what they were in the rest of Manhattan, so Harlemites invented a way to compensate. "Rent Party! Rent Party!" Folks were fanning themselves on the stoop and steps up to the five-flight walk-up.

At four in the morning, the joint was so torrid, the floor wax had melted. A Damballah line-dance of revelers slid across the wood grains—raisin' Cain, the roof, and the dead. Folks expected to get their money's worth, especially if it cost a quarter, a sum hard to come by for elevator operators, stevedores, Daughters of the Nile, and daughters of joy. "Let your Pap drink the whiskey, let your Mama drink the wine/ But you come to Florrie's, baby, and do the Georgia grind/ If sweet mama is runnin' wild and you lost your honeybun/ Come along and linger where the night is always young." Dancing on the table, skirt hiked up past her garters, Lizzie let loose her victory dance while a trio jammed in the corner, the sax player sittin' in the window, steady mopping his brow.

She sashayed into the next room to a hambone session of spoons, scat, and taps. Booze in the bathtub, collards n wings in the kitchen, making out on the toilet, throwin' up in the corner and, "Do you got some good food with some spice in it?" It was a jump, shout and strut, grindin', good foot good time. Harlem, which by day walked proud, was shameless in the wee hours of the morning. Imagine the wildest party you ever went to, and a little bit of it was there. Imagine Storyville, Beale Street, Central Avenue, and the Strand—brewed and bottled up, corked, and slapped with a fancy label. Pop!—Bubblin' Brown Sugar!

"Come on, Charleston, I need to git you home." Woozy himself, still sipping from his flask, Sparrow attempted to steer Lizzie down the steps.

"I cain't. My feet won't move."

"It's the reefuhs."

"The who?"

"Come on. There we go."

"How I'ma get to work tomorrow, muh feet won't move?"

"It is tomorrow. It was tomorrow yestiddy."

She got back to Elma's at seven in the morning. The sun was bright, the first wave of regular Joes already headed out to work. Midnight shift just coming home. Hands in his pockets, his head lowered in thought, Raymond strolled up the street in her direction. "Ray," she shouted, "I got me a job." Her arms extended, she leaned on her toes and hugged him, bracing her weight on his chest.

He bent away from her Tabasco, tub gin breath. "Doin' what?"

"Mayfield Turner, the Original Yamma Mama!" She swung away from Ray, steadying herself with one arm over his shoulder. "Stretch, this my brother-in-law. Raymond," she said very formally. "This my agent, Dakota Sparrow." She closed one eye and pointed to the open one. "Eye for talent."

Sparrow, still delighted with his discovery, glowed, "You shoulda seen her, blood." He shook his handkerchief fat with coins. "Look. She toah up the joint. Big Ed started jiggling. Broke the table! Got an audition with Tolbert 'n Cobbs. Do you know what that means? Ten percent, ten percent, ten percent." He looped around the lightpost in a jagged Kikuyu style.

Lizzie giggled and sat warily on the stoop. "Sparrow think I'ma be a star. Gon sell my songs . . . He think I got talent."

"For both your sakes, I hope he's right."

The trio was startled by the sound of the security grate flying up behind them.

"Mornin', Mr. Jolly!"

Drunk as he still was, Sparrow was wary. The eye for talent had an eye for deception, too. Raymond's hands, he noted, never left his pockets.

18

LIZZIE'S BREAK AT THE TURF CLUB DELUDED HER ABOUT
the realities of making it in New York. She thought to move up quickly
from the grinding late-night schedule at Big Ed's, to advance in classiness
and pay she didn't have to share. She got her first move up in street numbers, from 133rd to 141st with a gig as a background dancer in a new floor
show at Rhone's, featuring Queen Opal Roberts, the talk of Harlem for
her incredible record sales and her signature number, "Jazz Baby." Remembering how her sassiness turned off Black Patti, at the first rehearsal Lizzie
took the opportunity to approach the notoriously temperamental star.
"Miss Roberts, Your Majesty, I just want to say I am so honored to be working with you."

Although she was much better at improvisation than set patterns,
Lizzie concentrated to learn the routine and picked it up faster than the
other two dancers. She had it set after the first take, but saved her energy for
the run-through with the star. Midway through the set, Miss Roberts sent
a message backstage, "Tell the bitch I said turn it down seventy-five percent." In the third day, Lizzie lost the other twenty-five and was replaced.

"Fired from a show ain't even opened yet. That's great! That's just
great!" Sparrow grumbled, his jagged gestures emphasizing his dismay. He
kept her spirits up, though, preparing her for an audition with the col-

ored songwriting producers Tolbert and Cobbs. In the wake of the groundbreaking Broadway success of *Shuffle Along* by the rival quartet of Miller, Lyles, Sissle, and Blake, the duo Tolbert & Cobbs were thinking to make their own colored splash on the Great White Way. "The show called for fifty showgirls and live ponies," Sparrow told her as they entered the audition hall. "Surely you can manage not to upstage a horse."

Lizzie got her period the fateful day of callbacks. She knew her friend from down south's penchant for rendering no pain, then swinging back with a vengeance when she least expected. After sitting in a backstage hallway with a hot water bottle and slugging down a borrowed swig of modine, the cramps were still bad, sucking all of her thoughts and energy toward the pain. She balled her fist and determined to persevere.

She didn't make the cut of the "Shimmy Town Strut." She forgot the lyrics and sang scat, when it was not yet popular. More regrettably than that, she got the toss less for talent than her uncommon look—"Too short! And that hair," Cobbs scowled, "what color is that?"

The girl beside her scoffed out the side of her mouth, "Marhiney red looks to me. Put some bleach in your bathwater, baby. Get rid of some of them freckles. At least tone 'em down some. Lord!"

Lizzie blessed her back, "You honky-tonk, country-ass cunt!" and flew at the woman, grabbing a head full of hair as they tumbled off the stage. Sparrow jumped from his seat in the back of the theater and ran to pull her off in the first of his experiences with her explosive temper. His hand over her mouth, he strong-armed her around the waist, her legs kicking and arms flailing as she grunted every expletive she could conjure, waving the chorine's torn-off tap pants as a victory flag.

"What the fuck is buggin' you?"

"I got cramps, shit!"

"That still ain't no reason to go bananas!"

"If they didn't like my dancin' I can see it. If they didn't like my singin', well all right. But somebody say somethin' bout my color, I'll kick they ass."

"What are you talkin' about?"

"'What color is that? What color is that?!' I'll show him what color, I'll knock that muthuhfuckuh black and blue! I don't care who he is!"

"Sweets, he was talkin' about your tapsuit. Cobbs hates green." They sat in a café, sharing a cup of coffee. "Listen, when I hit the numbers, I'ma back your show, your very own, but you got to calm down."

"You bet too much. Waste your money."

"I'm bettin' on you. The Chestnut Filly. You're unique, Lizzie Turner. Takes time for people to understand that."

"Don't nobody else seem to think so. I'm so tired of people judgin' me."

"Then you in the wrong business, baby. Besides, you the worst judge I know."

"I am not."

"Got something to say bout everybody."

"Do not."

"How much you wanna wager?"

* * *

IT BEING Monday and her night off from workin' the Turf, Sparrow took Lizzie to the Crystal Palace weekly "Sashay," a transvestite ball competition, where the audience was the judge. Greeted by the male-clad pianist and singer Rene, their task would be not only to choose the most beautiful costume, but also to discern which one of the bevy of tall parading figurines was actually a woman. Sparrow thought the rowdy faux atmosphere would cheer her up. Her mind blurred by the morphine-laced tonic Sparrow had given her, Lizzie sat distractedly figuring out how to live on the two dollars a night and the tips she was making. Hardly enough to take care of the kid and still look for a place. Rents in Harlem were twice as much as anywhere else and she would still need childcare. Best make peace and stay with Elma, maybe get a bigger place together. *Even though I can't stand huh huzbin, Elma's still good with the kid. No way I'm ever gonna let Cinn stay with Mama and Mah Bette. Old clothespin lady.*

Over these thoughts, a melody floated in from the pit band accompanying the parade of sequin-clad performers. The tune was without lyrics, but Lizzie immediately recognized it. She blinked back to consciousness and looked toward the bandstand. *Osceola?* . . .

"Me and Ossie wrote that song!" When she stood up, Sparrow got a bad case of déjà vu. "Say! Where'd you get that song! Stop the music!"

"Lizzie . . . sit your ass down. You don't wanna make no scene in here. These is drag queens! Hey!" He caught the back of her dress as she flew toward the pit and snatched the sheet music from the nearest music stand. On the jacket: "The Cotton Patch Rag" by Mitch Jackson! The conductor reached up and grabbed the music back with one hand while furiously keeping time with the other, just as Sparrow spied two hefty bouncers headed their way, the tall bronze beauties strutting and fluttering, their eyes popping darts. Only his fast talking kept them from getting tossed out instead of "escorted."

"Look, you got to calm down."

"For what! That's my song! Me and Ossie wrote that—"

"You know if I had a nickel for every chippie come sayin' that's my song, I wouldn't have to play the numbers. I'd be a millionaire."

"You don't believe me?"

"I'm not saying that. But, but, but it happens all the time. 'Alexander's Ragtime Band,' Irving Berlin's biggest hit, his breakthrough. Scott Joplin swore he wrote that, tried to sue. What'd he get? Nothin', but the clap."

"I don't care bout that. That low-down, lyin' Mitch Jackson stood right up in my face when Ossie told him we—"

" 'That's my song! That's my song!' Ain't gon get you nowhere. You wanna do somethin' about it, write the publisher."

"I ain't writing nobody about my own damn song!" Lizzie jerked away from him and, turning her ankle, stomped, "Ow! Damn! You're fired!"

"I thought that was your specialty." Sparrow watched her hobbling zigzag disappear around the corner. "Go easy on the tonic, Slim."

* * *

SHE STAYED in the streets two days. Sipping the tonic until it was gone, a wandering nomad, she stumbled from speakeasy to dance hall to buffet flat, chased by her own memories, afraid to sleep. Through a haze of cheap booze and freely offered miscellaneous drugs, she searched a netherworld of anonymous bodies, looking for Osceola. A smell, a taste, a hand, a knee, eyes. "Wake up. Let me see your eyes." When she last saw Osceola's body, he looked asleep. The bleeding was internal, Roswell had said. "The wound just opened up inside." Hers was the same. *If only we had been able to talk, just to talk.*

She wouldn't let anyone else prepare his body. She told Diggs, her voice flat and determined, "I'll do this." When he asked, "Would that be appropriate?" she snickered. "People already presume we been inappropriate. I don't think a little bit more matters." Sensing her cousin's hesitancy, she softened, "I'm the closest he got to family," and added, "Osceola and me snuck in this same room to hear Jim Europe on your new Victrola." Roswell retreated, taking that last bit of laughter. The escapade had been their last joyful time together. So much had transpired for both of them in the thirteen months that followed.

His hair was cut different. His face had matured. Always so dramatic, never veiled, his face had never seemed conflicted until he saw her on the stoop that day. A face now without expression had been so alive, always with intent, alternately challenging and courting, their fighting mixed with play like young cubs wrestling to test and prepare. She picked up his hand and cupped it in hers. His knuckles were bloodied and bruised from the fight, but his fingernails were shaped and polished with a clear glaze. He had just treated himself to a manicure. She had envied those hands for their span of twelve notes. They had been her connection to the culture of men who made the music, the secret society of mentors willing to take on a youngblood like Ossie, dismissing her childhood aspiration as rebellion that would pass when she settled down. Ossie, the proselyte, defied the order and showed her the techniques just plucked from itinerant elders, willingly challenging his own mastery by exposing it to her boldness and innovation. She never appreciated the beauty of his hands until she held one feather-light and curled around her palm. Still warm. At Musicians' Hall he would have had the best-lookin' hands. She caressed his palm, kissed his lifeline which extended across it, then laid the hand back by his side.

She smiled to herself, remembering the last time they played at Pilar's dance hall, rousting Jocelyn from his favored seat, only time they beat him in a cuttin' contest. The Professor gloated as he bested the contestant before them, "Ain't a person alive good enough to beat me tonight." Ossie held back as she approached the bandstand, blurted out the challenge, "Yeah, but two of us is!" She had grabbed his hand, pulling him up.

They played as a duet that night, Osceola Turner and Lizzie Winrow, their four youthful hands with pint-sized virtuosity, making up for Jocelyn's famed long-fingered, thirteen-note stretch. It got so good, Lizzie lost her shoe. She kicked her right foot up and planted it on the keys, ticklin' the top notes with her toes. Osceola did the same, his left foot slammin' on the deep bass notes while he carried the boogie with his fingers. The crowd went wild, sloshing beer and throwing down shots, clamoring over their wagers, hootin' and carryin' on—a literal stomp. Jocelyn damned near jumped on the bandstand and slammed the key cover shut. "Puttin' yo dirty toes on my ivories! Get on outta here!"

"Took four hands and two feet, but we bested Professor Jocelyn that night, huh, baby? The two of us."

She removed his uniform, still pressed and proud beneath the scuffs and footprints of the brawling thugs he had battled outside the streetcar. She pulled his tee-shirt over him from behind. The clothing clung to him as the last trace of warmth departed his body, his weight falling into her. She held him to her, shook her head to dispel the expectation of a return embrace, then laid him back down. She was startled by the fresh scars from his war wound. Mimicking the explosion that caused them, the shiny, keloid welts of molten flesh crisscrossed his torso in jagged furrows of trauma and the rapid, sloppy sutures of a beleaguered base camp surgeon. She ran her hand along the filigrees of stitches. She could scarcely imagine, but then she could.

By comparison, the place where she had nicked him in the arm with her tambourine, a tiny, clean half-inch scar, seemed a mere birthmark. She had flung the instrument at him when he started seeing a neighborhood girl who was known for giving it up. He had stood Lizzie up for rehearsal, then tried to escort both girls home after their last set at the St. John's Island Harvest Social, dropping Lizzie off first. She screamed and cried a fury, less at the knowledge that he had a girl and more at his denial of it. Lizzie had no interest or enthusiasm for such activity. She fancied herself indifferent to human touch, instead finding sensuality in movement, the pulse of a rhythm in her body, a melody in her ear, the vibrato in her throat as she sang or the embrace of cool creek water on her naked skin as she dove beneath the surface. She, who loathed human touch, now found herself holding him with longing. He had kissed her just before he left, sending a shock of sensations through her body.

While Yum Lee washed and pressed his uniform, she searched Osceola's duffle bag for some good underwear. Beneath the dress he had brought her from Paris, she found a stack of music charts, their songs transcribed. She leafed through the titles—Zombi Stomp, Cotton Patch Rag, Tamarind Trot and the Geechee Town Ball, Gulley Bird Rag, Strut Miss Lizzie—her lyrics scratched beneath the mad scramble of notes, not simply for piano, but for a whole band. Osceola had learned to write music and arrange it! Just as he had vowed, he had gone off to war to find Jim Europe and returned a disciple.

She ran her fingers along the black flagged dots and measured bars, an archeologist of her own hieroglyphics or a blind man, understanding for the first time how the raised markings on a page represented a language and permanence that sound and memory could not offer. All her life, she had been the bold one. She had been the one to push, but now he was teaching her, leading her through the music they had made together. Here, in these charts, she could see his confidence grow with corrections and occasional splotches giving way to clear, unfettered, spirited strokes. Like the mirrored surface water of Oshun catching both her own reflection and a glimpse of Agwe's ocean depth, there was in the deep, rich India ink notations in his hand something of him and something of hers, indelibly intertwined.

As she sat there, contemplating a world without him, a slow bluesy rhythm slid from her lips, a song from deep within her body, a simple range of notes that flowed into each other, more a chant than melody, her voice floating on the wind. She rocked to and fro to her foot's slow scrape and step on the plain wood. An economy of gesture compressed emotion and held it taut till it broke over her in a wail. The sun well set, her sweat-soaked arms swept him into an embrace.

After she had washed him down, she swathed his body with scented water and oiled him with the treatment he used to like so much in her hair, trying to preserve the deep red hues of his graying skin. Her body heavy with life growing inside her, she heard only the quality of the silence—the archipelago of treble notes, water wrung from the washrag into a tin pail while outside the carpenter's hammer in fragmented four-four time crafted a new pine coffin. The baby stirred in her womb. She placed his hand on the point of pain. Where two children had snuck in to hear Jim Europe on a new Victrola two short years before, inseparable friends skipped lovers to become wife to husband. "I make this your child. Our child, Osceola Turner."

With the soft hiss of the radiator, and the tingling filament of a bare electric light, her memory of Ossie ebbing, she breathed in the morning and sat up in the strange apartment. The wallpaper was moldy with mildew spots, the bed creaking and stained. Except for maybe the slope of his shoulder, the young stevedore passed out beside her looked nothing like her love. *Wake up. Open your eyes.* She slipped into her dress and coat and broken shoe and walked out to a gray, empty street toward the subway. *Sittin' in the depot in the pourin' rain/ Waiting for anothuh mornin' train/ To carry me far from where I come from/ Carry me way from what I done done/ Nobody here even know my name/ Nobody here even know my shame/ Don't know how I keep goin' on/ When everythin' I done loved done gone/ I say, everythin' I done loved keep dyin'/ Seem even the day—Cain't stop cry-y-y-y-y-in'* . . . For the first time—doubt.

* * *

RAYMOND'S FIST clamped around the slingshot. "He says your sister taught him."

Elma sighed as she wiped her brow and continued stirring the evening meal of okra in tomato sauce, sipping it for taste. "I wouldn't put too much stock in that. Mrs. Marrano's kids are all a bit hooligan."

Ray leaned toward her and shook the makeshift weapon in Elma's face. "It's made outta his mama's garters."

Elma turned to him, bemused. "That's the way she used to make them, all right." She closed her eyes and breathed in the aroma familiar from her youth.

Ray walked away and returned. "One of her many talents. That kid coulda took my eye out."

"Taken, it's taken, Ray," she said softly as he paced behind her.

"Comin' in all hours of the night. Sleepin' through half the day." They talked over each other, the argument escalating.

"So do you."

"I work!"

"So does she. She works in a nightclub, Ray."

"That's what you call that two-bit dive? You don't see? Your ears too delicate to hear it?"

"What, Ray, what?"

Stuffing his hands in his pockets, he mumbled loud enough to hear, "Fornicatin' and whore mongerin', that's what!"

Elma slapped the serving spoon on the counter and turned with her hand on her hip. "Stop it, Ray! I won't let you say that. Lizzie's a sensible girl, a good girl."

"Oh give me a break. Dress hiked up to her knees."

"It's the style, 'sides, who says you should be looking?!"

"Parading around. It's disgraceful!"

"To whom?! Who in this neighborhood cares?"

"You said your sister needed a place to stay. All she was looking for was a place to dump her kid!"

"Leave Cinn out of this. She's no trouble. She's a help to Jesse, as if you cared a damn!"

"What are you sayin', huh? What are you sayin'?!"

"Lizzie's had no breaks, no money, no father!"

"She's a tramp! Your poor sister in mourning."

"What do you know about it?! What do you know about it?!"

"War widow hasn't shed one tear."

"Have you? Have you?!"

"This is my house!"

"Your house?"

"I'll not have it. Not under my roof. Walkin' around actin' the whore!"

He threw the slingshot in Elma's direction.

She whipped around. "That's my sister you're talking about. At least she's bringing some money up in here."

Raymond paused and laughed, ran his fingers through his hair. He walked away, stuffing his hands in his pockets.

Elma nursed her throbbing temple. "What is wrong with you?"

He had come so close to punching her. A trembling booze-laced swipe across the face. He couldn't believe how close he had come.

* * *

WHEN LIZZIE showed back up at Big Ed's, he didn't want to take her back. "Miss Big Time—too big for me! I got a business to run. Think you can show up when you want to?"

"Give me a break, Ed."

"I done gave you a break and you break mah heart. Already replaced you. Hot young thang from Kansas City Sparrow brought in."

"Sparrow?!"

"You think you the only show in town? Eye fo' talent got more n one eye. Toah up the place, she did." Big Ed walked ahead of her, talking over his shoulder, wheezing from his weight. "Juss gon run off, gon be a big star—told you I'd school you. Lesson number four hundred twenty-two." He turned and waved a fried wing in her face. "Nevuh spite the hand that feeds yuh. You can eat chicken or you can eat crow."

"Come on, Ed. I need this job."

"Like I care. I'm dockin' yuh pay. Twenty dollahs. You in the last set. We got competition. Rash of clubs. Coal Pit. Dreamland. Every nigga with a basement think he got a club. You all that, make it up in tips. Well, don't stand there. Get snappin'. Got fifteen minutes."

The hot young thang from Kansas City had taken Lizzie's spot in the dressing room. She would have pitched the girl's makeup on the floor had Sparrow not been there to intercede.

"What do you want?" Lizzie demanded.

"You might thank me for saving your spot."

"Yeah? How do you figure that?" She simultaneously rummaged through a heap of costumes on the floor and wiggled out of her street clothes. "Dog bite it, where my kicks?"

He dangled her silver slippers from his index finger. "Lookin' fuh these? Big Ed's main act, a complete no-show. You should be out of more than a pair of tap shoes."

She snatched them from him and leaned against the counter to put them on. He slapped his knee. Lizzie sucked her teeth as she looked away and contritely extended her pointed foot for him to fasten the buckle. "I . . . apologize, okay? I had troubles . . . of a personal nature. A row with Ray," she confessed as she proffered her other foot. "Boy, I would get outta that place if I could." She stood up and slipped into her costume, oblivious to Sparrow standing there.

He leaned on the door frame watching her. "I'm the one should apologize."

"How you figure that? I'm the one lost the gig," she said. "Can't seem to keep one."

"I shoulda warned you about the tonic. You ain't got the constitution. Ease the pain but cause some other. Make you do things you regret later. Don't wanna get yourself hooked on that. I worried about you."

"Well, don't."

"I can take care of myself," they spoke in unison, her serious, him mocking. She turned for him to zip her up. He whispered in her ear, "When I hit the numbers, gon set you up right. Back your own revue."

"Oh, please. You ain't got pot to piss in neithuh. You're addicted to them numbers. Just throwin' your money away."

"Take a chance on me, then."

"You need to see Miss Kansas City 'bout that. I already told you. I just shake my tail. I don't leave it nowhere."

Big Ed stuck his face through the change curtain. "Cops just come by. Don't come in tomorrow. Having a little accident. Stagin' a fire. Best take your costumes lest they get a little smoked up."

"First you wanna fire me for not showin' up," Lizzie protested, "then you tell me don't show up. Jesus, get me outta this joint!"

* * *

IT TOOK her an extra half hour to pack up her stuff. The morning was already bright when she curled up next to Cinnamon. With her knees pulled in, Cinn took up a full cushion's length of Elma's couch. Lizzie snuggled under the covers and tried to cradle her daughter in the crevice of her shoulder. Cinnamon frowned and grunted, stretched in her sleep and did a full turn. As her shallow breathing settled back into heavy slumber, her chubby fingers kneaded her mother's breast, still playing the piano game.

Lizzie had barely shut her eyes when Elma's morning kitchen clatter awakened her. Lizzie shielded her face from the brightness of noise and sunlight coming from the kitchen. Cinnamon stood in the door frame eating a piece of toast, the red jam decorating her cheeks. Her baby was growing. Her wispy edges had given way to full plaits, two stubborn ram's horns of hair. "She up, Mama El."

Mama El? Lizzie swung her feet to the floor. *When'd that start?* A wave of toxins sloshed across her brain. She pitched forward, lowering her head between her legs.

Elma bustled into the small living room, her hard-soled shoes slapping against the bare wood floor. She shoved a cup of black coffee under Lizzie's nose. "You nearly scared us to death! Gone two days again. Lizzie, I can't take this!" Cinnamon dawdled behind Elma, clutching a piece of her dress, sucking on two of her fingers.

"Can we talk about this later? I need to get some sleep."

"You need to get on your knees and pray."

Lizzie bounced to the floor on her knees, scrunched her eyes, and held up her hands in supplication. "Dear Lord, please let me get two hours sleep before auditions this afternoon."

"Go to church with me on Sunday."

"All right already, Jesus!" She turned her face to the crack in the couch and threw the coverlet over her head.

Elma started to speak, but held her tongue. "Come on, Cinnamon. Let your mama get some rest." Elma retreated to the kitchen, Cinn trailing behind her. Elma was encouraged by Cinnamon's interaction with Jesse. Her son now was making sounds, and movement, though slight and spasmodic, was evident in his arms and legs. His mouth still seemed lazy, staying open dripping saliva, but his eyes, which used to be expressionless, now followed Cinnamon's running form and even seemed, on occasion, to make and hold contact with her. She had found in the paper news of a specialist, "Neurology." Just a paragraph at the end of the article mentioned his work with premature infants, who were sometimes slower in development. She had not considered that Jesse's birth at seven months might have something to do with his condition. She didn't know if the doctor would even see them now that he was three—if he would see them at all, the family being colored—but she was determined to find out. An office on Park Avenue. She would need money for that. More than Ray was making. After the fiasco with Landry, he had managed to join the carpenters' union, passing for Irish again, but starting over with the least seniority. She had to find more money. She was thinking of asking her mother, but she was afraid. Afraid of Dora's response and of Raymond's.

Cinnamon and Jesse are getting along real fine. Elma composed a letter to Dora and Mah Bette in her head as she uncoiled her hair. *Maybe I should write Francina, too.*

She ran her fingers through the braid parts to loosen them and flipped her hair over the sink. She let Cinn stand on the stool beside her to watch. The ritual of washing her hair took hours. Snatches of thought flowed through Elma's mind as the water flushed through the rivulets of locks, which were thickest at the nape of her neck, the ends curling around the drain. Cinn's diligent little hands delighted in the silkiness and suds and the stories. "You should have seen it when I was a girl, Cinnamon. First year of college. We were forbidden to speak, not even to hold hands with a fellah. This hair, it ran down my back, so thick I could sit on it." The little girl's eyes widened with wonder, her fingers clutching the strands. Elma felt every move, remembering how Benna used to play with her braids and Gabby ask to comb it. She wrung the hair out like a thick slippery towel. *You're losing it, day by day. Broken bits all over the floor. Sweep, sweep it up 'fore somebody catch your soul, Mah Bette would say. Your crown and glory. Comin' in white.*

At the market that morning, maneuvering through the crowd, she had followed a young family, two women with several children, one child asleep in the second woman's arms. As Elma stepped behind the group at the curb, the sleeping child calmly opened her eyes. They were a deep dark blue like Eudora's. The women tried to steer the children through the crowd. Elma reached to help and felt dizzy, queasy, a slight pressure on her bladder. An elderly woman approached her. She spoke in another language, Polish perhaps. Elma didn't understand the words, but their substance was clear. She was pregnant again. The young woman gathered her chicklets together and instructed them to stay close, crossing the street. *This one will have eyes like Mama's.*

Dread mixed with hope. *I will go to the hospital for the birthing this time. Perhaps if I had before. This one will go right. No more death.* Mr. Rosario, from the family across the street, wore a red tie to protest his wife's inability to bear children who lived. He wore it like a banner of mourning, driving the poor woman to hysterics. But Ray was silent, distant, withholding of both love and condemnation. He simply stayed away. *Need to get on your knees and pray. You need to find yourself another church home.*

After the embarrassment of Ray's dismissal, Elma refused to attend Bethel at its new site. To her great consternation Ray swore he would never set foot in any church again. In concern for his hurt pride and in empathy with his anger, she had been lax in finding another place of worship. *I'll go to the Catholic church round the corner if I have to. Roof of God's house over your head.* The Madonna too had lost a child. Standing over the sink, she began to sing, "It's me, Oh Lord, it's me, Oh Lord, standin' in the need of prayer!"

"Think I'm kickin' up my heels, havin' a good time. Eighteen hours a day, two-three gigs strung together! No hot water, damn!" Lizzie's angry feet clomped up the stairs, the just opened bottle of bleach spilling over her hand, a towel haphazardly wrapped around her, the ends of her headscarf flapping in her face.

She found Elma combing through her long black hair, still damp, Cinnamon chattering beside her, "Tell me about the dance when you met Uncle Ray. When you paid the piano."

"It's played not paid, and why ain't there no hot water whenever I need it?" Lizzie shouted, her arms flailing, the bleach for her freckles splashing to the floor.

"Lizzie, you know how long my hair takes," Elma crooned plaintively as she tried to see her sister through the tangled mane over her eyes. "You know, forever. I used a whole bottle of soap." She pointed with the comb to the row of neatly torn muslin strips on the table. "Still have to wind in all those rags. Ray likes me to look like Mary Pickford."

"Oh grow up. That chippie is a hundred years old. You should cut it. Be modern!"

Lizzie stomped out of the apartment, slammed the door behind her, and sat on the steps. Miss Tavineer poked her head out of the lower apartment to see if the coast was clear. Cinnamon scooted from the apartment above and, balancing herself along the wall, quickly conquered the steep stairs winding toward her mother. Lizzie's frowning face rested in her fists. Cinnamon's strong, pudgy fingers tugged at her arms. "Mommy, Mommy. Pay piano on my tummy."

"Mommy don't wanna pay piano. Mommy cain't pay piano. That's the problem. But you know what? Your daddy used to say one man's problem is another man's opportunity. We gon get you a real piano, Cinnamon Turner. And a telephone!" she hollered over her shoulder at the shut front door. "Why I got to have the only fam'ly stuck in the nineteenth cint'ry?"

Lizzie regarded her recent calamities as a temporary loss of her luck, a missed fortune, as one would arrive at the subway platform just as the train pulled away. A dash of anger with a kick of her shoe, a few expletives, and complete confidence that another train with your letter on it would follow shortly. She didn't need prayer. A true god would not rob Osceola of his future. A real god would not snatch Jim Europe from his victory tour, wouldn't let her father vanish, or make her pregnant by a bastard like Deke Turner. A rightful god wouldn't give her a child she wanted to love and hated to look at. Any moment could draw her back in. To the rage. Any setting—a lonely crossroad, an abandoned depot, a crowded sidewalk, a department store counter, a bank teller's line, a bus stop—could set her off. At any moment—like no hot water! No burden of a three-hundred-pound cotton sack or lash across her back, but the wounds, nonetheless, could reopen and stretch into ugly, daggered, stinging gashes, emptying her of anything but fury. Toughened with methods minus the understanding, Lizzie kept moving. *Never slow down, never get caught, never surrender.* She stepped onto the street and hollered up to the window, "God helps those that help themselves!"

Her suitcase of costumes and sheet music weighed on her arm like a coffin. It was only mid-day, too early to head back uptown to Big Ed's. She told her feet to take her somewhere. They pointed downtown, discovering random Manhattan worlds along the way. She spotted the great Bert Williams standing beneath a Broadway marquee, deep in thought, his long arms laced behind his back. *Least I'm not the only one with troubles.* "Though his kind I wouldn't mind much havin'," she talked back to herself, "Ziegfeld Follies, now that I wouldn't mind."

The library was flanked with banners announcing a new exhibit related to the unearthing of Tutankhamen's tomb. "The Sun King, buried a thousand years," she read. "You and me both, buddy. Tut, tut, tut," she scatted. Her feet echoed with body music, a listless ball-and-jack blues. Miller and Lyle's Colored Revue *Runnin' Wild* had a matinee. "Best seats a dollah fifty . . . shit, a whole night's pay." She wandered on, contemplating her next move. "Tut, tut, tut. Lizzie May Winrow's inna rut, runnin' wild, goin' nowhere."

She noted Valentino had a new movie, *The Sheik,* but going to the cinema only brought back memories of sneaking into the Bijoux, poppin' redhots in the balcony, gettin' hot lips. *Oh Ossie, how I'm to do this on my own?* She was twenty-two and the world was passing her by. Other colored performers were making it. *Cars, jewels, and maids, and what am I doing? Still making my own costumes!* Sure, Sparrow always had an audition lined up, the next big revue. An out-of-town tryout like the last one. "Bombed royally in Camden, no less. Who the hell plays in Camden?" she said out loud. Like the rest of the crew, she had to make her way back to New York on her own. Back up to Big Ed's, beggin' for her spot. Just like her dancin', she kept spinnin' around and finding herself right back where she was.

The day was overcast and the air misty. Droplets floated upwards, the soft drizzle wreaking havoc with her marcel. "Damn!" She stopped to check the damage in the Macy's store window on 34th Street. The mannequins were bedecked in the new flapper styles, flat breasts and skirts halfway up the leg, bowed square-heeled shoes. Being modern was going to cost her a whole new wardrobe. She could alter the clothes she had. At least she knew how to do that. *Mama would be thrilled my sewin' skills come in handy.*

Through the glass she saw that copper, bouncing on his heels, across the street, just waiting to make his move. Ever since that day at Penn Station, he always had somethin' to say to her. Them both bein' redheads, each was easy to spot. She hurried along, weaving among the pedestrians, unconsciously arriving at her destiny, 28th Street, from the East to the West, the meat market of America's music—cannibals all we be! Tin Pan Alley!

From each gold-plate-lettered window, upright player pianos competed with crooners sampling their wares. From show tunes to shimmies, carnival barking pitchmen competed, enticing any would-be buyer with the next great hit. True to its name, the strip of publishers and professional pluggers of sheet music sounded to the untrained ear like the din of a thousand tin pans. Lizzie was baffled by the myriad company monikers. She wondered which one that foul Mitch Jackson had been to and how many other songs of her's and Ossie's he had hocked. *When if ever I see him, he'll get a piece of what for, for sure!* But she was hestitant. She battled with herself. *These are Osceola's and mine. How can I sell what belongs to both of us? Ours together.*

The internal debate resolved when she spied Lew Leslie, choreographer and stage manager at Rhone's and the new club called the Cane Break. He walked right past her into Axleton Bros., accompanied by three short, square-shouldered gents, their fedora hats pulled low over sallow white faces. *Gangsters! I shouldn't go up there without Sparrow. Oh what the heck! Everybody's a little illegal.*

She followed the quartet, catching the tail end of their conversation, "We gotta have new songs for the revue. The club just opening, it needs to be something the people ain't heard before. Somethin' Queen can cover. Snappy, like that," snap, snap, snap.

"'That be 'Cotton Patch Rag,'" Lizzie blurted as she followed them through the door. Two fedoras whipped around, flaring their jackets, each with a trigger finger to the rib, poised to draw a weapon from a side holster.

Lizzie froze and blinked a lot. The sidemen dropped their hands to their hips as she patted her bangs to the side, blotting her brow. Leslie, a short, cosmopolitan Jew, sat on the edge of the desk, glinting through a funnel of blue cigarette smoke.

"I'm here to sell a song," Lizzie continued. "I got just the one for you. Perfect for your revue." He had a high forehead, big ears, and one blind eye. The other, sharp and instantly assessing, made up for it. "Mayfield Turner." She stuck out her hand.

"This is Mr. Meeks and his associates, Mr. Edwards and Mr. McPherson. I'm—"

"Lew Leslie, I know. I auditioned for you once . . . a while back."

"Yes, I recall. Tolbert and Cobbs. You had that rather unusual brawl."

"Mm, well, today I have just the song you been looking for—as good as 'Cotton Patch,' if not bettuh." She launched into an a capella teaser:

> "Oh, oh, oh, baby
> I musta been a little bit crazy
> To think that I could talk to my baby
> When she been cryin' the blues
> Oh, oh, oh, baby
> My memory's just a little bit hazy,
> But I just was wonderin' if maybe
> It ever happened to you . . ."

"Not bad. I like it. Kinda snappy," said the one called Mr. Meeks. His skin was bilious, she noted without looking directly at him, and his nose had been broken several times. She knew this to be Cappy Meeks, the East Side thug who had muscled his way into Jolly's shop as well as much of Midtown and who now was huffin' and puffin' at Harlem. The former Calvin Murkowsky got his name for his penchant for capping his competitors and debtors in the knees. His clothes had gotten better and he had been taking skin treatments, but he had no lips.

Leslie flicked his cigarette. "That your portfolio?"

"My wh—? Oh, yes!" Lizzie responded and popped open the weathered bag and unbound her charts.

"Twine and waxpaper. Cute." They were leering, making fun of her. Her blood was pumping so heavy she could feel her temples. "We don't see too many chickies peddlin' music, doll," Meeks cracked. "How do we know you didn't just rob those off your boyfriend?"

Lizzie glared at him and said flatly, "I wrote these with my husband. He was killed in the war. The lyrics are mine. The arrangement is his. The songs belong to both of us."

"Touching," Leslie said as he picked up the song titled "Crazy Love" to examine it, the ash of the cigarette threatening to fall.

"The war," Meeks scoffed and sniffed, "that's ancient history, sistuh. Things gotta be uptempo—you know, jazzed." He snapped his fingers spasmodically.

"Tempo ain't nothin'," she clipped. "I mean you can always change that. One-step, two-step, foxtrot, tango—nothin' but time. It's the melody has to be catchy. Every single one of these is a hit. If you like 'Cotton Patch,' I know you'll like these. I been workin' 'em down at the Turf Club."

"Turf Club," one of the sidemen said without moving his lips. "They don't allow no whites. Too exclusive." His boss choked off his laugh with a glance.

"Open up a practice room, Lew." Meeks's off-hand command was crisp. "Let's see what she got."

"Anything for the war effort," Leslie added snidely. "It's Queen, you know, has to like it."

"It's me has to like it first. What's your name again, doll?" Meeks inquired.

"Mayfield Turner."

"Okay, May, let's see what you got."

She had not anticipated success. She had no clue of what she would perform. Their heels echoed on the marble floors. A dissonant array of sounds wanting to be music richocheted off the walls and collided with a clatter of noisy, urgent, loud-mouthed voices. All male. Beyond a couple of silent, suspicious, mascara'd secretaries wearing too much powder, she was the only woman in the building.

They entered a room at the end of the hall. The door glass was frosted, the room was musty and close. It contained only a beat-up brown upright piano and a couple of folding chairs. No dancin' routine here. One errant aerial kick and she'd be out the window. Instinctively, Leslie sat on the sill. His persistent cigarette ash folded over in an annoying defiance of gravity. The others leaned over the top of the upright as the last to enter shut the door behind him. She didn't like the closeness. Memories swarmed in on her. "I play standing up," she said, shoving the piano stool back toward them with her foot. "Have a seat."

Lizzie placed her foot on the pedal and her hands on the keys and called down Osceola's spirit. With the rhythmic, rising line and furious energy that would become her trademark, two hands turned into four. Lizzie Mayfield Turner blew them out of the room. The pure power of her sound surged with primary colors, a full orchestra jammed into eighty-eight keys. A wild left hand held down the bass line, while the right hooted, hollered, gurgled, and screamed. A trombone arabesqued and growled, the sax streamed diagonally across the keys. A muted trumpet whined over a clarinet's hypnotic trilling, while her left-hand traps kept the rhythm's frenetic pulse. When she kicked up her foot, her shoe flew off. The frosted door opened and its frame filled with astonished faces crowding in to see if they could believe what they heard. Lizzie Mayfield Turner coming into her stride, tickling the top notes with her toes.

When she finished, Meeks snapped his finger with impatience. "Shut the door, shut the door." The listeners scattered before his associates could oblige. The quartet of men now encircled her as Meeks stepped forward. "How many you got there? I'll give you fifty bucks for the catalogue. Fifty bucks." His voice dipped as if she should be impressed.

Lizzie folded her arms around her stack of songs and held them to her chest.

"Fifty bucks for this song, dahlin', plus royalties and a spot in your new revue at the Cane Break. As you can see, I can sing. I dance and I do comedy, too." She laughed, slipping her foot back into her shoe.

Leslie, still implacable, finally flicked his cigarette in her direction, indicating she had a deal. "Bring your stuff down to the Ninety-One. Four o'clock."

"Four o'clock . . . Say." She stopped. "How do I know you just won't walk off with my song and take it for yourself?"

"I'm a published songwriter, sweetheart. Sold over five hundred thousand copies. You want the job or not?"

"Four o'clock. The Ninety-One . . ."

"Forty-second and Ninth. So go on, get outta here before I forget how generous I can be."

She walked out quickly, got around the corner, and swung around the lamppost. "Whewwww! Thank you, Jesus! I'm sorry 'bout everything I said!" She could barely comprehend her dramatic change of fortune. Walking up and down the avenue, waiting for four o'clock, practicing what to say, *Don't bother—every time you practice, you get it wrong—just improvise*, she remained unnerved. *What to tell Sparrow? What other songs to pitch?* The afternoon sky darkened, and the anemic concrete-enclosed trees turned their leaves upward. The fine rain turned to pellets. Shielding her head with her suitcase, she ducked into the Times Square library.

She liked the floors—the banister's glide, the sound of her cleats on the marble, sand spins without the sand. "Shh!" The librarian made an eye gesture to the security guard. To calm her nerves and think, Lizzie found a seat and grabbed a thick oversized book on reserve about the recent headline excavations in ancient Egypt.

Facing the clock, she randomly looked at the pictures, pausing at one rendering of the perfect combo—two fluted horns, a guitar with a triangle base, drums, cymbals, rattles, flutes, and shake dancers—all of them women. She studied the features of the headdress, the elongation of the eyes, the hunched shoulders and elevated hips. *Oo, I could put charcoal around my eyes like Valentino.* A new tune began forming in her mind, her body instinctively moving to the swing tempo in her head. *Let's see Queen Cleopaterah/ Could do a shake or shimmy or tap or uh/ Brand-new dance to make old Pharoah prance/ And rise up from his tomb . . . Marc Antony of ancient Rome/ Never had such things as this at home/ Just one look in his girl Cleo's eyes/ And my oh my oh my oh my/ He knew that he was doomed/ Just one look at that Egyptian goyl/ Lathered and slathered in snake oil . . .*

Laughing aloud to herself, she borrowed a slip of paper and a squat yellow pencil from the book request box and jotted down the beginnings of what she thought a promising new lyric. *Talk, Camel walk . . . Sphinx, thinks? Oh, high jinks!* Her freestyle rhymes filled up sheet after sheet of the tiny slips of paper until the pencil was worn to a nub. The librarian looked over sternly. Was the girl going to order a book or not? A rumble of spring thunder underscored Lizzie's excitement. She wiggled in her seat and jostled her neck from side to side. *A whole new routine. I'll get my own spot, then my own revue!* The universe responded with a bright burst of sunlight streaming through the library's transom window. "The Devil was beatin' his wife and she run off leavin' a rainbow," Mah Bette would say. The storm had passed. It was a brand-new bright day!

Lizzie gathered her things to leave, but she wanted that picture for inspiration. *Who'd believe an all-girl jazz band in ancient Egypt!* "Reserved." Hmmm. She scanned the hall to see if anyone was watching and considered tearing out the page. *Just ask old Emperor Caesar/ Who did whatever he knew to please her/ But soon as he professed his love/ His bubble bath became a bath of blood/ But nothing seemed to harm her/ Indeed she was a charmer/ Who could resist that Egyptian goyl/ Lathered and slathered in snake oil?*

"Please, continue what you were doing." An ominous baritone voice bored into her from behind a towering stack of books. "I've been watching you for quite some time."

She froze, considering should she make up a story or bolt. The source of the voice emerged from behind the row of shelves. He was a short, dark-skinned, delicate man with huge, almost brooding eyes. He was dressed in a sleeveless cardigan with an open-collar cream shirt. Instead of a tie, a silk scarf loosely looped around his neck. A fitted tweed jacket, shoes that looked like slippers, and no socks completed the look. His hair was thick and pressed back in a series of tiny, rebellious waves. He surveyed the cover of the book she held. "Sprechen Sie Deutsch? You read German?"

She closed the book and crossed her legs. "Yeah, sauerkraut," she laughed. "A girl can't look at the pictures?"

"Please do." He placed another book on the table, pushed it in her direction, and gestured for her to open it. "I should introduce myself. But I think the proper thing is to wait for the lady to do so." He was oddly shy and self-assured.

". . . Lizzie May . . . Mayfield Turner," she extended her hand.

"Haviland Remick." He cupped both of his hands around hers.

High-toned to be so black. She liked that about him.

The book contained scores of charcoal and ink drawings, pastel sketches, and quick pencil studies. Faces, hands, shadows. Muscles moving swiftly. Head, house, light. A face in a window frame, a still-life bottle on a curb, a dancing couple, an estranged couple, the body proportions exaggerated. The work was not realistic, but sharp, with clean angles and curves, essential lines and emphasis where unexpected. As much as Lizzie wanted to talk to him, she didn't want to lose the strains of melody floating in her head. "These are really good."

He stepped backward, almost tripping as she complimented him. He was a contradiction, arrogant and insecure just like her. Lizzie liked that about him, too.

She turned the page. The last sketch was a half-finished, three-quarter charcoal profile of a young woman twisting a lock of her bangs and peering into a heavy tome, the open page of the book visible over her shoulder. The smudgings, line corrections, and scratching showed a tension between calculated labor and turbulence, a polish that erupted into a deliberate imprecision. Within the frame he had captured her movement, her thought, her essence. "You did all this in the little time I was sitting here?"

"One must commit like the flash of lightning on a darkening sky." His whisper traveled across the room. The librarian looked up again.

Lizzie examined the drawing more closely. No one had ever made a portrait of her. "You didn't have to make my lips so big."

"One distinguishing feature among your many. The unusual is the beautiful." He sat beside her, his shoulder probing her space. She shook her paper slips into a neat stack.

"I noticed you were writing," he continued. "Are you a poet?"

She laughed one short staccato note through her nose. "Hell no." The plosive startled him, but the thought had never occurred to her. "Uh, well I write songs. Show tunes, blues, rags and jazz n stuff."

"The triumph of this century—Negro music!"

"Excuse me." The librarian poked her pointy face between them. "If you two cannot be quiet, I'm afraid I will have to ask you both to leave."

He didn't blanch. "This is the public library, isn't it?"

"Impertinence!"

"Every day, if I can help it. We're New Negroes." Lizzie pursed her lips to smother another chortle. The flustered woman turned on her heel and marched back to her desk, a fortress of wood with its parapets of returned volumes. "I'm used to standing out," Haviland confessed. "It's rather an addictive habit." His voice tickled her ear. "I just got to New York yesterday. From Minneapolis. Friends are still putting me up on a couch."

"Shoot. That's an official New Yawk apartment. I'm sleepin' on a couch, too. And I been here goin' on two years. Where's that at, Minneapolis?"

He winced at her sentence construction, but recovered. "North, far north. Half the state's from Sweden," he imitated the Scandinavian lilt, two trochees and a spondee. He handed her a printed flyer. "You must come to my show next week."

"Show? Oh no!" She grabbed her things and flew.

* * *

LIZZIE GOT to the audition three minutes late, winded and wide-eyed. The band was sittin' around. Cappy had told the leader, "I got a new song for Queen."

"But Cap, the show's already set."

"Well, un-set it," he said, drawing his pistol. "I said, new song for Queen."

To the band leader's plaintive look, Leslie shrugged. His new silent partner was not so silent. "Give the kid a shot," he said diffidently, "she's got somethin'."

Lizzie, meanwhile, was in the bathroom, trying to fix her rained-on hair, which had ballooned into a mushroom. "Oh, forget about it. Lipstick. Stockings straight—Go!"

Queen sat, jawin' with her combo, the hot five. When Lizzie emerged, the seasoned players already had her music out, distributed and cleanly dissected. Queen looked up with her huge doe eyes. "I like that 'Crazy Day Blues,' and this Egyptian thing." She sifted through the slips of library paper. "It's different. Put a melody to that, I could do that," she laughed sexily, the combo concurring. "Got another one?"

And so it was, her sheet music had auditioned for her while she was frettin' and fussin' in the bathroom. Leslie agreed to take Lizzie on, giving her a little feature part in the second act. She was to start in two weeks. "I'll send my agent down to negotiate the details," she said as she shook Mr. Leslie's hand, barely able to contain herself. A little upset at the prospect of giving away her Cleopaterah, she was glad that Queen at least didn't take her Strut. *With that new gut the Queen's got to her middle, the tempo's too fast, anyway. Her speed-dancin' days is ovuh!* Lizzie was determined somehow to insinuate the Strut into her Cane Break debut. *And from there, in no time, my own revue. When the ritzy places all closed down/ The dukes and duchesses comin' uptown/ To see and hear the world-renowned—Mayfield Turner!* She nearly skipped out of the hall delirious.

After she left, Queen Opal strolled over to Lew and Cappy. "I know about that gal," the songstress cooed. "I tell yuh, if she act up just one time…" Miss Opal threw up her diamond-crusted fingers, then balled them into a fist. "Pow! I'll knock that redheaded heiffuh clear into Sundie!"

19

Lizzie didn't understand why Sparrow seemed to be backing away from her. Here she was, in two weeks opening at the first Midtown supper club to offer a black revue, ten blocks from Broadway, and he was testier than ever. "A tarbaby's jump away from the old minstrel shows—employing strictly black talent for a strictly white audience, a fantasy of slavery right down to the log cabin lobby motif," he blathered, "statuesque, near naked Creole chorines, and Queen Opal, the big, black Mama, beltin' the blues!"

"So what is it, Sparrow? You don't want me to take the gig just cuz I got it on my own?"

"I ain't sayin nothin'. You can go on the white time if you wanna."

"I ain't goin' on no white time." She jiggled in her thin coat and drew her collar tighter about her neck. The brisk March air nipped at her thin costume underneath. Trying out her new King Tut motif, Lizzie had wrapped a sequin halter top around her head, using the breast cups as ear flaps, the bodice tied tight to her skull. A halter strap smacked her in the face each time she turned to talk to him. She had employed twelve matchsticks to line her eyes with charcoal. "Here's the deal. I get what every other girl gets. Twenty-five dollars a week, seven a week for rehearsal. No muss, no fuss."

"No johns, no husbands, no babies, and no agents. I go up to negotiate your contract, Cappy Meeks stuck a pistol to my face with uh add-on, write-in clause—'I never wanna see your particular black ass again.' I neglected to tell you the finer details of the conversation."

"It's a job, Sparrow, and pays good. It's money, baby, and that ain't but one color. Greeeeen. Movie stars, dukes, and marquises come up in there. Give me a chance to be seen."

"Yeah, well, just lay low of the bootlegguhs, okay, Slim? Do me that favor." Sparrow blew on his hands and stuffed them into the pockets of his sports jacket. It was the first day of spring in name only. "I know a cat in the club's new band. He'll keep his eye on you."

"I don't need nobody keepin' his eye on me. I'm from Charleston!" Her black-rimmed eyes glowed like shields.

"What the fuck is this?"

"Villa Jualero," Lizzie slurped with delight. The total vamp, she teased, twirling Haviland's flyer in Sparrow's face.

"Welcome to the Black Palace!" announced the doorman wearing pantaloons and a powdered wig. They had been so busy talking they had not realized the line had reached the entrance. "Welcome to Mademoiselle Walker's Harlem Soiree!" The herald carefully scrutinized them. "The evening is strictly black tie, sir."

Sparrow glared back. "Is that before or after you jumped Red Riding Hood's grandma?"

"I knew I shouldn't of brought you."

"Admission is fifty cents."

Before Sparrow could retort, she shoved the flyer at the attendant. "We're guests of the artist. Mr. Haviland."

"You mean, Mr. Remick," the doorman said haughtily without actually looking at them. "Haviland is his first name . . . And yours?"

"Mayfield Turner."

"Starring, in two weeks, at the new Cane Break Revue," Sparrow pecked behind her. "That's her name right there, Minute Man." He poked at the ledger of invited guests in the doorman's hand. "In two weeks it'll be in lights."

"And . . . ?" the herald inquired with complete disdain.

"And guest, that's me. First name's Mystery."

"You'll find the gallery upstairs, Miss Turner. The buffet is on the first floor."

"I been to a buffet," Sparrow jabbed at the doorman as he passed. "Buffet flat right up on Hundred Thirty-third give any kinda food you want, and sex," he added, "cafeteria style."

Lizzie grabbed him by the arm and pulled him inside. "You act like you ain't been nowhere classy before." She had invited Sparrow so as not to appear too available, but now she regretted his companionship. Surveying the room, she felt a tingling in her body at the sight of so many successful show people mingling among Harlem's literati. Aside from a few exceptions like Rosamond Johnson and Paul Robeson, their worlds didn't mix. Most refined households still didn't play the blues.

Sparrow prattled on, "Millionaire heiress charging twenty-five cent for ice tea oughta be arrested." Mumbling fast in Lizzie's ear, "I'mo exercise my totin' privileges, that's what I'mo do," he scooped the petite salt and pepper shakers into his pocket. Lizzie slapped his hand. "Jumpy, jumpy."

He was right. She was nervous. Lizzie had not felt attraction for anyone. Big Ed's no-touch policy was fine with her. She could flaunt her body and taunt as she wished and still be in total control. Off the bandstand, she left quickly for the dressing room, avoiding the mashers with seductive dodges and darts. When push came to shove, she used humor. She was a cut-up, a show-off. That's how she made her living, but in this crowd, she didn't like the way she stood out. Despite her amazing skills with a scissors and safety pins, her outfit was clearly too flamboyant for the intellectual Renaissance crowd. Her outlined eye treatment was a whole fashion season ahead of its time. Everyone was staring at her. She knew not a soul.

Sparrow assessed the soiree set as they ambled. "Oooo-wee, sid and siddity's up in here. Defender of the race as long as it keep him among white people. He looks even whiter in person. Social activist especially fond of plump behinds. Post office runaway on the chickenbone express. Professional doll, her job to siddown and look good. That one built a sanatorium and was its first customer."

"Do you even know any of these people?" Lizzie asked distractedly.

"Read the paper sometime. You might learn something. I see why they call these things finger food," he quipped, holding a circle of shortbread topped with salmon and a whip of caviar-dotted sour cream. "Meal for your pinky."

"Look, if you wanna be mad at me, Sparrow, be mad at me. If you want me to turn loose the gig, say so."

"Shoot, baby. I cain't hold you back just to get my little piece. Go on. Take it."

Haviland entered on the arm of a gaunt white woman with a cape of wild foxes around her neck. Lizzie felt a tinge of irritation that he was not alone, but then neither was she. He had seen her. How could he not?

Like magic, Haviland appeared by her side, his arm cupping her waist. "Don't go anywhere." Voices faded, the air around her moving to his melody. "I want you to meet somebody." He squeezed her waist again. "Quelle ensemble," he purred, admiring her outfit. "Exotic and erotic, I love it!" And he was off again.

Sparrow didn't care for him at all. "Boss likes a little fruit with the fruitcake, seems to me."

She nudged Sparrow in the ribs. "He's artistic."

"I got the ick part. I thought you didn't like all that touchy feely stuff."

Lizzie turned to him, her hands on her waist, her hip jutting out. "You're upset."

"I'm not upset."

"You'll still get five percent. We still got a contract."

"No thanks, sweet thing. You go upstairs to Axleton and the sign says, 'Nigguhs, unless you singin', playin' piano, or shinin' shoes, there be the doah and it's closed.' I'll be right there when they fire your ass again."

Haviland returned. "They've put my pictures in the back. 'Too disturbing,'" he said with feigned dismay. Lizzie observed two well-heeled, pearl-clad Sugar Hill babies coming their way. Haviland casually put his arm over her shoulder. "Here come my couch nannies," he said slyly. "Do me a favor. Act like you're my girl."

"Haviland, there's something you should know. I dance and sing and shake my tail in a nightclub . . . Well, really, it's a speakeasy."

He looked at her in surprise and rapture. "Tonight?"

* * *

"OH, OH, oh, baby..." He was there every night. Sketching her form, kissing her neck, ranting in the cab rides to wherever, "To heck with all this genteel, never show the dirt routine. To prove humanity, you must strip it of anything false and pretentious, make it real and from the gut. When I paint a world is created. We need to radicalize the movement! New Negro—Show them the Fire of Black Folk! You do that with your dancing. You do that with your soul, Mayfield Turner." He kissed her and they both fell backwards.

That night and every night. Most often he came by himself. Sometimes he brought friends. To Haviland's Harlem crowd of poets and painters, Lizzie was exotic, authentic, and his effort to be egalitarian, noble. The mix was a floating crew of journalists, radicals, and mystics from the Village. Big Ed put his foot down at first. "It's policy. No whites allowed."

Haviland's friend Vee-Vee interceded, "But we're not white. We're Reds and pinkos, my brother—comrades in struggle."

∗ ∗ ∗

VREELAND HURSKMAN'S Midtown West 58th Street penthouse doorman announced them through the gold-trimmed phone receiver, all the while eying Lizzie because he knew Sparrow. The six-foot-tall, bucktoothed dirty-blond Dutchman greeted them at the door. His high round collar draped over a red embroidered kimono. "Ah, the Yamma Mama and the colored Corbusier."

"If you must call me something," Haviland responded as the couple stepped inside the spacious apartment, "at least make it original."

"My dear, ignore this young pug and come with me." Vee-Vee draped his long arm around Lizzie and like a strong Norse breeze scooted her down the hallway to the living room that looked out upon the glowing city.

"Fair weather friend," Haviland laughed.

"What do you want me to do? All of my old friends have been deported."

Lizzie's relationship with Haviland was easy from the start. Electric. Made the gossip columns. "Another cultural rising star lost to the cabaret life. The Hopeful and the Harlem Hottie!" She had grown to enjoy Haviland's absurd circle of radicals. *If you could see me now, Mama, you would prob'ly think this was the worst group of friends I could find. Well, good.* The woman in the fox cape from the soiree turned out to be rich, filthy rich, Southern rich. Her daddy's political influence was the only obstacle to Vee-Vee's boat ticket. To the consternation of her father, she had married an Indian, who now carried a smudge stick through the hall. Lizzie danced to his droning chant, dropping in on bits of poetry and inebriated conversations.

"You'll never get it published unless you're more fair-minded toward the white characters," Vee's companion, Anna, pleaded with a young, aspiring Negro novelist.

"It's not whites but blacks I want to reach," he protested while hoisting several clams casino onto his napkin.

"What are you, a moron? Did you not comprehend anything?" a downtown journalist hollered into the phone. "Perhaps if he didn't split his infinitives, you could explain yourself better! That's the heart of it."

"Lizzie, come close," Vee-Vee beckoned. "Tell your painter boyfriend about the music. Music is more in touch with the people. Painting just hangs on the wall. Holds you captive. Music you can listen to while doing something else. You can dance to it, can even join in."

"Music," she threw her hip suggestively, "is seduction."

"Brilliant! The brilliance of art, in a word, seduction. In the music seduction begins!" Vee-Vee put on a new plastic 78 of Louis Armstrong's Hot Five and lifted Lizzie clear off the floor. "Rhythm will change the world, Lizzie. Watch, I've been practicing my Black Bottom." His rumbling steps shook the chandeliers.

Lizzie led the party in a dance demonstration—ballin' the jack, grizzly bear, slow drag into a hug and rubbin' crawl. The revelers fell out on the couches and chaises in randomly formed couples and combos. "Rhapsodic!" shouted Vee-Vee, his pink face a glimmer of sweat. "Who wants gin?"

Fanning herself with a 78 record, Lizzie eased her way toward the open door off the kitchen. Haviland followed and laced his arms around her waist. She turned to him. He nuzzled her neck with soft sensual kisses. They danced away from the crowd, up the back spiral steps to the roof terrace and the crisp black night, the city dazzling around them. Her heart and body wanted him, but she was afraid. His warm hands grabbed her by the hips and slipped under her panty and garter, drawing her toward him, breathing her in with his kiss. Her arms wilted around his shoulders as he licked and bit at her neck and the small lobe of her ear. She caught his hand and drew it up toward her face, intertwining their fingers. He just as fluidly wound her arm around behind her and trussed it to her back, grabbing her ass. She couldn't move her arm. She started to panic. She couldn't move. *This is Haviland. He loves you.* But she couldn't move. Just then the door flew open from the kitchen. One of the waiters had stepped out for a smoke. They separated. She straightened her clothes.

The waiter eyed them through the cigarette smoke with a disapproving smile and tilted his head to get a better look. "Lizzie Winrow? That you? Cain't be!" She realized immediately that she knew him from down Charleston way. She thought she had put enough space between her and Charleston to forget it. Still, here it was back again, actin' familiar. "Thought that was you. Mighty my, livin' high you is. Wait'll I tell— How yoah mama doin'? How yoah—"

"I don't go by that name anymore," she interjected. "It's Mayfield Turner."

"Lizzie May Winrow!" the waiter continued, ignoring her correction, "I told 'em I knew you! Didn't b'lieve me. Lemme show 'em I know somebody. Know somebody highfalutin'."

She took Haviland's hand and followed the waiter into the kitchen. *Smile with too much knowin'. Best pal along and get this joker gone.* When they entered the kitchen, the West Indian cook was squawkin' over the sink, the pipes clunkin' back like drums. His scowl announced he didn't think too much of Lizzie and her kind. His preachin' confirmed it. "Tink you can make the world over wit poetry and paint. Change the world true culture. A&P got twenty-four stores, only treeee black errand boys." He held up three sudsy fingers, then plunged his hand back into the sink. "United Cigar Store with thirteen stores, got no black employees at tall."

"Hanaisse, what is you fussin' bout now?" the waiter pleaded, embarrassed.

"You people need to get serious. You piddle away your lives with idle talk, cavortin' wid the white man when you should be seeking independence. Come to the rally, my brethren. Marcus Garvey returns!"

"Yeah, from the federal pen." The waiter had a good laugh.

Hanaisse returned to his dishes, mumbling, "Our great leader was framed. Set up by the United States government. They deport him. You don't see them doin' nothin' to those pinkos upstairs."

The waiter leaned back against the counter, "Now, why you wan' say somthin' like that. Them pinkos is yoah paycheck."

The frenetic man paused. "That's the trouble with all of yuhs. Tink it's funny. Tink you got somethin', ain't got nuttin'. Mark my words."

Lizzie and Haviland took the opportunity to slip away. Standing in the door frame of the servants' entrance, she turned toward Haviland's touch and spied Ray unloading boxes from the freight elevator.

* * *

REHEARSALS FOR the Cane Break were a grueling eight hours a day, but until the show opened her big move downtown meant a cut in her income by two-thirds. *Seven dollah* and *NO tips!* So Lizzie kept working at the Turf Club. This time she wasn't going to give up her spot until she knew she had a bona fide hit. She found Sparrow lingering at her dressing room curtain. "Doorman at one of yoah Nordic friends told me, said, 'Saw your gal, hangin' out at the penthouse with the Communists, drinkin' Fifth Avenues.'"

She brushed past him and plunked herself on the dressing room stool. "What you want, Sparrow? And what's the idea, snoopin' on me?"

"Just checkin' up on my investment."

Stretching out her long legs, Lizzie flexed her ankles and grunted a dismissive laugh, then leaned over, exhausted. "Well, Mr. Biltmore, just gimme a bounce and get outta here."

Sparrow pulled a small vial of his custom elixir from his pocket and rolled it between his fingertips. "Only thing you seem to need me for now."

"Oh please." She snatched the vial from him and quickly snorted a couple of hits from the cap.

"So this fellah, Have-A Man," he continued.

"It's Haviland," Lizzie retorted, nearly throwing the vial at him.

Sparrow caught it agilely. "I'm just askin' does he know you got a shorty? Does he know you got a kid?"

"You wanna get me fired, nigguh?" Sparrow's eyes widened in shock.

Her sharpness had stung him. She began to change for her next number, softening. "You yourself told me the day I met you I can't get no work with no shorty. Mr. Meeks made that abundantly clear. He wants his yellah gals fleshy and fresh."

"I'm not talking about no job, or no Cappy Meeks. I'm talkin' bout your life, Slim. All I'm saying is that a man that loves you wouldn't care. Does this guy love you?"

"You're my manager, Dakota Sparrow, not my man or my father," she snapped. "Do me a favor, stick to show business and keep your nose outta mine."

He raised his hands and retreated in surrender as Lizzie turned to the mirror to check her makeup. The visage staring back at her was tense in the eyes, irritated at Sparrow's question, furious with her inability to answer. Truth was she didn't know how she felt about Haviland. She would see other chorus girls so easily seduced, so comfortable with their bodies, enjoying themselves with casual encounters or wild sweeps of romance. One married a horn man. One engaged to a preacher. Loads of sugardaddies, white and colored. Heartache to headache as far as she was concerned. She was fond of Haviland. She was with him almost every night, jostling from party to party. They would fondle in the corner, nibble on lips, dance a Southern grind or a hot speed ball and jack. He would sketch her form, visibly titillated by her near naked costumes and suggestive undulations. His hand was graceful and light with pencil and charcoal, but when grasping her arms, holding her, he was awkward, arrhythmic and fumbling. When it came to true intimacy she withdrew into herself, knowing this was not what she wanted, not who she wanted. How to love a man was supposed to be a natural knowing, but she didn't have it. This secret knowledge had been stolen from her. Deke Turner had robbed her of it. Runnin' off her father and truest friend, then catching her on the stair to the cellar, he had stolen her capacity to love. *Even my own child.* The heat of her dance belied the fact that she was hard, cold, and empty inside.

"Mayfield, tell me you ain't leavin'! Don't hurt me," a customer shouted as she strutted onto the Turf Club dance floor for the final set. "Doll, you breakin' my heart!"

"Baby, I don't break hearts," she retorted, "I collect 'em."

After the set, she took the subway to Midtown to get a couple hours sleep before rehearsal started at the Cane Break. She couldn't believe that two years after hitting New York she was still squatting with Elma and Ray. The arrangement suited her. Ray was rarely there, and Elma doted on her niece. Cinnamon's companionship had been a great help with Jesse's development. He was walking fine now, and even if Cinn was the only one who could understand him, he was at least talking—a slow warbling near baritone in that squat little body. He followed his cousin around like a puppy. Lizzie couldn't get a better arrangement than she had. Still Sparrow's query ate at her. That and his concoction wearing off made her edgy, her calf muscles twitching involuntarily. *You're tremblin', damn.*

The train made its way downtown toward Hell's Kitchen, each stop acquiring a new crew of day shift workers—porters, doormen, maids, elevator operators. Feeling the pulse of the tracks beneath her, watching the randomness of life like a movie at the Bijoux, Lizzie studied postures, expressions, relationships, imagining sketches and choreography to distract herself. A young colored man in clean pressed overalls boarded at 110th Street. His brown paper bag lunch in tow, he looked eager and ready for the new job. He held on to the pole and leaned forward as if he would drive the car faster toward his destination. His lean frame and Indian color reminded her for a moment of Osceola. Suddenly he bolted, his body seized, jumped backwards, and slammed onto the floor, his back arched, and his fingers curled into grotesque frozen sculptures. His irises rolled up and the whites of his eyes became slits. He convulsed wildly on the floor of the car as if shot through with lightning. The train halted in the darkened tunnel, the lights of the car flickering. The conductor ran from his booth. He was joined quickly by another entering from the adjacent car.

"There's a man here on the floor taking a fit," said one to the other.

"Well, can we move on to the station so other trains can pass?"

Passengers hurried away, sneaking glances over their shoulders, leaving Lizzie, the two train workers, and the helpless man. Unsure of the appropriate action, the conductors encircled him.

"Some kind of epileptic fit," the first repeated.

"Well, can we get him off the train?"

They were stuck just as she was, debating an action, while the poor young man continued to gyrate and froth at the mouth, his unseeing eyes fixed on her. She sat watching the strange dance before her, studying it. The man's body gradually slackened. How she wished she could shake like that, shake her body every part of it, shake off this demon.

She determined then and there that before the relationship went any further Haviland should know she had a near four-year-old child. She decided to introduce her high-class, legit beau to her family. Cinn's birthday was coming up. She would throw a party.

Elma immediately delighted in the idea. But for Sparrow occasionally fetching her for a gig, Lizzie had never brought any of her friends home. "Cinnamon will be so thrilled." The following Saturday, while the Cane Break finished up the costume fittings, Lizzie was to have the day off. She thought she would be able to sleep in a bit, but by the first light of morning, Elma dragged her sister to the teeming immigrant market of Delancey Street in lower New York, where they would get the first crack at the bargains and seconds.

Elma splurged on a new tablecloth and a porcelain-faced doll from Poland for Cinnamon's gift. Lizzie bought a Mah-Jongg set. The ancient Chinese game, a momentary rage in the city, had proven too complicated for American tastes, which tended more toward checkers. At the intersection where the Delancey market met Chinatown, there was an ample selection on display for resale. Lizzie wasn't actually interested in playing the game. Rather she thought it would lend an air of class and worldliness to the apartment. She didn't have much to make the place feel like her own. The colorful white, green, and red dragon tiles and the Chinese script reminded her of Yum Lee's awning and the markings on the shirt boxes she and Ossie had been charged with sorting by street address and delivering. To her touch the ivory tiles felt like the loose piano keys at Pilar's.

When it came to Cinnamon's party dress, Lizzie took the lead. "No hand-me-downs for my baby. Cinnamon Turner's gonna travel first class!" The two sisters headed to Macy's department store on 34th Street. As they headed up the escalator to the children's section, they twittered about their mother's story of her first day in Charleston, repeating the story in unison, "Yessiree, I saw that sewing machine and lost my mind. I had never even seen a department store, but that day, I walked right in the front door!"

"I can see her now," Lizzie continued, "nose stuck up and those country slew feet pointing east and west." When Lizzie got to the part about her mother's mistaking the screech of curtain rings for a chicken hawk, she folded her arms, flapped them at the elbows, and crowed. Elma simply shook her head in dismay. Even as Lizzie mocked their mother's lack of sophistication, she was more country and uncouth than Eudora Winrow had ever been. Customers turned and glowered at the two of them. Elma tried in vain to shoosh her sister's animated reenactment, apologetically acknowledging the silent rebuke coming from several corners. Lizzie put her hands on her hips and hollered at her detractors, "Can I help you with somethin'? Ain't you never seen a chicken hawk before?"

Elma discreetly moved to another row of dresses. True to form, her sister ambled over, contrite.

"They act like they ain't never seen a colored woman shoppin'."

Elma ignored her and held up a powder blue pinafore dress with a white organza collar and sash. "What do you think of this?" Then she looked at the price tag. "Oh. Maybe not . . . but the color would be just beautiful on Cinnamon. I do believe Mrs. Marrano's daughter still works here," she continued. "She might let us use her employee discount. She has offered before."

"I don't need no discount. This time next week, I'll be making plenty," Lizzie clucked. "Besides, you're only four once, right? That dress is way too dull. My baby likes color. How 'bout this?" Lizzie held up a red taffeta dress with a fitted waist and a ruffle-flounced skirt with a huge fabric rose stitched to the hip, a dress more suitable for Carmen than Cinnamon Turner.

Elma laughed, "Well, it certainly is red! But it's the wrong size." Elma proffered her choice again. "I think Cinnamon would like this one, it's more like a little girl. And," she was surprised, "it's cheaper."

It bothered Lizzie to think that Elma knew her child's correct dress size when she did not. It infuriated her that Elma believed that she knew her daughter's taste better than she did. Lizzie rifled through the rack to find the dress she liked in the next size up.

"Lizzie, you don't want to spend so much on something she is just gonna outgrow. You should be saving it for what's important."

"What's more important than turning four? Here's one. She could grow into it."

"Cinnamon's like a second child to me," Elma mused. "I'd give her the world if I could."

"Hell, let's get both."

As the salesgirl rang up the purchase, Lizzie knocked her leg involuntarily against the counter. She had not intended to get two dresses, but she was determined not to let Elma have the final say. Her sister was as good an aunt as she could ask for. She wouldn't have been able to make it without Elma's help, wouldn't have survived a month in New York, but Elma's closeness to Cinnamon made Lizzie downright jealous.

She knew her sister had her troubles. *Damn straight Ray ain't working no construction, but it ain't my place to say. Ain't my place at all.* She knew Ray was working the streets, moonshinin' like her daddy used to do. It pained her to keep the knowledge from Elma, but Elma acted as if she didn't want to know, accepting every explanation Ray cared to offer about his hours and the nature of his work. Jolly too kept a tight lip about his tavern turned grocery store, the basement of false-bottom crates, the Canadian labels trucked in from upstate New York or the Jersey Shore.

The clerk turned to Elma with the receipt. "Would you mind telling your maid to stop banging the counter?"

"Listen, sistuh," Lizzie glowered and put her elbows on the glass, "her 'maid' is payin' for all this shit, so why don't you just finish up?"

They exited the store, laden with their bounty from the day. "All I'm saying, Lizzie, is that if you comported yourself a little more—"

Lizzie cut her off, "Here we go."

Elma closed her eyes to calm herself. "I'm just saying—"

Lizzie cut her off again, "If I was to look and act a little more white, people might treat me more like they treat you?! This is the modern world, El. New Yawk! I don't have to take shit from anybody. 'Your maid.' She's lucky I didn't haul off and smack her."

"Fine." Elma stopped in her tracks. "Let's just go home."

"Nothin' doin'," Lizzie replied, walking ahead of her, "yoah maid's got a Saturday off and we got one more stop. Come on." Elma sighed and watched her little sister walk ahead, her two slew feet pointing east and west.

As they rounded Sixth Avenue, Elma followed Lizzie into a sparsely lit arcade off 34th Street. The corridor of small shops and booths smelled of kosher hot dogs, caramel corn, and musky bodies. Elma swooned, a combination of hunger and revulsion. *My head aches and my feet hurt. Where is that girl off to now?* Tucked away amidst the haberdasheries, tobacconists, jewelers, and fortune-tellers was Jolene's Salon, marked only by a small painted sign. Elma followed Lizzie up a narrow flight of stairs and emerged to a cavernous second-floor beauty shop with rows of young women all busily at work. There must have been fifty women getting their hair done.

Since adolescence, Lizzie had been experimenting with her hair, mixing her great-grandmother's jars of miscellaneous herbs and potions with various household items like eggs and milk and honey. Having inherited her father's African genes, she was perpetually aware of the tightness of the strands and their length. Lizzie's mother Dora ritualistically repeated the humiliating castigations to which she herself had been subjected. Yankin' and pullin' and cussin' and screamin'. Holding that hot iron over Lizzie's bobbling head like a branding rod—"Be still I say, be still." "Ouch, you burned me!" "I did not! Now look what you made me do!"—an absurd, terroristic tango, complete with lyrics, "I don't know why I married your father. Look at this kitchen! You hold still or I'll get that switch!" To many, Madame C. J. Walker's straightening comb was a stroke of brilliance, but the invention that appeared in a dream was for Lizzie a regular Saturday afternoon nightmare. Worse than the threat of physical torture was the verbal abuse. Her hair wasn't good, so neither was she. While Elma possessed a crown, Lizzie was instructed to bring that nappy head over here. By the time she reached ten, Lizzie would stop at no length to escape her mother's tyranny. A mad scientist in the kitchen. Dewdrops and rainwater, syrup, lard, butter, anything that would slicken.

So Lizzie loved the twenties. Suddenly, for the first time, short hair was the fashion, tight-fitting cloches and Valentino-inspired turbans were in. And she had discovered Jolene's. Most of the Cane Break chorus girls had hair that ranged from silken tresses like Elma's to crinkly ringlets, hair that one could wash and wear. To get her greased-down faux Creole took Lizzie a whole day and then another two for it to set. Still, when she performed, oil and sweat would drip down her neck and back, spoiling her costumes. A couple of girls had taken Josephine Baker's lead and had followed the male musicians to the barbers and gotten conkolines. She was contemplating this move when a white singer at one of Vee-Vee's throw-downs approached her. "Teach me some of them moves," she said, "and I'll turn you on to my hair place." Before Lizzie could respond, the woman shook her head. Her blond tresses bounced. "You'd be surprised, sistuh," she said, "how many Jewish girls got colored hair."

Jolene was a white-haired, smooth-skinned Egyptian Jew, a former rug merchant who realized that the more reliable market was women and their hair. He ran his shop, employing mostly relatives, like a Ford factory assembly plant, passing customers along the rows of swivel chairs from assessor to washers, perm specialists, dye artists, pressers, and curl girls. For ten dollars, colored women, Jewish women, Puerto Rican women, springy-haired Irish, and Beethoven Germans could join the great assimilation and emerge with the page boy, bob, or tint of the latest American movie star. Jolene loved show business as much as he loved hair. "I love to do this, love to, love this," he drooled as he removed the thick tortoiseshell clips from Elma's chignon, the raven locks tumbling down her back. Lizzie sucked her teeth as the entire salon clustered around her sister to marvel.

"It used to be so thick," Elma apologized as Jolene continued to run his nervous fingers through it, humming to himself as if he were anticipating a good meal or hot date. Elma looked toward Lizzie with consternation, then laughed shyly, "I've never been to a beauty parlor."

"You know how long it takes her to wash that hair, Jolene?" Lizzie said, twirling herself in a salon chair. "Gives her a terrible cold every time. Can't no colored woman know what to do with all that hair, talkin' bout 'It used to be so thick.' I'm giving my sister a glamour day."

"Your sister?" The Egyptian's eyes widened.

Lizzie rolled her eyes. "Can't you tell? I'm the modern one. I'm tellin' you, JoJo, make my sister look modern." Lizzie sat in an adjoining chair for a touch-up on her marcel as Elma disappeared into the back.

Two hours later, while Lizzie was bartering with a huckster for some bootleg records, Elma emerged with Clara Bow bangs and a neat clipped curl ending just below her ears. She held her crown and glory in her hand, waving it like a horse tail. "It's called a bob, just like in the movies," Elma smiled giddily.

Lizzie was aghast. "Elma, I say, what happened to yoah hay-uh?"

"Miss Tavineer's watching the kids. We better get home. Whew," Elma swooned, "my head's so light I feel like I ate a whole fruitcake."

"Well you should. Have you lost your mind?"

"For sure and about ten pounds!" Elma laughed.

Jolene primped about her, smoothing each strand, cupping the now cropped ends of Elma's new do with his palm. "Love this, love it. Gorjuice!"

Lizzie looked at him sideways. "How much do we owe you, JoJo?"

"Don't worry about that. I took care of it," Elma said. "We have a party to plan."

They gathered their packages and this time Lizzie followed Elma, or whoever that was walking in front of her. The crown and glory, the woman Lizzie knew as her sister, was gone. She had been jealous of that mane all her life. Now that it was gone, all she wanted to do was cry.

20

"The bad feelin' just got worse
Sometime I feel like I been cursed
I think my achin' heart gon' burst
And blow this blues away . . ."

WHILE THE VICTROLA PLAYED A SCRATCHY BOOTLEG
tune, a Ma Rainey knockoff, Lizzie dropped another dollop of beer into
her one and only specialty and frantically began to whip the batter for
her deep-fried shrimp. *Home-cooked sit-down dinner, conversatin' about
architecture and art? What in heaven's name were you thinkin'?* Lizzie's
marcel was not the only thing getting steamed. Ray had not shown up, all
night. This suited Lizzie fine, but Elma bustled about banging pots, fret-
ting with the decorations. The cake had fallen. The dress that she had
worn at the church groundbreaking two springs ago was tight around her
ribs and the neckline voluminous without the tendrils of hair. She kept
her apron on to conceal the stretch in the fabric, how the buttons zigzagged. Elma iced the lopsided cake with a fury, punctuating the sprinkles of coconut with a low, unconscious mumble, "Gingham apron and
my good garnet earrings." *Out all night, workin' a tunnel. Where's he dig-*

gin' to, China? Her hair, which yesterday had curved her jawline, the fraction of the curl that used to be, now frizzled about her head, each errant strand with a mind of its own. She had missed church worrying about her husband and now had the Lord's wrath on top of her own. The door opened. "Ray?"

Jolly entered without knocking. "Contribution to the festivities, bought a ham and a basket of biscuits." Without speaking the women looked up and went back to their tasks. Jolly watched their synchronized frenzy with amusement. The two sisters were alike after all.

"You didn't tell me you invited Jolly," Elma whispered.

"I thought you invited him."

* * *

AWAITING HER big day, Cinn sat downstairs with Jesse and Miss Tavineer. Cinnamon was so excited. Already she had received not one, but two dresses. The blue puffy one from Mama El made her feel as if she were sitting in a cloud, even if the crinoline pricked her legs a bit. The red shiny one from her mother made her heart beat fast. It was a little big. The cowl neck slipped off her shoulder, but she didn't care. A gift from her mother she was determined to wear. She had planned to use the blue one for church that morning, but they didn't go. She didn't want her Mama El to feel bad, her aunt was already so sad because somebody had stolen her hair. But her mother was giving her a party, her first birthday party. She would wear that dress. It reminded her of tulips, valentines, licorice, lipstick, and her mama's red kisses.

Cinn sat in her chair, clicking her new patent leather shoes. Swiveling her neck, she didn't dare move. Mrs. Jolly was just finishing up the three French braids with red bows, smoothing down Cinn's baby hair with the end of a comb. "You should wear your hair like that every day," beamed Miss Tavineer.

In her swishing taffeta dress, laced socks, and shiny buckle shoes, Cinnamon practically tapped up the steps. Little Jesse, his thick, stubby legs still managing only one step at a time, trudged behind her. They were met at the landing by the oddest assortment of people—a tall colored man, an Indian, a gypsy, and a buck-tooth ghost. Cinnamon clapped with delight. *Mama invited the circus!*

Expecting to find Ray, Elma opened the door instead to Haviland and his entourage, Vee-Vee, Anna, and the Indian, Chief Powahaton. "I know this address," Anna mused in her thick nasal New York Russian twang, "this is where my driver gets our gin. I didn't realize people lived here."

Vee-Vee loped into the room. "Mayfield, sugah, you didn't tell me you lived in a penthouse," he chirped. "What a lovely view! So colorful, all the lines of clothes. What is that smell?" he continued, ambling into the kitchen, lifting up the pot tops. "Yummy!"

Then came Mrs. Jolly with Jesse by one hand and Cinn by the other. "Miss Tavineer couldn't make it up the steps," she said as she entered, handing off the children. "I'll check on her directly."

Cinnamon pulled away from Mrs. Jolly's grasp and twirled around the room, her dress a whirl of color. "Look Mommy, Mrs. Jolly fixed my hair." As the room shifted about her, she saw a flicker of anger cross her mother's brow. What had she done?

The glower was intended for Haviland. "I didn't expect you to bring all these people," Lizzie slithered through her smile as Haviland pecked her on the cheek.

Haviland shrugged, "We're always with all these people. Who's 'Mommy'?"

The group collected awkwardly in the center of the living room. "We didn't mean to put you out," Anna said. "Hav said you were having a party."

Elma quickly recovered. "Of course we are. It's a birthday party. On account of Cinnamon 'Ceola Turner is four years old! Pot luck, buffet style." In fluid motion, Elma cleared the table of the six place settings and hurried to the kitchen to pull out the okra dish she was saving. "Lizzie? Lizzeeee," she prodded her sister, who stood like a stone, "make the introductions!"

"Mayfield," the buck-tooth ghost spoke again, "who's Lizzie?"

"That's me, or who I used to be," clipped Lizzie. "Mr. Remick, Powahaton, and Mr. and Mrs. Hurskman, allow me to introduce my family, my sister Elma Minor, my neighbors Mr. and Mrs. Jolly, my nephew Jesse. And this is my daughter, Cinnamon. Cinn, say hello."

"Sin? How delicious! How visceral and immediate and honest!"

"It's a spice," Lizzie sighed and plopped herself in a chair.

"How about some music?" Cinnamon's eyes followed the tall dark-skinned man as he threw his scarf over the lamp and looked around the room. Music started up. The skinny white lady bopped across the room like a jack-in-the-box, circling the Indian. "Louis Armstrong, I love it! Oh yes, let's. I've been practicing."

Haviland, who had been sifting through Lizzie's meager record collection, paused and turned to Lizzie. "Daughter? You did say daughter?"

"Yes. That's what I said."

The tall white man with buck teeth lifted Cinnamon high in the air. Specks of spit flew in her face as he spoke. "Oh, Vee-Vee. Just call me Vee-Vee. Mayfield, what a keeper of secrets you are and what an exquisite little human being!" His breath smelled of cigarettes.

"Down please," Cinnamon commanded.

The new knock at the door was Sparrow, his elbow linked round Miss Tavineer's.

"Uncle Sparrow!" Cinnamon ran to him. Finally a guest she knew had come to her party. Since their first meeting at the train station, she had often seen Sparrow when he came to the apartment to pick her mother up for a tryout. Though he would stay but for a minute, he never left without flipping a quarter over his knuckles and dropping it into her palm. "Hey, angel face," he greeted the child with his hand behind his back. She clapped with glee anticipating a bright shiny new coin. He handed her instead a gift-wrapped box she had to hold with both hands. "That's for your hope chest. Let's hope yoah mama act right this time."

Sparrow had been lurking outside the apartment, in case this soiree didn't go so well. He was familiar by now with Lizzie's tendency to disappear. He couldn't afford another slip like that, especially when Cappy Meeks was running the show. As Lizzie's manager, he knew his place and didn't want it to be in the East River. He had been jawin' with Hurskman's chauffeur, working himself up. Finally, when he couldn't take it anymore he bounded up the steps and ran smack into Miss Tavineer, doused with lavender water, her cheeks rouged like cherry lollipops. "Come on, doll face, you can be my date."

"Might as well come in," Lizzie greeted him coldly. "Just like old times. Grand Central."

Vee-Vee had decked himself and Jesse in triangular newspaper caps. Together the Norseman and the little boy were marching around the room playing soldier. Jolly squinted at the little boy's hat. "Hey, that better not be my stock section."

Vee-Vee shouted, "Halt!" and turned casually to Mr. Jolly, pointing toward the window. "Actually, I believe Havvy took that part." Sparrow couldn't believe it. Lizzie's beau was standing outside the window on a one-foot ledge four stories up with a roll of newspaper and a bottle of ammonia, washing the window glass of its late winter soot with exuberance. Anna continued to attempt to coax the intransigent chief into a line-dance.

Sparrow glided over to Lizzie. "Clearly, they all high as kites. I don't know why you bother to get stuff from me." When she did not respond he sulked, "Never invited me to your house."

"I didn't invite you now. I didn't invite any of these people but one and he's standin' outside, makin' out with the winduh."

Elma re-entered the room and announced, "In honor of my niece's birthday, I have prepared a light supper." With Jolly's ham and biscuits, some leftover cornbread, and an extra can of tomato sauce in the okra dish, Elma had worked some magic. The table setting looked like a feast and unfortunately made everyone feel right at home.

The room settled into idle banter. Jolly and the Chief traded stock tips. Anna and Hav jostled over the art scene. Vee-Vee held court with himself, disgorging fractured poetry punctuated by burps. "Talent, piercing resonance of simplicity, music of our collective past. In a random order, ancient sounds melded and amplified, sucking up the past and spewing it forth in a prism of sound. That space between the familiar, the comforting, and discomfort, the perfect excruciating tension, the slap of a shoeshine rag like a slap to the face, reminding us of the dusty trail we have trod, alerting us to the choices before us, the path we will all walk in the future."

"Do you mind if I pry," said Anna, the anthropologist, with no expectation of an answer. "You're all so different to be part of the same family."

"We are all part of the family of man, children of the Great Spirit," the Chief enjoined.

"Don't say anything," Lizzie cautioned Sparrow. "They're my friends."

"Really?"

Haviland approached her and squeezed her hand. "Found a new apartment," he began, "great deal, 267 135th, Niggerati Manor, all artists, low rent, sponsored by Iolanthe Holstein, Homer Holstein's daughter, runs her own Harlem employment agency . . . We gotta talk." Sparrow walked away, shoveling down a handful of peanuts.

Anna bustled about the living room from corner to corner. "Mayfield, dear, where on earth is the bathroom?"

"Down the—oh never mind, I'll show you."

Lizzie led Anna to the hallway and paused, confessing her plan and how it had gone awry. "I didn't mean for Hav to find out this way, but before this thing went any further, I had to tell him I had a child."

"But darling," Anna put her arms around Lizzie, attempting to comfort, "further in what way? Haviland is a homosexual."

When Lizzie re-entered the apartment, her mind was reeling. Cinnamon ran up to her, pulling at her arms. "Play piano on my tummy, Mama." Cinnamon had not asked to play this game in months, but these people were making her feel bad. If this was growing up, she was going to go in the other direction.

"Not now, baby." Lizzie watched Haviland as she spoke, lifting Cinnamon to her lap. "It's a game we made up in Raleigh."

"Train! Whoo-woo!" Cinnamon splayed her fingers palms up.

"Not now."

"Whoo-woo/ Chattanooga Choo-choo!" Cinn continued.

"I said not now!"

"Now it's time for the birthday girl!" Elma interjected, holding the crooked coconut cake with five bright candles, four for her age and one extra in the center. "Make a wish, Cinnamon Turner!"

I wish these circus people would go away so I can have my mama and cake to myself. Just as she blew out the candles, the key turned in the door. "Papa Ray!" Just in time to get the first piece!

While Elma fixed Ray a plate in the kitchen, Cinnamon opened her presents. From Mrs. Jolly barrettes and new ribbon bows for her hair. From Jesse a set of jacks and pick-up sticks. From Mama El, a porcelain doll, a princess with white hair. Haviland handed her a picture of herself on a napkin. From Mr. Sparrow a big book with nothing in it. "That there's a scrapbook, sugah," he said, "for when your mama gets famous. You can keep pictures, mementos, and all your memories in there. Even that napkin."

"How you know I'mo be famous?"

"I got the eye, baby. Surely you done figured that by now."

Cinn looked toward her mother expectantly.

"What?" Lizzie frowned again. "I bought you a dress and threw you a party."

"Lizzie." Elma appeared again. "We were so busy, I forgot to wrap the Mah-Jongg."

"What?"

"Go with me on this. The child is expecting a present."

"Oh, the Mah-Jongg!"

Raymond idled in the kitchen. *Overnight run to Buffalo. Caught a flat, dodged the feds, and I come home to this?* He just wanted to sleep. He had plumb forgotten about the party. *El cut her hair.* His beautiful wife had taken a hatchet and lopped off her hair. Bloated silly people sitting in his living room, Jolly silently mocking his complete lack of control. The ham was cold, the biscuits were hard, and he hated okra. *El cut off all her hair.*

Who does he think he is, comin' in here without so much as an explanation. Sittin' in there sayin' nothing, after worryin' me to death. Embarrassin' me in front of all these people.

Cinn sat fingering the ivory blocks of flowers, characters, and abstract designs; her tiny face was rapt as she examined each piece.

"Why didn't you just get huh some checkuhs? Mah-Jongg?" Sparrow cracked, stacking the pieces.

"Tiles would go nice wid the bathroom," added Mrs. Jolly.

"I bought it cuz we lived next door to a Chinaman most my life," Lizzie said, trying to wrest her daughter's attention from her sister. "My stepfather coulda been Chinese. I speak it fluently."

"You can count to ten," corrected Elma.

"I saw it at a party," Lizzie said, pulling out a cigarette. "Looked like fun."

Anna joined in, "I know the rules. It's similar to rummy or dominoes." She pointed out the various pieces to Cinnamon. "Three suits, Bamboo, Circle, and Cha-at. Four winds—East, North, South, and West. Three dragons. Red, White, and Green. The object is to build a great wall with your tiles and knock everyone else's down. The goal is to collect four sets of three. Kong, Chow, and Pung."

Sparrow made imitation Chinese, "This Pung is no Fung."

"Sparrow, expand your mind. Take in the world!" Lizzie scolded. "This is an ancient game. Thousands of years old."

"Took 'em five hundred years to learn the rules. Who wants whist?"

"I'm sure Cinn will grow into it just like she'll grow into this dress," Elma said as she nuzzled her niece.

"Come on over here, baby," Lizzie commanded, "we gon learn the Mah-Jongg. I bought this shit. We gon learn how to play it."

"Lizzie, no need for such language."

"Need for it tonight. Goddammit! Two orchids, a bamboo, and a pair of winds, hit me!"

"I think it's near the children's bedtime."

"Noooooo!" Cinnamon pleaded, pulling away from Elma. "I have a present . . . for Mommy. It's a game we made up. It's our game. Train time! Whoo-woo!" Cinnamon splayed her fingers, palms up. Lizzie approached and began playing out the chords and runs in miniature on her daughter's fingertips. "Woo-Woo/ Chattanooga Choo-choo/ Someone tell me Who Who/ Is ridin' in the caboose/ I need to be knowin'/ Where this train is goin'/ I simply got to find that sweet baby of mine/ So tell me where that Chattanooga Choo-choo/Is goin' this— time!"

Cinnamon, for her part, had to anticipate place or key shift as the song progressed. "Memphis, Nashville, New Orleans/ Jackson, Tampa, Tallahassee/Charleston, Durham, Kittyhawk/ Norfolk, Richmond, sweet New Yawk." Together they vamped the refrain. Each different note meant a different tickling spot and city. Cinn, even then a mockingbird, awaited where each tickle would fall, erupting in spasms of laughter that dwindled to a smiling sigh and an occasional hiccup of giggles.

Vee-Vee stood up, a cracker still on his lip. "That child has perfect pitch! . . . Ah, the talent of the Negro! A poem for Cinn. My Africa I kiss your soul." Vee-Vee rhapsodized, twirling in circles by himself. "I hear the language of your heart in distant drums. I put my lips to yours. We mingle tongues."

Elma's back stiffened. She grabbed Jesse and pulled Cinnamon up by the hand. "Say goodnight, children. Some man put his tongue in my mouth, I'd bite it right off."

Lizzie crossed her legs and remained on the floor. "So much for Miss Modern."

Anna broke the silence. "Vee-Vee, aren't we supposed to be in the Village for that reading?"

"Ah yes, of course. Great party, great fun, tra-lah." The tall Norseman saluted Jesse and bowed to Cinn. "My dear, you have the voice of an angel and the fierce spirit of a goddess. Cinn, my Cinn, you must sing, you must always sing."

Haviland pecked Lizzie on the cheek. "Talk later?"

She looked at him puzzled. "Why?"

The Jollys awakened Miss Tavineer and helped her down the steps.

The Chief turned to Elma standing at the cracked front door. "Do not let your eyes stay sad, Spring Blossom. The hair will grow back."

Sparrow too prepared to exit. Cinn approached him with a hug. "Thank you, Uncle Sparrow, for my scrapbook. I'm gonna keep it forever." Sparrow leaned over and said, "See, at least some people appreciate me." Lizzie just raised an eyebrow. "I'll let myself out."

* * *

MISS TAVINEER sat in her kitchen, crossing herself. *Grown folks hollerin,' Lord, Jesus, children screamin', floorboards thunderin' above my head.* "What was that crack—what crack—tryin' to embarrass me— You!—Usin' language like that in front of the children—Bringing those degenerates up here—Excuse me—Into my house—Stay out of this, Lizzie—Who the hell told you you could cut your hair—I don't need your permission—Get your hands offa—It looks like shit!—Mah Mahhhh!— Lizzie stay—I said get your hands—Let go of—You wanna see what it looks like, you wanna see—Ray, let go of me—Get your fuckin' hands offa her!"

Raymond had Elma by the hair, Cinn and Jesse latched on to her skirt, whipping around the room, Lizzie brandishing a frying pan.

Elma jerked away from his grasp and cradled the children in her arms. "Raymond Minor, what in hell's come over you!"

"This is my house and I won't have it sullied by this lowlife tramp!"

"You muthafuckin' asshole! That makes us even, don't it?"

"Oh for goodness gracious! It's my hair on my head, I should be able to do what I like!"

But Lizzie wouldn't let it alone. "You got your nerve callin' me a low-life. Least I ain't a liar. Liar! Carpenters' union, my ass. He's deliverin' booze all over town, Elma. Jolly put him up to it. That ain't no goddam grocery store! You're stashin' up booze for the Irish mob. Delivery boy!" He stepped toward her, then pulled back. "You think I'm stupid?"

Ray walked out of the room, Elma trailing after him, "Ray . . ."

Lizzie swooped Cinnamon up to her side. "Come on, Cinn, we don't need this."

Elma returned. "Lizzie, he didn't mean, Liz—"

"You need to get yourself together," Lizzie said flatly. "You need to be leavin' him. Crazy, lyin' . . ."

Ray returned with Lizzie's show trunk. He walked over to the window that Haviland had so nicely washed and threw her belongings into the street.

"Stop it, Raymond. Stop! Are you crazy?" Elma attempted to grab his arms but songs, costumes, makeup, phonograph records, then the Victrola, all went out the window.

Her child riding her hip, Lizzie turned on her heels. "All over some goddam hair?!"

"It's not about any goddam hair!" Ray followed her, his voice bellowing down the stairwell. "It's about you coming in here with your nigguh ways and that nigguh bastard, ruining my home! Get out!"

Shutters flapping, Elma screaming out the window, Jolly in his silk dressing gown, looking up at the sky raining someone's life. "Listen, Minor, I cain't hab dis."

"Hey, you goddam white-assed nigguh, you got my money!" Lizzie hollered up at the window. Her shoebox stash flew out next, the green bills falling like cherry blossoms. The window slammed shut.

Elma appeared at the door, her scruffy bathrobe pulled over her dress, now shorn of its buttons. She held the robe about her, bent over at the waist, pleading, "Lizzie, please come back inside."

"Loose me, Elma. I'll never set foot in that house again . . . Low-down, no-good son of a bitch!" Lizzie hollered at the night sky. Wilted and defeated, Elma stepped back into the shadows and disappeared inside. Lizzie looked at her child, standing there in silence, tears collecting in her eyes. "Don't you dare, don't you dare cry."

They salvaged what they could. Asa helped her collect the money. Mrs. Jolly gave Cinnamon a blanket and Lizzie some shopping bags. Cinnamon gathered a few Mah-Jongg pieces and her doll, which was now cracked and missing an eye. "Don't worry about that," Lizzie said, "just look for the money." Miss Tavineer sent down some gingersnaps wrapped in a napkin and Cinn's powder blue dress. "Leave it," Lizzie said coldly. "I'll get you another."

They took a gypsy cab to Sparrow's. Woke him up, interrupted some "private entertainment."

"Got no place else to go."

He looked at the frowning infant. "Hello, princess ... Wait, wait. You don't expect to stay here?"

"Just temporary. Bed share. Just till I get settled. I'll up your stake by five percent."

"Ten."

"Five." Both adults turned to the child swathed in a blanket, holding up her five sturdy fingers.

* * *

"I'm PREGNANT," Elma had said lying in bed beside Ray, her arm folded beneath her still-tender neck. "I sold my hair to get some extra money." He sat up and put his shoes on in the dark. "Oh go ahead just walk out! . . . Ray? Ray!" He walked out without speaking.

How had his life gone so terribly awry, drifting from one dream to the next, the slightest obstacle shifting his course? He was delivering downtown. The Palais du Strip, Second Avenue near Houston. The theater, like Jolly's, was a distribution center, storing illegal booze for neighborhood joints on the Lower East Side and the Village. Ray could hear the tinny voices of chorus girls in the background as he entered.

As usual, he surveyed the building, analyzing its construction. Right away he looked for exits, always aware that potential argument over the terms could lead to the delivery man being endangered. Fire escape, loose hinge, no bottom. Side exits chained shut. Made to look run-down, the building was heavily fortified, the girlie show just a front. Flimsy curtains. The building smelled of that vague lemon fish scent of two-dollar tricks between acts, old wood and mold. Scenes flashed before him— Lizzie's hard-earned dollars tumbling down to the street, sheet music dancing in the wind, children's clothes disembodied. *Elma . . .* disbelief, disappointment, disgust. The strip joint's owner sat in a back room, counting stacks of money.

"Got the load-in for the new show," Ray said, then followed the wordless man to the truck, noting the dandruff on his vest, the shine on the seat of his pants. The man inventoried the delivery, jabbing the air with his pencil. Ray stood in the door frame. His eyes drifted up to the rafters of the building. Fly space, no wings. *That damned Lizzie.* How had he exploded like that? Why did she so irritate him? She pursued her dream no matter what and what had he become but his grandpap, a failed old man, standing at the stage door. He counted the stage lights, assessed the crusted catwalk. *Wait, something?* High in the rafters, no bigger than a cigarette lighter. *A tiny blue flame? What is that?*

"Okay, stack 'em right here," the man ordered and folded his arms over his chest, standing over Ray like an overseer, rocking back on his heels. Ray followed the meandering corridor back to the truck and began the tedious process of loading the crates on the dolly, carting them inside and stacking. On his second trip, he felt a sting on his neck and saw a flash on the rim of his cap. Suddenly he felt burning fragments cascade upon him. He heard a "Whoosh!" and looked up. The curtains ignited in a sea of flames, the theater erupted in pandemonium.

"Fire! Raid!" Dancers ran helter-skelter backstage, musicians scrambled out of the pit, frantic customers tripped over each other in the aisles, falling into mounds of crooked bodies at the chained side doors. Ray looked at the crates of illegal liquor stacked against the back wall. *This building's going to explode.*

He grabbed the fleeing owner by the shirt. "Pull the box!"

"Ain't no box!" the frantic man cried, attempting to pull away.

"Get to the nearest fire house," Ray said, releasing him, "these crates are gonna blow!"

Pressure from the heat made the sound of cane thickets, the hollowed stalks bursting, the sound like gunshots. Ray pressed his body against the wall to keep from getting swept in the stampede of bodies on fire. He got down on his knees, panting and choking, *Dear God! Just give me another chance.* He made his way toward the cellar, dragging a panicked chorine by her feet. "Stay low! This way!" Others followed. He busted out the cellar door just as the world detonated above them and, with a plank of wood lain over the jagged edges of glass, he hoisted the hysterical group to the outside night air.

By then the fire trucks and police had arrived only to watch what was left of the tawdry dance hall tinderbox collapse into a charred and twisted, molten carcass. Ambulance attendants covered the dead and tended to the wounded, their bodies still smoking. Ray dusted himself off and lowered his cap. Fists deep in his pockets, he casually strolled away from the scene. "Hey! Hey you!" a copper hollered after him, but he kept walking.

Ray rounded the corner and dipped into a movie house. He sat low in his seat. A flashlight down on batteries scanned the aisles. He slid up the aisle and the side stairs to the balcony. Noticing the projection booth open, he knocked on the door and stepped in, then started up a conversation.

✳ ✳ ✳

WHEN SPARROW awoke the next morning, he found Lizzie strapping on his suspenders, his underwear, and his sock garters, substituting for her missing dance clothes. "I'm late to rehearsal," she explained, grabbing her still-sleeping kid.

"Damn," he mumbled and rolled over as she slipped out the door, "if you gonna take muh draws, least you could gimme some pussy!"

The YWCA wouldn't accept women with children. "But she's my niece," Lizzie protested, "I'm just taking care of her cuz my sister took sick. I've got a rehearsal at the Cane Break, damn it, and I gotta find somebody to watch her baby." Despite the cute young minister manning the soup line, the Abyssinian ladies in the basement meeting room would not accommodate her either. The home for unwed mothers didn't approve of Lizzie's choice of work. Such carryin'-on, they said, set a bad example for the other girls. The house matron at the Urban League expected her to be in by ten. "How's a woman spozed to work!"

Lizzie had to settle on a crib joint with pay up front, a neighborly Jamaican, who lived in the building next door to Sparrow. Lizzie was instructed to pick her child up promptly. "I has a day gig, me-self," the broad-nosed woman spoke pertly, looking over the rim of her smudged reading glasses. "Temple duties. And another set of children comin' from the day shift."

There was so much drama in Lizzie's real life that the revue opening passed without much fanfare. She was anxious to get back to some routine, a dance where she knew the steps, what comes next. Third week into the show run, when she arrived to pick up Cinnamon, she found her daughter tied to a chair with ropes and duct tape over her mouth.

"I tellin' you I won't take yerr child inny more. Screamin' all duh time. Soon as you leave, she ballin' and kickin' up a fit. Tellin' me what for."

Lizzie stooped to free her child, talking softly to those hysterical eyes. "Oh I'm so sorry, baby, hold on, hold still. I'm so sorry. Did she hurt you?"

The woman stood over them. "You need to put a hurtin' on her. You're too free with dot child."

"What are you talkin' about, you tied her up?!" Lizzie scooped Cinnamon in her arms, stroking her tear-stained face with her hands.

"You keep her. I don't care. That little nigger need to learn she place in dis world. You and she both."

Cinnamon held tight to her mother and pressed her cheek against her mother's warm neck. Lizzie straightened her shoulders and spoke calmly. "My daughter is a princess. My daughter is a goddess." Two pairs of eyes locked on the woman. "Cinn," Lizzie said, "anybody try to touch yuh, juss hollah loud as you can. You can yell as loud and fierce as you wanna. The way my daddy used to call pigs."

The matron folded her arms across her chest and looked through one lens of her crooked glasses. "Duh boat of yuh get your hinkty royal behinds out me house."

21

CINNAMON GOT TO KNOW ALL THE GIRLS. THE CHORUS line of Harlem cuties immediately adopted her and in their backstage camaraderie conspired to keep management in the dark. She hid in the back of the dressing room, in a customized bass fiddle case with padding and holes, in case they had to slam it shut if the need arose. She knew all of them, the Cane Break sisterhood. The Club as they called it.

In the first week she learned all of their names. By month's end, she knew all of their habits. Snowflake was just that, a little light and airy in the thinking department. Ada was the realist, "Auntie, hunh? Does yo' mama know where your auntie works?" Lois, a white girl from West Virginia, with her limited talent, realized she could get further passin' for colored. Doe-eyed Dream was always heartbroken, "Marry you a business man, Cinn, not no lowlife musician, horn-playin' bastard like I done. God bless the child that's got his own, and then some, I guess." Murtle dreamed of moving to the country with Diz even though she was allergic to everything under the sun, "Lord, just don't bring me no flowers. Who brought them flowers in here?" Gail loved to laugh. She could make anything funny. "I say, honey, the toilet's broke," she recounted to Cinn, "he goes out and comes back with a plunger in his overcoat. 'Stead of fixin' the doggone toilet, he looks at it and sticks it on the end of his horn! Wah-wah-wah-Waaah, wahduh yuh want from me?"

Each girl had her own hair and skin ritual—ice to the nipples to make 'em perky, shading the breastbone to give a small chest cleavage—and they all had their superstitions. "Who last touched my costume?" Nightly, Cinnamon was bedazzled by the manufacture of glamour and gossip in the tight galley dressing room.

"I hear Miss Opal gon' split."

"Cappy got trouble with Dutch Schultz."

"Girl, leave that mess at the doah. That's white folks business."

"It's our business if they close this show."

"What else you hear?"

But they kept her secret, this temporary family. In between numbers, Lizzie always checked back in.

"Mama."

"Lemme do somethin' with this hair first, okay." In the frenzy of her new life, Lizzie had run out of time to visit Jolene's. She had bought a supply of the goods herself, but had run out of the special rinse. She removed her feathered headdress to reveal a short helmet of brambles. "Lord, today!" She fumbled with her hair, looking for something to improvise, or at least to keep it from breaking off at the roots till she could figure out what to do. Selecting a red bandanna, she tied it haphazardly, talking to Cinn through the mirror, "You call me Auntie in public, you hear? Mama's just our secret name." She turned to Cinn and for a moment found herself staring into her own youthful face. "Remember our song though. Our song."

"Woo-Woo," Cinn looked up at her mother as they sang softly in unison, "Chattanooga Choo-choo/ Someone tell me Who Who/ Is ridin' in the caboose/ I need to be knowin'/ Where this train is goin'? Got to find that baby of mine/ So tell me where that Chattanooga Choo-choo/ Is goin' this—"

"Chorus up next! Congo number!" The stage manager stuck his mug through the door. "Get that kid! Is that a kid?" He moved toward them. Lizzie held her hand up, a shield.

"It's my sister's kid. Got no place else to take her. Just for today."

"Get that kid outta here! Go, go, go! Get my ass fired. You know the policy. Congo number! Places! Sunflowers up next!"

Lizzie threw a sequined cape over Cinnamon and trundled her to the kitchen. The cook she remembered from Vee-Vee's penthouse days agreed to help to watch her, "Just tonight." She hid Cinnamon behind a rack of dishes, "Stay here!" and flew toward her place on stage.

Lizzie got there too late for her entrance to the Sunflower number. Not only was she supposed to be in the center of a chorus line already on stage, she had put on the bandanna and forgotten the petal headdress. Already in trajectory, she threw herself onto the stage and tumbled into the line of dancing flowers, scattering them whither and nither. The music stopped. The audience roared. Lizzie unfolded her long body and shrugged, "Oops."

The music picked up again. Lizzie pretended to follow along, mimicking and exaggerating the choreography. For the unified kicks, she kicked her nose. Fan kick, she flipped herself over and landed on her butt. From the wings, the stage manager grabbed his forehead, sweating. "What the—pull her off, get that broad!" Crowned with a garland of ostrich feathers, Queen Opal awaiting her entrance stood behind him. "Leave her be. It's funny. That gal ain't got no bones."

Meanwhile, Cappy Meeks, owner and proprietor of the Cane Break and principal backer of Lew Leslie's new revue at the club, escorted some high-society guests through the kitchen, giving a backstage tour.

"I would love to take something like this to Paris, Mr. Meeks," said the group leader, a prominent old-money socialite. "What if I stole one of your girls, would you let me?"

"I would have to charge you. An arm and a leg or two," the gangster responded with a shallow laugh. The group didn't get the joke. "I'm sure we can work out some arrangement that will leave you still able to walk. Just kidding."

"It's ridiculous a bootlegger can afford Opal Roberts and I can't. Surely we can make some arrangement."

Cappy froze, then smiled. "I prefer to think of myself as an independent businessman. Everything's negotiable."

While Meeks and his company conversed, Cinn watched from behind the towel rack. The waiters picked up the final order. The cook staff began closing down the kitchen, the pots boiling on the stove before their scrubbing. A squad of Cappy's men bombarded the doors. The cook tried to say kitchen's closed, gentlemen. They pushed him aside. Two others dragged one Pinky Alvarez, still in his pajamas, by the neck and the wrist up to Cappy before his startled entourage. "Nice ring," Cappy said and turned back to his guests. The henchmen slid one screaming Pinky by the heels of his bedroom slippers toward the vats of boiling water. Atop Pinky's frantic squeals, a shrieking shrill high C scream cut the air like a razor.

"Jeez!"

"Coppers!"

"Raid!"

Quick time, boom, the guns flew out and like magnets all pointed in the direction of the sound . . . at this little chocolate kid, sportin' a tiara. Just as instantly a honey-faced Banshi appeared, her red bandanna pointing out like horns, shielding, ready to gouge anybody who came near.

Cappy walked over, his heel lifts digging into the floor. "What is this?"

"My sister's kid. I'm watchin' her. Took sick. Just temporary."

He liked her economy of words, her quickness. She didn't flinch.

Cappy cracked his neck to the side, a signal for his henchmen to loosen their grip on the fat Dominican. "It's your lucky day, Pinky. Won't be tomorrow." He bellowed at the assembled onlookers, "What's the ruckus in here? Get back to work! We got a club to run!" The crowd quickly dispersed. Cappy Meeks didn't move. Nor did his men. He pointed his manicured finger at Lizzie and Cinn and back again. "You sure this ain't your kid?"

"Does she look like mine?"

". . . Sounds like you. I never forget a song. Have her gone by tomorrow night. Or you be, too. It's policy."

* * *

LIZZIE HURRIED down 135th Street, pushing her way through the Harlem symphony, an open-air garden of wandering prophets, speculators, moneymen, race men, God's voices, governments, theories of luck, economics, and daily numbers. Snowflake had agreed to watch Cinnamon for the morning. Lizzie was determined to find an apartment and a place for Cinn before the afternoon pick-up rehearsal. She avoided the library across Lenox, looking like a courthouse. People were arriving for a poetry reading where she knew Haviland would be. Jolly had told her when she went back to collect the rest of her things that Ray and Elma had moved. "To the Bronx," he said like it was a foreign country. She couldn't stay with Sparrow indefinitely. She had to find something quick. *I got as much right to the Tree of Hope as anybody.*

The three-digit local lottery, based on the daily stock exchange, conceived by a West Indian businessman with the unlikely name of Sydney Holstein, grew exponentially in Harlem, sprouting several cottage industries and subsidiaries. Illegal until the practice was later appropriated by over twenty of these United States, "the numbers" was the largest private homegrown enterprise in the colored world—next to funerals, churches, and hair treatments, of course. Liquor stores would come later, the illegal Prohibition trade being strictly in the hands of first- and second-generation castaways and sharpies from Liverpool, Dublin, Sicily, and the Russian pogroms.

Sparrow was addicted to playing the numbers. When Lizzie complained of her financial straits, that was his solution. She would have none of it. "I told you I ain't got enough money. Why I'ma throw it away?" Yet here she was applying for an apartment from the Policy King's daughter. She didn't see any reason why Haviland's living there should keep her from getting a decently priced rent. The family sponsored literary contests, a black-owned recording studio, movies, and real estate. Why not an aspiring showgirl?

The rental office was crowded. Harlem was bursting with new arrivals every day. "Wait here," the receptionist said, appraising her. The way the woman smiled made Lizzie think she was not going to get the apartment. She looked down to pray. *Shoot! Dirty fingernails. Cuticles bitten pink and raw in places.* She sat on her hands. The young woman reappeared. "This way, Mrs. Turner, Miss Iolanthe will see you now."

The young woman led Lizzie down the hallway to a room with muted gray walls and stately mahogany furniture. Sunlight twinkled through a trio of stained glass windows. A tall, chiseled, even younger woman with large dark eyes greeted her, a slight West Indian lilt to her voice. "Mrs. Turner, please come in, sit down." Her broad mouth smiled without

showing her teeth as she took the chair beside Lizzie. The air stirred with
the scent of orchids. "I am Iolanthe Holstein."

*If the numbers racket can get alla this, I'm in the wrong line of work.
This chippie looks to be younger than me.* Lizzie clasped one hand over the
other and bent her fingers inward to conceal her stubby nails.

Iolanthe crossed her legs. Her long shins touched, one ankle neatly
gracing the other. "There are a few things I must ask you about your application."

Before she could be scrutinized, Lizzie went on the attack. "I hear you
got apartments for artists."

"Yes, for poets and artists." Iolanthe shifted in her seat, her eyes down-
cast, looking at Lizzie's hands. "I am a big supporter of the arts for Negro
people. We must support the artists."

*How 'bout artists who support themselves. Why she lookin' at me like
that?* "I write songs," Lizzie replied, conjuring her first conversation with
Haviland. "That's a kinda poetry. A painter told me that. One of your
tenants, Haviland Remick."

"Ah, you know Mr. Remick?" Iolanthe's eyes brightened. "A fine artist, great promise, if a little eccentric. You're friends?"

"I—we—well, I haven't seen him lately. I've been workin'. Down at
the Cane Break, the new club downtown, a new revue, they featuring one
of my songs. Queen Opal's gonna cut a record, got a great write-up in the
paper," she blurted in one breath. *Talkin' too fast, sayin' too much and
nothin' at all.*

Iolanthe folded her hands across her lap, tranquil as a praying mantis.
"It says here you want an apartment for two? Your husband?"

"No, I'm a widow. My husband died in the war. Well, just after. It's me
and my daughter, but she's no trouble. She's large for her age. Figure to
pass her off for five and get her into school." Lizzie's heart sank with regret. Why did she feel compelled to tell this arrogant, pampered woman
anything? She had expected an interview, not a cross-examination.

"I see . . . And your references? You haven't listed any."

"I just moved up from Charleston and started workin' the next day. I
ain't had time fuh references." Lizzie stood abruptly. Her shoulders jiggled
with irritation as if she could shake this woman's judgment off. "I've been
working two jobs, Miss Holstein. Was livin' with my sister until, but . . ."

Iolanthe leaned forward in her seat, "So is this the address you are living at now?"

"Look, Miss Holstein, I'm a hard-workin', decent woman and I need a place. If you can't see your way to rent me one, I got to be on my way."

Iolanthe stood and placed a warm hand on Lizzie's arm. "Mrs. Turner, I just needed to ask you some questions for clarity." She smiled and extended her other hand toward the door. "I'm sure we can accommodate you. I just need to check one more thing. Please, come with me."

With a breath of relief, Lizzie followed Iolanthe into a barbershop adjoining the realty office. The large, well-equipped room was lively with customers and conversation, each red leather chair occupied.

"Well, what makes you say that? You don't know that! You don't know that," the manicurist said as she filed the nails of her patron, the head barber circling with comb and shears. "I could be ridin' uh aeroplane," she continued, "I could do somethin' like that. Black Eagle did. You saying I can't cuz I'm uh woman?"

"Some Black Eagle," the barber laughed dismissively, "landed on a telephone pole! Powder blue jumpsuit, looked like a cholie inna Cotton Club show."

"You juss jealous!" chuckled the woman. "I work, Miss Holstein work. A woman can do anything. Ain't that right, boss?"

"All right, now, sh sh shshsh. Simmer down," said the man in the chair, "settle it down." He removed a steaming towel from his face with his left hand, the fingers of the right one sitting in a little bowl. The water started trembling to his laughter.

That voice. Lizzie knew that voice.

"Sweetheart, look who it is," Iolanthe said, putting her arm around the man in the barber chair and kissing him. "Tell me this isn't your brother Osceola's wife."

Deacon Turner could see her face in the mirror. "Good to see you, Lizzie."

Sound stopped. Shock waves traveled through her body. Her neck, her ear, her temple, her hand, her back, her eyes, her gut, her heart—all spasmed in pain. Lizzie backed out of the room and ran, then stopped. *I wrote down Sparrow's address! Damn!* She ran as fast as she could, grabbed Cinn from Snowflake's arms and ran.

When she got to Sparrow's apartment, Deacon's black Duesenberg was already parked outside.

"Your brother's wife," Lizzie spewed with disgust. She drew Cinnamon fast to her side, her fingers digging into the child's flesh. "Get away from me before I call the police and have them lock you up for what you done to me. Keep away from me! You think you can come up here and act like somebody. You ain't nobody. Loser, and always will be."

"I see you brought the child," Deacon said.

She scooped Cinn up so fast she snatched the child's breath and slammed the door in his face. *He won't touch her.*

"Hear me out." He spoke through the letter drop. "Open the door."

"Fuck you."

"For Ossie's sake . . . Fuh mine. Wasn't until Ossie was dyin' I stopped and looked around. A man came up and started talking to me, and that's how I met Mr. Holstein. I came and heard what he had to say. What he said I never heard it before, never understood. It made me think about my life. What I been till then. What I done with it, my life. What I had done to you . . ."

Cinn could feel her mother shaking. She could see the man's shiny buttons, the starch of his shirt, the smoothness of the skin on his hands. He smiled at her through the hatch and continued, "Lizzie, Lizzie, I'm running a business. Legit. Barbershop. Real estate. You met my wife," he laughed softly, then sobered. "Lizzie? At least let me . . . I'm in a position to do something for the child. At least let me do something for the child." He was scaring her mother. She was shaking, frozen. Lizzie held on to Cinn, held her fast by the mouth until the last scrape of his shoe hit the steps as he left.

* * *

SPARROW WAS spooked. He paced back and forth in his flat, his hands, arms, and elbows gesticulating panic. "Why Homer Holstein's head man, the one is married to his daughter, stalkin' my apartment? I would like to know. Why? Deacon Turner? Holy shit! This his kid?!"

"His brother's."

"Brother, brother, brother, you got to be kiddin' me. The third biggest nigguh in Harlem. The first be God, the second be his daddy-n-law!"

"He ain't who he says he is, Sparrow."

"That don't mattuh one damn bit, Slim."

Deacon's car remained parked outside. Near dawn, she snuck over the rooftops. Took Cinnamon to Elma's. Elma had finally gotten her lawn and trees, in the Bronx of all places. They were just striplings held up by poles, but they would one day grow into a fine oak walk. The neat row of red-brick apartment buildings had a wide front lawn and, Cinn noted, a playground and a park.

"Elmaaah!" Jolly had known the street but not the address.

"Is that my Lizzie," a voice said faintly, "is that my sistuh?"

They found Elma squatting on the second landing of her apartment's back steps, Jesse crouched beside her. She was holding her bulging stomach, a basket and clusters of spilled, damp laundry at her feet. "Just in time. You can help me hang this wash."

"Well, now, Elma," Lizzie said with her hands on her hips, "I think we gon go upstairs and have this baby. Unless you wanna have it right here on the stairs."

"Oh no no nonono, it's too soon. Lizzie," Elma grabbed her by the arms and squeezed with a vise-like grip as pain surged through her, "Lizzie, Lizzie, Lizzie, I can't lose the baby. I can't lose another child, Lord have mercy! Got to fetch the Reverend. I want the pastor here to deliver last rites."

"Sister, you talkin' crazy. Lizzie won't have it."

"We got to get me to the hospital. Columbia Presbyterian. Three to uh room, room. Not that colored ward."

"I don't think we're gonna make it to Columbia Presbyterian this mornin'," Lizzie said as she braced Elma and helped her to her feet. "You not gon lose nothin' but a couple of pounds, come on," Lizzie said calmly. "We almost there."

"That's right, that's right, th-th-th... A little bit higher, a little bit higher..." Elma began to sing, "I hear music in the air/ Just above my head/ Oh, oh, ohh, I hear music in the air/ Just above my head."

"Cinn," Lizzie said slowly, "get in front of us, baby. Now, run upstairs and make sure all the doors are open."

"I'll do it!" Jesse darted off.

"That's right, Jesse, you lead the way. Cinn, you go with Jesse and turn the covers down on the bed. One more stair, Elma. There we go. Come on now, come on. That's right, I hear music, too. I hear it."

"I hear music in the air/ Just above my head/ Oh-oh-ohh, I hear music in the air/ Just above my head," Elma sang. "Sistuh, I believe I'm havin' this baby."

"And just when was you expectin' to tell me? We'll get through this together, you and me . . . pretty as a picture."

*   *   *

CINNAMON SAT looking out the taxi window, trying to make sense of the morning. A glissando—stairwell, rooftop chimneys, sweet orange air at dawn, train, bridge, green trees, Mama El sayin', "That's my sistuh?" Her auntie had screamed, her face was all shiny and red and the clothes on the bed were soaking wet and red too. The ambulance came and took Mama El and the new baby away and Lizzie had taken her hand, hailed the cab and followed.

"Baby doll!" Lizzie exclaimed as she sat back, hugging Cinnamon tight, rocking, "what a day!" The cab crossed the bridge into Manhattan. Cinnamon's dreams rocked her to sleep, pretty as a picture.

By the time Ray arrived at the hospital, Elma and her new daughter were sleeping peacefully. Both would be fine, the doctor assured him. Cinn, too, and Jesse had dozed off. Ray found them in the waiting room with Lizzie, Jesse leaning on one shoulder and Cinn with her head cradled in her mother's lap. Lizzie looked up at him. Her eyes were sunken. Her voice cracked with exhaustion. "You got a girl, Ray Minor. I named her Memphis . . . I hope that's all right."

"Why Memphis?" he asked.

"I thought it was romantic. It's where you and Elma met, right?"

". . . Actually, that would be Nashville," he said as he picked up Jesse and sat down beside her.

"But they're both in Tennessee, right?"

He chuckled with her. "Yeah, they're both in Tennessee . . . I've seen her." *Hair like Gabby. Skin like Benna. Eyes like sky.* "She's kickin' up her heels like you. A good strong girl."

Cinnamon stirred. She sat up rubbing her eyes. When her uncle came into view, she reared back for a moment.

"Why if it isn't the spice of me life," he teased in his best "black Irish" brogue. "Hello, beautiful." She smiled, relieved. This was the uncle she remembered.

"Papa Ray's got a new job. Anytime you want to see a movie, it's on me. Projectionist," he continued, now talking more to Lizzie, "union card and everything. Back to being the straight man, again." He laughed to himself.

". . . Look, Ray," Lizzie began, "I spoke outta turn at your house. I didn't even know El was pregnant."

Ray put his hand up to stop her and, gently shifting Jesse in his arms, he leaned over toward Cinnamon. "You know, little bit, Jesse wandered around for weeks, looking for you." Cinn smiled and curled up again on her mother's lap to sleep. Lizzie stroked her hair, melody danced in her dreams, *Woo-Woo, Chattanooga Choo-choo* . . .

"Listen, Ray," Lizzie blurted, stoking up her nerve, "I gotta leave here. What you and El got, I won't never have that . . . I gotta go. Soon! I mean now. Elma said she'd keep the kid. I got two-three hundred bucks saved and I can pay twenty-five a week. Even more when I start work. Whatever it takes. Whatever you need. She's gonna be five in a minute. She gotta start school. She needs . . . a family. And I gotta go. I can't stay here. When I'm settled, then I'll, I'll, I'll, I can send for her." She looked at her daughter, curled up asleep, their fingers interlaced. "Tell Cinn for me. Tell her for me . . . Never mind."

* * *

LIZZIE WENT to Cappy Meeks and asked him to back her for the socialite's European tour. "That way you can keep Miss Roberts at home and still get a cut of the gate," she said.

"Why should I do this for you?"

"Now, I already asked you nice. Don't make me ask you naughty."

So Cappy went to the socialite and pitched Lizzie as the lead act and as a testament to her audacity booked her in a suite on the RMS *Mauretania*. Sparrow had decided to come with her. "Bath the size of my apartment," Sparrow marveled. Glistening white tiles, white soap, white robes and monogrammed slippers, but he couldn't enjoy himself. Lizzie had been crying behind a locked cabin door for two days.

"Come on now," he prodded, "open up the doah. I'm not exactly fond of this boat, you know. Colored people and boats don't have such a good history, but you don't see me cryin' about it." He leaned his forehead against the door. "Cappy Meeks, Deacon Turner, what is it, you just attracted to bad men? Bad man magnet!" Sparrow threw up his hands and started pacing. "Think I was gonna stick around for some six-foot, wide-angle nigguh to come at me," he mumbled, kicking at the stateroom carpet, "got me out here in the middle of nowhere, open duh doah!" He plunked himself down on the couch, all knees and elbows, and poured himself a glass of flat champagne. "Least we legal now. Cheers!" The door creaked open. Her coat thrown over her slip, Lizzie ambled into their shared central room. Her eyes were puffed into slits, her nose one red shiny ball. "She lives!" Sparrow teased. Lizzie grabbed his glass, poured some more champagne, and left. "Good mornin' to you, too."

The bow of the ship coasted atop the thick autumn waves, the slate gray contrasted by a thin strip of mauve and pink at the horizon line. Haviland appeared by her side. Haviland. Overcoat, silk scarf, and still no socks.

"Hello," he said. "Didn't think I'd ever see you again."

"No, I guess not."

"I looked for you."

"Not too hard."

"I'm with a group. Off to Russia." He laughed. "Going to make a movie. And you?"

"Paris. Finally got my own show."

"Good for you! I'll see you when I come to Paris, then?"

"Perhaps."

He left her alone on the bow. As the ship coasted, all around her was nothing but horizon. Her weight seemed to vanish and her chest swelled with the tart salt air. No boundaries. A lone bird struggling against the headwind circled back and, trying another route, disappeared into tomorrow.

✳ ✳ ✳

BETWEEN 1919 and 1929, the world exploded, expelling grief, death, and rage. The highways bled and flooded upstream with refugees from

Southern weevils, blight, and terror. Death Riders and riots swept St. Louis, Tulsa, Charleston, Chicago. Red Scare, Red Summer, Red—the age was hot! Burning the gut with liquor, feet slashin' up the dance floor. A perpetual party and ticker tape parade—on borrowed time and borrowed money. With underground economies propping things up, the Depression came as no surprise to the criminal class. Their trauma came later with the repeal of Prohibition.

They went down fast as the stocks on Black Friday. Asa Jolly got killed in a duel on 52nd Street. Paced off with a "customer" and they plugged each other. He finally made the New York paper, *New York Age,* page 22. You can't run a syndicate from the dance floor, Cappy Meeks found out. In 1929, somebody put a pistol hole through the gullet of one of his colleagues in the middle of Lew Leslie's favorite number. Word went out as to Cappy's liability, and he was gunned down in a Jersey City phone booth. Three months later, the Cane Break mysteriously burned to the ground.

Deacon Turner also died in a way. He retired from the numbers and adopted the name of his father-in-law. As Deacon Holstein and head of Holstein Realty, he became a noted Harlem philanthropist and Cinnamon's patron throughout her days at Juilliard.

Dakota Sparrow, when he returned from Europe, went out to Hollywood and because of his name was mistaken for a cowboy. Though he lost most of his fortune in a series of Ponzi schemes, his work can be seen in such minor colored indie classics as *Dusky Sunset* and *Kid Ory Rides Again.*

> "Why feel shame, when you should feel glorious?
> Why seek fame, when you could be notorious?
> So, come on folks, come on and join the band,
> All you boys bettuh settle up now,
> Cuz you're in Yamma Mama La-and!"

Mayfield Turner stood with her arms akimbo, a shimmering bronze statue of naked liberty, and launched into her signature.

> "Miss Lizzie Mae had her a way,
> Of walkin' down the street,

That would make the sidewalk,
Sizzle beneath her feet,
Yes, Lizzie Mae had her a way,
Of walkin' down the street,
That could make a hungry fellah forget to eat,
When she stepped in the lane,
All the necks would crane,
Just to name,
That way she had of wah-wah-wahl-kin',
Baby, when she hit the street,
Lemme tell yuh it was somethin' sweet,
When she what? Strut, Miss Lizzie, strut!
Say what! Strut, Miss Lizzie, strut!"

The club was a frenzy, the crowd wild, the air torrid with movement turned to vapor—another white-hot night of jazz—from London to Spain, from the Rhine to the Seine, Mayfield Turner had the world right where she wanted it, whirling and swirling around her.

Lemme tell yuh all now it was a four-alarm blaze,
The Joint was jumpin' for days and days,
Like water on a grease fire,
Those flames just shot up higher and higher,
Tell you bout the thing that started all the tawk,
Meet me at the junction where Charleston meets New Yawk!

The Jazz Age while it lasted was a blast! It was so hot—Pow! Pop! It sizzled/ Baby, just listen here/ It got so hot—Pzzsssst!—it fizzled. Hangover lasted nine years!

22

By now the photo album Elma pulled out was frayed and yellowed. She turned to the pictures of Eudora and Tom taken before the Great War. Then all of a sudden she came upon a photo of herself taken at Fisk and one of Lizzie by the sewing machine cutting out patterns for Eudora's blossoming business. Though Ma Bette didn't like getting her face "caught," as she called it, there were one or two late snapshots of her in her daily garb as a soothsayer with all her beads and turbans. Elma turned back the pages again only to find an image of Geechee women weaving baskets for God only knows what reason and, toward the front, a silvery daguerreotype of Ma Bette in her silks and lace, ready for the Master to come see his "fancy gal" at the cottage he maintained for her and their offspring. It was there that Elma decided to inscribe Bette's death, August 12, 1932.

Outside her window Elma could hear a group of itinerant colored gospel singers on the street praising President Roosevelt, "Tell me how ya like Roosevelt, he's our friend." Her mind wandered from the photo album to more recent newspaper items. Dusky, pasty-looking brown-skinned children sat blankly on the porches of shotgun shacks; older women with no life in them, not even longing in their eyes, leaned against newspapered walls—tent cities taking over the parks. Elma wondered how much suffering would be multiplied in the South. She wondered how much the Great Depression was affecting her mother.

Elma glanced away from the picture of her great-grandmother to take in the loss. Ma Bette had never seen any of Elma's children. Some part of Elma wondered if Mama Bette's spells might not have saved her two first-born, as so many Carolinian women swore by those charms, but she immediately pushed this thought away as blasphemy, a moment of weakness, yearning for a healthy child. She should count her blessings. She had three. Jessie and Memphis had lived long enough to have personality, and Cinn had become a part of the family, her other daughter.

Elma loved Jessie dearly. True, he had trouble learning to put words together to make sense, but her Jessie was a fine boy. If something was wrong with him, Raymond barely mentioned it. Elma could tell by the way Raymond ignored his son that her husband was still unnerved that Jessie had survived when their daughters Gabby and Benna had perished. *Lookin' at his son, seein' his own failures.*

"Elma, what are you doin'?" Raymond snapped at her. "Got no time for nostalgia. If we're going on this trip, you better get to steppin'. The trains don't wait, even for you, my lady." She closed the album and put it back in the drawer beside her bed. Raymond continued to pace and prattle. "I don't even understand why we have to go all this way at a time when a Negro can't rub two pennies together. Why, you were never that close to your great-grandma anyway, as I recall. You were embarrassed by her conjurin' as you called it. Now in the middle of this heat you want to take us to Carolina, where it must be burning up, to see the old lady get buried. For Christ's sake, she didn't even believe in God, just spirits and haints. We can't afford a trip like this now."

Elma softly responded, "Raymond, you're talking about my great-grandmother who lived through slavery, Reconstruction, and the Great War. What else could you ask of a soul, and how could we not pay homage to her? Sometimes you forget the heart of a matter and get all smothered in the dollars and cents of it. Relax, Raymond. She's only going to die once in our lifetime."

"Well, thank God for that. This is the Depression, you know. And when the white man sneezes, the colored man catches pneumonia. Thousands of people without jobs, more each day."

"Ray, what's all this bluster?" Elma said sweetly. "You still have a job, don't you? You make a decent living as a projectionist. Surely enough to see us through this little bit of mess. We've seen worse."

"Elma, isn't there any way I can take that calm and tranquility of yours and bottle it? Then we'd be rich colored folk for real." Raymond laughed. "We'd be goin' down there in style. Show your cousins, the Diggses, the real thing for a change."

"Come on now, Raymond, don't begrudge them their success. That's not Christ's way."

Jessie, who had been listening to this squabble, imagined that the family might not be able to go. He was a tall, rail-thin youth, two tones of color on his face as if his body after the infant fever couldn't make up its mind about the shade. His long-limbed awkward gait and his guileless slow-talking manner drove his father silently mad. "Mama, please don't argue with Papa," he drawled. "Papa, don't be vexed with Mama. She just wants to see her great-grandma and so do I. I never got to meet her."

"But she's dead, Jessie. You won't exactly be meeting her," Cinnamon quipped. At twelve, Cinnamon was a wry pragmatist. Conscious of her plumpness and color, how distinctly different she was from the rest of the family, she compensated with a stinging quick tongue and a compulsion to be right.

Elma put her arms around her son and niece. "Children, the dead just pass over to another world," Elma explained. "It's proper that we want to say good-bye."

"They don't go to heaven?" Eight-year-old Memphis pushed her face between Jessie and her mother's rib cage.

Raymond tustled his daughter's curly mop, his golden child. "See what you started, Elma? How you goin' to explain where an old conjure woman goes when she passes over?" he asked.

As jocular as her uncle was, Cinn never forgot that night of rage, the slew of invectives he had thrown at them, her and her mother both. As she watched her aunt and uncle bicker, she didn't know who to believe. She knew one thing. *Dead is dead. Gone is gone.*

"All right, Raymond, I've had enough. It's none of our business where the good Lord sets my great-grandma in His glory. We've no right to belittle her. Why do you want to turn the children against my family at a time like this? This conversation is over. If you don't want to go with us to Charleston, you don't have to. But we're going and we're going today. Raymond? Raymond!"

Whenever Raymond and Elma quarreled like this, Jessie tried to entertain Cinnamon and Memphis. Disturbances made him uneasy. He may not have been the quickest of Elma's children, but he was a sensitive child who watched over his sisters carefully. Of all the children, Jessie was most prone to following his instincts, like his great-great-grandma Bette. So while Elma and Raymond carried on about the failures of their marriage and Raymond's failures as head of household behind the closed doors of their bedroom, Jessie captured the girls' attention with a game of marbles on the kitchen floor. His thumb poised above his favorite veined silver-starburst, he prepared to obliterate his opponents with a three-ball knuckle knock-out when Elma appeared at the kitchen swing door, still wearing distress on her face. "Jessie? Girls? Why aren't you ready? Jessie, you're the oldest. Why don't you have your sisters dressed and ready to go? Lord, sometimes I just don't know what to do with you."

The children pummeled Elma with a thousand questions as she primped and plied their traveling clothes.

"Do we have to wear black? I don't have anything black."

"Are they really rich, Mama?"

"Will they be nice to us? Or mean?"

"Now, why would your own family be mean to you? Raymond, see what you've done? Scared the children half to death."

"Oh hush, Elma, I've got a right to my own feelings."

"Well, not right now. Right now, children, we're going to where your mama grew up. It's really beautiful. It's so green, and the folks are really friendly. We'll see cotton fields, rice paddies, indigo, and cane fields. Charleston is a beautiful city. Sailboats on the bay, fresh clams and fish to eat right out the ocean."

"You might even see a niggah or two hangin' from a tree."

"Raymond! Must you keep tryin' to frighten them? Keep your bitterness to yourself. I don't want to hear any more talk like that. I won't have it!" She turned to the children, enveloping the three in her outstretched arms. "The South is truly beautiful. You'll be surprised. All we're going to see is our Ma Bette goin' to meet her Maker."

"Well, let's get the hell on out of here! If we're goin', let's do it now before I change my mind and we stay right here."

"Nobody is staying here. We're going to Charleston."

"On a fancy train, Daddy?" Memphis exclaimed, jumping in place and clapping her hands.

Jessie sobered, serious, pensive. "Do you really think we'll see a lynching, Papa?"

Before either parent could respond, Cinn interjected, "You might see more than that. You're goin' south! You got to get off the sidewalk when you see white folks! You got to bow down to all the white folk you run into! You got to jump back and hold your hat!" Cinnamon threw her arms out, shoved her hips back, and slid one foot rearward to meet the other, making the other children burst into laughter.

"Cinnamon, stop that! Raymond, look what you've done! Filled their heads with foolishness."

"Dead niggahs are only 'foolishness' to you, Miss Mayfield of the Mayfields."

"That's enough, Raymond. I'm going out that door with my children in ten minutes. You can come with us or keep your damn self right here."

"Ooo, Mama cursed, she's really mad," Memphis whispered.

* * *

"COME ON girls, Jessie, let's go."

"Isn't Daddy coming with us?" Cinnamon blurted.

Trying to keep her temper, Elma answered, "I have no idea."

Once she had maneuvered her broad hips through the subway turnstile and had gotten everybody safely on the first car of the A train, Elma looked over her shoulder to see if Raymond had decided to come with them, but there was no sign of him. With a deep sigh she wondered what had come over her husband. When they first got to New York they had been so happy, and when they moved to the Bronx, it was a new start. Now, as they tried to make ends meet, all they did was fight. "Well, we're on our way, children. We should be in Charleston by tomorrow morning." They got to Penn Station and boarded the southbound train with no time to spare.

Jessie made quite a few friends on the train, helping people with their bags, inquiring about their travels. "He may be a slow talker, but he has no trouble doin' it," Elma mused. He met people on their way to Washington, Richmond, and Tallahassee. He told them that he rode the New York City trains almost every day, but he had no idea that his country was so big! Hour after hour the train roared by the makeshift shanty-towns along the tracks. Jessie was appalled but confident that his family would never have to live like that. His father took any and every job that came his way. Working at the movie house, neighborhood carpenter jobs, even hauling, trying to save as much as he could. Everybody in his family had a job. He was an usher at the Majestic Theater. Cinnamon was such a prodigy she gave music lessons at the settlement house and won singing contests every chance she got. Memphis was just Memphis, a professional baby as far as he was concerned, but pretty soon she would have to get a job too, even if she was only eight. No, his family would never be living by the side of a railroad track, with a blanket over their heads for a roof.

Once they passed Washington, D.C., the family was shuttled to a Colored car directly behind the locomotive engine. For the children's sake, Elma camouflaged the move. "I do believe I saw some people we know gettin' on in Washington," she told them, "goin' down to pay respects to Ma Bette, I believe. Let's join them up front."

"Colored car, just for us," Cinnamon quipped. She was old enough to realize that her aunt, without the presence of her children, could have ridden comfortably undetected in the Whites Only section.

Memphis skipped along. "Colored car? Do they have Crayolas?" She halted at the entrance. "Eww, smells stinky like cigars."

"You'll forget that soon as you get a whiff of my ginger cookies," Elma said as she settled the children. The seats were torn, the backs broken on some. The car was filled with smoke. Cinders danced in the fetid air. The windows were coated with a dull film. It was good that Elma had fried some chicken 'cause "Colored" weren't allowed in the dining car either. Jesse wiped the window with his jacket sleeve. Cinnamon leaned over and taunted her young cousin, "Oh yeah, we goin' south to see Ma Bette. Mixin' jars of flowers and herbs and goober dust. We gonna wear clothes-pins on our noses so we could talk to the dead. Ma Bette might sit up in her grave!" Cinnamon lunged forward and sent Memphis into a spasm of terror.

The conductor who checked their tickets wore a visible scowl every time he passed by. "He thinks you're white, Mama El," Cinn observed. Elma, who traveling alone would have masqueraded, only then felt the sting.

After sixteen hours of a long, hot overnight ride, the train finally arrived in Charleston mid-morning. The quaint seaside city looked charming from the train, but when Jessie bumped into a white man, Elma quickly pulled him out of the way and apologized. "See, told you," Cinnamon whispered in his ear. Luckily the family had come to meet them and Elma placed Jessie in their midst so he would attract no more attention. Eudora looked splendid, regal and well-groomed, with a broad-lace collar and a simple black dress that hung loosely on her gaunt frame, her blue eyes muted by the shade of her hat. Francina and Roswell Jr. were themselves. Francina was plumper than ever; Roswell, graying at his temples, looked drunk. There were lots of superficial kisses and hugs. Jessie was confused, not only by the relatives but by his mother's actions, jerking him sharply when that white man bumped into him. Jessie thought that the Diggses and Eudora looked wealthy, and his thoughts flashed back to the shantytowns they had passed. The world was a strange place. A place where some folks had nothing and others had everything they could dream of, and some were even colored.

Eudora beheld each of the children, one by one, and took pleasure in the inspection. She could tell by the girls' threadbare dresses and Jessie's worn jacket that the Minors weren't doing so well in New York. Though her nose was red and running and her eyes watery from grief, she managed to smile warmly at her family. "I can hardly believe Memphis is so big," she said, then frowned. "Where's Raymond, Elma?"

Elma just shook her head. "I have no idea, Mama. He was coming, but then he must have changed his mind."

"Oh, I see," Eudora said, quietly perturbed. "Well, you missed the wake. At least you made it to the funeral and brought the children."

Elma looked blushingly at her mother's fine linen dress and broad-rimmed hat. Who'd have ever believed that Eudora would end up doing so well! Elma felt embarrassed for herself and her children, embarrassed that after all her mother had sacrificed, she had done nothing with her education and had made so little of her life in New York. But when she looked again at Eudora's tense, rigid face, she immediately regretted her self-absorption. In losing Ma Bette, Eudora had lost the only real mother she had ever known. "Mama, I'm so sorry about Ma Bette."

"We've all got to go sometimes," said Roswell Jr. "That's how I make a living. Colored people seem to die a lot these days. Really good for business."

Eudora and Elma ignored Roswell as best they could. Francina called for their driver, and the whole passel of the Diggses and Minors were off. Roswell rode up front with the driver, while Elma, Eudora, and Francina as Ma Bette's nearest kin rode in the back seat, the children in the jump seat behind them.

As the late-model sedan sped along, Elma whispered to her mother, "Mama, I'm really proud of how well you've done for yourself. Everything you wanted for me and Lizzie you've earned for yourself, and you deserve it all, Mama."

Dora patted her on the knee. "Don't you just love these children, though?"

"I'm always telling them about Ma Bette and the farm," Elma said. "They all feel like they know you." Elma turned to the children, "Jessie, Cinnamon, Memphis, say a proper hello to your grandma."

"I'd rather they call me Nana if that's all right with you."

"Of course, Mama. Hey, you children back there, Grandma wants you to call her Nana. It's special, don't you think?"

"Nana, Nana, Nana," the giggling Northern children squealed.

Eudora grew serious and asked, "When's that heathen Lizzie coming home anyhow? She's not here for Ma Bette's funeral! That's terrible, shameless!"

"Well, Mama, she did send me a cable," Elma chided, ever her sister's defender. "She's in South America and would never get here in time. She didn't believe that Ma Bette wanted a Christian funeral, anyway."

Eudora was miffed, but she put her disappointment with Lizzie out of her mind. She looked lovingly at her grandchildren and said to Elma with concern, "That Cinnamon's a stocky one, but those other two children are skin and bones. Daughter, what are you feedin' them? I'm tellin' you now I'm gonna fatten them up like a good Southern Nana is bound to. That's part of my responsibility, to pass all the recipes down and get me some hearty-lookin' grandchildren. What you say to that, Elma?"

"Mama, that sounds just fine to me," Elma replied, happy that her mother wasn't going to let the news about Lizzie ruin the day.

Jessie had a million questions for his new Nana. "Where are the slaves, Nana?"

"Well, there aren't any more slaves now."

"Well, where'd they go?"

"Will you let me answer one question, boy, before you ask another? They're in our blood, son. That's where they are. They keep us strong. Your Ma Bette was a slave. The last generation to be slave, the first to be free." Eudora turned to Elma and said, "I just love this child, Elma. There's nothing wrong with this boy. I hate to say it, and you know I do, but I believe he's got a lot of Ma Bette in him."

Elma and Eudora spontaneously burst into laughter, thinking that Ma Bette, even from the grave, was ridin' right along with them.

Ever since the mention of her mother, Cinnamon had quieted. She had been too young when Lizzie carried her away from Charleston to remember anything but snatches. In the dance of morning sunlight, glimpses of memory came to her as the sleek polished automobile rode through the town. She noticed that people in the market stopped what they were doing and lined the streets, a glimmer in the eyes, slight smile on the lips, black skins shining, touching the ground as Ma Bette's descendants passed by.

* * *

THE AZULA Street Church was overflowing. At the chapel door Roswell began to greet the mourners and those who had come to pay their respects to Ma Bette. Charleston's aristocratic colored families showed up out of respect for the Diggses. Those who came to pay respect to Ma Bette were dressed in white and had a dozen white doves to let loose when the coffin came out of the church. Lijah-Lah had brought a boatload of old-timers from the island. They had goober dust, cowrie shells, and rice to throw into the air so that Ma Bette would pass on to the Other Side with food, money, and a free spirit. Elma smiled at Ma Bette's friends and patrons. Eudora ignored them. Jessie wanted to stay outside with the strange people in the white cotton dresses, so plain compared to the fancified folks going into the church.

When the service was over, some of Roswell's professional pallbearers carried the coffin from the church. The birds flew singing, the goober dust went lazily through the air, the cowrie shells grazed the coffin, and the people in white began a strange dance in a circle. Their feet never left the ground, but they rhythmically made a circle in the street and sang, occasionally shouting. They clapped their hands, made random turns, and closed their eyes as if they could tell where they were going through the Lord's eyes. Jessie was drawn to them. He wanted to sing and dance, too, but Eudora caught him by the sleeve and whispered that he was not to go over there.

"I'm going to keep you right near me, young man. That's not the path you're going to take. No sirreee."

* * *

BLANCHE DIGGS went out of her way to have a beautiful repast in honor of Ma Bette. Eudora and Elma were touched. In the same parlor that Eudora first beheld as a girl fresh off the island, her grandchildren sat wide-eyed, looking at the massive amounts of she-crab soup, crab gumbo and rice, okra and tomatoes, cornbread, and fancy liqueurs. The sweet tea even had strawberries in it!

Glass in hand, Roswell approached Elma. She braced herself for more rudeness. "Such an eccentric, that Ma Bette," he began. "She deserves a grand going-away fete, don't you think? I know you've never liked me, Elma, but I've got a lot of respect for you, your mother, and Ma Bette. Your people have real fight in you."

Elma was taken aback and puzzled. She had really thought Roswell held her family in contempt, less than trash. *Well, you never really know.* She thanked Roswell for his graciousness, only to look toward the front door and see Raymond standing in the threshold, his old confident self.

"Elma, my angel. I'm sorry I missed the funeral. I hope you're not too disappointed, but I did get here."

Elma was more disturbed than surprised. She prayed Raymond hadn't lost his job and regretted that she had pestered him so. "I'm delighted to see you, my diligent husband. Handsome, too."

Roswell, a bit uneasy with the two of them making eyes, asked Raymond if he'd like a drink.

"Why, yes, cousin Roswell, I'd love a brandy." Raymond rocked back on his heels with swagger. "A double if you don't mind."

Roswell motioned for one of the bartenders to bring two brandies to the handsome couple by the door.

"Papa, Papa!" Memphis came running to Raymond. He grabbed her and tossed her up like a bunch of colored balloons. Only Cinnamon was quiet, holding back, standing beside Elma.

"Look, Cinn, it's Papa," Jessie encouraged and coaxed the girl from behind her aunt.

Raymond greeted Eudora with a peck on the cheek. "So sorry I missed the service, Mother. Couldn't be helped. I had some very important clients with an emergency."

"Come on, darlin'." Elma took his arm. "Let's go see the rest of the family." When she had him aside, Elma lit into him with soft-toned ire. "Raymond Minor, what's the matter with you? Everyone knows about us. We're not fooling anyone."

"Elma, don't ruin this for me, for us. Nobody here thought we'd ever make it in New York. Let's not give them the credit for seeing it was just pipe dreams. Please, Elma, let me have this moment."

Elma looked into her husband's eyes, and nodded her head. "All right, Raymond, all right."

Not for a minute did Eudora believe the charade Elma and Raymond were playing. While Raymond's pressed white shirt looked new, the suit and jacket as well, the children's clothes were faded, their shoes worn thin, and Jessie and Memphis were just too skinny. It was then she began flirting with an idea. "Elma, honey," she began, "since you've got so many children in that one apartment in New York, why don't you let me keep Jessie down here with me?" Before Elma could open her mouth to respond, Dora pressed her case. "He could go to that fine new boarding school just opened for the Negro youth. The Avery Institute is a fine school for young men. Your cousin Francina's teaching there now. Our Jessie could really get his footing there. And you and Raymond could get yourself a fresh start."

Elma and Raymond looked at each other for a minute. "Mama, we don't need a fresh start. And that's that."

"You can't fool me, Elma. What'd he do, rent that whole outfit?"

"Mama!" Elma was incensed at her mother's outburst. Family was family, but if it came to a choice between her mother and her husband, she knew exactly where she stood. "We're going out to the farm now. Memphis isn't feeling well. Too many of Francina's bon-bons, I'm sure. We'll speak of this at home."

Eudora didn't say anything. She knew Elma was right. There was no need to embarrass her own child in front of the Diggses and the whole funeral party, but she still wanted Jessie. She had made up her mind. That was a boy with some get up and go. She could really raise him to be somebody.

✳ ✳ ✳

THOUGH IT was well into the night when the car arrived at the new farmhouse, everyone was still awake. Eudora worked ten years to buy back the land Tom Winrow lost and another seven to build a beautiful brick house on it. They didn't know when Eudora had found the time to cook, too. The children kept saying they'd never seen so much food in one day. Elma cautioned them sternly with a whisper, "That's private family business, not anybody else's." But Eudora heard.

"That's all right, daughter, I can see through all this. Raymond, don't you know I just want the two of you to be good to each other and raise these children up right? I know you're havin' hard times, but these children don't have to suffer, too. Let me keep Jessie, the boy, till you get your feet on the ground again. I can help you out some. Really."

"We're not paupers, Eudora," Raymond responded sharply.

"I'm not suggesting that, Raymond. I'm just saying there's nothing wrong with accepting help, either."

"Well, Mama, it's not as simple as that," Elma said.

"Why isn't it? I'm your mother, not some stranger doing a good deed. Francina and even Roswell were quite taken with Jessie. And I think Jessie took to me, as well. I think he'd like to stay with me."

Stoking his solitude, Raymond retreated to the corner of the parlor. Elma's mind turned to her children. *What Eudora was saying made some sense, but does Jessie want to stay in Charleston? How would Memphis respond to the absence of her big brother? And what about Cinnamon? Shifted and shunted from household to household, how would she feel?* "We'll have to ask the children what they want to do, Mama."

"Oh, no, you don't. You just tell them what's good for them."

Elma ignored her mother's admonitions. She walked over to Raymond. "What do you want, my angel?"

Raymond chose his words very carefully. He didn't want her to know what a failure he thought himself as a husband and a father. "Well, I . . . ah, I think your mother's got a good idea. Actually, I think we should give Jessie that one foot up on the world, like your mother said."

"What about Cinn? I can't see separating her from Jesse."

"Cinnamon might enjoy the farm."

Eudora overheard the name Cinnamon and felt a chill go up her spine. *Not Cinnamon.* She couldn't bear that. Her daughter's pregnancy had caused such a rift between them. *I lost my temper and cast my Lizzie into the wild and she has gone to naught.* Her daughters, she had failed them both, cut herself off. Even Elma, sometimes when she looked at that sweet girl, the long-buried rage at her unavenged rape passed through her body with a shudder. How could she feel these things toward her own daughters? *It wasn't their fault how they were born.* Trying to push these thoughts from her mind, Eudora retired to her bedroom.

She opened a heavy wooden chest at the foot of her bed. *Dress of lace made for a wedding that never was. Old pair of cloth-covered shoes.* Gingerly, she drew out an old Sears shoebox, though vintage, still pristine, the casing just frayed on the corners. Sitting by the light, she cradled the box in her arms and opened the lid. She held up a worn curled photograph. Acid had eaten away at parts. She squinted to make out the image, a ghost of itself. Her eyes widened as she remembered Lijah-Lah's words, "Oh yo mama could sing!" *Just to hear it once, just to hear her voice one more time.* The door quietly opened. Eudora turned and was looking straight into the eyes of the child she had wanted to avoid.

"Grandmother? Nana? May I sit with you?" asked Cinnamon, peeking through the entrance.

"Now there's a first. A relation who seeks my company." Dora held out her arms. "I'm teasing, child. Come." Cinn sat beside Dora, still fingering the edge of the photograph. She straightened her shoulders, laughing, "This here is our Ma Bette, when she was still livin' on that island, Sweet Tamarind. And this is your great-grandma Juliet, my mother. Only picture I have. You maybe favor her some, I think. People used to say she had a beautiful voice."

Cinnamon's embrace startled her. Dora had grown unaccustomed to warmth, but the child's gesture was so genuine and unfettered, Dora relaxed into it and drew strength from it.

Cinnamon gravitated toward Eudora as if Eudora had something just for her. "Why are you staring at me so?" Cinnamon asked. "Do I remind you of someone, Nana? Tell me about my mother. Am I like my mother, Nana?"

"Oh, goodness no, child," Eudora exclaimed, "you're not like your mother at all!" She leaned toward Cinnamon until their foreheads met. "Why, you're too graceful and well-mannered to be your mother's child."

"Can I tell you something, Nana?"

"Yes, child, you can tell me anything."

"My mother hates me."

Eudora's heart seized up like she was being stabbed. Softly she whispered, "Oh no, she doesn't," grabbing up the child like she wished she'd held Lizzie.

"Mayfields are just very mysterious folks. Your mama's just a mysterious woman, like our Ma Bette was, and you will be too. Ma Bette could talk to the birds, run with the horses, and read the moon. Oh, you're a Mayfield all right! And if you stay with me for a while I'll fill you up with gumbo and peach cobbler. Plus, all the magic you'll ever need to know."

Before long the family had gathered round. "Is this our grandpa?"

"Hmph. Tom Winrow, yes."

"Where'd he go?"

"To hell I most likely suspect. All I have to say on that matter."

"What's this?" Memphis chirped, holding up a small preserves jar.

"All that's left of Julius Mayfield, who your Ma Bette called her husband, while everyone else called her his slave woman, his fancy gal." She took the jar from Memphis and, squinting to make out the contents, held it to the light. "Ma Bette always said this was his big toe. Pickled like a pig foot."

"Eww!" The children already thought their mother odd for saving pieces of hair, and here their grandmother had a big toe!

Eudora laughed wickedly, then sobered. "Mayfield, that horrible man. Why my daughter has chosen to use it as a stage name is totally beyond me. Hmph, Ma Bette used to call it her proof!" Dora laughed and laughed, then started sobbing. "I made her to leave everything she held dear . . . She used to get on my nerves so. Now I can't stop missin' her. This house is so empty. Your father's people bought this place. Hoping their people would come back. Not a one ever did. No one ever come back. I bought it, built a new house, thinkin' it would give Ma Bette some peace, thinkin' my own children would come back. Not like this, not like this."

Intuiting her mother's needs, Elma approached Dora. "Mama, Cinnamon says she would like to sing something in honor of Ma Bette." Dora looked across the room at the tall pudgy brown-skinned girl. "Oh Mama," Elma crooned, "she has a better voice than I ever could claim."

"Come, Nana, sit with me at the piano."

"You know I will, darlin', you know I will." *Perhaps, my redemption.* Eudora took her seat by her grandchild as the rest of the family gathered round. "Your great-great-grandmamma, well, she held a lot of respect in this town. In the middle of this here Depression, people come from all over the country to honor her. Your Ma Bette's crossin' ovuh and she waitin' on your song. Sing so she can hear you, Cinn. Sing that song right on up to heaven."

"My name is Cinnamon Mayfield Turner. In honor of my great-great-grandmother Bette Mayfield . . ." As Cinnamon began to sing, a strength, a source infused her soul with both sweetness and power that swept all present into its orb. Eudora nodded to herself. *Hear that, Mah Bette? Lijah-Lah would say, like Ma Bette's mama and she mama before that. And Bette's daughter, my mama Juliet. Lijah-Lah could tell. A voice to make the birds take notice.*

Eudora turned to Elma and Raymond. "Let me keep Jessie and Cinnamon for a while. If they don't get on well here, I'll send them right back to New York for you to care for."

So Jessie and Cinnamon stayed with Eudora for a while, and Elma and Raymond returned with Memphis to New York to start their lives over. Both Jessie and Cinnamon flourished in the South. Jessie seemed to draw strength from the land and the slower pace of life there, while Cinnamon blossomed at Eudora's church, singing in the choir and, on many

occasions, playing piano and singing classics and hymns for the Negro
Society.

* * *

WHEN IT became time to think about college, Cinnamon returned
north with plans to attend school in New York. She returned with the
clipped proper drawl of Charleston's colored elite falling from her lips in
the dead of winter, like the start of spring when the air was fresh, the
trees bearing a small bit of green. She had grown three inches and her
body had slimmed into a tall Rubenesque bronze. With the Minors as
her guardians, she could go to Hunter College. The premier institution
for young women in the city college system offered a first-rate education
for five dollars a semester. Even then the cost was a challenge. Cinn still
had to find work in her off-hours and during the summer. She coached
the choir and the children's choir at the church and played piano at the
Wednesday evening service. She performed at weddings, funerals, and
teas, in the basements of churches, the lobbies of libraries and cafeterias,
and at summer gazebos. Bringing high culture to the Bronx and Harlem
also included supervising piano lessons *and* gym class at the colored
YMCA. "Roll call!" *How to arrange the junior choir. Three tan, three
crimson robes, two men one woman and two women, one man. Forty-five
students, three groups of fifteen for basics. Or four groups of ten?* Evenings
and weekends she took tickets at the Lafayette Theater. The job gave her
an opportunity to sometimes stand in the wings and watch the shows—
The Hot Mikado, Voodoo Macbeth, Mamba's Daughter. She didn't know
how she felt about George Gershwin's *Porgy and Bess* when the radical
all-Negro opera finally made its way uptown. The Catfish Row portrayed
in the musical wasn't anything like the Charleston she had come to know
while living with her grandmother. And she didn't even see how a decent
man like Porgy would ever fall for a triflin' heifer like Bess. *I loves you,
Porgy. Who talks like that?*

The Manhattan campus of Hunter College, in its new buildings, sat a
few blocks from Central Park. Cinnamon realized how much she enjoyed being at Hunter every time she walked past it. She had applied
herself so diligently that she expected to finish in three years, graduating
in June of 1939; yet as her senior year began, she missed being with the

friends she had made as a freshman and regretted that she wouldn't get to march with them. Already her visits to the campus were sparse. Having secured a part-time job as assistant choir instructor at Hunter High School, which was adjacent to the college, she was also still taking private voice lessons from her undergraduate singing instructor, Professor Olivetsky. She missed the camaraderie of her old college life more than she let herself know.

As she neared the campus, Cinnamon saw her friend Esther Mason coming from voice class, where they'd met. Esther was a charmer of a young woman with a fury of brown curls that enveloped her face.

"Cinnamon, what a serendipitous happenstance."

"Esther, don't put on so," Cinnamon laughed. "Where you goin'?"

"Just finished social studies. What are you doing here, Miss I-Can't-Wait-to-Graduate?"

"I was on my way to see Dr. Olivetsky. She left me a message that she had some good news for me," Cinnamon replied.

"Oh well, if Dr. Olivetsky says jump . . . we jump, huh?"

"Stop it, Esther!" Cinnamon started to blush. Everyone in the vocal department knew that Cinnamon thought the world of Dr. Olivetsky, who taught voice as vigorously as a Russian ballet teacher. "The Bolshoi of the Voice" she was nicknamed, with some reverence.

"Yes, I'm going to see Dr. Olivetsky. Why don't you wait for me? I'm sure my appointment won't be long. I'm supposed to meet Memphis here."

"Say, me too. What's your cousin cookin' up now?"

Cinnamon just shook her head and shrugged. "She'll be along any minute. I'm sure we'll find out. You know Memphis. Always somethin'." With that, she jumped on the elevator for the fifth-floor faculty offices. Cinn was a little nervous. Dr. Olivetsky wasn't the kind of teacher who called students at home. She had something to discuss that she could only talk about in person. Cinn prepared to be chastised. She was graduating early, but she was embarrassed that she had not yet found a permanent position. Cinn supposed she would teach music upon getting her degree. How long did she expect Olivetsky to be her private vocal tutor at no charge? She knocked on the door.

A gruff "Yes, come in."

Cinnamon brightened as soon as she saw Dr. Olivetsky, small and a little bent over, but the sparkle in her eyes was the same, and her arms opened for a big hug.

"Here's my girl, with a voice from the angels," her mentor said, her soft voice heavily accented. "Why must there be something as foolish as money keeping you from training your voice? Cinnamon, I have talked with a colleague at Juilliard who has agreed to audition you for a full scholarship, but you must be ready by tomorrow. Can you do that?"

Olivetsky's words were just sinking in. The Juilliard School of Music was world renowned, and the graduate school only for students of unusual talent with aspirations toward professional performance careers. "Well, I looked at *Madame Butterfly* and *Carmen* just the other day."

"Oh my darling, you must do more than 'look' at them. And you will also need an Italian aria from the eighteenth century or before, an art song in English, and a German lied. You must sing with all the control and passion at your command. Now here's the address. The appointment is at ten A.M. sharp. Plan to be there all day. There are practice rooms available. Get there at eight and we will go over your material. All right?"

"Oh, Madame Olivetsky, thank you! Thank you so much!" Cinnamon just about flew down the stairs. She ran past Esther and Memphis as if she didn't even know them.

"Hey, hey! Where you goin' so fast, girl?" Memphis shouted. Her high school classes just finished, she was still in her plaid skirt and bobby socks.

"Yeah, you sposed to meet us, not run us over," Esther said.

"Oh, oh, you won't believe this, but I've got an audition at Juilliard tomorrow."

"Great, we've got one tonight, my sister, in Harlem. Good luck all around, I say," Memphis beamed.

"I can't sing with you tonight."

"Hey, you promised. Friday night, remember? The Ebony Club? The Friday Night Talent Show? Helloooo?" The girls babbled on as they walked down the broad Manhattan avenue.

When they emerged from the subway station in the Bronx, the conversation had gone nowhere. "I have an audition tomorrow at Juilliard. I have a chance to get a scholarship."

"What better way to get prepared than to sing tonight?"

"But I can't sing that stuff you sing, Memphis," Cinnamon said.

"No, you mean that stuff I swing? Doo-ta-do-lil-da ta-do oh-yaaae."

"Yeah, that stuff. Can't do it."

"Hey, look," Esther said, hoping to deflect the argument as the trio came around the corner. A HELP WANTED sign was posted on the window of Walbaum's, the local variety dime store. "'Pianist Needed—Sheet Music Department,'" Esther read aloud. "You said you needed a job. Sounds right up your alley to me."

The Bronx apartment complex six-flats where the Minors lived was one of the few enclaves open to Negroes. The main thoroughfare and much of the surrounding neighborhood were still predominantly German and Jewish like Esther. Walbaum's dime store, still selling merchandise for the old neighborhood, had an abundant selection of classical, popular, and klezmer tunes.

"You're right, I should try and get that job," Cinn concurred. "Even with a scholarship, Juilliard's gonna cost. Train fare, books."

"Then you could help us and yourself out tonight. The contest at the Ebony Club. C'mon, Cinnamon, do it, just this one time," Memphis begged.

"Not singing what you sing. I sing lieder and arias."

"I know you, Cinnamon Turner. You can swing when you want to. You're still a Mayfield, sistuh," Memphis chided. "Hey, that should be our name, the Mayfield Sisters."

"We don't exactly look like sisters," Esther cautioned.

"Mayfield Trio, then. Nah, Sistuhs sounds better. So you're in, right."

Cinnamon paused. She could never resist her cousin's cajoling. "What's in it for me?"

"One third of the prize money, that's what. If we win! When we win. Cinn's been winnin' contests since she was five," Memphis boasted to Esther. "One third of a hundred dollars'll go a long way even at your Juilliard."

"A hundred?! . . . Okay, you two sing it to me. I'll learn it and then coach you and learn it as well."

Esther and Cinnamon began a song Memphis had written, a clear musical take-off of one of her Aunty Lizzie's big hits, "Egyptian Girl."

> "Come with us to Harlem,
> Where you'll surely meet a darlin',
> Feisty gals'll make some brand-new pals,
> Some dancin' and kissin' honeys, wow!"

"This is where we go into the scat," Memphis explained, launching into a spate of random syllables, "Ba da wowow uh huh so/ La-la-ta da dada papi," gliding into the refrain,

> "Come with us to Harlem,
> Come on along with me!
> Come with us to Harlem,
> Come on along and see!"

Memphis scatted through the bridge, and Esther joined in for the close. "How you like it? Tell the truth, Cinnamon."

"Well, I don't know if I can keep up, but you're both tending to flat on 'dancin' kissin' honeys.' Try that again."

"Well, you join in this time," Esther added.

"But I don't know the scat part."

Esther and Memphis laughed. "Nobody does, silly," Memphis chided her cousin. "That's the point. It's spontaneous."

"I don't know how you talked me into this, but I'll try."

The girls were a bit shaky as they tried to integrate Cinn into their rhythm, but the strength of Cinnamon's voice and her innate sense of melody carried her through.

"Aw'right. I think we're ready," Memphis said. "Now all we have to do is put on our outfits and we're cookin' with gas. C'mon over to our house. We can find somethin' to wear. Just like sisters, we can switch around." The girls caught the bus to the Minors' upper Bronx apartment.

* * *

"AS LONG as you're home by midnight."

"Midnight!" Cinnamon exclaimed. "I've gotta be home way before midnight! Mama El," she beamed, "I have an audition at Juilliard tomorrow for a full scholarship. Two arias and a German lied I've got to sing."

"Are you serious? Oh, how wonderful for you, Cinnamon!" Elma felt all her dreams come alive again. One of her brood was getting the chance, finally.

"That puts a whole new light on this, girls. You don't want to jeopardize Cinnamon's chance, do you?"

"Of course not, Mama, but what better practice for a tryout tomorrow than a contest tonight?" Memphis interjected. "And Cinnamon wants her share of the prize money, too. Isn't that true, Cinnamon?"

"Well, yes. I did say that, but I didn't know we'd be out till midnight. I need to know this material by tomorrow."

"How could you not know it?" Memphis complained. "You practice every day. Practice tomorrow. Practice on the way down there. You promised!"

"Okay, you're right," Cinn relented, "but we better win."

Esther and Memphis jumped with glee all around the parlor. "We're goin' to win, we're number one, we can't lose with Cinnamon!"

"Don't put all your eggs in one basket, now. We've got to sing as one voice, and you've got to carry me through that scat."

"Don't worry, we'll do whatever we have to, but don't you worry, you're holdin' your own. You just can't hear it yet. But the audience will," Esther chimed.

"Let's go pick out our dresses. Got to look good. Oh, Esther, I've got a red dress perfect for you. Cinnamon, you could wear that black crepe. And I'll wear my yellow silk dress. That way no one will be able to keep their eyes off us. That's half the battle."

The girls rushed to Memphis and Cinnamon's room, unzipping their everyday dresses to get into their best ones. Then they fiddled with their hair, hot combs and curling irons interfering with Elma's dinner plans. Finally, all of them had glorious pompadours and shoes that almost matched. The dresses fit. They got so giddy, they were getting late without even realizing it.

"Don't you have to get there to sign up before they close the list, girls?"

"Oh, Mama, you're right! C'mon, let's go. We really are late."

"Well, you look awfully grown up," Raymond said. "Maybe we should go with you."

At the look of panic on the girls' faces, Elma slipped her arm around

Raymond's waist. "You know you go with our blessings, girls. Sing your hearts out. I wish we could come, but we've got to stay here. Jessie is sposed to call tonight."

"I know how much you're rootin' for us, Mama," Memphis said with love.

"Of course we do, Mama El," Cinnamon added.

"Me too, Mrs. Minor. We all appreciate your support. And we'll be back by one, I mean, midnight."

"All right then, get going." Elma kissed each of the girls. "Wish the girls good luck, Ray."

Raymond gruffly kissed Memphis on the cheek and gave Cinn a thumbs-up as the trio departed.

* * *

ON THEIR way to the subway the girls practiced Memphis's song, and in case they were invited, an encore. Their spirits were high. They were certain they would win something. Esther wasn't sure how she would fit in, but she had always found that the Negro girls at school were friendly. She hoped she would be accepted at the Ebony, that she wouldn't be a jinx to the Mayfield Sisters, she, a Jew, singing colored music to colored people. Memphis was thinking maybe she should learn to tap dance as well, like her Aunt Lizzie in France. Memphis wanted this night to be the beginning of a whole life of entertaining people, all the people. Then the Depression wouldn't matter, her father would smile more, her mother wouldn't be so frustrated, wearing her hair so severely pulled back she looked ten years older than she really was.

Cinnamon's thoughts were on the aria from *Madame Butterfly*, the piece she had chosen to open the next day's audition, *"Ieri sono salita/ tutta sola in secreto alla Missione."* Cinnamon wanted to get to the beautiful, which she didn't find at all in the music her cousin lived for, swing. Cinnamon's sense of self was embedded in the tales that her Mama El had told her about the women in her family whose loveliness and guile had made slavery, for them, a time of reflection, passion, and introduction to all things European. Cinnamon's sense of self came from Elma's description of Black Patti, Sissieretta, bedecked in lace and pearls, stepping from her private rail car and bringing her bel canto to cotton pickers and cornfields. *Culture, uplift!* Cinnamon wanted nothing to do with that trashy loud colored improvisation.

Then it occurred to her that everybody had to defeat the Depression in some way, to make the ugliness of poverty less painful, less hideous, less all encompassing. People had a right to love whatever they wanted. Who was she to tell Esther and Memphis that what they loved was bawdy and noisome? Besides, who was she, a colored girl, to want to sing Puccini?

As the train crossed the bridge into Manhattan, Cinnamon turned round to Esther and Memphis singing, "Come with me to Harlem . . ." The other girls joined in, and they sang all the way to the Ebony Club. When the train stopped, somebody put a quarter, somebody else a dollar at their feet, as if they were singing for their supper. They laughed and then looked at each other inquisitively.

"Either they think we look beautiful or they think we look pathetic to be leaving us money for a bit of a song between stops—don't know what to make of that," Esther quipped. Cinn stood in place as if mesmerized as the coin spun on the subway floor, glimpses of memory like windows on a passing train . . . *"Look Cinn, that's what I'm missin'—New Yawk!"*

Memphis jumped into the silence. "It's like in Paris, like we're street entertainers, that's all, no shame in that." Esther and Cinnamon shrugged their shoulders and started up singing again. Memphis threw her arms around them both. "Harlem, here we come! Tonight Harlem, tomorrow the world!" The trio exited the station with smiles on their faces.

When they reached their destination, Memphis said, "Let me handle all the business, okay?" The other two nodded. Memphis was spunkier and bolder than Esther and Cinn. *Already underage. What I got to lose?* Memphis moved quickly and disappeared through the backstage door.

The acrid cigarette smoke curling through the corridor made Cinn's eyes wince and water. "Whew!" Cinnamon said, "I don't think I've ever smelled so much whiskey in my whole life."

"You probably haven't," Esther laughed.

Somehow they made it through the winding halls to find Memphis talking to a pudgy light-skinned Negro man with his hair oiled back.

"Oh, here's the rest of the Mayfield Sisters, Mr. Brooks. This is Esther and this is Cinnamon," Memphis chirped, batting her eyes.

"Well, if you can sing as pretty as you look, you might win this contest, gals," Mr. Brooks sighed heavily. He gave Esther and Cinnamon the willies, so they just smiled and left for the dressing room pointed out to them. They didn't hear him ask Memphis, "Say, how old are y'all?"

"Why, Mr. Brooks, you flatter me. We're all in our twenties, rest assured," Memphis said with all the aplomb her fourteen years of age could manufacture.

"Okay, but I've got to check on these things."

Memphis went searching for the rest of what she thought of as "her" group. She opened one door without knocking and ran into a female impersonator who not only gave her the evil eye, but asked, "What can I do for you, lil girl?" After that she knocked, but there was really no mistaking where they were. She heard Cinnamon's operatic voice from way down a narrow hall, "Spira sul mare e sulla terra/ un primaveril soffio giocondo." Memphis burst through the door, "We're not singin' *Carmen* tonight. We're singin' 'Come with Me to Harlem'!"

Cinnamon grew quiet. Esther said, "Well, I was enjoying it, Memphis."

"I have the most important audition of my life tomorrow and I came here to help you. Don't ask me to give up my dream. I'm not askin' you to give up yours." Cinnamon's frustration could be heard in her voice. "If you weren't my cousin, I'd walk out of here right now." She had nothing else to say to Memphis.

Esther decided the best thing to do was to leave Cinnamon alone. "Come on, Memphis, let's go see the rest of the contestants. Then, we'll know what we're up against." Without a word, the two girls left. Cinnamon finally was alone with Puccini. "No. È nato quand' già egli stava/ in quel suo grande paese . . ."

"Well, that was close. At least she didn't pull out," Memphis confided to Esther.

"Well, you did push it. Let her sing what she wants. She won't let us down."

"I hope not. As soon as she finds out we won't even be up til e-lev . . . vennn . . ." Memphis couldn't finish her sentence. She saw a man carrying a trumpet case. His chiseled chocolate face made her forget all about her troubles with Cinnamon.

"What were you going to say?" Esther asked.

"Nothing, I'll be right back." And Memphis hurried down the hall and bumped into the young man with the captivating face. "Oh, I'm sorry. I don't know what I was thinkin'."

The man picked up on Memphis's come-on and smiled.

"You didn't hurt, little as you are. I'm Baker, Baker Johnson."

"Hi, I'm Memphis Minor. I see you play the trumpet. Are you here for the contest?"

Baker laughed, "Oh, no. I'm with Fletcher."

"You mean Fletcher as in Fletcher Henderson?"

"Yeah, I'm first trumpet."

First trumpet? But he's so young! "Oh, I'm so sorry. I thought you were like me. I'm here to sing in the contest with a girl group, the Mayfield Sisters," she said, trying not to look stupefied.

"Must say, I've never heard of them."

"Well, we're new . . ."

"Okay then. Good luck to you. I'll be out there when you come up."

"Well, thanks so much. Baker, right? I do hope you like us." She winked and sashayed away, thinking herself very mature.

"No doubt." And Baker Johnson made his way to the music pit where a bunch of his cohorts were sitting in with the house band. They each smiled at Memphis, and Esther too, who'd caught up with her unpredictable friend, flirting from the wings.

"Who are they?" Esther asked.

"They play with Fletcher Henderson. You know, *the* Fletcher Henderson."

"Really? Oh, God!" Esther swooned. "They've gotta like us."

"I just know he better like me or I'll die. I'm tellin' you, I'll die."

"Don't be so dramatic, Memphis. Let's go see the show."

While Esther and Memphis made their way through the crowd, they missed Baker Johnson returning backstage. Looking for his wallet, he found it by the place where Memphis had bumped into him. "That chicky would make a good pickpocket," he chuckled, then he stopped in his tracks.

"Ma voi gli scriverete che l'aspetta/ un figlio senza pari!" A crystalline soprano melody lilted above the backstage din. Baker went looking for this voice singing an aria by Puccini. The closer he got to the sound, the faster he walked. When he reached where he thought the wondrous singing was coming from, he hesitated a moment, just listening. Then he couldn't help himself and knocked on the door. Cinnamon answered very quickly, abruptly, thinking Memphis had returned. When she saw Baker Johnson she was startled. Neither said a word. Cinnamon stepped back into the dressing room and Baker simply took a chair and sat down to listen. Cinnamon paused, looking into his eyes, and began to sing again, "E mi saprete dir s'ei non s'affretta/ per le terre e pei mari!" She glowed through the entire piece as Butterfly was proclaiming that her true love would come flying back to her as soon as he knew he had a son. She didn't know that Baker felt he could never stop hearing her sing or leave her side. It was magical!

Memphis stormed in, breaking the spell. "We're next, Cinnamon." She saw Baker and was puzzled. "I didn't know you knew my cousin."

"I don't yet . . ." Baker said softly, trying to let Cinnamon know he really did want to know her.

"This is Cinnamon Turner, one third of the Mayfield Sisters."

"Very pleased to meet you, Cinnamon Turner." His smile disarmed her. "I hope my intrusion wasn't disconcerting."

"Oh no, it was nice for someone to listen. But who are you?"

Memphis jumped in before Baker could open his mouth. "This is Baker Johnson. He plays with Fletch Henderson, only the hottest swing band in the world."

"I play the trumpet, by the way, and I prefer to call it jazz." Baker tried to take the conversation back from Memphis, but to no avail. Memphis spirited Cinnamon away just in time for them to hear, "The Mayfield Sisters!" The girls ran to the stage, so fast that Baker missed the disappointed look in Cinnamon's eyes when she heard he played in a jazz band.

✳ ✳ ✳

"LET'S GIVE the Mayfield Sisters a hand, ladies and gentlemen. Now we're going to bring all the contestants on the stage to determine the winner of the Ebony Club's Talent Show," Mr. Brooks proclaimed.

Out came the female impersonator with his boa, then the snake dancer, a group of young men who tap-danced, a big woman who sang the blues, and finally Mr. Brooks announced the Mayfield Sisters again. The winner was decided by audience applause. Mr. Brooks held his hand over the heads of all the contestants, and it was clear that only the female impersonator La Belle Harold with his cape of sequins and his fans, came close to the Mayfield Sisters. All the other groups left the stage except Harold and the girls. Mr. Brooks held his hand over their heads again and, sure enough, the Mayfield Sisters with their original tune "Come with Me to Harlem" won. One hundred dollars cash! The girls had never seen so much money. They hugged each other and jumped for joy. When they were leaving the stage the audience was still clapping.

Baker Johnson and his friends were impressed, too. The trumpet player leaned over. "Hey, man, even that ofay-lookin' gal can sing, but it's that soprano got the goods on all of 'em."

"I know," Baker said. "I know. And you keep your doggish self away from her, ya hear me."

"Uh-oh, I feel a jones comin' over Baker here."

"Oh, man, leave me alone. I know the girl. Just leave her alone."

"Well, what about the other two?"

"Far as I can tell, they're game . . ."

"Hey, fellas, Baker here is givin' us permission to go after the white girl and that gal who scats like a pro, but hands off the soprano."

Memphis was dividing up the prize money as she jabbered on and on about who was in the audience. "There was Sharkey McGee on trombone, Clifton Shaw on clarinet, and Melvin Grover, the drummer. Oh, can you believe it? The crème de la crème of Henderson's band saw us swing, baby!"

"It's past midnight, Memphis. We're supposed to be home."

"Oh, they won't be mad. We got the money! We'll share some with 'em."

"Are you forgetting, I have an audition tomorrow? I'm leaving."

Just then Baker Johnson and his friends appeared. "You can't go home now. We were goin' to take you out to celebrate," he said. "Stop by the Band Box and the Corner, play a little music, eat some barbecue."

Cinnamon was really getting annoyed. "That's very nice of you, but tomorrow is a very big day for me. I've got an audition at Juilliard. It's near one o'clock in the morning, and we still gotta catch the subway. The way that bus runs in the Bronx, we won't be home till two! I'm sorry, but I can't go."

"Well, we want to go," Memphis said eagerly, nudging Esther, who nodded her head in agreement.

"Let me put Cinnamon in a taxi and I'll be ready to go." With that, Baker whisked Cinnamon out the stage door. On their way out of the alley Baker stopped her. She turned around and looked him dead in the eye. Before they knew what they were doing the two were in the thralls of an embrace and a kiss. Cinnamon wanted to melt into Baker's arms, but her mind was on her audition.

"I'd love to go out with you all," she sighed, pulling away from Baker. "But I do have an audition tomorrow."

Baker took her arm. They began walking toward Seventh Avenue.

"Congratulations, by the way," Baker smiled.

"Oh, thanks," Cinnamon replied, "I did it for my cousin. I don't usually sing swing."

"Fooled me. Couldn't tell," Baker reassured as he helped her into a cab. "Can't let Madame Butterfly take the subway . . . I hope to see you again." He gave the cabbie money to cover Cinnamon's fare to the Bronx, then knocked on the window and waved as the taxi took off. *I could marry that woman.*

＊ ＊ ＊

"WE'RE READY to go now," Memphis exclaimed when she saw Baker walk back into the Ebony Club. Baker's enthusiasm had waned, but he felt like playing in a session, free-wheeling and improvised. There were sure to be other cats at the Band Box across the street from Connie's Inn. The music would get his mind off Cinnamon.

Memphis took Baker's arm. "Let's get on our way, shall we?"

Baker's bandmate had moved fast. Esther was now the flower of the trombone player's eye. "Yeah, man, let's hit the spots," he said, feelin' the mood come on him, "I wanna play. Let's make some noise." With that, they were off on the three-block walk to the Band Box.

＊ ＊ ＊

CINNAMON WAS up at five trying to prepare for her audition. She didn't get much done with Elma pacing and the memory of her recriminations, "You're the oldest. Why didn't you make her come home with you?" At seven A.M. Memphis and Esther stumbled through the door. They didn't get a chance to go on about their magnificent win, the hundred dollars, the guys they'd met or anything, before Elma roughly grabbed Memphis with a yen to slap her.

"Where in God's name have you been? I've been up worried all night long. I won't have this behavior goin' on in my house, Memphis. And, Esther, don't you think for a minute that this doesn't apply to you, too."

The girls murmured, "Yes, m'am." But Memphis did manage to pull her share of the prize money from her pocket.

"Look, Mama. This is what we won last night in the talent contest at the Ebony Club. A hundred dollars! We were the best. Professional!"

"That's true, Mrs. Minor," Esther blurted.

"Well, I don't care if it's a million dollars! You don't know what you're getting yourselves into. Just ask Cinnamon what it's like. Her mother, my sister, is as good an example as you can get. Traipsing around the world, ignoring everybody and everything near and dear to a decent woman!"

Cinnamon heard the reference to her mother and her back went rigid. "Mama El, would you please leave me out of this. Memphis made her own choice. I was home in time, so I'm not in this mess. Please, Mama El."

"Here, Mama, take the money. You and Papa go out for a fine night on the town or get something for the house. Don't you see I can help out now?"

Elma's face hardened and she felt her voice coming from the pit of her stomach, "We don't want your money. We want you decent! Now get out of my sight! Get to your room and get out those hussy clothes and face paint right now! You too, Esther."

Memphis decided not to fight with her mother. She put the money away and headed for her room. Esther thought it might be a good time to get to her own house. Elma pushed her toward the phone. "Esther, act like you got some sense and call your mother before she calls here looking for you again."

Cinnamon was amused at the terrible trouble her Mayfield Sisters were in. She waltzed downstairs to check with Elma about whether or not she was presentable for the panel at Juilliard that morning. "How do I look, Mama?"

"Why, you look lovely, Cinnamon. I've got salmon, grits, and eggs ready for you, right here."

"No thank you. I can't sing on a full stomach."

"Nobody said for you to eat everything in the pot, just enough to keep your energy up for the audition. You gotta eat somethin'."

"I'll eat just a little bit. Salmon and grits always reminds me of Nana and Ma Bette. That's a good omen. Yes, sirree. That's an omen. Don't you think?"

"I won't have you dragging me into the magic that Ma Bette haunted the Charleston wharf with, nor will I let you be putting spells on those jurors at Juilliard. Just trust in the Lord and the glory of your God-given voice and everything will be fine."

Meanwhile, Memphis and Esther, who were terribly hungry, came to the top of the stairs.

"Cinnamon, Cinnamon, can you come up here for a minute?"

"Not till I finish eating." She might have added not till I finish my daydreams about that Baker Johnson. Thoughts and tickles about Baker Johnson mingled with phrases from *Madame Butterfly* and *Carmen*.

"You want some coffee, Cinnamon?"

"No, Mama El, thanks, but I'd really prefer tea and honey. I've got a huge day coming up. Oops, I've got to go right now. I can't be late for Madame Olivetsky. She'll have a fit."

"Well, I think that woman works you too hard."

"But Mama El, she's the best. And she only takes the best. Doesn't care what color they are."

"I know that, sweetheart, I just hope she's done right by you."

"I love her, Mama El, but not as much as I love you."

"I'll be praying for you all day, Cinnamon."

Cinnamon rushed to gather her things and was out the door.

With Cinnamon tended to, Elma shouted upstairs, "You two come on down here for some breakfast. I want to hear all about last night." Memphis and Esther ran towards Elma's voice, hungry and full of chatter.

* * *

"OH, MY little black cherub, how glad I am to see you on this day of opportunity for you. Come, come, let's get you warmed up for this morning, no?" Madame Olivetsky was almost as excited as Cinnamon. After going through scales in virtually every key Madame Olivetsky could think of, she asked Cinnamon for her arias.

"Remember to breathe and enunciate, then bleed the next phrase into the last, like magic."

Cinnamon sang from *Madame Butterfly* and *Carmen*. Then . . .

"Excellent, excellent," Madame Olivetsky cooed. "I see no way they could deny you, a girl with such talent, such depth."

For once Cinnamon left Madame Olivetsky's with compliments ringing in her ears. She had a few minutes before the audition. The school was on Claremont Avenue, near the river in Upper Manhattan. She decided to walk a while through Riverside Park. The winter air would relax her, keep her lungs open and her mind clear. The bare trees swayed in the wind. Cinn could almost see the future spring blossoms dancing from their limbs, leaving halos of pastels round her head. She missed the comfort of the South, the warmth of her grandmother's parlor. Auditions and the waiting time before performance always riled her.

That first year in Charleston, the first time she was asked to perform at the highbrow Episcopal church, her grandmother, so proud, had made her a dress of powder blue chintz and organza. Set against her skin, it made her glow. She stepped in the powder room to sneak one more look at herself and overheard two girls chattering in the stalls.

"Songbird, they say, the bird girl. Look like uh ugly old black bird, uh fat black crow."

"Well, you know her mother was a tramp. Ain't no telling who her daddy was, black as she is, could be the Devil."

Her grandmother's spirit steeled her then. "What do you mean you don't feel like singin'. All these people waitin'? You look at me. You look at me!" Those piercing blue eyes, white streaks in her still-abundant hair giving her the countenance of the American eagle. "Don't you ever let anyone throw you off your course. These old biddies ain't worth nothin', ain't got nothin' to do but pick at you like some rice birds pickin' at grain. Don't know nothin', ain't been nowhere, ain't goin' nowhere either. You are from New York. Your mother is a star in Europe. Your father was a war hero. And your great-great-grandmamma held a lot of respect in this town. In the middle of this Depression, people come from all over the country to honor her. What those girls got? Nothin' but talk. You have a voice. Now go on out there. Everything gon be all right."

Buoyed by her grandmother's words, Cinnamon joyfully climbed the steps to the main building of Juilliard, wondering what kind of art the young men and women passing by were studying. *Imagine being surrounded by others seeking the best, the most beautiful, not pretty, but beautiful truth from themselves all day long.* Cinnamon was close to tears as she approached Room 311, where the audition was to be held.

Her performance went splendidly. All four judges were smiling as they took notes and whispered to each other. Cinnamon tried to cram her two years of study with Madame Olivetsky into each note. Her phrasing was impeccable, her passion great. The committee actually clapped after her performance. One of the judges said, "Miss Turner, you'll be hearing from us. And thank you so very, very much." They shook hands and Cinnamon was out the door, flying, it seemed to her, on the power of her own breath.

"You'll be hearing from us," that's what the man said. Cinnamon heard his voice in her head as she made her way through the crowds on Broadway. She wanted to tell everybody, everybody in Harlem, everybody in the Bronx, everybody in New York. Everybody! "I'm one colored girl who's going to sing opera. Yes, I am, I am." It occurred to her that she wanted to tell Baker Johnson more than anyone. *How peculiar. See a man one night and want to share your greatest joy with him.*

23

A FEW WEEKS LATER, CINNAMON WAS HEADED FROM ONE choir coaching job to the next when she walked by that neighborhood variety store—the HELP WANTED sign was still there! If only she could bundle all of her part-time jobs into one consistent position of employment. Confident and hopeful, she went to the personnel office to inquire about the position. If she was to go to Juilliard she would need a way to earn a living. The store clerk ignored her. Finally Cinnamon said, "Excuse me, I'm here about the pianist position in the sheet music department."

"What about it?" the clerk asked without looking up.

"I'd like to apply for it."

"Oh, you can't. I mean you might as well not. We don't hire colored. Except for the stockroom and ain't no openin's there."

Cinnamon looked quickly around the store. The clerk was white. All of the store employees were white, but all of the customers in the store at the time were Negro. "What do you mean you don't hire *colored*?" Cinnamon snapped.

"No need to get uppity, missy. It's company policy. Can't help you."

"Uppity?"

"Just fill out the form," the clerk sighed. "When there's uh opening for a sweeper or a cleaning woman," he said snidely, "we'll call you."

Cinnamon turned on her heel and stalked out the door, letting it slam behind her. Against her own will, Cinnamon pushed herself to go back into the store to buy something there for the last time: two cardboard sheets, some twine, and crayons. Right in front of the store, she knelt on the sidewalk and scribbled out a sign, then attached the two boards with twine and hung her handmade protest poster over her neck. DON'T BUY WHERE YOU CAN'T WORK! Inspired by the young Reverend Adam Clayton Powell's protest campaigns in Harlem, she staged her own picket line, repeating the words with vigor as she walked back and forth in front of the store. The day was nearing rush hour. As a few onlookers headed home from work began to gather, she added a personal touch to the campaign. She sang *Madame Butterfly* at the top of her lungs.

> "Davver? Non piango più
> E quasi del ripudio mon mi duole
> Per le vostre parole
> Che mi suonan così dolci nel cor."

People looked at her funny. Some stopped to listen and moved on. A few scurried by with fright. Others shouted for her to carry on.

"That's the truth, girl!"

"Sistah, you doin' right."

Another voice said firmly, "I didn't know you had it in you." It was Baker Johnson with his trumpet case, smiling with pride at this determined young woman he had met in the back halls of a nightclub. Baker unpacked his trumpet and began to echo her phrasing. Cinnamon's mood switched easily. What had been sung with a vengeance was now sung with tenderness. Baker Johnson surprised Cinnamon with his knowledge of the piece. So he wasn't just another jazz musician after all. Protesting injustice, the two were discovering each other.

While Baker took a solo turn, Cinnamon spoke to the small crowd. "Only allowed to clean and sweep, just because I'm colored? I'm not qualified to work in the music department?" She was about to launch into the next part of the aria when a colored woman looking quite grand approached. "Young lady, young lady, I don't want to interrupt your demonstration, but if you are looking for a place to work—well, my name is

Mary Cardwell Dawson of the National Negro Opera Company, and we'd love to have you and your accompanist here join us. We could use you. Why sell sheet music when you can sing opera like that? Here's my card."

Cinnamon brightened with disbelief—what a day! When the lights went out in Walbaum's and the locks were being put on, a policeman and a security guard came along to make sure those two crazy Negroes went about their business. Baker wanted to tell them where they could go, but Cinnamon calmed him. Said she had news. So he packed up his instrument and kept an eye out for any move the policeman and the security guard might make toward Cinnamon, but they seemed satisfied the two itinerant coloreds were moving on.

"Cinnamon, whatever got in your head to protest by singing opera?" Baker asked as he took her signs off and hugged her gently to him. "What did those people do to you?"

Cinnamon shrugged her shoulders. "Treated me like an ordinary nigger is what they did. It wasn't even uh they, it was a single old white man, wouldn't even look at me. But don't even waste a minute on that old geezer. Guess what happened? You'll never even believe it! I'm telling you, Ma Bette is working for me today! My Nana always said, 'Your own people will open more doors for you than any other folks.' My audition at Juilliard went perfectly, and then a woman tells me there's a Negro Opera Company she wants us to work with. Isn't that wonderful, Baker?"

Baker took a step back. "Cinnamon, I'm already working. I work with Fletcher Henderson, or did you forget?"

"Oh, no, I didn't forget, but this is something we could do together."

"If you'd listened to Memphis, we could be together. She talked Fletcher into givin' her a tryout spot. She's such a go-getter. Might be singin' with the band every night! The Mayfield Sisters," he laughed, "all three of you are somethin' else! Poor Esther's got Todd Lindsey so enthralled, he wants her to marry him and raise five kids. They hardly even know each other."

"Oh don't say that, Baker, cause then that would mean I hardly know you, and I feel like we've known each other forever."

"I know that's right, but we're married to our music and through the music we're married to each other, you see?" Cinnamon didn't quite see, but she let it slide. "Let's head back to Harlem to Wells' Restaurant," he said. "I'll treat you to some chicken and waffles, how's that sound?"

"That's just what I need. I need to celebrate, Baker, don't you think?"

"Nobody deserves it more, angel face."

At Wells', Baker and Cinnamon sat opposite each other, staring like one of them might disappear if they took their eyes off one another. They came up with a deal. If Cinnamon would sit in with him at the jazz club, then Baker would play with the opera company when his schedule allowed. Cinnamon agreed with this, thinking that Baker got the better part of the deal, but her heart wasn't letting her argue the point. They'd come to some kind of arrangement. Chicken and waffles, swing and opera, and what she wanted all along, Baker's attention.

Everything was going smoothly until Baker said casually, "I didn't know you were Mayfield Turner's daughter." At her look of surprise, he added, "Memphis told me."

"Yes, that's my mother," Cinnamon replied in a deadpan voice.

"Well, don't you have any plans to follow in her footsteps?"

"No, I do not," Cinnamon said in a voice suggesting that this conversation end quickly. *I like shoes. I have no intention of bouncing around barefoot and naked with a bunch of bananas.*

"I guess I've said something wrong, huh?"

"Yes. No, I mean—it's just very complicated. I tend not to talk about my mother."

"But Cinnamon, with a voice like yours! Why, yours is the sweetest of all the Mayfield Sisters. They should kiss your feet, carrying them the way you do. You're the natural lead. Even when you sing backup, your voice stands out. It seems to me you'd want to shout your mother's name. Let the world know there's another Mayfield Turner comin'."

"But that's just it. I don't want to be anything like my mother."

"The great Mayfield Turner who turned all Europe on its ears? Cinnamon, I bet folks would give their eyeteeth to see her daughter. You should be proud."

"She doesn't even act like she has a daughter. There, are you satisfied? I may as well not have a mother. Now are you satisfied? Excuse me for a minute, please." On the verge of tears, her face blazing red, Cinnamon ran toward the ladies' room and put cold towels to her face. The wall she hid behind protected her from nothing. *From the great Mayfield Turner—cards, money, checks. From Lizzie, my pal, my mama, nothing—no dolls, no visits to the zoo, no bedtime stories, no kisses good night, no "I love you, Cinnamon."* Pushing her feelings about Lizzie deeper and deeper down in her soul, Cinnamon decided to forgive Baker the inquisition. He simply didn't know. To him, Mayfield Turner was an icon, a music legend. To Cinnamon, Lizzie Turner had left an excruciating void, better left in peace.

Cinnamon couldn't bring herself to smile, but as she approached Baker she let him know she was not angry with him. "I'm sorry, Baker, I don't know what got into me. When I talk about my mother I don't know what'll come out of my mouth. Forgive me, please."

"Cinnamon, I just didn't know. I won't say another word about your mother, I promise."

"You don't have to be that dramatic, Baker. I need to let go of childish memories, that's all. Besides, I already know that my life won't be involved in that gaudy, vulgar Negro jazz life my mother's chosen for herself. No, that's not for me."

When Baker heard these words, his heart sank. What else did he have to offer Cinnamon, but exactly what she said she didn't want—jazz? But oblivious to the sting of her remarks, Cinnamon went on as if she had not meant that at all. "I intend to sing opera. Everyone laughs when I say that—everybody! But you don't laugh at me, Baker. Maybe that's why I love you so. What do you think?"

She sounded like she loved him, she acted like she loved him, but clearly she was confused by her intentions toward him. "I think you are lovely, and I still say you've got the voice to top Memphis and Esther. Really," he said, deciding he was up for the challenge. Cinnamon laughed and leaned toward Baker to kiss him, when he looked at his watch. "Time to go, honey, I'm almost late for the gig at the Savoy."

"Uh-oh. We'd better figure out how to adjust our schedules or we'll both be out of work. Let's get goin'," Cinnamon said.

He hugged her tightly as they zigzagged down the street. Dodging and shouting at passersby, he joked, "From opera to swing, we swing! From Puccini we swing over to Verdi, from Verdi we swing to Wagner! We swing!" Cinn's bell-like laughter in counterpoint.

* * *

AT THE stage door everybody was looking for Baker, and the surprise of Cinnamon took the band members aback. They had just gotten used to seeing him with Memphis. The impertinent teen ran right up to Baker and fell into his arms. Baker tried to untangle himself but to no avail.

"Baker, what on earth happened to you? Tonight is a Battle of the Bands. Chick Webb himself. So, where've you been, huh? Tell me or I won't let you go."

Baker tried to let Memphis know her cousin was there right next to him, but Memphis could only see Baker. Finally, Cinnamon said, "Hi, Memphis. How you doin', darlin'?"

Without missing a lick, Memphis replied, "I'm just fine, how you?" then whispered, "Don't you dare say anything about my age, don't you dare." Since the night of the contest, Memphis had been cutting school to hang out with the fellahs. To push herself forward, compare, learn, affirm. Now that Fletcher Henderson had let her sit in a few sessions, she considered herself a featured singer. She took all kinds of liberties and never stopped flattering or endearing herself to Baker no matter how he responded. Finding her schoolgirl crush amusing, he indulged her.

Baker took out his horn, fingering it deftly. "Come on, guys, we gotta warm up."

Honoring her bargain with her beau, Cinnamon squeezed his hand and said, "I gotta go have a conversation with your band leader." As she left, she could hear Memphis chattering all the way down the hall with the rest of the brass players.

Cinnamon came upon Fletcher Henderson at a delicate point in conversation with the trombone player Todd and Esther. "I'd love to take you back in the band, Todd, but we can't have a white girl traveling with the band. Half my guys will get lynched or beaten to death in the towns we play in if there's an ofay chick with us. Esther, if you really wanted to sing, you shoulda picked Whiteman, Miller, Dorsey, anybody, but not a Negro band."

"That's so unfair, Fletch. If I could sing with you, I'd be with Todd all the time."

"That's what I mean. Todd would be one dead nigger, too. Think, Esther!"

Esther ran off crying. Fletcher Henderson turned back to his charts and shook his head. "Sometimes I just can't believe what people think goes on in the world doesn't go on in the world. We'd lose half our gigs, if I carried a white girl around with me. Jesus . . ." He caught sight of Cinnamon.

"I didn't mean to eavesdrop, Mr. Henderson. Didn't think I should interfere in your talk with Esther."

"That's all right, doll, what can I help you with?"

"It's Cinnamon, Cinnamon Turner," she interjected. "Baker says you enjoyed my performance at the Ebony Club. I came to ask for an opportunity to sing with your band."

"Well, welcome aboard, Cinnamon Turner," the dapper, soft-spoken band leader said. An impish look came over his face. "You and Memphis together will be a blast. We'll give Chick Webb and his little chicks a run for the money."

"Well, thank you, sir."

"Call me Smack. Smack is fine."

"Thank you, Smack," Cinnamon said, puzzled. "I'd like to tell Memphis, but I don't know where she is."

"Oh, that's no problem. She's probably in the dressing room. Do you know where that is?" Henderson asked offhandedly.

"No, but I'll find it. Thanks again."

Cinnamon made her way through the halls ablaze with musicians warming up their instruments: trumpets, clarinets, flutes, saxophones, bass violins, and drums. Everyone was getting ready for an evening to remember. The Savoy with its wild blue and orange–colored walls, the marble stairway and revolving stage, mirrored walls and dance floor the size of a football field, for years had only had one king. Drummer Chick Webb's Harlem Stompers reigned at the Savoy. The diminutive drummer and band leader compensated for his crooked spine and truncated legs with a Shango-blessed upper body that pumped out rhythms, vanquishing every challenger, Harlem lindy-hoppers stompin' 'em into the dance floor. He had thrown down the gauntlet to Henderson, the cool gray-haired patrician whose band was heralded as the tightest on the scene and whose arrangements were sought after, copied, and covered by every big band there was, black or white.

This was a serious challenge. More serious than Cinnamon was up for. She felt herself in the way. Everyone seemed to know where they were going except for her. At last she reached the brass players' section, only to find Memphis on Baker's lap. Baker nearly dropped Memphis to the floor when he saw Cinnamon. But Cinnamon prevented what could have been an awkward moment by blurting, "It's okay. I can sing with the band. I just can't call him Smack, though. I gotta call him Mr. Henderson."

Baker grinned with pleasure and Memphis jumped for joy. "Oh, see, I told you so! I knew you'd come around, Cinnamon. I'm so happy. Now it'll be just like when we won the contest. This is just great. C'mon, I'll show you what we're doin' tonight, so you can catch up."

"Well, Memphis, I was just going to watch tonight."

"Watch, my foot! If Smack says you're in, that's what he means. Here, come look at the charts, you'll do fine."

Baker was busy warming up his trumpet and his lips while the other guys, especially Todd, were teasing him.

"You in a real mess now, my man."

"Right, if Cinnamon is goin' to be singin', too. Man, you're too hot for me."

"Bold, if I do say so."

"Y'all got it all wrong, fellas. My heart belongs to Cinnamon and always has. You know that."

"But does Memphis know that? That's the question!"

"Memphis is just a kid, be serious."

"Oh my, oh my, and they in the same family, too. Baker, you must be out your mind."

Baker was getting riled by his compatriots' joshing and turned around to them. "Listen, there's nothing, not a thing, going on between me and Memphis."

"Well, my man, you better watch your back, 'cause Memphis is a slick lil ol' thing."

"That's enough! Y'all got that? That's enough talk like that!" Baker retorted.

"Fifteen minutes!" the stage manager announced, sticking his head in the door.

Memphis had hurried Cinnamon to her dressing room, where she busied herself picking out something for her cousin to wear.

"Don't make such a fuss, Memphis. People aren't really here to look at us. They're comin' to dance! I doubt if they even know we're here."

"Oh no! When I open my mouth to sing, folks goin' to know the name Memphis Minor. I'm goin' to turn heads and be proud of it. There, this ought to look good on you, Cinnamon." Memphis held up a scarlet silk pleated dress with a small Asian pattern. "This will look perfect. Here, try it on."

Cinnamon took the dress from Memphis and held it in the mirror in front of her. *Pleats? Print?* "Memphis. Are you sure?"

"Nothing's too good for my cousin. Maybe after the gig tonight you, me, and Baker can go out together?"

"Sure," Cinnamon said, "that'd be fine." Cinnamon quickly changed, and Memphis brightened her makeup for her.

"Places, everybody!" The stage manager made his final rounds.

Although Chick Webb was frail and often ill, he held his band together, and at the Savoy the challengers never underestimated him. With his two new singers, Memphis and Cinnamon, Fletcher Henderson was determined to fare better than the last time he had been up against the Chick Webb Orchestra. At that duel, Webb had introduced a new weapon in his arsenal, the young Ella Fitzgerald. Fresh off a recent win at the Apollo Theater's amateur night, Ella that night was astonishing and since then had become a permanent fixture in the band, as respected as Webb himself.

Henderson hoped that tonight he would have similar luck with the two chippies he caught at the Ebony Club. Memphis begged Henderson to give her a shot. If her pipes weren't anywhere near as good as Ella's, at least she was a looker. He was just about to chalk up another victory to Webb when that other one, the tall brown-skinned girl, showed up. *We might make this, might give Chick a run for his money.* Still, Cinnamon and Memphis had their jobs cut out for them—singing against the one and only Ella.

"Love and Kisses" was the tune Webb started out with, Ella scatting and exhibiting her astonishing vocal range, over three octaves. Cinnamon's operatic training came in handy on "Dicty Blues," which Fletcher set up against the second Webb piece. Baker led the brass section on "Sugar Foot Stomp," and the crowd that Webb usually had in his pocket was beguiled. Throughout it all, the dancers competed against each other as much as the bands did, the crowd, always the crowd determining who was the best. Cinnamon's solos were daunting; Memphis hung in with her improvisation and sense of timing. But in the end, it was the dancers doing every kind of movement possible, tossing each other in the air, turning like there was no tomorrow, that was the crowds' main attraction to the Battle of the Bands.

The dancehall's hollers for the King of the Savoy returned the crown to Chick Webb, but there was no animosity between the bands. Benny Carter, Edgar Sampson, and Jimmy Harrison all shook hands and hugged their cohorts in Henderson's group. Cinnamon and Memphis went over to Ella and complimented her without fawning. Memphis just wanted to keep singing until she could wow a crowd like the great Ella Fitzgerald. After all, Ella was proof that age didn't matter. She was an "under twenty" diva, and Memphis's dreams were fueled by this. Sensing that the strength of Cinnamon's voice might overshadow her, she worked even harder. Cinnamon on the other hand was always listening for a chance to show off her own three-octave range without showing Memphis up. Baker was right, she was the stronger of the two vocally; but she didn't have Memphis's yearnings to live the jazz life, to exploit her mother's name. Actually, Cinnamon was bored with the whole swing scene, but she would do anything for Baker. As the musicians left the bandstand for their fifteen-minute break, Baker went over to Cinnamon to sneak a kiss. Memphis, always looking for him, missed this.

"So Baker, where are you taking us tonight?" Memphis said when she returned, "Let's go somewhere hot and bluesy, okay?"

"How's that with you, Cinnamon?" Baker asked.

Cinnamon was confused about what was going on between Baker and her cousin, but she decided Baker was just looking after Memphis, giving her some guidance, keeping those doggish jazz musicians away from a young girl. For her part, Memphis thought that Cinnamon needed encouragement to be more outgoing. Cinnamon was obviously comfortable hanging with the two of them, and Baker got along with a lot of fellas, any one of whom might be interested in Cinn if she lightened up.

Baker found it hard to shake Memphis to get a few minutes alone with his true love. Memphis was so enthusiastic about the music, she was so eager to learn, he could never say no to her. She was a sweet kid, after all. Cinnamon thought of Memphis as a young girl infatuated with the jazz life, fame, and adulating fans. Memphis longed to be what Cinnamon abhorred. The next Mayfield Turner.

Even if Memphis didn't, Cinnamon and Baker thought of themselves as a couple. In between sets they often spoke of life together and the marvels of music, any kind of music. Baker was constantly edging Cinnamon to see the world through his eyes and ears—swing. He knew she could see it, 'cause she could sing it. But every Monday night he was off with Cinnamon to the opera rehearsals. He didn't know how long this was going to go on, creeping down some lonely church steps to an auditorium with children's drawings of Jesus, Moses, and David and Goliath decorating the walls. He knew he could play anything Mrs. Dawson put in front of him. The question in his mind was, why? *Why play any of this at all? There were plenty of white folks dying to play it, so let 'em.* But Baker would do anything to keep Cinnamon happy. They were practicing a section of *Aida* when he missed a cue. Mrs. Dawson nearly burst her lungs screaming about how "This isn't going to work, young man. Your heart isn't in it. I'm sorry, Cinnamon, but it's obvious that Baker here is not a devotee. Hush, don't take up for him. Now everyone's awake, let's take it back to the coda."

* * *

ELMA WAS doing Memphis's hair. The curls she could do with a twirling comb, but those edges needed some heat. Elma had yet to meet this Baker of whom both her girls spoke so highly. It puzzled Elma. Cinnamon and Memphis were usually on opposite sides of any issue, but this Baker Johnson had both her girls humming.

"You know what, Mama, Baker just looks so sharp in those slick suits the bands wear. Why, when the horns rise up to do their chorus, he looks better than Duke Ellington. You see, different sections rise and sit down when they're featured in the music. Oh, Mama, I can't see how they can play so well and actually do choreographed movements with their horns. They look so good and move so smooth, high style! Really, they do!

There's more to playing swing than just picking up an instrument. You've got to feel it, live it, even dress it. You've got to respect the power of rhythm and jump up when the feeling gets to you. Wait till you come see me and Cinnamon, Mama. You comin', Papa?" she shouted to Raymond, who was down the hall listening to the radio.

"We're comin', darlin'."

Then Elma, still ambivalent about this "swing," nodded yes. Memphis turned her head to see what Elma's response was, and the hot comb in Elma's hand nearly burned her.

"Gosh, Mama, I didn't mean to upset you. I just asked a question."

"Then sit still so I can finish up this head, all right? You told me there's going to be photographs of the whole orchestra this afternoon, and I want you to look nice," Elma reassured her child.

"That's not the most important thing I told you, Mama. Always worried about how I look. Ought to be worrying yourself about how I sound. We're recording this afternoon. That's what's important. Where's Cinnamon anyway? She should be getting herself ready, too."

Elma knew where Cinnamon was. She was on the roof practicing her opera exercises, but that was of no concern to Memphis. Memphis thought the whole world revolved around Baker Johnson and Fletcher Henderson.

"Well, I'm going to be on time and look like a princess, huh, Mama? Think Baker will notice?"

"If he doesn't he's blind and walks backwards, baby," Elma said, smiling at her handiwork.

Cinnamon entered, buoyant and gleeful. "I got that note. I tell you, Mama El, I got that note. *Vedi? Di morte l'angelo radiante a noi s'appressa. / Ne adduce eterni gaudi sovraaaaaaah!* See, didn't I tell you?"

"Sounds beautiful to me, sweetie, but Memphis says you've got a big day today. Want me to do something real quick, while I've got the comb in my hand?"

"Yeah, that would be nice, Mama El. I keep thinking about the music and forget all about how I look. And I don't want to do that. Not today, too much to do. Too many folks to see today."

Elma started to work on this second head of hair just as she'd always done for her two girls. Raymond came into the kitchen and smiled.

"One of these days I'm going to hear you on the radio. You both are going to make me so proud. I know it."

"I'll do my best, Papa," Memphis glowed. Cinnamon didn't say anything. She just wanted to be good, not necessarily famous. Admired was enough for her.

✳ ✳ ✳

WHEN THE recording session began, Cinnamon and Memphis were stationed at the mike to the left of the horn section, so they could both see Baker. He nodded to them and blew a kiss to Cinnamon that Memphis thought was for her. The band started off with "Queer Notions," but the recording people kept asking them to do more takes and the hours slipped by without a break. They had just started "King Porter Stomp" when Cinnamon looked at the clock and realized she was about to be late for a lesson with Madame Olivetsky, who had invited an important operatic figure on a visit from Milan to hear her sing.

Cinnamon signaled to Henderson and the engineer to stop the session. Baker looked over at her and couldn't believe she was trying to interrupt the recording. Studio time cost money and there were a number of pieces left to be done. Finally Cinnamon just picked up her things and ran out of the room. Henderson saw this and stopped the session. "Take ten!" he announced. "Baker, go find out what in the hell is going on with that woman."

Baker immediately put his horn down and ran out the door, trying to catch up with Cinnamon, who must have lost her mind, running out on Fletch like that. This was her big break. Didn't she get it? Finally he saw her going down the second flight of stairs. He shouted, "Cinnamon, wait. Wait! Talk to me." Out of breath from following her, Baker questioned her fiercely. "Where in the hell are you running off to in the middle of a session? What's the matter? Are you sick, or crazy?"

Cinnamon indignantly responded, "I've got an important lesson with Madame Olivetsky—"

Baker didn't even let her finish the sentence. "Are you going to be a fool forever? I indulged you as much as I can, maybe I shouldn't have done that, but there is no life for you in no goddamn opera. You must be crazy to think these white folks are gonna let you sing opera!"

Now Cinnamon turned on Baker. "I am singing opera. I sing with the

National Negro Opera Company. And I'm going to continue to sing opera. I'm not going to wallow in the gutter with this swing, this 'jazz,' like you and Memphis. Don't you see there's nothing hallowed about swing? It's colored folks doing what colored folks have always done, making things up as they go along. Just noise and pelvis grinding is what it is . . ."

At that point Baker raised his hand to slap her, but didn't. "So, that's what you think of me when you get down to it, huh? I guess I might as well go on back upstairs."

At that moment, Memphis came running up to see what was the matter. She'd heard the two yelling all the way from the fifth floor.

"Nothing's the matter, Memphis," Baker said quietly. "Come on, Cinnamon has something else she wants to do." Baker put his arm around Memphis the same way he used to hold Cinnamon and turned to walk back up the stars.

"Baker!" Cinnamon called out.

Baker turned his head toward her. "No, don't say a word, I'm not an artist, I'm just some colored man makin' thangs up as ah goes 'long. Leave me alone, Cinnamon. Just go."

Memphis slipped her arm round Baker's lean body, about to ask what happened, but Baker put his fingers over her mouth gently, saying, "C'mon, baby, let's go make some music."

Cinnamon stood alone on the stairwell, her heart flooded with sorrow. Baker would never come back to her now. All because of what he called music and what to her signaled abandonment by one Lizzie Turner. She had lost not only her mother but the only man she would ever love to jazz. She gathered her thoughts and made for Madame Olivetsky's, where she sang till she wept. Madame Olivetsky said, "My little black cherub. Your heart is broken. It takes a broken heart to sing the opera for the people. You must make them cry."

Signor Grapelli, Madame Olivetsky's visitor from Milan, showered her with compliments. "We shall see you in Milano, my dear . . . if our countries will behave, yes?"

Cinnamon left, headed nowhere in particular. She thought of the songs she wasn't singing, of Baker's gestures toward Memphis, and called herself a fool for not recognizing what was going on between them earlier. But maybe nothing had been going on. She had thrown Baker into

Memphis's arms. He hadn't left her, she had disrespected him in a way that he could not tolerate and be a man. Memphis was just there. She had underestimated her cousin, and had not seen the precocious teen as a competitor. As she tried to make sense of it all, Cinnamon made her way through Manhattan to Harlem, where she and Baker had been so happy. She realized she had lied to herself and to him. She couldn't stand jazz, the jazz life. She had simply wanted that man who made her feel so special. He seemed to accept her for who she was, while she had not accepted Baker for who he was and what he represented. It was her own fault. No more Battle of the Bands, no more lindy-hoppers, only the heroines of the great operas. That's what she was left with, so she would make that enough. Eventually Cinnamon made it to the Bronx. Her head was clear. Elma wanted to know why she was home so early.

"I guess you could say I got fired, Mama El. I wasn't what they were looking for after all."

"Well, where is Memphis?" Elma asked. "Didn't she quit too, since they fired you?"

"Oh, no, Mama El, that's not at all what she did, but I'm going to lie down now, all right?"

"Well, don't you want something to eat? I've got some okra and rice to heat up."

"No, Auntie, I just need to rest. I walked a long way today."

✳ ✳ ✳

MONTHS LATER, Cinnamon grew used to Memphis skipping off to be with Baker and the band. Some of the fellahs even came round to visit with Raymond and Elma. Only Raymond felt the tension between his niece and his daughter over the one they called Baker. Elma was just happy for Cinn. Her niece had found a working calling with some class and talent in it. She prayed the response from Juilliard would be positive. She hoped her Memphis would find an interest of equal value. She took joy in their dreams, when her own dreams had slipped from her fingers.

Raymond, too, knew the frustration of wanting to practice a fine art and being shunned by one's own. He tried to spend more time with Cinnamon, listening to her sing arias as if he were the only member of the audience. He thought his attention would help Cinnamon to keep going.

Keep going to Madame Olivetsky, keep going to the National Negro Opera, keep going in spite of Memphis and Baker. The Negro Opera Company's production of *Aida* was coming up, featuring Cinnamon in her first lead role. Plus there was the final word from Juilliard yet to come.

* * *

CINNAMON SAT very patiently in the anteroom of the Office of Admissions at Juilliard waiting to be called before the committee. A tall blond girl came rushing out crying and slammed the door. Cinnamon was intimidated by her hysteria and tried to calm her own nerves. Finally an aristocratic-looking woman stepped through the door and nodded at her. "Cinnamon Turner?" Cinnamon rose and followed the woman through the heavy mahogany door. There was a group of four seated behind a long table with pitchers of water and glasses set beside them.

"Well, Miss Turner, it's been a while since we've seen you," said a man with heavy eyeglasses and a mole on his nose.

"Yes, sir, it has been," Cinnamon replied.

"We have come to a unanimous decision concerning your application for admission," a woman in a herringbone suit injected.

One of the others added, "Yes, this is very true."

Cinnamon was coming out of her skin. Why didn't they get to the point—was she in or not?

"But Miss Turner, there's one major mitigating factor," the man with the heavy glasses said somberly. "We noticed that there are no Negro spirituals or work songs in your repertoire."

"No, sir, there aren't."

The herringbone woman interrupted her. "We're very interested in admitting young Negroes who are committed to exploring the beauty of the Negro's music and song."

Cinnamon felt her blood rushing to her head. Her fingernails were plunged deep into the flesh of her palms. "I want to sing opera, ma'am," she said as respectfully as she could. The committee members smiled those sick little smiles that the powerful often have when someone challenges their perceptions.

"Well, Miss Turner, unless you will concentrate on your own race's contributions, it would be cruel of us to admit you to our school, as well as a waste of money . . . for wherever in the world do you think you would sing?"

When she heard that, Cinnamon reached into her purse and pulled out flyers for the *Aida* featuring Cinnamon Turner. "Here, you might be interested in attending this production by the National Negro Opera Company." Then she turned and ran out of the door the same way the tall blonde had just before her. Cinnamon fought back tears, sobs actually, but she was angry as well. If Mary Cardwell Dawson was her only option, so be it. Somewhere in the world, she would sing what she wanted. Of all places, it was Harlem!

> "Vedi? Di morte l'angelo
> radiante a noi s'appressa.
> Ne adduce e eterni gaudi sovra i suoi vanni d'or.
> Già veggo il ciel dischiudersi,
> ivi ogni affanno cessa.
> Ivi comincia l'estasi
> d'un immortale amor!"

Amidst a rousing applause Cinnamon took her bow as roses showered the stage. Elma and Raymond were clapping heartily. Cinnamon noticed that Memphis wasn't there. She saw Baker wasn't either. But she held her head high. This was her night. Thank you, thank you, she waved to everyone as she headed toward the dressing room. She looked in the mirror and said to herself, "I am an opera singer no matter where I sing."

Elma was the first person backstage. "You were magnificent, sweetheart!"

Then came Madame Olivetsky and Signor Grapelli with kisses and hugs. "Oh, my little black cherub has made me so proud, non, Grapelli?"

"Yes, yes," the petite man replied, smiling. "If she will have you, Signorina Cinnamon will make a fine addition to your graduate opera program. She might even force me to reconsider whether I teach in America."

Before Cinnamon could respond, Madame Olivetsky handed her an envelope embossed with the Juilliard logo. Her wizened and faithful teacher patted her on the shoulder. "Full tuition. Congratulations, my dear. The maestro has come to you."

Cinnamon had difficulty accepting so much praise, but she did her best. This was going to be her life. Now she knew it was possible, the world opened up for her in a new way. Still Memphis's absence weighed on her. Finally she relented and asked where her cousin was. Elma quipped with disapproval, "She's runnin' after that band. I'm sorry, Cinnamon, I know you miss her."

So Baker and Memphis were together somewhere away from her. Cinnamon thought of the implications of their absence, but gathered her roses to her face and took heart. She could make the audience cry. Baker and Memphis had given her that.

The rush of well-wishers parted as a handsome stately couple approached. The man was tall, round-chested, and dark like her. The woman on his arm, a willowy sylph swathed in silk and the scent of orchids. The woman was a mystery. The man she had seen before . . . the day her mother disappeared.

"Cinnamon Turner?" he queried. "You aren't by any chance related to a Lizzie Turner from Charleston?"

24

LONDON, BRUSSELS, MOSCOW, SHANGHAI. WITH THE REST-
lessness of an oceanic storm, Mayfield Turner had to be on the move. She
had traveled by train, by car, small plane, milk wagon, motorcycle, gon-
dola, even an Arabian stallion once. Since abandoning her native U.S. of
A. more than a decade ago, she had circled the globe a few times. Place
took on an illusory quality. She might awaken to a bronze sunrise over
the Alps or to a Flanders merchant peddling fresh, steaming strudel or to
a Tehran urchin offering the finest Persian weave—"Qalicheh, Kilim!"—
the languages percussive, plodding, pleading, a kaleidoscope of sound.
All over the world she had performed her sacred dance, an undulating
body without bones, a winding, whirling, rubber-legged dervish of light,
the "apricot dipped in honey," flaunting herself to her nation of birth,
anointed by the denizens of the cabaret life "divine!" Barefoot and, but
for a few strategically placed feathers and sequins, butt naked, the former
Harlem chorine had become an international sensation. Still, she was a
gypsy, a migrant worker with sore feet and a wrenched back.

Holding the money pouch tightly in her lap, Lizzie reviewed the tour
earnings in her head. "Band, chorus, manager, porters, whiskey—man!" *I
shoulda converted the take to francs while I was over there.* "Some measure
of success, sistuh!" she spat to herself. "Tryin' to make that little bit of

money 'fore they close the border nearly got us all killed." Her last night in Berlin, a gang of brownshirts had stoned the club she was playing and pelted her sidemen with eggs, cursing the long-haired German youth who had crammed in to see her act, her "Negermusik!"

All she wanted to do was get across the border back to France and the safety of Paris, but the train had stopped again. She arched her spine against the stiff leather cushion of the cabin seat, then stood up and stuck her head out the train window to see if Haviland was on his way back to report on the holdup. She gripped the moneybag tighter and stuck her hand deep into the pocket of her russet fox jacket and wrapped it around the cold, smooth pearl handle of her derringer just to feel safe. "Haviland! Hav!" she hollered up the platform. He turned casually as if annoyed. She watched him jockeying with the border guards. *Dog bite it, he's givin' away my cigarettes.* Avoiding the black expat village in Montmartre, Haviland had been strictly a Latin Quarter guy until his Harmon Fellowship ran out. Then, like so many others, he came easin' over to Lizzie's Banana Club looking for a job. She hired him as a companion, passing him off as an African prince. Haviland had a facility with languages and a seductive grace with which she was all too familiar. Every day she regretted her nostalgia. He sauntered back, his collar up, his hands in his pockets. The train still had not budged.

She stood up, pacing the cabin, a profusion of epithets, slurs, and curses punctuating the frigid air with percussive clouds of vapor and puffs of tobacco smoke. She wouldn't tolerate it. Not here. Her laundry was picked up and delivered. She had exclusive vendors just for her show clothes. Her apartment got cleaned, the walk swept, pets pampered, and plants watered in her frequent absences. "People work for *me!* Goddammit! People wait for *me!* I don't wait for them!" She swayed, intoxicated by the remembered scent of green orchids and a thousand roses at her dressing room door, the sound of the crowd wrapped around her like a lover, her fingers bedecked with yellow diamonds and around her neck a priceless choker of pink pearls. "Women burn their skin trying to get my color!" she fumed, "steal my bathwater!" She would not be treated this way! "What's the holdup now?" Mayfield Turner bristled at the frosty chill of the morning and a train stuck on the tracks in the middle of nowhere. "Happy New Year!" she barked as Haviland entered the cabin.

"They're checking everyone's papers," he said.

"Damn Nazis," she hurled under her breath, offering Haviland her already lit opium-laced cigarette. "Just my luck." Haviland nervously took the cigarette from her and, darting his head out the window to see how close the patrols were to their cabin, attempted to put it out. She wrested the thing from him and flipped the flame around as if she might burn him, then plopped herself on the seat, taking a long drag. As the nicotine and narcotic took effect, she leaned back in the corner and began improvising a song, "It's a sorry thing when your luck done gone/ You start worrying and everything goes wrong/ My daddy lost his luck/ Now it's mine I'm missin'/ Some joker took my luck/ Like it was his commission . . . Just put it in his pocket/ Weren't no way to stop it/ Now everything's gone wrong/ Cuz my luck done gone . . ." Haviland's look of anxiety completely annoyed her. "What are they gonna do? Shoot us?"

She missed Sparrow. In fact, she blamed the downturn of her fortune on Sparrow's departure. Sparrow yearned for the rhythms of a Harlem snap apple, bobbing in the breeze. "The unique smell of lard, biscuits, and hair oil. Dixie Peach, Brilliantine, and Miracle Grow Palm-Made!" he said. "I wanna stand in the shade and watch Easter hats float atop round rumps rolled into their clothes. All that Parisian stuff. Act like they doin' you a favor to stop and listen." She couldn't believe he just packed his bags, bopped and dipped around the joint, kissing everybody on both cheeks, dusted off his spats, and stepped. "Say baby, I got to go. I know you like Europe and everything, but I want me some decent grits. And I don't want to search all over town for 'em." On a drunken whim, they had married aboard the ship that first brought them to Europe. Ten years later he just up and announced he was leaving. "I hear we can get a divorce in Reno quicker than it took to get hitched. I'll stop there on the way to Los Angeles. Think I'mo try my hand in Hollywood. See if I still got the eye."

She had blessed him out then. She missed him now, his wiry clickety-clack manner. "Listen, come back with me," he had said, but she declined. *Never that, never back.* Europe was supposed to be a fresh start. "No stoppin' us!" Ossie had said. *Europe, Asia, the Greek Isles, Egypt. No past. No claims. No ties. No shit.* On the road half the year, the permanent exile found no world to her liking. Paris at least was a life of her own design. Paris was where she was staked and where she was going to stay. *My worthless friends, my sorry club, my lousy bookings, but mine.* She was tired of runnin'.

When she arrived at the Banana Club, the shutters were down. She found Mitch padlocking the club door. More often than not, he ran the club when Lizzie went on the road. Twenty years of knowing each other, a nod of her chin sufficed as a greeting. He was agitated, blowing her tenuous high.

"Damn Nazi goons pelted my band with eggs," she said. "Train held us up for six hours. I ain't seen shit like this since Charleston! I swore I'd never let it happen to me again!"

"We gotta talk," he said.

Her voice ricocheted in the empty street as she waved him off. "I'm a French citizen, goddammit!" She squinted at the gray overcast morning and she walked wearily around the corner through the alley to the back of the club. She was tired, bluesed up, and mad, her sorrow rising with each step. Her platform heels that buckled at the ankle tracked up the steep winding lane with its crooked streetlights and broken cobblestones, the dog shit and bouquets of garbage.

In its day, the Banana Club would still be going strong, a center of action right along with the Duc's and Bricktop's. *Free thought, free love, free imagination. Everything free. No wonder I didn't make no money.* The shipping heiress and the black pianist, the flying champ and the countess, the dashing young writer and the sheik—she had danced and sung for them all. Fitzgerald, Hemingway, even posed for Man Ray. *The toast royale of the modernists. Wrapped in aluminum foil for a Dadaist!* Dalí, Duke, Louie, Calloway—the rich radical high-life fringe had been her Paris. Now near abandoned, her club was still the hotspot of sorts—for Communists, anarchists, down-and-outs, hookers, and spies. *Prostitutes, pimps, gigolos, and gypsies.* Would-be fortune-tellers, speculating on where the world was headed.

In its day, her little patch of Paris was a French-speaking capsule of Harlem's 135th and Seventh, a bustling, hustling intersection of music, cultures, and classes, but her beloved neighborhood was no more. Paris was no longer a city of light but a city haunted by shadows, the Lost Generation replaced by a constant traffic of lost souls. The Americans began disappearing first. Their casual newspaper gigs evaporating and patrons jumpin' off buildings, they had come, like Haviland, asking Lizzie for loans, looking for a way back home. Then came Russians—poets, painters, musicians—fleeing theirs. And constantly Jews, spilling in spurts and gushes from Austria and Germany, crowding into the already teeming, labyrinthine Montmartre, staying in flats, ten, twelve to a room. While everyone who could leave already had, Lizzie remained among a small and diminishing group of colored musicians, who had collected among themselves, still making their home in the gritty winding streets of the hill district beneath the white-domed Sacre Coeur. Lizzie was barely hanging on, and that was in 1938. The year ahead looked even grimmer. *Sparrow would have at least seen me to my door.*

The narrow wooden staircase's uneven steps and rancid smells gave way to a temple of tapestries awash in candlelight. The inviting smell of Mediterranean spices and the warmth of the communal dining room and oversized kitchen of Mitch and Genya's attic flat softened Lizzie's mood. A gash of purple ink on her cheekbone, fingernails blue-black on the cuticles and rim, Genya greeted Lizzie gruffly, "Algerians are the niggers of France, you know that?" Genya crunched her body over a rustic mimeograph as her thick muscular arms unwound another stencil sheet of her weekly neighborhood newsletter. "Worthless piece of shit! The roller is stuck again!" she said over her shoulder to Lizzie as she dodged the zigzag clothesline strung across the kitchen and motioned to her two daughters to come collect the inked sheets. "Quick, quick before I have to type the copy all again! Lee-zee, I ask you, why I'm still a student? Thirty-eight with two grown daughters! I tell you why," she fussed, "I fall for that American musician! That is why!"

Lizzie chuckled to herself. She had always collected the strays. Crook School kids in Charleston, leftist intellectuals and gangsters in New York. In Paris, it was the colored musicians, of course, and Corsicans, gypsies, Left Bank leftovers like Haviland and Genya's bunch, French colonial students, colored of another variety. Genya was Algerian. She and Mitch had met through her brother Farid, who supplied Lizzie's club with contraband drugs and caviar. Farid also ran a brothel on the nearby Rue Pigalle, which he stocked with country colonial girls from the shanty zones on the outskirts of the city. When Genya arrived, on a scholarship to the Sorbonne, her days off from studying, she spent organizing the Algerian factory workers. She and her brother were having words about her activities the night she met Mitch. Fifteen years later, Genya had lost none of her fire. Lizzie rolled herself a cigarette as Mitch sat down beside her.

"We need a plan to get to Lisbon, Genya," Mitch said. "Tell her, Lizzie, what happened to you on the train. It's not safe."

"You want to go, go! I am not leaving Paris," Genya insisted. "Took me ten years to get here to study, fifteen to get to the point of dissertation. Now you want me to go?"

"At least let's get the girls out of here," Mitch pleaded.

"Where are they going to go? With you? You're on the road, sometimes gig, sometimes not. Strung out, sometimes yes, sometimes, no. No!"

Bruria whined, "I want to go with Papa."

"You hush and get ready for school," snapped Genya.

Rachel said nothing, but swept a few spilt sugar crystals with the corner of her napkin. Mitch got up from the table. "I don't understand you. I'll be downstairs."

"Try not to miss the vein," Genya hollered over her shoulder without turning around.

"I got no time for your shit today," he said and left.

"Walk away! Always your answer? Hey, and put the records in the jackets. What do you think, I'm American slave?" Genya turned from the mimeograph and threw the shuttle onto the floor, her hand to her head in frustration. "He never bothers to put the records back in their jackets."

Lizzie found in Genya a rhythm that was sisterly without any of the hurtful ties. It struck her as amusing how a strung-out musician and a radical Marxist could somehow have an otherwise ordinary, contentious marriage, when she had never found anyone with whom she could bond more than a few months at best and that was with effort. She expressed this opinion to Genya, who laughed, "I tested out a theory. The idea of going to bed with a black man is no more extraordinary than with a white man. Now I know. But I guess I keep him. But I will not run away from German bluster." A perpetual student and ardent Communist, Genya was also a fierce patriot, loyal to the principles of equality, liberty, and fraternity. "Do you think they will stop with Austria? Spain and Ethiopia were dress rehearsal, how you say, an out-of-town tryout. I will not allow the same to happen to France." Genya placed a bowl of steaming lentil soup on the table. "That's the last of the lamb." Lizzie sniffed at the slices of curled meat and the intricate blend of spice. She would never get used to Genya's notion of breakfast. Bruria sat in the corner, silently sheathing a stack of 78s in their brown jackets, then randomly in album covers. Rachel sipped from her glass and nervously kicked her leg under the table, rattling the place setting beside Lizzie's untouched bowl.

"They rounded up the patrons at the club I was playin' and took em away . . . just kids," Lizzie said off-handedly. "They say they're rounding up Jews. I've seen that look before. It's more than bluster."

"The hell with it," Genya spat. "Mitch should go ahead to Spain then. But I stay to finish this course work. If war does come, God only knows when I will get done. I will send the girls to him when I know he is safe." Lizzie looked at Genya and her two silent girls, then slipped off the kitchen stool and shimmied out the creases in her skirt. "I better get downstairs. We gotta talk over this new ordinance. Musicians' union demanding we only hire Frenchmen! It's hard enough keepin' my band together as it is. Gotta see what it means."

"I'll tell you what it means. More lentils. Stale bread."

Lizzie took off her pearl choker. She now wore all of the expensive jewelry she had. "See what Farid can fetch for this."

She ambled down the steps and entered the club through the back door off the kitchen. She could hear a faint improvised solo emanating from the bandstand. Just as he sat now was how she first spied Mitch, tinkering on the piano. She had just arrived from the States with La Danse Negre. During the break, he sought her out hoping to sift through memories. He had seen how much Osceola loved her, how he had risked his life and lost it to save her. Initially, she wasn't having any of it. Mitch had made presumptions about her and, by claiming Osceola's music as his own, betrayed him and stole from both of them. Mitch insisted she listen. He took her to a nearby café to explain.

"I didn't know about any song. I don't know how they got it. Damn scam artists, the lot of them."

It had never occurred to her that Mitch was unaware that his name was on Osceola's sheet music. He sure hadn't made any profit from it. She could see even then, when Negroes were the thing in Paris, his pant knees were shiny, his figure gaunt, but he looked content, at home. Mitch had immersed himself in the ethos of France. As if he had opened the pores of his skin and breathed out color, a musician learning a new key, he had picked up the language, its musicality, the movements of the body, the rhythms of the day. In the Great War, the French army had embraced him, awarded him the Croix de Guerre, and when the band played, the people threw garlands at their feet. He had no desire ever to go back. "Back to where? The place that killed my boss? The place where my best friend was stomped to death? Steal a song off a dead man. America? You can have it. Put me in the army of a foreign land rather than accept me as a fightin' man? To hell with 'em for real! Vive la France!"

She watched him, these many years later as he hunched his shoulders over the piano, anticipating his solo. He had long ago lost the edge. He didn't play loudly anymore and barely went to late-night jam sessions. His one method of holding on was his religious purchase of any American albums he could get his hands on to keep up with the flow from the States. Lizzie joined him on the bandstand.

"Really thin house for the New Year," he noted, barely moving his lips. "Mostly Farid's girls at the bar. What we gonna do bout the fellahs, they sayin' we gotta hire half French?"

"Shit, I don't know about you. I am French. Got papers to prove it," she chortled as she rolled her eyes. She took a long drag, then put her cigarette to his lips. "We'll add that accordion player and that guitar, the gypsies, they must be French. Cut the combo down to five."

Like Haviland, Mitch, and Genya, Lizzie had found Paris a comfort to her rootlessness. New start. No past, no ties. Except now she had made them.

* * *

FOR DAYS, months, even years after, Cinn's ears would be keyed to the sound of arrival. She would look toward a door opening, the rhythms of footsteps, the crescendo of an approaching car motor. Often she would stare out the window with an involuntary expectation and predictable disappointment. She and her mother had been on the run it seemed most of her young life. That had been Lizzie's way. "Wait for me, wait for me here, you hear?" her mother Lizzie, her pal, had said, spending longer and longer times missing until finally, she just never showed up.

"That is done," Cinnamon told herself. She was a young woman now, the same age as Lizzie when she had given birth. Cinnamon Turner was her own person. The daughter had chosen her own path with her own song, one totally distinct. *Lizzie Turner, Mayfield Turner, Aunty, whatever she wants to call herself, we're done with that.* Cinnamon vowed her voice would never be used for loose, lowlife entertainment, but as a beacon of dignity and class and a champion for the voiceless. She saw that her voice had power, that standing up for what she believed produced results. Just as she had pursued the job at the five and dime, just as she had defined her own repertoire of songs for admission to Juilliard, the picture of poise and rectitude, when she sang *Aida,* she embodied the role and became an ancient African princess, battling injustice on and off stage. Incensed to learn that Harlem's National Negro Opera Company as a "Negro unit" of the New Deal's Federal Theatre Project would only get half the resources provided the white theater companies downtown, she wrote letters to the press demanding that the Negro ensemble get equal support. She stood with the protesters against the city unions to demand that Negro construction workers be hired to refurbish the cavernous Harlem dance hall that was to be the opera company's home. She had even gotten her Papa Ray some much needed work, helping to bring the old dance hall back to life, transforming the decrepit freezing ballroom into a respectable amphitheater.

Unbeknownst to the young singer, the National Negro Opera Company had not gotten its supplementary money for the full orchestra at rehearsals, the glorious lush costumes, and the moving scenery for the production of *Aida* from the U.S. government, but through a private contribution from the Holstein Realty and Trade Company run by the late founder's adopted son and heir, Deacon T. Holstein. It was he who had persuaded the whites-only construction and theater unions to back off of their hiring demands. She would often see the production's anonymous benefactor looking over the workmanship on the building repairs or lingering during rehearsals. He was a striking, square-shouldered man, always impeccably dressed from hat to shoes, his dark face broad and implacable. She thought him an odd stage-door Johnny and found his staring inappropriate. The cast would often whisper, "That's Mr. Holstein," as if she should be impressed.

Opening night, she discovered that same Deacon Holstein was her relative—an uncle, her father's brother. "My name used to be Turner," he said haltingly. "When I married into Mr. Holstein's family, I took the name on—for the sake of the business."

"My father is old-fashioned," the woman beside him said. "He so wanted a son, I had to marry one for him." She was beautiful, willowy, moving ever so slightly as if stirred by a breeze. She put her arms through his, their fingers intertwined. "I'm Iolanthe," she said. "Deacon, what a gifted young woman your niece is!"

"We lost track of you when your mother went to Europe," he added with a single chuckle.

Cinnamon suddenly remembered. *That voice . . . the man on the steps.*

"We presumed Lizzie took you with her," the man continued, speaking slowly, searching for the proper words. "Didn't realize till this day, till I saw your aunty sittin' in the audience," he smiled. "Then I knew for sure who you was."

I have family. Other family. I had a father. That was in February. The revelation stunned her still.

The week after the final performance of *Aida,* the Holsteins invited Cinnamon and her aunt Elma to tea. The Holsteins. Refined, with delicacy of movement, the strict staccato speech denoting their British-influenced West Indian origin, the Sugar Hill brownstone four-story home, uniformed servants, everything in its place. Deacon T. Holstein had come up mightily in the world from bootblack and pickpocket to Harlem kingpin. Rackets into respectability. Marrying into the Holstein family, he now controlled grocery stores, clubs, hairdressers, barbershops, and real estate up and down the Northeast, not to mention the Policy Wheel in three-quarters of Harlem. Yet, he looked awkward in his own house. His body seemed oversized for the imported ornate furniture, his color too bold against the muted pastel walls.

"This is your father with the Great Jim Europe, third from the end, his helmet tipped to the side," Deacon said proudly with a heavy baritone laugh, pointing out the pictures in an album Iolanthe had made for him. Sitting beside him on the divan, Cinn slowly flipped through the pages. "Orange Street Gang," "Verdun, beside a cannon," "Welcome Parade on Sullivan Island," the captions read.

Deacon occasionally looked over to Elma. He asked after her mother Miss Dora and was sorry to learn Mah Bette had passed a few years back. He laughed, reminiscing, "I usedta pester Mah Bette and your grand-mamma somethin' awful. They set food out for me just the same. Miss Elma remembers. She could set the plate down for me, but was forbidden to play. Had a little marchin' band back then. Your father was the star. Could play everythin'."

Cinn slipped one photo out of the jacket and held it up. Standing be-side a fellow soldier, a smiling Osceola in uniform. *He has such a young and open face, my . . . father.* Lizzie had never spoken of him. "Mitch— the most terrific guy I ever knew," she read aloud the writing on the back of the photo. She did not see Deacon's face wince at the words. Her fin-gers graced over the script. *My father's words in his very own hand.* "How did he die?" she asked. He paused before putting the picture back in the album jacket. "Got caught up in a riot just after the war, two days home . . . A gang of white sailors kicked him to death. He died pro-tecting your mother. A hero twice over in my book."

Cinnamon blanched, suddenly unable to breathe, her throat con-stricted. She excused herself from the room, her mind dizzy, her heart pulsing shocks of grief. Elma and Iolanthe followed her to the powder room. The two women held her between them, Iolanthe apologizing for her husband's matter-of-fact delivery, Elma telling her it would be all right, but the news was too much to comprehend. She had found her fa-ther and lost him that same day.

"Your father was a great guy all around," Deacon told her when she returned to the parlor. "He woulda been a great musician. You got music on both sides."

"Perhaps, you could honor his memory with a song," Iolanthe sug-gested.

"Of course," Cinn replied. She chose the German lied that she had prepared for her Juilliard audition, the melancholy *Die Winterreise* by Schubert. Cinnamon accompanied herself on the piano while she sang, her black hair coils catching glimpses of indigo and purple in the shafts of window light through the stained glass. At the selection's end, she ex-tended the last note and slowly introduced a timorous vibrato that trailed off, leaving the pitch still ringing in the soundless room.

Iolanthe watched her husband's new charge closely. The girl certainly favored her husband more than she did the pictures of his brother. *This might be Deacon's child.* She was tempted to come right out and ask, but since he had never spoken about it, she did not. Iolanthe had no offspring of her own and was not intent upon any. Her marriage with Deacon was designed for convenience, not conception. She had no inclination toward intimacy with a man. Birthing was not a notion she had considered. *But a beautiful young ward, related by blood? This could work.* Iolanthe told Deacon, "Because she is part of you, she is part of me. I will do for her as I would my own daughter."

Cinn could tell her aunt Elma was none too pleased. Elma fidgeted with her finger sandwiches and adjusted her body position on the couch far too many times. The ruffle of her dress fluttered about her face. For the occasion, Elma had altered an old dress, alas, with none of her mother Dora's artistry. Her hair, which had never regained its fullness, was haphazardly pulled back and laced with gray. Compared to Iolanthe's refined stillness, Elma seemed provincial, old-fashioned, and old. Cinnamon felt closer to her new aunt, who was so stylishly attired and closer in age.

For her part, Elma went along silently. Clearly this haughty Harlem couple had taken a shine to Cinnamon. Elma determined not to tell Dora or Lizzie about the liaison until she saw better where it was going. Intending to reciprocate the lovely afternoon tea and to investigate this relation further, she inquired, "What are you all planning for Easter?"

"We're going to see Marian Anderson at the Lincoln Memorial," Iolanthe replied. "We're sponsoring a delegation from New York. I was about to ask you if you would care to motor down with us? It would be a perfect way to celebrate Cinnamon's admission to Juilliard."

Elma immediately saw the look of delight in her niece's eyes and how easily they came under the sway of these strangers.

* * *

EASTER SUNDAY was already a momentous holiday in most Negro households. This particular Easter, April 9, 1939, was for Cinnamon Turner triple-fold excitement. Saving every penny she could for her graduate study at Juilliard, she had only hoped to hear the great Marian Anderson's performance on the radio. The thought of seeing the famous contralto in person made her dizzy with anticipation. The weekend was already jammed with activity. Not only was she overseeing two church choir rehearsals and a Sunday school pageant play, she was also studying for her last set of exams before graduation from Hunter. Having scheduled an extra-long Saturday rehearsal to make up for her absence from the actual Sunday performance, she got home to the Minors' Bronx flat well past midnight and fell into bed. Iolanthe had promised to pick the family up at seven o'clock Sunday morning, allowing plenty of time for the drive to the nation's capital.

The six A.M. elevated train squealing round the corner awoke her. "Dog bite it!" She sat up in a panic, unfolded her body, and flew toward the bathroom, the scrape and flap of shrunken feet in oversized slippers just behind her. The door opened without a knock, a wisp of white hairs poking in. Miss Tavineer in her disheveled robe, one withered breast hanging out and a towel draped over her shoulder, looked wounded with irritation. "Who in there?" Then just as quickly, she shuffled off with a "Jesus, have mercy!"

"Hey, skyscraper." Jesse knocked with a trill and poked in his nose. "Some people got to go. Shake a leg, sistuh, 'fore the old lady guh-gets back." Their Nana had allowed Jesse an Easter week vacation to visit his parents. Ever since he got back, he was a pest, bossier than she remembered. Distance had changed their relation little. He had become a young man. Slow of speech, he was no longer bashful. He had an easy manner, ribbing her with disarming wit. Tall and gangly, he would forever be her brother and buddy, tagging along at her heels. "Hurry it, huhn. People got things to do." Cinnamon held the warped door shut with her foot. *WHEN is Poppa Ray gon fix that!* Clearly, she was just going to have to live with the stomach. The knots would have to work their way out. *Relax. The choir will be fine. They've rehearsed enough. They know the material. You won't be missed.*

She was a large girl. Tall for her age, taller than Jesse, who everybody in the neighborhood now said favored Jimmy Stewart. She pulled at her hair in the mirror, a thick tangle of kinks and curls, five different textures. The longest hairs grew on the top of her head. The back never seemed to grow at all. *Kitchen. Someone's in the kitchen wid . . .* She pinned two fat braids across her skull with an arsenal of hairpins to prevent their penchant for popping loose into what Jesse had deemed "the Bronx view of the Manhattan skyline," then stared at herself for one more moment, searching for approval, her eyes piercing as a couple of new pennies. The style accented the wideness of her face and flat broad sweep of her nose. The pins were prickling her already. Miss Tavineer appeared again, more plaintive and urgent.

Cinn sidled down the narrow corridor of her aunt and uncle's two-flat, now home to a vague carnival of strangers—random boarders, Great Migration strays, island refugees, and stranded intellectuals. After the economy crashed in '29 it crashed again in '38. Hence, Miss Tavineer and her nephew Mr. Lohar, Mrs. Lohar, their adopted son, and, in what used to be a walk-in closet, Miss Hadjo, the Ph.D. who had found her belongings cast onto the street by the city marshals. Adelle, a young West Indian woman Elma had taken in ostensibly to help out, shared the bedroom with Cinnamon, Memphis, and Priscilla, Elma and Ray's youngest. Sissy she was called, the surprise who came along once her parents had stopped trying. Her mop of curls peeked in just as Cinnamon returned to their room. "Mama says you two better hurry up. What do you want for breakfast?"

Cinnamon Turner longed for one thing, "Deliverance!" She tickled Sissy, who scooted from her giggling, then turned and shook her older sister roughly. "Memphis, get up, you'll be late, sleepyhead!" Memphis grunted and pulled the covers over her head.

"Memphis, come on," Cinn echoed, "we overslept." Since Baker had gone on the road, there was an uneasy truce between them. After all, he had left them both. Memphis swatted her away. "I didn't sleep at all, you kickin' me like that. Leave me alone."

By the time Cinn reached the kitchen, Elma and Raymond were already on their second cups of coffee. Elma bustled around the table and bellowed as if straight to God, "Grea-eat Day! Great day, the righteous marching! Gre-eat Day! God's gonna build up Zion's wall!"

Jesse was halfway out the back door. His eyes widened as he stared at Cinn's hair.

"Wow! Don't tell me . . . the Statue of Liberty!" He clucked his teeth and darted, deftly catching the dishrag Cinn threw in his direction.

"Jesse, you are going to church today, aren't you?"

"Yeah, later. First gotta help Papa with the truck," he hollered over his shoulder, his heavy boots pummeling the back steps.

"Don't hold that clutch!" Raymond admonished. He had lost yet another job. Inspired by his niece's New Deal activism, Ray stood in solidarity with the Harlem Negro projectionists against their job cuts. In short order, the then all-white International Alliance of Theatrical Stage Employees discovered that card member 372 was not quite "black Irish." With his severance pay, Ray bought a used truck from one of his old bootleg connections to pursue independent contracting. Jesse, on his visits home, always gave the engine an overhaul. Ever-faithful Elma starched and pressed his overalls with the same attention to detail she would give a dress shirt.

"Somebody in this house needs to go to church," Elma fussed softly. "To tell Pastor Hawkins why we're not at the service." Elma sat Priscilla between her legs and began pulling the girl's wavy dark hair into plaits, Sissy yelping like a puppy dog with each yank of her mother's unforgiving comb.

Grand Hotel, thought Cinnamon as she peered out the window. "Mama El, why didn't you wake me?"

"Well, I did, child, two or three times. I figured after you came in so late last night from work, you needed that little bit of rest. Mornin' to you, too, by the way," her aunt said without a smile. Cinn folded her hands around a steaming cup of lemon slices in water and blew impatiently on the surface.

"Papa, me and Cinn are going to hear the great Marian Anderson!" Sissy chirped as she wiggled away from her mother.

Raymond clanked his spoon against the saucer, imitating the rhythm of his daughter's nervous motion. " 'Me and Cinn?' What kinda language is that? . . . D.A.R., hmph," Raymond grunted. "They're not a bit concerned with Marian Anderson's singing. Only with colored folk flocking to see her. What did they think we were going to do, bring chicken bones to the theater? The color rub off on the seats?"

"Raymond, shoosh," Elma cautioned. "This is a great occasion, a great day, whatever the reason. Cinn, you gotta have more than that tea. Can't live offa lemon juice. Have some breakfast. It's going to be a long ride."

Cinn remained glued to the window, ignoring the chaotic morning.

Adelle, who sat beside her in the windowsill, continued to study the leaves that collected in the bottom of her cup.

Her eyes half closed and still in her bathrobe, Memphis ambled in and behind her Miss Tavineer. Elma immediately rose and ushered her old Hell's Kitchen neighbor to a seat. "We have some fresh coffee for you, Miss Tavineer, and some hominy and a bit of salmon if you like. It's the Lord's day. He has risen!"

"How could he not? Even Jesus couldn't sleep round here," Memphis snapped.

"Don't you blaspheme in this house, young lady," Elma scolded. "Why aren't you dressed? Those people will be here any minute."

"Not going," Memphis answered with a yawn.

"If you're not going with us, you should be going to church. You can take Miss Tavineer."

"As soon as you all leave, I'm goin' back to bed." Before her mother could respond, Memphis, the small-boned, sallow child, now grown into a long-legged, amber-eyed bronze filly colt, slinked in a diagonal across the floor with her signature Lindy Hop shuffle, waggin' her finger in the air.

Always mischief. Always the party, Cinnamon thought, then said, "There's still time for you to make it, Memphis, if you hurry."

"I'm not interested in ridin' in some old crowded car for seven hours to hear some woman warble that stuff like you every day. Besides, you're all going to freeze in your Easter hats."

"You are so ignorant."

"It's better than being ignored."

"Girls! Not today." Elma's exasperation at the testiness between her two girls had no limit. She had warned them never to let a man come between them, between blood, yet here he still was, that Baker fella, though the body was long gone, still a lingering blues. "Memphis, if you're not going with us, you can escort Miss Tavineer down the street to the church like I told you. And when I get back, your smart-aleck behind better be right here."

"Pappuuhhh?!" Memphis stomped over to her father.

She attempted to hug him. He kissed her gruffly on the forehead and pushed her away. "Hey, hey, do what your mother says. Maybe you can pray your way out of high school."

"No use playin' to your father," Elma admonished, "we're together on this."

"Your cousin is going to *Juilliard*," Raymond added. "You should be happy, you should be proud. You go to the concert, or you go to church."

Memphis didn't need to hear anyone's opinion today of what she should be doing with her life. She was blue, hiding her disappointment that Baker had just skipped town without so much as a "see yah." And now all the attention was focused on Cinn. Memphis bounced hard onto the kitchen chair, her bare heels thumping the floor. She folded her arms, imagining random expletives under her breath. "The same darned scales over and over."

"They're called arpeggios."

"Cinn can sing all the day long. You'd do well to follow her example." Raymond continued, "Can't build a career, bankin' on winning a couple of contests."

Memphis stomped off to the bathroom. "I sing when I want to."

"That's pretty apparent." Her father's words stung. She slammed the bathroom door.

Cinn followed and knocked gingerly with a truce offering. "Memphis, you can still go if you hurry." Memphis turned up the sink water full blast and bellowed at the top of her lungs her own rendition of her latest Billie Holiday favorite, "Why Was I Born?" Knowing her practice-perfect cousin was standing at the door, Memphis would deliberately go off-key, recomposing the melody and lyrics as she went along. She imagined the improvisation would drive her cousin mad.

"They're here!" Cinnamon shouted and ran off.

Cinn reached the front parlor window first. The whole family gathered around her to see. The Minors, who had been impressed with Eudora's late model Ford, gazed upon the Holsteins' car that was bigger than their kitchen, a chauffeur-driven Cadillac with brilliant chrome fixtures and a polished navy blue exterior shining like patent leather. The car door opened and from the plush leather seats emerged a driver in a customized caramel gabardine uniform, black riding boots, and a smart black cap.

"You think they know there's a Depression goin' on?" Raymond mused. "I shoulda stayed a bootlegger."

Sissy turned to her parents, her mouth agape. "Papa was a bootlegger?"

Elma cut her eyes toward her husband. "No dear, he's just seen too many movies in that old job of his."

Still wrapped in her towel, Memphis tried to poke her head over the crowd. Immediately she regretted her decision not to go. She saw a glint of satisfaction cross Cinn's face.

Sheathed in a light green knit suit with a fur-lined cape and matching muff, Iolanthe greeted the family at the front door to the flat. She blinked quite a bit. Hoping to disguise her dismay that her newly found niece lived in a walk-up, she pretended that an ember had flown into her eye. The young socialite noted Priscilla's thin coat and Cinnamon's short jacket. Across the street, a rusty old pickup backfired with a gunshot bang as Raymond and his son pulled off waving. Iolanthe stared with dismay at the hand-painted sign on the truck's side—MINOR REPAIRS: WE FIX ANYTHING!—a cloud of smoke billowing behind. "Well, shall we get started?" she asked pertly.

* * *

THE HOLSTEIN car joined a steady caravan of pilgrims journeying to Washington from all points of the country. Because she was a Negro, the Daughters of the American Revolution had refused to allow the great contralto Marian Anderson to perform in Constitution Hall. The D.A.R.'s insult to Miss Anderson had made poignantly clear the nation's disrespect and intransigence toward the Negro people. Among black folk and progressives, the rejection had sparked a quiet revolution of its own.

"So President Roosevelt arranged for her to sing in front of President Lincoln's statue," Elma explained to her youngest child.

"The greatest voice of the century and these ridiculous women think they have the right to reject her?" Cinnamon fumed. "Against the Daughters of the Revolution stands one lone daughter of the race," she added, "and we stand with her."

The brisk spring day had chilled by late afternoon. Cinnamon shivered in her seat, as much from the cold as from anticipation. Because of the Holsteins' stature, the Minor family found themselves seated in the row behind the officers of the New York Urban League and the NAACP delegation. Cinn could see Mrs. Roosevelt clearly. She admired the First

Lady almost as much as she did Miss Anderson. Mrs. Roosevelt counseled her husband to be responsive to the needs of Negroes and was vigilant in pressing for equity in his policies. That took gumption. Now she was defying the D.A.R., the defining organization of America's power elite. That took courage.

Iolanthe took Cinnamon by the hand and began to introduce her to the important New Yorkers in their section. Looking up into her face, the squat powerhouse mayor of New York, Fiorello La Guardia, shook her hand vigorously. "My niece and protégée," Iolanthe cooed, "on her way to Juilliard. That was she playing Aida in the Negro Opera Company production."

The young Reverend Powell eyed her like she was a chocolate drop. "Are we perhaps looking at a future Miss Anderson?" the dashing Harlem leader inquired. Cinn blushed, speechless before the handsome, self-assured activist. The soon-to-be first Negro congressman from New York was as white-looking as her Aunt Elma and tall like she was. "You must come sing before my congregation," he insisted. Cinnamon stared at him as if hypnotized.

Iolanthe came to her rescue. "Music runs in the blood. Her mother is Mayfield Turner."

"Really?" Powell's attention spun away from the daughter, breaking the spell. "Mayfield Turner. Haven't heard that name in ages. Quite a sensation for a while."

His look changed, the tone changed, everything changed. The look of admiration had turned into a leer. Cinn took Iolanthe aside. "Miss Iolanthe, I prefer you not mention my mother's relation, I'd prefer that you introduce me as myself."

"Of course, dear," Iolanthe replied, her face querulous. The conversation left both women on edge.

It was shortly after five o'clock when, dressed in a heavy wool overcoat, Secretary of the Interior Harold Ickes took the podium. There were slight hints of frost from his breath as he began, "In this great auditorium under the sky, all of us are free . . ." Sitting amidst congressmen, Supreme Court justices, and cabinet members, the image of her father's murder at the hands of a white mob still fresh, Cinnamon felt anything but free. Miss Anderson stepped forth in a full-length fur and hat. Her signature high cheekbones and strong arched eyebrows, her defined, proud, sculpted lips, gave her the countenance of one's favorite Sunday school teacher. Her tranquil silence settled the crowd of seventy-five thousand as if they were a group of small children. She began the evening's performance with "My Country, 'Tis of Thee," emitting a tone of such warmth and purity, her stance so dignified and serene, that it set Cinn afire. With each note of Miss Anderson's performance, Cinn's faith in the power of voice to draw people, to awaken them, was reaffirmed. More than speeches, more than protests, more than marches and movements, the authority of a single voice could rise above them all, to stir the winds of change. "Let Freedom ring!" Miss Anderson sang, the *r* rolling off her tongue like the call of a celestial being, opening the heavens to a common plea. The colored contralto's voice soared above the crowd, commanding all to rise with her above the pettiness of human life, beyond the differences toward a unified humanity, aching, longing for the divine. She proceeded to sing Donizetti's "O mio Fernando" from *La Favorita* and Schubert's "Ave Maria" with perfect diction and modulation. The woman was majestic. Cinn stood amidst the mesmerized throngs, rapt in silence, moved to tears, but her tears were of a different sort. Before the magnificent Miss Anderson, Cinn felt herself an impostor, undeserving. Her determination now seemed brittleness, her voice trapped. "Cast out from Constitution Hall!" she lamented aloud, when in her heart she became that child again, cast out from a little apartment in Hell's Kitchen, pages of sheet music dancing in the air along with her clothes and toys, jacks and Mah-Jongg ivories, broken into pieces on the asphalt, her mother screaming, grasping her wrists so tight she thought they would break. "That voice, that great woman! That beautiful voice, still shackled!" she seethed.

Anderson then offered a medley of spirituals, beginning with "Gospel Train." When she got to the second selection, Cinnamon's rage erupted. *They can't be asking her to sing 'Trampin'?' 'Trampin'?' What's spiritual about that??!*

Cinn determined from then on that her mission at Juilliard would be to go beyond even the grand concert performance career of Miss Anderson to sing on the world's great stages of opera. Forget Constitution Hall! Cinnamon Turner set her sights on La Scala, the London Opera, and the Met!

The Norwegian composer Dvořák in 1893 had declared American Negro spirituals the root of truly new American music. Since the end of the Civil War, the Fisk Jubilee Singers had stunned the world with their repertoire of these indigenous songs by anonymous composers. The great baritone Paul Robeson and tenor Roland Hayes in concert performances across the globe had through their renditions of American Negro spirituals become social and political ambassadors not only for the struggle of black Americans but for the plight of workers and the oppressed everywhere, linking the resistance of American slaves to resistance struggles throughout the world. But when Miss Anderson launched into that dulcimer spiritual "I'm trampin', try'na make heaven my home," Cinnamon Turner could not hear these things. She could not hear the song of resistance. She could not hear the coded message detailing an escape route. She could not hear the determination of a vanquished and impoverished people to have their glory. She, who had gotten her training in the South, who was steeped in the tradition, chafed at the expectation that it would be in every black singer's repertoire. She herself, who wanted so much to be free, could not bear the longing. There was too much emotion overwhelming her, the wail of all those souls, threatening to sweep her away. She could not hear hunger for freedom or feel the abiding faith that it would come. She could only feel the sting of degradation and passivity. For her these were not the songs of liberation and beauty, but the cobbled-together mumbo-jumbo of slaves, of a people without value or pride, the persistent reminder of a past she would sooner bury and forget.

The South had given her an advantage. Stressing the value of enunciation, clipping her sentences, Eudora had told her, "You carry the responsibility for the Negro people with every step and every breath. Everywhere you go, you set an example." The church had given her opportunities to perform, even financial help, passing the plate. She was asked often to sing for weddings, settin' ups, and funerals. Midnight burials, waiting for the spirit to go home, 'fore the stars finally fade. The people would sit up all night. The walkway lined with torches, a steady stream of visitors, ragged and bedraggled Holy Rollers, the droning rumble of their feet standing in for ancestral drums. The worst one, the last, a young child had died. The mother got up—dancing, got happy, jumped up, body gyrating and bouncing, shifting into hysterical spasms, up and down the aisle of torches, her skirt flying dangerously close to the flames, the people unable to contain her body, buoyant with the light of the spirit come upon her. "Don't get tired, don't give up . . . Lord, take my child!"

On the car ride back to New York, while everyone chattered on about the historic day, Cinnamon bowed her head and cried big heavy tears. "Why did she have to sing spirituals?"

"Spirituals?" Elma inquired, genuinely perplexed. "Why shouldn't she sing them? What better day to sing them than the Day of Resurrection?" At that very moment, the woman who was most like a mother to Cinn plunged into her abundant inventory of Negro sacred songs and erupted, swaying back and forth, bellowing out the car window, "Oh Jesus, come before my face!"

Iolanthe patted Cinnamon on the knee. "Your real recognition will come in Europe."

25 ⌒

As a present, they said, for her admission to Juilliard, Deacon and Iolanthe offered Cinn that trip to Europe. Elma initially resisted the idea. "Being to tea and a concert doesn't mean you can go traipsing across the ocean. These people are almost strangers. And there's so much carry-on going on over there. Don't know if it's wise."

"If I don't go now, who knows when I'll get a chance."

"Well, your uncle and I say no."

"I'm nineteen years old. I can make my own decision, thank you," Cinn replied. "He's my uncle, too, Mama El. They're just as much family as you."

"Well, I don't believe that," Elma said, holding back tears at the sharpness of Cinn's response.

Cinn softened. "I didn't mean that the way it sounded, Mama El." She approached her aunt and put her arm over her shoulder. "You and Uncle Ray and Nana are my family, but Uncle Deacon and Iolanthe don't have anyone but me. It makes them happy to be a part of my family. It would make me happy if you saw them that way, too."

"Have you let your mother know you'll be coming?"

"She didn't come to my graduation. She hasn't been to see me. I'm not going to Europe to see her. Madame Olivetsky's colleague who came to see

Aida will be meeting us, and she has provided me with letters of introduction to people who can advise me on my career. Prague, Vienna, and Salzburg are already off-limits because of the war. The maestro has offered to make some introductions in Paris and London while there was still time."

"At least let her know you're coming."

"Fine, be my guest. But I don't plan on having the time."

* * *

"I HAVE been trying to get your uncle to go for years," Iolanthe said as she busied herself about the stateroom, instructing the redcaps where to dislodge the last trunk from the dolly. Deacon flipped a ten-spot to the beaming porter, impressed that a Negro family was traveling first class. "Europe will appreciate you," Iolanthe added. Not until they were well out to sea did Deacon confide in his wife that he was in a bit of trouble with the law again. "Police bustin' the policy wheels, downtown mob on my ass, the mob's invadin, trying to retake Harlem, again! City Hall diggin' into my pockets, indictments coming down." By their leaving town for a while, subpoenas couldn't be served. Hence Cinn's graduation present, her first trip to Europe, and theirs.

The trip was a disaster. The week they arrived, Germany invaded Poland, and Britain and France declared war. Air raid drills in the middle of the day greeted them, soldiers in uniform everywhere. As soon as the trio landed, like the Hellfightuhs comin' back, all hell broke loose. Gas masks selling on the street, everywhere furtive looks, hurried steps and scuffles, the exit ports stuffed like sardines. Cinn with her statuesque height, her uncle immaculately pressed, polished, spiffed, and Iolanthe, her cloche a russet cashmere, stood out like three beacons.

"This place is absolutely dead," Iolanthe quipped with shock. Cinnamon didn't notice. She was in Europe! The home of Puccini, Bellini, and Mozart! The land where her father was wounded and got a Medal of Honor. "Ma princesse! C'est vrai que je serais avec toi ce soir?" a young pup hollered from the back of a motorbike. "Jamais!" she responded. "Comment osez-vous parler comme ça!" At the sound of her immaculate French, he melted, clutching his heart as the bike sped away. "Je t'aime quand-même, ma chérie!" She laughed, delighted with the feel of the language on her tongue.

The maestro, Signor Grapelli, who had oozed rhapsodic over Cinn's Aida, met them at the Paris station. Wiping his brow of the sweat, he apologized for the rush of people. "The French," he chirped, his shoulders tight as his body jiggled. "The whole country takes vacation in August." He looked around nervously. "You could have perhaps picked a better time."

"It's convenient for me," Deacon said blandly, surveying the scene, without looking at the man. The maestro was hoping to get a visa to accompany them back to the States, back to that job offer at Juilliard. Iolanthe blinked. "Sweetheart, my husband's a gangster. He can't help you. He can't help himself." She turned to her husband, pouting. "Deacon, you brought your mess with you. People everywhere leavin' however they can, and here we come!"

Neither Deacon nor Cinnamon wanted to see Cinn's mother, but Iolanthe insisted on it. "The opera's closed, the museum's packing up. Montmartre's the only night life left," Iolanthe softly fussed as the taxi made its way through the blackout, the city in mourning for itself. Blue streets. Black curtains. The City of Light shrouded. The driver shouted over his shoulder, "Oui, le Club Banana, je connais l'adresse," then giggled.

"You sure it will be open?"

"Oh yes, la rue Pigalle is always open. Toujours ouvert."

The taxi pulled up to what looked like a small pocket of squalor. In the blackout, there were no front lights, the sockets just empty husks. The Banana Club. A squeaky clarinet, an accordion, and a gypsy guitar wafted from within. Cinn, brown child of amber light, opalescent like red ochre of clouds at dusk, watched her mother descend from the eaves and glide as if suspended in space through a star-strewn sky. Her voice was huskier, the tone languid, the vibrato still quick,

> "Comment suis-je arrivée à cette chanson lancinante?
> Et pourquoi personne ne me répond?
> Bien que j'en ai cherché la réponse de par le monde entier,
> Je ne chante que cette chanson lancinante.
> De nouveau, je suis seule,
> Et ce soir, je m'envole,
> Pour voir si demain je rencontrerais,

Quelqu'un qui me liberwill de cette chanson lancinante
Quelqu'un qui me liberill de cette chanson lancinante . . ."

Honoring her dual nations, she continued the song, this time in English,

"You ask how I come by this sad, haunting song,
My friend, that's a song all alone on its own,
I have searched the world,
Still I wander alone,
Searching no matter how long for my song,
Yes, I search the world for that crying song . . ."

Her body shimmered, white feathers covering her breasts and sequined wings, Mayfield Turner . . . descended from the rafters of the tiny club on a silver trapeze. Cinnamon had not seen her mother in fifteen years.

✳ ✳ ✳

DURING THE intermission, Cinn walked toward the dressing room. Deacon and Iolanthe held back, Iolanthe sensing that mother and daughter might need some time alone. Lizzie had seen the trio from the stage. Elma had wired her that Cinnamon was coming to Europe, but her sister had said nothing about the traveling companions. "Well, look at you! You're beautiful! Ray always said you was gonna grow into your beauty." Lizzie sat down and crossed her thighs with a sigh, a bouquet of feathers her halo, smelling of sweat, funk, and Chanel, her veined hands belying the youth in her face. "Tell me about yourself."

". . . Well, I just graduated from Hunter College. And I'll be attending Juilliard this . . ." Cinn smiled, dying inside. *Why am I doing this? What am I doing here? Tell me about yourself? she says.*

The preshow flurry began. Lizzie changed costumes and spoke at the same time, looking at her daughter through a squint of cigarette smoke, a smile on the other half of her lips. "I seen you ain't spent none of that money I sent yuh."

Farid poked his head in the dressing room. With the downsized staff, he was now acting as house manager as well as pusher and pimp. "Cinq minutes, Madame." He stopped, noticing Cinn. "Ohh la lahh!" Lizzie lifted her leg and landed the toe of her shoe on his chest, and let the spiked heel rest on his gut. "Monsieur Farid, this is my niece." She spiked the cigarette as she spoke. "You must stay till the end of the show. We got lots to catch up. Promise me you'll stay!" She disappeared with a trail of folks swishing behind, Cinn the tail of the entourage again. "Picked a devil of a time to come to Europe." Cinn left a note with the hotel number.

The next morning, Cinn awoke to a U.S. Marshal pounding on the door. All Americans were ordered out of France immediately. Paris was a zoo! Pouring down rain. Carloads of dazed Americans stuffed into buses bound for Cherbourg.

"What about my mother? Does she count as an American?"

"Cinnamon, Cinn," Deacon reassured her. "Your mother will be okay. She's a survivor. Now get your bags ready. You've got five minutes."

"I won't leave without her! I won't! You can go on ahead, but I'm going to find her."

Deacon grabbed Cinnamon by the shoulders and told her to sit down. Iolanthe sat beside her holding her hand. "I will go to find your mother," he said.

He left the women at the hotel and went to see Lizzie. The moment he stepped through the door, she reached for her pistol. Deacon stood in the door frame and threw up his hands in a gesture of peace. "That was a long time ago, Lizzie. I am a different man from then."

"Don't you say that to me, don't you call me by my name!" He had held the conversation many times over in his head, but now as he looked at Lizzie, her face still remarkably like it was twenty years before, a wild, wide-eyed beauty made more stunning by hate, his words vanished. He had not intended to harm her. He had come to her for help. Even then. How could he explain that? "Cinn sent me to come after you. They're telling all Americans to—"

"Farid!" Her eyes motioned to Farid standing silently in the doorway behind him.

Deacon was startled by the Arab's stealth. *How he done got the jump like that?*

"Cet homme doit quitter—maintenant!" Lizzie leaned back in her chair and blew smoke in Deacon's direction. This was her club. These were her people. She had nothing to fear from him.

"What shall I tell your daughter?"

"I have no daughter."

"I give you permission to tell her."

"Permission? Your permission? . . . Get the hell away from me!" He had mocked her. Her spindly legs, the spray of loud freckles cross her broad nose, big mouth and brazen speech, mocked her in the street. He had threatened her, "You say anythin' about this and I will kill you. Say somethin', anythin' and I will tear your face off." Through the mirror, Lizzie stared at him standing in the door frame. "Tell her your damn self!" It took all her power to keep her back to him. He had stolen everything that was dear to her. Given her a child she never wanted. He knew this. Deacon lowered his head and stared into his hat, then left without speaking further.

✳ ✳ ✳

DEACON STOOD in the middle of a foreign street and let the rain wash over him. Like the river rapids that carried him away from the prison camp, a mighty stream hurled him down to someplace he didn't need to be. In the thunder squalls between the lightning, voices mimicked the raging, rippin' water, claps of driftwood cracking beneath its steam— around him everywhere bodies, faces, hands pullin' him down. The stranger on the bank, Riley, Win, the men he had killed or ruined, grabbed at him, desperate. Lizzie scratchin' at him, whirled away from his blow, fell over, rollin' in the hard dirt, faintin', legs splayed to the sides, cryin', cursin' him. Osceola, his own brother, fightin' him, tryin' to kill him, then dyin' like that. Ossie had marched toward him, grimfaced, heels dug in the ground and took a wild swing. Deke was shocked at how quick he was. The blow grazed his jaw. Nobody did that.

"Keep away from her."

He laughed. "Or what?"

Ossie charged him and they were in it—fightin' when the mob come round the corner, swooped down on 'em like locusts. They fought their way back to Sully's, but Ossie was done by then. Just breathin' out his life, sittin' in that barber chair as if waitin' for a shave. Slippin' away without a sound, slippin' under . . . His brother had looked at him with such hatred.

Finding his way back to the hotel on foot, leaning into the rain, Deke's mind wandered from then. *Chesapeake, Chambersburg, Chester.*

Small time, layin' low. Rolled into Harlem, past a tent show. *Summertime. Old time, Revival.* He thought, *Holy Rollers! A parade!* But it was women, tall and straight in crisp white, men in high-button black uniforms and boots, their leader in an admiral's cap, riding high in a gold and sable carriage, a team of black horses drawing it. All of them black, their faces eatin' up the sun, glowin' themselves. He said, "I got to see this."

"Please remove your hat, brother." Deacon remembered a face black as his, smiling but looking firm. He went in, stood way to the back in a sea of people. Black pearls of Africa in a sea of new pressed, starched white cotton. The Leader talkin' about a ship, a fleet of black ships to Africa, to the Kingdom. Talked about how black minds had been twisted into not knowing who they were "because we been slaves who was Kings. We didn't belong to ourselves, so we don't know ourselves and what we do!"

Instantly he had seen it. What his life had been. The cuttin' and gamblin', killin' and stealin'—*hurtin' my own people, makin' it all strife, makin' it all pain.* From that time, that day, that moment, he turned around. Walked different, thought different, felt different from that time. He had mocked her, he had threatened her, he had hurt her. He was a different man. But Lizzie would never see that, never. *How do I undo all that I done?* The father. The brother. The daughter. The wife. He had sinned against them all.

He put the conversation out of his mind and headed back toward the hotel, shards of rain pelting his face. Cinn charged him at the hotel entrance. Deacon tried to speak, "Cinn, your mother wouldn't come. I'm sorry." She collapsed in his arms. "She doesn't love me. She doesn't love me at all." He leaned in and cupped her hands in his. "Come on. We have to get ready. We have to go." He couldn't bring himself to be despised in her eyes, couldn't risk it. He was a coward. He could live with that small casualty.

✳ ✳ ✳

THE HOLSTEIN party was herded onto a rustic British freighter that had been pulled into emergency service. They disembarked in Canada. From there, they took a train to Chicago, where Deacon decided to do a sleepover and conduct some business. New York still being too hot for his return, this would give his favorite girls two more days of their vacation, a little Chicago-style fun. He hired a Duesenberg and let the girls have the car for the day while he got a manicure and shave, saw the tailor and later the Jones brothers at the Club De Lisa.

After three hours at the Art Institute, Iolanthe begged off from the afternoon with a headache. Riding in the back seat, still trying to make sense of the recent events, Cinn got to see the city with two of the Joneses, henchmen Deacon knew from back in the day, driving her around. Fingers and Snook went all the way back with him to Crook School. They always took care of him when he came through Bronzeville. The trip to the museum had taken longer than anticipated. They didn't know the boss had a goddaughter. They swung west to make a pickup before heading back south to the De Lisa. The car slowed on a bridge, then stopped completely. Snook rocked and strained his neck, beeping the horn! "Come onnn! Dirty Commies! Some sort of protest march down the street," he explained.

She had an uninvited opportunity to review her nineteen years of life and stop in a few places. *New York, Charleston, and a brief jaunt to London . . . Paris, Chicago . . . Never expecting no one.*

A young man appeared by the car and tapped on the window. He seemed to look right over the dashboard, straight into her eyes, startling her from her memory.

"Just thought you gentlemen and you, young lady, would be interested in supporting the working people of America."

"Hey buddy, move along." Fingers nudged him with a hand missing two of its digits. "Damn Communist! Git your hand off the dashboard, I said git your grubby mugs offa duh kah!"

"I assure you, I'm no Communist. I'm democrat, small *d*. All we ask is that you blow your horn in solidarity with the demonstration. We're the Woodlawn Improvement Association."

"Your friggin' fingers? You wanna keep em!?" Fingers hollered as Snooks furiously rolled up the back windows.

"Mr. Snooks! Stop that!" Cinn admonished her driver. Snooks reluctantly lowered the window just to her eyes. "What is the rally about?" she asked.

"The shipbuilding plants here on the South Side tell the Negro workers they're not hiring," he explained as he walked alongside the automobile, maneuvering through the crowd. "Then they bring in a whole white crew from Indiana. This equipment is being built to help England and France in their fight against Fascism. I ask you why should Negroes fight Fascism abroad when we are battling those same forces over here?"

"Get outta here, you crazy Commie," Snooks snarled. "You're un-American."

"What's un-American about democracy?"

"It's subvoy-sive," Snooks said with emphasis, "you lousy nigguhs just don't wanna work."

"How can you say that about your own kind?" the man asked calmly, with no hint of malice or ire, more a teacher than agitator. "Two hundred fifty major defense industries refuse to employ Negroes. That's subversive! Discrimination in Selective Service, in the training. The Negro wants a job just as badly as anyone else. All he wants is a decent chance to get one." A riot of colors swept across the young man's face; he had wild eyebrows as if his thoughts had set them afire. "Negroes need to join forces to fight for justice and equality at home."

"You got a death wish, bub?"

"Liberty or death!" he laughed. "We can accomplish great things if we stand together."

"I went to see Marian Anderson," Cinn spoke up. "On the steps of the Lincoln Memorial. They say seventy-five thousand people attended, but I think it was more. The finest voice of the twentieth century, faultless timbre, made your body vibrate just to hear it." Then amidst great protest from her guardians, Cinn got out of the car.

Defying his proletariat impulses, the young man took her arm and escorted her toward the parade of picketers blocking the street. "This protest is just the beginning. Imagine a March on Washington, a hundred thousand people. A hundred thousand people demanding justice, equality! A. Philip Randolph, Adam Powell, all the Negro leadership is talking about it."

"I've met Reverend Powell," she boasted, finding herself eager to impress the brash interloper. He walked with perfect posture, perfectly comfortable with her being a shade taller. Fingers trailed behind them like a Sicilian grandmother, Snooks driving the car two miles an hour alongside. As the couple's walk proceeded, the protesters began to part. Word quickly spread that the car was on loan from the Jones brothers to a big shot from Harlem. Cinn spied a woman, one of the marchers, skitter up, then skitter away like a snow crab. After a few moments, her escort smiled. "I'm told I am in the presence of royalty. The ubiquitous grapevine has it that your father's a policy king."

"I beg your pardon?"

"I'm brutally honest. It's a flaw of mine."

"My uncle is a respected businessman, a respectable, legitimate businessman."

"I stand corrected. He's your uncle."

"What business is it of yours?" She started back toward the car. "I didn't come to Chicago to be insulted."

"Please don't get back in the car," he blurted. "You haven't told me why you are here. What brings you to our fair, unfair city?"

"... A short, a very short trip to Europe," she laughed. "A graduation present. Hunter College. I'm on my way to Juilliard. It's a—"

"Music academy. Juilliard! I'm impressed."

"You know it, then."

"I'm from Chicago, not Neptune," he joked. "What are you studying?"

"Uh ... music?" she said. "Please don't ask me to sing blues, or jazz. Please don't ask me why I won't sing spirituals."

"Well, what do you sing?"

"Ballads, art songs, lieder. I sing opera."

"When the world is at war?"

"Opera is the only art form capable of that scope of human drama."

His eyebrows perked. "Ever sing a union song?"

"Okay, that's it," Fingers interjected and grabbed Cinnamon by the arm. "Back in the car, missy." He was a stocky man with a muscular clawlike grip. Before she could speak, she found herself unceremoniously shoved into the back seat, the car door slamming angrily behind her, the locks bolting shut with an exclamation. Snooks leaned on the horn, pounded it until the protesters began again to disperse. Cinn put her hands up to the closed window as the young man ran alongside the car. "At least tell me your name," he said through the glass, "so I can tell people I met you when you're famous."

As the car sped away, Snooks looked at her through the rearview mirror. "Sorry about that, miss, but Deacon, he don't do unions."

* * *

BY THE time Cinnamon got back to New York, she had missed the first week of class. The pacing at Juilliard was fierce. Languages and diction classes, piano, music theory, lieder, intense choral work, even dancing the first year, and a bedeviling course entitled "The History of Singing"—all prerequisites before her beloved opera classes could commence. "Restate the rules—identify the composers and period pieces by ear—music history from Greek to Baroque—compare your notes again." Cramming for her first semester review, Cinnamon closed her eyes to commit melodies to memory. Gregorian chants danced around Beethoven, then stumbled. She jolted. "No, no, no tritones! Better go over the translations again." She attempted once more to synthesize the jumble of textbook highlights, sample questions, and class notes she had devoured the night before.

The Minor household was still crowded. Although Dr. Hadjo had moved on, and Adelle had taken over the walk-in closet space, Cinn still shared a room with Sissy and Memphis. The Lohans were moving soon to the new Abraham Lincoln Homes, but they were leaving Miss Tavineer.

The outside world kept intruding. She dreaded the daily subway ride to Manhattan. Ironically, the nearest stop to her exclusive school on Claremont Avenue was in the heart of Harlem. The rain seeping through her coat, men with their hands, she couldn't stand it. *Just because I'm Negro, they got cause to think I'm loose, there for the pickin', that they got cause to put their hands on me. Buddy, you better not even think about it.* Cinn bounded the steps to the train platform and paced the length of the walkway, her short breaths punctuating the brisk fall air. When she reached the opposite side, she would rake herself for her seeming incapacity to control her volatility. *Hop the train to Toogalou. Or roll on over to old St. Lou.*

When she actually got to Juilliard, she was stunned by the competition. Just like Hunter, practically everyone was on scholarship. All had been the local favorites, hand-picked by private vocal teachers; winner of the Texaco contest and the Wolfe Fellowship, recommended by Toscanini, sang for Shostakovich. *Ballet training, stagecraft.* Her well-heeled classmates were paying five hundred dollars' board while she was still taking buses and subways.

The Manhattan-bound train navigated the corner screaming like her insides. She had slept three hours, two and a half maybe, and now she was going to be late. *Of all days, German diction class.* "Ah, yes, our Aida." She could anticipate his mocking tone. It was no secret, her German language professor, Dr. Marintz, thought her ambition misguided. "Your physiognomy is not suited, your articulation sloppy." She sensed his Aryan irritation at her very existence. There were two other Negro students in the entire voice program, she the only brown-skinned one. A fourth youth disappeared after the first week. Marintz didn't want her to be there and let her know it. She was too ugly, too dark, and too tall. Duet work was impossible. No tenor wanted to sing with her. They all wanted a white partner. The cafeteria staff was smug. She bagged her lunch. It was her duty to endure.

Her full scholarship came at great cost to her psyche. She had to be excellent at everything. Under Madame Olivetsky's tutelage, she had become fluent in Italian, French, and German—all phonetically—then studied them in college. She had been performing since childhood and had entered her first opera competition at fifteen, yet she could feel it. *No one wants me here. Why did they admit me?* She loved the singing, but she loathed being judged. The experience roiled her every time. No matter how many medals, how many ribbons and certificates. *Always the same. The only Negro.*

She read through the assigned chorus part, talking to herself, "I need to keep working. I have to lose these pounds. Get down to size—brown dress, purple, green? Which will make me look smaller?" If she lost some weight, perhaps there would be less of her to cause irritation. Though she was well beyond her classmates in her grasp of Italian and French, Marintz seemed to think her African mouth incapable of clearly enunciating German. Before the whole class, he would stop and correct her at every turn of phrase. He would spend minutes suggesting how she should work her lips to attain the correct fineness of tone. Really he just wanted to possess them, to wallow in their succulence, but she just didn't get it—a pass for a pass. She didn't perceive herself as attractive. It never occurred to her that anyone else would. Nor would she allow that men of culture might confuse their authority with sexual privilege. Being a Negro opera aspirant at Juilliard and the daughter of "the apricot dipped in honey" were liabilities enough. Marintz's cutting remarks made her even more competitive.

The afternoon session with Madame Olivetsky did not go well either. The department had announced the spring student opera would be *Carmen*. All year, she had taken secondary assignments in the choir, the perpetual understudy in the yearly recital. *They know I could ace out Notrovny and Gordon and any other soprano in the department.* She was determined to land Carmen. *What excuse could they have? She's a gypsy for Christ's sake.*

Cinnamon hated to displease her mentor, to be reminded that she was a special case, yet again. "I said I was not taking any more students. Certainly, no colored. I'm not taking any new students, I say, but I will hear you and I marvel. Where does a voice like this come from at sixteen? I say . . . And where has it gone, enh, where is it today?" The old woman patted her brusquely on the arm. "Once more, please."

Cinnamon practiced her introduction, hands neatly folded one over the other, her spine snapped penny-bouncing straight. "Cinnamon Turner. Today I will sing a selection from Bizet's *Carmen*."

"Ah! J'étais vraiment trop bête!" *Ah! I was really too dumb! she sang.* "Je me mettais en quatre et je faisais des frais." *I put myself on all fours and I went to such pains.* "Oui, je faisais des frais, pour amuser monsieur!" *I went to such pains!* "Je chantais! Je dansais! Je crois, Dieu me pardonné," *I sang! I danced! I believe, may God pardon me, that a little more, and I would love him!* "Taratata! Taratata!" *That bugle!*

"Stop, stop!" The old woman interjected. "Baroque you can sing with all that precision, but Bizet you must feel! Carmen is a woman who refuses to give up her way of life for the man she loves. She risks her life to be free." Madame Olivetsky almost lost her balance. Cinnamon caught her by her thin, birdlike elbow as she jostled the music stand. Suddenly, her faithful teacher broke into tears. "I'm so sorry, my dear. My family in Prague, I have lost touch with them. Things are happening in Europe, frightening things. I am afraid I may never see them again." Cinn had not thought of Madame Olivetsky having a family. She was embarrassed by her self-absorption and her obliviousness to her mentor's growing concerns. Affairs in Europe she had tried not to think about. *What does she mean, never see them again?* Regaining her composure, Madame

Olivetsky patted Cinnamon on the arm. "My dear, you are technically proficient, but you are not letting through your spirit. You must release it to find your power. You cannot approach Carmen with technique alone. Bizet was passionate! Bizet wrote only one great opera, died at thirty-six. If you insist on singing Carmen, please do not sing it if you cannot find its soul."

The fortune-telling theme in *Carmen* made Adelle come into her mind. Adelle, sipping her tea in the corner windowsill, studying the leaves collecting in the bottom. She told the girls once that she could read the future. "Until I seen my own mother's death," she whispered in her ominous Jamaican lilt. Adelle had said to Cinn, "You tink you an artist?"

Cinn stopped by her uncle's barbershop. It was full of customers. She felt distance, never comfortable with the working-class language. "So I told the nigguh . . ." Deacon smiled with pride as she entered. "Gentlemen, this is my niece, Cinnamon Turner. She's a student at Juilliard." The audience grunted that they were impressed, if only by his intonation. "She is my brother's child—Osceola. Her mother's a big star in Europe."

Cinn blushed, disheartened by the reference. She had put the abysmal European trip and her encounter with Lizzie out of her mind. "I just stopped by to say hello."

"Come. Sit awhile." He put his arm around her and beckoned an assistant to take over for him.

She confided in him how she didn't feel like she belonged. "Anywhere! At school the white students are always yapping at me, whispering, wishing I weren't there. In the Bronx, I stood on the corner singing Madame Butterfly! People thought I was a lunatic. They called the police! At home, even at home, it's not my home."

Iolanthe proposed that Cinn take an apartment in one of the buildings she and Deacon owned. "That way you would be right down the street from us and one subway stop from the school. Our driver could drop you off. You could even walk."

Elma and Raymond wouldn't have it. "A young woman? Livin' alone? In Harlem?"

"Mama El, Uncle Deacon and Iolanthe are willing to sponsor me. It wouldn't cost you anything."

"How do you really know he is any relation but by his sayin'? Haven't you been happy here with us? No!"

"But Mama El, I really do need to be able to concentrate. Other girls at the academy have their own apartments." After much cajoling and pleading, with Cinn's sincere efforts to seem her most mature and confident, Elma folded one hand over the other and rocked on her heels. "We'll see."

* * *

SHE MOVED over the winter break. Elma and Raymond came along to inspect. Doorman, marble lobby, sleek, crisp art deco design. She left behind the scrapbook Sparrow had given her at her one and only birthday party. For a while Lizzie had sent back pictures. For a while Cinn had pasted them in the book along with random articles, notices, and water-stained postcards. She took only the few pages of Osceola's sheet music that she had collected on the sidewalk that cold birthday night. Left behind in the room she shared with Memphis and Sissy, the dusty leather-bound album now bulging with withered yellowed tongues.

* * *

CINN GOT home to her new apartment the second Saturday and found even more people than at the flat back in the Bronx.

"That'll be twenty-five cents please." The pert chocolate drop with the wide, smiling dough face handed her a flyer. PRESENTING, MISS MEMPHIS'S MID-DAY DELTA THROW-DOWN. "I said that'll be twenty-five—"

"Listen, sistuh," Cinn pronounced, "I live here." She found Negroes with rumcokes in parts of the apartment she didn't know existed, conversatin' in the bathtub, surveying the dumbwaiter, dipping into the pot of okra and rice Mama El had prepared and which Cinn had planned to ration for the weekend. In the center of it all, Memphis!

"Isn't it great?"

"Memphis, what's going on here? Miss Tavineer?!"

"Cinnamon, darling! Great partay! Woohoo!"

Memphis scrunched her shoulders and giggled as Miss Tavineer slunk by, her skinny flat hips swiveling in a paisley print dress. She waved coyly at the girls with two fingers, the others wrapped around a Dixie cup, and smiled through her glasses askew on her nose, a pair of false eyelashes applied upside down.

"I had to bring the old lady," Memphis confessed. "I was supposed to be watching her while Mom did her civil defense class. We were doing makeup lessons."

Cinn tugged up both sides of her brassiere, preparing to give Memphis a piece of her mind, just as a partier grabbed her and swung her around. "Don't worry. I take control. One two, one two," as if she couldn't count. She pulled herself away.

"Memphis, these people have got to go."

"Oh come on, Cinn, lighten up. They're just gonna crash till gig time."

"Memphis, have you lost your mind? I just got this apartment."

"Oh, nobody's going to do anything to you. You're everybody's angel. This is art! This is the, the, the hottest small combo in New York. Why shouldn't we have them in the house?"

"The band, Memphis? Or the whole club?"

"Isn't it hot? A genuine jam!" Memphis finished just as the trumpeter took his solo—Memphis's ear peaked as spirit awakened in him colors he could not touch—blues, church music, the beauty parlor, Porgy courtin' Bess in a call and response. He ended in a cadenza, then slid into a fast groove, "Ain't gon fool yuh/ Poppa gon school yuh." This fast-livin' crazy cat, cross-dressin' the music, raised the bar with a composition vamping off pre-existent melodies and such harmonic ingenuity, the notes just jumped off the page. Finding melody without, within, molecules of sound, the particles not mass, but energy. Visceral, cerebral head music, traveling up and down her spine like light. To Cinnamon Turner it sounded like radio static. "What is that *noise*?"

Memphis begged, "Come on, Cinn. It's a party!"

"At ten o'clock in the morning?"

"Cinn, we just got off work."

"What we? And what work? You're supposed to be finishing high school!"

"Why you have to harp on things? If you got an idea, you never let it go and never present it as if you understand it to be an opinion, that you might be wrong. I just don't need to hear your opinion today of what you think I should be doing with my life. Cinn, Cinn, Cinn, that's all they talk about. We expect great things," Memphis ranted. "Best thing I ever get is a 'That's nice, dear.' I'm gonna go out and shake my tail. 'That's nice, dear.' I'm cuttin' school. 'That's nice, dear.' I showed my drawers at the Savoy last night. 'That's nice, dear.' Everybody can't have a rich uncle or get a scholarship like you."

"I can't believe you. I worked hard to get where I am. You have a beautiful voice. You could get a scholarship if you wanted to."

"I don't want to hear all that. That's okay for you, but not for me. I just want to sing."

"Sometimes you sound so ignorant."

"Just cuz I don't like that white folk shit makes me ignorant?"

The last number of the set, the trumpet player slid in with a fast tempo, spare, liquid, melodic line, punctuated by irregular, dissonant chord changes, the linear melody metamorphosing into something rapid, precise, yet unpredictable, crisp, and intense. The trumpet soared, a cupped hand over the bell, pressing the structural limits of sound till the room was airborne.

Taratata . . . It was *Baker* . . .

As he leaned to put his mute away, his bandmate Preach teased from up front, "Buckwheat cakes with blueberries, like Grandma used to make for us, buttermilk oven-warm pound cake with a delicate, toasted French-made crush. Better watch out, Junior. That's a whole lotta woman there."

Cinn found Baker in her bedroom, looking over her father's charts with a cigarette in his hand. "Say, these look interesting," thinking, *Overlapping influences—club scene, Grandma's spirituals. Textural interplay of sounds. Modern composition.* He had changed his hair and grown a beard, a chiseled stripe on his chin.

"It's called a goatee."

"I know what it is," she said as she took the charts from him. "They're my father's. I've been using them for inspiration." She stiffened. "Baker, I don't know what my cousin told you, but you cannot stay here. You can't be here. I'm sorry."

She resisted her desire to fall into his arms while he stood there with all of his gentlemanly grace. "You need to relax," he said.

"Excuse me?"

"Your shoulders. You're trapping the sound. May I?" He turned her to face away from him, then began kneading her back muscles between her shoulders. "I learned this technique while I was in Hong Kong." She could feel the knots popping loose under the firm steady pressure of his fingers and thumb. His deep baritone voice with a slight gravel whispered in her ear, "Only thing I ever regret leavin' was you."

He worked up her neck to the base of her hairline, his touch so gently cradling her skull. "See, that's not so bad—touching."

"Yes, that's delightful." She turned, momentarily recovering her composure, and faced him, their noses almost touching, "But you still have to . . ."

Blouse, skirt, tie, shirt, pants, shoes flew away from them and they fell onto her bed, impatient with passion. Garter belt unsnapped, she caught his hand at her hip. She was no easy thing, this soprano. She was complicated. He liked that. They moved like music, a comic duet. Flirting, wrestling, arousing. What she lacked in experience, she made up for in ardor, a complete surrender until he got to the bra snap or the edge of her panties. Enraptured, her body vibrated, the sensation of him thrilled her all over. Even the simulation was rapture. Melody filled her, all the movements of a song. Even through her underwear, she found her first notion of sex totally captivating. *This is why they call it forbidden.* They fell back from each other. He had come in his shorts. Laughed. Not since high school. She was quiet, glistening, her eyes fixed on him, adoring. She played notes on his chest with her left hand, caressed his brow with the fingertips of her right. From the placement of her fingers he could hear the melody and chord changes. They rolled over each other dragging the bedclothes right onto the floor, laughing and loving, finally falling asleep. When they awoke, the apartment was quiet. They were alone, the two of them, in that room, just the two of them in the world. He kissed one breast, which she gingerly put back in her bra.

"I'll get it off eventually."

Their lips met again, entwined like a couple of clef notes.

* * *

LATER WHEN they emerged from her room, they discovered the party had pared down to Baker's small combo of friends. Reno on sax, Waxby the drummer, Inglewood on bass, and Preach on stride, a new set of musicians who were edgier, rough-cuts of his former swing band comrades. Preach rubbed the tips of his fingers together, flexed, sat forward, and sprinkled some dewy green grains of marijuana over fresh tobacco and rolled a new joint. In between hits they had been regaling Memphis with tales from the road. Baker and Cinn rejoined the set, with Cinn trailing in a wobbling two-step behind him. Miss Tavineer had long ago passed out on the couch. Not wanting to compromise her mood, Cinn scurried around the apartment opening the windows.

Preach observed the young couple and mused, "S'wonderful. S'marvelous. S'got to be volatile." Both looked stunned, Baker even more than Cinn. Nothing like that had ever happened to him. He had been with the bandstand girls, townies, and background singers before. He had seduced band leaders and record producers with his virtuosity, gangsters, pushers, and narco cops with fast talk. He had many a hallway roster of women, and here he had only kissed the girl and made out like a teenager. Sensing the change in status, the inner sanctum of the round table all rose when the black prince and his lady entered, but they weren't going to let the youngblood bask too long. Waxby was practicing paradiddles with his hands. "Hey, Baker," he said without breaking the rhythm of the slap and slide of his palms, "they talkin' bout you bad, man."

Inglewood continued his anecdote. "Youngblood comes to the club. Winter. Kansas City. Two degrees. Freezing like uh— We got uh old brokedown, beat-up bus. It's two degrees *inside* the club, and he come wantin' uh cuttin contest. Introduces himself as uh Baker Johnson Junior." Inglewood manipulated his voice to be a perfect parody of his friend's accentless Midwestern English. The elder band members laughed.

Preach stuck out his tongue and patted his toes with glee. "Ask him, ask him ain't, ain't he, ain't his real name uh Bubbuh or somethin' like that."

Baker wanted to respond with a clever, poetic remark. He wanted to control the situation, to impress her. This was *his* band. Junior or not, he was making a name for himself. "So he got up on the bandstand with all this flourish," Waxby picked up, "fingered the pedals, jerked his shoulders, Preach playin' a furious medley of notes, finding every change within the melody, flyin! And here come Baker up underneath, 'Beep, beep-deep.' No vibrato, no nothing, but three little notes with a mute. Little did we know, nigguh was inventin' a whole new style." The entire combo broke into spasms of laughter.

Baker smiled and continued rubbing down his horn. "S' cool, man. Cool. Less is more. I'm just gettin' started."

The paradox: As much as she irritated him, Cinn had shown him somethin', challenged him. Because of her focus and the clarity of her pursuit, he demanded of himself, "How true are you to what you hear? How true are you to what you've been called to do?" Talkin' through the mute, notes falling like dew onto petals, a flower by her ear, his solo came up beneath her. *What's the good of me all by myself?* Though they had collided over the music, their heartstrings were still perfectly attuned. They fit, the harmony so close it hurt. Snatches of melody, strange groaning harmonies, rhythms delicate as wings breaking toward a headwind.

They came to a truce on the music. He saw her between gigs, cramping her into his already heavy schedule, doubling his own drive. "Baby . . . What is happening is happening out here in the world, not in some class. We don't need anybody else's validation. We're the only original sound in America," he said. He took all of his old charts, threw them away, and started anew. He never wanted to sleep. Something was happening. "A leap in the music," he said. She heard it in Baker's voice, sensing the surge, the urgency. The Baker Johnson Quintet of trumpet, sax, piano, bass, and drums was a lean machine, playing the smaller clubs that dotted midtown Manhattan's 52nd Street. Mixed crowds. No trouble. No dancing. It was all about the sound. People come to listen to the music.

Cinn, for her part, surprised herself. *Taratata!* After her travails at school, she bore Baker a new respect for striking out on his own. Since discovering her father's charts, she had developed a new interest in music theory and composition. Haltingly she had even begun writing some original compositions of her own. Her first sonata . . . she couldn't wait to tell him. After class, she took the A train down to the Village, where he kept a little basement studio apartment. As she came up the subway stairs, she almost decided to turn back, then ran toward his block, singing, slipping like a schoolgirl on the wet cobblestones. The spring rain was banished, the sun was bright. Peering into his window, she shielded her eyes, squinting to adjust her view. Beyond the window's half-shade, Baker was embracing a woman on the bed. *Memphis.*

He ran after her and grabbed at her. She pushed him away and unleashed a fury, the volume knocking him back—in the middle of the street, passersby making way for her bleeding rage. Waves of pain and tumultuous tears ricocheted through her body. Baker became the jazz life—the bandstand girls, the disrespect, cigarette smoke scratching her eyes and throat, the leers, bandmates' hands slipping middle fingers down her palm, the women again, the secret society of drugs—the sound itself, its lack of boundaries, its insulated indifference to all but itself!

"You must think you're my woman!" he shouted back in assault and defense.

She ran until she couldn't hear him anymore—"Cinn, Cinn, I didn't mean . . ." and disappeared down the subway stairs.

A mask of tears, she rode around in that car for hours. *How stupid! How stupid could you be!* Regardless of who got on or off, she cried hysterical crazy chords. Mama El's caution, "Never let a man come between you and your sister," seized through her brain. "She's not my sister!" she shrieked, her voice reduced to rasps. "If it weren't for me, she wouldn't even exist! Argh! How could I be so stupid?!" She finally got off at 145th Street, headed blindly toward her empty apartment. She wound up sitting outside Deacon's mid-Harlem office.

✳ ✳ ✳

HE COULDN'T believe Cinn had caught them. She had been to his apartment all of twice. To top it off, Baker actually had been telling Memphis that there was no hope for them because he was in love with Cinn. Memphis was a kid, but she loved the pants off of him. He was just setting her straight, letting her down easy. Now Cinn never wanted to see him again, wouldn't return his calls. *Well to hell with her! Dames!* But he was missin' her already. Hoping to console himself with a little pick-up purchase between sets, he patrolled the alley behind the club. "Doc, that choo?"

A large square-shouldered man stepped from the shadows, accompanied by two associates. "Yeah, we makin' a house call," he said. "I knew a trumpet player once. Had uh accident. Broke all the fingers in his hand."

"Tsk, tsk," said a voice from behind, "imagine 'at."

"Is that supposed to scare me?" Baker quipped coolly, his knees buck-ling beneath him.

With lightning speed, a boulder struck his rib cage, pressed through his stomach, and rattled his spine, folding him in half. "I got a crystal ball to the future, and I don't see you in it."

Just then, Preach bounced through the narrow walkway, tiptoes scrap-ing the uneven brick, balancing a flattened brown bag and a new pork pie hat. "Oh, sideeze, excuse me please. Can I interest anyone in some Parn Bhaju?" He held the bag in the air and sniffed with delight.

"You are an occasional pop-the-cork junkie on his way to a slide," the menace whispered in Baker's ear. "Git your narruh black ass outta town. Tonight." The man straightened his coat, cracked his neck, then disap-peared. The trio of footsteps echoed down the alley.

Baker told Reno to get him a piece. "A piece of what?" the tenor laughed. "Don't need a piece, baby boy. That's Deacon Holstein's niece and heir?! You need to get you some exit capital. Just a chick. Get over it. Live to fight another day."

Baker left on the midnight Chicago Limited, bound for Kansas City and points west.

Cinn sat in her apartment for three days. "Snap out of it," she told herself. "Exams begin tomorrow. You've worked too hard for this recital review. Pull yourself together." She plunged her face in ice to reduce the mottling and swelling, dressed, and headed for the subway. The day was gray with a light drizzle, threatening to become rain. The sky rumbled ominously. She had forgotten both raincoat and umbrella. She bought a newspaper to shield her hair and froze upon reading the headline. "Ger-man Troops Advance, Holland Falls, Paris Orders Evacuation."

26

IN THE SPRING OF 1940, UNDER THE WEIGHT OF A MASSIVE
German invasion, the nation of France collapsed like a child's toy box.
The French army retreated in disorganized scampering bands and the
government fled the capital, leaving two million Parisians in its wake. In
less than a month, Nazi troops overran Paris. The newly installed rulers
wasted no time in dividing the country into a Gestapo-run northern sec-
tor with Paris as its center and a "Free France" southern zone overseen by
a puppet regime holed up in the former resort town of Vichy. With some
bread and cheese slung over his shoulder, Mitch managed to pedal a broken
bicycle to the southern border and slip across the Pyrenees to the Spanish
frontier. From there he made his way to Madrid to petition the American
consulate to get his family out and to sign up with the Free French army
in exile, which galvanized around the tall, implacably patrician General
Charles de Gaulle. With every crooked pump of the one pedal he had,
Mitch cursed his crazy wife Genya, who had resisted his pleas to leave for
a year. "France will never surrender!" she said. At least, they agreed on
one thing, to hide their two black Arab Jewish girls in a local Catholic
convent.

German street signs replaced the French. For the citizens of Paris who
remained, every imaginable commodity became scarce. No butter, no

milk, no sugar or petrol. Bicycles converted to taxis, one half a car chassis attached to the back. To feed the German homeland and support their war effort on multiple fronts, the Nazis commandeered French produce, manufactured goods, machinery, and labor and deflected them north. Yet Paris was spared the crushing assault experienced by Warsaw, the relentless bombing of London. Paris, it seemed, the Reich desired not to destroy, but to possess. Paris, the white slave, the comfort woman. Preaching Aryan purity and austerity at home, in Paris, the occupiers daily displayed their excess. Rare cheeses, fine wines, vintage champagne, prostitutes in silk stockings, cigarettes, and chocolate were plentiful for officers. The city was the furlough destination of choice for the troops. Meanwhile, ordinary Parisians were issued ration cards for bread, meat, and milk. Thinking her two girls safely hidden away in convent school, Genya turned her organizing efforts entirely toward the Resistance.

The Banana Club remained open. Lizzie survived through the patronage of an SS official who had admired her when her show played Berlin. Karl Von Arendt, a decorated officer in the omnipresent black-shirted Gestapo, had a secret love of jazz and a secret passion for Mayfield Turner's bronze flesh. Before the war, Von Arendt was a modernist and a well-connected socialite. During the war, he turned pragmatist and used his pedigree to secure the plum assignment of commandant to Montmartre. While the official Gestapo headquarters were on Avenue Foch off the magisterial Champs d'Elysées, Von Arendt's undocumented office was just off the scruffy Rue Pigalle, specifically the corner table by the bandstand. The general often used the club to entertain emissaries from the Italian consulate and to vet potential turncoats from Britain and other mangled nations. Most Parisian nightlife performers were banned from working. Mayfield Turner's little underground spot was just about the only place one could get a taste of the once infamous and now forbidden demimonde. It was the last place anyone would think a hotspot of the underground.

While Lizzie entertained her commandant, her girls, under the tutelage of Farid, gathered bits of information from the soldiers they picked up. In the attic, above Genya's old flat, the perpetual doctoral student pieced together the strands of idle conversation into intelligible information— troop movements, naval schemes, aerial strategies, supply schedules, prisoner records, travel patterns, odd habits and proclivities. Using her own urine as a cheap and accessible form of invisible ink, Genya would then transcribe the notes onto the back pages of sheet music. A little heat to the tune and the message could be relayed by radio or courier. Lizzie told Von Arendt that she had to keep her show fresh. She changed her musical numbers often, ensuring that as her musicians left for the night, they carried a steady flow of information to the Allied forces.

She suffered the silent watch of women and old men. Mothers gathered their children and crossed the street to avoid her. She met their stares without apology. She did what she had to do. She ventured out less and less. Her caramel complexion began to fade, even her freckles. Her hair had gotten used to the damp, cool climate of France. She wore it short. It curled around her face like young Octavian's. When she gazed in the mirror, she didn't look so colored anymore, but downright Mediterranean. *Who the hell are you?*

The spying arrangement had worked successfully for almost a year when Genya's daughter Bruria came running to Lizzie. Genya and Rachel had been arrested.

Lizzie sat outside the SS office. She hated enclosed spaces. She didn't know why Genya had been arrested or if her own position had been compromised. She had been waiting for two hours. Her anxiety was not eased by Von Arendt's arrival. When he came to her club, he most often appeared in civilian dress. He stood before her in his field gray uniform of the Schutzstaffel. His eyes darted about with concern, his posture the soldier and enemy. "Mayfield, you should go. You cannot get involved. These people are foreign nationals and they are Jews."

"Their grandfather was Jewish, their mother's Arab," she argued. "Their father's—"

"I can release the girl for now, but you should go south to the free zone. I have a place near Marseilles."

"But—wh—"

"Lizzie, the woman is dead. Your friend is dead."

Lizzie sat down, immobilized, unable to process the casualness of his comment. Von Arendt gripped her by the arm and pulled her close to him, his intonation unchanged. "It is not safe for you to remain in Paris. You I can protect. They are foreign nationals and they are Jews."

That night she took the girls through a basement passageway that Farid had used for years in his black market enterprise to a nearby house, out the skylight into a neighbor's balcony window, onto a back street, down to the sewers beneath the streets. The trio made their way to the outskirts of west Paris to La Ronde, the ancient ring of gypsy wagons, always poised to flee. "Gypsies . . . loyal to nothing but their freedom," she said. She found Farid among them. With conditions increasingly precarious for foreign nationals, the Romani were already planning to head south. Farid convinced them that Lizzie's papers from Von Arendt would help. The caravan became her company of players. Farid was silent on the death of his sister Genya. But for his ashen pallor and black arcs beneath his eyes, he exhibited no grief.

Movement between the occupied zone and the Free France zone to the south was highly restricted. There were three exceptions, German and Vichy officials and the circus. Waving papers from her commandant, with her money stuffed in her undergarments, the soles of her shoes, and the lining of her hat, Lizzie said that she was on her way to the Mediterranean to develop a new review with a circus theme, "Une carnivale pour élever l'esprit des gens!" Ferrying the girls in a false-bottom truck full of circus gear, she told the patrols that Cocteau had promised her a ballet with a circus theme. The gypsy caravan of old cars and covered wagons hopscotched through Vichy-controlled southern France. After a significant conversation, Lizzie convinced Farid that a slow passage would draw less attention. Making their way to the coast, the convoy stayed with miscellaneous friends of Lizzie's—holdouts, renegades, and leftovers from the Left Bank. Man Ray took her picture, Simone trimmed her hair, Trudy and Miss T. served the entourage cucumber sandwiches, Matisse begged her to don one of her feathered costumes for yet another speed painting. They sweltered in a hothouse, and shivered through the night hidden in a wine cellar. The meandering trip gave her time to reflect. She had lived by magic. By all rights, she should be dead by now, a few times over.

Paris to Lyon to Marseilles was the plan. From Marseilles, they were to cross the Mediterranean to Algiers and Free France. Belying the appearance of a pastoral bucolic countryside, there were signs of war everywhere. Deserted villages, empty farmsteads, crops left unattended. The caravan ran into three nuns, their habits a colorful pink. One of them whispered hysterically that, to protect a Jewish family they had been hiding, she had killed a soldier. Lizzie calmly decided that the group would have to join their party. Just outside Avignon, they came across two children on the side of the road, squatting in a rain puddle, drinking the filthy water. Lost children, abandoned, separated from their families, Lizzie couldn't resist. A third child, a toddler with dark, sparkling eyes, she scooped up herself. "The boat trip will be cold," she said, "best get them coats." Farid hit the roof when he saw this new brood. Lizzie insisted, "When the war is over, we will find their families. For now they come with us. The children can sit on our laps."

They were stopped again just outside of the town. Lizzie flashed her papers. The regional inspector, bedeviled by the local underground, bore no goodwill toward Von Arendt, whom he considered a decadent son of privilege lounging in Paris while he swatted at peasants in the French hinterlands. When Lizzie presented her papers, he insisted she demonstrate a preview of the show.

Lizzie May Turner had been putting on shows since she was six, but two hours to mount a circus? "Sorry, sistuhs," she told the nuns, "you got to lose the habit. Prepare to go to confession." She taught the children some simple acrobatics—cartwheel, backbend into a elephant walk. She stacked them by weight in squatting positions. "Okay, on the count of three, everybody stand up. Un, deux . . ." The toddler on the top began to cry. With no way to get him down, she volunteered Farid to catch him. With a little gypsy music, a side booth for fotune-telling, and three very angelic-looking shake dancers, Le Cirque Mayfield magically appeared. Lizzie topped the show with a comedic, German rendition of her old-time signature. "Say what? Strut, Miss Lizzie, strut! Sagst was? Gehe ab, Fraulein! Gehe ab!"

The inspector and his men were delighted. Kicking up his heels in imitation of her, the hard-nosed SS official begged Lizzie to return when the show was complete. Shortly after the entourage had set out on their way again, Farid threw down his hat. "You marry colored scarecrow, sleep with German SS, fool around with cuckoo photographer, what is wrong with me? You no like Arabs?"

Lizzie stared at her old friend in disbelief. His lips were tight, his brow protruded. His hands were on his hips and his chin jutted out. His tawny, aquiline face was red with rage. "How are we doing with the coats for the kids?" she said slowly.

"Kids are goats," he replied, turning on his heel. He got a few paces away and pivoted. "You never think why I do this for you? You never think of anyone but yourself."

* * *

DESPITE MASSIVE Nazi sweeps that rounded up thousands of French Jews and hundreds of gypsies, Lizzie's colorful caravan somehow meandered unmolested. When they reached the sea, the waves were the Aegean blue of her mother's eyes in summer, the sky tangerine. The old fisherman who agreed to transport them was a Haitian. As he prepared the boat he sang an ancient song to amuse the children.

> I had a girl in Puerto Prince,
> I loved her so and was convinced,
> She was the only girl for me,
> Then I first saw you . . .

The sweet merengue reminded Lizzie of Osceola laughing in the harbor breeze, his deep brown skin reflecting tints of ochre like her daughter. *Cinnamon.* Farid was right. *Pah, Dora, Ossie, then El . . . and Cinn.* People she wanted to draw near, she only managed to push away. *Fresh start. No past. No ties.* The skiff set sail. The boat slipped across the smooth Mediterranean waters toward the edge of the world.

They landed safely in Oran. The drone of flyers overhead pierced the morning fog. When the plane formations came into view, they bore the ensigns of the British Union Jack and La Croix de Lorraine of the Free French. Her escapades made the cover of the *Harlem Herald,* "Mayfield Turner Rescues Lost Children. Stages Concert for Allied Troops."

In short order, Lizzie rented a spot and opened a club in Algiers. She offered Farid a partnership—"Une petite boîte, just you, me, and piano, my friend." Imagining the lush fecund shores of Mah Bette's Sweet Tamarind, she christened the dry dusty sand trap Le Tam-Tam. "The only joint in the quarter with an unlimited supply of ice," she boasted and joked with the press, "Roosevelt and Churchill come here to chill." By then, Mitch had secured passage from Spain. She gave him his old job on piano so she was free to circulate. Both Bruria and Rachel volunteered as aides at the Allied field hospital. It is there that Bruria met a young Algerian doctor, who spoke of a further resistance, a North African alliance, forming in the mountains. Rachel hung around the club, often serving as hostess for American GIs on leave. They brought her chewing gum and tales of the U.S.

Mayfield Turner made a new recording of "Le Chanson Pleurante" and was frequently asked to sing it. The tune became a favorite on the mainland, often sung in cafés and dance halls, by peasants and shop girls, and a battle cry for fighters still holed up in the mountains, all yearning for elusive liberty. "Recherchons, n'importe comment longue pour cette chanson . . ." *We search, no matter how long, for that song . . .*

✳ ✳ ✳

CINN HAD the sanctity of her own apartment, a full scholarship at Juilliard, and her choir jobs. She wanted for nothing material. With Baker's departure she swore off any more romantic distractions. Memphis had also disappeared—out the fire escape with her suitcase. Cinn figured they were probably touring together. *So be it.* She awoke in the morning hearing children outside her window, a family going to school, the bustle of people going to work. How solitary she was, betrayed by her own ambition! She resisted the heartache with a near maniacal focus on her voice. For a full year she poured herself into her studies. For her final concert recital at Juilliard she prepared a grueling repertoire. She practiced relentlessly, choosing some of the most challenging selections in the classical canon. After hearing and seeing Miss Anderson, she had set an impossible standard for herself. Madame Olivetsky cautioned that, like a good wine, singers needed their time to mature, but Cinn was impatient to succeed and paralyzed at the thought of failure.

She told her family that the graduate performance recital only allowed a few guests. She wanted no big to-do. She didn't know how she would be received, and she wanted no witnesses in case the recital went badly. Seated in the back of the small unassuming recital hall, only Dora and Raymond, Madame Olivetsky, and Deacon. Iolanthe, who was invited, was absent. Cinn kept looking toward the door. She caught herself wondering if Baker might surprise her.

The roster of judges included her nemesis Marintz, van Giesen, Sachse on stage technique, Vaillant to test her French, the famed conductor Bruno Walter sitting in as a guest. Her graduation and future career depended on this performance. Small consolation they would inform her of their assessment and her status that day. She breathed deeply and steeled herself as if making ready for battle. She would play no colored divas. No Carmen, no Butterfly, no Aida, no Bess. No fickle fortune-teller, no suicidal concubine, no doomed Nubian slave, no stranded whore down on her luck. Today she would dazzle them with surprise or be a disaster. Beethoven's *Fidelio* provided the required German selection. In her private protest to Marintz's dismissive treatment, as Leonore she cursed her prison tyrant in a perfectly intonated venomous German. She chose Massenet's sacred *Rêve Infini* for her French melodie, imbuing the Virgin Mary's grief for her son with the passion of one abandoned. From Mozart's *Idomeneo* her Elettra descended into madness with perfectly modulated pitch. Bellini's impossible *Norma* was her eleventh-hour offering, convincing everyone that she was a Druid princess standing with her people against ruthless invaders. For her English art song she chose her own arrangement of a classic in the making, Duke Ellington's "Sophisticated Lady," her one bow to blackness and modernity, a gauntlet to Baker. *I can do this if I want to. I'm not afraid of you.*

Marintz came to her in tears. "This Hitler," he said, "we must stand up to him like your Leonore . . . You think that I was hard on you, Miss Turner. Only to make you your best, your best. We trust you will be entering the Opera School. Consider this an invitation."

Despite her ardent preparation, Cinnamon couldn't believe what she was hearing. She had succeeded, and on her own terms. The Opera School was Juilliard's pinnacle program, equivalent to a musical doctorate. Only ten percent of the graduate vocal class. In Juilliard's rarified environment, that translated into fourteen students, and she would be the first African American. Her aunt and uncle insisted on taking her out to celebrate. Begging off, Deacon kissed her on the cheek and apologized on behalf of Iolanthe, "Some stuff with the business."

"Surprise!" The family greeted her as she opened her apartment door.

"First in the family to go to college and now graduate school!" Elma beamed. "You didn't think we were goin' to let you get by with that little bit of to-do?" she teased and hugged her niece, "We're so proud of you, baby. A model for Memphis, I pray." Papa Ray chomping on his glory carried on, "Never let you through, build you up only to dash hopes. Going up to that school," he said, "we gave them a piece of our minds, we did!" Madame Olivetsky clasped hands of jubilation. "Finally, emotion!" Deacon looked on, curiously silent, yet always there. Iolanthe bustled about. "I'm so sorry I missed the recital, my dear," she quipped while refilling champagne glasses, "someone had to plan the party." Among them Sissy and Miss Tavineer, now a fixture with the family, Iolanthe's colleague, the social columnist from the *Amsterdam News,* Mrs. Dawson and some members of the Negro Opera Company, and Jesse, who drove up with their grandmother Eudora. "My first trip to New York! My grandbaby, a graduate from graduate school!" Her grandmother's business partner Yum Lee and her cousin Roswell had come along for the ride. Jesse alone was comforting. "A gift from God the way you sing. No one can take that from you." Cinn couldn't take their joy.

Dora didn't much like the idea of having to share her prize with someone she used to feed with scraps from her table. *Deacon Turner or whatever his name is now.* Cinn's father's people. Even if they were well placed in New York society, he was still wharf trash to her. Dora was dismayed that Cinn seemed more enamored of them than herself. She thought her granddaughter might return with her to Charleston, but clearly Cinn was on her way to new and bigger thrills, leaving Dora to her loneliness. The grandmother consoled herself that she still had Jesse. At least he was loyal.

Elma called Cinnamon to the phone. "Sweetheart, it's for you." The line was full of static. "I hear congratulations are in order. How's my girl doin'?" It was Lizzie. "Got the general to put me through. Callin' from Casablanca. Just like the movie—Hello?"

"The line went dead," Cinn said, holding the phone like a sleepwalker.

"Dog bite it," Elma fussed, taking the receiver back. "It took me two days to set up that call." She pounded on the drop hook and held the receiver to her ear. The phone rang again. "Thank, God! Hello, Lizzie, that you?... Well, who is it then?... Lawrence, Lawrence who?" her aunt continued.

"Mama El, let me have it." Cinnamon took the phone from her distraught aunt and spoke into the mouthpiece. "You have the wrong number."

"Tell him to get off the phone. Your mama's callin' long distance."

Cinn shooshed Elma off. "I don't know any Dr. Walker . . . Chicago?" She turned to her aunt, then back to the receiver. "How did you get my number?"

Elma fussed in her ear with that chicken rhythm she acquired when she got nervous, "Well who is that what does he want tell him to get off your mother's trying to call—long distance!"

Cinn hung up the phone in a daze. "It's a guy I met in Chicago last year, Mama El. He wants me to meet him."

"On a date?" Iolanthe peeked in between them. "A doctor?"

"Isn't he comin' to the house?"

"No time. I'm to meet him. Curtain's at seven thirty," Cinn replied, still perplexed.

"It's a date, Elma. Don't quibble," Iolanthe assured with a quick survey of the room. "If he's worth anything, we'll meet him later. Go, get dressed."

"At least let us know where you're goin'," Elma insisted.

"He's got tickets to . . . the opera."

* * *

STANDING BENEATH the marquee of New York's Alvin Theater, Cinnamon was wearing a pewter satin sheath that clung to her body, a stardust tiara, taupe gloves, gossamer shawl, and silver slippers. She was ecstatic, then worried, then panicked. He was late. She didn't know a thing about him, not even his full name. Just as she was about to bolt, he hobbled up on crutches, his left eye swollen like a plum. "Miss Turner!" he said with a huge smile. "The last time we met, I didn't get a chance to introduce myself. I'm Lawrence, Lawrence Walker."

"Cinn, call me Cinn. It's short for Cinnamon."

"Hmm," he said, as if tasting something delicious.

"How did you find me?" she asked.

"Social science research, University of Chicago Ph.D. I can find anything." He had lost nothing of the confidence or fire she remembered.

They had to excuse themselves over a whole row of people. "Got knocked out playing squash, imagine that," he joked to a snarling patron, bumping knees. He explained as they finally took their seats, "Ran into a little union-bustin' goon squad back home. They accepted the platform, but not without a little explanation of the fine print," he babbled. "I would have waited to let it heal a bit, but I couldn't wait to see you. These were the best seats I could get." He turned to her as if the rest of the room had simply vanished. "My God, you're beautiful." She flipped through the program to hide the blush. A Kurt Weill piece, another side of Gershwin. "*Lady in the Dark*," he said, looking at the tickets, "only thing I could get on short notice. It's opera, right?"

Cinnamon rolled her eyes. *My, he's nervous.* "Well, it's musical."

"I have to confess, the only other one I've seen is *Porgy and Bess*," he said. "I thought it was pretty good."

Porgy and Bess has as much to do with Charleston as I do. I know Cabbage Row, I've seen Goat Man. Why do we always have to be low-down, old-time, lowlife, no-count? We have nobility, we have class. Where's that story?

The lights went down. The overture began. Despite her reservations, Cinnamon found herself pulled in different directions, intrigued by this man, intrigued by the music's modern composition and characters, the concepts in the dream sequences. Danny Kaye's recitation of Russian composers, rattling off fifty in one minute, reminded her so much of herself cramming for exams she laughed out loud.

During intermission, Lawrence escorted her to the lobby, hobbling on the one crutch. "Excuse us, sorry about that, pardon us, please," he said with a smile to the irritated white patrons as they made their way back to their seats. The audience was not used to seeing Negroes among them, especially in the choice orchestra section. Lawrence spoke with a smile, disarming the frowning faces, "Good evening. Magnificent performance, don't you think?" Reading her dismay, he chuckled. "Have to use every opportunity to educate these white folk. We have as much right to be here as anybody. And you! You need to be up there—center stage!"

When the show concluded, they exited the theater. Lawrence balanced precariously on his crutches, bouncing on his foot. "May I offer you some dinner? A drink, perhaps?"

She shook her head. "The music was meal enough. Fills you up."

He leaned toward her with an impish whisper. "All right, I confess, I don't know a thing about opera, except you."

Walking down Broadway with no particular destination, they got quiet. Memories for her—52nd Street, where Baker used to play, the Cane Break, Mr. Jocelyn's, an apartment above a saloon and stairwell where she used to sit waiting.

He stopped and turned to Cinn again. "I went off and did this crazy thing," he said, laughing. "I enlisted . . . in the air force, can you believe that? I know it doesn't look it, but I'm supposed to report for duty in a week."

"Lawrence! I thought you were against the war. The protests."

"Protests to make the country more American, not less. Democract small *d*, remember? This war can change the whole policy toward Negroes, Cinn, change the whole world. I leave for training next week. It's only a matter of time before the country's at war. It occurred to me, I might not come back. I didn't want to risk the chance that I'd never see you again."

She had just met the man, yet just as fast as he had entered her life, he too was leaving.

* * *

PICTURE ROY, Waxby, Reno, and Inglewood, in their swing through East St. Louis, sittin' round a fire extinguisher on a curb outside the pawnshop waiting to get their instruments out of hock before the ten o'clock train pulled in. Maybe the music was hot, but the Baker Johnson Quintet was still ridin' rough and ready. The manager stiffed 'em on the gate and the band had to pawn their instruments to get a place to sleep and something to eat that night. Now they were just waitin' on the pawn-broker and on Preach, who was pulling an all-night poker game to get them square again. Just as Inglewood started up a scat Memphis Minor appeared from around the corner, switchin' barefoot in the street, her high heels slung over her shoulder. She eased her made-up lyrics onto Inglewood's improvised tune. "Sneakin' out the window for the very last time/ She was finished with a life that was nickel and dime/ She was lookin' for a high life that was pretty and fine/ She was lookin' for the high life, but she couldn't read the signs . . ." In her opinion, the Baker Johnson Quintet could use a singer. "Even if it is music you can't dance to." She saw Baker look up at her warily. "I'm just here to sing, brothuh. I come all this way, the least you can do is hear me out. I've been practicin'."

The band toured the Midwest to Cali, small club circuit. Sleeping in the back seat of a sedan or upright on the bus, cokin' through the long hauls, heroin to mellow out, drinkin' to balance and disinfect. With Baker Johnson on trumpet and Memphis Minor as his featured jazz singer, the combo blew city after city away, and swept their competitors into debris. A way never heard he played, a sound never heard, her melody following the chord changes, Waxby skating on cymbals and snare, Preach's piano polyrhythms strattling lead and percussion, Inglewood grounding the sound with an amplified bass, they spoke a new urbane language, stirring the guts and brain faster than the most complex jitterbug. Fingers snapped, heads bopped, feet pulsed, knees bounced, keeping time with the high hat, curls of smoke and clinks of highball glasses. People came to listen and danced in their minds.

The music had been great that night. They wanted it to go on forever. St. Paul, they were shooting up in the boiler room when the feds blew through. Everybody thought it was for the dope! Flushed it, tossed it, good stuff straight into the snow. While her bandmates scooted out the window, Memphis stuck hers in her bra and threw her hands in the air. "They went that way!" she shouted. Still looking the naïf, she pointed the police in the wrong direction.

Memphis had to run through a cornfield to catch em. "Draft notice? You've got to be kidding."

Memphis was good to him, but driving through the late-night fog, Baker still found himself thinking about Cinn and those broad Asiatic eyes, so fierce and unforgiving. He hated himself for bowing to Deacon's pressure. Maybe a military stint would do him good, toughen him up, give him a chance to get himself straight. He begged off in Kankakee and hopped a train. Joined an air force pick-up unit in Michigan and began training as a mechanic in the fall of '42.

* * *

LAWRENCE WAITED at the platform, uniform buffed, white gloves and aftershave. "I didn't know you were going to bring your whole battalion." Behind Cinnamon stood her grandma Dora, humming to herself, and beside her, Yum Lee with a basket of fried chicken, biscuits, homemade jam, and her grandson Jesse's favorite—*stewed cherries*. Dora poked out her ruffled chest and arched her back, steadying herself with both hands on her cane. Elma flanked her other side, as Papa Ray collected their bags. Cinn laughed and turned to Lawrence playfully, her hands clasped behind her. "My uncle insists I have a proper chaperone." Priscilla popped between them. "Cinnamon says you're a pilot. Can I go on an airplane?"

Dora poked her cane in the direction of a new uniform striding across campus, soldiers saluting him. "An officer! Praise Jesus!" she exclaimed and threw her arms open as her grandson Jesse approached.

"Nana, staying with you sho' paid off," Jesse beamed. "After seeing me leading a prayer meeting, the captain made me a chaplain. Imagine that." He leaned over, giving her a peck on the cheek.

"That's no way to greet your Nana," she said and hugged him fiercely. Dora drew back and patted her grandson's chest, speechless with pride.

Before his grandmother could settle herself, Jesse cupped her delicate wrists. "Nana, I should tell Mama, Memphis is here," he said. To his grandmother's look of consternation, he countered, "She seems good, Nana. Lead singer. Working with Mr. Sparrow. You remember him. I think she's happy, but better tell Mama. Got something else to tell you, too . . ."

The family piled into a taxi, Lawrence and Cinn in the jeep ahead with an enlisted man as their driver. Lawrence threw his arms out, framing the bare dusty fields. "So what do you think of our airstrip?"

"Way too many trees," Cinnamon teased.

Memphis arrived with a four-car cavalcade, DAKOTA SPARROW'S EBONY TALENT SHOWCASE emblazoned on the sides. The show had been hopscotching military bases in the South with a medley of comedy routines and variety acts for the Negro troops. Finding her stranded and heartbroken in L.A., Sparrow had bailed her out with a gig. She ran into Private Baker backstage. "Hey you."

"You know this sorry-ass suckuh?" Baker's drill sergeant barked.

"I see you ain't heard him play," Memphis smiled.

"The band is the only outfit where officers and enlisted meet on equal terms," Baker said wryly. "Tonight they need us mere mechanics."

"Arrogant roughneck, act like he know something bout music."

"Yeah, yeah."

"You got something to say, Private?"

"No sir." *Not yet. I'll speak through my horn.* About some things, Baker was still cool.

*   *   *

"WHAT? WITHOUT telling us? Without our meeting this girl?" Elma's eyes were round as saucers.

"Mama, it was the right thing to do," Jesse said flatly.

"Lord, don't tell me you got her pregnant?"

"I hope to, but no! I married her because I wanted this woman to be my wife," he said with the earnestness that he had always possessed. "Mama, this is Mabel. Mabel . . . this is my mama."

Mabel, a thin-framed young girl with a round face, dimpled smile, and button nose, pushed a lock of her simple pageboy cut behind her ear. She was clear-eyed, bright, and direct. Her grasp firm with faith, she shook her new mother-in-law's hand, then, slightly embarrassed, she pulled Jesse away. "You told me that you weren't going to be able to see your family and that's why we should marry. Two weeks later, here they all come. Jesse Minor, you wanna tell me about that? What's it gonna look like?"

"Mabel, May—May—Mabel. Stop, listen to me. I didn't know Cinnamon's uncle was going to pay for the trip. My family couldn't afford to get down here. Honey, I promise, that's the truth. Mabel Minor. You are my wife, that's all that matters."

She laughed as they clasped hands. "Yes, Reverend."

Cinnamon was the only brown-skinned date at the dinner dance. She spied Baker in the pit, Memphis leaning over the music stand, wigglin' her behind and singing alongside him. Salt gnashing old wound.

Sparrow checked out the cantina audience from the bandstand wings. "Hi ho, the gang's all here." His USO show was the headliner. The warm-up featured the officers' house band, the Rhythm Kings, vs. the King Pins, comprised of enlisted men. The only place they all could congregate was the bandstand. The friction was natural. For black men battling for equality so long, the inequality of rank was bound to rile some. Sparrow still had the eye. *Brothuh, brothuh, brothuh. Someone itchin' for a fight.*

Tuskegee was to be an experiment, the crown jewel of the military's efforts to offer black men an opportunity to fight as equals, but the atmosphere was tense. In Houston, Negro soldiers had been court-martialed and executed for a blow-up with local whites from the town. There were incidents in Jackson between Negro soldiers and MPs. Charlotte, Fort Huachuca in Arizona, Fort Dix in Jersey, all had seen trouble. In Chicago, a munitions loading dock blew up, killing seventy-nine colored dock workers. Harlem had exploded in a riot.

A skirmish broke out at the ticket booth and spread inside, tumbling toward the bandstand. An MP swung at Baker. He backed up toward the stage and threw up his arms to avoid the blow. Lawrence saw in a look that Cinnamon loved someone else.

* * *

COOPED UP in the jailhouse, Baker Johnson had a holy conversion. Out there something was happening, a new music takin' off, threatening to leave him behind, standin' on the ground. Bird, Dizzy, and Prez—pressin' past the boundaries of sound—squeezing notes outta nowhere. Mad scientists, huddled in their secret laboratories, surviving on a diet of salt peanuts. In their pork pie hats, long waistcoats, tapered trousers and berets, horn-rimmed glasses and snakeskin shoes, they seemed an alien species, speaking in a language all their own, generating an afrocentrifugal force reducing sound to smaller and smaller components, generating unstable, unheard-of radioactive elements till the notes were like pieces of string, powerful enough to pierce through black holes and emerge on the other side. Another Manhattan Project, cookin' up the recipe with a fusion of traditions and a fission of the rules, splitting apart the known sonar universe.

And there he was—in lockdown! *For what? Tryin' to prove some damn thing to some gal you ain't seen in a year!* Baker let loose a howl, wailin' to the record down the hall, he pursed his lips and conjured up his horn. The notes traveled on a trade wind. He imagined they could hear him in Tunisia and blew into the night.

> monk crunched over the piano keys,
> always with his hat on,

diz workin' up to light speed,
splittin' notes like they was atoms and electrons,
bird blastin' so fast and precise
he could flyyyyyyyyyy . . .
for miles and miles and miles and miles and miles . . .
from five a.m. at minton's to a carnegie hall convention,
in uh five—six—seven dimensions,
these black argonauts of sound,
discovered that space had elastic bounds,
long on talent, short on shellac,
these black magic radical cats,
disgorging their galactic scat
just couldn't be stopped,
once the formula unfurled,
they rattled the world,
with be-bop, be-bop be-bop!

"Shut up that noise!"

"That's the sound of the future, my man, *Straight, No Chaser!*"

"This isn't a bandstand break, buddy." They gave him thirty more days for insubordination.

Lawrence came to see him just before his unit shipped out. Baker was right about one thing. They needed their mechanics. "You gonna have trouble fixin' my plane?" Lawrence asked, sizing up his adversary.

"Having trouble flyin' it? . . . Sir?"

"Private."

"Yes sir."

"Get ready to ship out and get yourself shined up."

✳ ✳ ✳

MEMPHIS TOLD Jesse that she was going overseas with the USO. "It's a bad idea, sis," he said. "Niggas ain't seen a woman in five month and a shower in six. They don't treat those girls with any respect."

She didn't want to hear it. "I can take care of myself."

"Startin' when?"

"It's my patriotic duty."

"You just followin' that nigguh."

"You would say that. None of you ever supported me and what I wanted to do. I got talent."

"Here we go again."

"Cinn's not the only one can sing, you know. I might not have a voice like hers," she argued, "but I can take a colored song to your bones, and that's something she'll never do."

Elma didn't approach until they were all standing at the train platform. She was conflicted. Her son had become a man. Married. A preacher. Her daughter was troubled. *Both my daughters.*

"Hey Mah, what's cookin'?" Memphis smiled that devilish grin, still dimpled. "It's regular work, Mah. A job."

Elma couldn't stay mad at Memphis. *That child was a mess of trouble from the very beginning, but so full of life, so full of yearnin'.* Elma hugged her daughter, not wanting to let go. Memphis, so skittish, relished the moment before plunging back into the whirl. "You a mite skinny, Memphis Minor."

"Better for the camera, Mah. When I come back from the tour, I'm goin' to be in the movies."

Quiet Mabel, a preacher's daughter, surmised that the best and quickest way to become a true member of her husband's family was not through its very formidable women. She and Papa Ray made great friends, especially when she mentioned that her father had hoped to build a new brick church. The revelation gave her new father-in-law the entrée to speak of his great architectural achievement, the landmark Harlem church which did not bear his name on its cornerstone. Everyone else's eyes discreetly rolled up at the all too often recited lamentation. Mabel's fascination allowed Raymond a touch of that ambition he once had for himself.

Dora, in the interim, took the opportunity to pull Jesse aside. "May I borrow my grandson for a minute, m'am?" She had gone out to Sweet Tamarind and talked to Mah Bette. Her grave might have been in Charleston, but her spirit had never left the island. She asked Mah Bette to put the light round her grandson and protect him overseas. She scooped up some dust from the grounds of the old slave cemetery and put it in a pouch. She handed it to him now and patted his chest. "Now, you'll always come back. You carryin' a piece of your home with you." He promised not to open the cherries until he got overseas. He didn't have the heart to tell her that he wasn't really fond of cherries. He shared the jar with his bunkmates on the ship and was surprised at how fast the compote was devoured. Too late he discovered his Nana's secret ingredient, homemade brandy.

✳ ✳ ✳

CINN REALIZED that she had not been listening. Lost in thought, she had wasted fifteen minutes of a very expensive hour. "Think of a time when you were singing," the doctor counseled. "Go to that place when the music first captured you." A flurry of memories spun in her mind, the good and the bad colliding. Watching that turntable go round, she heard Mahalia, Dinah, Ella, Ethel. Singing everything. Her big voice. Summers at Nana's, solo in the children's choir. Elder Miss Mary, saying, Have you thought bout getting her some training? Shaking her head to the offer, wanting to so bad, but hearing the laughter, the gawkers. Papa Ray bringing home the radio. Mimicking everything from her grandfather's famous sow call to high C. Cousins, boarders, neighbors beggin', Shut up! Papa Ray shoutin' back, Let that girl sing. Leave her alone! Her first talent show, Jesse's delight, We won five dollars. Here's your cut, twenty-five cents. Big money for the big voice! The hawkers of Delancey Street, two subway stops to the other end of Manhattan. Good stuff, great stuff, cheap! The air smellin' of harbor and garlic and chestnuts and fish and sweat, old clothes and ambition. Elma sayin', You got a good eye for quality. The sound of fabric, sifting through a bin of odds and ends. "Sissieretta." Her aunt spoke reverently as she stared over Cinnamon's shoulder. "Your mother and I went to one of her concerts. You shoulda heard her voice, Cinn." Elma sighed. "Like Marian Anderson, beautiful, brown skinned, like you. Black Patti. The night Ray proposed. The last day we saw our pah." *Everything—Everything . . . How to remember a moment when it was everything?*

Disto—what? *Dystonia.* She noticed something was wrong. A scratch in her throat didn't heal, a tightness in her larynx felt like, sounded like . . . her voice was dying. *What did I do? Who do I tell!* The street was a flurry of people. Jumping up and down, shouting, yelling. But her world was completely silent. *What?*

"Victory! The war's over. We won!"

"Oh, Mama . . ." Broken. Ambition and hurt, love and disgust, longing and rage fracturing her song into a million discordant pieces, her dreams swept away in a pan of dust. Her voice was gone.

El took her by the hand and pulled her close, rocking her slowly. "We gon pray on this one. Pray with me, Cinn. The body may fail us, but the Holy Spirit never will."

Cinnamon sat straight-backed, defying the soft contours of the chair, fingers of her left hand laced round the right, trying to hold them both still, squeezing until she could feel the tendons bulging and sliding from the bones.

"Ridicullous!" Dora's voice popped into her head, followed by a typically pragmatic pronouncement. "So you can't sing. Do sumpin else." Simple as altering a pattern or letting out a seam. But it wasn't.

Private coaches in singing, acting, and languages, university and conservatory, first to crack the junior circuit. Better than the white girls. Invited into Opera Studies. She had trained hard, she had powered through with intensity, but now everything, everything, was gone. Perfect pitch? Now she couldn't even approximate. Over a period of a few weeks, her sonorous Verdian power began to diminish, then simply vanished. Approaching even the smallest crescendo, her larynx went into horrible spasms and she thought she might die, gasping for breath.

Iolanthe sent her to specialists in New York, Los Angeles, Chicago, but the small fortune in train fare and doctor fees left her without a diagnosis. *Nowhere.* They could find nothing physically wrong with her vocal folds. Following her aunt Elma's ardent faith, she then sought counsel at her church. The Reverend's warm hands were not consoling. *"Those whom I love, I chastise.* You should thank Him for the hardship, for it is a blessing. If things hadn't gotten worse, they wouldn't have brought you back to the Lord. Trust that He will deliver you." She had prayed, repented, and endured a year, a whole terrifying year as if she were preparing to be hanged.

Thirty seconds. The episodes only lasted thirty seconds. To a singer that was a lifetime. If she pressed on, attempting to force the note, she became a cipher of herself, her voice a whisper or vapor, escaping or stolen. The prospect of never singing again—she didn't know how to cope with that. *What am I to do? What am I supposed to do?* Panic made the condition worse. Sometimes she dared not speak for fear of the sound, a grating rasping hoary thing that she could not recognize as her own voice.

Medication—she had a paper bag full. Muscle relaxers, pain relievers, throat coaters, antidepressants, stimulants, and the "experimental" injections, to which Madame Olivetsky had strongly objected. "That stuff could go all through your body, you don't know where. You must heal organically." Needles in her ears. Crystals to her throat. "You have time. You have time," her aged mentor advised. "You are only in your twenties. Thirty-eight is young for an opera singer."

She was young, but no fool. Opportunities for Negro opera singers were beyond rare. Anne Brown took the revival of *Porgy and Bess* in '42. Then the Muriels, Smith and Rahn, stole the role she was meant to play, Carmen in Billy Rose's Broadway-bound production of *Carmen Jones*. Her blood boiled. *Dim light mezzos, think you can out-sing me? I'll meet you again in the next world!* It took two Carmens to withstand the passion she was born to play. On any good day, the timbre and color of her voice would have reduced all three of them to ash. But she had no good days. *Just when the door opens, can't speak to say I'm standin' here.* Singing had been her life. Now she had to sit by and watch others live it.

Frustrated with the pointless prodding and the questions that always seemed to come when a tongue depressor was halfway down her throat, she was driven to search on her own. She found her diagnosis at the 42nd Street library. Dystonia. *Dystonia, what makes your big head so hard?!* Laryngeal dystonia. No known origin. No known cure. Neurological disorder generally affected people of Ashkenazi Jewish descent. *Well, we can rule that out.* "Disease of the mind . . . a form of psychological hysteria." She resisted believing that this affliction was only in her mind. If that were so, why could she not will it away? Last stop, psychiatrist. *How bad can it be? I'm already sticking needles in my ears.* She hated reliving the trauma to her body and spirit, the ritual humiliation of recounting her disorder to yet another stranger. Remembering the first notice of shortness of breath, the creeping strangulation, withdrawing from competition, standing before judges she had impressed enough to make her the exception, a gaggle of pink-faced girls in pink ribbons, pressing their noses against the door pane to get a peek at the so-called colored prodigy. "From the Bronx, not even Harlem!" She sat perfectly poised, feeling still too proud. *God said, This is my beloved in whom I am most pleased. Not proud.*

Lawrence came to see her as soon as he got back. "I can't imagine losing something as precious as that, something that fills you with so much passion—except when I think of not having you in my life. I can't offer you a New York stage, and I might not have a job once the college gets my letter of protest about the housing situation, but I would very much like to marry you, Cinnamon Turner. I have a firm teaching offer in Chicago. They have some of the finest hospitals in the world. We can get them to see about your voice there, see if they can fix it, however long it takes. Will you marry me?"

She didn't want to answer him. She didn't want to hear herself. *However long.* "How long is that?"

Oh Lord . . . I wanna sing like the angels sing, Lord I must go, Oh Lord, give me eagle's wings, Lord I must go/ I wanna pray like the angels pray, Lord I must go/ Carry my soul to Judgment Day, Lord I must go/ I wanna shout like angels shout, Lord I must go/ Carry me off to your Great House, Lord I must go . . . "Look at that, Cinn, look at that! That's what I'm missin' . . . Charleston, Durham, Kittyhawk!/ Norfolk, Richmond, New Yawk!" That melody. Just a rush and it was gone. Runnin' to catch the steamer, jumpin' the rail cars in Philly, hidin' backstage at the Cane Break, flyin' over Harlem rooftops, then finally collapsing exhausted, dippin' ankles in a cool blue creek 'longside the long day, Lizzie massaging her fat toes. *"You ever hear the Winrow howl, call a sow clean over to another state? I'ma show you how it goes. My pappy taught it to me. He played the trumpet. But he dint play trumpet good as he could hollar. I'ma now teach it to you just like he taught it to me and his pap taught it to him. If ever you need me or if ever you get lost, you just call it like this."*

* * *

CINNAMON AND Lawrence were to marry in Jesse's new church in Alabama, not far from the old airbase. Mabel was pregnant. Several of

Lawrence's fellow airmen showed up. Deacon and Iolanthe arrived in a limo from New York. Cinnamon left Lizzie off her list. Elma and Dora had a big fuss about it. "Mama El, I appreciate your concern, but this is my decision. It's for the best."

"And how is that? Not to have your own mama to your wedding."

"This is my day, not Mayfield Turner's." She turned and brushed down Raymond's lapel and straightened his tie. "Uncle Deacon's only walking me to the first row. You're giving me away."

Dora tried one last time. "Your mother should be here."

Cinnamon embraced her and held her tight. "My mother *is* here."

Only Sparrow knew. Sparrow asked Deacon if he had told Cinnamon the truth about Lizzie. "Get outta my face," Deacon replied, knowing Sparrow hadn't the nerve. How to explain who he was then and who he had become? Her wedding day certainly wasn't the occasion. He would wait.

Memphis arrived just in time to help set up the party. She had married a second cornet in Sparrow's band named Calhoun. "Yeah, baby, I got to Paris. Baker's sittin' up in your mama's club with his arm around some Algerian chick," she reported. Even if it wasn't Baker, she damn straight was showing up with a husband. If she showed up with a husband, she figured all would be forgiven. She had followed her dream and she had lived it. She patted her round tight belly and danced up the wooden steps of the modest white-framed chapel. "Talk about, talk about, talk about it!"

* * *

AS CINNAMON dressed in Jesse and Mabel's small cottage, random thoughts danced in her head. Rain was threatening. How to fit a hundred twenty people at a garden party into a house. The wedding cake was decorated with sparklers. Would they work in the rain? Dora had made her dress. It was more baroque than she would have chosen herself, but in the delicacy of design and the care with which her grandmother had sewn each element in its place, she felt comfort. In the rustle of a veil, the song in the trees, the wind . . . she was content. *No more intrigue, settle down,* she thought. *College professor.* The backyard was festooned with lanterns.

Lawrence and his airmen buddies were corralled at the town's juke joint and café. Flush from the war, they joked easily about their future, primed to take their place in Negro Society. Bolstered by their performance in World War II—providing tactical air support and aerial combat, never lost a man—they were the fulcrum of the new elite. Access to higher education through the GI Bill insured the successful push for desegregation beyond military into everyday life. Not without a fight, but they were ready for it. Civil rights talk was constant among them.

"Had to sleep over with friends. No accommodations. This has got to stop. I'm sick of this crap."

"Passed a GI Bill for me to buy a house, but I can't get a mortgage and when I do, can't buy where I want to."

"Wiley got his teeth knocked out and nose broke for steppin' off the train in uniform. He's gon be late."

But they agreed. It was a joyous day. The last of the radicals was going traditional. Lawrence Walker was jumpin' the broom and gettin' hitched!

Preceded by Sissy, the maiden of honor, and escorted by her two fathers, Cinnamon Turner walked down the narrow aisle, past her friends and family, a radiantly pregnant Memphis, and her ever faithful Mama El, toward her husband to be. She squeezed Raymond's hand and joined Lawrence at the altar. This is what she wanted. This is what she wanted as her own. Her own family.

At the garden reception, the rain held back. Memphis was first to toast the newlyweds, "Never seen her happier!" Via Calhoun, she then produced her wedding present, "As advertised, an almost brand-new portable record player!" To the room's silence, she prompted Calhoun, who held up a little brown tweed box with a red bow hastily taped atop. Memphis glistened. It was her most precious possession. "So that the music may always dance between you."

Sissy got hold of the record player almost immediately. Sparrow just happened to have a box full of sample 78s in his car. While a few adults lingered in the living room with the classical pianist Cinn had found through the local college, the party was on the porch. With an extension cord slung through the window, Priscilla and company popping their arms to a new sound, making the very floorboards shake, rattle and roll.

Sparrow offered Memphis a job in L.A. "A new thing called teevee," he said. "They want to put me in some colored comedy show." Jesse, as usual, saved his announcement for last. Mabel's father's congregation had asked him to stay on and pastor their church.

The record player clicked on a new 78. Lawrence swept his new wife into a mean boogie-woogie, her veil flying around as she spun, the guests all laughing. Who knew they were such good dancers? Everyone was jamming as the stack of records dropped a new cut on the turntable. As soon as the needle hit the groove, the whole party was on its feet, jookin' to a hot blues stompin' electric guitar from Chicago, a new R&B label called Row House Records. "That's my song, that's my song!" Sissy squealed as the whole party erupted in a sing-along. "Tell yah what I'm gonna, what I'm gonna do/ It's somethin' my Papa taught me, and now I'm teachin' it to you/ When you're feelin lost, when you're down and blue/ Ain't nuthin' left at all/ Nuthin' you can do/But howl, howl the whole night long/ When you howl like that/ Baby I'll come runnin', Say I'll come runnin' along!"

Elma looked on the party with some dismay. *I don't trust our Memphis, shakin' her hips that way, belly all out. Calhoun seems a nice man, but still.*

Mabel offered, "Stay here and have the baby, then go on out there to L.A. Our little Joshua would love some company. A baby's no good for the road, Miss Memphis."

There they were, crowding her again, telling Memphis how to live her life, but, four hours later, her baby was born at the county hospital not five miles from her brother Jesse's place, so last-minute, the kid almost made her debut in the back seat of Calhoun's car. Memphis with her little Alelia, upstaged her cousin Cinn again—at her own wedding!

She and Calhoun didn't last long. Split up by the time they reached Los Angeles. After Sparrow's television show tanked, Memphis wound up running a boardinghouse for broke musicians. "Anyone with a hard luck story, a sad song, and cash."

Christened Alelia, the daughter answered also to Lia and Leelee, depending on whose house she was in. Rotating from Nana's to Grandma El to Uncle Jesse and Aunt Mabel, and then to Aunt Cinn and Lawrence, she became another migrant child, a visitor even at her mother's.

* * *

CINNAMON MOVED with Lawrence to Chicago, where he began his teaching position at his alma mater the University of Chicago, one of the few elite universities in the country allowing Negro faculty. She got pregnant almost immediately and had three children in rapid succession, much to Dora's dismay. "Can't you two do anything but make babies?" Cinn's second was hangin' low in the belly. Dora pronounced it a girl.

Deacon came to see her that spring. "Doctors say I got cancer in the blood," he said.

Cinn reached out to him and held his hand. "There are doctors at the university hospital, the finest doctors in the country."

"Too late for that. Didn't come here for that." He was impatient. The rackets had moved on. Younger men in the game. Harlem real estate had plummeted. Tax troubles. Iolanthe had bought a house in New Jersey. "I'm settin' my affairs in order," he said, "I'm leavin' what I have to you and the boys . . . I'm dyin', Cinn. But before I do, I must tell you somethin'. I have wronged your family. Run off the father, deceived and betrayed my brother, but the greatest wrong was to Lizzie. Broke her body, her heart, warped her spirit. I cannot undo that. I cannot give these things back to her, but maybe I could give her back her daughter.

"When I was a young man, I was a wild one, a roustabout—got so the police arrested me before the crime, sayin' 'I know you gonna do it.'" He chuckled softly and coughed, holding his hat in his hands. He lowered his head to shield the grimace of pain. "I was wild then. Didn't know." He waited for the words to sink in. Cinn did not stir. "We both loved Osceola. Competed. I came outta prison, took your mother by force. Your mother. Hurt her, hurt her bad. Most likely, you my daughter."

"Most likely?" She shrank from him.

"Please, please. Hear me out. I cannot rest while there is distance between you and Lizzie, distance that was caused by me. When she left, she wasn't runnin' from you, she was runnin' from me."

The words cleaved through her torso. "You tell me this now? Why now?"

"I cannot undo that night. Would not want to. You are my pride, Cinn Turner. I have done my best to do right by you."

✳ ✳ ✳

CINNAMON NEVER regained the full power of her voice. After Tokyo's birth, she stopped seeking treatments, stopped trying to discover the root of the dysfunction and techniques to overcome it. Standing at the cash register with a shopping cart filled with groceries, she would sometimes absentmindedly begin singing, a soft voice, concealing the cracks.

"What's that tune?" a customer would say.

"Excuse me?"

"The song you were singing just then. It was beautiful."

Her laugh was disparaging. "I didn't even realize."

"You have such a lovely voice!"

Cinnamon blushed. "Used to be."

She turned to teaching, encouraging singers to pace their growth. Her daughter Tokyo later credited this early training for her heralded vocal power and range, for the maturity of voice in one so young.

Cinnamon masked her memory of ambition with pride in her daughter. The interviewer's question caught her off guard. "Why *Tokyo?* . . . Why did I name my daughter Tokyo? Oh, I don't know," she said, gently tapping her fingertips on the table to some internal melody. "It was shortly before she was born. I don't know, I just had a whim. I used to play this game with my oldest son, all my children, really." Tokyo crossed her eyes and sighed with embarrassment that her mother was telling the story on national television. Cinn continued, "Teaching them the scale and geography with a tickling game. What's your favorite tickling spot, I would ask. For my oldest brother, it was Tokyo. 'St. Louis, Denver, San Francisco/ Hawaii, Manila, Tokyo,'" she crooned softly and giggled. "A spot right here on the left side made him laugh with such joy." She smiled, remembering. Snatches of memory, snapshots, a nibble of dialogue, pretty pictures, distant harmonies, and sunlight so warm . . . singing . . . somewhere she could hear someone singing.

27

IN 1959 AUTUMN CAME EARLY TO CHICAGO. THERE WAS A
nipping chill in the air as the Walker children waited for the special bus
picking up the Negro students assigned to a pilot program integrating a
new public school on the city's southwest side. The children were wearing
the thick wool sweaters Cinnamon had knit for them all summer long.
Abbott, Tokyo, and James felt the air on their faces and knew it was summer no longer, but thanks to their mother, they were warm as kittens by
the fireplace. Three nervous little brown bodies lifted themselves onto
the bus, jostling with other colored children playing hand games and
shouting greetings or riddles. They were riding with some enthusiasm
and some trepidation. They'd seen other cities in violent crisis because
"the niggahs" were coming.

As the meandering vehicle approached the school building, looming
very large, loud, and treacherous to their right, the three Walker siblings
crouched on the floor and covered their heads with their hands, trying to
block the sights before them. Bottles broke the windows, followed by
eggs, tomatoes, vile curses, and screams of "Niggahs, go back! Get back,
niggahs. No spooks round here! This is for white people. Go, get away
from here!" Irish, Italians, some Jews, and plain poor white trash were
furious that some eight- to thirteen-year-old colored children were where

their children were going to be. This was driving them crazy, making them rabid and terrifying the Walker children along with the other students, and even the newspaper, radio, and TV men.

It was an ominous fall morning, like a heroin haze kind of day, like a lazy Charlie Parker day, taut, delicate, and spiraling to God knows where. Trash dropped into the gutters was thrown at the lil mess of colored children. But the Walker family was prideful, and Abbott, the oldest, was tending to the safety of his siblings. He saw a darkened doorway and drew the weeping Tokyo and a pale James to him. Eventually the police came to carry the colored children back to their various neighborhoods. The Walker kids wandered through Hyde Park, the cloistered neighborhood near the University of Chicago where the father worked, with frozen eyes, walking as if Charlie Mingus held them all on his back with a strong unyielding spine that could straighten up and face any man. They'd seen burning crosses and KKK parades before, but this was different. It was their backs that carried the weight of the race and nobody had said a word. Abbott's eyes were steady and piercing. He would never again be spat upon by no white trash, ever again. He'd either die first or take down everybody around him. That he knew for sure. And he kept on walking toward home with his near-hysterical baby sister and the befuddled James, now running to the doorman of their building, the Sutherland.

They loaded onto the elevator, whispering among themselves. "What are we gonna tell Mommy and Daddy?" Tokyo whined. They had been so proud just this morning and here they were now, disheveled and soiled. How could they explain that the white grown-ups just didn't want them there? That any Negro youth found west of Halsted was imperiled? The first day of school—turned away at the door. They hadn't done anything. Just being colored and trying to learn. What could they possibly say? They were now the ones to be ashamed or beat with a cat-o'-nine-tails, that's how fearful they were of messing up their parents' dream.

When Cinnamon let them in she forgot all about the new Wagner album she was playing. She only heard Billie Holiday painfully crooning "Strange Fruit." When the trio told her what had happened, their voices falling and tumbling over each other's, she thought of one of the images she had seen as a child in her grandmother's book by Ida B. Wells, a black man dangling from a cursed tree with his tongue hanging from his mouth, body twisted and left unknown till the sun rose. She could still imagine the small group of coloreds letting him down with tight jaws and angry eyes. Now she must hold her children close to her bosom, for blind hate had pelted them into three centuries of pain and humiliation. She wanted to ask why, but she knew already. Jim Crow followed and mocked them, his jagged dance like their very own shadows. The KKK's burning crosses could not be seen, yet the fires were out of control.

Cinnamon gathered her brood, saying, "Sometimes, white folks just act like that. There's nothing we can do about it. I am simply determined that you all have a fine education. White folks may ruin your new clothes, even find pleasure in your pain, but you've got to learn to get used to them and the fact that sometimes they can't stand the sight, the very breath, of the colored folks, the Negroes, or any of us steppin' up to claim what is rightfully ours."

"But Mama," Tokyo whined from her special corner in the kitchen, "they were callin' us niggers," and she wept.

Abbott coldly echoed, "Somebody should go on ahead and throw rocks at their white trash kids."

Exasperated, Cinnamon held her head in trembling hands, undone by her own children's anguish and rage. Not being able to soothe them, she called Lawrence to quell this mess, to talk some sense to all of them. Hearing Abbott shouting to the walls all the wretched things he could do to torment white folks with his saxophone, she urged her husband to hurry, "I don't care if you've got a class. Come home now!"

As soon as Lawrence arrived Cinnamon rushed into his deep brown arms, grabbing on to him, as though he were an armored jeep at Little Rock. Lawrence held her close and let his fingers massage her head through her hair, rearranging the style every which way. He could feel her breathing slow as he rocked her in his arms. He wished his wife didn't shudder so at the weight of white folks, though he understood. "Cinnamon, it's gonna be all right. Sweetheart, believe me, we'll weather this."

At that very moment they could hear Tokyo screaming, "I'm never goin' back, never!"

And James was right behind her saying, "They ain't gonna hurt me no mo', no sirree!"

Abbott was laughing cynically, throwing a basketball against the kitchen wall, his face implacable. Entering the kitchen both Lawrence and Cinnamon caught this and held each other closer. They'd seen this look before. On the faces of Max Schmeling fans as the Brown Bomber was defeated, on the nightly news footage of Little Rock, in the press coverage of Emmett Till's mother walking passed her son's killers, alternately smiling and snarling at her. The hatred their son had just experienced he now wore on his own face. It was the look of hatred so deep there is no passion, like strangling a man and not breaking a sweat.

Cinnamon abruptly jerked her head up from Lawrence. She wanted an aria of solace to grace her ears, but all that she could hear was Marion Williams and Mahalia Jackson, their voices colliding, the rhythms out of control. With a rollin' stride and Hallelujah wig flyin' off, Lord take my burden, she jumped up and flew toward her son with fear and rage. "Abbott! Of all times to be playing ball! You know I don't allow ball playing in the house. Now is the time for you to be an example for your brother and sister, not act like some street hoodlum."

Feeling her husband's hands on her waist, Cinnamon calmed a bit. Abbott chuckled softly in a quiet disregard and threw the ball again. Lawrence caught it mid-air and slapped the hide hard with his palm. "When your mother speaks to you, young man, you mind what she says! You hear me?" Abbott didn't answer, but sat down hard on the kitchen stool, his legs sprawled out, his head buried under his arms.

Everybody was in such emotional disarray, Cinnamon could only think of food. Only something inaudible, undeniable, and known could bring sanity back to her family. She could almost smell her grandma's magical gumbo and all the other pots of the delicious stew brewed by Mayfield women way back to Ma Bette's Sweet Tamarind time. Cinnamon looked around at her children in various degrees of shock and announced, "Hey, I'm going to the store and pick us up some things for a great big ol' gumbo. How's that suit you?" Tokyo and James immediately smiled. Abbott rubbed his hand over his close-cropped hair and stared straight at his father like Frankie Lymon looking at his dealer before the buy, as angry as he was hungry. Simultaneously, his parents decided to ignore him.

"C'mon, Tokyo," Cinnamon coaxed, looking for an ally, "let's you and me run to the store 'fore it gets too late. Let's leave the men here to set things up, all right?" Tokyo jumped at the chance to go with her mother and away from the dense tension in the room. Without looking at anyone, Cinnamon bustled her only girl out of the apartment. When they boarded the crowded elevator, Tokyo wiggled her way to the back through her neighbors with their laundry and their dogs until she could go no further. Huddled in the corner, she wished she could simply vanish.

The grown-ups somberly nodded to Cinnamon. "Was a terrible thing those white folks did to those chirren today," said Mrs. Weathers. "Already on the news."

Mr. Hubert shook his head grimly. "Now, we are in the very gospel itself. White folks actin' like ravin' maniacs, goin ta hurt the chil'ren so. Jesus say, 'And now a child shall lead them.' Yes Lord, we gotta praise those lil chil'ren for standin' up to 'em."

Tokyo listened intently. She had thought that she and her brothers had embarrassed their parents, but now these adults were singing their praises. None of it made any sense. She sighed to herself and clutched her mother's hand.

At the co-op supermarket, Tokyo watched her mother wordlessly roam the produce section picking the best okra, tomatoes, onions, garlic, peppers, and celery, then sniffing at the spice jars of clove and filé powder. "Hmm. No tamarind, well, we'll have to make do." In the meat section, Tokyo broke the silence. "Mama, did you hear what those grown-ups were saying about us?"

Cinnamon kept rolling their cart and smiled. "I do believe they were praising you and your brothers. They think, just like I do, that you all were mighty courageous this morning."

As her mother pointed to the sausage preferred, Tokyo could almost taste her Grandma El's gumbo simmering in the pot, but at the sound of the butcher whacking at the row of short ribs, Tokyo reeled back on her heels and saw fear toddle round through the blood on the butcher's floor, the clap of the meat cleaver striking the bone reminding her of the tomatoes hitting the windows of her bus. Tokyo lifted her head finally, and followed her mother over to the seafood section. She watched curiously as Cinnamon hummed along with an Elvis Presley tune on the supermarket sound system. "Why are you singing with that poor white trash, Mama?"

Cinnamon tried to look irked, saying, "Tokyo, we don't talk about people like that. White people actin' ugly at your school doesn't make 'em all ugly, and trash is garbage, not people."

The child was not pleased with that response.

"Besides," Cinnamon softened, "it seems like Mr. Elvis Presley didn't hear much but Negro music when he was growing up. Sometimes I just hum with him to let him know whatever kind of 'King' he may be, his blue suede shoes can't just walk away without stuff. If he can sing our music, I suppose I gotta right to sing along with him."

Tokyo thought for a minute, figuring her mother made sense in an odd sort of way.

Once Cinnamon and Tokyo arrived home, the whole family pitched in to clean and chop what the two had bought for dinner, all layin' on their hands. Pretty soon, the meats and fishes, vegetables and seasonings all heated up together to make a savory magnolia and gardenia Southern night rise up out of Chicago. For generations, the Mayfield women could bring scents to soothe and nurture the same way they handled music. Like a vigorously blossoming orchid, fragile but fiercely alive, the gumbo pot bubbled and simmered, undulating colors of green, pink, bright red, and white in a thick russet-hued roux. Like a grandma rocking a child back and forth, the exotic aroma of Cinn's famous okra gumbo brought the whole family's temperament back to equanimity. With one bite everyone's mood lightened and their faces shone. Cinn and Lawrence glanced around the table. The varied chocolate and caramel tones that were their children brought proud and romantic smiles to their faces. Yes, it had been a turbulent day, but that's all it had been, a day.

The Walkers drifted into a Jackie Wilson, Billy Eckstine smooth defiance. Then Smokey Robinson for the kids. Cinnamon succumbed to their pleas, "No opera!" She, too, had had enough of Europe today. She settled on Count Basie in white tails and Duke Ellington's sensual orchestrations, his "Daybreak Express" leading the Walker children off to bed. With a new Art Blakey cut wailing from the front room, Lawrence closed the evening with one of his professorial overviews. "This, the music of our forebears, has survived everything, and because it exists, it tells us that we can survive anything. Jump back slavery! Jim Crow better lay low! Today we welcome the Walker children to the Movement. Be ready for school tomorrow," he hollered down the hallway after them, "the bus will be here at seven o'clock."

Lawrence saw his youngest son, James, still huddled by his bedroom door. James had his hands over his ears as if he couldn't hear the music or didn't want to, as if he would shut out not only the music but his father's words. Thinking how he might embolden the child's spirit for the next day, Lawrence walked quietly toward his son, but when he reached to touch James's shoulder, the boy ran away. Lawrence remembered very distinctly telling his children, "All of you are children in the battle for your race. No matter what those white folks try to do to you, you'll show them they can't stop us." He wondered what had not gotten through to James. "What's the matter, son?"

James stood still for a minute, then broke down in tears and finally sprawled on the floor screaming and kicking. "Daddy, I don't want to be colored anymore, never, never again! Daddy, I want to be white . . . I wanna be white!" he pleaded until exhausted.

Lawrence gently lifted his son off the hardwood floor and carried him to his bed. "So you want to be a little white boy, do you?"

James nodded his head an emphatic and tearful yes.

Tenderly Lawrence caressed his son, saying, "Hmm, that would mean I couldn't be your father anymore. And we would have to find you another mother, of course. Abbott and Tokyo wouldn't be your brother and sister anymore either."

James looked astonished. "We could all be white, Daddy. If we all turn white, then we wouldn't have to lose anybody."

Lawrence heard Gene Ammons vaguely in the background and told his son that he wasn't sure the rest of the family ever thought about being white.

"Daddy, I hadn't either, not until this morning. I swear, Daddy, it's the Lord's honest truth. But all those people cursing at us and all the time shouting 'Niggah this' and 'Niggah that.' Next thing you know there'll be shooting and lynching, Daddy."

Lawrence hugged his son, not really sure how to express himself, but he said soberly, "Do you honestly want to be like those people and scare and injure nice Negro children like you and your sister and brother?"

James shook his head.

"Do you want to hurt other little colored children, like you were hurt today?"

James shook his head no again.

"You know, I think you're one of the finest Negro boys I've ever known. And your mother and I love you so much just the way you are. For all that you are and because you are. Why, if you became white, you would be someone else and we would miss our little colored child for the rest of our lives." As Lawrence hummed an old Pearl Bailey blues, James fell asleep faster than Ella Fitzgerald scats.

✳ ✳ ✳

NEITHER THE tribulations of integration they faced that whole autumn, nor the freezing lake winds that followed, were allowed to hamper the Walkers' Christmas holidays. The children had wrapped fruitcakes and special letters for all their family down south. The apartment smelled of cloves and Jack Daniel's as Cinnamon cooked for their grown-up friends and Lawrence played bartender. The adults danced to Brook Benton and Johnny Mathis, sometimes Ruth Brown or Big Mama Thornton, depending on how high they got. Abbott, Toyko, and James made themselves comfortable way in the dark of the longest hallway, mimicking the grown-ups, making believe which instrument each would play on which song. Abbott always had a tenor horn in his hands, his fingers feverishly pouncing upon imaginary keys not unlike Dexter Gordon. Tokyo played at warbling notes like Dinah Washington and teasing the ivories like Hazel Scott. James fell languidly over his knees banging out drum beats as though Mongo Santamaría himself had settled in his body.

Eventually the adults turned to doo-wop and the sounds that enticed them to do the dances their children had vainly tried to teach them. "This is how you do the mashed potatuhs," Lawrence joked and proceeded to embarrass both his wife and children. From Lee Andrews and the Hearts to the Flamingos and the Olympics, the Walker home was, as they say, jumpin'. The children didn't miss a moment of their mother, the opera aficionado, flinging her lithe body the same way most colored women did. They fell over themselves laughing until they fell over themselves sleeping. Cinnamon and Lawrence began untangling their offspring from one another to put them to bed safely and then went to their own bed-room to finish that dance.

Savoring Eddie Jefferson's languid sensual vocals over Coleman Hawkins's husky sax, Lawrence began undressing with no particular haste. Cinnamon caught her husband in the midst of his crooning and giggled out loud while she bounced on their bed. Lawrence looked askance at his wife's taunting and flirting, her thinking to get him all hot and bothered. "Well, now you know how I feel when you're up here by the mirror being all of Tina Turner and then some."

"My sweet thing, if you want to be Bo Diddley, I most surely am your guitar."

As they lay across the bed, Cinnamon wrapped her arms round her husband, feeling his weight and warmth. She thanked the Lord again that he'd come home unscathed from the war, giving her a chance to discover how much she loved him. How precious his life was to her! When she lost her ability to sing, he had stood by her through the sorrow and anger. The emptiness had been filled with love and laughter and three rambunctious children. At the same time Lawrence hoped his wife understood that while he couldn't play a horn or a piano like most of her family, he had tried to surround her with creativity. Works by Negro artists: Richmond Barthé, Jacob Lawrence, Lois Maillou Jones, Charles White, and Elizabeth Catlett. Music from Cuba, Brazil, and India. He would read to her a sonnet from Shakespeare or in French from Senghor's "Poèmes Perdu." True, she had founded a Chicago branch of the Negro Opera Company, which performed at local society clubs, and she offered private instruction it seemed to any aspirant who knocked on her door, but she missed her own voice. He knew that. Still, to him, Cinnamon's music was never lost. It lingered in the way she walked and laughed and smelled, in how she loved. She was every woman Ellington ever composed for, every lady Prez ever serenaded, every girl Smokey ever crooned to. Even if he couldn't give her that one thing she craved, "Everything, you're my everything," he whispered in her ear. Fervently embracing, their bodies melted into a jazz-laced adagio.

✳ ✳ ✳

AS THEY grew older, the Walker children developed their own idiosyncratic musical obsessions. Tokyo belted out every blues and R&B song she could lay her hands on, from Bessie Smith to Aretha Franklin. Often, she would dip out of her Presbyterian Sunday school and sneak over to a Baptist storefront, where she could wail until her hair came loose. James, when he wasn't reading Baldwin or Yerby, caught himself dabbling with chords on the piano. Abbott was rarely seen; the young teen was now both the treasure and bane of old blues men come up from Mississippi, Arkansas, and Alabama, he and his high school cohorts challenging the older fellows with what they called the Chicago sound. In the big brassy, funky new sound, Abbott's screeching saxophone was a standout. "Bring it to me, youngblood!"

All was well with the Walker family, but Chicago's desegregation issues remained unresolved and there were rumblings all over the South. Lawrence and Cinnamon were constantly going to NAACP, CORE, and SCLC meetings and taking the family to rallies. They waited with hearts pounding for the next syllable from Martin Luther King's lips. The Negro people were preparing themselves for a struggle that Denmark Vesey and John Brown never dreamed possible. The adamant sounds of Coltrane beat against the wind. Max Roach and Abbey Lincoln set the pace for the determined steps of the colored marching anywhere they'd been swindled, lynched, tarred and feathered, or seen their house burnt to the ground. Archie Shepp propelled the songs of the freedom brigades with his wildly lyrical horn, his voice and words indefatigable. All this quivered and roamed the blood of the Walker family as they reflected Sunny Murray's skillful brushes and cymbals, leading the Negro people to James Weldon Johnson's roaring seas of "let earth and heaven ring." Liberty was a taste on the very tongues of the colored, their appetite for freedom unquenchable. "Ain't gonna let nobody turn me round, turn me round, turn me round/ Ain't gonna let nobody turn me round . . ." echoed at the all-white lunch counters and general stores, in polling booths and on campus steps, and through the televisions of the world. Couldn't a livin' soul escape what Alain Locke prophesied some forty years before. "The New Negro" had become a people suddenly turned Black with Power, embodied in the symbols of a clenched fist and the crouched stance of a panther. "We Insist!" they said.

* * *

IN THE summer of '62 Memphis's daughter Alelia was still living with her adoptive parents, her Uncle Jesse and Aunt Mabel, in Jefferson County on the outskirts of Birmingham, near Bessemer. Their little homestead beside the church was surrounded by forests so thick light found a hard time getting to the roots of plants and trees, tripping the feet and bodies of any remotely unfamiliar. Through this formidable foliage slaves escaped or didn't, were chased by raving dogs and their masters carrying white-fire torches and cursing the niggahs what dared for a new life. Amongst these memories and the dense near-jungle of unharnessed Alabama lived Jesse and his family.

Alelia sat at the kitchen table and begged her parents to let her join the sit-ins being mounted in North Carolina and Tennessee, or to enlist in the freedom rides that were spreading throughout the South. She wanted to be on the front lines of what people were calling the Movement like her brother Joshua. Jesse and Mabel's natural-born son, she argued, had already participated in several demonstrations. He had written them all from his school about efforts to desegregate a lunch counter and to integrate the public library—all as practice he said for a major voting rights campaign across the South. Jesse and Mabel were adamant that Alelia should not leave. Yes, she was nearly the same age as Joshua, but clearly he was more mature. His having graduated and gone off to college while she was still in high school was testament to that.

"Besides, Joshua is a man, and you are a young lady. It's too dangerous," Mabel scolded. "You don't know these white folks like I do." The whole congregation for weeks had been talking of the buses pulling up to stations engulfed in flames, the buses themselves reeking of smoke and fire, screams of the freedom riders rising above the crackle and harsh bursts of gasoline booming from the engines. Mabel simply forbade her to go.

Jesse, ever the preacher, tried persuasion. "Alelia, my child, the struggle elsewhere ain't no more urgent than right here. You got plenty of work to do right before your very own eyes. If you wanna do some organizin', you can help right at home, helpin' me to cover all the little black enclaves and farms 'tween here and Bessemer."

Mabel's mouth flew open in astonishment at her husband's suggestion. Alelia sighed with frustration. She didn't want to stay in some backwoods hamlet, working out of her father's church. She wanted to be part of somethin' new. She wanted to be with the college students at North Carolina A&T or Fisk or Orangeburg State, not chattin' up the congregation of Reverend Minor's Gethsemane Baptist. Jesse just patted her hand and chuckled, "Your mother will tell you, you'll be in as much danger as any soul ridin' some bus, or sittin' at a drugstore counter, waitin' for their eggs insteada ketchup and oil spillin' over their bodies. You don't need to look for no trouble in the South. It'll come find yuh. You young folk act like we ain't done no battlin' before. It's just your turn, that's all."

Mabel rose from the table in anger. "You mind what I say, the both of you! Bless my soul, what they riskin' is they very lives, jus' like you'd be doin' right here. You listenin' to me, Alelia?"

Jesse shrugged and bit his tongue. Some part of Mabel knew Jesse was right, but another part—well, she just shook her head and rubbed her hands together. Alelia squared her shoulders and stretched her long neck, a tacit sign that she accepted her father's vision that the struggle was anywhere the Negro was.

Alelia retreated to her attic bedroom, which she had converted into her studio, the prize centerpiece a portable record player her birth mother, Memphis, had left behind the day her Aunt Cinn got married, coincidentally the day she was born. Her favorite refuge was the voice of Odetta with its thick, fully rounded body and mournful or challenging words. Odetta, thought Alelia, was the epitome of a true Negro folk singer. That's what she wanted to be, a musical descendant of Marian Anderson, Mary Lou Williams, Nina Simone, and above all, Odetta—colored women whose voices were impenetrable and fearless. With song she could bring her folks toward her and get them to trust her. Then she would speak to them of voter registration, literacy, and the strength to stand up to white folk no matter what. She would talk to them of freedom, but first she would sing it. She didn't actually want to be a lone soul traipsing the backwoods of Alabama, and there would be no band of white and colored college students to help, but she would heed her call. The next day, she slung her guitar over her shoulder and got on her bicycle and pedaled down the dirt road toward the hamlet of Bessemer, the county seat. "Gather ye baskets where ye may," her father had said. Her confidence left no space for misgivings or self-pity. She too was a freedom fighter.

Sun-streaked and sodden with her own sweat, she arrived in Adger, population four hundred, near sundown. She crossed the railroad tracks to the colored part of town, a cluster of tin-roofed shacks and a one-pump filling station. Being sure to address everyone as m'am and sir with a smile like she belonged there, she asked for a Mr. Goodenough, whom her father had said was her contact. Folks had just started to gather on their porches after a hard day's work. They hummed songs of the gospel, seeding the way for Christ, a chorus of mostly womenfolk singing their way to heaven. Having grown up in the church, Alelia naturally joined them. Nods of heads and glasses of sugar water assured her that she was welcome. Suddenly a rich baritone filled in the bottom harmony, then launched into a solo. This, it turned out, was Mr. Goodenough, whose presence emboldened the women's voices. At the end of the praise song, Mr. Goodenough said to Alelia, "You must be Reverend Jesse's daughter. We've been waiting for you. Isn't that right?"

A group of women uttered in unison, "That's right, yes, Mr. Goodenough."

Mrs. Wilder inquired, "Ain't this the chile come to help us to learn to vote and such?"

Goodenough rubbed his shaven chin, already showing a late-in-the-day stubble speckled with white. "Yes, she's the very one."

The women nodded their heads in approval. Some had their slippers on, others their support hose, rolled up to their knees. All together Alelia figured these women were fierce churchgoers, the caretakers of children and culture, as much as they were tillers of the soil, tenders of their flock. What she wanted to ask of them was to change their whole way of living, to banish the fear and end being complicit in their own exploitation. Dignity was too scarce and life too precious for a people not to know it freely lived.

What she said was, "Good evening, everyone. My name is Alelia Minor, and I've my guitar, too." Silence followed. She scrambled to recover. "You all know my father, Reverend Minor." She heard a whispered "Amen" and "Ain't she speaking the truth," and continued, "Actually I have a mission to carry out down here. I've come to register all of you. For the vote." Silence. "Not just us womenfolk, but husbands and gentlemen callers, too."

A slight rumble of laughter went through the crowd. "Lissen at that, 'Womenfolk.' She ain't nothing but a gal."

"I've come to change how we been treated all this time."

Miz Butler's eyes rolled and then focused on Alelia. "Damn you, gal, Lord forgive me. Damn you, gal." Her heavy body lumbered quickly down the wooden porch steps as she mumbled to herself, flinging her arms as if to cast the girl's spirit far from her, "Come to get us kilt is what you done come heah for, to bring those Communists down on us 'long with the Klan and plain ol' angry white folk."

Alelia rubbed her chin out of nervousness and answered her critic quickly before anyone truly heard what Miz Butler was saying. "I hear tell that during Reconstruction colored folks voted fine as a summer day. Had plenty of colored representatives—congressmen, even senators."

"A hunnerd years ago!" someone exclaimed, not knowin' it to be the truth.

"I'm just here to insure that we get represented again. Today."

The women shared puzzled looks as well as frightened gazes. "But lissen, gal, now we got to own land as well as know how to write in order to vote and cain't everybody do that. Then when you get up there, they test you on the Constitution. Say it's the law."

Alelia strummed her guitar casually, trying to put the group at ease. "Well, that's sorta what I'm here for, to help you to prove those old tests unconstitutional. See, I'm here representing the real law. How you've been livin' is lawless."

An audible gasp went through the gathering. Seeing the unintended response of these churchgoers, Alelia corrected herself, "What I mean is how you been forced to live is lawless." Thinking it was time to engender a little of that trust her father had talked about, Alelia pulled her guitar close to her and began to strum. "I've come all the way almost from the county line, and I brought this guitar, too, so I could sing with you like the Christian soldiers that we are. We're workin' against Satan, yes we are. Those who have us slave all day with little if anything to show for it, those who keep our children in the fields three quarters of the year so they can never better themselves, those who keep you from voting and from having say in how your town is run, those who tell you that you are less than, lower than any other human being that walks this land—they are his followers and it is our duty as Christians to stand up to them, powerful with God's love and fearless in his Glory!"

Alelia heard a whispered "Amen" and "Ain't she speakin' the truth now." And the whispers turned to claps and shouts of affirmation. "Well, she sure is the Reverend's daughter, that's a fact," said Mr. Goodenough.

Miz Butler let loose a sigh and a grumble, while eyeing her latest handiwork hanging on the clothesline and over the fence. "White folks come round hyeah lookin' for my quilts, missy. Is all this you plannin' on doin' gon' mess that up? What you 'spect a vote gon' do?"

"Well, it'll give you a say, and with that, you can make your lives better and you won't be fearful. I'm talkin' about a new world, where people walk together in peace and equality."

Miz MacGraty and Miz Pearl rolled their eyes at each other and laughed. Alelia was startled when Miz MacGraty said, "Chile, that there, what you talkin' bout, awreadly exists. It's callt Heaven, the Rapture, or the Ecstasy." Now all the ladies were chuckling at the neophyte organizer. Alelia did blush some, her cheeks matching the rose panels Miz Butler had begun to work on. Not knowing what else to do, Alelia decided to play her guitar gently and softly at first, then more vigorously. Even if she couldn't get these women to believe her this minute, she sure would get them to remember her.

Mr. Goodenough asked who would house this young woman come all the way from the Gethsemane. Miss Halihan, a withering lanky woman, claimed her. "What do folks call you again, chile?"

Alelia looked around so that she might address the group of women all at once, including every single soul. "I'm callt Alelia, that's my given name." At the look of raised eyebrows, she quickly added, "But please feel free to call me Lia."

"Well, we might as well get to know you, Miss Lia. Folk don' usually bide much time here. Don't rightly think a bicycle gon make it to Bessemer."

* * *

REVEREND JESSE'S household was like the Atlanta train station. Folks coming and going with signs or paintbrushes. Mabel was loudly coordinating the chaos while, with his inkstand perched on his knees, Jesse sequestered himself in the bathroom to finish his sermon for the march the next day. Emboldened by the progress made by civil rights groups across the South, Bessemer had become a new focal point in preparation for a full campaign in Birmingham, the county seat. A planned march had been in the works for weeks. Jesse had to find a way to capture the community's excitement in his sermon. It wouldn't be his congregation's first march, but Jesse hoped that, with the newcomers from Talladega and Montgomery, it would be their largest. *Ordinary people are about to make history. Pedaling down those dusty roads, Alelia turned into quite a freedom rider on her own, even without Joshua.* He dipped his pen in the inkwell again, and laughed to himself as he corrected a line. His adopted daughter thought him so old-fashioned, still writing his sermons by hand with a fountain pen. *And Joshua!* His son, who had brought some classmates home to participate in the march, had taken to not speaking. "As a symbol for the voiceless," Joshua wrote on a sheet of blue-lined school paper.

Jesse shook his head at his children's impatience. *Their ideas.* Just then his quill broke and an ink blot spilled on the page in a jagged splatter, staining his hands and shirt. He sobered. *Blood will fall this morrow.* He shook his head to block the images, rejecting the sign, and tried to pull hope from his soul. Suddenly, a commotion startled him—Mabel banging on the door and behind her a tumultuous clatter.

The Walker family had arrived from Chicago, singing a Supremes song. "Baby, baby, I hear a symphony . . ." Mabel banged on the door again. "Reverend, get on off the throne and come on out here! Joshua and Alelia, come on and help with their luggage. Lord have mercy, they done brought a trailer!"

The Walker teenagers tumbled out of the car, stunned by the rich density of the thick forests and a real stream, the water so clear, they could see the fish in it. The trio had begged their parents to take them south, but now they felt some doubt. This really was the country. Strumming her acoustic guitar and singing a Joni Mitchell tune, Alelia strolled onto the porch. Her cousins were astounded, for she had cut off all of her beautiful hair and had let it grow into a bush as wild as the forest around her.

Alelia stared at her cousins and listened to the casual banter with their mom and dad, their parents encouraging them, fussing with them. *A whole family.* She was surprised she felt envy. It wasn't that she didn't love Jesse, Mabel, and Joshua, but her real mother, Memphis, whether living in L.A. or singing in Europe, had refused to take her, ever. Every once in a while, some token or souvenir from Budapest or Oslo, that was the extent of the relationship. Or worse, an autographed glossy publicity photo. "Just like your great-aunt Liz," Cinnamon once told her. "Memphis always did want to follow in her footsteps."

Cinnamon took one look at Lia's hair and silently went inside to console her sister-in-law and see if she could be of some help in the kitchen. Lawrence succeeded in unlatching the trailer from the back of the family Buick. He opened the trunk and started unloading the luggage just as Jesse stepped onto the porch. "Jesse, got a rip-roaring sermon ready for tomorrow?"

Still wiping the ink from his fingers, Jesse smiled slightly, nodding his head. "If it's the Lord's will, I surely do."

"Welcome to the Walker Family Band!" A mere station wagon wasn't enough for the Walkers. They needed a U-Haul to accommodate the children's musical passion. While their father and uncle struggled with the bags, the Walker teens unpacked only their instruments and abandoned the adults immediately for Lia's attic. As soon as the hatch was down, Abbott picked up his saxophone, Tokyo set up her electric keyboard and amplifier, and James assembled his drum kit and cymbals. In no time, they were ready to hit it.

Now, while his parishoners weren't dyed-in-the-wool holy rollers, Jesse thought for a moment, listening to the din above his head, that the Walker children's musical talents might be just what his congregation needed to rouse them for the very serious and dangerous march ahead. After supper, he called the young people to him and asked them if they knew "We Shall Overcome." With their urban antennae piqued, the Walker youth quieted. Somebody inside the house started singing until everyone joined in, even the Walkers who really didn't believe in "some day."

Alelia found her relatives fascinating. With her hair in two bushy pigtails, and dressed in a pantaloon sunsuit, Tokyo was a jabberwocky in constant motion. Yet her childish antics belied the powerful trajectory and command of her voice. Abbott in his stovepipe polyester pants and stocking-cap pressed hair was too cool for everyone, except during his awkward attempts to coordinate the group's choreography. And James, the different drummer, sometimes would just close his eyes and rock his head to a rhythm that was totally his own. They talked constantly about music, but not the music Alelia loved, the torrent of protest songs from Max Roach and Abbey Lincoln on *Freedom Now*. She preferred John Coltrane's *Love Supreme* to the Supremes. She looked askance at all of Tokyo's electronic accoutrements. For Alelia the guitar itself was enough, surely. Tokyo couldn't understand how she could survive without an amp. "Acoustic? That's like the Middle Ages!" Still Alelia gravitated toward her younger cousins. Joshua had come home for the march, but spent his time with the classmates he had brought with him. When she tried to tell them of the organizing she had done throughout the county, his friends patronized her or ignored her. Her brother was different, introspective, removed. She took his vow of silence as a personal affront. *At least you could talk to me.*

With a nod from Mabel, Alelia led each of the Minor children to their sleeping spaces. There were bodies everywhere. Fortunately, the Walkers were flexible. It wasn't like anything the children had ever seen—all these strangers and strange-looking folks coming to support their uncle Jesse and his march against segregation. "Even white people!" James exclaimed. The Walkers, coming from one of the most segregated cities in the country, were taken aback.

Abbott mumbled, "We gotta get the hell outta heah."

"Naw, Abbott, these folks came to help us," Tokyo responded as they all settled down in their makeshift beds, Miz Patrick and Miz Butler's downy quilts on loan.

Early the next morning Mabel rang the triangular bell on the porch to alert her houseful of guests that breakfast was ready. Alelia came by each visiting soul in the midst of some kind of sleep to tell them that it was time.

Lawrence complimented Mabel on her organization skills. "Breakfast for twenty people, and the hotcakes are still hot!" Everybody got grits, eggs, biscuit, sausage, and preserves, to boot. "So this is Southern hospitality!"

Cinn took a moment aside with Jesse. "I'm so proud of you," she said. "All that you've done."

"If I didn't have you to push me at first, I wouldn't have got this far," he mused and looked at his little church now teeming with folks, the scattered groups about the grounds—all waiting on his word. He put his arm around his cousin, who was more than a sister. "You were the first one to get me to say anything. Now cain't shut me up."

Abbott, Tokyo, and James all wanted to participate actively in the march. Young James had the idea that they should bring the instruments they could carry and accompany the march with music. Abbott suggested that they could play rhythmically to keep the march full of spirit. Tokyo asked Alelia if she'd join them. Alelia hesitated at first, but finally she softened at the joy and openness she felt in Tokyo's entreaties. All four of the young folk approached Jesse, who guffawed, then chuckled slowly and said, "I was thinkin' you might wanna perform some at the church rally aftuh. But children, I don't know if you should be carryin' anythin' but the signs to the march. Those instruments look expensive. Lord knows we don't want 'em to get wet. They might turn the water hoses on us. And I'm sure the dogs might like to get a nice bite outta that drum hide."

No one had seen much of Joshua, Jesse and Mabel's son. It turned out he was painting placards, END SEGREGATION. FREEDOM NOW! 1861–1961, A HUNDRED YEARS IN LONG ENOUGH. While the signs were drying around him, the sounds of Ray Charles, Nina Simone, and Charles Mingus danced in his head. When Joshua overheard the children's entreaty to his father, he grabbed for James's big bass drum and began to mark a rhythm. James took the cue instantly and began a counterpoint on the snare. Not to be left out, Abbott swiped Aunt Mabel's triangle and added a treble part. Joshua nodded, and the three boys marched off to gather the student marchers who were milling about the Reverend's home. "Amen, Amen, and the child shall lead them," Jesse said as he looked upon his son, and when Jesse saw Joshua and his nephews were in place, he motioned that the march should begin.

Alelia watched as the men gathered to lead a march that she had largely helped to organize. *Will you look at this? I've been relegated to just someone in the crowd.* She felt Tokyo take her hand. "Come on, Lia. Don't pay them any mind. I like your hair." Led by Tokyo, Alelia jockeyed through the group to be with her family up front.

Over the rhythm of the drumbeats, Jesse bellowed, "Do not err, my beloved brethren. 'Wherefore, my beloved brethren, let every man be swift to hear, slow to speak, slow to wrath.' James chapter one, verse nineteen. Do you understand what the Lord is saying to us?"

The crowd of about seventy folks responded, "Yes, Lord!" "Amen!" "Hallelujah!" "Preach, brother!"

Jesse continued, "We're gointa march to Bessemer Town Hall. We march in peace to let the world know we want to vote, we want to sit anywhere we please on the bus and the trains, we want to eat in decent restaurants and to walk in the front door of every public place. We want what every other American citizen wants. No more, no less! Just equal to the rest!"

From the moving crowd came voices muttering, "Yes!" "Speak on it!" "Tell the truth!" Voices picked up Jesse's closing couplet, and turned it into a chant, "No more, no less! Just equal to the rest!" Their steps were rallied by the percussive rhythms provided by Joshua, James, and Abbott as Jesse went on with his sermon, "But brethren let me remind you, we come in peace, we are not a rageful folk. 'For the wrath of man worketh not the righteousness of God. Chapter one, verse twenty. We want our rights, and neither the heat of the sun nor the might of the sheriff will turn us away from our goals. In the face of fear, we have faith. In the face of power, we have truth. In darkness, we have the light. Wrong-doers, we got the right."

In a short time the deep green of the Alabama forest gave way to the public square of the town of Bessemer. Alelia boldly stepped forward, parting the line of men, and linked arms with her father. As Jesse smiled pridefully, she began a strong "We Shall Overcome." The congregation assembled from the nearby towns of Midfield, Lipscomb, Kimberly, and Leeds joined in as they approached a formidable assembly of state troopers carrying loaded rifles and holding back a fierce pack of dogs.

Jesse paused about fifty yards away from the courthouse steps and raised his hands for the chanting and drumming to stop. In the silence, pregnant with intent, he directly addressed the sheriff. "Sheriff Campbell, we've come here in peace to register to vote. If you let us by, there'll be no need of trouble."

The sheriff took a couple of labored arthritic steps down the granite stairs with a great grin on his face. "Ya nigras best be goin' on along. This is not the day to register and sides ya'll ain't eligible. I'd advise you to go on away now."

In the silence that followed, Jesse's flock remained still. "Sheriff, we'll come every day till it's the right day," Jesse responded ruefully, "and we'll stay heah today in case the person in charge shows up."

The sheriff's face turned reddish orange, his voice filled with bitterness and disgust. "I tol' y'all to git. Now git!" No one moved. "Ya ain't got business heah, git goin'. The first person who comes nigh these steps, I'll shoot. Do you nigras understand?"

No one moved. In the quiet, Joshua put his drum down and walked alone. Stepping ahead of the marchers, he walked boldly toward the courthouse. The sheriff signaled the troopers, who cocked their rifles, but Joshua kept moving. From somewhere in the right flank a shot rang out. Joshua fell to his knees, but kept on moving, bracing his body, dragging himself with his arms. The sheriff acted as if he didn't see the newspapermen or the cameras. He nodded and another shot rang out. This time Joshua fell flat, gushing blood. Alelia and Mabel ran toward his body and cried his name.

In disbelief, Jesse walked toward his son. Praying the whole time, he lifted the boy from the ground. His congregation surrounded him, his son's blood spilt upon the ground.

Pandemonium ensued. Some marchers scattered, some stood stunned. Some troopers advanced, others hesitated, the sheriff calling for order through the bullhorn. A group of the students hoisted Joshua up and put him into the back of Mr. Goodenough's car. Miz Patrick and Miz Butler tended to Mabel, who fell backward, then ran to the car where her son lay dying. While Cinnamon shielded the children and tried to push them back, Lawrence gathered Jesse, who remained crumpled on the ground, and bustled him into the car. Then it sped off toward Birmingham. "Joshua honey, please don't die, hang on, chile!"

Tokyo and Lia stood together in the dusty street, watching the bedlam as if in a dream. Not knowing what to do, Tokyo took Lia's hand and sang out, "Amazing Grace, how sweet the sound, that saved a wretch like me . . ." She didn't even know she knew the song. Didn't understand the words. But it seemed to calm the square. The remaining marchers gathered in a cluster and, following the two girls, retreated back to the church. No ambulance came. In Jefferson County, they were for whites only. No doctor appeared. The nearest emergency room that would admit Negroes was in Birmingham. The Walkers, together with the marchers, took solace in song. It had always saved them before, but there would be no victory that day.

* * *

FOR YEARS, Abbott struggled gravely with what happened to Joshua. These feelings he dared not speak to his family. Instead, he found a place for his yearnings in the mournful music of Ben Webster and the frenzied wails of Albert Ayler, and even Maceo. For hours at a time he locked himself in his room with his horn, his cry. His saxophone signaled a different attitude, a dissonant, impatient, and furious resistance.

After that fateful trip South, such a riff was running through his mind when Abbott was casually walking through the South Side of Chicago, catching the trail of sounds from rehearsal sessions at the jazz and blues clubs that lined 47th Street. A voice on a loudspeaker disrupted his reverie. "Listen, my brothers and sisters, the white man is the manifestation of Yacub," the strident voice declared, "in Biblical terms, none other than the Devil. Do you understand me?" A crowd had gathered around a van bedecked with speakers. "Amen" and "Speak Brother," "Tell the Truth!" The young serious men with clean pressed suits and bow ties, who meandered through the crowd selling copies of *Muhammad Speaks,* amused him. Just for the hell of it, Abbott bought one. He found mention of the Republic of New Africa, Robert Williams arming poor black people with weapons to defend their homes from the Klan. He was surprised by the international news coverage of people of color, but was most intrigued by the column by a Malcolm X.

His head swirled with a whole set of possibilities he had never even considered. When Abbott arrived home, he heard Thelonious Monk's piano and above that his mother shouting for Lawrence to turn off that "awkward two-fingered piano playin'." He'd heard these squabbles all his life and they were never resolved. His parents loved each other so much, yet they were complete opposites in taste. They had grown tolerant and laughed at each other. But he was in no laughing mood. He had bought a bunch of *Muhammad Speaks* as well as *How to Eat to Live* by the Honorable Elijah Muhammad himself.

"Dad, I've got to talk to you. There are Negroes out there who don't believe in that 'turn the other cheek' mess. They believe we should fight for our rights and separate from the white people."

Overhearing, Cinn was taken aback. How could her son be voicing such foolishness? "Abbott, we've been through this so many times. We're full-fledged Americans and deserve to be treated as such. Those folks you're talking about want a revolution or an uprising or something that's never going to happen. Don't you see what happened right here to the Black Panther Party? They'll get killed is all."

"Like Joshua?" The venom in Abbott's voice stunned his mother to silence. "I watched Uncle Jesse try to scoop his son's guts off the street. You don't have to worry about me. I won't go down like that. Time comes, I'll be carrying a gun."

As he stomped out of the room, Cinnamon started right behind him. Lawrence caught her by the arm.

"I'll talk to him."

"Talk to him? When?"

Abbott could hear Tokyo flipping from one colored radio station to another in her bedroom, her voice drowning out the records. The Motown sound and Chicago's Chess Records had monopolized the national market. Abbott thought of his sister Tokyo and her aspirations and just shook his head. *Baby love feel-good music, they preferred dancin' in the streets to organizing and protest.* For his part, he was ready to leave the planet. With a deep sigh he thought of running off to play with Sun Ra's Heliocentric Arkestra. There was so much he could learn from John Gilmore and Marshall Allen. He could hear June Tyson's voice luring him into galactic adventure and imagined Tokyo in her place. Just then, Tokyo knocked softly and entered. "Hey, Abbie. I got a new song. Wanna hear it?"

28

As pigeons skedaddled over the tiled roofs of Paris, Raoul was bleeding from the nose and mouth, his hands bloodied with the blood of others. Three French hoodlums had attacked him, ruined his amplifier and threatened his guitar, but Raoul was not one to give in easily, especially while they shouted, "Sale Arabe, sale noir! Dirty Arab, filthy black!" This made Raoul furious. He knew he had a knife in his leather jacket. *But where?* They laughed as they tried to break his fingers, but Raoul Johnson miraculously got out of their hold and found his knife. "Sale Arabe, sale noir, enh," he seethed as he jabbed at them. *Dirty nigger* rang in his ears. He protected his guitar as best he could.

He was worried lest these hooligans follow him from the Métro station at Les Halles to the Twentieth Arrondissement where he lived with his parents Baker and Raschel. But the fellow with the stringy brown hair didn't budge when Raoul pulled the knife. The other two laughed some more.

"Isn't it just like a filthy Arab to have a knife?"

Suddenly Raoul lunged forward and slashed his sharp blade through the cheek of one of the blond bigots. Then he was ready for the other two. As they backed away, he grabbed his guitar and boarded the Métro. His hands were covered in blood, but his guitar was safe. *I'll have to stay away from Les Halles for a while.* He decided again to speak frankly with his parents about his desire to move to the States. As the train zoomed down the tracks he improvised his own rendition of Jimi Hendrix's long-fingered electrified psychedelic bluesy rock. *That's the sound of the future!* He kept telling his father this, but Baker Johnson, whose jazz combo was a Paris institution, would hear none of it. Nonetheless, he would have to listen to his battered son this night.

Raoul's mother, Raschel, was Genya's daughter. He had grown up hearing of how his grandmother Genya had battled against the Nazis in Paris and how Raschel's sister Bruria fought for the independence of Algeria. Raschel busily tended to her wounded son, all the while asking questions about the brawl. How many? What names did they use? How had he succeeded in fighting them off? She was proud of him, three against one! Just as Raschel finished wrapping Raoul's torso, her husband's key rattled the door.

Raoul jumped away from Raschel's protective care and ran up to his father. "Papa, I'm so glad you've come. I was attacked tonight by three dirty Frenchies. They tried to break my fingers. They called me 'sale Arabe, sale noir'! How can I be both, Papa, a filthy Arab and a filthy nigger? I was born here. I'm a Frenchman, just like they are, I told them and I cut them, all three!"

Raschel was piqued. "No, you are not a Frenchman just like them. You are black, American, Arab, and Algerian. You must carry yourself like that. Always, mon fils."

Baker set down his trumpet case, embraced Raoul, and sighed, "Son, I settled here to escape what you just went through, but it looks like racism just keeps showing its ugly face. But you've got to stop carrying that knife. That will land you in a French jail for a very long time. Now give it to me."

Raschel cried out, "You're leaving him with no protection."

Baker said, "I'm leaving him with a future. That's what I'm doing. So you beat them, three to one, huh?"

"Oui, Papa. They didn't get a chance to touch my guitar."

"That's my man, that's my man, Raoul, but no weapons."

"What revolution was ever successful with no weapons?" Raschel scoffed.

Raoul was often totally confused by his parents' conflicting ideas. He grabbed his instrument and took refuge in his room where he could still hear Raschel and Baker accusing each other. Raoul put on his headphones and pumped up the volume on his electric guitar. He'd heard this dispute all his life. *Black, American, Arab, and Algerian.* He didn't feel like he belonged anywhere.

* * *

ON CHICAGO'S South Side the crowd at the Regal was as wild as the ticket: Sly and the Family Stone, Patti LaBelle and the Bluebelles, and, opening for them, the Walker Family Band. Tokyo looked vampish in her sequined stockings, head feathers, and mini-mini dress. Abbott and James were in Temptations-style two-toned tails. Leading the band of twelve musicians, they rocked the house, but it was clear that Tokyo was the real star. Her brothers were just her sidemen. She had the power over the people that night. With her renditions of Diana Ross, Tina Turner, Justine "The Bells" Washington, even Billie Holiday and Dakota Staton, it was Tokyo the crowd wanted, and she knew how to work them, too. She had done her studying and it had done her well. She cruised through a medley of the group's local hits, but it was her song they wanted, and she knew how to sing it. In flaming red satin and stiletto heels, Tokyo approached the footlights barely whispering; the whole hall silently attentive. Then she belted out a note like Etta James, and launched into the party groove that everybody had been waitin' for, "Jump Up!" Number 12 on the R&B charts with a bullet.

> "Jump up,
>   You been givin' me the runaround,
>   Jump up,
>   But I got no time for none of your messin' round,
>   Jump up,
>   I'm tired you tryin to put me down,
>   Jump up,
>   Listen to what I'm throwin' down,
>   You're through tellin' me what to do,
>   Cuz I'm through with you!
>   Jump up,

Right now like I'm tellin' you,
Jump up,
You're through tellin' me what to do,
Jump up,
Wait, wait, here's the breakin' news,
I through messin' around with you,
I'll dance all night, dance all night, dance all night if I want to!
Jump up,
Come on everybody now,
Jump up,
Up on your feet and party down,
Jump up,
I'm gonna show you how,
To dance all night, dance all night, dance all night if you
    want to!"

While her brothers led the eight-piece backup band in synchronized choreography, Tokyo was shakin' and bakin', kickin' her taut muscular legs as she slithered from one side of the stage to the other, seductively tossing her head forward so her cluster of curls fell over her eyes just so. The song she had written after a petulant tantrum, thrown when her parents wouldn't let her go to a party near the projects, had become a defiant teenaged anthem of sexual rebellion. When they finished, the crowd wouldn't let 'em go. They shouted "Amen" and "Go girl" till the lead act in the wings was getting impatient. The teenager threw up her hand and sang ever so sweetly into the mike, "Now way-ay-ait uh minute . . ." An encore of the Isley Brothers' "Shout" left the audience roaring for more.

Waiting in the wings was a white girl with curly hair and hippie clothes. She tried to catch their attention. Tokyo and James ignored her, but Abbott stopped to listen. "My name is Bethany Cooper," she said. "I represent one of the anti-war groups. A week from now we're having a coalition of all the anti-war groups to stage a citywide rally. Will your group play? 'Jump Up!' That song could be powerful."

Abbott began to feel uneasy. He was against the war, but had planned on going if called. "I understand your position, Bethany, but I'd have to check with the whole group before I give you an answer."

"All right, that's fair," Bethany smiled and followed him.

Abbott went to walk into the dressing room, but found it locked. "Open this damn door, y'all. I got to talk to you two." Abbott heard some noises and repeated, "Open this damn door or I'll break it down!"

Abruptly Tokyo opened the door, her nose powdered with cocaine. James was straightening up the mirror and razor blades where they were cutting the rock. Abbott knocked James out with no compunction. He shut the door in Bethany's startled face and grabbed up all the drug paraphernalia he could find. Then he took his sister's face in his hands and wiped it clean. By now Tokyo had begun to weep, her frail body shaking in her big brother's arms.

James pushed himself up from the floor. "You don't understand, man, she needs that snow. She can't stand all the pressure, the press, the money. I was helping her, I swear."

"Some help you are, now look at her, an ordinary dope-fiend! Come on, Tokyo, I'm taking you to get some help."

"But, Abbie, we're booked solid. The agents will—"

"Did you hear me, James? You did this, now you clean it up."

Abbott got Tokyo out of her stage makeup and into some street clothes. They went swiftly out the stage door toward his VW bus, where Bethany was faithfully handing out anti-war pamphlets. Once Tokyo was in her seat, Abbott started the bus. He asked seriously, "Tokyo, is there any more of that coke on you? I have to have an honest answer."

Tokyo shifted her eyes a little. "Maybe a little," she said meekly and reluctantly handed over the last of her stash to Abbott, who threw it out the window.

"You'll be fine, angel. Don't worry about a thing."

"But what about the tour, Abbie? We got a hit. Did you hear that crowd?"

"Don't worry about the tour. You're going to get well."

"And just where am I supposed to do that?

"Don't worry about that either. Uncle Jesse and Aunt Mabel will be happy to see you."

"Oh no! Let me out this car!" she said, her knee spasmodically jerking. "Well, can I at least have a drink?"

Abbott thought a minute and figured maybe some alcohol might bring her down from the agitated high she was on. He was still on the South Side, so he slipped into a corner store and picked up two bottles of Cuervo Gold Tequila, then he was back in the bus. He'd gotten two go-cups and poured one shot for Tokyo and one for himself. "All right, easy now," he said as he watched his little sister start to guzzle her drink as if she were already a seasoned pro. "Not too much. We've got a long way to go." He thought of all the things he could have said to James and Tokyo, that the only freedom for black people was liberation and they were busy enslaving themselves to cocaine and booze. But he could hear Tokyo sardonically replying, "How you gonna be liberated when you're headed for the white man's army?"

He tried not to focus on his low draft number. *Focus on a battle you can win.* He needed to get Tokyo to Alabama. If she could stay clean for six months, maybe she could learn to live another way before she returned to the stage. "Springtime in the South will do you good," he said as he looked over at her. She had already nodded off, her mouth open and her head leaning against the pane.

It was April. Abbott got his sister out of harm's way in the nick of time. That summer grim-faced police with helmet shields and bullhorns and trucks stacked with troops in battle fatigues, their rifles drawn, patrolled the city's broad avenues, flying glass crackling under their feet, everywhere fire and the ricochet of bullets. Beneath busted streetlights, preachers and civic leaders pleading with people to go home. The mayor screaming, "Shoot on sight!" (A command never rescinded.) Whole blocks ablaze, the hospital floor so slippery with blood, the mop couldn't sweep it up fast enough. The jails couldn't keep track of the scores of looters, the stores picked clean, the alleys strewn with plunder—shoes, liquor, pork chops, radios, cigarettes, and busted canned goods snaked through them. Futile sirens and false alarms screamed from all directions block to block, the fire hoses' white arcs of water like spit in the wind. From the South Side neighborhoods of Woodlawn and Inglewood to the West Side communities of Lawndale and Humboldt Park, Black Metropolis was ablaze. And through the broken panes of project windows, Tokyo Walker's number one hit "Jump Up!" bellowed with new meaning.

* * *

ALELIA ARRIVED from Birmingham just as Tokyo was on her way there. Alelia had decided to stay with her aunt Cinn and uncle Lawrence while she finished her studies at the University of Chicago. Her uncle, who was on the faculty, convinced her that a history degree was a wiser choice than folk music. Her parents, having already lost Joshua, thought her increasing militant style too dangerous for her to stay in the South. As Ma Bette would say, "Out of the fryin' pan into the fire." She wound up more often on the streets of Chicago than in class. She found the Chicago-style architecture invigorating and the style of the people even more fascinating. She loved the museums and long strolls down Michigan Avenue. That's where she made her spending money. With tie-dyed hand-cut tee-shirts, embroidered bell-bottoms, and a cup, she camped out on the steps in front of the Art Institute, mixing all kinds of popular folk songs with those she had written herself. In between song sets, she passed out anti-draft and anti-war flyers. Some folks smiled, others spat at her as unpatriotic. To some, a freedom fighter, to others, a traitor.

Her activities worried her aunt Cinn to death, until Lawrence reminded his wife of her own youthful street-singing stint as Madame Butterfly at the five and dime. He championed his niece's commitment, and when she led a campus protest rally, he brought the whole group deep dish pizza.

When she'd first arrived Alelia had looked for traces of her mother, Memphis, in Cinnamon, but couldn't fathom any. Alelia imagined that her mother's house would be jumpin'. Cinnamon was constantly, quietly poring over operatic scores or giving private voice lessons in search of the next Leontyne Price. Her aunt was bewildered and annoyed by her vegetarian foods and her back-to-nature white friends, who conserved water by not flushing the toilet. Occasionally, Cinn tried to tell her about her mother. How she saw Memphis being born, their singing group, the Mayfield Sisters, but then Cinn would drift off. She didn't have many pictures. A group shot from the wedding. No recent ones. Lawrence stayed out of it. "I like studying our people's history in a general sense," he said, "not specific."

So Lia sang on the streets of Chicago and found a kind of family there. She thought she'd find an ally in Abbott or James, but James was desperate without Tokyo and the band. And Abbott would soon be off to the war. She got Abbott alone once in a café off Madison. Low draft number or not, she had to convince him that he had alternatives.

"Abbie, how can you consider killing people you don't even know?"

"There is nothing for me to do but get these white folks off my back. They shot Malcolm, they shot Joshua, they shot Fred Hampton."

"Abbie," she interjected, "they did not shoot Malcolm. Two black men did. You can't blame all white people for—"

"How can you say that, Lia, when your own brother was gunned down before our eyes?"

The question stunned her. *My brother, my beautiful brother . . .*

"If I stay here, they'll shoot me, and I them," Abbott continued. "I have no choice, Lia. If I'm just another nigger for their cannon fodder, so be it. All I want is to play my horn, and I don't want to do it in jail." Only then did Abbott look up. Lia had not been listening. "It's all right. Joshua's all right," he said, softening. "Nobody can hurt him now. And I'mo be all right, too! Grand-Nana says I got the luck. Mah Bette done marked it so!'" he joked, capturing his great-grandmother Dora's inflection. "Come on . . ." he coaxed his cousin to smile. "There's a big AACM concert tonight, you know." At Lia's look of ignorance, Abbott took on his father's stern professorial tone, "Art Ensemble of Chicago? Only the cutting edge of avant-garde jazz, born and bred on the South Side. We could still get tickets. I got a few weeks of freedom left and I wanna make the best of it."

Alelia thought a moment and said, "Only if you promise to come see Richie Havens and Taj Mahal with me."

Abbott rolled his eyes, but nodded yes. His huge Afro bobbed in the wind like the smooth jazz rhythm of Ramsey Lewis's left hand. There were things Alelia and Abbott shared. They sometimes quibbled about Johnny Taylor or Stevie Wonder, not bitterly but with humor, about what black music should sound like and why. In the days and weeks before Abbott was deployed, they wandered South Side Chicago jazz clubs and West Side blues bars, cruising through smoke and sawdust. One night, the blues guitarist Buddy Guy, seeing Lia's guitar case, invited them to sit in. Alelia took in a good deal more of what she thought folk singing was that night. She decided while listening to Guy's meteoric chord changes and his wailing plaintive call, conjuring all that she knew and loved of the South and her journey in a riff, that the blues was in fact the penultimate folk music, music of the folk, acoustic or not. She heard, too, in the mournful trepidation of Abbie's horn, a foreshadowing of his coming orders to Vietnam.

Tokyo was on a wholly separate journey, as was James, now her manager. *Tokyo is becoming an R&B star, "Jump Up!" still toppin' the charts. James has become a businessman. Abbie's becoming a soldier. Joshua's gone. Where does that leave me?* Alelia had a dream that night that she walked toward the east, toward the morning sun and jumped into it. When she awakened she had made a decision, the same decision her great-aunt Lizzie had made so many years before, *Paris!* In Paris was her destiny.

✳ ✳ ✳

ALL ALELIA had to do was find an empty corner and begin to sing and francs dropped into her guitar case like manna from heaven. She was staying in a hostel which suited her needs and was meeting people at an alarming rate. One day she walked through the Tuileries Gardens and four handsome Senegalese fellows stopped her and invited her immediately to a nearby café, where they were soon joined by some Haitians, Congolese, and Ivorians for a grand salon. Though everyone spoke French, there were several side conversations in Swahili, Mende, Hausa, and various patois. Lia thought the African students delightful, though a bit aggressive. She decided to sing, using her guitar for both accompaniment and shield. Her performance was such a hit, the group insisted she accompany them that evening to a Martinican nightclub. "Il y'a une bande superbe, qu'il faut que tu l'écoutes et qu'ils t'écoutent à toi aussi! Quelles mains splendides, et cette voix—si belle ta voix!" they told her. "There's a great band, which you simply must hear and they must hear you! Viens, viens avec nous, c'est la première fois que tu fréquentes la boîte! Le Club, viens! Come!"

Just before her night out on the town, Alelia made up her mind to go to see her mother and her great-aunt Lizzie. *My very own mother after all these years!* Memphis would see her and they would talk, no matter what. The bright sun belied the nervous tension in Alelia's soul. After changing at the hostel, she grabbed an album Abbott had given her by the Art

Ensemble of Chicago, *Les Stances à Sophie*. She would ask her mother's opinion. A prop to ease their first encounter.

Memphis was house-sitting at Lizzie's apartment near La Place de l'Opéra, that much Cinnamon had told her when she gave her the address. Alelia had done her best to look nice. She put henna on her hair and she had done her chestnut eyes in exotic colors. In a pastel striped A-line mini-sundress, she rang the bell labeled Mayfield. When the buzzer rang and the door opened with no questions, she simply walked in. The doorman momentarily glanced up from his newspaper and went back to reading. The wrought-iron elevator door was exquisite but the ride was very, very slow. As she went up floor by floor she felt herself sweating, her mouth dry, but she and her guitar finally made it. Alelia knocked delicately on "Appartemente #8," the entire eighth floor. Without so much as a "Who is it," the door swung open onto the most opulent of environs. Velvets, silks, and oriental rugs, mahogany tables, mother-of-pearl inlaid chests, a grand piano, a harp, and wonderful light. The woman who opened the door, Memphis herself, took one look at Alelia, grabbed her and held her tight. "Alelia, child," she whispered, "I knew you'd come for me one day."

Memphis stepped back from the bewildered Alelia and made a full circle around her, eyeing every aspect of the young woman. "My, you are just as Cinnamon told me, a wholly new creation and so lovely."

Alelia thought she should say something and blurted, "Mama, I'm a singer."

Memphis smiled and made her way to an easy chair near a decanter of burgundy. She gestured to Alelia to take a seat and have a glass with her. Alelia could hardly find her seat in the chair she was so busy looking at the photographs on the wall—Mayfield Turner with all the jazz greats for decades, from Louis Armstrong to Josephine Baker, Brick Top, Bud Powell; literati—Langston Hughes, Baldwin; heads of state—wearing Ike's helmet, standing on her tiptoes with de Gaulle. It was Lizzie's collection, half a century of memories. She set down her untouched drink on a finely carved glass table and just sat there staring at Memphis.

"Why don't you take out your instrument and sing, child? Let me hear you."

Alelia mustered a small smile and glowed. She took her guitar from the case and tuned it, cleared her throat, and adjusted her lanky frame to the plush velvet divan. She sang Nina Simone's "Safronia" and Joni Mitchell's "Both Sides Now." Then she threw in a blues song 'bout the 1927 flood that hit New Orleans. Memphis closed her eyes and felt her daughter's voice seep through every vein of her body. *What more could a mother ask for than a child of conviction and a creator of beauty?* Then Memphis moved to the piano and played a few notes from "La Vie en Rose." Immediately she and Alelia sang together and the spirit of Piaf filled the room. Memphis jumped to her feet shouting, "Brava, brava! Come, you must have dinner with me."

"I can't tonight, b-b-but soon, yes!"

"Yes, darling, and Lizzie will join us. She'll be back in Paris in a couple of days. Your Aunty Liz will love you!"

With that said, Alelia soberly took her leave, hugging her mother like a newborn with tiny warm tears welling in her eyes.

Later that night she met her new friends Mamadou, Zaid, Doudou, and Malik and off they went. She'd seen small cobblestone streets in Charleston, but it was nothing like Paris. The group turned off a thoroughfare into what Alelia surmised was an alley and stopped abruptly, as if they had arrived somewhere and were looking around to find it. Just as she began to question the rashness of her actions, her newfound friends pushed open a thick wooden door that looked like the entrance to a cellar and were met with damp intense heat and rhythms that were irresistible. Down, down, down they went, many, many stairs, around curves and into a darkness that approached Zaid's skin tone, Alelia simply trusting this was the right thing to do. At last she caught sight of figures dancing, the moves ever so sensual and so familiar her face brightened.

The Africans spread out like fireflies in search of partners. Alelia headed toward the sound. In every sense of the word, the music was live! She had to get closer. She wiggled and smiled her way through the sweating crowd, meandering through what seemed the entire African Diaspora, and came upon the wildest-looking band she had ever seen. It was like Jimi Hendrix's Band of Gypsies, only they were black and French. Alelia couldn't stop smiling. She was especially taken by the guitarist who sang "All Along the Watchtower" and played like a genius.

Raoul Johnson was angry that night and he played with fury. His father Baker and he had just had a huge row over his wanting to quit his studies and leave France "to find himself." "First you say I'm not Algerian. Then you say I'm not French. I can't be American. I've never been there. I'm black, you can look at me and see that. You think it's safer for me in a Paris subway than one in New York?" he ranted. "I don't want to be everybody in the world. I want to be someone from somewhere!" He played one of his own compositions to close the set, "Another Dienbien-phu for You," he said in English. The crowd, only there for dancing, barely heard him, but Alelia did. During the band break, Alelia, who was not shy, asked Raoul in her best Parisian French if he'd care for a drink, which he slyly agreed to. "A song like that deserves a toast," she said with a seductive Southern accent. Raoul's smile widened. *Not hard to look at and she's American!*

"You know, you're quite remarkable on that guitar," she said as they sipped on two Belgian beers. "I play, too, but folk songs, anti-war songs."

This intrigued Raoul. He was truly delighted by a woman who knew something about who she was and about the music. They had another beer, and soon Alelia had him looking for one of Tokyo's pop hits on the jukebox. Though Raoul's band played till daylight, Alelia waited and danced with many strangers, her body taking on whatever African beat was set. Raoul was plotting. He was a man. He was Baker's son.

After the band had been paid and had packed up, Raoul asked Alelia where she was staying. When she told him a hostel, he laughed and said gently, "Not tonight."

Raoul walked Alelia to a presentable *pension* where they got a room. Though the sun had risen, the full moon was still rising in their souls. Raoul asked her to sing something as he began to undress her. A bit taken aback, she protested she hadn't brought her guitar. He offered her one of his. She softly sang Miriam Makeba's "Thula Thula Mama." Raoul's body melted as if the lullaby were for him. He took Alelia in his arms and lifted her to her feet. Naked in the austere *pension,* they were a kaleido-scope of passion. Eventually they found themselves against a wall, the table, the bed, the floor, lust without boundaries, more a coming together of seekers. They felt they'd been looking for each other all their lives. Two separate journeys became one. They could make music and they could make love in secret humorous unmasked ways. Alelia vowed to herself she'd never leave Raoul's side and he promised to never let go of her. And they didn't.

Alelia joined Raoul's band. She worked on her own songs and began studying the electric guitar—she'd finally realized the power that Tokyo loved. Living their lives in the moment, they were excited and at peace. In a week they had already set up house and decided they should meet each other's family. Raoul's mother gave them her blessing. Alelia impressed her as a fighter who was joyful. They laughed a lot. *This is a good woman for my son,* Raschel thought. Baker, still smarting over his son's belliger-ence, was taciturn much of the evening. Raschel told her grim-faced hus-band to get over himself. "Your son has found his American, whether you like it or not." Not wanting to further irritate Raoul's father, Lia said very little about her family.

Raoul was a mite nervous at meeting Memphis and Lizzie. He was shocked to learn that Lelia's Aunty Liz was the legendary Mayfield Turner. Her mother Memphis, too, was popular all over France, if more for her aplomb than her singing. But when they arrived at the Place de l'Opéra apartment, the housekeeper gave Alelia a letter. "My Dear Daughter," Memphis had written in a large lazy jagged scrawl, "We didn't know how to reach you. Tokyo has been nominated for a Grammy Award and for the first time in decades Aunty Liz and I are headed for the States. Please try to make it. The whole family will be there. All my love, M." The enve-lope was stuffed with cash. Alelia was devastated, standing there in the new dress she had bought for the occasion. Raoul consoled her. There was enough money for both of them to fly to New York.

Raoul wanted Alelia's last night in Paris to be African, Antillean, and Arab. They went from Moroccan to Mauritian restaurants, they sat in with a Congolese band, and they drank Jamaican Red Stripes. When they were actually emotionally incapable of dancing any more, they left for the airport to jump the first flight they could find. They were in love no matter what.

* * *

WHILE ALELIA was having the time of her life in Paris, Abbott had been in Vietnam's living hell. He constantly dreamed of the Four Horsemen of the Apocalypse, yet he'd become what the army wanted, a good soldier. But he was a good soldier with an ax to grind. He kept seeing black and Latino youth manning the front lines while their white compatriots were in the rear. When he was finally discharged, Abbott went to New York City to play music. He went to Slug's, the Five Spot, the Vanguard, the Blue Note, and made the loft scene where cutting-edge artists had ensconced themselves. Vampin' with Lee Morgan, Clifford Brown, Cecil Taylor, Ornette Coleman, Sam Rivers, Mongo Santamaría, Mario Bauza, Orquesta Broadway, and Willie Colon, Abbott tried everything.

He got a small one-bedroom apartment on the Lower East Side with the tub in the kitchen, but he didn't care. He had his costume ready for Sun Ra's Arkestra as well. As fellas made their way to New York from Chicago, St. Louis, and Oakland, Abbott made friends with the new guard—Chico Freeman, Joe and Lester Bowie, Abdul Wadud, Sunny Murray, and Phillip Wilson, the new band of troubadors, challenging the generation before, even as they studied them. The scene was hot. Livin' was not. Playin' music all night, he was a cabbie by day, a gypsy.

He was terribly proud of his sister, Tokyo, though, who had stayed clean and had one number one R&B hit after another. She was the darling of Chicago-based *Ebony* and *Jet*. Even *Billboard* had to acknowledge her dynamic ascent. Abbott finally forgave James, who had become a respectable record executive. All was well, plus Alelia was coming home.

※ ※ ※

THE GREATER Mayfield family had taken adjoining suites at the Waldorf Astoria, where Tokyo was staying for the awards ceremony. The staff there felt she was one of their own. Cinnamon was at a loss for words. She'd never really known her daughter in her child's own element, though she could have. It was probably her fear for her daughter that had distanced them—the wild tales of Tokyo's life left Cinnamon no shelter for her grief. But now all was well. Tokyo Mayfield Walker was a nominee for the best R&B album of the year and she was sober. Cinnamon's heart was gleeful and light. Lawrence, too, was moved by the qualities of his daughter's voice and her studied style. All those years next to the record player with his daughter close by had paid off. Even in her most rambunctious blues, he could hear the Nancy Wilson or Betty Carter albums he cherished. *Yet she's barely touching her talents!* Lawrence had nothing but confidence in her.

Before the record label's reception for Tokyo, Cinnamon presided over a private pre-Grammy gathering for the family so that all the Mayfields could be together for the first time in many years. Memphis and Lizzie's appearance alone was reason enough. Cinnamon had never approved of Alelia's being left with Jesse and Mabel in the South, but she had said nothing, fearful of her cousin's biting tongue and ambition. When Memphis absconded for Paris and moved in with Lizzie, she had said nothing again. Now with the two of them returning, she didn't know what to say. After all, Cinnamon had never fulfilled her operatic dreams, while Memphis had lived the jazz life she quested. *If it was at the expense of her daughter, it's none of my affair. Then again, maybe it was for the best. Mama El rescued me, and Jesse and Mabel were there, not just for Lia, but for my Tokyo, too. Losin' their own child, healin' someone else.*

When her own daughter Tokyo appeared in a stunning black and beige beaded, form-fitting, backless gown, Cinnamon was speechless. This time she had nothing to say because her child simply looked too gorgeous for words. *Why, she has the glamour of Dorothy Dandridge, imagine that!* Her rambunctious child had become a woman. Her rebellious teen was now a firecracker femme fatale, exhibiting all of her grandmother Lizzie's startling sensuality and charisma.

"Tokyo, you've got to win tonight! You look like una bella donna, a true diva. I'm telling you, sweetheart, this is your night!" She grabbed her daughter up in her arms ever so tightly. At the same moment Lawrence swept them both in his arms and kissed Tokyo on the forehead, whispering, "You've got it all, baby. You make us proud."

Toyko burst from her mother's arms, loudly beseeching, "Everybody, have some champagne and somebody get me some sparkling water, please."

With a clamor at the door, Elma and Raymond walked in with Sissy and her college-bound twins. The last of her generation of Mayfields, Sissy had settled in Minneapolis right after college and married a real Irishman to go with her father's invented one. While one son had the straight hair and countenance of a young Abraham Lincoln, the other had started to dred his spiky blond locks. "Pray for me, sistuh," she said, hugging Cinnamon tightly. "Would that college were five dollahs a semester again." Sissy had never gone into music. "Too much competition in one family already," but the younger of her fraternal twins played a beautiful piano and was more interested in music than college. Unbeknownst to her, he was very anxious to talk to his famous cousins.

Out of the corner of her eye Tokyo spied Elma and Raymond walking in, looking almost angelic in appearance, Raymond in a powder-blue tuxedo and Elma in a finely crafted crepe gown of navy and a shock of silver hair. They approached Cinnamon first, which left Tokyo free to greet Alelia and Raoul, who had entered just behind them. The young women were so excited they barely caught their breaths in their conversation, but Tokyo did catch, "And this is Raoul." Before Tokyo got a chance to assess her cousin's beau, Lia was on the move, pulling her young man along. "Have you seen my mother?" she asked, her eyes scanning the room.

"No, Aunt Mabel and Uncle Jesse aren't here yet." But that's not what Lia meant.

"Oh, my God, that's right! Your mother is here, your other mother, but no one's seen her yet," Tokyo replied, catching up with the couple. *Yeah, I'm getting a Grammy, but it would be nice to have a date.* "Raoul, it's so good to meet you," she said, taking his hand and speaking loudly. "I understand you and Leelee have been doing some interesting things together in your band. I can't wait to hear about them. And I would love to meet some of your band members." *If any of them look like you.* "Get a little intercontinental conversation goin'."

Alelia put her arms around both of them and smiled benignly. "He's French, Tokyo, not hard of hearing. Come on, Rah. You have to meet all the mothers. I have three."

In the meantime Abbott had wandered in, sucking on a saxophone reed like a Tootsie Roll Pop. When he saw his sister with Alelia and Raoul, he stopped in his tracks and whistled. That Alelia and Raoul were possessed of another aesthetic was obvious. Alelia's dress was a strapless golden chiffon thing, clinging to her body like fairy dust, and Raoul's Nehru jacket put all the tuxedos and cummerbunds in the room to shame. They were definitely together. *In both senses of the word.*

Abbott was ever so proud of his sister. "I knew you could make it, baby," he said to Tokyo as she approached him. They hugged while Alelia came over to introduce Raoul. The Frenchman's English was startlingly fluent.

Alelia walked over to Cinnamon and Lawrence with Raoul in tow. "Aunt Cinnamon, Uncle Lawrence, this is Raoul. I sing and play with his band now."

Never before had Cinnamon seen Memphis in Alelia, but noting Lia's new, slightly French accent and the cut of her dress, Cinnamon felt herself blushing. This wasn't Memphis, but this was surely Memphis's daughter, svelte and sensual in ways she would never be. Cinn had gone all out for her daughter's celebration and already she felt dowdy, her cultured reserve sinking into awkwardness, her broad shoulders and hips suddenly too wide for the room. Lawrence felt the sudden tension in his wife, and understood once he glimpsed Alelia.

"Oh, Uncle Lawrence, it's so good to see you again! This is mon cher, Raoul. I'm sure you all will get along. He's quite the jazz historian, though that's not what we play."

"Well, I'm delighted, Raoul. We must get together in Chicago. Alelia, you *are* coming to Chicago?"

"Uncle Lawrence, we're going *everywhere*. Raoul wants to see America, even the South."

Just as Lia said that, in walked her adoptive parents, Jesse and Mabel, straight from Alabama, that was the unavoidable conclusion. Mabel's dress fit a bit too snugly and Jesse's tuxedo was obviously rented. Alelia ran up to them and smothered them with hugs and kisses. She was so engaged in greeting them she forgot about Raoul for a moment, but not for long. When she realized she'd lost track of him, she quickly turned, thinking he must not be far away, but she was mistaken. James had Raoul in the eye of his video camera, interviewing him about God only knew what. The family had remained suspicious of James ever since Tokyo's addictions became public. Even after he had started his ascent in the music industry, he had a ways to go before he could redeem himself with the family. That's one of the reasons he decided to hide behind the camera—that way he could talk to everybody and control the conversation. Only Tokyo had really forgiven him. She rushed over to embrace him and started jabbering into the camera, as if they were children again, fooling around, putting her nose right up to the lens.

Suddenly the room quieted. James panicked for a second, thinking all eyes were on him again, judging him. Then there was a real "Ahhh," the kind one hears in Hollywood, accompanying a trance-like turning of heads toward the door. There she stood in all her glamour, Lizzie Mayfield Turner, the myth of the family in living color and in person. She seemed to embody the very essence of Paris in appearance, in a tight black sequined gown with a train and a full ostrich boa, her platinum wig perfectly coifed. And with her, looking nearly as alluring, was Memphis. Alelia's eyes lit up, glistening. Elma downright started bawling, tears streaming down her heavily powdered face. Her sister and her daughter had come home.

"Good evening, everyone," Lizzie announced, playing for James's camera.

Elma and Raymond, Jesse and Mabel, Tokyo and Abbott almost ran over each other trying to get their taste of the great Aunty Lizzie. There were plenty of hugs and kisses for everyone. In a crowded moment with her mother, Alelia took the opportunity to introduce Raoul. While niceties were exchanged in French, Memphis couldn't keep herself from staring at the young man. There was something very familiar about him, something in his eyes and carriage. Then she saw the joy in Alelia's face and embraced the young couple, inviting the rest of the family to celebrate the coming together of the late-twentieth-century Mayfields.

As Cinnamon looked on, her self-image tottered. She smarted at these interlopers, and didn't know which one she found more irritating. *I'm giving this party. This is our suite! What are they doing comin' in here acting like they're runnin' things.* From behind, Lawrence put his arms around his steaming wife and nestled his chin on her shoulder. "Ever sing a union song?"

She laughed despite herself. He looked at his wife adoringly, "You got three beautiful kids and you got me! That's not bad."

Although there was little time left before the group had to leave for the official reception, Jesse felt compelled not only to pray for Tokyo to win, but also to invoke the names of Ma Bette, Eudora, and seemingly the rest of the entire Mayfield line who had passed through this life.

James roamed with the camera to capture every moment: Alelia, Raoul, and Memphis; Lizzie primping over Elma's hair; Raymond pontificating with his daughter-in-law Mabel on building a new church; Abbott circling Tokyo, trying to ease her to the door.

Cinn went up to Memphis and took a deep breath before she spoke. "You know I owe you an apology, Memphis. All these years I been mad at you, but I had it all wrong. I should be thanking you, Memphis. For the best thing that ever happened to me. If it hadn't been for you runnin' off with Baker, I never would have found my wonderful husband."

"Comment?" asked Raoul. "Did I hear someone say Baker? My father is named Baker."

"Baker Johnson?" the two women asked simultaneously. *Of course, that's why he looks familiar. Taratata!* Lizzie, who had observed the interchange, jumped in, "Hmph, hmph, hmph. Seems some kinda way, Mayfields always gotta have a trumpet playuh in the family." With a tap to her crystal champagne glass, she called everyone to attention. "I have come from across the waters to deliver a secular benediction. Tokyo Walker will be walkin' away with this award tonight!"

Jesse lifted his glass, then sobered for a moment, missing his son Joshua and his grandmother Dora, who had passed three years before. *Just yesterday . . . Oh, Nana, I wish you had lived to see this.* Feeling their presence with him, Jesse felt a calling to jump in with Psalm 95, "Oh, come let us sing unto the Lord; let us make a joyful noise to the rock of our salvation."

Virtually on cue, Abbott voiced an Ayleresque crescendo imitating his saxophone. Cinnamon in spite of herself slipped in, lilting an improvised melody, sounding very much like a spiritual, "And we haven't forgotten where we all come from . . ."

With some laughter the clan shouted in unison, "Sweet Tamarind, South Carolina! And Ma Bette Mayfield! To the seventh generation!"

For a moment, their eyes met, Lizzie and her pal, a mother and daughter. Memories danced between them. *So many years lost, so many years ago/ Too many years lost, too many years ago . . .* Bent over giggling and laughing, sportin' capes of velvet and coats of fur, tweed jackets and pea coats, the family left for the party. But just as she was walking to the door Memphis got the last words to James's camera, "Slavery leaves telling marks lasting generations, still every word out of our mouths is a song."

Coda

S OUND CHECK, ONE, TWO, ONE, TWO." LIBERTY JOHNSON stepped to the turntables beside her spin partner De Spain, his wild locks tied in a chignon atop his head. *Work boots and stilettos.* She laughed at the juxtaposition—she in a black turtleneck more suitable for a SWAT team, he in loose raw silk pants and imported square-toed snakeskins with two-inch heels. She felt privileged that he had asked her to join him. *Honored. Nearly five months down.* He didn't have to do this. De Spain already had street cred. Five years ago when she started at fifty dollars a gig, he was pullin' five hundred, and his last set overseas drew ten grand. She was anxious about the blend, her readiness. She had started out subbing for him. This was the first time he had asked her to partner.

"No favors, Dee."

"None offered. You the one with the pedigree, professor."

He still teased her about graduate school. She had originally started deejaying to help pay the tuition, then quickly realized that, more than cataloguing artifacts, she enjoyed curating sounds. But De Spain, being among only a handful of people who knew her lineage, was speaking the truth. She had the pedigree all right. Billed as "Lia and Raoul," her parents had been on the counterculture circuit for two generations, folksinging to world music. Her grandfather Baker Johnson was an elder statesmen of be-bop in Europe. Her R&B diva aunt Tokyo, counted down and out more times than anyone could remember, was on yet another comeback tour. And Mayfield Turner, her great-great-aunt, was a show business legend. "At a hundred and four, she was still showin' her legs! Aunty Liz wasn't just famous, she was downright infamous!" she joked with De Spain. "Grandma, grandpa, cousins, aunts, uncles, greats and great-greats. Wherever they be, the Mayfields and music go way back. 'To the seventh generation!'" Music was always there, mixing geography and melody.

She felt a twang in her left breast. Memory of her Aunt Cinn playing the piano game. *Charleston, New York, Chicago* . . . the place above her heart, now a snarled spiderweb of scars. *To the seventh generation, then what?*

She kept telling herself that she was deserving of life, deserving of happiness. "Take it slow," De Spain had said. She couldn't move her arms after the surgery, had to teach the muscles to reconnect. "Just feel the crowd," De Spain coaxed her, coached her. "Same as your grandpop takin' a solo. Same as your aunt finding her blues in a slow jam. Find your music, Lib, find your groove."

She thought it ironic that, but for the technology and perfect pitch of her computer, she couldn't sing a note. The turntables were her instrument and voice. "Supposed to get thirty-two bars, Dee," she said wryly. "The blues only got twelve."

"Still rocks, just work off the moment." He smiled. "When you're ready," and with an expert combination of control and surrender, he glided into Tina Turner's sultry "I can't stand the rain . . . against my win-dow-oh-ohhh . . . Bringin' back sweet memories . . ." She chuckled at this inside joke. They both used the Rane Serato program. With her combination of turntables, CD players, and laptop, she was fully digitalized. Still she understood the purists saying "If you've never touched vinyl, you're not a real deejay." But she had to be able to move, to adapt. Versus taking an hour to load twenty milk crates in a truck, with the new technology she could stuff her overnight bag in fifteen minutes and hop a plane with ten thousand songs.

Sweet memories . . . Each generation had its collector. For her Great-Nana Dora it was swatches of fabric and buttons, photos and shoes. For Lizzie it was costumes and posters, a kaleidoscope of stuff from her ragged, rollicking life. Rare LPs from Uncle Ray and her grandmère Memphis. *Always the music. Aunt Cinn's precious librettos.* The last time she had visited her beloved Cinn, the woman was just a grip of shaking bones, the skin soft, holding fast to her hand. *Memories dissolving, even her beloved arias. Aida, Carmen, Butterfly, the heroine always dying. Cinn* . . . clinging to her with desperate fingers, one last grasp at life. Liberty had gone to confide in her, seeking that quiet solace she had always found. *I can't do this alone.*

She reminded herself that she wasn't alone. *You got De Spain.* When she finally had allowed him to see her and to touch her, he had cupped the palm of his hand over the scar on her breast with such tenderness, like a lover. Though her blood family was scattered all over the globe, she had family. People who loved her for all of her eccentricity.

"No reason why you can't live to be a hundred and four," her doctor had said, "just like your great-aunt Lizzie." Liberty had found it hard to believe that the birdlike creature she knew as Aunty Liz had been such a powerhouse. Still insisted on driving her car when she could barely see over the dashboard. "And walked really slow, Dee. 'Wheelchair?' she'd say. 'Oh, please, honey, 1921, I walked from Baltimore to Philly, with you on my hip. No, no, wait . . . that was, that was Cinn . . . What's your name again?' " A hundred and four and twenty-four, both staring death in the face.

"Liberty, comin' fierce and fabulous with a House/World/trip-hop mix of her own styling, a hybrid form of Electro, Goth, Punk, round the world to round the way." She pumped herself up, talking in a soft drone over the mix. *You can do this.* She grabbed De Spain's checkered scarf and slung it around her neck. "I need some color." Though it wasn't her thing, she braced herself for '90s and '80s remix requests that she knew would be coming, especially after Michael's death. Same year the King of Pop dies, his body blanched, cloaked in as much mystery as Robert Johnson, the same week Emmett Till's grave is desecrated and more kids died in Chicago than Baghdad, the President watched his daughters walk through the Door of No Return. She had to get her mind around the contradictions. *Life, Liberty . . . or death. All of this rich history, this past I'm supposed to be able to stand on and draw from. Instead I'm already part of the past even before I've begun. The Seventh Generation. The what?*

The club was cavernous, reminding her of a tomb. *Catacombs.* Underground caves where the faithful secreted their dead. The brick walls were still damp, the stone floor uneven, warped by the metric tons of water that once coursed through. She started up a Tibetan chant with her left hand, looped in a JB holla, layered a piece of her uncle Jesse's sermon and a plosive Berber's call, haunting Islamic harmonies into a Badu lick, thence to that twelve-bar blues she was carryin', pullin' heavy with the bass, that Zulu club that shakes the bones.

"What's your name again?" Liberty . . . what a name to live with. Congress just now apologizin' for slavery. Wasn't an apology she sought, but recognition, a celebration even, for the music. For the weave of Spirituals and Blues to Rock 'n' Roll that let freedom ring from one generation to the next. For the Jazz that defined modern. For the root music from Bebop to R&B to Hip-Hop, pushing the boundaries, giving the world permission to syncopate, improvise, and integrate styles, to synthesize and sample, make somethin' fresh. The music always the music, as soon as it's born fading away, giving birth to somethin' else and somethin' new. Shedding skin like Damballah. *New life. To the seventh generation. What then? What now?*

De Spain looked over, one earphone off his ear, listening to the room and the track at the same time, between their two sets of hands and the six instruments between them, every sound in the world, his beat in sync with hers, eyes locked, looking for the hand-off. Liberty had chosen life, but what then? How much time to bend it, stop it, speed it up, slow it down, slide or let it rumble? Startled by its syncopation, the shift in accent, holdin' back on the strong beat, leanin' heavy on the weak, producing the unexpected—surprise—this night, this dance, this song into the next into the next, she laid down a groove that surged into a wall of sound, that gospel effect irresistible, the crowd catching the spirit, erupting with an Ahhh . . . responding to her spin, the whole club her partner, conjuring souls with stomps and slides of their feet, the collective naturalized Soul. Everyone is there, in call and response, callin' up the ancestors and wakin' the yet to be born, the notes dancing in the air, a world without bounds at the tip of her fingers, *the music, always the music.*

* * *

THE TRANSVAAL'S vast Drakenberg Mountains on the horizon, the two-wheeled cart toggled up the road. On the scenic Sani Pass, the car had broken down and rolled backwards on the winding road. After two hours in the blistering sun, they had been rescued by a donkey cart driver. Tokyo Walker just shook her head. *I could just as well be in the eighteenth century as the twenty-first.*

Her career was down and out. Her R&B "classics" covered and sampled to death, but she couldn't buy a gig. Her big hit, her signature, was a theme song for the presidential campaign. *Think they'd let me sing it?!* Who was she kidding? Back taxes and a reputation for bad behavior had trailed her all the way to Botswana. *This was Jimmy's cockamamie idea . . . I oughta fire my brother—again!* Her comeback needed a new platform, James had said. "Broaden your outlook. We gotta go global." She still had some presence on the world music market, he argued; blue-collar Liverpool white girls were forever copying her licks. Her backup band was already international, hailing from Morocco, Senegal, South Africa, and Brazil. Only the bass player and keyboardist were American, and they were both white. Her '70s hit "Jump Up!" was a staple all over the continent.

"Tokyo Walker's Africa Tour." It sounded like a good idea. *Right! Twelve cities in three weeks. Rumbling planes, obtuse airport officials, from rain forests to sandstorms the size of Manhattan.* Ostensibly she was on tour to raise awareness about Africa's lost children, orphaned by disease, poverty, and war. While half the money she would make would go to settle the million-dollar debt she owed the federal government and she got to keep ten percent, the rest was to be entrusted to private, not-for-profit organizations her brother had identified. "Get you a couple of celebrity TV shows," but she needed a charity. *All I need right now is a drink.* She had been straight for ten years, but still savored the memory. She was tired, broke, and alone. Funny, Alelia, her radical, hippie cousin, had settled with Raoul into a relatively ordinary, stable life. *House, husband, daughter, named Liberty, of all things. What you got?* Her Grammys, her fans, memories. *No man. No children.* She had never imagined that. Here she was at fifty, schlepping up a mountain in half a buckboard. She removed her tour logo baseball cap and held her face to the white noonday sun. *The music has fed me. No cause to feel sorry for myself.*

Her escort, Dr. Kwetana, a young pediatrician from Umtata, looked like a child himself. One leg braced on the side of the cart, he talked over his shoulder. "This is one of twelve safe houses of the Pathways Organization," he said in a thick South African accent that bespoke Xhosa origins. "These children, products of the mines. Men far from home, women. The stigma of an orphan is unfortunately still a bad thing. Parents drink, use drugs, abuse the children—or their parents have AIDS. Once they know they're going to die," he said matter-of-factly, "they leave the children alone. They think, why spend money? It's not going to do any good." He shrugged, clicking his teeth.

The cart slowed at the top of the hill and pulled up to an enclave of corrugated tin structures, squat, plain prefabricated buildings. *The other side of the world.* "They touch your hair, play with your ears," he forewarned her as they disembarked. Despite herself, Tokyo was heartened by his earnestness. Suddenly the seemingly empty settlement came alive. "Bayeté! Bayeté! She coming!" A choir of barefoot children in navy blue and white uniforms, and their teachers, a gaggle of children, gathering around her, pressing in to touch her.

"They just want somebody to love them," Kwetana said as they entered a small room lined with cribs. "Here we are. Our latest arrival." Before she knew it, the young doctor had picked up a swaddled infant and placed her in Tokyo's arms.

The baby was a golden hue, her face a glowing amber, her black eyes a cubist picture of reflected light. "Hello there . . ."

"Her name is Monday," Kwetana explained. "That is the day she arrived, so that is the day she was born to us."

Tokyo cradled the infant's head in her elbow and sat in one of the clinic's fragile folding chairs. "Monday?" Tokyo cooed, "Where you from, chile? Charleston, L.A., Chicagah?" and tickled the baby's stomach, playing her piano game, "Abuja, Nairobi, Umtata!" With each changing note, the baby scrunched her tiny belly and gurgled with laughter. She fidgeted madly, her little fists in constant motion, her delicate graceful hands a miracle of architecture. Suddenly she grabbed Tokyo's finger and held on, the eyes seeming, trying to focus. Tokyo gazed into those eyes, in those eyes all that had ever been and all that would be, and she began to sing.

A Note on the Vernacular

Capturing the nuances of African-American speech is always a challenge, and the particular voice patterns of the Carolina Sea Islands' Gullah people—Geechee in our family—especially so. The patois on the outer, isolated islands off the coasts of South Carolina and Georgia derived from the blending of various African tongues with West Indian influences and the overarching lingua franca of Southern English. In earlier segments of the story we have tried to create a vernacular reflecting some of these influences without being too severe. Linguistic studies suggested using "em" for all third-person pronouns; however, since the Mayfields straddled house and field, giving them some exposure to standard English, we deferred to the use of the third-person pronoun without the possessive and the occasional dropping of the *h* from *th*. The choices could be maddening. In our matrilineal family tradition, we were always told that we were Geechee descendants. In contemporary studies, scholars of Gullah culture have decried the term "Geechee" as a derogatory expression. Thus we were faced with a dilemma at the outset of the tale. Do we honor the respected academic research or the testament of our grandmother and the truth of the story she told? In this fictive landscape of ours, how do we get to the truth of the language, the truth of the story?

Since music is a theme, we thought it important to approach spoken passages with sound in mind and let the spelling follow. Hence, readers will encounter changes in language through time and in different situations. Characters modify speech patterns depending upon whom they are addressing and the emotions of the moment. Many early characters are emerging from pre-literate and semi-literate enslavement and Jim Crow constriction. We have allowed ourselves to hear what they say and let that guide the spelling; thus the dialect/dialongue is not standardized. For instance, "something" may appear as somethin' and sumpin; "everybody" as ever'body, ev'body, eb'body; "brother" as spoken by the Reverend may appear as brothuh in the barbershop and brothah to signal a labor recruiter's New England Yankee twang.

We debated both going without dialect and standardizing it. We decided instead to allow for variation in hopes that the many voices we encountered would suggest the fluidity of language these people lived in as they made their way from enslavement to liberty and from the countryside to the city—as they struggled to find voice and to carve out and discover their identity. This fluidity is reflected in character names as well. A character's family name, nickname, and outside name may change as individuals literally try on new selves with nomenclature. Betty is Miz Bette, Mah Bette, Ma Bette, Mother Betty, Bette, and Mauma. Eudora is Dora and Dora May. Alelia is also Leelee and Lia. And since two sisters wrote this book, our voices closely related yet distinct, we saw no reason to force a linguistic uniformity onto this family story. The small discrepancies in names and style may be read as tell-tale signs of individuality within the family, both the Mayfields and ours.

In most sub-Saharan African languages, sound is paramount. As another character of mine once said, "L'epellation n'est pas importante. C'est le son qui est la verité." Spelling is not important. The sound holds the truth. When in doubt, read aloud. It is a story meant to be spoken and sung as well as read.

—IFA BAYEZA

A Note on the Composition

My sister Ifa and I have heard and felt and tasted and saw many of the same things for a long time. As children, we went to different schools yet always returned to the same colored household. We were the product of the South as well as of Northern education and worldly experience. Our ears are open to all kinds of dialects and manners. With *Some Sing, Some Cry* we traded off sections as if trading verses of a song or trading eights in blues or jazz. It was as natural as changing partners for turns during a mambo. The story is told in a voice that is the voice of the Mayfields as heard by two sisters listening carefully to their tune.

—NTOZAKE SHANGE

A Bibliographical Note

For a fictional work spanning nearly two centuries, we consulted numerous sources. To set the timbre of various decades, we relied heavily on contemporaneous newspapers, journals, and letters. We also gleaned much from studying photographs and images, and from listening to the music when recordings were available. While the core of our story is based on the lore of family and friends, colorful and mysterious oral histories, our efforts got context and grounding from many excellent scholarly sources. A few tomes stand out in their invaluable specificity: James D. Anderson, *The Education of Blacks in the South, 1860–1935;* Leon F. Litwack, *Trouble in Mind: Black Southerners in the Age of Jim Crow;* Elizabeth Fox-Genovese, *Within the Plantation Household: Black and White Women of the Old South*; Dorothy Sterling, editor, *We Are Your Sisters: Black Women in the Nineteenth Century*; Bernard E. Powers, Jr., *Black Charlestonians: A Social History, 1822–1885*; Reid Badger, *A Life in Ragtime: A Biography of James Reese Europe*; David A. Jasen and Gene Jones, *Spreadin' Rhythm Around: Black Popular Songwriters, 1880–1930*; Jeffrey Melnick, *A Right to Sing the Blues: African Americans, Jews, and American Popular Song*; Rosalyn M. Story, *And So I Sing: African-American Divas of Opera and Concert*; Tyler Stovall, *Paris Noir: African Americans in the City of Light*; Gregory A. Freeman, *Lay This*

Body Down: The 1921 Murders of Eleven Plantation Slaves; Luc Sante, *Low Life: Lures and Snares of Old New York*; and W. E. B. DuBois's *Black Reconstruction in America, 1860–1880* and David Levering Lewis's *When Harlem Was in Vogue,* which remain the definitive texts on these two vital eras.

Acknowledgments

First and foremost I want to thank my parents, Eloise and Paul Williams, who passed before this book reached publication. Without their stories and sense of history, I would not have been able to create the many characters in *Some Sing, Some Cry*. I hope they are as happy as Ifa and I are with the project's completion. I especially want to thank Ifa Bayeza, my sister, for her remarkable creativity and diligence while working on this project. My sister Bisa Williams and my brother, Paul Williams, were patient and full of suggestions that Ifa and I took to heart and that enhanced our journey in bringing this story to life. I want to thank Cora Ledet for her wonderful work on the manuscript; I would like to give considerable attention to Claude E. Sloan's meticulous care of the manuscript long before we went to print. As in all his work, Michael Denneny has assiduously applied his craft as an editor to every word in this novel. Thank you, Michael. And then there's Lindsay Sagnette, editor at St. Martin's Press, who pulled together all the various genres that make up the whole of *Some Sing, Some Cry*. I want to thank my agents Tim Seldes, Joy Azmitia, and Jesseca Salky for seeing me through the many years of this novel's evolution. They hung in there with me. I'd like to graciously thank Mr. Witte for having kept the faith in us. And lastly, I want to thank my dear Savannah for her sense of humor and her deep appreciation of our rich and complex cultural history.

—NTOZAKE SHANGE

* * *

INDIVIDUALS TO thank, especially our editors: Michael Denneny, who took us on the maiden voyage, believed in the project, and fought hard to bring it to life over many years, never losing patience or the grander vision. My gratitude also to everyone at St. Martin's Press, especially George Witte, editor in chief, and our editor, Lindsay Sagnette, for their palpable excitement about the work, as well as managing editor Amelie Littell and copy editor India Cooper for their tender treatment of the manuscript. To literary agent extraordinaire Tim Seldes, and the entire staff of Russell & Volkening, Inc., especially Jesseca Salky and Joy Azmitia.

I cannot express enough gratitude to our sister Bisa Williams for her wise comments and good counsel, with a superb eye and an ear to match. She pitched in for any task from proofreading to translation, and had unwavering faith and encouragement. Appreciation also to our brother, Paul T. Williams, Jr., for his wry, steadfast support and for recommending such great counsel in the form of Craig D. Jeffrey and J. P. Benitez at Bryan Cave.

I owe specific thanks to a few folks for their informed conversation: Lyndia Johnson on the operatic path, Johnny Lee Davenport on coon can and man stuff, Yolisa Madulo of South African Translators' Institute on isiXhosa naming practices, Mrs. Margaret Allen on her Hunter College memories, Sadie Woods and Adam Green for deejay reminiscences, Shawn Wallace for musical terminology, Mickey Davidson for dance history, and Alma Baeza for her amateur-night stories. Jeni Dahmus at The Juilliard School Archives was extremely helpful with back catalogues and class schedules.

A special note to Mrs. Gwendolyn Elmore and the Arna Bontemps African American Museum in Alexandria, Louisiana, for fellowship assistance in 2003 and my first public audience for the work. Thanks also to Jane Saks and the Ellen Stone Belic Institute for the Study of Women and Gender in the Arts and Media at Columbia College in Chicago as well as the SonEdna Foundation of Mississippi for their ongoing support of this work and of my writing in general, and to Gracia Hillman for offering me that lovely summer house by the beach as I reached the final stages of the book's preparation; also to Arnold Newman, my wonderful landlord, a true and patient patron of the arts. A special note of appreciation to Howard Rosenman and Lauren Shuler for their early enthusiasm.

We have many ancestors to thank far and near. We've borrowed snips and snapshots from both sides of our family to make this musical quilt: maternal grandparents Viola B. and Frank Eugene Owens, who braved the Great Migration; Vi's father, Benjamen, who worked the railroad, and her Sea Island–born mother, Victoria Mack; great-aunts Carrie and Marie with their stories and secrets; Grandma's sister Lizzie with her fire and iconoclasm; and Aunt Emma with all that hair, a beautiful spirit, and tickets to the theater every time we came to New York; on Dad's side, Grandma Ida Williams, the community seer, and Charles, who fixed violins; and with their beautiful voices and musical prowess, all of my father's sisters, my paternal aunts Thelma, Barbara, Ora, Blanche, Dottie, and Britomarte, the world traveler. To my great-great maternal grandmother, Filis, I thank you for leaving us a trace of you; and to my niece Savannah, I am always grateful for your insight from the future.

To our parents, Paul T. Williams and Eloise O. Williams, a debt of thanks always. Magician and conjurer, visionary and raconteur, they were extraordinary parents, rooting us in spirit, imagination, intellect, and commitment. Zake and I both chose the artist's path. Our parents gave us everything we needed for the journey. Such drama! Such wonder. . . .

Last, but surely not least, I would like to thank my sister Ntozake for her remarkable brilliance and for inviting me on yet another adventure, hand-dancing along the way.

In the course of writing a narrative covering roughly two hundred years, we consulted myriad primary and secondary sources. We are indebted to the many, many scholars and historians who labor so valiantly to bring our illustrious journey to light. For those intrigued by the history detailed in *Some Sing, Some Cry*, we are preparing a detailed bibliography that will be available online.

Surrounded on all sides by music, while writing this book we discovered again and again how vast and varied the music of African-American people, how vital. There are so many antecedents, it's impossible to name them, so rich is the panoply. With our collage of characters we can only suggest the singers, players, composers, writers, dancers, and producers;

the theaters, churches, living rooms, and sidewalks, the cabarets, juke joints and dance halls; the solo artists, big bands, and combos—the heavenly choir of legendary and anonymous voices that have filled our nation and world with song.

—IFA BAYEZA